Sorcerous Moons

Books 1–3

BY
Jeffe Kennedy

Thank you for reading!

Credit
Editor: Deborah Nemeth
Production Editor: Rebecca Cremonese
Back Cover Copy: Erin Nelson Parekh
Cover Design: Louisa Gallie

Hello!

Welcome to the print edition of *Sorcerous Moons*, books 1-3. This volume contains the initial three books of the series: *Lonen's War*, *Oria's Gambit*, and *The Tides of Bàra*. They were originally published separately, available as eBooks only, in July, August, and October of 2016. The fourth book, *The Forests of Dru*, came out in January 2017, and I anticipate two more books after that in 2017. Those three will be packaged for print together also, so there will be two print volumes in the end.

Unless things change.

I don't *think* they will, but you never know with me…

At any rate, there won't be fewer than six books total, with at least two print volumes like this one.

These first three books made sense to bundle together for print. They were too short individually to make the costs worth it, and together they complete the initial arc of the series. I chose the cover of the third book, *The Tides of Bàra*, for the print volume simply because it was my favorite one.

Many thanks to all the wonderful readers who've made this series so successful! I paid most of our household expenses with the royalties from these books. Food and shelter are wonderful things. Getting to write this story the way I wanted to—a true slow-burn romance that takes a long time to build—has been even better.

Best wishes to all of you and thank you for reading!

Jeffe Kennedy
Santa Fe, February 2017

Table of Contents

Lonen's War

Sorcerous Moons – Book 1

By
Jeffe Kennedy

An Unquiet Heart

Alone in her tower, Princess Oria has spent too long studying her people's barbarian enemies, the Destrye—and neglected the search for calm that will control her magic and release her to society. Her restlessness makes meditation hopeless and her fragility renders human companionship unbearable. Oria is near giving up. Then the Destrye attack, and her people's lives depend on her handling of their prince…

A Fight Without Hope

When the cornered Destrye decided to strike back, Lonen never thought he'd live through the battle, let alone demand justice as a conqueror. And yet he must keep up his guard against the sorceress who speaks for the city. Oria's people are devious, her claims of ignorance absurd. The frank honesty her eyes promise could be just one more layer of deception.

A Savage Bargain

Fighting for time and trust, Oria and Lonen have one final sacrifice to choose… before an even greater threat consumes them all.

Dedication

To Sassy Outwater,
who wanted a fire-breathing guide dog.
Close enough?

Thank you for reading!

Credit
Editor: Deborah Nemeth
Production Editor: Rebecca Cremonese
Back Cover Copy: Erin Nelson Parekh
Cover Design: Louisa Gallie

~ 1 ~

ORIA SQUINTED INTO the heat shimmer rising in the distance beyond the high walls of the city. Maybe if she looked long and hard enough, the weapons of the clashing armies would give off a telltale glitter or the shouts of the men would echo back. But, even though her high tower gave her one of the longest views in Bára, she remained blind and deaf, stuck in her chambers, remote from the battle underway.

Just as she'd lived most of her life isolated from the rest of the world.

Despite the lack of other evidence of war, the hot wind seemed to carry an unfamiliar smell to her rooftop garden. Layered among the scents of sand, the brackish bay, and distant ocean came something new. Something like roasting meat, redolent of rage, despair, and determination. An unsettling combination unlike anything she'd ever experienced. But until this, no one had attempted to attack Bára in her lifetime. Not for a long time before that either, according to the histories.

She paced the gilded balcony as Chuffta, perched on the rail, watched her without moving, green eyes sliding back and forth as if he were watching a xola match.

"You realize you walk much and get nowhere," he said in her head.

"Yes, yes—the story of my life," she snapped at her Familiar. "Besides, it's not as if I need to conserve my energy just to hide in my rooms while the city falls."

"Bára will not fall," Queen Rhianna said in a mild tone. Her nimble fingers never faltered as they wove seven needles threaded with different colors in an intricate embroidery, a casually powerful exhibition of her magical skill, her the golden metal mask that covered her face without eye holes demonstrating her ability to see in other ways. "It has not these many years and there's no reason to believe it will now. Don't put attention on a result you do not want. You know better than to articulate such thoughts, lest they manifest in truth."

Oria frowned at her mother. "I don't know any such thing, but let's try it out. Everything is fine! The Destrye army has vanished into thin air and we're no longer under attack."

Queen Rhianna sighed, leaking the barest hint of exasperation through her carefully cultivated calm. "Your casual attitude toward powerful forces beyond your ken will be your undoing, daughter. You should know better than that, too, by now."

"If they're beyond my ken, how can I respect them?" she grumbled.

"You've never met a Destrye and you fear them, so your logic is faulty," Chuffta pointed out.

She did—and fear of their ancient barbarian enemy drove her to rudeness, as Chuffta obliquely noted. Sometimes her Familiar's wisdom grated on her. Okay, a lot of the time, but he offered sincere advice and helped her when no one else could. *True growth is uncomfortable, even painful*, the temple taught. She made herself stop and stroke the winged lizard's soft white scales between his eyes. "You're right. I apologize, to both of you," she added to her mother.

"What is Chuffta right about?" her mother asked.

"That I'm afraid of the Destrye without knowing any, so my logic is bad. Though there are plenty of stories and illustrations to inform *that* opinion." Oria's longtime morbid fascination with the warrior race that shared their continent had led her to ignore the texts she was meant to study in order to linger over the vivid drawings of the Destrye with their big bodies, darkly gnarled hair, black-furred garments, eyes wild in their cruel faces. So unlike the

Bárans.

"As there are similarly many stories, diagrams, demonstrations, and *lessons* on how magic works," her mother was saying in a placid yet pointed tone. "You may not yet have access to all of the temple's knowledge, but you know the basic laws. If you paid as much attention to those as to the gory histories, you might be making more progress than you are."

"Yes, but they never really *explain* anything. Like 'you'll understand *hwil* only when you master *hwil.*' How in Sgatha is that remotely helpful?"

"Some things may only be understood through experience. You know that we would tell you if it could be put into words."

Oria did know that, not that it helped. "None of this has anything to do with my original question. How can you sit and *sew* not knowing what's going on out there?" She flung an impotent hand at the desert beyond the city walls.

Her mother raised her featureless mask toward Oria. "Is pacing about like a wild thing giving you information on how the battle goes?"

"Maybe not, but it makes me feel better than sitting still does."

"I know it's difficult for you now, but once you master *hwil*, all will become clear. You'll understand that there's infinite motion in stillness, and you'll be able to channel the energy that makes you so restless into its intended purpose. You will find great relief in channeling your sgath to the common pool And, following that, you can begin to seek your perfect partner and perhaps find a temple-blessed marriage. Once connected to him, you will be able to express your magic to its greatest extent, as Sgatha intended."

Oria turned to stare into the distance again, choking back her impatience. Queen Rhianna, like the other sorcerers and sorceresses of Bára who wore the masks of their office, exemplified *hwil*, the art of peacefulness under duress. *Sgath only flows through a calm mind*, Oria's teachers explained again and again. Though they never said it out loud, in the last years their featureless golden masks seemed to hold disapproval—and the resignation of those who'd given up on her.

Oria could never sit through a full meditation session. Her body unfailingly thrummed with restlessness to get up, to do something. Her mind dashed from thought to thought, like the jewelbirds in the garden, pausing in its mad flight only to hover over the worry that she'd never find the key, never qualify to receive a mask of her own. Never realize her mother's patient hopes.

If course, the possibility that she ever would grew less likely with each passing day since she'd never even glimpsed this perfect state of *hwil* where all became clear. Of them all, only her mother remained confident that she could.

Would it be so terrible if she didn't, beyond disappointing her mother's unshakeable belief? Her three brothers had all passed the final testing, each possessing enough power and control to succeed their father, needing only marriages to solidify their positions as heirs. They'd all taken their masks before they were twenty—including her baby brother Yar the year before, a prodigy at sixteen—while Oria trailed miserably far behind, facing her twenty-second birthday within weeks.

Truly, the blow to her pride rankled. And in her secret heart, more than a little unbecoming jealousy, nursed all those years as her brothers practiced the showy battle magics below her tower, so she could at least watch. They'd meant to entertain her, not deepen her envy.

Oh, her teachers could go on about how the male grien magic was easier to learn; that it burgeoned in young men, pushing up from the ground below Bára like the sap in the trees in springtime. How they only had to practice restraint, focus, and release, and that such things came naturally to men, while women's magic worked in the reverse. Instead of exploding outward, sgath drew in and received.

Thus the emphasis on meditation, calmness, and peacefulness. A woman should be like a serene lake, always refilling from those deep wells, so she could nurture with her magic. The sacred blessing of creation belonged to women, a divine obligation that provided Bára and her sister cities with the blessing of fruits, greens, and grains in the desert.

In the most exalted partnership, a sgath sorceress and a grien sorcerer married with temple blessing, their magics complementing and enhancing each other in a perfectly balanced flow. She to receive and grow magical energy, he to focus and release it. For this reason, the temple frowned on same-sex partnerships as not ideal, though they weren't strictly forbidden. Many settled for lesser marriages, not temple-blessed, and every person regardless of gender possessed some sgath and some grien, in different measures. Even the purest and strongest sgath carried a seed of grien, just as their parent moons, Sgatha and Grienon, waxed and waned, one around the other's orbit. Diligent study led a sorcerer or sorceress to develop his or her best self, all the better to serve Bára.

And that best self would be reflected in a temple-blessed marriage, such as her parents enjoyed. An ideal none of Oria's brothers had yet achieved. Something she could be first in, if only she could find a way to be still long enough to grasp the essence of *hwil*.

If only.

As the partnered sorceresses of the city did their half of the work of defense, the halcyon shimmer of women's magic pooled below Oria's tower, radiating from their stations on the walls, flowing out like a reverse bore tide. Queen Rhianna would have been with them if she hadn't elected to keep her daughter company. As it was, between the immense power of her sgath and her temple-blessed marriage with the king, she could be anywhere and feed him magic, a constant vital flow Oria sensed but could no more access than she could the battle taking place leagues away.

Thus it remained the sorceresses' job to stay within the protective circle of Bára while the men went forth to battle the Destrye with their powerful grien, fueled by sgath.

"This system has worked for centuries," Chuffta told her. *"In this*

way the cities have survived many onslaughts."

"Like you've been around for any more of them than I have," Oria retorted in a dry tone, but scratched Chuffta's wing joints where he couldn't easily reach them. He arched his neck, purring as she relieved an itch.

Her mother had no trouble following that thought. "Chuffta may be young, as you are, but the derkesthai have stood by and advised many a queen and princess of our line while our armies fought in the distance. I know you'd fret less if you could be directing your energy to feeding power to our sorcerers, but your time will come. The women in our family are like—"

"Like the fruit that ripens in the dry season, long after the rains have passed," Oria chimed along with the familiar adage. "I know, I know. Unless they don't bloom at all." Like her various aunts, exiled to live in other walled cities, far from the temple and the source of all magic.

Queen Rhianna tilted her face up, as if looking at her daughter, though she wouldn't be literally. The smooth golden mask of the sorceress gazed at her with eyeless serenity. "Or all the more powerful for the slow ripening. I would not have made the journey to invite Chuffta to be your Familiar and guide for when you take your mask unless I believed you would find your magic. Nor would you be able to hear him if you were mind-dead."

"Nor would I have agreed to put up with you for any other reason," Chuffta teased in his dry mind-voice.

"I know you love me. You think I'm charming, brilliant—and funny." She stroked the winged lizard's softly scaled hide, always soothing with its sueded texture. Of all her fears, the possibility of losing Chuffta worried her most. They'd been together since her seventh birthday. He was the greatest gift she'd ever received. If she failed to take her mask, he'd have no reason to stay with her. She could deal with a life without being a sorceress, even with a mind-dead half-marriage without magical completion—though what an unhappy life that would be—but living without the rustle of

Chuffta's thoughts in her head? A desolate prospect, indeed.

"What people believe becomes real." Chuffta echoed her mother's advice.

If only it were that easy. Like a jewelbird going to the wrong blossoms, Oria's thoughts seemed to forever return to the worst-case scenario. The dreadful potential outcomes of any situation filled her head far more readily than any other. Unbidden, they sprang to life in her mind. So much so that she diligently hid the extent of them from Chuffta, her teachers, and especially her mother. A woman's sgath magic could turn toxic, undermining as easily as it nurtured. If they knew how poisonous her thoughts could be, they'd stop training her altogether. The techniques they taught were far too potent to chance in irresponsible hands.

Another warning repeated far too often for comfort.

It all came down to this: She must learn to calm and quiet her mind. To be like her mother and live serenely behind the mask of a priestess, with no desire to pace in restless agitation, only happy thoughts running through her mind, not dread of the future.

Focusing on positive images, she determinedly rehearsed them in her head. The Destrye would go back to their sterile and magicless land. The battle would be won, perhaps so soundly that the fierce warrior people would never come after hers again. Bára would be safe and her father would peacefully hold his throne for many joyful years to come. Her brothers would continue the elaborate courtship and testing rituals to find their ideal wives among the priestesses of the temple, which she wanted for them with all her heart. (Never mind that little corner blackened with jealousy—she'd excise it.) *Focus on the result you want.* And she, herself, a paragon of peaceful maturity with vast powers of concentration, would find her *hwil* and receive her mask. Somewhere out there, her perfect match awaited, too. Perhaps she already knew him, and he only needed her to grow just a bit more so they could join in a blissful, eternal union.

A fine hope. Though more unlikely with every passing day.

Especially with the Destrye attacking.

"When will they send news?" she muttered at the horizon.

This time, no one answered her.

~ 2 ~

LONEN SWUNG HIS iron axe with grim determination, ignoring the sweat dripping from his soaked hair into his eyes. This land of burning sun roasted a man as surely as a slow fire tenderized a haunch of meat. The golem dropped, halved by his axe, and three more took its place while Alby, Lonen's first lieutenant, followed to chop apart the fallen one. Emotionless, thoughtless, the monster creatures advanced in relentless, silent waves, tearing with long, saber-sharp claws, rending Destrye flesh with crystalline-fanged mouths if they got near enough.

For too many years his people had superstitiously feared engaging the golems in battle, terrified by the things that felt no weapon, that kept coming with implacable strength, shredding every living creature between them and their goal. Until Ayden the Great had discovered by happenstance—and via the dire necessity of being trapped and alone when golems attacked his camp—that iron affected the creatures as nothing else did. The legend of Ayden, all on his own, killing a squad of the invincible golems with only the iron pick he used to clean his horse's hooves was told and retold among all the Destrye.

The epic tale replaced despair with hope—and had been the turning point in the war, just as Lonen had been old enough to shoulder his iron axe and help with his peoples' defense.

With the discovery that iron could take out the lifeless puppets the Bárans employed, King Archimago had implemented new strategies. But despite their early exultation at being able to fight back, the end of the conflict remained a distant dream and, unfortunately, plenty of despair remained. The hope wore thin quickly enough under the grind of what turned out to be the beginning of actual war, with the Destrye fighting back instead of hiding from the golems' raids and eerily quiet rampages.

They'd reduced the incursions for a time, but the enemy rallied, sending more golems until there seemed to be two for every one that fell. And forcing the Destrye to abandon Dru's lakes, one after another to be drained by the golems' unquenchable thirst and the endless chain of wagons taking the water away in barrels that held far more than seemed possible.

Finally, it became clear that all of Dru would wither and die, and the Destrye people would erode to nothing under the relentless onslaught. For every step they took forward, the enemy set them back two. So the king had sent his best trackers to follow the supply chains and find the source of the monsters. By dint of years of effort and many lives lost, they'd located the puppet masters, those who stole the Destrye's most precious and lamentably finite resource. The scouts had brought back the first descriptions of the crimson-robed men who wore smooth metal masks and commanded tremendous—and impossible—magics.

Getting within reach of them had taken more months of slow effort.

Alby cut apart two of the golems Lonen had cleaved with his axe, while Lonen hacked up the other. No more immediately surged into the space, not with the way his men had moved their perimeter. Lonen took advantage of the momentary lull to study the flow of the battle, beyond the center section under his command.

They'd come farther than the Destrye ever had before, reaching the apparently placid shallow brackish bay where a once mighty river had once emptied to the sea. The sudden treacherous bore tides had drowned a number of Destrye and their mounts, too entrenched in the silt to escape the onrushing surf that arrived with a roar like thunder. Finally, though, they'd learned to time their crossing to the moons, then found this strangely hot and barren land on the other side.

The plain of battle might be teeming with the featureless, waxy, pale golems as always, but for the first time their troops had cleaved through enough of them to come within sight of the golden-masked sorcerers who directed the monsters, and the towers of the walled city of Bára beyond.

King Archimago had thrown everything into this conflict, and the battlefield showed it, teeming with bold Destrye warriors. He'd even committed his sons, Lonen fighting shoulder-to-shoulder with his three brothers. After all, of what use were a king's heirs if all their people died?

They'd done well, pressing the enemy ever back, drawing within sight of the distant walled city that spawned the foul magic users. But then they stalled against the bulwark of those cursed sorcerers, who'd turned out to wield even more devastating magics than the scouts had reported.

To the right, a legion of Destrye surged, making swift inroads. Too swift, it turned out, as they drew the attention of one of the sorcerers. A tall man in a golden mask raised his hands and fire flew from them, forming a blazing ball that shot into the merciless blue sky, then rained down on the Destrye troops. The men screamed, hair and clothing catching fire, then disappeared from view as they fell.

The battle mages only seemed able to send the fireballs within a certain distance, not unlike an archer's range. They also avoided singeing their golems, which had a distressing tendency to melt into a viscous substance that clung and singed Destrye flesh if a fighter remained too close. It became a tricky proposition as more golems fell before the Destrye's iron, opening a gap between the front line of assault and the long phalanx of golden-masked men on their platforms—and creating a clear path for the fireballs.

Taking heed of the lesson, Lonen gave orders to draw his men back. "Keep it tight and steady!" he shouted.

Under Lonen's feet, the earth rumbled and shifted, making him stumble to catch his balance. Relieved of the incessant need to hack through the golems, Lonen observed what he could as they withdrew. He scanned the Báran mages and, sure enough, another had his arms upraised, his faceless mask pointed off to the left, where Lonen's older brother Nolan led his forces. Another rumble, like thunder from below, and the ground cracked open, a jagged black lightning bolt of doom. Destrye and golems alike spilled over the crumbling edges like precious water through the bottom of a broken bucket, plunging into the great crevasse.

The despairing cries of falling Destrye added to the screams of those burning, though the golems remained, as ever, eerily silent. Lonen fought a similar plunge of his heart. Not Nolan, his laughing dreamer of a brother. Surely he'd stayed well back and remained safe.

His older brother Ion forged his way through Lonen's line of sight from the other direction, a line of blood dripping from a score down his temple and cheek. Lonen set his own men against the wedge of Ion's battalion to hold a perimeter against the golems surging from the fore, and to cleave a larger path for Ion's men. Lonen himself took down five more of the things, chopping them with his axe like so much firewood, ignoring how the pieces feebly plucked at his boots as he stepped on them.

Spiking the warriors' boots with iron nails to further decimate the golems had been another of King Archimago's strokes of genius.

"We have to take out the mages or we'll be entirely lost," Ion gritted once he got close enough. "Father says pull back. The closer we get, the more easily they employ those greater magics."

Lonen bit down on an argument. To come so near and withdraw felt very much like defeat. But of course they were right. It made no sense to destroy the golem army only to dash themselves against the implacable forces the battle mages wielded.

Nodding, he set his men to creating a new perimeter, fitting them against the forces on his other flank, directed by his brother

Arnon. Ion moved on with his battalion, taking over those between Lonen and the great crack in the earth, all that remained of Nolan's section of the battlefield.

Was Nolan even now clinging to a crumbling lip—or writhing broken at the bottom of the chasm? He couldn't bear to contemplate it.

Fortunately, the press of battle, of staging their retreat while holding a firm line at their backs, required all Lonen's attention. If his brother had indeed died, there would be time enough later to mourn.

If Lonen even survived that long.

THEY GATHERED HOURS later, wearied, covered in smeared ash and blood, in King Archimago's tent: Lonen, Ion, and Arnon, and their father.

Nolan had not been found. He was lost, along with an entire regiment of brave Destrye.

Their father leaned his head in his hands, visibly aged since they'd engaged in battle that morning, on top of the years he'd already piled on in the past months of fighting to get within striking distance of their faceless enemy. Ion dismissed the retainers, the captains of other regiments. This moment was for family.

Stepping around the table, he put a hand on their father's shoulder. "We don't know he's dead."

The king laughed without humor, a sharp crack like the one that had rent the earth. "Would you wish him alive and trapped below ground with those monsters? Perhaps captured and tortured by those sorcerers?"

A dismal thought that hadn't occurred to Lonen. Nor to his two remaining brothers, by the expressions on their faces.

"It could be I was wrong to bring us all here," Archimago said into his palms, his voice weak, nothing like the robust warrior who'd taught Lonen everything he knew.

"We couldn't know their powers would be so enormous." Ion gripped their father's shoulder. "There was no way to know, short of this battle."

Lonen leaned his axe against the table, shoulders tired and aching now that he'd stepped away from the fight. His men would be exhausted, too, and they'd soon have to rotate out the ones holding the defensive line around the encampment. Two hours of rest at a time, no more. So far the sorcerers hadn't pursued their forces, which made no sense. True, the golems continued to attack, but why not open the earth beneath the Destrye tents and rain fire and storms on them from above? Had Lonen been in their position, he would have pressed the advantage, eliminating his enemies from under the sun forever. If only.

"There wasn't any way for the scouts to assess a thing that never showed until now," Arnon added, catching Lonen's eye. "We had to walk this path to discover what we now know."

"Besides"—Lonen took his cue from his younger brother—"you made the only choice you could. We were forced into the offensive. Had we stuck to the old ways, the Destrye would have surely perished."

Their father raised his head, eyes dark in his weathered face. "And now we will be decimated in one fell swoop, immediately instead of through slow erosion."

"Even if we all die on this battlefield," put in Arnon, always the philosophical one, "the Destrye are not destroyed. This assault has at least provided a diversion for the rest of our people to escape to a new place. A land where they can live in peace."

"A caravan of women guarded by boys and old men." The king shook his head wearily, staring at his hands on the scarred wooden table covered with maps of all the territory they'd crossed. "If only I'd sent Nolan with them. He would be still alive and the Destrye not scattered to the tides."

Lonen and his brothers exchanged looks over their father's head. It wasn't like him to second-guess his decisions. None of the choices had been easy ones—even though they'd seemed simple, forced on them by their ruthless enemy. But now the king seemed already defeated, as if they'd lost the war instead of the day's battle.

In truth, they'd lost a great deal that day. Perhaps more than they could recover from, and yet—

"Why haven't they come after us?" Lonen found himself saying aloud.

Arnon frowned at the change of subject, but Ion, their father's heir, nodded in approval. "It's a good question, and we should take that into account in planning our next strategy."

"Our next strategy?" Their father looked from one of them to the next, his blank black eyes seeming to see only the grief-filled images that haunted them. "There is nothing more we can do except attempt to flee. They've destroyed half our forces."

"But why only half?" Lonen persisted.

"*Only* half?" Arnon echoed incredulously. "That's ten thousand men who died in our service that you're dismissing."

"They died to protect our people," Lonen growled, "for the very same reason you and I fought today. Not for a throne but for their wives and children who were forced to flee even as they marched away from them. And yes, I say 'only' because they could have killed us all. The fireballs, the earthquakes, the thunderstorms—you saw the power of their magic. Why aren't we *all* dead?"

"Because we pulled back," Ion said, looking thoughtful. "We're out of range now."

"Exactly," Lonen replied. "And something is keeping them from pursuing and keeping us within range. What?"

The king sat up straighter. "We need to find out. That could be the key to emerging from this debacle victorious after all."

In the silence of his skull, Lonen thought victory might be a little much to hope for. Forestalling total destruction of the Destrye, however, remained a hope, however slim. With his mother, his sisters, and his beloved Natly on their way to who knows where, he'd resigned himself to never seeing them again, never feeling the kiss of Natly's lovely lips, the silk of her darkly oiled hair. If he could buy them a better life with his death, then it would be well worth paying.

"Yes." Ion sat at the table, nodding at his brothers to follow suit. "Call in the captains and every scout we can recall. We need to pool our information and plan our strategy."

~3~

AT LONG LAST, the next morning, the Báran army returned.

Oria held vigil from her tower as always, Chuffta beside her, though Queen Rhianna had long since descended to greet her victorious husband and sons. Somewhere in the cheering throngs below, beneath the shredded flowers tossed from high towers all around, they'd be embracing and celebrating the joyous day.

"You'll see them soon enough, and it would be difficult for you to withstand that level of energy."

"Yes, yes—I know." Yet another drawback of not yet mastering *hwil*. Oria, like all those gifted with sgath, tended to absorb any and all energy around her. She'd always been excessively fragile. Without the skill to ground the sgath and feed it to another, she overfilled, which resulted in shameful meltdowns. Chuffta served as a buffer for her, but he could do only so much. Living within the walls of Bára helped, of course, and being up in her tower made a huge difference, something her mother had known and insisted on since Oria was very young. She couldn't remember any other life.

Mostly Oria had played alone or with perfectly *hwil* nurse-priestesses, and even as an adult she descended from her tower only on the most tranquil days for brief appearances as the sole royal princess or to attend critical temple ceremonies. Otherwise, only those with perfect control of their emotional output were allowed to visit or wait on her. Thus she spent most of her days on the sunny terrace with a nearly complete view of Bára, biding her time to suddenly understand *hwil*, watching real lives from above.

"Princess." Alva, her lady-in-waiting, came out and curtsied, no whisper of emotion emanating from behind her smooth mask. "Her royal highness Queen Rhianna asks me to tell you that the family will convene for the midday meal in the second-level salon so that you may join them."

"Thank you, Alva. Tell her I look forward to hearing the news." Oria had already bathed and dressed for the day, so she had nothing to do but wait. And pace around her small perimeter, observing the jubilation of the city. Hours yet to kill. If only she could fly like Chuffta, she could zoom into the sky and circle above everyone, at least able to see the victory parade.

"Perhaps use this time to practice meditation?" Chuffta suggested in a gentle tone.

Oria sighed. The last thing she wanted to do was sit and attempt to calm her mind. But as always, her Familiar offered good advice. Her family showed thoughtfulness in coming to her; they all had excellent control, and naturally, all were masters of *hwil*. Energy would likely still run high in the room—particularly as a meal of the royal family required more than her few servants—and she'd handle it better if she at least attempted to ground herself beforehand.

She plopped herself down onto the sun-heated tiles, folding her legs and arranging her skirts around her so the raw silk wouldn't wrinkle, forcing a change of clothes.

"Would you like me to guide you?"

"Yes, please." With Chuffta's help, she could go deeper, get closer to mental stillness than she could without. Not that it was enough to come anywhere near the state of *hwil* others described, something she failed to do, over and over.

"Shh. Let go of those thoughts. You are who you are. I love you as you are. Forget the expectations. Hwil *is different for everyone, and you'll find your path to yours. Now, imagine a deep blue lake. Lovely, pure, and warm. You're standing on the shore, warm water lapping your toes. It is peaceful, restful. You step in, the water lapping around your ankles. You go deeper, the water surrounding, embracing, accepting you. With each step,*

you count backwards from one-hundred. Ninety-nine. Ninety-eight. Ninety-seven..."

Oria followed along, seeing and feeling as Chuffta suggested. Absorbing the directions from his mind-voice was easier than when her teachers guided aloud. Mostly because they always seemed to have that *tone*. Though they offered her the deference due her rank, they still condescended to her untutored ways. Especially High Priestess Febe.

"With each step, your thoughts dissipate into the water. The cool, deep blue water fills your being, giving you peace, joy, calm."

Chuffta didn't judge her, and she calmed, sinking into the deep waters. Still, part of her stood aside, wondering if there might be fish in the lake. If so, what kind would they be? She'd never seen a lake, of course, but she'd read descriptions and pored over the illustrations. Bigger lakes and oceans had fish that lived in them, apparently. So there could be many of them, schools of fish brightly darting about. Flashing here and there. Then scattering at the approach of a predator. Large and sharp toothed, it arose from the depths of the water, an immense shadow that resolved into the hard face of an axe-wielding Destrye warrior. What had happened at the battle? Had the Bárans vanquished the enemy entirely, banished them back to whatever wilderness they'd emerged out of? Impatience to know rippled through her. How much time had passed—would lunch be soon?

"Nearly," Chuffta said. *"And that's enough for now."*

Abruptly Oria recalled that she was meant to be meditating. The same thing happened every time. She always started out with the best of intentions, then got distracted along the way, her thoughts turning to more interesting ideas than a pure, deep lake, enticing as that image might be. "Sorry," she said, chagrined. Sometimes it seemed she'd spent her life apologizing for the same failure, over and over.

"Then don't apologize. This is not a failure. The window will open for you when you're ready."

"I'm ready! I don't know how to make myself be more ready than this."

Chuffta laughed in her mind. *"You cannot force this. It must come in its own time."*

"Wonderful. Just like lunch." She stood and offered her forearm for Chuffta to hop onto. "We might as well go down and wait for them."

The lizard spread his wings for the short flight from the balustrade to her, his claws sinking into the leather padding of her sleeve, his sinuous tail winding around her wrist. All her gowns were made with thick shields on her left forearm and shoulder, so he could accompany her everywhere. Ironic, as she so seldom left her tower, but it spoke to the eternal optimism that she'd take her mask at any moment and be free to walk about Bára like everyone else.

Alva fell in beside her, then opened the double doors to her rooms that always remained closed, though the buffer they provided was primarily symbolic. Guards kept watch over the tower at the base and at several intermediary levels between, but almost never ventured to the top three floors. And any priest or battle mage who'd achieved enough *hwil* for Oria to tolerate his nearness could be better used elsewhere in the city, for the many magical feats that kept Bára running with such beauty and efficiency. Or, more recently, for defending Bára against the Destrye.

Chuffta, too, acted as a formidable bodyguard.

They wended down the wide circular stairs to the next level. Large windows let in light and air, keeping the interior fresh and breezy. She wasn't the first princess of her line to spend a good twenty years sequestered in the tower—her mother had done the same—and generations before had gone to considerable lengths to make it a pleasant place to live, if one could get over the seething restlessness. Sometimes Oria fancied she sensed the fidgety energy of past residents in the stone walls, radiating out like the residual heat of day lingering long after sunset.

"The victory is most welcome news, Princess," Alva offered in a smooth tone.

Oria gave her a speculative glance. "Is that verifiable information, or assumption?"

"Assumption. Would there be cheering and a parade without victory? And no enemy is pouring through our gates."

"You were on the walls for the battle yesterday—couldn't you sense how things went?"

Alva shook her head, smooth mask gleaming. "Without a husband, I only feed sgath into the common pool. It feels much like being a vessel that knows not who drinks the water it pours."

Suppressing a shudder—something about that image crawled under her skin in an unpleasant way—Oria didn't reply. She had no good reason to think it, but something told her the return of the army signaled only a pause in the conflict. The breeze coming in the wide windows carried that scent, of something carnal, full of rage. It hadn't gone away. Not far enough.

"Trust that intuition."

"Do you sense it, too?" she murmured to Chuffta.

"No, silly. You *are the sorceress in this relationship. I don't sense exactly what you do—I only taste some of it through you. Being sensitive is a gift as well as a curse. Of course you sense what others do not."*

Of course. From meat-filled scents to the echoes of restive ancestresses in the very stones of the tower, all very reasonable and rational to pay attention to.

Chuffta mentally snorted. *"I never called you rational."*

"Gee, thanks."

Alva, long accustomed to Oria's one-sided conversations, remained quiet, pausing to open the doors to the salon with a studied sweep of her graceful arms. Shouts broke through, slapping Oria like a physical blow. She gasped, clutching the doorframe lest the energy knock her backward.

"Steady." Chuffta hopped up to her shoulder, only the tip of his tail remaining around her wrist, the rest winding down her arm like a decorative band, and stroked her cheek with his angled head. *"Let*

it pass through."

"Calm down, please." Queen Rhianna's voice remained mellifluous, but nevertheless carried the tone of maternal command they all responded to without thought. Even though the reprimand had been directed at Oria's brothers, it worked on her, too, steadying her as much as Chuffta's stabilizing presence in her mind.

If only her mother could follow her around all her life, chiming gentle reminders.

Oria smothered a grimace at the thought and cooled her expression into a facsimile of serenity. *Hwil* might remain out of her reach for the moment, but she'd mastered the appearance of it. The smooth golden masks of her family all turned to face her.

"Forgive us for startling you, Oria. We arrived earlier than expected," her father said, holding out his hands. "You look lovely and peaceful today, flower of my heart."

She took his hands and let him draw her into his strong embrace, inhaling the feel of him. With her parents, being flesh of their flesh, born of their magical energy, she could enjoy physical contact without reserve. Always so welcome. He'd bathed and changed into fresh clothes for their meal, out of the crimson priest's robes he and her brothers would have worn into battle, and into the light, beige ones that better forgave the midday heat.

In turn, each of her brothers embraced her; some of their young male excitement buzzing through their *hwil* like a displaced swarm from a broken hive even though they carefully touched her only over her gown, so she kept the contact brief. They all treated her as if she might break apart, which irritated even as she appreciated the consideration her parents had drummed into them regarding their delicate sister. Still, there was nothing wrong with her physical body. The healer-priestesses pronounced her strong as a desert pony.

It was inside that she remained as fragile as a blown-glass figurine.

"Let us sit." Queen Rhianna spread her hands at the table, the waxed wood gleaming gold. They arranged themselves around it, her father at the head, her mother at the foot, her eldest brother, Nat, at their father's right hand, the second eldest, Ben, at his left. Oria sat at her mother's right hand, her younger brother, Yar, across from her. Her mother linked hands with her, but Ben hovered his palm over hers, symbolically sparing her the stress of skin-to-skin contact. It impacted her less from her siblings, but they were different enough from her not to be in as perfect harmony as her parents.

"We give thanks for the gift of *hwil*," the king intoned. "Which both protects us from the power of grien and sgath and allows us to draw from their blessings, to share with all the world. Here, in this safe place, we remove our masks and take the sustenance of food and drink with those we love best."

Oria folded her hands in her lap while servants stepped forward with dainty silver knives, one for each royal, and cut the knotted ribbons of their masks. Her family held the masks in place, then removed them as one, setting them reverently on the mats to their left, placed there for that express purpose. They accepted damp cloths, perfumed with menthol herbs, to cool their flushed faces. Alva gave a cloth to Oria also, a long-established courtesy to include the royal children who'd not yet taken their masks.

They meant well, but the rest of her family actually *needed* the cloths. So instead of playing the game of wiping away nonexistent sweat in exaggerated gestures as she had growing up, Oria set hers aside, making a deliberate effort to let go of the feeling of being excluded. Chuffta sent her an affectionate thought. Giving back the cloths, her family relaxed and smiled at one another, her favorite part of the ritual. Though she knew their faces well, it warmed her heart to see them again. The king accepted a flask of wine and poured for them all, the servants bringing them first to the queen, then to Oria, and then to her brothers in reverse age order.

She held her glass until her father raised his. "To my beautiful family."

Not to victory, as she'd anticipated. The wine, kept chilled on ice in the cellars even through the hottest season, tasted lightly sweet as the fragrance of day-blooming flowers, but the faint scent of roasting meat drifted through her head nonetheless. Her father and brothers all smelled on the surface like the honeyed soap the men preferred, and yet it seemed the smell of carnage clung to them, tingeing the flavor of the wine with the bitterness of char. Oria swallowed back against it.

"What news of the battle then?" she asked as the servants brought out the first course, a cold berry cream soup.

Her brothers all glanced at their father, though Yar gave her a cheeky grin first, clearly pleased with himself. King Tav's expression remained calm, revealing nothing. "Always so impatient, my gifted daughter."

A mild reproof, but one that stung. Yes, yes—if she had *hwil*, she wouldn't have prompted them for information. Still, they all knew she struggled with impatience, so it didn't need reiterating. Oria blew out a retort without speaking it and focused on her soup. Delicious, a perfect complement to the wine. But not enough to distract her from the undercurrents beneath the apparently peaceful meal. Her brothers might have silenced their voices, but their emotions ran high. Their bright energy tugged at her, eroding her hard-won calm like a receding tide dragging at the sandy shore.

Her father let the silence stretch out and finally Oria set down her glass spoon so carefully that it made no sound. "I can feel that things aren't right and it's getting to me. Would you please tell me what happened before I have to excuse myself?"

Her mother gave her an approving smile. Much as Oria hated confessing to crumbling control, she'd finally agreed that was better than melting down because she wouldn't admit to it.

"Tav," Rhianna said, "there's no need to push her. Not today."

Her father's eyes rested on his wife with burning warmth, a slight smile breaking the calm of his visage. He gestured to his man to remove the soup. "As always, you are wise. This, then, is what occurred. The Destrye had indeed made their way to within leagues of the city and seemed determined to storm the walls."

"Unfortunate," Chuffta commented, the irony settling her thrill of fear. Her mother, naturally, showed no reaction, but it seemed not all the dismay belonged to Oria.

"But we were victorious!" Yar burst through, that cocky grin cracking his unfortunately still-pimpled cheeks. "We halved their numbers and sent them scrambling. They were still retreating this morning. Let the cowardly barbarians run with their tails between their legs!"

"And us harrying them with golems all the way," Ben added with a thin smile of triumph. Of all her brothers, Ben had been the oldest when he took the mask. Not as old as Oria was now, but they'd at least shared the struggle to find *hwil* that Nat and Yar had escaped. Privately Oria thought the trial had tempered him, made him less impetuous than her other brothers—and that he'd be a better heir than Nat because of it.

Nat…he had a meanness to him. She'd stopped mentioning it because everyone told her that older brothers always give grief to their little sisters. Chuffta didn't like him either, which validated her unease.

"I don't have a good reason, though," Chuffta mused. *"He reminds me of those sand mites that get under the scales."*

She smiled a little at that and found Nat watching her with cold eyes, as if he somehow knew she discussed him. "Don't be afraid, baby sister," he said. "Unfortunate that you're too fragile to leave your tower more often than a few times a year, but we're here to protect you. Those meat-headed warriors ran away, squealing like little girls."

"They did!" Yar crowed, clearly delighted. "And now we'll be able to return to the business of finding our ideal wives. I bet I find mine first. Pretty Priestess Jania seems likely."

"You don't even know what she looks like under her mask," Nat scoffed.

"I can see the shape of her body well enough. Besides, her face doesn't matter. It's the matching of sgath and grien that does." Yar rubbed his palms together. "So far we match."

"You wish you could find a temple-blessed marriage," Ben muttered, a bitterness to it. From what Oria gathered, his testing and courtship went as slowly as his qualifying for the mask had. Though he didn't discuss such things with her. "You'll be beyond lucky to find a priestess who can barely tolerate your touch."

"He does, because he wants to tup someone besides—"

"And if the Destrye don't continue to retreat?" Queen Rhianna interrupted Nat.

"Well, they will," Nat replied, with a confident nod. "Why wouldn't they? We decimated them."

Their father waved off his half-eaten salad, leaned his elbows on the table in its place, steepled his fingers, and met his wife's gaze. Their magical connection clicked into place, the cycle of their regard flowed between them, warming Oria like the rising sun on a frosty morning. Like her father's embrace and the cool calm of her mother's presence, the perfectly balanced partnership between her parents grounded Oria more than all the meditation and mental discipline lessons.

"If they don't, we will have to take other steps," the king said slowly, speaking only to the queen. "Tell the priestesses to build all the sgath possible. We may need it."

~ 4 ~

LONEN LED HIS men across the sand, which swirled like so much soft shadow with Sgatha not yet risen to shed her rosy light and Grienon—in the sky as he nearly always was—falling into his darkest phase, then to slowly wax to full white in the next few hours.

The sleeping city loomed ahead, shrouded in dim lights and traces of fog rolling off the ocean in the chill night air. How it could be so cold at night when the days blazed so hot made no sense. Thankful for his black fur cloak, both for the warmth and the way it helped him blend into the night, Lonen pulled the hood closer around his face, paying close attention to his footing.

They'd waited for this night, this hour, charting the moons for the best shrouding darkness. The golems moved by night as well as by day—as Ayden the Great had discovered to his sorrow and Dru's triumph—but low light confused their vision. It had been a considered gamble, waiting so long, giving the Báran sorcerers time to replenish the golem ranks the Destrye had painstakingly hacked their way through. Of course, the entire war had been a calculated risk, betting the potential future of their people against their certain destruction. Not much of a choice in the end, put in those terms.

So far events had played as predicted. The Destrye had fully decamped and marched away from Bára for days at a time, allowing just enough golems to pursue unharmed to convey back to their masters that the rout continued in full force. The army withdrew to the far hills, which at least held enough game to replenish their food supplies, though far less than even Dru's declining forests.

When the moons' phases allowed, Lonen and Arnon had peeled off with small troops, seeing them through the silent lines of their pursuers, then releasing the men under trusted lieutenants to creep back to Bára's environs in secret. Lonen and Arnon then returned to the main force to ostentatiously march again the next day.

None of their scholars could be sure how intelligent the golems were, if they could recognize the faces or scents of the human leaders, but it didn't pay to be careless. Lonen's hunting dogs knew him from his brothers—why wouldn't the golem hounds belonging to the Báran sorcerers?

In this way they left behind pieces of the Destrye forces, like the goddess Arill scattering seeds across the land, orchards growing in her wake. Except the Destrye seeded the Bárans' destruction, carefully building over days and weeks.

Finally, Lonen rejoined all those men he'd scattered to the winds, taking several days to travel at night and hide himself during daylight, timing his crossing to avoid the blazingly fast and lethal bore tides of the bay before Bára. Somewhere out there Ion, Arnon, the king, and their best captains did likewise. They'd form a net around the desert city and draw the sorcerers away from the walls. Scattered thinly enough by attack on all sides, the defense would have to fail at one point or another—allowing the crack Destrye squads into the city with a single mission in mind.

Destroy the source of the sorcerers' power.

Another gamble there, that the sorcerers had not pursued beyond a fixed range because they dared not go too far from the source of their magic. In a perfect world, the Destrye would have spent time on feints, testing the theory, determining the range.

But the world had stopped being perfect the first time the golems raided.

As Lonen and his men slipped through the wandering golems who milled about, ghostly white in the darkness, in a loose defense around the city, he prayed that his squad would make it through the walls. Not for glory—there would be no glory this night—but to spare himself the grief of losing another of his brothers. Or his father. There'd been no word from Natly or his mother and sisters. No message from any of their dispersed people on the Trail of New Hope. They hadn't truly expected any. King Archimago thought it best to leave no connection between the refugees and the warriors who went after their enemy. The other half of their people were as safe as any could make them.

Still, Lonen's mind insisted on imagining their gruesome deaths at the fangs and claws of pursuing golems. Defended by only a few, the women, children, and elderly would be easy pickings. They carried little water with them, relying on the old maps to guide them to oases, so the golems should have no reason to pursue, but there was always a chance...

Too many gambles, too much reliance on luck: a fickle goddess at best and a vengeful bitch at worst.

In the distance, shouts went up. Ion's men, judging by the direction. They'd engaged the enemy and as agreed, upon running afoul of the golem net first, were sending up as much noise as possible. The battle mages, inevitably alerted, should focus their defensive efforts there.

Time to move quickly, before their enemy realized they'd been stealthily surrounded—as much as a walled city with rock spires at her back could be. Signaling to his men, Lonen broke into a ground-eating lope. They fanned out, iron axes and knives swinging in a pattern to intercept the golems that loomed up out of the dark. Lonen's axe bit, his momentum taking him into a sickening collision with the creature's slick, resilient body, a foul parody of a lover's embrace. Claws raked his back before Lonen yanked back the axe to slice through the golem from the other direction. Gritting his teeth against the pain, he finished the thing, then ran to catch up with his men.

He passed a few, wrestling their own monsters here and there, but kept going. That was the rule of this engagement—any man who could get to the wall, should. No stopping to help anyone. They weren't out to survive the night. At least not past getting into the city and destroying the source of the sorcerers' power.

Whatever it might be.

Fireballs flew through the night, heralding the arrival of the mages. The magic fire lit the sky to nearly daylight brilliance; illuminating Lonen, his men, and the entire area. A miscalculation there, as the golems, upon seeing them so clearly, gave chase from all directions. Fortunately for Lonen's chances, unfortunately for Arnon's, most of the golems moved toward the brightest light, leaving Lonen and his men relatively unfettered by the mindless creatures.

Lights also flared into life on the city walls, moving in a progressive wave, voices carrying through the thin desert air. This time there would be no retreat. They'd committed utterly. King Archimago had left some forces in reserve, to send after the refugees on the Trail of New Hope should this attempt fail, but otherwise he'd bring the remainder of the army up behind them with the intent of slaughtering first the golems then the hopefully incapacitated battle mages.

If they all died, they'd do it knowing they'd given everything to the effort.

Lonen and his men reached the shadow of the wall after a long slog through the soft, still-hot sand dunes massed against it. Destrye scouts had noted during the previous disastrous battle that various gates studded the walls. A large main gate faced the road, big enough to admit wagons and other conveyances. As it had in the previous battle, that gate opened, vomiting out a torrent of battle mages on wagons pulled by golems, the sorcerers' golden masks shining as brightly as the torches they reflected as they moved into position. No going that route.

Though that had never been the plan. Instead Lonen and his squad ran for the smaller gates. The first they came to was, of course, tightly closed and barred. That was fine. They didn't intend to go *through* it. Lonen would use it as a platform to lever up. Gripping his knife between his teeth, his axe secured to his back, he clambered along the bars of the gate. He reached the lintel above, hauling himself up.

Pausing there, he set a spike between the stones, pounding it in with a hammer from his belt and looping a rope through it. He dropped the free end, waiting for Alby's tug to confirm he'd grasped it.

Then Lonen climbed.

The towering wall wasn't the trees and cliffs of home, but it offered a similar set of chinks and handholds. Back in the deep shadow cast by the wall, Lonen felt his way, the old habits from boyhood kicking in. The adage advised not to look down, but really, for climbing like this, it was often better not to look at all.

Fix the feet. Reach, fingers smoothing along the stones. Seek. Find. Grasp.

Then set another spike, connect the rope, wait for the tug. Repeat.

Fix. Reach. Seek. Find. Grasp.

Fix. Reach. Seek. Find. Grasp.

His world narrowed to only that. No thinking about the explosions, the spike of lightning and roar of thunder, the rumble of earth and the harrowing screams of men. All that dimmed as the trance-like focus on the climb took over. Later he'd notice the trembling muscle fatigue, the scraped hands and broken skin bearing testimony to the all-consuming attention to survival, to gaining the victory of the summit. But in this moment he might be in the forest, bark rough against his cheek, the rustle of green leaves above and the chortle of the creek below.

He was suspended there, peaceful again. Carefree.

Fix. Reach. Seek. Find. Grasp.

Fix. Reach. Seek. Find. Grasp.

Fix. Reach. See—

His scrambling hand hit something wrong, bright bruising pain in his knuckles. A limb? No, no—the parapet overhang at the top of the wall. He'd made it.

Inching up his footholds, he gathered himself into a crouch. The next bit would have to go fast. He found a grip with one hand, then another as high as he dared. It felt like it could be the flat surface of the top, but who could be sure? Tensing his thighs, he sprang, praying he wouldn't launch himself directly into a swarm of the enemy.

His hands caught, held.

Slipped.

And he fell in a sickening arc, hands flailing for purchase. The rope around his waist grabbed hard, catching all his weight, vising the air out of his lungs, and slamming him into the wall with a brain-rattling thud.

At least the knife between his teeth helped silence his grunt of pain.

"Prince Lonen!" Alby hissed from several lengths below. "Are you all right?"

They'd climbed together enough times for Alby to know to stay back. Lonen waited to be sure the spike would hold, then tugged the rope below three times in their all-clear signal.

Resolute, he made himself climb again, forcing himself to go as slowly as before. *Don't assume the handholds will be the same.* That made for careless mistakes.

He didn't count the fall as a mistake—it had let him glimpse the top of the parapet. Plus, he hadn't been spotted. The flat top had been a false perception. Next time he needed to reach higher and deeper. Now that he had it in his head, he could do it.

And he would be ready to take out the crimson-robed sorcerer standing a short distance down the wall, golden mask facing the tumult in the distance. That priest had been still, no upraised arms spewing battle magic, so perhaps he channeled it from whatever foul source they tapped.

Lonen found his final spike again, checked its stability, then reached for the top once more. Not there. Just past it. There.

He sprang. Caught. Slipped. Held.

With a mighty kick, he launched himself over the top. The priest turned in surprise and Lonen knew his gazed fixed on him even though the golden mask had no eyeholes. No time for the shudder of revulsion, the instinctive fear. Every moment he hesitated the priest could raise his hands and end Lonen's life, along with the hopes of all the Destrye.

No time to pull his axe. Yanking the knife from his teeth, he charged, fast and silent as a golem.

The blade sank deep into the priest's heart, the slight body falling back, a woman's gasp of shock rattling from behind the smooth metal. Her hood fell away and her hair, a mass of blond silk, spilled over his hands along with the hot blood pumping from her rent chest. He pulled the knife away and lowered her body to the walkway below the parapet. Putting her out of easy sight of her people, yes, but also…

He'd never killed a woman before.

Lucky for him and the Destrye, he hadn't known before he dealt the lethal blow, as he might have hesitated. The woman gasped, lungs frantic for air that would do her no good, with her life's blood pooling around her, but he found and cut the ribbons holding the mask on her face anyway. Dull eyes in a once lovely face, already going slack with death.

"I'm sorry," he told her. The words echoed in his memory. Back to the forest of his youth and a doe he'd brought down with his bow. The arrow had been enough to drop her, but fell short of a clean kill. He'd found her in the soft leaves, glistening eyes dimming exactly like this as her life soaked into the forest loam, instead of pooling on hard rock, running in black streams in the cracks of the stones. "I'm sorry," he said again, as he had then.

And cut her throat to finish it.

"Their women fight?" Alby breathed next to him, a world of astonished horror in his voice.

"I don't know, but they're complicit." Lonen pointed his blade at another crimson-robed priest stationed farther down, also facing the battle. Still and rapt, unaware of them as if focused out of her body. "Kill as many as you can."

"I can't kill a woman," Alby said, horrified gaze still fixed on the dead woman's face.

Deliberately callous, Lonen wiped his blade on the priestess's robes. "They came after us and have killed *our* women, our children, even our hound dogs and house cats. Forget your sympathy. They're the monsters. This is a sorceress, not a woman. Pass the word to the men who reach the top. Kill as many as they can find who focus on the battle, then get back."

Alby swallowed back a retort, one that gave him a look of quiet agony as it went down, then went to obey.

Lonen steeled his gut and went to kill more sorceresses.

~ 5 ~

"ORIA, WAKE UP."

"Hmm?" Oria stretched, then frowned up at the flickering shadows playing over the high ceiling. The city walls must be ablaze with torches. Was it that early in the night still? No, because she'd gone to sleep well after they'd been doused to night levels. She'd sat out in the terrace garden to savor the fragrance of the night-blooming flowers and the sight of the white bats that came in like ghosts to drink from them.

"Wake up. Bára is under attack."

Chuffta peered at her from beside her pillow, eyes catching the orange gleam of flame, turning the calm green mad.

"The Destrye?" She sat up, threw off the down comforter, and shivered at the sudden chill. Yanking off her sleeping gown, she pulled on underthings and a casual gown of sturdy cotton. "Where's Alva?"

"On the walls. All the high-level sorceresses are on the walls."

Chuffta's mind-voice dripped with sorrow and an unusual blankness behind which something else wailed with grief.

Oh no. *Mother.*

"Tell me what's going on," she demanded, striding out to the terrace and the balcony overlooking the city. The walls blazed, as did the plain beyond. Thunder boomed through the sky as lightning forked through it, her father's magic, alive and well, which meant her mother should be also. One of Nat's fireballs raced out, then fizzled into shivers of descending flame that quickly winked out.

"I think some of the Destrye have climbed the walls and are killing the sorceresses." Chuffta gave it to her fast.

"But why would—" She cut off her own foolish question. Somehow they knew. The Destrye had discovered the battle magics would sputter and die without the priestesses feeding it to the men. Even now the mages were exhausting themselves, only her father's storm magic still going strong. Because her mother would be somewhere near Oria, and not on the walls.

"Where are you going?"

"To find my mother. She must be nearby."

"The city is in chaos. People dying and grieving the dead. You cannot go down there—it will be too much for you."

No news there—her head already pounded with the overload, even this high up, from the miasma of emotion rising like heat off the desert floor. It would be worse lower down, among them. But not worse than being slaughtered by the cruel Destrye on the walls of their own home. Why wouldn't they just go back where they came from and leave Bára alone?

"I can't stay up here while my people, my own family, are suffering and dying."

"What can you do that others cannot?"

She flinched at the sting of his caustic, but accurate point. "Maybe nothing, but if I stay here then I'm certainly contributing nothing. It's bad enough that I can't fight. Don't ask me to be more helpless and useless than I am." Due to her own failure to learn. If she'd exercised some simple self-discipline, she might not have been slumbering in peace while others died.

"You can't blame yourself. And if you'd been on the walls with the others, you might be dead as well."

A harrowing thought. She didn't argue with Chuffta, simply held out her forearm for him. With a sigh that sliced disapprovingly through her mind, he flew to her and dug in his talons. They pierced through the padding to her skin, demonstrating the displeasure that seeped from him. Deserved, no doubt, and yet…

"Don't punish me," she gritted through her teeth. "I can't bear for you to be angry with me on top of all the other emotion."

"I apologize, Princess." His mental tone layered contrition over the cuts he'd made, soothing and steadying. He hopped up to her shoulder and rubbed his soft-scaled cheek against hers. *"I am upset also."*

"The great guru Chuffta, ever placid and master of all things *hwil*?" She ran down the steps, only then realizing she'd forgotten to put on shoes. She so rarely wore them, only donning slippers for the few court occasions and city celebrations she all-too-briefly attended. As she passed each window on the spiraling downward journey, she looked out, searching for signs of priestesses on the walls and battle magic in the sky.

"Watch your step or you'll break both our necks," Chuffta chided, spreading his wings for balance, catching one in her hair.

"Like you couldn't simply take wing instead of tumbling." But she slowed and kept her eyes on the stairs. She couldn't see much through the windows, regardless.

"I'd never abandon you to save myself."

She nearly threw some of his oft-repeated advice back at him, not to make promises he couldn't keep, but the possibility of separation from him loomed too close, edged too sharp with blood-drenched Destrye blades. Pausing on a landing to catch her breath—had she ever run so fast for so long?—she stroked the long tail he'd wrapped around her waist for extra stability. "Promise me you will. If the Destrye get to me, you must fly away and warn the other cities, the other temples. Tell them what happened here. That the enemy knows to kill our priestesses to disable the mages. That Bára is in enemy hands."

"I pledged my loyalty to you and—"

"Exactly," she interrupted him. Something that surprised them both, as she never had done so before. "Consider this a last service to me. If I fall, fly away. Warn them or not, but save yourself."

With an unhappy mental mutter he agreed and she continued

down the endless stairs, going more slowly to stave off at least physical exhaustion. Outside, the night had gone quiet. No more rumble of the earth or crash of thunder. Silence had never been so ominous.

She reached the ground floor without encountering any of the usual guardsmen. They'd all been called away, apparently. Good that they'd gone to help, but daunting to contemplate that if the Destrye made it to her tower, there'd be no one to stop them from killing her. Or worse. The history books held tales both dire and vague of what happened to women who fell into enemy hands. She'd gone through a phase in adolescence of gruesome fascination with those sorts of tales. None related *exactly* what befell the women, only that they suffered terribly and it had to do with sex; sorceresses tormented by intimate flesh-to-flesh contact with men not only incompatible, but entirely without magical sensitivity.

The heavy bar on the door gave her some trouble, Chuffta regretfully unable to help. While he could grasp things well enough with his prehensile tail and feet, being aloft gave him no leverage to help lift something that weighty. On his somewhat helpful advice, Oria bent her knees and wedged a shoulder under the bar, pushing up with her legs as Chuffta flew circles over her head, admonishing her to try harder.

Apparently, now that he'd agreed to this plan, he was all in.

The bar lifted out of the slats by slow degrees, then tilted and fell with an alarming clatter, Oria barely scooting her bare toes out of the way in time. At the noise, the door flew open and Renzo, one of her usual guards, crashed through, sword drawn and eyes wild. At least they hadn't left her entirely alone.

"Princess Oria!" He pulled back several feet, visibly calming himself, which she greatly appreciated as his battle-ready aggression, anxiety and frustration swamped her with a wave of frenetic energy. Chuffta landed again on her shoulder, touching her skin with his, which helped dampen the overload considerably. "What are you doing down here?" Renzo demanded, all normal protocol discarded.

"It's not safe. You don't know—"

"I do know," she snapped, and his eyes widened at her brusque tone. Normally Oria remained subdued and quietly withdrawn when he escorted her. On those occasions she'd been working on her balanced calm, not soaking in the bristling emotions of a city under attack. "Do you know where Queen Rhianna is?"

"Ah..." He shook his head, then nodded. "Yes, Princess."

"Take me to her."

At least he adjusted to the changed reality quickly, saluting smartly and taking the lead—sword still drawn, eyes scanning the shadows—to guide her through the echoing empty hallways of the palace.

"Have the Destrye penetrated inside the city, do you know?"

Renzo shook his head, light brown curls shifting with the vigorous movement. "I don't know for sure, but I don't think so. The enemy attacked an hour after midnight. The king called for the princes, emptied the temple of the most powerful priests and priestesses, and mustered every guard who could be spared. The priestesses took to the walls and the rest went to meet the Destrye. Only the queen and her personal guard remained behind—and me, to guard your tower."

And they hadn't even bothered to wake her. The only person in all of Bára who'd slept through it all.

"Not all of it," Chuffta reminded her.

She sent him an affectionate thought, envisioning a hug that was impractical in reality, in gratitude that he'd awakened her, but didn't speak it aloud. The nonmagical tended to be disconcerted by her one-sided conversations with her Familiar. They did much better in her presence if they all pretended Chuffta was a pet, nothing more. No one else in Bára had an ivory-scaled winged lizard for a pet, though derkesthai populated Báran children's tales. Amazing what the ordinary person would accept in order to cope with the existence of magical gifts they didn't possess.

They reached her mother's favored salon quickly, as it lay not far from Oria's tower. The queen's guards bristled, then gave way as they recognized Renzo and snapped to attention at the sight of Oria. They didn't attempt to stop her, but opened the doors for Renzo to pass through first, speaking to the guards inside the doors. Renzo's tall frame blocked the narrow opening and Oria chafed to push him aside, craning to see past him. Chuffta simply took off and flew over his head.

"She is in a deep trance," he reported. *"She does not look well."*

Renzo and the queen's guards were arguing about whether Queen Rhianna could be disturbed, the discord jangling through Oria's skull, all that much worse without Chuffta's buffering contact. She balled her fists by her sides, reaching for some measure of calm, and failed worse than usual.

"Enough!" she screeched, the sound grating to her own ears. The men all fell silent, Renzo spinning to gape at her. In his astonishment he allowed the door to swing wide, so Oria plowed through them all, slamming through the interior door before any of them recovered enough to prevent her.

Lit by a few candles that burned low, her mother sat in a chair by a window that looked out on the city wall a short distance across the chasm. The way the palace ranged over the steep hillside, the ground floor of Oria's tower stood stories high over the sheer drop to the wall's base on this side. The parapet of the wall stood nearly level with the window's view, though a significant distance separated them.

"Mother!" Oria cried, rushing to her and taking her hands. Cold and limp. Such a deep trance. "Should I remove her mask?" she asked Chuffta, who perched on the window ledge. Temple law and custom of privacy strictly forbade removing anyone else's mask, except in dire emergencies. Surely this counted? Still, Oria hesitated, looking to Chuffta for his advice, since he hadn't yet answered. His sinuous neck curved so his head reversed from his body, he sat motionless, staring with reptilian interest at the view out the window.

At a man running along the parapet, illuminated by the blazing torches.

Destrye. Wearing a dark fur cloak that swirled heavily around him, he loped in a half-crouch, a dully gleaming knife in one hand, an enormous axe strapped to his back. Furred boots rose to his knees, crossed with leather, his muscular thighs bare except for black curls that matched the thick locks of his wildly tangled hair and beard. He melded from one shadow to the next, and Oria might not have seen him if Chuffta hadn't spotted him.

As if feeling their attention, however, he froze mid-step at the rim of a pool of light. Still but for the swivel of his wolfish head, he scanned his surroundings, thorough and unhurried.

Then locked gazes with Oria.

~ 6 ~

LONEN HAD SEEN many strange things in the past weeks. Impossible magic and horrific deaths that would take him years to purge from his nightmares, if he ever could.

If he lived that long.

The sight of the woman in the window hit him with enough force to unbalance him. Through the blood-drenched night, he'd kept focus on one kill after the next and only on that, much the way he'd climbed the wall, except that he slit the throats of defenseless women, one after another, instead of reaching for holds. They died so easily, seeming oblivious to his approach, focusing their placid attention outward to the battle where the booming assault of the sorcerers diminished and ceased as their sisters succumbed to the blades of Lonen and his men.

The fact that they didn't fight back, that they remained so vulnerable, sickened him, each death layering on unclean guilt that he'd ignored until the vision of the woman in the window knifed into him like an unseen blade. Maybe it was because her fair coloring was so much like the first woman he'd killed. After that one, he hadn't looked at their faces, taking the dispensation offered by their featureless masks.

For whatever reason, the sight of her gripped him, standing in the open window, illuminated by candlelight in an otherwise dark tower that rose from a deep abyss. Her hair shone a copper color he'd never seen on a living being, like a hammered metal cloak that shifted with her startled movements. She put a hand to her throat, eyes dark in her fine-boned face. A creature from children's tales perched beside her, staring at him intently. He would have thought it a statue carved from alabaster, but it swiveled its head on its neck to look at the woman, then back to him.

Lonen had seen illustrations of dragons in his boyhood books, but they'd been huge and…fictional. This thing looked very like those, only smaller—maybe as long as his forearm, not counting the tail. All white, it shimmered in the bright torchlight from the walls much as the woman's hair did. It sat on its haunches, taloned feet clutching the stone windowsill, bat-winged forearms mantled. Large eyes with bright green shine dominated a wedge-shaped head with a narrow jaw and large ears. It lashed its long, sinuous tail against the stone, as a cat watching birds would.

Beautiful, both of them, and as fantastical as if they'd stepped out of one of those storybooks. The wonder of the sight swept away all the bloody horror. She was the bright face of the terrible magics—something lovely, pure and otherworldly. Something in him lunged at the prospect of such beauty in the world, a part of him he hadn't known existed. Or rather, a part he hadn't thought survived from childhood. That sense of wonder he'd felt looking at those storybook illustrations, long since lost to the grind of the Golem Wars. He lifted a hand, not sure what he meant to do. A salute? A greeting?

"Prince Lonen!" Alby ran up, bow in hand. "Why do you—a sorceress!" He reached for an arrow and notched it, a smooth, practiced movement that Lonen barely stopped in time.

"No," he commanded. "Stand down. She wears no mask. She isn't one of them."

"They're all the enemy," Alby insisted through gritted teeth, resisting Lonen's grip. "She's seen us."

"It doesn't matter." Abruptly weariness swamped Lonen. Far too soon for him to wear out, as much remained to be done. That bright bubble of the fantastic had distracted him, the shattering of that brief moment of childlike wonder more painful for the sudden loss of it. He'd have been better off not feeling it at all. "Her people are largely dead, their defenses falling around them. Look out at the plain."

Alby followed his nod. Grienon, enormous and low in the sky, waxed toward full, shedding silvery light on the quiet field. None of the magical fireballs or earthquakes thundered through the night. The golems had dropped like corn stalks after harvest. The Destrye forces moved in a familiar cleanup pattern, groups of warriors methodically searching the field for the dying, to either save or dispatch, depending on which side they'd fought for—and if they *could* be saved. Other groups remained in pitched battle, but the Destrye had the upper hand. Without their magic, the Bárans would eventually fall.

For as many years as they'd worked towards this day, Lonen had expected to feel jubilation, triumph, the roar of victory. Not the drag of exhaustion and regret. Their plan had worked far better than any of them had dared to hope—and yet only bleakness filled his heart.

The copper-haired woman's fault, for showing him a glimpse of a dream of something more than monstrous death and destruction. He'd been better off hoping simply to live to the next moment, or not to die in vain.

Hope and the promise of wonder could destroy a man's spirit more surely than a well-wielded blade.

With one last look at the woman in the window, he turned his back on her and her false promise. "Come, Alby. Let's find a ladder or stairway down to the city inside the walls, so we can open the gates." One that wouldn't plunge him into that dark abyss. "There must be stairs or ladders that the sorceresses climbed. By sunrise, Bára will be ours."

Soon he would be done with this evil place.

"STUPID TO STAND in the window like that. You made a perfect target."

"Advice that might have been useful in the past and is irrelevant to the present is best not offered," Oria replied with one of Chuffta's favored adages, the oft-repeated words all her shattered mind could pull together. The impact of the Destrye's energy and high emotional state had pushed her even closer to the edge of control. He had no mental discipline, not even a shred of control over his raging feelings. They'd doused her with a bewildering range—wonder, hate blended with an odd joyfulness, horror, despair, soaring hope, and surprising regret. Not at all how she had expected a barbarian warrior to feel, but then she'd never encountered one before.

Yet despite their scope and potency—especially at such a short distance—his emotions hadn't overloaded her. Just left her a bit battered.

She sank to her knees, both because her weakened legs wouldn't hold her and to better chafe her mother's cold hands.

Blood pulsed weakly in her wrists, a faint flutter of butterfly wings. The two warriors had been speaking to each other, though she'd heard them as clearly as if they'd stood in the same room, the thin cool air transmitting their words. Had the Destyre been speaking the truth? Everyone dead, Bára fallen. The night had gone ominously silent, so it seemed so.

"It doesn't matter," the Destrye warrior had said of her, of whether she lived or died. The other man had called him *prince* and he'd taken her measure and declared her not worth killing, a strange tinge of betrayal to the bitter emotion. She should be grateful for the reprieve from imminent death, though the old anger burned at her worthlessness. Something even a Destrye prince could recognize across the gap of a chasm.

Enough thinking about that rough man who'd so strangely grabbed all her attention.

"Mother!" She spoke sharply to penetrate the trance. Deeper than Oria had ever seen. If all the sorceresses on the walls had gone so far into sgath, no wonder they'd all died. Still no response from the queen. Enough of this, too. "Chuffta—use your talons to cut the mask ribbons."

"The temple forbids—"

"I think all bets are off tonight. It's not as if Priestess Febe will be looking for trespasses against holy law to punish in the next few hours." If the high priestess of Bára's temple had even survived. She might have been on the walls, too.

"Lift me then."

Oria held up her left forearm for Chuffta to land on, his feet gripping as he used his thumb talons to carefully slice the ribbons at Rhianna's temple. Holding the mask with her right hand in a numb parody of the usual ritual, Oria kept it in place while her Familiar sliced the other two sets of ribbons at cheek and jaw.

When the mask loosened, she drew it gently away, then tossed it on the floor. Not proper treatment for the sacred relic, but the sight of her mother's wide open eyes, dull and spiritless in her deathly pale face, sent a fresh rill of terror through her and Oria forgot all else.

"Oh, Mother," she moaned, patting the queen's cold cheeks. "Come back to me, please. I need you. Don't leave me alone."

"You're not alone. I'm always with you." Chuffta, on her shoulder again, stroked her cheek with his own, his tail looped around down around her arm to her wrist in reassuring affection. *"Don't cry, Oria."*

She brushed impatiently at her tears. "It's not all mine."

"Yes, you're overloading. We should go back up the tower."

"You heard the Destrye. There's no one left in charge. I might not be a priestess, but I can't be so fragile that I leave Bára without direction. My father and mother would expect that much." Her mother, who still stared without moving or blinking. Perhaps dead inside a body that yet lived. "I'll get through somehow."

"And if you break?"

"Then I break."

"You won't do Bára any good if you're broken."

She wrenched her gaze from her mother's blank eyes to

Chuffta's worried ones. "Look—either I do no good because I break doing my best to serve Bára in her hour of greatest need, or I do no good because I'm sitting in my tower preserving a potential, something that may never manifest. The choice seems clear. If I can just wake up the queen, she can take over."

"Oria, she may be..."

"Don't say it," she replied fiercely, taking her mother's face in her hands. Wishing for *hwil* more than ever before, she tried to calm her mind, then she deliberately reached for any glimmer of emotional energy. Strange and awkward to go in a totally different direction—to move outward, to attempt to receive instead of vigilantly defending herself. It opened her to the crashing terrors, angers, and sorrows around her, but she focused on her mother, letting Chuffta do his best to screen the rest of it.

And there. A thread of soul-killing grief, dark but potent. Oria fastened on it, pulling it up and out.

"Oria," her mother breathed.

"Oh, thank all the stars!" Oria gripped her mother's still-limp hands. "Are you all right?"

Rhianna's eyes filled, then overflowed, a waterfall of tears flowing down her face. "He's gone. Tav is dead. There's a hole where he was. Oh no, no, no. Why did you bring me back?" She collapsed into sobs, not seeming to hear or feel Oria's reassurances.

Oria's heart bottomed out. Her father dead, her mother beyond reason. Likely her brothers dead, too. This wasn't how it should be. Oria wasn't the strong one. Of them all, she had the least ability to cope, much less to lead. She wanted more than anything to crawl into her mother's lap and be comforted, but that wouldn't happen. Maybe never again.

Not many made temple-blessed marriages, so the nature of such relationships were long on myth and romance, but short on facts. The ballads and tales always told of the sorcerer and sorceress dying together—either in sweet old age, in each other's arms, or, tragically, battling some dire foe. Never did one survive the other.

Maybe her mother's total and shocking loss of *hwil* hinted at why. The world quivered under Oria, spinning into a new pattern. One where her unshakeable parents were no longer the fixed points in her life, her mother no longer the single person who believed in Oria. Her father was gone forever and her mother this sobbing, hysterical wreck of a person.

Feeling sorry for herself accomplished nothing, however. Though it felt as if the world had ended, it no doubt continued hurtling headlong into disaster.

"Stay with her, Chuffta."

"No, you need me more."

Too tired to argue, she pulled herself to her feet, a monumental effort. Her legs leaden, she went to the door, opening it to find Renzo and her mother's guard waiting with expectation so bright and dread so thick that she had to grip the door handle to keep from bowing beneath the onslaught.

"Take the queen to her chambers and call a healer for her. Send word round the city for anyone still able to attend that there will be an emergency meeting in the council chambers—"

"At least have it in the tower, so you'll reduce some *of the input. And it's more defensible if the Destrye enter the city."*

She nodded wearily, no longer spending the energy to protect the sensibilities of the guard. She wasn't thinking clearly. "All right, that makes sense. Emergency meeting in the third-level salon in my tower. I'm going there now. All of you—get as much information as you can about what's going on. Send messages as soon as you know anything. I believe the Destrye have plans and the means to open the gates and let their warriors into the city. There may be no one left to stop them."

They made sounds of protest, but subsided when she shook her head. "Find out if I'm wrong. Make sure someone stays with the queen, should worse come to worst."

"I'm staying with you, Princess," Renzo said, face grim.

"No, I—"

"Begging your pardon, Princess, but if what you say is true, it's possible you are the last surviving member of the royal family. Who is capable," he added, carefully not looking toward Queen Rhianna. Hating that truth, Oria cast one searching glance at her shattered mother and queen as one of her guards gently picked her up and carried her from the room.

"We must protect your life at all costs," Renzo urged quietly.

With no energy to argue and no thoughts to muster, Oria nodded. Then went to drag herself up the long climb to her tower, to find out whether any pieces remained to be put back together.

~ 7 ~

BY THE TIME Oria reached the third-level salon, the sky beyond the open windows had brightened with dawn. She went to the window; the view wasn't quite as good as the one from her garden several floors above, but there was little to see of the conflict. Bára lay eerily quiet.

Most likely any citizens who hadn't been summoned to the battle were barricaded in their houses, and any who had answered the call to defend Bára would still be trapped outside the walls. The main gates weren't visible from her vantage point, which came as something of a relief, though that might be the wrong response to have. A good leader would want to see everything for herself. But it might be more than she could withstand, the sight of Bára's gates hanging open like a wound, Destrye barbarians streaming through it to spill more blood, to finish the job of crushing her people.

And her. So far she hadn't broken, had withstood more input than ever before in her life, but it felt as if one more blow would do her in, leaving her shattered beyond repair.

"You're doing very well. Besides, there is no 'beyond repair.' Where there is life, there is always the possibility of healing."

"But where there's death, there is no healing, only corruption of the flesh." She sounded bitter even to herself and Chuffta did not reply. The image of her mother as a corpse in her chair still filled her head. She couldn't quite grasp that her father might be dead. Perhaps her brothers, too. All that seemed far away, muffled behind a curtain she dared not draw back.

A scuffling sound at the door made Oria turn from her morbid thoughts, and High Priestess Febe entered, leaning heavily on her walking stick of carved bone, accompanied by her aged husband, Vico. Both wore their golden masks, both alive, if not necessarily well. Vico had earned his mask fairly, of course, but expressed the merest trickle of magical power. He served Priestess Febe well enough to siphon off her powerful energies when needed, but theirs was far from a perfect marriage and he couldn't muster any of the greater defensive or offensive magics. No one had worried about it, because the high priestess used most of her sgath to sustain Bára, with the help of the junior priestesses. Vico mainly functioned to keep her balanced.

"I've sent word to the head priestesses of the temples in the other cities, Princess," Priestess Febe said, sitting heavily. "I don't know if they'll be able to help—though they owe us—but they will at least know of Bára's peril."

"Thank you, High Priestess." Oria hadn't thought of that. So much she didn't know, such as why or what they owed Bára. Except she did know that Bára was the capital of them all for a reason. None of the others sat atop such a potent and constant source of magic.

A few other priests and priestesses arrived, a dozen or so, all similar in magical power and physical strength—which was why they had survived the night. All were too elderly or not useful enough to have been called to battle the Destrye. The only others would be those too new to their masks to have ascended the walls or taken to the field, or those of the noble families who'd not yet qualified to take their masks at all. Who knew how many among them would find *hwil* and become useful?

Folcwita Lapo arrived, breathless, for once not perfectly assembled and groomed. Pausing in the doorway, he surveyed the small gathering, then scrutinized Oria. They'd interacted very little. Mostly she'd seen him at court functions, but as someone unmagical and not at all trained in *hwil*, he'd kept his distance from the sensitive Oria. Even though it felt as if she could absorb no more, his prickly energy hit her from across the room, forcing her to breathe through it. Ambitious, ruthless, and determined, the folcwita had served her father well in managing all nonmagical aspects of running Bára, and by all accounts did it well. Oria should be grateful to have his assistance at this time.

If she could stand to be in the same room with him.

"Folcwita," she greeted him. "What news do you bring—are we invaded?"

"Obviously," he bit out.

"Not quite, Princess," Ercole, captain of the city guard, answered, pushing through the doorway. "The main gates remain closed, but only because a few of the faithful city guard hold them. There's intense fighting there, both inside and out. I have to say, without the battle mages, we're bound to lose. Our numbers are not great and their warriors exceed our skill."

"Then why are you here instead of there?" the folcwita demanded.

Ercole shook his head, his lined face gray with exhaustion and despair, his once splendid uniform soiled with blood and other matter Oria couldn't identify and didn't care to examine too closely. "One man will make little difference at this point, though I will go back as soon as I'm released. I'm here at your summons, Princess. To give you the information you requested. What do you need to know?"

Oria fought back a headache, an aura forming at the edges of her vision such as she hadn't experienced since early adolescence, when her hormones and burgeoning magic collided and conspired to send her to bed for days on end in a darkened, soundproofed chamber, with only Chuffta's quiet thoughts for company.

"I'm still here."

"What of—" not just her brothers "—the sorcerers and our forces still outside the walls?"

"We don't know for sure what their status is." Captain Ercole looked at his hands, scrubbing absently at the bloodstains. "It's certain that they cannot return with the gate closed, so they're likely in dire straits, pinned between the wall and the Destrye forces. With the priestesses dead, they're down to their own reserves of magic, if they have any left at all. The golems have all fallen, which surely means Priest Sisto is dead. They have no help there."

Priestess Febe, Priest Vico, and Folcwita Lapo all startled at that—not at the news of his death, but something else. Through the roar in her head, Oria tried to parse what upset them. Something they didn't want her to know.

"Priest Sisto's golems were outside the wall?" But Ben had said something, hadn't he? *"Harrying them with golems all the way."* She'd only partly listened at the time, concentrating on keeping her brothers' bristling grien out of her head.

Captain Ercole rubbed a hand over his face, chagrin oozing off of him. "They'd become the mainstay of our defense."

Oria hadn't known that, but why would she? Aside from the occasional family meal, she had rarely participated in discussions of the particulars of Bára's defenses. She'd only encountered Priest Sisto's golems a few times, the most salient during a demonstration at the temple, as part of her lessons, probably a good ten years before. With an otherwise minor magical ability to manipulate silicates, the priest had refined his art to ambulate creatures made of the stuff. Nasty things with no intelligence, the golems did not move quickly or with any agility. The lesson primarily demonstrated how even minor magics manipulated with inventiveness and ingenuity could produce large-scale results.

They'd become useful for menial work around Bára, she'd understood, particularly for unpleasant tasks that humans preferred to avoid, such as clearing sewage pipes of blockages. Her father and Nat had discussed it once.

"I know of the golems, but how are they useful for defense?" she asked.

The folcwita stepped in, preempting Captain Ercole. "Why use human men when the golems served the same purpose with no loss of life? The golems made far superior soldiers."

The captain glared at the floor, obviously disagreeing but not arguing.

"Priest Sisto gave them fangs, Princess," Priestess Febe explained into the gap. "And long, very sharp claws. They served as a solution to several problems."

"Most of which are not relevant at the moment," Folcwita Lapo inserted with a quelling glance at the priestess.

"I imagine I have no time to learn about them with the enemy literally at our gates." Oria's eyes throbbed, focus blurring in and out, and she pressed her fingertips to them. "But I will want to hear about them in detail later. Your advice, Captain?" she managed to say.

"Open the gates, Princess."

"What? Are you mad?" Folcwita Lapo roared, slamming his hand on the table.

The literal and emotional impact drove through Oria's temples with knifelike intensity. Green fire rolled across the table, sending the folcwita reeling backwards, frantically batting at the silk sash of office that had caught flame. Everyone stared in astonishment at Oria. No—at Chuffta on her shoulder.

"I will protect you." His mind-voice came through with grim certainty.

"Watch your volume, Folcwita. The princess is fragile." Priestess Febe said, with sgath that nevertheless reverberated. It spread through the room like a cooling balm, easing Oria's pain considerably.

"That...that *creature*," the folcwita sputtered, his fear palpable.

Oria understood his reaction, though she judiciously hid that thought from Chuffta. The derkesthai Familiar had never shown aggression like that, typically saving his fire for roasting bits of meat and vegetables. But then, they'd both been pressed far that day.

"So far as we know, Princess Oria is the only functioning member of the royal family we have left," Priestess Febe continued. "Let's do our best not to sacrifice her this bloody day also. If her Familiar even allows it."

"Apologies, Princess," the folcwita gritted.

Oria nodded at him, saving her energy. "Explain your reasoning, Captain Ercole."

He spread his hands, palm up. "We've lost. The gate will be opened. If we fight, every man who does will die and the gate will still be opened. As long as the gate is closed, our people outside are trapped away from shelter and succor. They will be killed and the gate will still open. We might as well offer our surrender."

Folcwita Lapo choked out a sound, but subsided with a wary glance at Chuffta. "I disagree," he said softly enough, though his emotions raged. "King Tavlor would never surrender, Princess. Think of your father, out there battling for us. Bára cannot simply throw open her gates to the Destrye and offer her tender belly to the enemy for them to rend and tear. We must fight with all we have. What would he say upon entering Bára only to hear you already gave it away?"

"My father is dead." Oria hadn't meant to state it so baldly, but she lacked resources to cushion the words. As it was, they echoed with hollow finality in the salon, the morning sunlight pouring in with ironic cheer, a playful breeze fluttering the sheer curtains framing the windows, hung there to be drawn on hot afternoons.

"You can't mean it, Princess," whispered Priest Vico. "Queen Rhianna yet lives, I'm told, and she wouldn't if…"

"My mother felt him die and, yes, it nearly killed her, too. I don't know about my brothers and the other priests, but we must prepare for the worst news there also. Captain Ercole is correct. We've already lost. Now we must decide what to do about it. I say we offer surrender."

"There is another alternative," the folcwita said. "We can invite the Trom."

"That's hardly a viable option," Priest Vico retorted. "We might as well throw ourselves in the chasms."

"The Trom?" Oria groped for the information, her mind stupid with overload. Captain Ercole looked similarly baffled. She recalled the word vaguely from some long-ago tale. Some sort of mythical elder race?

"These teachings are sacred to the temple and those who've taken the mask," High Priestess Febe said, her featureless mask making the order resonate with hollow echoes. "I discussed this eventuality in a general sense with the folcwita of the council once news came of the devastating losses of our priestesses. The Trom are ancient guardians who can be summoned in times of extreme need. Many are the cautions against calling on them lightly, as the price they demand is high. That's all any of you need to know."

"What is the price?" If Oria hadn't squandered so much time not learning *hwil*, she wouldn't be scrambling to assimilate all of this new information. She'd be privy to the temple's sacred knowledge.

"I know some and will share that with you."

"The specifics may be shared only with those who have achieved *hwil*. The inherent power is far too dangerous otherwise." High Priestess Febe nodded, several of the priests and priestesses echoing the gesture knowingly. "Suffice to say that the price is different every time, chosen to suit the time and place. I urge we look at every option before we choose this, only at the hour of extreme need."

"Aren't we there already?" Folcwita Lapo demanded. "Look around you!"

"No," Captain Ercole said quietly. "Not if we surrender."

They all looked expectantly at Oria.

"Don't give them more opportunity to argue. You are queen for the moment."

"Princess Oria, you are inexperienced, fragile by your own admission, have no mask, and can't know what a grave step—"

Oria cut the folcwita off, happy to also shut down the frustrated rage he sent her way. "I am also the royal princess and, in the absence of anyone who outranks me, my word is law. Captain Ercole—how do we go about offering surrender?"

Folcwita threw up his hands. "Without my help, I can tell you that. I'm not eager to die."

"We need an emissary," Priestess Febe said. "Someone brave enough to approach the enemy within the walls, to make the offer to discuss terms. The folcwita is correct—the risk of death is high. They may not wish to listen. The Destrye are a bloodthirsty and barbaric people, who live to destroy. It's entirely possible they won't withdraw until they've slaughtered every one of us."

Captain Ercole nodded. "I will do it."

"No." Oria smiled at him. If they survived, she'd remember his stalwart loyalty and courage. "We need you to continue to lead the guard. I will do it. They won't kill a woman under flag of surrender."

The group exchanged uncomfortable glances. Finally, Captain Ercole said, "Princess—we believe they won't hesitate. They murdered the priestesses on the walls in cold blood."

But not her. *She wears no mask. She isn't one of them.* "They will recognize me as no priestess. I have the the best chance of speaking to them of any of us."

"It's too great a risk, Oria," Priestess Febe said in a gentle, insistent tone. "You may be no sorceress and perhaps can never take the throne, but we cannot afford to squander your potential, just in case."

Oria shook her head, pressing her lips against the regret. "Such is the fate of a figurehead." One about to collapse at that. "You have Queen Rhianna. She is strong and will recover. Perhaps my brothers yet live. It's worth the risk to my small life to perhaps get them back and save what we can of Bára and her people. To protect the magic well beneath the city, as is our sacred legacy."

A short silence settled over the room, no one mustering an argument against her logic.

"Prepare a horse for me, dress it in white tack. White is for surrender, yes, Captain?"

He nodded unhappily, but with respect in his eyes. "I'll prepare a banner for you also. Would you like some help with the words to speak, Princess?"

"Yes. Thank you. I'll don white also and be down as soon as I am able." She hesitated. "I hate to ask, but with Alva gone, I'll need someone to help me dress."

"It would be my privilege to assist, Princess," Priestess Febe said with a grave nod.

It seemed they all would be taking on new roles that day.

"I'm going with you when you ride out, Princess," her guard Renzo said from behind her. "I won't let you be completely undefended."

"Thank you." She stroked Chuffta's long tail. "But I have my own defenses, too."

"Yes. We will do this together."

She smiled at the lizard's fierce thought. And maybe felt a little fierce, too.

~ 8 ~

IN A WAY, fighting human men came as a relief. Though the guard inside the walls put up a fierce fight, fueled by the desperation of men defending their homes and families, Lonen understood it better. And though exhaustion dragged at him, that bleak despair no longer clouded his mind. This kind of battle at least made sense.

These men would not give up easily, either. Though the sun had risen to midmorning, making him entirely too hot in his furs, with no opportunity to doff them beyond shoving his cloak behind his shoulders, the Báran guard showed no sign of flagging. Lonen and his men had formed a defensive wedge inside the gates, holding it in the narrow passage against the city guards who came at them, but they hadn't yet found a way to open the massive doors. Could be magic, knowing these sorcerers.

Destrye from outside arrived to supplement their forces, finding the ropes and scaling the wall, then dropping over. But more Bárans joined the guard attacking them—common folk by their dress, mingling with the brightly uniformed guard. The Destrye who added themselves to Lonen's defense were men separated from their units, still doggedly following the primary mission of getting up and over the wall, then throwing into Lonen's fight for lack of any other objective. None had news of the rest of the army, at least not that could be transmitted between pitched skirmishes.

Much depended on the Destrye forces outside the walls, because they had arrived at a stalemate within it. It sounded like utter chaos on the other side of the doors and, if Lonen's people weren't going to make it through soon, it could turn his occupation of the gate into a long-term proposition. Something they had meager supplies to outlast. At least the narrow alcove just inside the gates made it relatively simple for a small group to defend.

They might as well implement rotations and settle in.

Sending several of the recently arrived men to push the line of defense forward, to gain them a bit of breathing room, Lonen stepped back behind them. Then he shucked the damn cloak, grateful for the immediate cooling. Too bad he couldn't discard it altogether, but he'd need it if they found themselves still outside when the cold night settled in on them again.

"Alby!" he called, waiting for his man to disengage and similarly take refuge behind the wall of fighters. Alby also immediately doffed his furs.

"What kind of monstrous land has burning days and freezing nights?" Alby panted, leaning hands on knees to take full advantage of the breather.

"I begin to understand why they came to Dru for water, brutal as this place is," Lonen agreed. "We need to set up shifts. Only enough men to hold the gate, rotate out the ones who've been fighting longest, fresher ones to the fore."

Alby eyed him wearily. "There's not a man here who *hasn't* been fighting all night."

"Best judgement then. And find me whoever's come over the wall most recently. I need to know what's going on out there."

"Yes, my prince, but—" Alby's eyes widened just as a trumpet pealed. "Holy Arill incarnate!"

Lonen spun to follow the direction of Alby's gaze, tired muscles singing into life as he lifted his axe to meet the challenge, then lowered it again in slow bemusement. A white banner rippled over a blaze of copper hair. The woman from the window. Another dream made flesh in this nightmarish and impossible place.

The clank of weapons fell from cacophonic levels to bearable. Enough for the men to hear Lonen as he called the command to desist but remain alert. He pushed to the fore, ready for a trick. If she did wield magic she might be able to obliterate them all, and he'd be responsible because he could have killed her at her window.

All for youthful idealism and a soft heart he'd long since thought shredded by the golems' claws.

Quiet spread outward, reverse ripples that stilled the fighting, bringing a welcome respite as she approached. Men continued to face off, holding their poses, ready to reengage at the slightest hint of betrayal.

She rode a pale horse, decked out in exotically smooth fabrics that caught the sun and shone with reflected light like Grienon, all in shades of cream and crystal white. The gown she wore distorted the slight frame he recalled from her silhouette, an impressive display of wide shoulders and voluminous skirts. It put him in mind of a small cat arching its spine, every hair on end to appear bigger and more ferocious. She dripped with laces and shimmering pearls, jewels from the sea he'd only read about or seen in illustrations.

That bright rain of copper hair was the only color about her, a stubborn note of resistance against her vigorous demonstration of surrender. That and the armed guard who walked at her stirrup with a determined mien, and desperate emotion in his eyes. He loved his mistress, whoever she might be.

The white dragonlet on her forearm moved, spreading its wings and blinking at him with those green eyes so brilliant they vibrated against her vivid copper hair.

Lonen tore his gaze away from the mythical creature and forced himself to focus on the woman's face, to read her intent. Though if she opened the earth beneath them, there was precious little he'd be able to do. Rationally, he should not let her approach.

But he seemed to be far beyond rational thought.

Normally her skin would be golden-kissed by the sun, he guessed, but something had made her unnaturally pale. Lines of strain rode her forehead and bracketed her mouth. She looked to be in pain, possibly injured in the fighting? But she didn't look like a fighter, all soft limbs and graceful slenderness. Young, too. Younger than he'd first thought, when he'd glimpsed the curves of her woman's body in the candlelight.

Barely more than a girl, in truth, especially to be apparently negotiating a surrender.

But then he wasn't that far into his own majority. Only last season his father had scolded him about flirting with girls more than he practiced with his axe. How things changed in a short time. Look at him—war-weary and in the position to discuss terms for the Destrye armies. War had aged him far beyond the demands of daily life. What he wouldn't give for those irresponsible days.

The woman reined up before him, her eyes narrowed. Another sign of pain.

"I believe you can understand my words?" she asked in an accented but clear use of the trade tongue.

"I do. What is your intention?"

"I will speak with the leader of these men—is that you?"

"Yes. I am Prince Lonen, son of King Archimago of the Destrye. In his absence, I may speak for him." He hoped. His father was in no position to disagree and Lonen would pass off negotiations to him soon enough.

"I am..." The woman swayed a little in the saddle and her guard cast her a concerned glance. She recovered, however, straightening her spine. "I am Princess Oria, interim ruler of Bára. I wish to negotiate a surrender."

A susurrus of surprise ran through her people. Not what they'd expected, despite the banner she carried. Probably, in their arrogance, they'd never witnessed or even contemplated such extremity. Well, they would now.

"Total surrender," he stated, his voice harsh to his own ears. "You, your people, and your city agree to complete subjugation to King Archimago of the Destrye. In exchange for your lives, you will yield everything else."

Princess Oria looked to the lizard on her arm, her lips moving ever so slightly. Talking to the animal? Perhaps they'd dressed up a crazy girl to bargain, to distract them from a sneak attack. Backing up a step he summoned Alby. "Keep out a sharp eye, in case this is simply a ruse."

"Yes, my prince."

Oria fastened her gaze on him. The same color as her hair, her eyes gleamed brighter with shrewd intelligence. "You offer death, not life, Prince Lonen. Abject slavery is no way to live. The people of Bára might as well expend all our effort and the last of our lives taking as many of you barbarians with us as we can."

Her people cheered at that and Lonen kicked himself for the misstep. No cause inflamed people faster than that of the martyr. He should know. "Who do you call barbarians?" he challenged, his men shouting in accord. "You sit in your fine city draped in jewels and send your monsters to slaughter our children. Who is barbaric in their behavior?"

She flinched—though she covered it well—more color draining from her face. Her lizard mantled, hissing at him, eyes burning with green flame, as if he'd injured the princess in some way. She soothed the creature, stroking a hand along its scales, and Lonen suppressed a shudder of revulsion. Oria's eyes flicked up to his again and a small smile twisted her lips, as if she'd somehow read his discomfort and found it amusing.

"Look around you, Prince Lonen. It is you who attack us, our people who are dying. We can debate the specifics later. For the moment it seems to me that it gets us nowhere to hurl insults and accusations at each other. The fact that we are enemies has been well established." She waved a graceful hand at the scatter of bloodied bodies on the stones, and Lonen didn't miss that she averted her gaze. "The challenge is to find common ground for setting terms to end this conflict."

"I offered grounds for your surrender," he all but growled. It rankled that she remained so calm in the face of utter destruction.

"No, Prince Lonen." She emphasized his title with the same

mild reproof his mother might have in correcting his manners. "You flung out the most extreme ultimatum, likely to challenge how easily I'd fold. I can tell you quite plainly that yes, you have cornered us to the point where we offer surrender, but we are not defeated. Given the choice between utter subjugation and death on our own terms, the people of Bára will choose death—and we have the means to take you with us." Her people broke into cheers again, raising their weapons.

She was bluffing. She had to be or her sorcerers would have hurled magical weapons at them already. Still, he had to give her credit. Young princess and interim ruler or no, she had a gift for rallying her people. Something about the way she held herself communicated her commitment to that path. She *would* rather die than give up entirely. The sudden image of her white gown bloodstained, her throat cut and those brilliant copper eyes going dim with death raked at him. He had no wish to see her dead.

He'd had plenty of death already. In fact, it suddenly felt as if he might agree to anything to be able to set down his axe, wash off the blood, and sleep for a few days. Could she be that sort of witch, to influence him that way?

"What terms do you propose then, *Princess?*" He made the question hard and sneering, so she wouldn't catch on to his weakness.

She steadied herself, raising her eyes as if reading from a mental list. Someone had prepped her. Not a fool then.

"We will agree to cease all fighting, both in and out of the city. You and your men will be granted safe passage. We will open the gates and you will inform your forces that a temporary truce is in effect. We will similarly inform our forces of such. At a date and time we agree upon, the highest ruler of each of our peoples who yet survives will meet to discuss further terms."

It sounded reasonable, though his tired brain could be missing a loophole. Or whatever she was doing to cloud his intentions and incline him towards sympathy. "The truce includes the use of magical weapons against us."

"Of course."

"Including any witchcraft you or your creature may be working on me at this moment."

She cocked her head, ever so slightly, but he noted it. He'd surprised her. "I'm working no magic on you at this moment," she said. "And Chuffta is magical by nature. He cannot cease being who he is. However, I offer my personal guarantee that so long as you do not violate the truce, magic will not be used to harm you or your people."

"And your personal guarantee is worth how much, exactly?"

A shadow flickered across her face, beyond whatever pained her, something hard behind that pretty oval face.

"I might ask the same of you, Prince Lonen, you who wears the fur of animals and is covered in the blood of my people. I am not the one with a battle-axe in my hand and hatred in my gaze."

No. If anything, grief and exhaustion clouded her eyes. She had no right to play the high moral card, however. She might be pristine in her garments, but her people's hands were bloodstained with the guilt of causing this war.

She must have read something of his anger in his face because she held up a hand, as if to ward him off, briefly closing her eyes. "I cannot offer more than my word. Either you and I trust each other enough to stop the fighting long enough to set terms or we might as well all go back to slaughtering one another."

Once again, she set him back, had him feeling chagrined. Fine then. Lonen lowered his axe, wiped it ostentatiously on the uniform of a fallen guard of her city, then sheathed it on his back and held out his bloodied hands. "You have your temporary truce, Princess. Open your gates. You, however, will go through them with me."

~ 9 ~

ORIA MANAGED TO keep her expression smooth, drawing on years of faking enough *hwil* to escape lessons. She couldn't let this Prince Lonen—if he was indeed a prince, as that seemed a lofty title for such a brutish man and people—perceive how much he frightened her. Up close the Destrye were every bit as vile, ferocious, and bloodthirsty as the worst of the illustrations she'd pored over with such sick fascination.

Even the wild dark hair that hung to his shoulders was matted with blood, indistinguishable from the black fur vest he wore, which left tanned arms as bare as his thighs. He bled from a half-dozen wounds and seemed not to notice. It must be abhorrence that transfixed her, that made it so difficult to look away from the play of corded muscle as he sheathed that enormous axe.

And now he expected her to go with him through gates she'd never passed through in her entire life.

"You likely cannot withstand it. You are already close to collapse."

"I've been 'close to collapse' for hours and hours," she muttered at Chuffta. "So far it hasn't happened."

"That doesn't mean it won't. You've been able to forestall it through strength of will, but even you will reach a breaking point—and it will be all that much worse for pushing yourself so far."

"This is not helpful advice."

She'd tried to keep her lip movements small, but Lonen frowned at her, black suspicion on his face and angry revulsion pouring off him like the stench of a decaying animal. It made her stomach lurch.

Several of his men made hand signs at her, hate and fear oozing from them.

"Cease stalling," Lonen sneered at her. "Do we have a deal or not?"

"I cannot go through the gates with you. I can stay just inside the doors and—"

He cut off her words with a chopping hand and furious glare. "Then I can only conclude you are without honor and mean to betray your word. Do your men wait outside the gates to slaughter us the moment we step out? Perhaps the earth will open beneath our feet or a wall of fire will immolate us? No deal, *Princess*."

Oria sighed. "There is no such plan, but I understand your fear."

"Fear?" He visibly bristled. "I am not afraid. I am a warrior of the Destrye, a prince and my father's son. I am simply not a fool to be tricked so easily."

Instead of retorting that she could sense his fear as palpably as the sun on her skin—and that it made her want to empty her guts except she hadn't eaten in so long that nothing sat in her stomach—she nodded in resignation. "I shall go through the gate with you."

"Oria, don't do this."

She didn't reply to Chuffta, partly because there was nothing to say and partly to forestall more of that glowering hatred from the Destrye. Not that she cared what he thought of her, but the toxic energy dragged at her fragile control more than any other variety. In a better frame of mind, she might appreciate how much she'd learned about her own capacity to endure various energies in the past hours.

"Renzo, would you help me down?" She held out a gloved hand to him, not trusting her legs to hold, especially in the heavy court gown meant for sitting and looking impressive, not walking. With a mental grumble, Chuffta climbed to her shoulder, winding his long tail around her waist.

"Princess, I can't let you walk among armed enemy soldiers with no protection," Renzo whispered, harsh and adamant, as he handed her down.

She dipped her chin at him, doing her best to ignore the way the ground squished beneath her silk slippers, moisture soaking in along with the violently fractured energy shed by the dying. Perhaps she'd reached a similar saturation point, where she simply couldn't hold any more energy, so it ran off an overflowing roof cistern in a good monsoon year. That would be helpful. Chuffta snorted his opinion of that in the recesses of her mind.

"My man comes with me, to guard my back," she said, hoping she sounded firm.

Lonen acknowledged that with a grim twist of his lips. "Mine, too, then." Another man, equally shaggy and blood-soaked stepped to his side.

"They need to form an aisle," Renzo murmured to her, "and lay down their weapons."

Lonen overheard the quiet words. "Not happening."

"You can't ask Princess Oria to walk a gauntlet of the enemy," Renzo snarled at him.

"If they wanted to cut me down, they could have already," Oria said in a mild tone, letting Lonen overhear that, too. She held his gaze with her chin high. "My people are largely dead, our defenses falling around us. One more death would hardly matter." She'd surprised him with that, enough to abate his fury, the relief like a cool evening breeze after a sweltering afternoon. "I shall walk your gauntlet."

He eyed her, gaze slipping to Chuffta. "Leave the dragonlet behind."

A laugh escaped her, shocking and raw. Mostly at her Familiar's indignant and inarticulate reaction. She shook her head. "Not happening." It gave her some satisfaction, too, to throw his words back at him.

They locked eyes and wills. His, densely fringed with black lashes, were a dark gray, like the granite their sister-city to the north, Arvda, sent in trade. Surprisingly lovely, they would have made him look feminine but for the angry line of a recent scar that dragged from his forehead, skipped his eye, and continued down his cheek. Nearly missed losing that eye to whatever had sliced at him, something thin and sharp by the look of it.

"Every moment we waste allows more of both our people to die," she said softly. "Chuffta remains with me or I don't go. Give your men the order to let us through and I'll give the order to open the gates."

With a grim nod, he turned to face the gate, standing on the side of her away from her Familiar.

"Dragonlet," Chuffta fumed.

She ignored him, knowing perfectly well that he was attempting to distract her from the trial of stepping beyond the boundary walls of her world. She didn't understand how it worked—yet another temple secret that would be shared only if she fully realized *hwil*—but something about them buffered the wild energy of the larger world just as her tower did. No sensitive who hadn't taken the mask even came close to the gate, much less set foot outside.

All she had to do was get through the next minutes and remain conscious long enough to get the message through to stop the fighting and get word to her brothers. Hopefully at that point at least one of them lived and could take over.

"And plan your funeral," came Chuffta's sour thought. His worry came through clearly or she might have been annoyed.

"Don't put attention on a result you do not want," she told him. Then, before Lonen could say anything or make that sign against evil, she called out in a louder voice, "Open the gate!"

Lucky for them that Priest Vico had enough magical ability to do that much, with Priestess Febe feeding him from her still vast reserves. It seemed a grave miscalculation to Oria to have left the city without sufficient sorcerers to even open the gates again. Why had the king committed *all* of the most powerful to the battle? It didn't bear thinking of at the moment, but if she survived and didn't end up a Destrye prisoner, she resolved to learn more about strategy.

She'd wasted a lot of time pretending to meditate and chasing elusive *hwil* that she could have spent studying useful knowledge.

Magic streamed in a thin swirl past her, then burgeoned, touching the massive doors. Without a sound, they slowly opened, admitting the roar of battle that had been muffled before.

Frenetic, fragmented energy slammed into her like a physical assault.

Chuffta loomed large in her mind, soaking up what he could, but she swayed on her feet. A hand grasped her wrist, where the lace cuff bared her skin, burning with raw, undisciplined energy, scorching her unmercifully.

"Princess Oria?" Lonen peered at her, much too close.

"Don't touch me." The request came out ragged, nearly begging him, and he snatched his hand away, eyes firing with renewed offense and fury. She turned away from it, feeling top-heavy and bottom-light, a festival cake piled too high. The doors opened enough to show a raft of Bára guard just outside. They turned, swords and spears ready.

"Stand down," Oria commanded, fastening her gaze on one she recognized. "Lieutenant. We have a temporary truce."

The men sagged, their exhaustion and despair swamping into a kind of dreadful relief that blackened the edges of her vision.

"Bring my brothers—or the highest in command who's still alive. I've offered surrender in exchange for cessation of hostilities." She got all of Captain Ercole's words out, though it seemed she heard them from a vast distance, down a long tunnel. "Someone needs to take over negotiations."

She pushed the final instruction through the onrushing black. Then succumbed as it crashed over her and washed her away, Chuffta's mind-voice a wail in the distance.

"Oria!"

LONEN CAUGHT ORIA as she fell, an instinctive grab he would have stifled if he'd had a beat more to recall her hissed directive not to sully her with his touch—and to consider her reptilian defender. As it was, she passed out so precipitously, as if that last word uttered took her final breath, that he nearly didn't catch her before she hit the paved road. The dragon creature took wing.

Bemused to find himself holding her as he would a Destrye bride, but dressed in white, he kept one wary eye on the man Oria had called lieutenant and the other on the dragonlet circling his head. He'd throw the princess to the ground if either of them attacked. He owed her nothing, not even this courtesy. Except…

Except she'd said she couldn't exit the gate and he'd insisted on it. Perhaps it hadn't been a trick or missish timidity. What did he know of magic? He'd thought of her as a puffed-up, spitting cat before—holding her this way now, she seemed like one soaked that turned out to be skin and bones beneath a wealth of fur. She weighed practically nothing and most of that had to be the gown.

He nearly did drop her when talons sank into his shoulder. "Gah!"

Bright green dragon eyes stared fiercely into his. "I'm not hurting her, curse you, beast," he hissed. Amazingly the thing seemed to understand because the wicked points retracted some. Not entirely, but less painful. The thing's long tail curled up like a snake about to strike, then wrapped around the bare skin on Oria's forearm, a slight strip of creamy flesh, slightly darker than her glove and sleeve.

A moan sighed out of her, a faint hint of color returning to her death-pallid cheeks.

"Let me take her from you," her guard said. "She'll do better inside the gates."

Lonen hesitated. They could cut him down without her, but a

Destrye didn't use a woman as a shield. No more than he already had, to his chagrin. Hopefully her faint didn't indicate she carried a disease.

He held her out and the dragonlet hopped from his shoulder onto Oria's chest, folding its legs and wings to curl up there, gaze intent on her face, evincing an unnatural intelligence and affection that made his skin crawl. As her man took the princess away, Lonen noted how her formerly pristine gown bore blood smudges in the shape of his arms and hands, the shadow of his grip like an injury. The crimson, both bright and drying, on her white dress looked like a bad omen.

But for her people or his, he didn't know.

Possibly both.

~ 10 ~

TO LONEN'S VAST relief, his father and Ion soon arrived at the gates, the Báran guard parting for their passage with hard faces but lowered weapons. Much as Lonen wanted to embrace them and pound their backs in the great good consolation at seeing them still alive, he held himself back. And told himself Arnon must be out commanding the Destrye forces, in case of treachery, not fallen in battle.

Before they could converse, another two men arrived wearing the crimson robes and eyeless golden masks of Báran sorcerers.

They ranged into sides. King Archimago and Ion flanking Lonen, and the two sorcerers standing shoulder to shoulder across from them. How could they see to walk in those masks? A silence stretched between them, neither side willing to concede by speaking first.

"Where is the Princess Oria?" one of them finally demanded, the metal mask making his voice echo like the ghosts of campfire tales. "We were told she was here, outside the gates, but she clearly isn't. We won't fall for the tricks of barbarian scum."

Lonen clamped down on a childish quiver of fear. It was only a man wearing a golden mask, nothing supernatural. And one with his magic fled, bled out undefended during the night on the high walls above. Anger surged through Lonen that this man hid behind a mask, flinging insults when they'd been the ones who'd forced Lonen to commit the unthinkable, the murder of women.

King Archimago turned to him. "I understand a princess of this city gave formal surrender and we are to negotiate terms."

Lonen nodded. "Yes, my king. Princess Oria approached us and offered peace if we would allow her people outside the walls to return within, with no further fighting or fatalities."

"Oria?" The other, slighter masked man sounded incredulous and young enough that his voice cracked a little. "Our sister outside the gates, offering terms? I find this so unlikely as to be impossible."

Lonen bristled at the dismissal in the boy's tone. He hadn't much cared for the witch, but she'd met him with bare-faced bravery. "She recognized the gravity of your defeat and conducted herself with honor in an attempt to salvage what she could—including your cowardly lives. She accompanied me here, gave the order, and then was...overcome by some sort of fainting spell. Her man carried her back within. All here witnessed it. You can ask your own guard."

"It's true, Prince Nat," the lieutenant confirmed, addressing the older man. "The Princess Oria, in the flesh, rode to the gate under banner of surrender. She asked that you take over negotiations." The words he didn't speak, of what occurred after, rang with quiet significance.

The featureless mask seemed to glare, the man's bony shoulders stark lines beneath the draping robe. Not a lot of muscle there. Not a warrior then, not like the Destrye. No wonder they relied upon magic and the golems to fight their battles.

"We do not honor the promises of a girl made under duress," he said. "There shall be no surrender."

The younger sorcerer started, glancing at him.

King Archimago, surprising them all, laughed, the harsh, hoarse sound that rattled in his voice ever since Nolan was lost. "And I do not negotiate with a mere prince. Where is your king?"

They both lost their bluster at that, the formerly brash boy turning his masked face down in apparent grief, the one called Nat going slack before regaining himself. "I am the king now. As my father's heir, I step into his place."

A murmur ran through the people, a sound of further defeat, and—surprise? Another moment that should have been triumphant and fell far short of the mark.

"Very well," King Archimago said. "You have two choices, boy. You can honor the terms of the surrender offered by the Princess Oria or we can finish the job of killing you, your family, your leaders, and any of your people still wishing to fight, until we reach a true surrender. I have no wish to destroy your people, but I will if you force my hand."

"No wish to destroy!" the younger man burst out. "*You* attacked *us*—unprovoked!"

Oria had said much the same thing. A strange defense, this protestation of innocence. One that the heir did not echo, however.

"You think you can defeat us so easily," Prince Nat snarled.

"Look about you! We *have* defeated you," Lonen put in, surprising his father and Ion, judging by their sidelong glances. But he'd had enough of it all. Had since the dark hours of the harrowing night. "Your sister nearly killed herself to make this truce. I don't pretend to understand your ways, but she and I agreed to terms at some cost to her. Would you throw that away?"

"She had no right." By the sound, the young Prince Nat spoke through gritted teeth. "It's not my fault the idiot left her tower."

"Your family politics are nothing to us." King Archimago gave Lonen a quelling stare. "Choose, heir to nothing. You agree to Princess Oria's surrender of your city and we negotiate terms, or we recommence battle. Before you answer, you may have a moment to speak to your lieutenant. So your understanding may rule, rather than your pride."

Leaving the enemy prince no choice, King Archimago turned his back. A deliberate insult that the Destrye, at least, would understand. Their forces had—against all probability—seized victory over the dreaded golems and sorcerers, and they deserved to know it.

"Lonen." His father beckoned Ion and him closer, for a low-voiced conversation. "What is your relationship to this Oria?"

The question took him by surprise. "None at all. I met her not an hour ago when she rode up to offer surrender." He left out the previous sighting as not relevant.

Ion gave him a strange look. "Why are you defending this woman then?"

The king dipped his chin at Ion, confirming the question.

The sun beat way too hot on Lonen's scalp, the blood drying and drawing the skin tight, an irritating harmony behind the growing chorus of aches and pains from various wounds. "I found her bravery in the face of defeat admirable. And…there's been enough death this night and day. But for a vain princelet blinded by his pride, we could be done."

His father clapped his shoulder, squeezing. "You did well, my son, breaching the wall. I won't ask what you had to do, for I see the shadow of it in your eyes, but we know you won this battle for us. Much as I do not wish to censure you in this moment, I must caution you to harden your heart against this princess."

Lonen gaped at him, scrambling for a reply.

"It happens," his father said in a softer voice. "Some part of you thinks that by saving her you can expiate this guilt you carry for whatever dark deeds haunt you. But she is the enemy as much as any of them. When we are done here, you can make sacrifice to Arill. The goddess will lighten your heart."

"My king, I don't—"

Ion, who'd been leaning in, trying to overhear, broke in. "He means don't let a bit of foreign pussy make you think with the little head instead of the big one." Ion grinned at him. "There. That manned you up again."

"That is not what—"

"We have a decision," Prince Nat called out, sounding considerably less arrogant. "If you will, King Archimago."

They returned to face the two sorcerers. "We agree to the surrender," Prince Nat said, defeat and sullen anger manifest in his voice and shrouded form. "What now?"

"Now, I will send men to occupy the city," King Archimago said, "to ensure continuing peace. My son, Prince Ion, will accompany them and remain in charge of the Destrye forces within the walls. Your men may reenter the city and see to your dead and injured. We shall do the same, camped outside the walls. We shall agree to meet just after dawn tomorrow morning, to discuss terms going forward. The least hint of hostility toward my men will result in immediate cessation of the truce. We'll finish what we started and there will be no further pause for mercy. Tell me you understand."

They didn't like it, the desire to protest clear in the tense lines of the princes' shoulders. Lonen himself barely squashed the urge to speak against Ion's assignment to command the occupying warriors. After all, he'd been the one to establish diplomatic relations with…with Oria. *Don't let a bit of foreign pussy make you think with the little head instead of the big one.* Ion was wrong on that. Oria might be exotically fascinating, but the strange witch held no attraction for him. Not like his lovely Natly. He simply wished to—what? Be assured of the princess's well-being, perhaps.

As if by making certain that he hadn't harmed her irreparably, he could wash the blood of all the others from his hands.

His father, always wise, was right. He needed to purify himself and make sacrifice to the goddess to begin to shed this terrible guilt. The sooner away from this place the better. Somewhere out there, even at that moment, Natly and his real life, the normal peaceful one, moved step by step away from him.

Perhaps he could take solace in that aspect of victory. They'd nearly reached the end of their consuming quest to free the Destrye of the golem incursions. With this crushing defeat of the enemy, they could return to the fertile forests and meadows of home. The place he'd marched away from, certain he'd never see it again. Suddenly, it seemed he might.

The prospect gave him unexpected hope. Enough to banish the unfortunate Oria from his thoughts and firmly replace her visage with Natly's. As was good and right.

~ 11 ~

THOUGH A BATH wasn't in the stars for him in this sunbaked, goddess-forsaken land, Lonen scrubbed away the worst of the bloodstains with sand, while a medic cleansed his wounds with alcohol—a fiery purging he welcomed as the beginning of his penance. He bore more injuries than he'd thought, but far fewer than he deserved, having slaughtered so many.

The wide, wounded eyes of the first woman he'd murdered hovered in his mind, overlapping with that long-ago doe, then overwhelmed with Oria's grief-dark copper ones.

But he didn't speak of it. Not to Alby. Certainly not to his father. Nor to Arnon, who had indeed survived the gruesome battle. Odd that he didn't want to say anything to Arnon about meeting Oria, even when he shared a flask of hogshorn with his younger brother. Arnon had listened many times to Lonen's trials with the elusive Natly, always offering a patient ear and decent advice when asked. Though this…encounter—really only the one, because the semi-vision didn't count—had nothing to do with pining as he'd done for Natly.

No, it was as his father had said—a product of guilt and post-battle nightmares. It would remain between him and Arill, all part and parcel of the peculiar shameful guilt he carried, hopefully to be relieved in time. But even after he shoved food into his aching belly and toppled onto his sleeping furs, naked but for his many bandages, Oria's eyes haunted his dreams.

IN FRESH GARMENTS, his hair oiled and tied back, if not particularly clean, Lonen, with Arnon and their father, made the trek up the road to the city gates at dawn. Destrye guarded them now, saluting and then bowing—acknowledging their commander and king—following with broad, even jubilant, grins. Lonen wasn't the only one who hadn't expected this day to come.

Within the city walls, a far more morose atmosphere prevailed. Ion, who met them at the gates to escort them in, had of course stationed Destrye throughout Bára, which looked desolate otherwise. Most of the population must be keeping indoors. Unless more had perished than he'd thought.

Occasional denizens observed their passage, the lightly clad and slender people, mostly fair-haired, a clear contrast to the occupying Destrye. With the leisure and daylight to pay more attention to the city itself, Lonen found it surprisingly attractive for a place constructed of so much stone.

Like the high rocks behind, the towers of the city speared up in rounded shades of gold, rose, and gentle browns. As if the people had taken the harsh colors of the desert and blended them into something gentler, more forgiving. Window openings laced every building, often giving glimpses of blue sky beyond through yet more windows. White net fluttered in many of them—some drawn across completely, some were tied to the sides. Open-air balconies and terraces held all manner of plants and trees, with flowering vines draping over the edges. Between the towers, arched stone bridges traversed dizzying drops, both spectacular and fearsome. And yet other paths that bordered the canyons were studded with benches, presumably for people to sit and enjoy the view.

Combined, it all gave an impression of delicacy, verdancy, and peace at odds with the forbidding city walls, deep chasms, and dry salt plain that encircled it.

They'd mentioned a tower in reference to Oria, as if it were a specific and special one. Which seemed unlikely, given that the lion's share of buildings in Bára could be called towers. Could it be the tallest among them? It wasn't so easy to judge relative height from below—rather like trying to pick out the tallest tree from the forest floor—but one seemed to tower above the others, fat in circumference, with a profusion of balconies and what must be an extensive garden at the very top.

"Looking for someone?" Ion's tone was snide, his expression forbidding.

"Observing the city," Lonen replied, as if the question had been sincerely asked, not barbed with innuendo. "It's lovelier than I expected."

"For the home of rapacious monsters? I suppose it is."

"Is this the behavior of my heirs?" King Archimago asked in a mild tone. "Now that the enemy has fallen, must you fight amongst yourselves?"

"I don't even know what they're poking at each other about," Arnon protested.

Ion didn't comment, so neither did Lonen. Odd how, with the battle crisis over, they so quickly reverted to old roles and arguments. Except that Nolan should have been there to act as peacemaker, cracking jokes instead of lying broken at the bottom of one of those dramatic chasms. The thought brought grim reality crashing back. They might be walking through a city that could have been drawn from storybooks, but they traveled over the corpses of too many people.

As if they felt it, too, the other men fell silent until they crossed one more bridge over the deepest chasm of all and entered a complex of towers near the one Lonen had picked as the tallest. Tracing the line of the surrounding outer wall with his eye, he reconstructed the encounter from the fragmented images of that long night of assault, deciding that it could indeed be the spot where he'd stood and seen Oria in the window.

"Is this the palace then?" he asked Ion, figuring it for a reasonable question.

Ion nodded brusquely. "So far as we can discern. We haven't been sitting around chatting. But apparently this is where their council meets and makes decisions. Prince Nat sent me a message—a surprisingly deferential one—that this would be the logical site for negotiations, as they had the room for plenty at the table and for as many guards as each side felt comfortable bringing. He offered to accede to our wishes for an alternate meeting site, but as I had no better to offer..." He glanced at the king.

"We shall see when we arrive, but I imagine I would have chosen the same." King Archimago put a hand on Ion's shoulder, gripping it much as he had Lonen's the day before. "I'm proud of you for how you've handled this occupation. Of all three of you. And of—" He broke off, not naming his fourth, lost son.

The council chamber occupied a vast space indeed, with many windows, a cross-ventilating breeze blowing between them, fluttering the pale curtains made of sheer, shimmering cloth reminiscent of Oria's white gown. Destrye guard ringed one side, the Bára guard on the other.

The two priests, masked and in their crimson robes, sat at one end of a long table, a dozen other Bárans, mostly elderly, ranged along the sides near them. Though women made up part of Prince Nat's council, some of them in golden masks and others not, none had Oria's distinctive hair. King Archimago took the seat at the far end, Lonen and his brothers taking the chairs to the sides.

Just as well. It would be a long day, hammering out a lasting agreement. Not that Oria's presence would have distracted him, but the less trouble from that direction, the better.

SHE FLOATED THROUGH a gray mist.

Amorphous, numbing, it calmed her for an endless time. She felt nothing, sensed nothing, was nothing.

Restful nothing.

But after a while, as she became aware of the passage of time, the nothing began to bother her. The dragging muck of sleep went from comforting to cloying to confining, keeping her wrapped tightly like the silkworms succumbing to their lovely cocoons. Only she would not emerge into a night-winged moth. She'd remain trapped in this place, blind, deaf, without touch or scent of anything. She struggled against it, wanting to scream and finding that, too, entirely missing.

Was this death? She was alone, bereft of the world.

"Oria. Oria, you're alive and I'm with you. I'll never leave you."

She didn't know who that was or who Oria was, but she clung to the calming voice, as if it were shelter in a sandstorm.

"Yes. I will shelter you. Rest. Heal."

No longer so afraid and alone, she allowed the sleep to rise up, grateful for the black to replace all that clinging gray.

"...WHAT TO EXPECT..."

"...never before..."

The disjointed phrases cottoned through her mind. At first the words held no more meaning than the soughing of an afternoon breeze just before sunset stilled it. After a while, they began to retain their shape, sticking longer, with edges that signified something. "...no more mind than an infant's..."

Hot rose light beat through her eyelids, burning away the last of the mist that had obliterated her senses, and she registered a breeze on her skin, the scent of day-blooming lilies.

"...prepare yourself for the worst."

"I've already lived through the worst," a voice she knew well cut through. She reached out for it, blindly seeking.

"Mama?" No sound came through her stiffened, dry lips, which cracked, bringing bright pain that she actually welcomed. She *was* alive. She fought to make that final escape. There were things living people did—opening their eyes, moving their limbs.

"She's here, Oria. We're both here. Try harder."

"Mama!" she called, some part of her remembering that time when she'd been unable to feed herself, calling for this woman who—oh yes. There. That cool hand on her forehead, then slipping behind her neck, dribbling cool, sweet water between her lips.

"I'm here, baby girl. Wake up now."

"It may not be wise to—"

"I'll care for my daughter. Leave us now."

The room went blessedly silent, of both sound and a certain anxiety that had strummed unpleasantly. A smoothly scaled tail wrapped around her wrist, caressing, affection flowing in as restorative as the water in her parched throat.

"Swallow the water, Oria."

"Can you open your eyes? Come on now. Wake up for me. Chuffta is here."

It took a monumental effort. One she had to carefully think through, finding the old nerve pathways, cranking at them like a servant girl working a well pulley. That helped, to imagine the stiff wheel turning, the rope pulling, tugging at her lashes painfully.

"Wait a moment, baby. Hold still." The hands went away and Oria whined an inarticulate protest. They came back, a cool cloth on her eyelids. So much better. "There. Try again."

They moved more easily this time. The light hurt, but she squinched against it, seeking her mother's face—unmasked and lined with worry. "Mama."

"Yes." The familiar brown eyes filled with tears and spilled over, running down her face, choking out her next words.

"Why are you crying? Don't cry." The words only came out partially, mostly in a voiceless whisper. She tried to raise a hand to wipe the tears away, but couldn't.

"She is happy, Oria. Grateful to have you back with us. As am I."

"What happened to me?" The words came better this time, but with effort. She managed to move her eyes, though not her head, to spot Chuffta on her pillow, green gaze intent on her face.

"It may be best for the moment not to try to remember too much. Just know you've been ill and must recover. Slow and steady wins this race."

She didn't like it, the not knowing. But it also made her head hurt to think about it, a much less welcome pain.

"Swallow a little more water. You need to drink," her mother urged.

Oria obeyed because it was the easier choice, and because she suddenly discovered a raging thirst, as if her belly, too, had only just awakened.

"Not too much. Not at first." Her mother set the cup aside, then wiped her tears away. "Sleep if you can and I'll wake you in a bit for more."

Succumbing to the suggestion—or, more truly, giving up fighting the onrushing darkness, she did. "Love you," she muttered before she went under.

"We love you, too, Oria. We're with you."

She sank again, with her mother's hand stroking her forehead and Chuffta's firm presence in her mind, tail wrapped around her wrist.

And a puzzling fragmented memory of granite eyes searching hers, asking some question she couldn't answer, before strong arms swept her up, holding her close against his heart.

~ 12 ~

THEY'D BEEN TOO many days at the negotiations. Stalled, in the most galling way.

The young king, hastily ratified by his people the evening of Bára's crushing defeat, so they'd been told, proved cagey and stubborn in his arguments. Far too much so for the ruler of a conquered people. To Lonen's ongoing puzzlement, his father seemed to be losing ground in this war of words. Certainly King Archimago had never had to debate in these subtly insidious ways before. Among the Destrye, his word was law—none argued with him, on the battlefield or off.

These sorcerers and priestesses, however, with their expressionless masks and endless picking apart of details—they wielded arguments as the deftest warrior would a set of sharp blades.

And the Destrye king…well, he wasn't the man he'd been when they set out on this quest, much as Lonen hated to acknowledge that much, even in his darkest thoughts.

He'd learned a great deal in the past few days that would serve him well should he ever have to take the crown, an unlikely event with Ion heir before him. Still, he'd never expected Nolan to perish and leave him one step closer to the burden of rule, so he filed the lessons away as a precaution, trying not to fret over how his father seemed to fade with every passing hour under the desert heat. Beyond that, the disquiet of wondering what had happened to Oria nibbled at his peace of mind like the biting insects that came in the open windows in late afternoon, until someone thought to summon servants to draw the sheer curtains. He needed to step away from it all, clear away the nattering worries. So when they broke for a midday meal, Lonen went walking instead.

He followed the path along the gorge that separated the palace complex from the other parts of the city. Clearly some long-ago ancestor had set it up so the bridges could be quickly destroyed in case an enemy breached the walls. If the people supporting Oria the day Bára fell had been smart, they would have advised her to do just that, and to remain in her tower. Maybe they had and she'd ignored the advice—she seemed stubborn enough for it, even on brief acquaintance.

It's not my fault the idiot left her tower.

Indulging himself, he squinted up at the structure, reasonably certain she must be up there somewhere. He hadn't seen her at all since the surrender—and her subsequent collapse—and he couldn't exactly ask after her health. Giving it up, he resumed his walk, nodding at the Destrye guards stationed here and there.

The Bárans had begun to emerge more with every passing day, slowly taking up the business of daily life again. Another strangeness, seeing the Destrye warriors and their enemy interact over such things as putting the city back to order, or even bartering for pretty objects to take home to their women. Lonen should think about getting something for Natly. Maybe some of that fine fabric that gleamed with its own light, for a gown or scarf.

Hopefully they'd hear from the Destrye women soon. Fast-riding messengers had gone out but had yet to return with word.

A few young Báran women passed him, bare faces tanned and hair streaked with sun, though none with Oria's distinctive copper. Nor did anyone he'd seen have a pet dragonlet like hers. They nodded to him cautiously, one eyeing him with more boldness, then fell to whispering among themselves after he'd passed. King Archimago and Ion both had been firm in orders that the women of Bára were not to be touched. They'd leave no Destrye blood behind to be fouled with their witchcraft and magic.

To his surprise, he encountered Ion approaching on the path from the other direction. His brother lifted a hand in greeting, as if they hadn't parted less than an hour before. "I see we have the same idea."

Lonen nodded ruefully at an elderly priestess he knew from their meetings by her tower of platinum braids, and who sat on a nearby bench, unmoving, nearly a statue in her stillness, only the midday breeze stirring her crimson garments, sun reflecting painfully off the golden mask. "I can't bear to sit any longer. How do they stand it? I feel as if I've been moldering in my grave."

Ion cocked his head in the other direction, indicating they should move away. After they made it a short distance down the walk, he said, "I'm concerned about how long this is taking."

Lonen blew out a short breath—both relieved that he wasn't the only one to be disturbed and bothered that Ion felt the same. "Do you think they could be deliberately stalling, that they've somehow called for aid that could be on the way?"

"It's what I would do." Ion had his hands clasped behind his back, brow furrowed. "We know next to nothing about these people. The Destrye have—or had—allies. Why wouldn't the Bárans?"

"That's my take, too." Lonen hesitated before broaching the difficult question. "Then why is Father allowing them to drag their feet?"

Ion flashed him a dark scowl and Lonen braced himself for his older brother's withering scorn. He should have known better than to question the king aloud. But Ion's forbidding expression crumpled and he rubbed his brow with a sigh. "I don't know," he finally admitted. "The same is bothering me. Arnon has noted it, too, and pulled me aside last night with the same concerns."

At least they all three agreed. "Do you think," Lonen ventured, tentative in this new territory of being aligned against their father, "that they could be working some form of mind magic against him? Something subtler than fireballs, thunder, and earthquakes, but just as powerful?" If they could do such things, it might explain the way thoughts of Oria clung to him.

Ion's dark brows rose as he considered that. "It hadn't occurred to me. Arnon and I thought to blame it on Nolan's death. That grief is still fresh."

"It is for all of us," Lonen pointed out, taking a moment to choke back the black emotion that wanted to rise at the very mention of his brother's demise.

"Harder, though, for a parent to lose a child, a king to lose an heir, than for us to lose a brother."

Was it? Ion had sons out there with his wife on the Trail of New Hope, so perhaps he understood something Lonen did not. In many ways, he had a hard time coming to grips with Nolan being truly gone. For long spaces, he could forget about it. Until moments like this one.

"Perhaps so." He hesitated, then voiced one of the ideas he'd been mulling. "We've had no opportunity to say the prayers to Arill to guide Nolan's feet to the Hall of Warriors. With his body lost in battle, it could be that his shade wanders until we do. It's a plaguing thought."

"Do you—" Ion cleared his throat, gazing into the chasm. "Has it occurred to you that he might not be dead? He could be down in something like that, hoping we'll come find him. He could be hurt and…"

Lonen put a hand on his brother's shoulder when Ion's voice choked off, his own throat going tighter. "Yes," he said. "In dreams, I see him, falling, lying there broken, calling to me." A pall settled over them. Lonen had thought he'd be the only one to be plagued with such morose phantasms. Ironic that he and Ion should bond over this, of all things.

"Remember when he was seven?"

"And fell in the river? Yes." Lonen shook his head, a smile alleviating the strangling grief. "And you jumped in after him, fully dressed, sword in hand."

Ion laughed, which was better. "Father nearly skinned me alive for that one—for ruining good boots, nearly dropping my sword, and because I was supposed to be watching all of you, not flirting with that girl. I can't even remember her name." He'd gone back to sounding bleak.

"Nolan wasn't a little kid, Ion. He was a grown man in charge of a battalion of Destrye who fought bravely to save our people—including you and me and that girl whose name you can't remember. It's not your job to watch us anymore." A strange place to be, offering such comfort to his eldest brother.

From Ion's sidelong glance, he thought so, too. "That's not how it feels. But enough of this. Tell me why you think they're working some form of mind magic on the king."

He absolutely would not mention Oria. "I don't have any good reason. More…a feeling?" Lonen waited for his brother's disdain, but Ion said nothing, only listened. "I've told you how it was, killing the priestesses who stood on the walls that night."

"Yes." Ion's voice and face were grave. None of them liked that they'd won the battle on the broken bodies of women.

"It seemed—this will sound strange."

"Can any of this be stranger than it already is? We've already witnessed the unthinkable. Stop dithering and tell me straight."

Lonen had to smile. Ion, back to being himself with his didactic ways, but also a changed man, wanting to hear the strange thoughts of his fanciful younger brother. Once Ion would have rubbed his face in the dirt for saying such foolish things. In a sudden glimpse, Lonen could see his brother as king after their father's death. Something that had once been unthinkable. Now it seemed not only possible, but that Ion might make a good king.

"When I killed the first one, not knowing she was a woman, I did so because she faced out toward the battle. At least, I told myself it was only that. But—thinking back to that night, I must have felt something else at work. Something about those masks and… Have you noticed the way they seem to glow sometimes?"

"A reflection of the light," Ion offered, but not dismissively, simply as an alternate argument.

"I thought that, too. Metal reflects and the gold is bright, highly polished." Oria hadn't worn a mask. So far every man and woman of higher rank who'd spoken in the negotiations did, while the bare-faced denizens of the city all seemed to be of lower status. But everyone who spoke of her freely acknowledged her as a princess. As if of their own will and not his, his eyes strayed to her high tower. He wrenched them away before Ion noticed. "It makes me wonder is all. Why do they wear them? It seems they shouldn't be able to see, but they behave as if they can."

"It's cursed unsettling, I can tell you that." Ion pursed his lips behind his thick beard. "He hasn't said, but it could be that Father meant to leave them some measure of dignity by allowing them to retain the masks."

"Or because none of us really wants to see what lies behind them," Lonen said, before he rethought the jest.

Ion nodded to that, however. "That could be part of their trickery. Like the Xyrts who paint their faces blue to frighten their enemies."

"It makes it more difficult," Lonen said slowly, thinking it through, "to guess at their intentions when we can't see their faces. I'm not adept at negotiations, but that bothers me."

"None of us are skilled in this arena, which is why we shouldn't have accepted their surrender and simply continued the battle until they could no longer fight."

Lonen bristled at the implicity accusation. "I know you think you wouldn't have done the same in my shoes, but—"

"But nothing," Ion cut in, more the brother Lonen knew well. "You were swayed by a pretty face and a sorrowful smile."

"What makes you think Princess Oria is pretty? You've never laid eyes on her and I certainly never said so."

"You didn't have to. It was writ all over your face when you defended her actions—to her own people, I might add. Besides, plenty of Destrye witnessed your conversation with her and described how you saved her from falling, all noble and full of concern. You have a soft spot for females and always have. Didn't you consider how it might look, that you showed such care for one of the enemy?"

Lonen clenched his teeth, keeping his response measured. "No, I didn't think at all. She fainted and I caught her. Any man would have done the same."

"Not any man. I wouldn't have. But that's always been your problem, Lonen. You follow your heart, not your head."

"The big one or the little one?" Lonen snapped back, tired of this old argument.

Ion clapped a hand over the back of Lonen's skull, hard enough to make his ears ring. "The one is empty and the other attached to your heart. See if you can figure it out. Still," he said, while Lonen fumed, "your points are well taken and I will bring them to Father's attention. We should demand they remove the masks or we will rejoin the fight and see who wins."

"And if they don't agree?"

"They will, because even their proud and stubborn boy king will see that they cannot prevail against us."

"Unless they have aid coming," Lonen replied, full of the foreboding that had plagued him these past days. Ion called King Nat a boy, but he was their age. He might seem younger and softer, not being a warrior, but that did not make him foolish or without weapons of his own.

"All the more reason to insist on this measure immediately."

~ 13 ~

ORIA LIVED IN a world of alternations. Asleep. Awake. Dark. Light. Drink. Sleep. Eat. Drink.

Sleep.

Sleep.

Sleep.

Every time she awoke, her mother and Chuffta were there, ready to offer her a glass of cooled water and affectionate reassurances. A bouquet of lilies sat in a vase on the table beside the bed, wafting a sweet, thick fragrance. She'd gaze at their vivid colors, feeling as if she'd forgotten something, but she always fell asleep again before she could determine what it was.

Eventually she stayed awake long enough to string several thoughts together. Her mother attended her constantly. No one else did. Where was Alva?

"Don't worry over these things. You have one concern—to rest and heal."

"I've been doing that."

"You've been doing what, baby?" her mother murmured. "Have some broth."

"I don't want broth. I want to know what happened. Am I sick?"

"Yes." Her mother looked away as she said it. "You've been very ill and you must take care not to relapse. You must rest and heal."

"That's what I just told Chuffta—I've been doing that."

"He's wise and you should follow his advice. That's why you have him. This is not something to be quickly overcome. Recovery follows its own calendar."

Oria struggled to sit up, to look around, not sure who or what she sought or why her body responded so sluggishly. Then realized her mother was holding her down by the shoulders, the slight pressure more than Oria could muster the strength to resist.

"Why am I so weak?"

"Because you've been ill," her mother replied with strained patience. "It's not good for you to become agitated. Sleep. Rest. Heal."

The familiar calm of her mother's soothing energy spun through her. Reminding her of something. Her mother, face creased with devastation, unresponsive. In a chair, overlooking the wall, where a Destrye warrior covered in blood, carrying an axe, paused in a pool of light, just as in those lurid paintings that had aroused the fascination of adolescent self. So vividly real and—

With a choked gasp, her eyes flew open. "The Destrye!"

Her mother winced in regret. "Don't think about it. It's done. You must—"

Harsh reality cut through. "Father is dead. What of Ben, Nat, and Yar?"

The queen passed a shaking hand over her face. "Nat and Yar are fine."

Oh no, not Ben. Not her gentle brother, who'd never once teased about her lack of *hwil*. Who'd taken his mask after his little brother and never showed bitterness or any kind of grudge. She'd secretly hoped Ben would even things out by finding his ideal wife first. Now he never would. She lay back, letting the deep and formless grief move through her. Something else. "And the Destrye?"

"Try not to—"

This time Oria managed to struggle up to a sitting position, mostly because her mother seemed unable to resist further. Oria's body protested, stiff as a corpse and weak as a newborn's. What in Sgatha had happened to her?

"I have to know." The memories came back, jagged, sharp-edged scenes, and her head began to throb. Descending from her tower. Her mother unconscious. Enemy within the walls. Her brothers without. Meeting with what remained of the council.

The granite-eyed Destrye prince. Something in her shied away from thinking past him.

"You were overcome," she said, touching her mother's arm. "Are you all right?"

"I will live. Thanks to you." Something in her tone made it sound more like an accusation, but only sorrow showed in her mother's face. "Though I shall always regret that I failed you in your hour of need."

"Failed me?"

"I'm so, so sorry, my baby girl." With a broken sound, she stood. "I need a moment."

Oria watched her mother, the unflappably *hwil*, ever cool and composed queen and priestess, as she hastened out to the terrace, a hand over her mouth to muffle the sobs that nevertheless blew back in on the breeze. Chuffta remained on the light blanket beside her, the tip of his tail lightly clasping her wrist. Steadying her. As he always did.

"She believes you would not have fallen ill had she remained cognizant," he explained with great gentleness.

"What does my being sick have to do with..." But the rest came back, reverberating through her skull. The excruciating agony of stepping through the gates, the cascade of energy and emotion, along with vibrations she'd never before encountered, one upon the next, until—

"Stop it." Chuffta's sharp thought cut through the rest. *"That's in the past. You survived it. But thinking of it can recall the damage. Exercise some self-discipline and cut it off."*

Gaping at the lizard, whose green eyes sparked with unprecedented ferocity, she wrenched her thoughts from that moment. The pounding in her head receded, a welcome reward. "Tell me what happened after." She put a finger to her temple to stop the distracting pulse beat. "Are they—gone?"

A pair of stone-gray eyes in a scarred, blood-spattered face.

"Will you promise to remain calm? Let me walk you through a meditation first."

"I don't want to meditate." Her voice came out too sharply impatient, a bit of wobble beneath. She let out a long breath. "I'll be calm, just tell me."

Chuffta appeared satisfied and folded back his wings. *"The Destrye accepted your offer of surrender. They occupy the city, negotiating with your brother, who is now king."*

Nat was king? Why wasn't her mother ruling in the waked of their father's passing? Nat had no wife yet, not even an imperfect one to feed him energy. He couldn't be king.

"The Destrye king does not know your laws. Nat and the council stall for time."

"Time? What good will more time do?"

Chuffta's hesitation was palpable. *"They have invited the Trom to Bára."*

That memory came back with force. Folcwita Lapo arguing that they should send for help from the Trom. The fear and heightened excitement some of the others felt at the suggestion. "But we decided not to send for them."

"It appears your decision was overruled." Queen Rhianna, composed again, stood in the doorway, framed by brilliant sunshine. "Something else I blame myself for."

"Why?" Oria frowned, more for the fact that she'd suddenly realized she'd never before seen her mother so often without her mask of rank. "You didn't call them, did you?"

"No. High Priestess Febe did."

"With…Priest Vico sending the call? I didn't think he was powerful enough."

"He's not. I think—" She sighed heavily, sagging against the doorframe. "I think Nat must have done it. Had I been cognizant, I would never have allowed such a drastic, foolish move." Moving like a woman twice her years, she came to sit beside Oria on the bed, gripping her forearms over the long sleeves of her sleeping gown, preempting further questions. "Let me resume my apology. I regret, so very much, that I failed you. I lost *hwil*—an unforgivable breach. I apologize with all my heart and will spend what is left of my life trying to make it up to you."

The bed seemed to sway under Oria, the sense of dislocation, of the bottom falling out of her world so profound. "You can't lose *hwil* once you find it."

Her mother wouldn't meet her eye, squeezing her hands too tight. "I did. It's…it's thought that when your father…" She choked on the words.

A chill of horror-filled grief dragged over Oria, followed by beads of cold sweat down her spine.

"Steady," Chuffta murmured.

"That I broke," her mother managed to get out. "Thus I no longer deserve the mask of a priestess."

"They took your mask away?"

Her mother nodded, weeping again. No composure at all. "When Tav fell, I—" She couldn't continue, her wild grief, despair, and a black rage beneath it all pouring into Oria. Gasping, she reeled under it, aware on one level of Chuffta's tail winding between their hands, breaking her mother's grip—too much, even through the silk. As soon as the contact broke, Oria could orient again, begin to separate her mother's grief and anger from her own—though they had so much interface, like mirrors of each other, that she couldn't disentangle all of it.

"Rhianna." Juli, a junior priestess, new to her mask, was suddenly there. "Come away. This isn't good for Oria."

"I let him die," Rhianna sobbed. "I wasn't enough. The union cracked and…" Her words devolved into a garble as Juli led her away.

Stunned, Oria lay back, trying to process it all. Letting the emotional energy drain away. "Why does she say she let him die?"

"Because her failure resulted in his death." High Priestess Febe entered the room, golden mask implacable, hands tucked into the billowing sleeves of her crimson robe. "A priestess's responsibility, even more so a wife's sacred obligation—particularly in a temple-blessed marriage of perfectly matched partners—is to keep her sorcerer husband fed with sgath. Queen Rhianna failed in this, no matter the reason, and her husband died. How are you feeling, Princess?"

Chuffta bellied onto Oria's chest, folding his wings so he rested his pointed chin on his thumb claws, eyes green and shining as the leaves of the fruit trees in her garden.

"Listen," he soothed, no doubt sensing Oria's ire. *"Perhaps we shall learn something."*

"Better, but I don't understand, High Priestess."

"Of course you don't. Had you achieved *hwil* and taken the mask before all this happened, you would be better prepared." The high priestess sounded weary, on top of the eternal stain of disappointment. "Knowing what we know now about Queen Rhianna, perhaps we erred in letting her have such a strong influence over you."

Though Oria, of course, could not see Febe's eyes, she nevertheless felt certain they rested on Chuffta. Much as Oria wanted to bristle, it seemed that the High Priestess emanated something through her careful *hwil*. Uncertainty?

"Anything you can tell me that the temple will allow would be helpful, High Priestess Febe." Oria pulled off the humble tone reasonably well. Chuffta agreed with a mental snort of amusement.

Febe paced over to a window. "Some of it, naturally, is a question of whether your mind and spirit have the maturity to understand. However, the situation is grave enough that I believe I should endeavor to teach you, though it may be pouring water into a bucket with no bottom."

Fortunately, the promise of information had Oria restraining a smart remark in response to the not-so-subtle insult.

"Despite all that has been studied on the flow of sgath to grien, there is a great deal we do not consciously understand, that lies in the realm of *hwil*. Testing showed your mother and father to be a perfect match. There were no indications otherwise, else the temple would not have blessed their marriage. To all appearances, she'd always provided him an unending source of sgath, which made him a powerful sorcerer and king."

"I know all this," she muttered softly enough that the high priestess could not hear. Chuffta, however, heard clearly.

"No, you know what you've always believed. What your parents believed and taught you in turn. Listen to a new truth."

She didn't want to. Stubbornly, she stared at her ceiling, the mosaic of clouds and sky not as restful as usual.

"Or, if you are not ready to hear, if you need to rest, we need not do this now. Tell her to keep her secrets for later."

Chuffta's mind-voice, while solicitous, held enough reproof that she unbent. At the gate, facing down that bloodied warrior prince, she'd resolved to improve her knowledge. That included the painful things.

"Particularly the painful things, some would argue."

"We've since learned that perhaps some individuals are able to falsify the appearance of *hwil*, of compatibility with a mate." Febe's voice held suspicion, stopping short of accusing Oria of faking *hwil*. Though Oria had never claimed to have reached that miraculous state. Had others done so? Simply said so without really doing it? Had her own mother? It had never occurred to her to pretend, and yet...what a simple answer that would be, to gain access to the temple knowledge, to buy time to cultivate control of sgath in secret.

"King Tavlor relied on that bond heavily," Febe was saying, "believing it to be unshakeable, that with his temple-blessed marriage and the combined pool of power from all the priestesses, the sorcerers could not fail. Then the Destrye began killing the priestesses, an unprecedented event, at least in recent memory."

That was why he'd committed nearly everyone to the battle. Her father had believed they couldn't fail. Had he realized the truth before he died? She hoped not. What a horrible thing to realize, then to die without being able to rectify such a terrible mistake.

"We knew killing a priestess would obviously sever the bond between her and the sorcerers. We did not predict what might result if a number of priestesses died in rapid succession because it never occurred to anyone that it could happen. The walls of Bára have never been breached in such a violent and sudden way. Now that you know it could and did, knowing what you know of sgath magic, what do you predict? Think it through."

Oria quelled her stubborn impulse to disobey the high priestess's pedantic instructions. Her obstinacy had held her back in the past and she needed to learn to do better. She tried to calm her emotions. One of the clouds in her ceiling mosaic had always looked like a winged horse to her, ever since she was little. She found it and traced its lines with her eyes while she thought about it. "Priestesses absorb energy from all living things, particularly the focused and purified magical sources, as below Bára, and transform it into sgath."

"And some nonliving things. Perhaps an exacting point, but an important one for this puzzle," Febe said. "What are some examples?"

"Magical energy also comes from the sun, from Sgatha and Grienon, and from certain kinds of rock and heated gases in the earth below Bára. Depending on her nature, a woman might absorb one kind of energy more than another." Oria had no idea what her nature tended toward, which had always been part of the problem. Without *hwil*, the energies just piled up into in a meaningless jumble. "A priestess releases sgath ideally to a priest who's her perfect mirror. Through their bond, he converts that into grien, supplementing his own and repurposing it into whatever element his nature dictates."

"And for those without marriages, let alone without temple-blessed ones?"

"Those priestesses direct their sgath into a kind of pool that all sorcerers can dip into." The logic began to take shape. She wrenched her gaze from the winged horse in the mosaic sky to Chuffta's discerning, somber gaze. "When they died, if they were effectively bonded to the pool of magic, then all their energy poured into it, one after another."

"Yes. One life, even with the violence of murder, would not have made a difference. That energy would have been diluted into the rest. But, with so many powerful priestesses dropping their entire life energy into the Báran pool, within minutes of each other…" Febe sighed, her sorrow palpable.

"The priests overloaded. I can see how that would happen, though I don't think they could."

"No one imagined that scenario. But then, never before have so many priestesses been so actively contributing to a common pool, nor so many sorcerers drawing from it so heavily. The battle magics consumed so much that the priestesses offered more and more to sustain it."

"So what happened?" Oria asked, mouth dry with dread.

"It's difficult to explain to one without *hwil*, and the framework of teachings to support your understanding. But what you need to know is that King Tavlor overspent himself and died, which left Queen Rhianna unmoored. She should not have survived." There was a question there, an expectation, and Febe's mask faced Oria, scrutinizing her with uncomfortable intensity. "How is it that she did?"

"I—I don't know." She hadn't expected to feel accused of something, especially not knowing what she'd done, right or wrong.

"You were alone with her. Think back. What exactly did you do?"

"Nothing." Oria tried to think, so much of that a blur. Aware also that maybe telling the exact truth would not be the smartest step. "I chafed her wrists, called her name, and she woke up."

"That can't be all." Though Febe remained serene, an impatience crawled through the room. "Tell me, moment by moment, how you—" Her chin snapped up, head swiveled to the window. "I must go. Don't leave the tower, Princess."

She swept out so abruptly that Oria frowned after her. "When she says 'overspent,' does she mean they broke?"

"Sounds that way to me."

"I didn't think men could break, because they can always release the grien."

"Now we know they can. Like you, they lost consciousness from the overload. Many of them died immediately."

"Did I… For a while I thought I was dead."

"We feared as much." His mind-voice became a gentle stroke. *"I couldn't sense you at all. I suspect that… Well, it's not relevant."*

"It is to me. What do you think?" She studied the jade-deep eyes, full of some uncharacteristic emotion.

"That perhaps you did die, that your essence departed your body, but then returned. Much as your mother's did."

"Why did I come back?"

To her surprise, he sounded vaguely amused when he replied. *"I don't know—why did you?"*

It took her aback, to contemplate that she'd somehow made this choice and caused it to happen. She'd think about that later.

Shouts reverberated outside. A new energy sliced through Oria's mind, unlike anything else she'd ever sensed. "What is that?" But she knew. That was why the high priestess had rushed out so precipitously.

"Unless I am mistaken, that *is the arrival of the Trom."*

~ 14 ~

THE DESTRYE DEMAND that masks be removed had not gone over well. King Archimago had agreed with the wisdom of the strategic move—though Ion couched the proposal in terms of transparency of expression—with no mention of magical influence. Their father balked at discussions of magic.

All of them did, really, despite all they'd seen.

A rapidly heating argument seemed to be headed directly toward renewed combat, a prospect Lonen actually welcomed as it would be far better than this endless debate—killing a few of them would go a long way to releasing the building tension—when Ion's first captain ran into the room. He whispered urgently to Ion as Lonen's stomach dropped. And as shouts rose outside.

He didn't miss the way the young king, his adviser, Folcwita Lapo, and Prince Yar all exchanged glances that radiated smug satisfaction, even through the blandness of their masks. Most of the Bárans, however, looked confused and uneasy. As did many of city guard, who drew their weapons.

Shouts turned to screams.

Ion surged to his feet, his chair falling from the force of it, King Archimago a beat behind him. "You betray our truce!" Ion roared.

King Nat stood also, facing them down the long table. "You attacked our city. Are we not meant to defend ourselves?"

"You are a people without honor," King Archimago gritted out. "We should never have accepted your surrender."

"A surrender offered under duress," Nat snapped back, "by an untried girl with no mask and no authority to commit Bára to any treaty."

"She is a princess," Lonen said, before he thought better. He would never live down that decision. "Your sister."

"You know nothing of us, barbarian." Nat's sneer oozed from behind the mask. "And you never will because you'll all die under Trom fire."

"We waste time here." Ion signaled his man, sending quick orders. "Seal them in. No Báran leaves. King Archimago, we must move you to safe quarters. Lonen, Arnon—with me."

They jogged behind him, leaving a small crew of men to guard the city elders. At least they'd gathered conveniently in one room. The Destrye could ensure they'd remain there. All but the high priestess of their temple. He'd last seen her sitting on that bench by the great chasm, apparently meditating. Where had she gone?

"I'll stay with you," King Archimago said, drawing his great sword. "I won't cower behind my sons."

None of them argued. The king's word was law and they could not defy it at that moment any more than they ever could.

"What's the situation?" Lonen asked.

"Monsters," Ion replied, terse words shot through puffs of breath. "Attacking from the sky."

Indeed they were.

At the gut-watering sight, only hard years of training made Lonen continue his headlong rush to battle the impossible. He recognized the creatures, however—giant versions of the dragonlet he'd spied with Oria. He still hadn't mentioned it to his father and brothers, though their men had seen it also and could corroborate his story. On top of everything, it had seemed…too much.

And not relevant until that moment.

Batwinged and bellowing fire, the dragons roared through the sky, barreling between towers and roasting Destrye and Bárans alike.

"Why would they call upon a savior that kills their own people?"

Arnon cried out the question as they skidded to a stop at the edge of the chasm surrounding the palace. The confection of a bridge that Lonen had walked over less than an hour before had disappeared, cutting off the palace from the rest of the city. At whose behest?

"We cornered them," King Archimago said with weary resignation. "They saw no other way out. Desperate men take desperate measures."

"We could have come to an agreement," Arnon protested. "We only wanted to be sure they wouldn't come after us again."

"He's too young to be king." Their father shook his head. "I should have seen it before this. He'll sacrifice his people to retain his pride, to keep his grip on a throne he never earned. His people have become my responsibility now—unless we all perish together."

Helpless to do anything—not that any of the Destrye within the walls could do much to battle the giant monsters—the four of them watched from the brink of the chasm as people ran, some to the safety of the stone buildings, some in flames to collapse in heaps, burning into ash. Much as he wanted to look up to Oria's tower, Lonen forced himself not to, to bear grim witness to the destruction and terror before him. After a while it became clear that the beasts never crossed the chasm that surrounded the palace, though they could easily have flown over. Nor did they cross outside the walls, save for one section, toward the high mountains, where more streamed in.

If she was in her tower, Oria would be more or less safe. Along with her brothers and the others who'd so thoughtlessly sacrificed their people to destroy their enemy.

Within a short time, nobody remained outside shelter, the city as deserted as that first morning Ion and his men had walked them through. Less so, because no Destrye warriors could be seen. Not alive, at any rate.

A winged beast flew up, hovered, then landed on the far rim of the chasm. It looked like a snake with its unwinking black eyes, but with hind feet and leathery bat wings affixed. Talons the height of a man dug into the edge of the precipice, rocks falling way as they crumbled beneath its grip. Perched on its neck where it narrowed above the wing joints sat a creature that, while human in shape, bore no resemblance to any man or woman Lonen had ever seen.

The dragon creature snaked out its long neck, pointed chin coming at them like a spear. The four of them scrambled back, weapons drawn. Foolishness, in truth, as the dragon could have roasted them where they stood. Instead it laid its triangular snout on the ground, opaque eyes fixed on them. The man-thing on its back stood and walked with preternatural grace along the sinuous neck. As it grew closer, more detail resolved. And yet Lonen still struggled to make sense of what he saw, even as the hair rose on the back of his neck.

It looked like a corpse that had been dried in the sun, skin shrunken over bones. Moving with a strangely articulated movement, almost insectile, it possessed no room in its angular body for the organs of a normal man. Black lidless eyes gazed unseeing out of the sockets of an overlarge, mouthless skull. Lonen had thought nothing could be more of an abomination than the golems. Another lesson learned.

"Arill save us," Arnon breathed, horror in his tone. "What is that thing?"

"If it lives," Ion grated out, "it can die, like any living thing."

It walked precisely, the way the forest cats do, one foot aligned exactly in front of the other, following a straight line between the giant lizard's eyes and down its snout, onto the rock of the palace promontory. Ion could very well be wrong, as the thing didn't seem to be living, beyond the fact that it apparently moved on its own initiative. A puppet on strings did the same. No expression showed on its smooth face, unnervingly like the masks the sorcerers and priestesses wore. A deliberate imitation of these monsters? If so, the Bárans were even sicker, more twisted than Lonen had believed.

King Archimago stepped forward, crowned by a wreath of bronzed oak leaves glittering in the sun, sword high, the polished steel bright. An impressive sight, though Lonen preferred the solid wooden haft of his iron-bladed axe. This creature could well be magically animated, like the golems, which meant the coarse iron would do far more than the king's sword.

"Halt!" King Archimago commanded, in the steel tones that had left more than one hardened warrior leaking into his boots. "This land belongs to the people of Destrye. You trespass uninvited. State your purpose here."

That was the king and father Lonen had always known—brave, commanding, the sun of his universe. With righteous wrath fueling him, King Archimago no longer looked old or worn. He blazed with glorious purpose. Protecting even the Bárans he found himself reluctantly responsible for. Lonen's heart swelled with pride. Despite all the terror and despair, the world also held honorable men who stood up for the good and the right.

The desiccated thing continued forward, expressionless and undeterred, easily a head taller than any of them. Nothing more than skin stretched over bone, it walked smoothly up to King Archimago.

Onto the point of his sword.

And kept going.

Somewhere Ion shouted a warning. Lonen sent slow messages to his muscles to raise the axe.

All moved as in a dream. The man-thing continued forward as if the sword didn't exist, the metal slipping through him like a hot knife through grease, the point emerging out its back. The moment spun out forever, a long, sticky summer's afternoon. And yet Lonen couldn't lift his axe in time to stop it.

Like a mother lifting her hand to test the temperature of her child's brow, like a lover caressing his beloved's cheek, the thing stroked spidery fingers over King Archimago's face.

And watched him fall.

King Archimago crumpled into a boneless pile of empty flesh, the sword and oak leaf wreath clanging down with him. Lonen's axe arced through the air, but Ion had been moving first.

Always first to defend, to protect, Ion swung his iron broadsword, releasing the battle cry of the Destrye warriors.

It went through the thing as if it didn't exist. A brush of light fingers and Ion, too, collapsed.

Somehow a sense of self-preservation kicked through Lonen's wild horror and he checked his swing.

"No!" he shouted, his voice taking up Ion's still-echoing warrior cry as Arnon lunged past him.

~ 15 ~

ORIA FLUNG HERSELF through the doors to the garden terrace and pelted for the balustrade, gripping the stone with shaking fingers as her mind caught up with the sight that greeted her.

Derkesthai filled the skies—only they were hundreds of times Chuffta's size, and darkly shaded instead of white. When they weren't silhouetted against the sun, their deep metallic colors gleamed bronze, copper and gold. Their fire, though, blazed the same green as Chuffta's, and even more lethally, incinerating on a proportionally grander scale.

One swooped below her tower, broad-winged and chasing a squad of city guard who ran for the bridge to the palace. The men nearly made it across before the bellowing fire that chased them—so beautiful, like leaves fluttering in a cooling breeze—immolated them and the bridge, too. They plummeted into Ing's chasm, becoming floating ash as they fell, their death wails rising up to Oria.

It took her to her knees, the bruising pain of hitting the stones barely registering above the agony of so many lives pouring through her, with all their desires, sorrows and unspent wishes.

Chuffta landed on her shoulder, tail winding over her sleeve to wrap around the bare skin at her wrist, the pain receding. Not gone, but less intense, like the sun's heat fading behind a rare haze of clouds.

"You can't save them—at least spare yourself the burden of suffering along with them."

"Why?" The question sobbed out of her. She laid her palms flat against the softly gritty carved balustrade, peering through the openings, aghast at the scene playing out below, Bárans and Destrye alike running before their attackers, then vanishing into clouds of ash. "If Nat called to them for help, why are they attacking *us*, too?"

"That's why calling upon the Trom is a dangerous proposition, why the temple warns against it. They follow their own code. Once invited, they are as a beast released from confinement—killing indiscriminately."

"So they'll destroy us all. After everything we've suffered to try to make a peace, we'll simply all die at the hands of your brethren."

"Only distant brethren and those you see serve the Trom. We are similar, yes, as you are to the Destrye, but even more unlike. There are tales from long ago of a Báran mating and producing children with a Destrye. A derkesthai could no more mate with the Trom steeds than a Báran cat could with its larger, wilder cousins."

Obscurely that comforted her, that her wise and gentle Familiar wouldn't someday grow into the monsters that terrorized a city full of defenseless people. Angry as she was at the Destrye for bringing this blight upon Bára, she couldn't revel in their agonizing deaths. When Lonen dashed out from the palace entrance, recognizable even from her great height by the massive double-headed axe he carried, she cried out an involuntary warning.

A useless one, as he couldn't possibly hear her. Three other men accompanied him, one wearing some sort of golden crown and carrying a bright silver sword. Like the other Destrye, they'd abandoned their heavy cloaks, likely as a concession to the Báran heat, but still wore their furred vests and leather-strapped boots. They seemed as stunned as she, watching both peoples die in great numbers. Though she looked for them to appear, her brothers did not emerge, nor did any of the rest of the council.

She prayed that they remained under shelter.

The immense derkesthai never crossed Ing's Chasm that isolated the palace and temple, however, as if an invisible wall prevented them.

"It could be the temple's magic acts as a barrier, though I'm not sure."

How could Chuffta remain so calmly speculative?

"I don't even understand how that would work," she muttered, mostly to herself, stewing with frustration.

"Probably one of the many secrets they intended to teach you."

"Information that could be critical to know if we're not going to be incinerated. But no." She was as far from attaining *hwil* as she'd ever been in her life—and never likely to reach it under these conditions. The trials of the past week dragged her emotionally to the opposite pole of where her mind and spirit were meant to be for *hwil*. Instead of calm detachment, she jangled with death energy and despair. She became aware that her Familiar hadn't replied and turned her head to look at him. Chuffta also gazed at his giant cousins, soaring through the sky, a pensive look in the quiet green of his eyes. "Chuffta?"

He replied without looking at her. *"Maybe it's a time for rules to be broken. Perhaps also..."*

"What? Perhaps also what?"

"I hesitate to say too much, but they might have been wrong about you." Chuffta's mind-voice held regret and Oria tried not to let it dig at her. She'd long suspected the same, of course, that she would never don her mother's mask, take her place among the least of the temple's priestesses, much less as a power of her own. Small and unimportant problems to have, in the face of such great ones.

With no one left in sight to char, many of the great lizards peeled off to make lazy circles in the sky. One, however, landed at the edge of the chasm, snaking its sinuous neck just as Chuffta would, creating a living bridge across. Something stirred at the wing joints that had blended in before that. A person?

"That is a Trom," Chuffta said with quiet emphasis.

"How do you know—have you seen one before?"

His trepidation leaked through the long pause. *"In dreams,"* he finally replied. *"Though I didn't know what it was when I dreamed it."*

Oria suppressed a shudder as the Trom stood, then walked along its steed's neck bridging the chasm to the palace side. "Why can they cross now?"

"The invitation might have been worded as such, to allow that individual Trom entrance, if no one else."

"And what will they—" She broke off with a strangled croak as the Destrye king first confronted the Trom, then fell to its touch. Then another man. Lonen aborted an attack he'd launched, dragging the third man to the side. Faint shouts rose up from them, audible in the silence of the empty city.

The Trom seemed to ignore them, walking on and disappearing into the palace.

"We have to go warn my mother, my brothers." Oria dragged herself to her feet and made for the inside, Chuffta spreading his wings for balance at her abrupt movements.

"How can they not know? Everyone in the city knows what you know."

"Then I can't simply stay up here while they all die." She pushed through the outer doors, rapidly descending through the long spirals.

"What will it profit for you to die with them? Remember what happened last time. And you were at peak strength then. The last collapse weakened you severely."

"I don't care. I'm sick to death of being weak. If I die with them, at least I won't have to suffer the pain of outliving them all."

Chuffta said nothing more, though his disapproval—and fear for her—wafted through her mind. Or perhaps that was the smoke from the burning bodies carried by the afternoon breeze through the tower windows.

It seemed easier to lift the bar at her tower door this time, though she should have had more trouble, being weak from her days as an invalid. Perhaps having done it once before helped. This time no guards at all remained outside, not even Renzo. Shouts echoed down the hall, from the direction of the council chambers, and she ran towards them.

Then skidded to a stop.

Renzo lay in a heap, sword drawn, handsome face crumpled like an overripe fruit. She crouched, reaching out a tentative hand. Not to test for life, as he couldn't possibly be alive. Even with her inexperience, the lack of any animating force in the abandoned flesh before her was obvious. Rather, she struggled to understand what had happened to him. No evident wound and yet...

"I've heard it said that the Trom can dissolve that which makes bone strong."

"They chew the bones of their enemies," she whispered, remembering how the Destrye king seemed to simply collapse at the Trom's touch.

"Apparently more than a metaphor."

Needing to reassure them both, for Chuffta sounded unsettled, too, she reached up and stroked the silken scales of his breast, where the powerful wing muscles flexed. The shouts from the council chambers had faded, though voices harsh with anger occasionally echoed through, too vague for her to make out words. No clash of weapons.

Feeling her defenselessness, she took up Renzo's sword, easing it from his pulped fingers with the burn of nausea in her throat. It was heavier than it looked, dragging at her shoulder and elbow.

"It's not too late to go back. You walk into great danger."

"I wouldn't be able to lift the bar into place again. We'd be trapped up there while the great danger came after us." And she wasn't sure if she could climb all those stairs. Her body still didn't feel right, the enervation of her collapse exacerbating the poor condition brought on by her soft existence. Another fruit of Bára to be bruised and discarded. Too sweet and overripe.

Determined to be more than that, she headed to the council chambers, skirting the crumpled bodies—both Destrye and Báran—strewn about like the discarded skin and gristle from one of Chuffta's carnivorous meals. Nobody guarded the council doors, not even the ceremonial guard who'd remained there day and night all her life. The sucking sensation of crashing loss pulled at her, leaving her as boneless as all those dead.

Time enough to grieve later, if she survived.

She straightened her spine, imagining it lined with steel the Trom could not dissolve, and edged into the room.

And got her first close look at the Trom.

Not benevolent in appearance by any stretch, the Trom looked like the reverse of the kills it left in its wake, as if it took their bones to make its own, then coated them with a layer of finely scaled skin.

It stood before Nat, who wore his mask and robes—and their father's crown. The sight shouldn't have made her angry, but it did. War must change all the rules, for none of the Báran or temple laws provided for Nat to be crowned king. Yar stood at his right shoulder. Both of them simmered with grien, drawing from the pool that must have been slowly rebuilding as High Priestess Febe put the junior priestesses to work. Nat seemed to be speaking to the Trom in low tones, gesturing to the group of Destrye.

She picked out Lonen easily—not for his double-headed axe this time, for he was barehanded—but because he was staring at her with a hard, even mean, expression. Perhaps the face of a man who had just watched his father and brother fall boneless to the ground in less than a heartbeat. He stood at the forefront of his men, not bloodied as he'd been the day of surrender, but no less intimidating for that. He pointed at her—no, at the sword she carried—then at the floor.

Feeling stupid as well as weak, she gripped the sword tighter, as if he could take it away from her from across the room. Even though her arm muscles already wept with fatigue so much that she'd love nothing better than to cast it away.

Nat's raised voice carried across the room. "I command you! Kill them all, now."

The Trom's reply slithered across the polished stones, like dry husks rubbed together, reverberating on a mental and emotional level that sawed across her raw sensibilities. "The Trom do not answer to you."

"I am King of Bára and I summoned you for this purpose," Nat proclaimed in ringing tones that nevertheless evoked his teenage arguments with their father. He'd never done well being thwarted, had always been too prideful and easily frustrated.

"You are not the Summoner," the Trom replied, without heat or interest.

"Princess Oria." The hissed whisper dragged her attention away. Lonen and his men had edged closer. She turned, struggling to point the heavy sword at him. He shook his head at her. "Drop the sword. It won't hurt you if you're not a threat."

Uncertain, she surveyed him. "Do you think it's a trick?" she asked Chuffta.

"It could be. But none of the Destrye hold weapons, so they must believe it to be true."

"Do as I command as King of Bára or face the consequences!" Nat's voice grew louder, along with the palpably building tension of contained magic and incipient violence, buffeting Oria like the hot desert winds that brought late summer sandstorms.

"Oria! What in Grienon are you doing out of your tower?" Yar had spotted her and sounded overexcited, his voice cracking with it. "Get over here now."

"Be careful," Lonen said, no longer bothering to whisper, holding her gaze, his own urgent. "If you offer threat of any kind or point a weapon at that thing, it kills with a touch. Blades pass right through it—even wielded by someone who knows how to hold one correctly."

"Oria! Attend me," Nat thundered.

Something changed in the tenor of magic in the room. The Trom looked at her now, matte-black eyes boring into her from even that distance. "Oria," it said. "Princess Ponen."

Her own roiling energy, still boiling over with all those death agonies, surged within her at the Trom's words. Swelling up the way grien was said to, an irresistible force that yearned for release. If only she knew how. The Trom stepped away from Nat and Yar, turning in her direction. It lifted a hand that seemed to have no palm, only long, articulated fingers, like the desert spiders with bodies so small they seemed to be all leg. A kind of greeting? No more emotion showed in its still face than in the golden masks of the temple. With a start of near revulsion, Oria realized those masks must be modeled on Trom faces.

"Put down the sword, Oria." Lonen sounded less commanding than imploring. He might be her enemy, but she didn't think he wished for her death. A great deal of emotion surged through the room, liberally mixing with the barely leashed magical energy, but his stood out from the rest, something leafy, cool, and ancient to it. Not violence and anger—not toward her, anyway—but grief and keen-edged fear.

Following intuition and because her arm muscles begged for it, she bent her knees and laid the heavy sword on the floor. Lonen had seen through her on that—she wouldn't be able to swing it anyway. Straightening, she faced the Trom, refusing to be cowed by its remote, alien visage. "Greetings, Trom. Why do you slaughter the very people who asked for your aid?"

"Oria!" Nat surged forward, halting abruptly when the Trom pivoted its head to gaze at him. Though her brother wore the mask, nerves showed in the lines of his body. Behind him, Yar clutched white-knuckled hands together. The flavors of their barely restrained grien coiled and lashed. They planned to unleash something huge. "Don't presume to question our distinguished guest. Go back to your tower. I command you, as your king."

She nearly spat at that, mouth full of bitter grief that Nat would presume to command her, only days after their father's death, knowing as they both did that he could not have been truly crowned. All of it a ruse. He meant for her to move away from the Destrye, who faced certain death as soon as she did. A demise they richly deserved, so she should not interfere. She couldn't stop herself from glancing back at Lonen, though, not sure what she expected, but still feeling somehow as if she were abandoning him. If nothing else, she'd be breaking her word. He was still staring at her with a kind of ferocity unique to the Destrye, his eyes gritty and bleak as unpolished granite.

"I think it wise to move out of the line of fire." Chuffta sounded unusually subdued.

She made herself look away but did not leave the room. Instead she joined the group of masked junior priestesses, a brace of city guards protecting them. At least they'd learned that lesson. The Destrye warriors might have sheathed their weapons, but they looked as if they could kill with their hairy, brutish hands.

"Kill the Destrye, Trom," Nat said clearly. "It's why you were summoned."

The Trom had been watching Oria all this time, with skin-crawling focus. But at Nat's command, it swiveled its attention, not to the Destrye, but to Nat. "That may be why the Summoner called us, but it's not why we are here," it said, voice scratching over Oria's consciousness like a dull knife.

"Then we shall compel you." Nat raised his hands, magic pouring from the priestesses to him and Yar, who echoed their brother's movement. "In the name of Grienon, I command you to—"

As he spoke, as the magic sprang from his hands, the Trom lifted a languid hand on an impossibly long arm and caressed her brother's cheek.

He sagged, crumpled, and fell in a heap.

~ 16 ~

If Lonen expected Oria to scream—or perhaps faint again—at the sight of her brother's abrupt demise, she surprised him. She seemed vastly changed from the girl he'd glimpsed, candlelit in the window, or the young woman who'd ridden bravely to offer her city's surrender.

The last days had honed her. She'd lost weight, though she could hardly afford to lose any, her cheekbones and jaw line stark under her pale skin, copper eyes overbright in violet-shadowed sockets, her formerly shining hair braided back and dark with oils. As if she hadn't washed it in some time. As if she'd been abed all this time.

He should keep his attention on that foul creature the Bárans had so foolishly summoned, but his gaze kept going back to Oria, the white lizardling fierce on her shoulder, tail wrapped down the arm of her gray gown like a shimmering series of bracelets.

She didn't scream or faint. Instead she impossibly—showing incredible foolishness, not bravery—thrust herself in front of her remaining brother, taking his hands by the wrists, forcing them down. And turning her back on the monster.

He hadn't realized he'd stepped forward, fists clenched, until he became aware of Arnon's strong forearm around his throat. "My turn to save you," his brother hissed in his ear. "Don't be an idiot. She makes her own grave."

The last years of Lonen's life had become a study in helplessness. His inability to stop the increasing golem rampages. The final, agonizing decision to send the women and children away, to abandon their home to the enemy's raids. That goodbye to Natly, certain he'd never see her again. The devastating losses of their forces. Nolan gone. His father dead. Ion, too.

Each death had carved another chunk out of him, as if every one of them took a piece of Lonen away to the Hall of Warriors. It seemed a man couldn't survive being gutted so many times, which explained why he felt so empty, so beyond the ability to feel anything.

And yet the sight of that slender, exhausted girl putting herself between her brother and a monster who killed with a caress filled him with a desperation that demanded action.

Oria stared up into her brother's gold mask, saying something low and urgent. Lonen's heart thudded in his empty chest as the monster raised its hand.

Closed the distance easily.

Drifted to touch her bright hair.

"No!" he shouted, the cry choked off by his brother's stranglehold.

Oria turned, still holding her brother's wrists, and flinched back at the spidery fingers hovering so near her cheek. Her cur of a brother wrenched free, backing up several hasty steps, and Lonen's heart shredded into panic as the thing made contact. Traced her high cheekbone, followed the line of her jaw. Brushed one deadly finger over her full lower lip.

And she remained standing.

The thing spoke to her in some incomprehensible language. It had a voice like an old warrior Lonen had known as a boy, a man who'd taken a sword wound to the throat. He'd lived, but spoke in a rasp, a cawing whisper.

"Nothing else." Her clear voice rang through the room without wavering. "Except to go, all of you. And do not return."

The thing caressed her cheek again, and she surely restrained a shudder, her slim frame tight as a drawn bow string, as it spoke to her again, at some length.

With that languid, unhurried, and jointless movement, the thing turned and strode away, out of the chamber. All in the room watched it go, silent, frozen in place, as if afraid even a loud breath might attract it back again.

Then erupted in chaos.

Prince Yar shouted something incoherent at Oria, then dove on the late king's pulped body. The princess reeled a bit, but caught herself, bolstered by the masked priestess with corkscrew red curls, who carefully supported Oria by the shoulders, saying something in her ear that made Oria nod sorrowfully as she gazed at her brother. The city guard advanced on Lonen and his pitifully small force of Destrye, who quickly scrambled for their discarded weapons. They were few in number—only the handful of warriors who'd been occupying the palace itself and guarding King Archimago, and who'd managed to evade the monster's touch. An amazingly simple strategy, to lower weapons and not attack the thing. It seemed to ignore everyone otherwise.

Except for Oria. Who alone had survived the thing's touch. Two exceptions at once.

"We have to recover Father and Ion," Arnon was saying in his ear. At least he'd released his throttling hold. Lonen supposed he should be grateful for it, but he burned with resentment—and an odd sense of betrayal. So many dead to that thing's foul touch, and nearly Oria, too. Not that he cared for her fate exactly, but it grated that she'd protected her brother instead of the other way around. Even now her brother paid more attention to a dead man than his living sister.

Or, rather, to the crown.

"Lonen!" Arnon urged.

"Their bodies are going nowhere," Lonen replied, his voice surprisingly even, given all that churned inside him. "Let's turn our attention on those still living—with the goal of keeping them that way."

Prince Yar stood, the heavy jeweled crown of Bára in his hands. "I am king now," he proclaimed.

"You are not." Oria overrode his words before he finished, making the boy turn to her in shock. If Lonen could have seen his face, the young prince would be gaping slack-jawed, an image that amused him greatly.

"Then who is in charge, Princess Oria?" Folcwita Lapo demanded.

"There are laws—both secular and prescribed by the temple—that decide such things, Folcwita. You know this as well as I."

"We are at war." Lapo thrust an angry hand at the Destrye. "We are invaded, occupied!"

Oria's chin held a stubborn tilt. "And yet we are not animals. We choose a ruler by writ of law."

"Surely, you don't think to claim the crown." Yar was still holding it, his voice full of anger. "You have no mask and are too frail to be—"

"Not me," she cut him off. "Our mother, Queen Rhianna holds the right to rule. At least in the interim, until protocols are followed."

"Oria, she..." The priestess who'd supported Oria trailed off, with a cagey glance at Lonen and his men. Following her gaze, Oria pressed two fingers to her temple, looking pained.

"Why are you holding blades at each other? Haven't you all had enough of death today?" Her voice wavered. "We need to get people out there to restore order to the city. Some of the burned may yet be helped. Others in hiding should be told it's safe to emerge. Why is no one thinking of these things?"

"We need to use this opportunity to evict the Destrye from Bára once and for all," Prince Yar said to her back, his snarl unfortunately a bit too much of a whine.

"We promised a truce and broke it," Oria said to Yar, but she looked at Lonen. "Will the Destrye accept a renewed truce, at least for the next few hours, so we may all tend our dead and wounded? I realize you have no reason to trust my word a second time, but it's all I have to offer. I shall remain here to see that it's kept." She threw a significant glare at the folcwita.

Yar and Arnon both burst into protest—a strange pair of bedfellows there—but Oria held Lonen's gaze. She kept her spine straight and chin high, both proud and humble at once. Her eyes held a special plea, as if she somehow asked this of him personally. He who'd risked himself to implore her to drop that ridiculously large sword she so obviously had no skill or strength to wield. Despite the hollowness of grief, the image of her straining to carry, much less lift the thing and point it, nearly had him smiling.

Even so, she seemed to be one of the only sane one of her entire tribe. Which was saying something, given she went everywhere with that white dragonlet that she seemed to believe understood her when she spoke.

He found himself inclining his head, a slow nod of acceptance that had his brother rounding on him. Tempting to knock Arnon upside the head with the haft of his axe, to silence him. But they needed every able-bodied man the Destrye could muster. Until they assessed the casualties, it could be that the balance had changed enough for the Bárans overpower the Destrye forces inside the walls. A daunting thought, even though the Bárans weren't warriors.

"Princess Oria, you have no authority to—" Folcwita Lapo started.

"In my mother's absence, I do. And I'm older than you, Yar."

"You wear no mask, Oria," the prince grated.

"And you have no wife," she retorted, then turned back to Lonen. "I'm asking for a few hours."

"You have them," he found himself saying.

"Lonen, you—"

"I'm older than you, Arnon." Lonen nearly smiled to be echoing Oria. It hit him like a physical blow that, with Ion and Nolan dead, along with King Archimago, that he—the dream-filled third son—

would have to assume the Destrye crown. If they ever got out of this cursed walled city. "Let us tend to our people, Princess Oria. A truce until we can convene here again at sundown? I promise that any Destrye who lifts a weapon in violence to one of your people will die by my own hand."

"I promise the same, that any Báran who attacks a Destrye will be tossed into Ing's Chasm. Blades down, gentlemen, please." Oria seemed to sway a little on her feet, recovered herself. "Let the Destrye go about their business and us to ours."

Her guard bowed to her, sheathing their weapons. With another nod to his unlikely savior, Lonen returned his axe to its place on his back, mustered his men, and went to see about dealing with yet more dead.

~ 17 ~

ORIA WAITED FOR Lonen and his warriors to clear the room, then succumbed to Chuffta's chiding—and the sapping weakness in her limbs—and sank into a chair at the council table, cradling her throbbing head in her hands.

Nat dead, too. Only her mother and Yar left of their family. Her mother acting crazy, bereft of her mask and *hwil*, and Yar… What was this infection of power madness that had overtaken them? Her father had raised her brothers to be ambitious, true, and prepared them to rule. And Yar had been ever the most impetuous of them all, but everyone had laughed at that, saying he'd grow out of it. She'd never imagined her brothers would be so quick to claim the crown, especially with them so untried. Of course, never in her worst imaginings had she imagined such a vacuum on the throne of Bára.

Even so, everyone knew no one not stabilized by a marriage bond could rule Bára, or any of her sister cities.

"Perhaps that is the problem," Chuffta pointed out.

"Good point," she murmured to her Familiar, watching Yar and Folcwita Lapo argue, Nat's crumpled corpse at their feet. Somewhere in the mad jumble of emotions sandblasting her there had to be grief for her brother's death, but for the moment she couldn't find it. She'd passed into some state of callousness where she felt everything and nothing at once. High Priestess Febe entered the room, pausing to take in the scene. Her mask, naturally, gave nothing away, but she seemed unsurprised. Aha, it turned out anger still ran strongly in her heart. Oria called Febe over.

"Yes, Princess?" The high priestess emanated calm, her hwil unshakeable, which only fueled Oria's ire with the woman.

"We need Queen Rhianna here."

"Is that wise, Princess?" The high priestess's mask turned towards the fallen prince. "Can she withstand another death, the loss of her son? You saw how fragile she—"

Sick to death of talk of fragility, Oria fixed Febe with an imperious glare. "It's happened, whether she can withstand it or not. She is the queen and we need her. Please bring her here."

"But Princess..." Priestess Febe hesitated, her voice going kind in that tone Oria knew all too well. "You may not be in the best frame of mind to be making decisions since your unfortunate incident."

Just charming how the priestess said that, as if it were a tale written in illuminated letters and taught to children: *Princess Oria and Her Unfortunate Incident.*

Chuffta snickered in her mind. That at least remained the same.

The priestess noted something of her poor attitude, because she drew herself up, a thread of...something leaking through her cultivated calm. "There are things you should be aware of, Princess. Without *hwil*, however—"

"I'm aware of a great deal," Oria interrupted her, beyond done. "Mostly I'm *aware* that many people have lost sons and daughters today, while still mourning the thousands lost only days ago. I'm *aware* that my mother is also the queen of Bára and not even the temple has the power to strip her of her responsibilities, even if she did lose her mask. If there's precedent to remove a widowed ruler from the throne, that should be put before the Council of Law and judged accordingly. Until that eventuality, she is needed and she will step up to serve Bára as she's always done." Oria discovered she'd risen to her feet and that High Priestess Febe had taken a hesitant step back. "I may not be a priestess, but I am a princess who might be Queen of Bára myself someday—perhaps sooner than you think—and you *will* do as I command."

"Yes, Princess Oria." The priestess's voice sounded odd, but she hastened away with enough speed to set her crimson robes swirling.

"Well done, Oria."

She sat again, pressing her face into her hands, muttering into them. "Do you think so? My temper got away from me."

"Anger will fuel you in a way that despair will not. Use it."

"So much for seeking the calmness of perfect *hwil*."

"It occurs to me that one can only beat one's head against a wall for so long before determining that the wall is harder than one's head."

"Is that supposed to be a profound teaching? Because I have no idea what you just said."

"Oria!" Yar shook her shoulder.

She lifted her face to narrow her eyes at him. This shouting of her name was getting old. A minor irritation in the face of all that had occurred, and yet…

"Stop nattering at your derkesthai and face reality. Either look about you or go back to your tower."

"I'm looking," she replied as evenly as she could. "I'm taking a moment to meditate while we await the arrival of Queen Rhianna."

"Our brother is dead!" Yar shouted the words at her, as if she somehow didn't understand.

Oria took a breath and counted, trying to exercise patience and compassion for her obnoxious little brother, as her parents had always counseled, and her gaze strayed to Nat's jellied corpse. Her gorge rose along with grief that he'd never juggle fireballs for her again. Funny, the inane things that you remembered about a person. She should be mourning the loss of Bára's best heir to the throne. Not his cocky grin. Had his teeth dissolved, too?

"It's not him. *Only a shell he left behind. He does not suffer."*

"A lot of people are dead," she told Yar, swallowing back the sorrow. "Have you looked outside?"

"What are you saying?" Yar sounded young and uncertain. More the Yar she preferred, the adolescent boy overwhelmed by his formidably precocious powers rather than insufferably arrogant about them.

"The Trom arrived on giant derkesthai."

"As dumb as they are large."

"But not intelligent, like Chuffta," she added, to please her Familiar. "They burned everyone in sight, Destrye and Bárans alike. I saw it from the tower. And the halls are strewn with corpses like...like Nat's." Her throat grabbed on his name. "That Trom who walked in here dropped anyone who attacked him."

Yar sat heavily. "I didn't know. The Destrye kept us trapped in the council chambers, under guard."

"Well, now you do know. The bridge over Ing's Chasm was burned to nothing. I imagine the Destrye are working on something to allow us to cross into the city, to help all our people. But magic might come in useful, if you have some to spare." She allowed a little doubt to leak into her voice, to prick his pride.

Yar spread his hands, palms up, as if he knew she could see the grien in them. Perhaps everyone could do that. One of the temple's many secrets—but the temple did publicly teach that sensitives perceived magic differently, depending on their natural affinity. "We were building it up," Yar said faintly. "Priestess Febe and the junior priestesses had been feeding us sgath for days while we stalled negotiations. Nat said... He and Folcwita Lapo said the Trom would kill the occupying Destrye in the city and we'd take out the ones in here with one focused blast." His mask raised to face her, forlorn in its featurelessness. "It was a good plan."

Oria put a hand on his forearm over his robe. It was not the time to point out the utter foolishness of a plan that opened Bára to the Trom—not the least because Nat's poor judgment got himself killed. "We can only do our best, going forward. One step at a time. Go find Prince Lonen and help them bridge Ing's Chasm."

"You want me to work with the enemy?" Yar jerked his arm away, the moment of uncertainty gone, replaced by the brash pride of the arrogant young man who'd declared himself king over his brother's corpse. "I won't do it, Oria."

"We have no choice," she explained with more patience than she'd thought she possessed. "We have a truce until sundown and not enough people left to waste in fighting each other. Go help build the bridge, Yar. Use that grien you built up to help Bára. To help us, not the enemy."

"Okay." He nodded. Then stood. "Okay," he said again. Straightened his shoulders and left the room.

Folcwita Lapo glared at her from a cluster of council members near the windows, but none of them approached her. Which was fine with Oria. Nat's menservants arrived with a litter and managed to move him onto it, by dint of lifting his robes, then covered him with a pall. She didn't envy them that job. Or all the servants of the palace doing likewise with the casualties of the Trom's lethal caress. A further punishment for the survivors, having to cope with this horror.

She shuddered, for that and at the memory of that thing's touch, how it penetrated to her bones, touching intimate places that should belong only to her. The peculiar sensation of being…tasted. In all her life, only her mother and father had touched her skin-to-skin, besides accidental encounters. And Prince Lonen. The contact with him, however, while searing and possibly contributing to her collapse, hadn't unsettled her the way the Trom's did. But it hadn't hurt her, either.

And those things the Trom had said to her. *Princess Ponen. We have satisfied the call of the Summoner. You do not yet command our obedience. Perhaps you never will. I look forward to our next meeting. Thank you for the invitation.*

She hadn't liked it a bit.

"I did not like it either, even filtered through you."

"Why didn't I die?" She asked the question with hesitation, certain she wouldn't like that answer either.

"I don't know." Chuffta sounded apologetic. *"Logically, however, there are two explanations. Either the Trom can control the result of its*

touch, deciding whether to kill or not with it. Or you are in some way immune."

"Both of which would be followed up with the bigger question of why."

"Agreed. But…"

"But what? Be straight with me, Chuffta." She'd spoken a bit too loudly, one of Nat's servants starting towards her, then backing away when she waved him off.

Chuffta hopped off her shoulder and onto the table, keeping his tail in a loose bracelet around her wrist, gripping the wooden edge with his talons and straightening with mantled wings, so they looked eye to eye. *"Oria—I don't know everything either. Your mother visited my flight when you were a little girl and asked for one of us to be your Familiar. I agreed because I was young enough to bond with you and my family said such service to your line could be a great honor, if you turned out as your mother hoped."*

"What does that mean?" Oria's throat had gone dry.

"It means you're special. Your mother knew it. My family knew it. Maybe it's related to this."

"Well, if we're waiting for me to find *hwil* to get answers, we might be dead before that happens. It would be very helpful if someone would share a secret or two before it comes to that."

"Perhaps it is time to ask your mother."

"Perhaps so. But—you left others that you loved to be with me?" The question had never occurred to her. Chuffta had always been there, from her earliest memories. She'd never considered that he'd had a life outside of being her Familiar.

An odd conversation to be having at that moment, but she'd make no further decisions without the queen's approval, and at least this helped calm her.

"Family, friends, sure. But my flight is still there. We are a long-lived people and I will see them when I return. I thought it would be interesting to wander in the world of humans for a while."

"The way things are going, that might be sooner rather than

later," she told him seriously, then stroked the curve of his neck. "But I'm grateful for you, now more than ever."

"I'm glad to be here, now more than ever. And I fervently hope I won't have cause to return home for a long, long time."

~ 18 ~

TO LONEN'S SURPRISE, Prince Yar appeared to help bridge the chasm. At first the Báran prince stood to the side, managing to be both arrogant and diffident, watching them build an anchoring assembly in tandem with the Destrye team on the other side. Wary of the prince's intentions, Lonen detailed Alby to surreptitiously observe him.

But when the opposite team brought out arrows to carry ropes across, Yar stepped up. "Ah...Prince Lonen?"

"Yeah?" First time the kid had used his title. Interesting. Too bad it was now out of date.

"I can make the bridge—with stone."

Arnon bristled. "We don't want any part of your foul magic, you—"

Lonen held up a hand, swallowing his own knee-jerk revulsion. "Yes, we do. If we can spend effort elsewhere, I'm all for it. There's plenty to do." On the other side of the chasm, groups of Destrye and Bárans edged around each other as far as the eye could see. Observing the truce but not embracing it. He wanted to get over there as soon as possible, to start everyone coordinating for the few hours they could. He didn't care who built the bridge. "We'd appreciate it, Prince Yar."

The unsettling mask turned to him for a moment, and he thought the boy might ask a question, but he didn't. Just squared his shoulders and faced the chasm, raising his hands as they'd seen the sorcerers do in battle, the sight giving Lonen a habitual rush of terror before he reminded himself that it wouldn't be directed at his men this time.

"Clear your men away," Yar commanded. "So there are no accidents." The addition came in a less certain tone, revealing a young man's anxiety. Much like a young warrior still learning to trust his skills.

Lonen passed the word, using hand signals to the men across the chasm. Bemused, they obeyed, standing back to watch the sorcerer work, for the first time able to observe without the duress of battle. It seemed that nothing happened immediately and Arnon shifted restively, then stilled as he saw the same thing Lonen did.

The edges of the chasm seemed to blur. Lonen narrowed his eyes, searching for the illusion. Then the stone actually moved. Like the soft clay worked by Destrye potters, the rocks transformed as if under a giant hand. Extruding from each side, thickening as more stone flowed to join in, then extending again, the two fingers of stone met in the middle, blending seamlessly together into a low arch very similar to the bridge that had been burned away, though devoid of ornamentation.

It took only minutes, but Yar lowered his hands with a long breath, sweat streaming down the sides of his face at the mask's edge as if he'd exerted for hours. Then he faced Lonen. "It's solid. They can cross. It takes more, to build a thing, so I kept it simple." He sounded apologetic, but also hopeful, a puppy hoping to be petted.

Lonen gestured to his men that it was safe, grimly amused to see Destrye on both sides pause to knock fists against the stone and slide their feet to test the surface. Caution paid off, to be sure, but their doubt stemmed more from distaste for the magic of the Bárans than from concern that the structure would fail. The stone bridge looked as solid as the sharp rock edge of the chasm, all of one piece. It might, in fact, be difficult to take down again without the help of a sorcerer. But that would not be Lonen's problem.

"An impressive feat, Prince Yar." He nodded his respect, willing to throw the boy a bone.

The boy actually shrugged. He might be younger even than Oria. In fact she'd said as much, hadn't she? When she set him back on his heels. An intriguing glimpse of fiery spirit in an otherwise gentle-seeming personality. "Earth is my affinity and I'm unusually strong," Yar was saying. "But breaking it open is much easier than molding it."

A rock of angry grief plummeted through Lonen. Those cracks in the earth, like the one that took Nolan. Still, it might not have been this boy. "Is it…usual," he asked, trying to sound neutral, "to have that 'affinity'?"

"Oh no." The prince shook his head, sounding proud. "It's a rare gift. I'm a prodigy, in fact."

Full of himself and oblivious to the impact of his words on Lonen, who curled his fingers into fists to stop himself from wrapping them around the sorcerer's throat to throttle the life from Nolan's killer. *Haven't you all had enough of death today?* Oria's weary voice echoed in his head and he loosened his fists. Yes. Yes, he had.

"Perhaps you'd best go help your sister," he suggested, turning away.

"She doesn't want me." The prince sounded far too petulant. "She sent me out here to help you."

Ah, that explained a great deal, and he couldn't really blame her. "Then let's go see to our people."

CLEARING AWAY THE dead took less time than tending to the many injured. That is, once both peoples resigned themselves to collecting a small portion of the ashes that were all that remained of their friends and loved ones, identifying them by jewelry or metal weapons, which was all that didn't burn. The remaining ashes they swept onto wagons and dumped into the seemingly bottomless chasms.

Expedient, if nothing else.

And filthy work, too, both physically and spiritually. Lonen's soul would be begrimed beyond purification by the time they made it back to Dru. His body certainly was. They experienced a bad moment when the Bárans brought out golems to assist. His men cut three to quivering, gelatinous bits before the protesting Bárans explained these would help with the uglier tasks. Only then did they note that these had no fangs or claws as the ones outside the walls had.

The Báran healers also surprised them by offering to tend to the Destrye injured as well, citing the truce and that Lonen's warriors had helped so many survive to reach the hall where the healers worked. Still, Lonen assigned to them only the Destrye who seemed unlikely to survive the short journey out the gates to their own healers with the encamped army outside the walls.

In a stroke of good fortune, the Bárans' dragons had only attacked inside the walls, so the already much-reduced Destrye army outside had escaped further losses. Especially welcome as most of those men weren't stationed inside Bára because they'd already been too severely wounded. While speaking to the Destrye captains, Lonen relayed the news of King Archimago's and Prince Ion's deaths, along with the remains of their bodies, such as they were.

A curse of this benighted land, that death took his family without leaving bodies to properly anoint, to guide their steps to the Hall of Warriors. He could only pray they'd find their way regardless. Surely Arill would not be so cruel as to turn her back for a technicality of ritual.

They would burn the Destrye dead that they could, and decamp the next day in stages, dividing the army into groups by travel speed. There would be no more delays in negotiation. Lonen intended to put as much distance between the Destrye and Bára as possible. They'd be done with this place if he had to browbeat Oria and Yar into staying up all night. And this Queen Rhianna, if she showed herself. She had not thus far.

The sun was declining to the flat horizon by the time Lonen walked over Yar's stone bridge to the palace, weary in mind and body, and filthier than he'd been in his life. His skin itched to be rid of the ashes of the dead, but he'd made an agreement. The Destrye kept their word.

To his surprise, Oria met him just inside the doors. She'd changed from the gray dress she'd worn earlier, and had washed her hair. No longer braided, it floated around her like a cloak of copper, contrasting with the slim outline of the deep green gown she'd donned. The white dragonlet sat on her shoulder, iridescent scales catching the firelight from the sconces in the dimming hall, reflecting back Oria's colors.

He scrubbed a hand over his eyes and looked again. "Princess Oria," he acknowledged. "It seems the sun is setting."

"As it does every day," she replied, in the manner of someone returning a ritual greeting. Then shook her head slightly and gave him a rueful twist of her lips. "I think I don't want to know what grime coats you. I've arranged for you all to have access to the palace baths. Several of your captains, your lieutenant and your brother are already there." She gestured at a young serving boy. "Bero will show you the way."

"Thank you." It took a moment for his numb brain to process. "The truce—"

"Can we agree to extend it until you are not soiled with the remains of all our dead?"

"Yes." As much as he longed to be clean, he lingered a moment more. "I appreciate your thoughtfulness."

"In turn, I appreciate your long afternoon's toil on behalf of my people," she returned gravely. "I've heard many reports of your efforts and a proper bath seems a small favor in return. Go bathe. There are clothes for you to wear while yours are cleaned. I'm having food and drink brought to the council chambers. Everyone can eat freely."

"So we can stay there as long as necessary to come to an agreement."

He must have sounded harsher than he meant to because she flinched. The dragonlet's long white tail snaked around her wrist, coiling and uncoiling.

"I think it's best," she said, in a reasonably smooth tone. "Then we can all be done with each other."

As if it were so easy. "That will depend on you, Princess. We'll go when I'm satisfied with the terms."

"You and I made one agreement before. I feel confident we can come to another."

"Perhaps so." Uncertain what moved him to do it, he bowed—a slight incline—but a concession Ion would have smacked the back of his head for. Ion, however, now walked with the dead and Lonen lived. "I shall return shortly and we will find out."

~ 19 ~

ORIA LINGERED IN the entry hall until she felt certain all the Destrye who were going to had returned to the palace and found the baths. Thankfully all of them had been appreciative of the consideration and none had argued. She'd been uncertain how they'd receive the courtesy, as they were hardly well groomed at the best of times. Apparently being covered in the ashes of human bodies crossed the line, even for them. Or they were too exhausted. The cleanup efforts had been grim, all the men emanating dark thoughts. Some angry, some in despair.

Lonen, in particular, was a tumult of rage and guilt, all underlain with a grief that matched her own—energy he projected as forcefully as he swung that axe.

"He will not go easy on you," Chuffta observed.

"I don't need easy. I need them to go. We'll agree to their terms, watch them leave us be, and then set about rebuilding." She didn't want to think about the Trom's promise to return.

"You don't know what terms he'll ask for."

"Does it matter?" She sounded bleak, even to herself. "We are a decimated people. Prince Lonen already understands that we wouldn't agree to total subjugation. Anything else we can live with."

"Perhaps he'll ask for that again."

"If so, we'll ask Yar to build that bridge when we come to it." She smiled a little at her own joke, making her way down the hall to the council chambers. In truth she was proud of her little brother.

She'd expected him to pitch in with heavy lifting, at best, and stay out of her aura at least—not create an entire bridge. And then he hadn't returned immediately, instead staying out and assisting with the cleanup. Something he wouldn't have stooped to before now. But then, before now she wouldn't have possessed the audacity to send him off on a task, either.

The temple taught that the crucible of crisis built character. *True growth is uncomfortable, even painful.* Of course, the priestesses meant by testing the strength of *hwil* under intense pressure, but perhaps the horrors of this week would mature both her and Yar. A small benefit for all they'd suffer—and would still face in the days to come.

Yar had dragged himself back to the palace before Lonen did, but not by much, exhausted and utterly defeated. Witnessing what horrors he and Nat had wrought affected him enough to agree to let Oria handle the negotiations, saying he no longer trusted himself. Then he shuffled off, uncharacteristically despondent, to bathe and eat in his own rooms, then to sleep.

More than a little weary herself, Oria envied him the respite. She wanted nothing more at that moment than the remote isolation of her tower. But she'd slept for the past several days—she could make it a few hours more.

"You were unconscious for days because your body shut down to keep your spirit attached. It's not exactly the same thing."

"I feel all right. Nothing like I did before I collapsed. I'll ask for a recess if I feel it coming on."

"Did you feel it coming on before?"

She didn't bother to answer as they both knew she hadn't. Yes, the pressure and input had been building to unbearable levels—and blew up exponentially once she stepped outside the city gates—but she'd expected to feel the onset of actual collapse. Instead she'd simply blanked. Gone from agonizing consciousness to clawing her way out of that gray fog, days later. Not something to dwell on.

A number of people waited in the council chambers and she

hesitated outside the doors, not ready to go in. Lapo, along with several other folcwitas, had Priest Vico in one corner, arguing in low voices. Priestess Febe sat nearby, apparently meditating. Freshly washed Destrye warriors prowled the laden food table. Even in the pale silk trousers and loose shirts of Báran men they stood out with their dark skin and wild hair. No sign of Queen Rhianna. She'd said she wouldn't come, though she'd received the news of Nat's death with her former outward calm.

She and Oria had spent an hour together while the queen's handmaidens washed Oria's hair and fetched her a clean gown from the tower, so Oria wouldn't have to make the climb. The queen had put her off when she asked why the Trom called her *Ponen*, though Oria thought it wasn't that she didn't know, but rather she couldn't bring herself to care enough to muster an answer. Her mother also listlessly refused to advise Oria, telling her that whatever terms she set with the Destrye didn't matter to her.

With Oria on her feet again, her mother seemed to have again lost the brief spark of her old self.

"She may yet recover," Chuffta comforted her.

Oria fervently hoped so.

Folcwita Lapo spotted Oria and waved her over. "Does he think I'm a servant girl to be summoned?" she muttered, irritation crawling up her spine.

"Don't go then."

"I'm not going to." Instead she waved him off in the same preemptory fashion and ambled to the buffet table, picking up a plate and filling it slowly, deliberately dawdling. The Destrye gave way, nodding with more courtesy than she would have credited such rough men with. Ironic that she'd rather be in their company than the folcwitas'.

"Princess." Lonen greeted her with a nod, taking up a plate of his own and scowling at the table. He'd tied his still-wet hair back with a piece of leather and trimmed his beard to a neat scruff. Between the two, the hard line of his jaw stood out more, along with the scar that dragged down his cheek. He shouldn't look so appealing, nor should she be battling an unsettling urge to run her hand over his beard, to discover if it felt soft or scratchy. She never wanted to touch people, as it only led to disaster.

Lonen noticed her intent stare and raised dark brows. "Problem?"

"I didn't expect you so quickly, Prince Lonen."

He tilted a wry glance at her, a glint of something in his slate-gray eyes. "Your baths were such a treat I thought it best not to linger, lest I get too comfortable and fall asleep. A strategy of yours, perhaps, to incapacitate me before the negotiations."

"I'm sure you must be exhausted." She clutched her plate, glad of something to do with her hands, and focused on not stepping back, though the Destrye stood much too close for her to screen out his emotions. A great deal going on under that remote expression, but…a flicker of humor there, like a blue flame licking up from banked coals of darker feelings.

"As you must be also," he returned. "We have not had the opportunity to speak since you fainted in my arms, but I believe you've been unwell since."

"I did not faint, certainly not in your arms." She used the excuse of making room at the table for new arrivals to put a bit of distance between them. That was better.

"Actually, the Destrye did catch you when you collapsed."

"Not helpful," she muttered through clenched teeth.

Lonen stepped back also, the scar on his cheek pulling with displeasure. "Is there no meat?"

"Meat? Animal flesh?"

A ghost of a smile twisted the man's lips, the frown smoothing. "Generally, yes—meat is animal flesh. The Destrye are rarely cannibals."

"No," she replied a bit tartly, feeling the sting of embarrassment that she'd implied as much. Surely they weren't really and he was teasing her. "Bárans eat only fruits, vegetables, grains. There's some cheese you could try."

"No wonder they're all so weak," one of the nearby warriors said to another, to a crack of laughter.

"Don't try it—that stuff is rancid."

"Stand down," Lonen snapped. "Get your food and go. If I want to hear from you, I'll say so."

They bowed and hastened away with admirable discipline while Lonen peered doubtfully at the round of cheese. He took a bite, then spit it out with a grimace of distaste. "It *is* rancid. Do you mean to be rid of us with food poisoning?"

Oria risked drawing near again, reaching a hand around him to snag a piece of the cheese, biting into it and chewing. "No. We don't think of it as rancid. It's more…cured over time."

He frowned at her in such consternation that she nearly laughed, an odd bubble rising through all the dark despair. "Did my brothers bring in meat for you before this? I didn't think to ask the kitchens for it. We don't have much, but…"

Lonen was slowly shaking his head, expression opaque, but a tendril of curiosity winding through his bleak emotions. "You are the first of your family to offer us food."

Oh. Maybe she'd erred in doing so. Probably a conquered people didn't play host to their overlords. She made a terrible diplomat. Another course of study to add to the list, should their lives ever return to normal.

"You're doing fine. I'll tell you if you make a real misstep."

Holding her gaze, Lonen bit into the cheese again, a smaller bite this time, chewing it thoughtfully. He swallowed, the ridge in his throat moving with it. Her fingertips tingled to touch him there, too. "An acquired taste, perhaps," he said and she had to drag her thoughts back to the subject at hand.

"Try this," she said, not certain why she felt hot. Though the curtains lay slack along the windows, no breezes to catch. Reaching for the crock, she dabbed some honey on his hunk of cheese, smiling as he bit in, his brows raising in pleasure.

"It's sweet. We have something like this made from the sap of trees in winter."

"Ours comes from insects. They make it to feed their young."

He made such a grimace at that, setting the cheese down and pushing it aside, that she realized she shouldn't have told him. It did sound odd, put that way. "I can ask for—"

"It was thoughtfully done—" Lonen said at the same time, a faint smile for their mutual gaffe. Surely he wouldn't be as nervous as she? "Thank you," he continued, "but we have meat at the encampment, if the men wish to find some."

"Oh." She had no idea what armies ate. "Where did you get it?"

Two lines made brackets between his thick brows, a definite sense of puzzlement coming from him. "We brought some with us, dried, and we've been sending parties back across the bay to hunt for more."

"Oh," she said again, feeling like an idiot. Hunting. Of course. She had no idea what animals lived across the bay, but would not ask and further reveal her ignorance. Averting her gaze, she noticed Folcwita Lapo prowling the other side of the room, throwing her black looks. The force of his displeasure crawled over her sensitive nerves even from that distance, a headache pounding into her temple.

"Careful, Oria."

She was sick to death of being careful, of being so cursed weak. But she really did not look forward to sitting at that table and having everyone's anger shout at her for hours. How could she make good decisions under those conditions? Especially when only she and the Destrye prince need agree to the terms, as they both spoke for their people at the moment. The rest was courtesy and she had used up her quotient of that commodity.

"An excellent idea."

"Right." So great was her relief at the suggestion that she forgot herself and spoke out load, reaching up to scratch Chuffta's chest.

Lonen gave her a startled glance, then scrutinized her Familiar, distaste wafting off of him. That time she didn't care. She took a physical step back, bringing his stormy gaze to hers again. "I have a suggestion, Prince Lonen. Is there any reason you and I can't sit down alone and discuss terms one on one—do we need all these people?"

She'd surprised him, which at least backed off the worst of the disgust. "My brother will be annoyed," Lonen said slowly, thinking it through, "but I outrank him. What of your advisers, your council?"

"They will also be annoyed, but I outrank them." She nearly smiled at the flicker of amusement that lit the stormy gray of his eyes. "Arguably they have had their opportunity for days now to make their opinions known."

"Believe me, Princess, they have. Repeatedly."

She didn't ask why the Destrye had tolerated the obstructionism. From the resolute set of Lonen's jaw and the determined anger rising out of him, he, at least, was done with it.

"Then I see no reason you and I shouldn't sit down privately to discuss. Come. I know a place." She set her plate down, not hungry in the first place, and beckoned to Juli. She liked the junior priestess, who possessed both a solicitous nature and discretion, and asked Juli to relay that Oria had withdrawn to her tower and should not be disturbed—after a suitable delay. They'd see how long that lasted before Folcwita Lapo and the others realized she'd circumvented them. She started to go. When Lonen didn't accompany her, she turned back. "Problem?"

"Shouldn't we include a guard of some sort?"

"Why—are you afraid of me?" She regretted asking it, because his reaction stabbed at her, that severe distaste, shaded with suspicion and distrust. His eyes flicked to Chuffta and away.

"I don't know." He paused for a long moment. Then his mood shifted and he smiled in truth, a bright emotion echoing it, a flash of who he might be when not at war. "It depends on if you have that sword on you. My life could be in danger."

"A risk you'll have to take, Prince Lonen." She made herself stay somber. And did not further draw attention to Chuffta by mentioning his ability to guard her well-being.

~ 20 ~

"It's King Lonen, by the way," he told Oria as he followed her out the doors. The dragonlet had swiveled its head backwards on its neck, keeping those bright green eyes fixed on him, unblinking, reminding him uncomfortably of its enormous lethal cousins. He wouldn't let it unsettle him. Or her, with her uncanny gaze that seemed to see more in him than he liked.

Could she read his thoughts? It would be interesting to test it. Something to discomfit her from that unshakable poise. Like working up a vivid image of tossing up her skirts and ravishing her until she screamed his name and—

"When did that happen?"

He nearly asked what before he caught himself. She cast him a questioning glance, which at least seemed to prove she hadn't eavesdropped on those prurient thoughts. Something that felt like a reprieve, after the fact. Still—what witchy powers did she possess? He wanted to pose the question, but it seemed…intimate. Not appropriate for the conversation they needed to have. About politics. So the Destrye could finally leave this cursed place and go home, find their own women again.

What Oria—or any of the vile Bárans—could or could not do should no longer be his problem. A fine goal for the negotiation.

Oria frowned slightly, and the dragonlet leaned into her, tail coiling so much like a snake that he fought the impulse to throw it to the ground and stomp on it. "*King* Lonen?" she prompted, emphasizing the title.

"As soon as my brother the heir died," he said shortly. "There's no need for discussion, ceremony, or…law committees, among us, as it seems you Bárans have."

She nodded, looking thoughtful, neither confirming nor denying. They arrived at a set of closed doors, two of the city guard outside it.

"Admit no one but Queen Rhianna," she told them, and they bowed, opening the doors for her. She began to ascend a winding set of stairs, but Lonen paused, taking a moment to observe the weight of a large metal-clad bar settling into place behind them, as if by magic.

"Operated by a secret external mechanism," came her explanation, and he turned to find her copper gaze on him, again discerning far too much. "But it can be lifted from the inside with a bit of effort. I managed it, so I'm sure you could."

"Ah." He restrained a comment that her slim arms looked barely able to lift the weight of the dragonlet, much less that bar.

"I hope you don't mind climbing," she said as he joined her on the step. "It's a bit of one."

"Not a problem." He took in the spiraling stairs, made of stone and clinging to the curved outer wall of the tower, circling an echoing space from the ground floor to the dizzying heights above. Flaming sconces studded the walls at intervals, but failed to illuminate the ceiling that must be there, somewhere, high above. Open windows looked out on the city, though the night seemed too still for breezes. "Do you intend to be queen?" he asked, earning a startled glance.

"Is that one of your terms?"

"No." He didn't know why he'd blurted out that question. "I don't care about your government, as long as you keep it far away from the Destrye."

"Then why do you ask?"

He gestured at the endless rise of stairs. "Making conversation. It looks like a long walk."

"I apologize for that. But it's the best place for me to be for a number of reasons."

"Why's that?"

"No one will be able to interrupt or interfere with our conversation. I want a solution, not more arguing and delay."

"I meant, why won't they be able to interrupt?"

"It's my tower." She shrugged. "No one may enter without my permission, by sacred law."

"Interesting. To protect your virtue?" If so, he shouldn't be alone with her. Certainly the thought shouldn't give such a punch to his gut.

He surprised a breathy laugh out of her. "It's more complicated than that."

"Try me."

She threw him a repressive glance, all humor sapped from her expression. "None of it is relevant to our negotiations. To answer an easier question—no, I have no desire to be queen and there are…reasons I should not take that role. Suffice to say, we have a queen. My mother is alive and well. There will be decisions to make depending upon what you and I agree the Destrye role in our government will be."

He mulled over her words—both spoken and what she cagily withheld. When she'd first offered surrender, he'd proposed total subjugation because he'd been thinking in battle terms. Fighting made things simple. You won or you lost. Usually if you lost, you died. Or wished you had. But this would not be so straightforward. He had no desire to rule Bára from afar. During that interminable wrangling, his father had never gotten to the point of giving his vision for the future of the two peoples—one of many things Lonen would give a great deal to know that his father would never be able to relate.

None of them had discussed what would happen if they managed to stop the golem incursions, other than a vague idea of going back to a way of life already thoroughly destroyed. But King

Archimago had died in part because he'd taken responsibility for the innocent portion of the population of Bára. Rage at the injustice of it all boiled through Lonen. Against all odds, they'd triumphed…and yet, what had they won?

Oria paused, putting a slim hand against the stone wall. She'd paled, her breathing labored.

"Are you well?" he asked, though clearly she wasn't. The dragonlet peered around her hair at him, the stare oddly accusing.

She raised her eyes ruefully at the remaining stairs. "I am not in condition for extensive exercise, to my great chagrin. Also, as you observed, I've been unwell these past days."

Something told him that wasn't the entire truth, but before he could question her further, she pushed away from the wall with a grim set to her jaw, gathering up her long skirts, and set to climbing again.

"Why pick a place so far then, that takes so much effort?"

"I'll need to get up there eventually tonight, it might as well be now. And…I'll be able to think better." She hadn't been looking at him, but did then with a slight grimace. "I should probably not admit such things to my enemy."

She was likely right, but for a few moments—to his own chagrin—he'd forgotten that about them. Also he wasn't entirely sure what she'd admitted. "I could carry you," he found himself offering, then regretted it instantly.

Already shaking her head, she brushed him off. "Really it's better if you don't touch me."

Don't touch me. Her desperate command of before still rankled. "I'd hardly rape you," he replied, stiffly furious. "None of your Bárans have been bothered that way."

"I did not know that," she said quietly, perhaps because she lacked the breath for more. "But that's not what I meant. I intended no offense, King Lonen."

Feeling like he should apologize but unwilling to, he remained silent for the rest of the ascent. Better for her not to waste breath talking anyway. Finally, they reached the very top and she led him through a series of rooms to an open-air terrace full of flowering trees, blossoms luminous in the night, and the rustle of trailing vines. Oria lifted her face to the sky, Sgatha high and rose-colored, sighing in what could only be relief. No sign of Grienon, so he must be in his dark phase.

Lonen wandered to the balustrade, struck by the view of Bára below, all falling away beneath her eyrie. Beyond the high city walls the Destrye camp blazed with campfires, the long dry plateau moonlit around them. Oria's tower. It tugged some emotion from him, a strange tenderness that felt misplaced amid all the rage and grief.

"You live up here, all the time, alone?"

She joined him at the edge of the balcony, though still a good distance away, well out of touching range. As if he'd try after she'd sounded so horrified by the possibility. "I go down sometimes. And I'm not alone. I have—had—attendants, teachers. My mother, too, spends time with me here. A few others. Also, there's always…"

When she didn't finish the thought, he turned his back on the staggering—and stomach-dropping—view. The torchlight made her hair even more coppery, if possible, and the moon gave a pinkish cast to her fair skin and the winged lizard's white hide, both more otherworldly than ever. How she could both fascinate and repel him, he didn't know. Unless she practiced sorcery on him as he suspected her brothers had been doing to his father. What he needed was to get away from her unnatural influence and this place of monsters and death.

Superstitiously, he moved away from that dizzying drop. She might look fragile and become sickly climbing stairs, but he knew firsthand how powerful the Báran magic could be. He did not care to sample what a long fall that would be.

"There's always what? That lizardling you cart about everywhere?"

"His name is Chuffta." She sounded stiff. He'd annoyed her,

insulting her pet. Good. Better than feeling that strange tenderness.

"You don't really believe you can talk to that thing, do you?"

She gave him a long look, then went to a set of low chairs around a table with a freakish violet fire burning in the center of it. Pouring from a pitcher into two transparent goblets, she nudged one in his direction, then sat back, cupping the other and drinking deeply. She heaved such a sigh of relief that he couldn't restrain his curiosity and went over to pick up his. The goblet was made of something very thin that felt as if it might shatter in his grip. He sniffed at the contents. Fruity and sweet. He tasted it. Juice, not wine. Figured.

"Shall we get to the subject at hand?" she suggested in an even tone.

"You didn't answer my question."

"Because the answer doesn't matter. What I do or do not believe has no bearing on our negotiations. We could argue all night about our differences and it seems both our peoples have wasted enough time doing that already. What terms do you propose?"

"You don't have an offer?"

She actually made snorting noise, at odds with her regal poise. "No wonder you all spent so many days discussing. If I'm not mistaken, you're in the position of power. It seems to me that this conversation should consist of you, the conqueror, giving terms to me, the conquered—at which point I attempt to weasel out whatever concessions I can."

Abruptly tired, he sat across from her, dangling the goblet between his knees, reminding himself to handle it gently. He felt strangely naked wearing the soft garb of the Báran men, the loose material of the shirt and trousers so thin he barely felt it on his skin, but also grateful for it in the overly warm night. Something about sitting there with her, with the softly burning fire—pretty, even in its strangeness—and the moonlight turning the night-blooming garden into an oasis in her stone city surrounded by an unforgiving desert, made all the war and politics feel far away. For a wild moment, he entertained what it might be like to be there under other circumstances, to be courting her as he would Natly, seeing if he could make her laugh and—

He shook off the romantic notion. That was exhaustion getting to him, and being so long away from feminine company. Natly was waiting for him to return, a normal, beautiful and spirited woman of his own people. One with a strong, lush figure and vitality to run and ride with the best of the Destrye. And he'd be returning as king, which should be enough to finally persuade her to marry him.

"Mostly I just want this done." His turn to be admitting to the enemy what he shouldn't.

"Why don't we start with what you came here for—were you after the source of Báran magic?"

"Arill, no!" The shock of her suggestion had him rejecting that foul notion too brusquely, because she physically flinched, making him feel absurdly guilty, as if he'd punched her. "No, we want nothing more than to keep clear of your magic," he said more smoothly, rolling the fragile goblet between his palms. It reminded him of Oria, in a way—both easily crushed but also exotically lovely, unlike anything he'd seen or touched before. Not trusting himself not to shatter it carelessly, he set it aside.

"Why did you attack us then?"

Glancing up sharply, he opened his mouth to retort, but her expression, wide, wondering, and without guile made him pause. An act perhaps, but… "You attacked us first, Princess."

She shook back her hair, frowning. "How can that be true? Our peoples have battled in the past, I know, but the peace has lasted for centuries now. The Destrye live far from here. *You* came to Bára. We only defended ourselves."

It could be that she truly didn't know, isolated in her manmade fancy of a garden. He gestured to the trees, the lavish vines with their hand-sized pearlescent blossoms, faces turned towards Sgatha and visited by pale-winged moths that hovered over them as they drank. "Where does the water come from for all of this?"

Her frown deepened and she looked around, as if seeing it all for the first time. "Well, servants haul it up, but I gather that's not the answer you mean. They bring it from stores, cisterns below the palace. All the city buildings have them, as reserves for dry weather."

He gazed out at the sere, moonlit plain. "Is it ever not dry weather?"

"We have a monsoon season, though it's been very light the last few years. When it does rain, we have roof cisterns to gather it. A good monsoon season gives us water to last until the next."

"And if it's a bad monsoon season, very light, as in the last few years?"

She shrugged. "Well, obviously we've had enough stores to be getting by. My trees aren't dying so we haven't run out."

"*Or...*" He held her gaze. "You've been sending those unnaturally puppeted golems of yours—only equipped with fangs and claws—to steal our water and kill any living creature that stands in their way. Mothers, children, livestock." A bleakness washed over him at the memories.

To his surprise, Oria's expression echoed that.

She looked horrified, even. "You mean, similar to the ones we used to defend the city when you attacked?"

He barked out a laugh and swallowed some of the juice to salve his dry throat. Too sweet, but the flavor was growing on him. "They didn't just look like them, Oria. They were the same. They've been attacking us for years, decimating our people and driving us out of our homeland. We tracked them back here to make it stop. We had no choice."

That last came out too forcefully, too defensive. She needed to know the truth, though. He ran his hands through his hair, remembering belatedly that he'd tied it back in an attempt to look more appropriate for a meeting with her in her lavish gown. Impatient with it, he tugged off the leather tie and tossed it on the table. She might find him brutish and unkempt, but what did he care?

"Everyone has choices," she said, as quiet as he'd been loud.

"You have to understand, Princess of Bára. You—or maybe not *you*, I don't know, but your people—you drove us to this. Yes, we had choices. We either had to stop you, die trying, or die by the claw of your golems."

"I see. A moment, please." She rose, seeming restless, moving back to the balustrade and gazing out. The quiet murmur of her voice drifted on the night air like the heavy scent of the moon blossoms.

She must be talking to that dragonlet. The absurdity annoyed him, but weariness softened the edges of the irritation. Oria was right that they'd argued enough to last years. Along the rim of the fire table, a series of animal figurines paraded, made of the same delicately transparent material as the goblets, catching and reflecting the violet firelight. He picked up one that reminded him of one of the forest cats of Dru. Amazingly lifelike, the cat seemed to be stalking something.

The white lizard hopped off Oria's shoulder, wings unfurling for balance and catching Lonen's eye, then took a perch on the balustrade, green eyes glowing. Oria ran an affectionate caress down the thing's neck with long, slender fingers that stirred Lonen in deep places that felt long forgotten. She turned her back to the drop, facing him with hands folded over her belly, chin high and steady. "So, if this is the case—and I know nothing of it, but have no reason to disbelieve you—then you've succeeded."

It took him a moment to drag his thoughts back and she tilted her head, with a wry smile. "Your men killed the sorcerer who created the vicious golems," she explained. "That was a singular gift."

Anger burned through his stupidly besotted brain. Perhaps Ion had been right about his lack of judgement—and now Lonen could never tell him so. "A singular *gift*?" he snarled.

She held up a hand, both fending him off—though he hadn't moved toward her—and acknowledging his protest. "A poor choice of words, I apologize. That's simply how we refer to the magic. *Affinity* might be a better word. At any rate, no more of those golems will be sent against you because the man who piloted them is gone."

"We've seen others of those golems around the city."

"Piloted by others with far less ability, as manual labor only, and…it's something I cannot explain, but if they go too far, they lose their animation and collapse. I don't know exactly how the late Priest Sisto was able to send the water-seeking golems all the way to Dru, but I do know—from conversations among us—that we have no one else in Bára who could. I can also assure you that we won't launch attacks against you of any other kind, if you agree in turn to leave us alone."

He wanted nothing more. "How can you guarantee that?"

"What else can I offer?" She held up her palms, copper eyebrows forking as she thought. "I'll add a personal promise. If you are attacked by anyone or anything of Bára, I vow to do whatever it takes to protect the Destrye."

"A sweeping promise."

She smiled, ever so slightly. "Easy enough to make, as I can be sure Bára won't attack you again. We have other problems than warring with the Destrye."

"And you…have the ability to protect the Destrye?" Seeing her in that violet and rosy light, he believed that perhaps she did.

The brief moment of amusement fled. "I hope so, because Bára will need that, too. I can only promise that I'll do my utmost for the Destrye, as I would for Bára."

"I'll have to settle for that, then."

She nodded, crisply. "So that's agreed. You say you have no inclination to govern us. What else do you want?"

Nothing, he realized. His father, Ion, even Nolan might have sought to take more, but he himself would be hard pressed to simply put things back together again. Still… "You must agree to keep those other things away from us, too. The dragons and the monsters that rode them."

She folded her hands again, expression shadowed. "I have no control over the Trom, but I believe them to be our problem. They came at our call and have a long history with our people. I don't think they have reason to pursue the Destrye in any way."

He nodded, wishing that made him feel better. The way that thing had caressed her cheek… "What did it say to you—and why didn't its touch kill you?" he asked, unsure if he wanted to know for her sake or his.

"I don't know. It's something I shall have to discover more about in the days to come." With her body silhouetted against the moon, the violet fire not quite enough to reveal her expression, he couldn't read her reaction to his ill-advised question. Some tremor in her voice, though, made him think she was afraid.

"You don't know what it said, or why it didn't kill you?"

"Why it didn't kill me. The words were…an old dialect, and were not important."

She was lying about that, which shouldn't annoy him as much as it did. "Are you in danger from it?"

She cocked her head slightly. "If so," she said in a measured tone that revealed he'd pricked her pride, "that also would be my problem, not yours, King Lonen. Do you require anything else?"

He searched for the words to express it. He wanted his youthful idealism back, to know that magic could be wonderful, the way he'd imagined it as a boy, the way it seemed possible in her enchanted garden. Not watered with the blood of countless Destrye dead. He wanted to be rid of the crushing grief, to rewind time so none of this had happened. Except that he would never have met Oria. Which didn't matter anyway as this meeting sealed their goodbye. He'd return to Dru elevated in station but impoverished in heart and spirit.

Nothing Oria could give him would change that.

"No," was all he said.

"All right." She scrubbed her hands briskly, as if shaking off dust. "Let's write it down and end this terrible day."

He agreed. Though once again, the final victory felt lacking.

~ 21 ~

ORIA STOOD AT the balustrade, the rising sun scalding her eyes as she watched the Destrye army decamp. Chuffta perched on her shoulder, similarly fascinated by the spectacle. She should be feeling a sense of triumph. She'd achieved what she'd wanted all those days ago, standing in that same spot, straining for any sign of the battle.

Don't put attention on a result you do not want.

For the first time, the import of that lesson came clear. She'd wanted quite desperately to know more about the battle, to see and hear and experience it up close. She'd gotten exactly what she'd wanted, hadn't she? And it had left her an empty shell, able only to feel grief and regret.

"A fine sight this is." High Priestess Febe said, stepping up beside her. "Who would have believed even a day ago that they'd leave so easily?"

"It was hardly easy," Oria replied, toying with the strip of leather Lonen had used to tie his hair. He'd left it on her fire table and she'd picked it up, first out of curiosity, not sure what it was, this foreign object in her otherwise unchanging world. Then she'd held onto it for no reason other than it gave her something to do with her hands. "It only took the near total destruction of our people." A destruction brought upon them twice over by her own family, something she still didn't know how to reconcile. A destruction that still loomed in their future, if what Lonen had said was true. If Bára had gone to such lengths to steal so much water for so long, did they have any reserves at all? The cloudless sky and heating plain mercilessly glared in confirmation of her worst fears.

"The arrival of the Trom frightened them." The priestess's mask inclined as she nodded at her own insight, oblivious to Oria's point—and probably Bára's dire circumstances. "Else they would not have agreed to terms so speedily afterwards. However you managed that, particularly without the advice of the council, at least they are gone."

Oria bit her tongue, keeping her opinion on that to herself. There would be time enough to sort out all of that, once the Destrye left. Already Bára felt different with none of them in it. In exchange for her promise that they would not be attacked or pursued, Lonen had withdrawn every last warrior the night before. Perhaps the vacancy in the usually humming energy of the city could be attributed to the loss of so many lives.

Or perhaps to the long shadow cast by the advent of the Trom. The people of Bára looked to face a rapid extermination by fire and bone-crunching, or an extended demise by starvation and drought. Removing the threat posed by the Destrye had only changed the cause and the timeframe—Bára still stood to fall as surely as she'd predicted the week before.

But if Oria had learned nothing else, she understood now that fretting changed nothing. Her mother would be proud. If she could see past her mourning.

Resolutely, she put her mind on next steps. "What can we expect of the Trom now, High Priestess?"

"That's not something for you to worry about, Princess Oria. This is a matter for the temple."

Chuffta made a snorting sound in her mind, one she'd love to make aloud. She wouldn't, however. Though she'd lost much of her respect for the temple in the past days, she would not demonstrate it overtly.

"I disagree. The Trom indicated that it would be back to visit me, personally."

"Surely the Trom meant the temple, where the priestesses are trained to interact with them. Without having received your mask, without *hwil* and the teachings that follow, you are ill-equipped to deal with such an important entity."

Oria turned with angry incredulity on the woman. "The important entity that dropped my brother with one touch, that killed him and countless others for no reason at all?"

The priestess's mask gazed back at her with equanimity. "I understand that such emotional outbursts are difficult for you to control, as you have no *hwil*, but do try to restrain yourself from wild accusations, Princess. Clearly Prince Nat, while seemingly worthy of his mask, was in truth lacking."

Back to "prince" for Nat, demoted again, if he'd ever been truly elevated to king. "By that logic, I was not found lacking because the Trom's touch didn't kill me," Oria snapped back.

The priestess didn't reply, turning her face back to the Destrye army. Aha.

"Indeed," Chuffta echoed the thought. *"Something there."*

"It called me Princess Ponen," she said, noting how the other women tensed, ever so slightly. Not enough to break *hwil*, but a lick of bright emotion leaking through.

"I don't know that word," Febe said, voice blander than the gray fog that had cocooned Oria. A lie. Oria felt it in her bones.

"I need training," she told the priestess. "If I'm ill-equipped to deal with the Trom, then it's the temple's responsibility to teach me what I need to know."

"You know the rules, Princess. Only those with *hwil* can be taught. The knowledge is too powerful to be entrusted to the unstable." Priestess Febe attempted to sound regretful, but the untruth radiated off of her. Did she not know how easily Oria could sense that?

"Perhaps not." Chuffta sounded thoughtful. *"I don't have access to anyone else's experience, so I don't know how they perceive magic. We know yours is unique, with your unusual sensitivity. We've learned much*

about your magic in the last days."

She really wanted to be able to discuss this with Chuffta, a surge of excitement lifting her spirits from the morose depths. It seemed wrong to feel hopeful when they faced so much mourning and such severe trials ahead. And yet the prospect that there might be an alternative solution to her problem, some other way to access her sgath—maybe without all that endless and futile meditating!—to end this crippling sensitivity and maybe have a weapon to fight that loathsome Trom, to find other sources of water for Bára…

The possibility gave her reasons to keep going. She sorely needed those.

Once Lonen had said goodnight and goodbye, she'd expected the relief of aloneness. Having his jangling, angry, and grieving presence gone should have given her a whole other level of palliation. Like stepping into the rooftop garden after all the chaos.

And his departure *had* given her some of that respite. But it left her with an odd feeling that had taken her time to identify. She'd even let Chuffta guide her into meditation so she could sort it out before she tried to sleep. Finally, she'd identified the emotion.

Loss.

For the first time in her life, she experienced real loneliness.

You live up here, all the time, alone? His incredulous question kept rattling back through her brain. That and the feelings he'd emanated, sensual and rich, that heated her inside as if the sun's midday rays penetrated her. Waking feelings she hadn't tasted outside of those illicit illustrations of the Destrye that had so fascinated her.

They'd lingered long after his departure, touching her even in her sleep. She'd wakened from an intense dream of impossible sensations—of his hair in her hands, his mouth on her body, and their skin slicked together. Things she was unlikely to feel other than in dreams, as she'd never be able to bear such contact with anyone other than an ideal husband, which the temple wouldn't grant her even the opportunity to test for until she earned a mask.

Certainly she would never be able to touch Lonen so intimately, even if he wasn't gone from Bára forever.

She wrapped the leather band around a forefinger. Perhaps she kidded herself that she only held it to give vent to her restless fretting. The scent of the leather, maybe something of the man's energy, lingered in the tie. The Destrye king was such a creature of the larger world, with his exuberant masculinity. She'd watched him from her tower, greeting his men, slapping backs, and shouting happily about going home. The words had echoed clearly even to her heights.

Unable to sleep after those restless, unsettling dreams, and telling herself she was only performing her duty to the Bárans, she'd kept vigil all night, watching them pack up and go, just as she bore witness as they streamed away into the rising sun.

It had all left her strangely bereft, which seemed impossible on top of all her other sorrows. So this renewed purpose would put her back on track to do what she needed to serve Bára and her people, however she could. No more wallowing in grief over the past or of what would never be. The next step would be to get real answers.

"That would be helpful, indeed," Chuffta agreed wryly.

She scratched his chest in silent solidarity and gratitude that he didn't comment on or judge her preoccupation with King Lonen.

Not without some petty pleasure, she broke the cloud of smug satisfaction surrounding the high priestess. "Tell Queen Rhianna and Prince Yar I'd like them to meet me for breakfast in the salon, as soon as they can manage it."

Febe stiffened. "Am I your handmaiden, Princess?"

"The temple has not yet seen fit to supply me with a replacement for Alva, and *you* seem to be available." She let the pause hang, tasting the woman's rancor, learning what she could from it. If they wouldn't teach her, she'd discover her own truths. How had the first sorceress learned, after all?

"An oversight, Princess," Febe replied. "With all the tumult and you being an invalid all those days. We believed you near death, not in need of tending from one of our few remaining priestesses. A pity that your fragile psyche cannot withstand the company of someone less trained. They are a precious resource, not to be squandered on frivolous whims."

Oria ignored the escalating barbs, easier to do with the promise that she might not be so fragile forever. "An excellent point," she said in her mildest tone. "Fortunately, I don't require a great deal of tending, especially as I will be out and about in the palace and the city."

"Is that wise, Princess? Your fragile condition—"

"Grows no less fragile for this sequestration. I faced the worst and survived."

"We don't know that for sure."

"You can't be sure of that, Princess. Perhaps your condition is more akin to those sensitive to the sting of the honey-makers—the first reaction is merely a shadow of successive ones."

Oria flashed Chuffta a glance for sounding so much like the priestess. He resettled his wings, a gesture remarkably like an irritated shrug.

"If that's the case," she told Febe, "then I shall find out. In the meanwhile, a junior priestess to come by from time to time will suffice. While I'm away from my rooms, regular servants can assist with upkeep."

"I could carry messages for you," Chuffta offered, *"if you would like to see how you fare without me for short times. That might be a good test of your endurance."*

Gratitude for her Familiar's understanding welled up. That felt good, too. Enough to disperse the feedback from the high priestess, who seethed with that buried something. Nevertheless, Febe inclined her head. "I shall see if any junior priestesses will volunteer to be assigned to you."

"Thank you. On your way to take care of that, you can pass along the message to my mother and brother."

Without another word, the high priestess glided out, her fulminating resentment swirling in her wake.

"Well, that made her a bit angry," Oria commented.

"You sensed something else, too, beneath the resentment and irritation."

Had she? She sorted through it, as she had the night before, peeling away the layers. "Fear?"

"Yes, a kind of alarm. And maybe… jealousy. You unsettled her. I wonder why?"

"We'll see if my mother has answers."

~ 22 ~

THE QUEEN AND Prince Yar arrived together, she leaning heavily on her son's arm. When she saw Oria already waiting, Queen Rhianna opened her arms, a sad smile breaking over her face. "Oh, Oria."

Oria slid into her mother's welcome embrace. Even filled with the ragged shadows of grief and failure, the cool serenity of the woman felt like a balm on sunburn. "Mother," Oria whispered.

Yar waited stiffly, his mask of course impassive, control in place. She sensed nothing of his state beyond a faint burn of…more resentment and fear? After he'd been so much better the night before. And she'd had such high hopes that he had matured. Something had happened, she sensed it in the rapid shift of his emotions.

"Let's sit and eat," Oria said, gesturing to the table. The sight of the greens and fruits gave her pause. How much longer would they be able to grow food?

"I already ate in my rooms, where I'd intended to stay and rest, but I was *summoned*." Yar stalked broodily over to the window. "And we shouldn't be breakfasting while the Destrye army might yet turn around and attack us."

She didn't point out that resting in their rooms would be no better in that case. "Should they do so, our watching them will change nothing. We've reached treaty agreeable to both sides. Let it go."

"I'm only relieved to have them gone," Queen Rhianna said,

sitting and nodding to her servant to fill her plate.

"Yes, and for so little on our part." Yar paced the room restlessly. "It makes me wonder what my lovely sister promised—or gave to—Prince Lonen in exchange."

"Oh, of course." Oria stabbed a berry, wishing it could be her brother. Never mind that her illicit dreams and their lingering effects made Yar's sally rather closer to the mark than it should have been. She felt sure he'd eaten, or lied about having eaten, because he didn't want to remove his mask. He was definitely hiding something. "I can barely stand the most casual touch from a carefully shielded and trained masked priest or priestess, but you believe I bedded the enemy so he'd take his army away? I suppose I should be flattered that you think my charms sufficient to accomplish such a great task."

"Then why were you closeted with Prince Lonen?" Yar retorted. "Folcwita Lapo is furious. I wouldn't have gone to bed and left things to you if I'd imagined you'd exclude the council! I thought you'd be smart and let them handle things. You were supposed to be only a figurehead."

She bit back her frustrated response to that. "What do I care if the folcwita is angry? I accomplished what he could not—what you and the council didn't, I might point out. Besides, I invited our mother. She did not attend."

"I couldn't have offered anything. Without my mask, without Tav, I am nothing." Queen Rhianna focused on her plate, eating methodically but without relish.

"Exactly." Yar paced over. "Which is why Oria, who also has no mask, should have left the decision-making to the council."

"Yar…" Their mother sounded infinitely weary and wounded. "We're still family. Sit with us and eat."

"Is that a command from my queen—or should I say, former queen?" he snarled.

Their mother's face crumpled, and she stared at her meal, a tear rolling down her cheek. Oria leveled an accusing glance at him, which must have worked, because he finally sat, if sullenly, but still did not remove his mask.

Probably better to direct the conversation away from the erratic bore tides of personal issues and onto the problems Bára faced. "So, did both of you know that Bára had been sending golems to raid Dru for water?"

The queen set down her fork, pressing her fingertips to her eyelids. "I warned Tav that would come to no good."

"What water?" Yar shifted in his chair, restless and unhappy. He'd never been much for politics, even at his best. "Why are we talking about this now?"

"Bára's water, all of it," Oria explained patiently. "Priest Sisto sent the fighting golems to Dru to bring back wagonloads of water, because we'd run out. That's why the Destrye attacked."

"The Destrye attacked because it's in their nature. They're barbarians." Yar got up to stare out the window again.

"We were desperate, Oria," her mother said, at least sounding bolder, more alive. "So were our sister cities. The drought has gone on for too many years. Dru was the only place close enough with plenty of fresh water still."

"So we slaughtered the Destrye for it—even their children?" Oria couldn't keep the incredulity out of her voice. Her mother opened her mouth but swallowed the reproof Oria expected.

"The Destrye weren't supposed to die," she said instead. "We never intended that. Sisto claimed he'd found a way to create the golems with a kind of ongoing spell. It acted like a packet of sgath. He embedded them with both the command to carry out the task—to fill the barrels with water and bring them back—and also provided them with the magic to keep them animated. No one realized that would result in them going through anything—or anyone—who stood in the way."

"But you knew," Oria whispered. "You and Father, Vico and Febe—you knew afterwards."

"Not at first. Not until the Destrye began to fight back. They discovered that iron would kill Vico's golems by neutralizing the packet of sgath. He felt them die."

"So you—" no, Oria shared the responsibility as a member of the ruling family of Bára "—*we* sent more."

"Yes." Queen Rhianna looked sick with it. "We chose our children over theirs. It was supposed to be only for a short time. Until the monsoons returned. But they never did and then, before we knew it, the Destrye had traced the golems back to Bára."

"Oh, Mother."

"Do you hear yourself?" Yar sounded incredulous. "Were you even listening? It was us or them. They made the same choice—only we won in the end."

"That's highly debatable," Oria said without looking at him. The question applied even more to him. "Though the Destrye let us off lightly, Bára still faces utter destruction. Do we have any reserves of water left?"

"Enough to last a few months," the queen replied, poking at her salad. "Longer if we stop trading it to our sister cities, but that will create backlash from them."

Oria rubbed her temple. "Because of the goods they trade in return?"

"Food we don't grow here, yes, but also because they will see us as weak with no one on the throne, with our temple so depleted. Why not simply come and take the rest of our water? They need it as badly as—probably even worse than—we do."

Fragments of family dinner conversations turned around and fit together to make a new pattern. Her father and Nat boasting of Bára's power, how the other cities sent wealth in tribute, that King Tavlor ruled them all, with Nat gleefully planning to follow in his footsteps.

"It wasn't just about keeping our people alive, was it?" Oria laid her hand over her mother's. "Maybe at first it was, but then it became about the wealth and power."

Her mother turned her hand to grip Oria's. "Your father was a good man. He only wanted the best for us and for Bára. We cannot leave our cities, not now, after so many generations living above the source of magic. If we go outside our walls for very long, we'll die. Some of us waste away, effectively starving. Others, like you…"

Blasted apart by it. Her mother didn't have to say it. Yar sat still, finally, absorbing the conversation.

"Then the answer is a strong front," he said. "We have water reserves. We have the Trom, which means we have more power than ever before. We can get more water and force our sister cities to continue to pay tribute to us."

"We can't do that—"

"There is no *we*," Yar cut Oria off, popping to his feet. "I will do it because I will be king. Our mother cannot be queen, not without a mask."

"The law doesn't say that."

"He's right, Oria." Her mother withdrew her hand, patted Oria's once, then settled it in her lap. "The law may be silent on the issue, but only because no king or queen has survived the death of their temple-blessed spouse. I've spoken with High Priestess Febe. She, the temple, Folcwita Lapo, and the rest of the council no longer consider me to be the queen. The throne of Bára belongs to a matched, masked husband and wife. As we sit, there is only one candidate."

Yar held out his hands, as if expecting congratulation.

"But Yar cannot be king—he has no wife."

"I'm one step closer than you are, sister dear. At least I have a mask. If I cannot find a match here—though I'm testing a few of the junior priestesses—I'll command our sister cities to send theirs for testing. There's a perfect wife for me out there somewhere. In the meantime, I'll act as king."

"Our sister cities know perfectly well that you won't qualify. One of their matched couples will come here and claim the throne."

"Not with me as their sole source of water—thank you for that solution."

"We have only a few months left!"

He shrugged. "We'll get more from Dru. I'll command the Trom to do it."

"The treaty prevents us from attacking them again, Yar. You can't do that."

"Oh yes I can." Yar prowled over to her. "And it's all your fault. Your treaty means nothing because *you* had no power to sign."

Oria glared up at him. He'd always been precocious, and the baby of the family, so spoiled for both reasons. But she'd never imagined he'd be so foolish. "You saw the Trom. What they did to Nat, to so many. They do not serve us."

"Correction. They do not serve you, but they do serve me. *I* summoned the Trom, not Nat. That's why they didn't listen to his commands. I realized the answer when I awoke this morning."

"Why—what happened?" Oria rose to her feet. Grien, bright, nearly uncontrolled, rolled off Yar, along with a kind of triumph twisted together with sheer terror. This was what had changed from the night before. "Is that why you won't remove your mask?"

"Why are you obsessed with me removing my mask?" Yar snarled, clenching his fists, impotent rage and fear billowing through his *hwil*. Oria nearly flinched, anticipating the blow to follow.

"He'd better not." Chuffta's fierce thought bolstered her courage.

"What are you hiding behind it, little brother?" Oria replied, all reasonableness to his tumult.

"If you must know." Without waiting for a servant, Yar wrenched the mask from his head, the ribbons leaving wild tufts of hair in their wake. Oria and her mother both gasped, Rhianna putting an involuntary hand to her throat, as if choking back further words.

Yar's eyes had gone entirely black, like the Trom's, matte and without pupils. Horrified, Oria extended a trembling hand to her brother, not sure how to help but moved to try. He yanked out of her reach.

"Can you see?" she asked, for want of other pertinent questions.

"Only with grien, just as I always do with the mask on. It's no loss. Especially compared to what I've gained. You! Come tie this on me again." The servant scuttled over, taking the mask with shaking fingers.

"When did this happen?" Oria asked.

"I noticed when I awoke this morning, when I washed, before I donned my mask."

"Did the Trom do it, touch you in some way?"

"You know they didn't. The Trom touched *you* and you're fine." Yar oozed bitterness. "I'm the one who performed the summoning ritual. It should have been me the sacred one paid attention to. Not my magicless, maskless sister."

Oh, Yar. "What was involved in the summoning ritual?" And why had Nat put their brother up to it? But she kept it to the one question. Not that it did any good, as Yar exploded out of his seat.

"You look to steal my secrets, my power—but I won't let you!" Yar's unmasked fury poured out and Oria staggered back from it. Chuffta spread his white wings, wrapping them around her in a shield as Yar's grien followed his shout. Green fire shot out, incinerating the blast.

Yar's turn now to fall back with a thin scream as his robes caught fire. His valet rushed forward to put out the flames, but he pushed the man away with an incoherent roar, patting them out himself, featureless face fixed on Oria. "How can you do that?" he whispered, hoarse. Frightened. "You shouldn't be able to do that." Then he ran from the room, the valet in his wake.

Oria met her mother's stunned gaze. The queen had both hands around her throat, horror in her brown eyes.

"What did I do?" Oria asked her mother, though the queen didn't answer. "It was Chuffta who breathed flame."

"But you dissipated Yar's grien. You neutralized it."

She sank into the chair, pressing fingertips to her temples. Out of habit, though, because her head didn't hurt for once. It should. That amount of fury should have sent her screaming to the shadows.

"This is what I mean—you stopped it."

"How?"

"I don't know. But it would be most useful to find out."

"As much as I knew this might be," her mother said slowly, the quiet words slipping past her hands, "I never truly believed. And here we are."

"That what might be?" Frustration roiled up. "Ponen?"

Her mother closed her eyes, nodded ever so slightly.

"Explain this to me, Mother. I need to know."

Queen Rhianna nodded again with more conviction, finally dropping her hands. For the first time since her husband died, something of her powerful sgath welled up. "Yes. I have things to show you. Perhaps there is yet another way out of this mud trap."

Oria could only hope. Though through no fault of her own, she had still broken her oath—and she would do everything in her power never to be forsworn again.

~ 23 ~

WITH RELIEF, LONEN left the Báran desert behind him. It had taken days of slow travel to reach the dry scrublands, which then gave way to the cactus- and evergreen-studded border country, populated by neither Destrye nor Bárans. Much as he wanted to ride ahead with the faster scouts, he sent Arnon instead and kept himself to the back of their decamping army, moving with the slowest of the injured.

Ion might have made a different choice, but their father wouldn't have abandoned their many injured and Lonen hoped to be something of the king Archimago had been. If nothing else, he owed his father that, and the Destrye his father and brothers had died to save. They'd be remembered with honor, certainly. Already the musicians and poets among the warriors called him the Savior of the Battle of Bára. Several tales of the various battles with the Bárans—including increasingly more lurid descriptions of the golems, dragons, and Trom—were passing up and down the caravan of men and wagons and circling the campfires at night.

None of them mentioned Oria or her dragonlet, which suited Lonen just fine. The strange princess continued to plague his thoughts in worrisome ways, sometimes walking through his dreams, her hair copper fire, gaze full of some question. Sometimes her eyes were the bright green of the lizard's, her teeth the same sharp fangs as she hissed. Once she flew at him, white leathery wings capturing him and holding him still while she feasted on his liver, murmuring love words all the while, her avid mouth then fastening on his cock, milking him until he ruptured.

He woke from that nightmare in a cold sweat, his seed ignominiously filling the furs as it hadn't done since he'd been a randy adolescent. Too long away from women, from his lovely Natly. It seemed a king shouldn't be subject to such human frailty. He'd never expected to wear the Destrye crown, so he hadn't imagined exactly what it would be. Shinier and more noble, somehow. Without the disturbingly sexual dreams of a foreign sorceress or the persistent runs of the campaign trail.

Or the endless consultations on every matter, great or small.

The slow pace gave him time, at least, to learn the tasks of being a king, which seemed to be mainly making one decision after another, few of them compelling—a mountain of gravel, like the sands of Oria's desert, relentlessly piling into dunes. He longed to switch places with Arnon, to be riding fast and furiously to reunite with the rest of their people. The greatest irony of becoming king was learning that he'd lost a freedom he'd never fully appreciated—and would never have again.

BY THE TIME Lonen and the tail end of the returning warriors and litters of the injured sighted the forests of Dru that filled the deep and wide valley between the Snowy Peaks, they'd received word of those who'd been on the Trail of New Hope. The good news was that the refugees had turned around and traveled back to their homeland also, in another long caravan, spearheaded by the strong, followed by a long, straggling tail of the weak and wounded.

The bad news was that the women, children, and elderly had run afoul of more golems, suffering additional losses. Indeed, said the scouts who reported to him in the squalor of his inherited tent, much worse for wear from the long campaign, had the golems not inexplicably fallen dead one night, the refugees would have been decimated.

As it was, less than half those who'd set out returned to their emptied city. They turned out to welcome the final dregs of the Destrye army. They lined the road and drawbridges over the moats surrounding Dru, cheering with the forced enthusiasm of traumatized survivors, pitiful in their reduced numbers.

Once the Destrye had lived in cabins scattered throughout the lush deciduous forest of trees that towered as high as Bára's many towers. Some Destrye preferred to live alone, others in small family groups occupying one cabin, still others in extended families and communities in compounds of connected buildings. None had walls like Bára. Networks of roads had connected them, allowing for travel and commerce—all feeding into the broad, main road that led to Arill's temple.

Some holdouts lived in those outlying cabins and communities still, but the bulk of Destrye had fled their homes following the golem incursions, building new homes to cluster under Arill's sheltering wings. King Archimago had devoted considerable resources to digging wide, deep moats around the burgeoning city, filling them first with sharpened wood spikes, then iron ones to foil the golems. Those moats looked like a child's ditch compared to the chasms of Bára.

Never once had it occurred to them to build walls.

Lonen brought up the rear, riding over the last drawbridge through the gates of the city at the end of the column. Odd to see wooden buildings and leafy trees instead of stone balconies and towers, people with dark hair instead of light. The slapdash, panicked construction around Arill's temple had only deteriorated during the period of abandonment, but it had been ramshackle to begin with. One hastily assembled dwelling piled on top of another, the city was a hodgepodge of materials and design—except for Arill's centuries-old temple and the adjacent palace of governance—and nothing like Bára with her meticulously arranged and airy towers.

Still, the similarities shone through. The defeated Bárans had also been determined to cheer the smallest victory. The two peoples had chewed on each other's livers, it seemed, both cities crippled husks of what they'd once been, simply in different aspects.

Who had won what?

A woman broke from the throng, running up to him, long dark hair streaming like the tears running down her lovely face. Natly.

Though he was filthy, soiled in body and soul, Lonen dismounted, making his startled horse sidestep, and caught Natly up in his arms. She was both sobbing and laughing, her words incoherent. He held her close, inhaling the scent of qinn spices, the warmth of home. This. This was what he'd fought for, what so many died to protect. What his father and brothers had given their lives to rebuild. Through the exhaustion, a thin ray of hope wormed its way through. He'd made it home. Alive and mostly well.

Natly framed his face with her long fingers, her once elegantly jeweled nails short and broken. "You're king now," she managed to say, her gray eyes full of tears. "And returning victorious. I'm so proud of you. I love you so much, Lonen."

He kissed her, mostly to stop himself from saying this was no victory. All that time he'd waited for her to say those words, to be proud to be his woman—and now she said it because he'd simply managed to survive where others had not. And by committing unspeakable acts. "It still feels like dream. A long and terrible one."

"For me, too," she said, kissing him again and again. "But it's over now."

"Yes." Her mouth strange against his after so long apart. He threaded his chapped and dirty fingers through her black curling hair, grounding himself in Natly. His lover with dark eyes, not copper, who smelled of qinn and possessed no uncanny magics. She would make a good queen for the Destrye. "It's over now," he echoed her, wishing he felt that in his heart. Over her shoulder, a movement caught his eye.

Arnon stepped forward with Salaya, her hair shorn short in grief, holding the hands of her young sons, who'd never see their father Ion again. Natly made a sound of protest, clinging to him tightly when he tried to disentangle himself. "I have to talk to Salaya," he told her, and Natly also looked over her shoulder, thrusting her lip out in a bit of a pout that he'd always found so sexy.

"Do you have to? Talk to her later. Come with me and I'll bathe you." Natly scratched the back of his neck with her nails, a trick that had always made him crazy for her. But the devastation in Salaya's face, the haunted look in her eyes that reminded him strangely of Oria, cooled any desire he might have felt.

Gently, he unwound Natly's hands from his neck and kissed her nose. "Go prepare the bath. And food if you can find any—I'm starving. I'll talk to Salaya and meet you shortly."

"You'll have to make it quick, Brother," Arnon said, gaze dipping over Natly and away. "I have a list as long as my arm of things for you to deal with as soon as possible."

"He's only just arrived home." Natly put her fists on her voluptuous hips. "Surely a conquering war hero—our new king!—deserves a bit of rest and celebrating."

Arnon shook his head wearily, squinting at the sky. "He'll be king of nothing if we don't figure out how to feed everyone. The first frost is only weeks away and it seems wolves scattered the herds we left behind. Not to mention we drained our water supplies when we left and the nearest source is at least a day's journey. We've brought some in, but it's slow going and not enough to keep up with everyone returning. Plus there's squabbles over housing and accusations of theft that have already caused several fights resulting in injuries."

"You're full of good news, aren't you?" Lonen scrubbed hands through his hair, slick with oil and dirt. He'd last bathed in Bára and it didn't seem as if he'd have another one any time soon. It would be unconscionable with their supplies so low.

"A fine welcome home for the King of the Destrye," Natly

hissed.

Arnon only shrugged with a wry smile. "The good news is that we're alive to come home. The rest of it is pretty bad. We've got a lot of work to make it livable again."

Looking at his city made of wood, however ugly, Lonen let the weight of responsibility settle on him, heavy as Salaya's imploring gaze. He owed so much to his father's legacy, to Ion's forsaken family, and to Nolan's unrealized dreams, along with all the lives cut short, Destrye and Báran. He'd find a way to rebuild. His people needed him.

They needed a good king and he'd be that. Or die trying.

~ 24 ~

WRAPPED IN A cloak of night, Oria followed her mother to a place she'd never known existed, much less been to. Still within the city and somewhere beneath both the palace and the temple, they descended a set of stairs that seemed to be the mirror of the ones to her tower, spiraling around a dark pit that echoed with odd whispers, winding into the earth, possibly as deep as the chasms that cracked through Bára. Climbing these again, plus those to the height of her tower, might very well kill her.

Something to worry about later.

For the time being, feeling crushed beneath the earth occupied most of her attention.

"It's no different than being in a cave." Chuffta chirped the observation far too happily. *"I used to live in a cave. Cool in the hot weather, cozy when the chill winds blow. You'd like it."*

"So far I am *not* liking it," she muttered at her Familiar.

Her mother glanced over with a wry smile. "I found Chuffta in a cave. Is he telling you that?"

Surprised that her mother mentioned it, Oria latched onto the question. "Yes. Will you tell me about that? How did you find him and why? How did you convince him to come with you if you can't hear him now?"

"He can hear me, though, can't he?"

"Of course. I'm not stupid."

"I will tell you," Rhianna continued, "as we still have farther to go, no one to overhear, and all of this is a piece of what I wish to show you. Perhaps I should have told you more to begin with, but that's sand long since blown away."

Though she privately agreed, Oria kept silent, lest she stem this flow of long-awaited answers.

"Nat and Ben were but young boys when you were conceived. I knew right away that you would be a girl, the daughter I longed for, and more—I sensed that you might perhaps inherit the secret legacy of our family."

"The secret legacy?" she echoed.

"What my great-grandmother possessed, called *ponen*."

"That's the word the Trom used with me—I asked you about it."

"I remember. I wasn't ready then to explain it to you."

"Why now?"

"Circumstances have forced my hand. Yar is not ready to be king. He is far too proud and impetuous. The city guard agrees. They fear we'll be conquered by one or more of our sister cities if Yar takes the throne of Bára."

"Then you'll fight him for it—remain queen."

"Not me." Her mother flashed her a wry smile. "You."

Oria nearly stopped in her tracks, then had to hasten to catch up. "Are you saying you can help me find *hwil*?"

"Not exactly," she temporized, "but I can help you get your mask, which at least puts you and Yar on even footing."

"But…how?"

"*Ponen*," her mother said, as if it answered Oria's question, "is an ancient word, known primarily to the priestesses of our family, and recorded in only a few place. From the tales passed down, it's no easy burden to bear—as you've experienced in your life thus far. All of the women with ponen, however, had derkesthai to help them withstand the power of their affinities."

"What are my affinities?" Her question echoed with hollow immediacy, signaling the end of their journey. Indeed, the amorphous shadows of the center well showed blacker. They'd hit bottom.

"That is still your journey to discover."

Wonderful. It had been too much to hope that she might finally know that much. At least her mother hadn't advised her to meditate on it.

"Meditation is a useful exercise. You gain benefit from it when you exercise the self-discipline to truly quiet your mind."

"Yes, well, I gain benefit climbing up and down all these stairs, but that doesn't mean I enjoy it."

"What is Chuffta advising you?"

"To meditate, as always."

"No, I'm merely pointing out its benefits."

Her mother paused before an ironbound door set into a stone arch. The cool, sweet, and intense magic so characteristic to Rhianna swelled, swirled, and the door swung outward. Oria raised her brows at the nontraditional use of sgath. "Would High Priestess Febe approve?"

"The temple may govern most modern-day magical law," her mother replied crisply, striding through the doorway and into a dark hall, "but magic itself predates the temple. So does our family."

"And yet you allowed them to strip you of your mask."

Her mother faltered and Oria regretted the words. "I'm sorry, I—"

"No. You're right. I let them take my mask because according to temple law I no longer deserve it. However there are other, higher laws. The sorceresses of our line have had good reason to subject ourselves to the discipline the temple teaches. That is something for you to remember always. This knowledge is powerful—and can go badly if entrusted to the unstable."

The door behind them swung closed, plunging them into utter darkness. A breath of air against her face told Oria the other door had opened. That was why Oria shivered, not at the echo of Febe's words.

"Coming? If you're afraid, say so now, because it will only worsen." Her mother's voice held a hint of impatience.

"I can't see." Oria bit back the bitter words that begged to follow. No *hwil*, no ability to control her magic, no seeing in the dark. Or from behind a mask.

"I apologize." Her mother sounded chagrined, her hand touching Oria's sleeve, then guiding her to wrap her fingers around her mother's elbow. "Take my arm."

"I can't see either." The irritation in Chuffta's mind-voice perversely cheered her.

It bolstered her on the strange journey through pitch darkness, trusting to her mother's guidance. She kept wanting to put a hand out before her, to stop anything from smashing into her face, but it felt like that would be cowardly.

"There are no lamps or sconces in this section or I'd light them. I'd never before considered this a barrier to one who cannot see without eyes," her mother continued, apologetic, yet also thoughtful. "There are various guards set to prevent this knowledge from the wrong hands, and this must be one."

"Are you sure mine are the right hands then?" Oria joked.

It fell flat, however, because her mother didn't immediately reply. Finally she said, "I'll be honest with you—I don't know. That's another reason I hadn't yet shown you this path. I hoped you'd find *hwil* first and then I could have been more certain you'd survive this. That's why we do this now, brutal though it may be."

"Do…what?"

"Face the test. If you survive, you'll understand."

"What do I do?"

Her mother softened, took her hands. "Oh, my brilliant daughter, if I could tell you, I would. But I am not ponen. I honestly do not know what you'll have to do to pass."

"Oh." Had she ever felt so small and afraid?

"But I do know that if you're not brave enough now, you won't have another chance. You're out of time, Oria. *We* are out of time. I wish it wasn't so, but it is what it is. You don't have to do this, but if you want to gain your mask in time, this is the path. Just…follow your instincts."

She wasn't brave enough. It made her angry that the cowardice sabotaged her.

"And if I fail, I'll die?" she asked.

"Yes." Her mother's voice echoed hollow in the dark. "Or you might as well be, as when you broke, sleeping the rest of your life away. Don't do this if it's not important to you. You can find another life, a quiet one, perhaps in one of our sister cities."

It sounded possible. Grim, and unlikely to last long, with Yar taking them back to war, and the Trom promising visits.

"Oria…" Her mother sounded hesitant. "I don't say this to sway your decision, but I believe you can do this. The magic is in you, powerful and consuming. You used it to repel Yar when he attacked you, and to bring me out of the pits of grief. This is your birthright, if you're strong enough to claim it."

She took a steadying breath. She might not be strong enough, but she wanted to be.

"You can be. Look how much you've done these last days."

"Thank you." She scratched his scaled breast.

"Chuffta must stay here, however."

"What—why? You said he helps me with the ponen."

"Exactly. And this you must do alone or not at all."

Chuffta had promised never to leave her.

"And I won't. I'll be with you, in your thoughts, in your heart."

With care, she unwound Chuffta's tail from its loops around her arm. He leaned his head against her temple. "If I don't survive sane, promise me you'll return to your family."

"No promises, other than that I'll wait for you always."

"All right," she said, her voice barely audible. "I'm ready."

Her mother's magic built again, like water filling a tub, and a faint blue glow glimmered ahead. Growing stronger, it outlined yet another doorway.

With an indigo blaze it opened, searing Oria's eyes and mind.

She felt suddenly supremely unable to rise to the task. Was that a shape within?

It was one thing to face her own death in the abstract, to offer surrender to the Destrye prince, knowing she might be struck down. Oddly, the memory of Lonen's granite gaze steadied her. He wouldn't be afraid. Or rather, he might feel fear—she'd sensed plenty of it in him—but he hadn't let that stop him. She could do no less.

She stepped over the threshold.

Freezing blue seized her with agonizing brilliance, and she flailed, without reason or purchase. A bony hand caressed her cheek as the Trom had done, another rising to join it on the other side, framing her face. Something stared into her. Black, unwinking eyes, full of intelligence and entirely lacking in compassion.

She writhed mentally, her body no longer her own.

"Who?"

A mind-voice like Chuffta's, yet entirely unlike. Unforgiving, uncaring. It asked the question she couldn't answer.

And yet she did give an answer, her deepest heart opening like a night-blooming blossom to the fruit bats that plundered their nectar. It all poured out of her, the jealousy of her proficient brothers, all the bitter restlessness, the shame of failure and inadequacy, the rancor of her thoughts echoing in the walls of her tower, the bitterness of breaking her word to Lonen—and the eroding fear that he'd blame her if Yar sent the Trom after the Destrye.

It shouldn't be so important, but the possibility of losing his good opinion festered in her heart and poured out to this alien consciousness's indifferent scrutiny. All those princesses before her, also trapped by their own inability to rise above, to live up to their vows.

She wanted out with fierce ambition. Not to be forever subject to her little brother, to forswear herself because she didn't have the strength to back up her promises. She wanted to live. To live and burn brightly. *She* would find a way to save Bára.

The determination rose in her, strong and vital, much like the frustrated impatience that had always plagued her. It wanted to burst free, to release and whip about, as it had when she faced off with Yar. And yes, as she'd felt trying to reach her mother. Not only absorbing and calming, but also pushing out, striking and hooking.

This is who I am.

"Ponen," the being whispered. *"Ponen Trom. You are of us and we of you. Welcome."*

~ 25 ~

"WHAT WE NEED," Arnon said, sitting down with a rolled-up parchment and an excited mien, "is a better, faster way of getting water to the crops, if we have any hope of one more harvest before winter."

"The king is still eating his supper," Natly informed him, grabbing the wooden wine carafe before Arnon could and pouring more for Lonen, and then for herself.

A measly meal it had been, too. Lonen almost wished for Bára's odd array of plants and grains over the stringy meat from an aged animal he didn't want to try to identify. He even had a yen for that cheese of Oria's, with that tangy-sweet honey complementing the smoky rancid flavor—a contrary combination that shouldn't appeal but somehow lingered in his mind. Much as the woman did.

"The king is done eating," he said, schooling his face not to return Arnon's amused grin. Natly had a short temper for such teasing and Arnon seemed to be entertained by poking at her. One would think they'd have other things to worry about, with all the problems on their plates—besides sparse and unappealing food—but apparently not. "Better and faster water to the crops would be excellent, but how?"

Arnon pushed aside the plates, Natly protesting at his lack of manners, and spread out the parchment. "Aqueducts," he proclaimed.

Lonen studied the neat drawing. There was Arill's temple in the center, the squares of residences surrounding it and the palace, then the rings of moats—all circumnavigated by lines that reminded him of the old network of paths that had once connected the cabins and compounds. Indeed, several followed along historic roadways that led to the settlements farther down the valley, where the forests had been cleared to make fields for farming.

For the past weeks since he'd returned to Dru, Lonen had thought about food night and day—how much they needed, how little they had, even with the greatly reduced population, how they could grow, barter, or buy more. Livestock needed grain to eat, too. Slaughtering them all for meat instead of feeding them apparently wouldn't work because then they wouldn't have enough to make calves, kids, and what-have-yous in the spring. Even chickens needed grain to lay eggs—both for eating and hatching to grow into more chickens. The formerly abundant game in the forests had moved with the water sources, so the hunters came back empty-handed or with squirrels and rabbits that made for watery stews. The fisheries had dried up with the drained lakes. They were exploring harvesting fish from the sea, though the tides made that a daunting and dangerous effort.

Lonen had learned more than he'd ever wanted to about animal husbandry and population dynamics, not to mention farming practices which turned out to be far more complicated than planting seeds and cutting down the plants when they were ready. It made him weary to contemplate the mountain of obstacles facing them. By contrast, mowing down golems with his axe seemed far simpler.

Perhaps one reason why men turned to war when farming failed. A sobering thought.

"What am I looking at?"

"See, with Lake Scandamalion more than half empty"—Arnon indicated on the map the closest remaining body of fresh water a day's journey away—"we need to access the more distant lakes or we'll just be facing the same problem again before we know it. But that would take a lot of bodies and time, hauling water from that far—bodies we need in the fields or here in the city, patching up the treasure boxes for winter."

He and Arnon had taken to referring to the ramshackle collection of falling-down construction that made up the refugee houses clustered around the temple—and now outside the moats, too—as *treasure boxes*, for their own lackluster creations when they'd been boys. With cold weather looming and what little resources the Destrye still possessed concentrated around the city, people stayed, throwing up whatever shelter they could manage. Or fighting with their neighbors to take theirs.

"So we dig…ditches?"

"No—this is better. Jordan brought this idea to me, from Arill's teachings. We build big troughs, essentially, on stilts and let the water roll downhill from, say, the Seven Lakes here, all the way to where we need it." He traced his finger along the lines to the farmlands, then another to the city.

A rill of excitement burned through Lonen's fatigue. "We build them out of wood?"

"Exactly! A good thing that the sun here doesn't scorch as it does in Bára, or we'd have to put a cover on it." Arnon frowned at the plans. "Otherwise there'd be none left by the time it reached its destination."

"And good that we have no golems or fire-breathing dragons to combat," Lonen added, meaning it as a joke, though it fell flat, Arnon wincing at the reminder.

"You and those tales of magic and dragons," Natly teased, slipping her arm through his. "I never know what to believe anymore. Warrior's stories, where the battles grow bolder and more glorious with each telling."

Out of habit, Lonen covered her hand with his, smiling down at her as she expected. She'd begun to look more like her old self, before the Trail of New Hope. No longer careworn, her nails once again sparkled with jewels, her hair elaborately coiled and gleaming with oil rather than hanging down her back in tangles. The people needed hope and to look up to them, she insisted, so they used water to bathe at least weekly. She wanted to look the part of Queen of the Destrye, to make him proud, though they'd made no plans to marry. She'd mentioned the midwinter celebration as the perfect time. As that would be well after any further efforts could be made to supplement the late harvest, Lonen hadn't objected outright.

Actually, he hadn't said anything either way. He'd teased her about marrying him long before the Battle of Bára, and she'd always put him off. Now she behaved as if they'd been engaged all along.

It wasn't that he didn't want to marry Natly, but it felt like a moot point if they were all bound to starve. She didn't understand his reticence to make plans, though, and to press the issue she'd stopped warming his bed after the first few nights. She claimed his nightmares kept her awake, with his thrashing about and yelling, but she'd made it clear that a wedding date would be sufficient to entice her back. Lonen, however, was frankly relieved to sleep alone, and not only because so many of those dreams that drove Natly away involved Oria.

Guilt and a level of mortification chewed at him, that his fascination with the sorceress continued to plague him, making him imagine the scent of night-blooming lilies even with Natly's qinn filling his head, with her supple body pleasuring his. It made him irritable, which Natly put down to the pressures of kingship. But her pride in him, and the delighted plans she made to become queen, rankled more than the sand dunes of decisions that piled up daily. She hadn't been so enthusiastic to wed him before he was king.

Something that proved as impossible as Oria to forget.

"How long to build it?" he asked Arnon.

"That depends. There's a number of options and decisions to make on prioritizing."

Of course there were. "All right, walk me through it."

"You're not staying up all night talking again," Natly protested. When Arnon made a choking noise and Lonen raised a brow at her, she folded her arms, pushing up her luscious bosom. "You need your rest. And I thought perhaps we could…spend some time together."

She looked so disappointed that Lonen regretted his uncharitable thoughts. Of course the nightmares bothered her. She needed her sleep, too. He cupped her cheek and kissed her, inhaling the qinn to remind himself that Natly was the woman he craved. Was supposed to crave. "Perhaps tomorrow night. If we're to build these aqueducts to irrigate the late-season harvest in time to keep our plantings from dying, Arnon is right that we need to start right away. You go to bed."

"All right." She pushed out that lower lip and gazed at him through lush black lashes. "But you know where to find me. Don't keep him up all night." She pointed a jeweled nail at Arnon and flounced off.

Lonen watched the sway of her hips that once so beguiled him, missing that feeling and disliking the creeping realization that Natly would make a terrible queen. She was nothing like Oria, who would have wanted to learn about the aqueducts. Which he needed to focus on, as thoughts of Oria being his queen instead of Natly were not only impossibly distracting, but impossible, full stop. He studied the aqueduct lines that went to the farmlands. A longer distance, but more critical than getting more water to a people already accustomed to rationing. "So, if we build these first, then would—"

"Lonen." Arnon put a hand over the map, covering the lines and forcing Lonen to look at him. "You can't marry her."

Lonen blinked at him, dragging his eager thoughts from the logistics of building aqueducts. Had Arnon somehow read his thoughts? "Who—Natly?"

Arnon gusted out an impatient breath. "Of course Natly! Who else would I be talking about?"

Who indeed? "I'm not marrying Natly. Not anytime soon, anyway," he amended.

"That's not what she thinks. Nor what she tells everyone."

"I don't control what she thinks and does."

"Exactly the problem. Natly does as she pleases, always has and always will. She would have made a decent princess, but she won't make a good queen. Don't do it, brother of mine."

"She's strong as a horse, can bear many children, understands and loves Dru and the Destrye—what's the problem?"

"The problem is that being queen means *not* doing as she pleases. It's more than wearing pretty dresses and sucking your cock, Lonen! These are dire times. Better for you to lead our people alone than be distracted by her."

The words prickled and Lonen burned to lob back a few of his own. But Arnon had that much right—being king meant not doing as he pleased, either. "I thought we were discussing aqueducts and building schedules."

Arnon held his gaze, then nodded, accepting the truce. "Good. I've made a timetable."

~ 26 ~

"YOU COME BEFORE the temple as a supplicant," High Priestess Febe intoned, "sponsored by our daughter, former priestess Rhianna. Do you, Princess Oria of Bára, plead to be granted the mask of priestess yourself?"

"I do, High Priestess. You have tested my *hwil* and see that I am ready to wear the mask," Oria replied, her face serenely composed.

"Indeed, remarkable as it may seem, none can find fault with your *hwil*." Febe sounded sour, a bitter complement to the irritated—and suspicious—energy she emanated.

As well she should, as Oria no more had achieved *hwil*, whatever it truly felt like, than ever. But she faked it perfectly well. Nothing the priests and priestesses had attempted to shake her composure had rattled her. At least, not that she showed. It rankled deeply that, for all their pride in their personal magic, the masked ones could not truly see into her heart. As her mother had predicted, once Oria came out the other side of the harrowing test of scrutiny in the heart of magic, nothing less could frighten or upset her.

After that, passing the simple tests of *hwil* proved quite simple. In fact, those challenges had been easy enough, after the horrors of the Destrye Wars, that she could have passed them before, had it ever occurred to her to lie about achieving *hwil*.

How many priests and priestesses of Bára and her sister cities had hit upon that solution? In her most cynical moments, Oria suspected most of them, perhaps all. She hadn't met anyone who didn't leak emotional energy. Over the past weeks, practicing with her mother and Chuffta, she'd refined her ability to sort through what she sensed—and to release it again.

Both sgath and grien flowed in her. Ponen. Not something for anyone else to know, however.

"But the final test resides in the mask itself." The High Priestess took up a golden mask, newly minted, from a stand on the altar. She anointed it with oils, holding it up to the assembled priests and priestesses, who took up a low chant. "Rhianna."

Her mother moved behind Oria where she knelt on the hard stone before the altar. She kept calm and unmoving as Febe pressed the metal mask to her face. It burned her skin, hot from the candle flames and warmed oils it had rested in, but Oria didn't allow herself to flinch. Her mother took up the first of the three sets of ribbons, weaving them through Oria's elaborate braids and tying them tightly.

"Show us you possess the second sight," Febe demanded, her hope that Oria would fail coming through quite clearly. The chanting rose in volume, climbing to deafening levels, to prevent an aspirant from using sound to navigate. Oria stood, walked around the altar, opened the door behind it and stepped inside.

The others followed her, their chanting a drumbeat that accelerated her heart rate. To unsettle her also, then. It would take more than that to distract her.

"Because you are more powerful than all of them," Chuffta said, sounding both smug and proud.

"Shh. You'll make me fall." She enjoyed focusing the thought at him, though—something else that had become easier with the thick walls of resistance removed.

Men and women saw the obstacle course differently, her mother had explained, though she only knew how she perceived it. Using sgath, the narrow beams stood out to a magic user from the background. Apparently her father had confided to Rhianna that the men used grien much the way bats did, bouncing the magic off surfaces to detect the edges and pitfalls. It went against temple law for him to have told her that, or for her mother to have told her any of it, but it seemed any number of rules had fallen by the wayside in her mother's—and other allies'—determination to see Oria on the throne of Bára.

Careful to use no grien those present might detect, Oria let the sgath flow and walked confidently along the narrow path, careful not to shuffle or appear to feel her way. Though the room was brightly lit enough for the shine to leak around the edges of her mask, the way the metal curved close to her skull kept her from seeing the beams she walked along. The route—which changed for each supplicant—twisted and turned, changing angles, but still fell short of the ones her mother and Juli, the junior priestess assigned to Oria, had designed with diabolical mischief for her to practice on.

She still had bruises from falling. But they'd been worth it, for this moment.

At last, she stepped off the end that narrowed to a needle-thin point, showing her mastery by not breaking it. And that was all. To advance to higher levels in the temple, she'd need to demonstrate sgath, but that would be for the future.

The priests and priestesses surrounded her, kissing their masks to hers in ritual congratulation, the clinks like the chiming of wineglasses. Chuffta landed on her shoulder. His physical presence still worked to bolster and balance her, though she managed more of that on her own, through understanding the interplay of sgath and grien through her being. He tapped her mask with his nose.

"I bet I could melt it if I tried," he remarked.

She tweaked his tail. *"You'd be sad when I blasted you with my amazing magical abilities."*

He snorted mentally, with which she ruefully had to agree. So far she hadn't been able to do much with the grien besides use it as a release valve. No thunder, no fireballs, no earth-moving. Of course, as her mother wryly noted, most men learned their affinities from other wielders of grien. Oria wouldn't be asking for lessons in that, so she'd have to figure it out on her own.

The story of her life, it seemed.

She felt her mother's aura before Rhianna's soothing embrace surrounded her. With a sigh, she leaned her masked face against her mother's shoulder. "It seems odd for me to have the mask and you to be barefaced," she said.

"I don't mind," her mother murmured. "Those things get cursed hot."

Oria huffed a laugh at that, though she already believed it. She'd look forward to those cool, herbed face cloths now.

"Now," her mother said, releasing her, "to deal with the council. And Yar."

"I don't like that we have no idea what he—and the rest of them—have been up to these last weeks. If only I could have gotten my mask sooner."

Yar had walled her out of all discussions. Neither she nor her mother had been able to find out many details about the city's water reserves or communications with their sister cities—and without masks to allow them entrance as representatives of the temple, they were banned from the council meetings. Folcwita Lapo had turned Oria down with ill-concealed glee when she'd asked to be admitted as a citizen. She hadn't sensed the Trom, but the giant derkesthai glided in lazy circles in the thermals high above Bára, from time to time.

"At least we'll know soon." Her mother patted her arm. "You've done all you could."

Perhaps so. But that still might not be enough.

~ 27 ~

"HOW LONG UNTIL we have the final sections in place?" Lonen shaded his eyes against the angled autumn sun, to better see the lay of the aqueducts through the distance.

"We'll do the stretch to connect to Dru itself last." Arnon pointed at the direction it would take. "It might mean hauling water all winter, but you wanted to prioritize crop irrigation, and the sections to the farthest fields will be done in the next few days. Even manually carrying water from the finished aqueducts to those, the time savings has allowed us to grow a respectable harvest, enough to last through the winter. You've done it, King Lonen."

"We did it. All the Destrye. And thank Arill for the unseasonably warm weather."

Arnon cast a judicious eye at the landscape. "Except for the danger of fire. Everything we haven't watered is tinder dry."

"Perhaps we should be watering more things then," Natly spoke up. "There's plenty of it now, after all." She pointed at the staged aqueduct platforms, painstakingly built into the foothills, funneling water in a series of manmade waterfalls to the ripening crops of fast-growing alfalfa.

Arnon didn't glance at Natly but his shoulder muscles bunched. Lonen suppressed the absurd urge to apologize for her, especially knowing how much Arnon disapproved of their engagement. He also—more ruthlessly—cut off the disloyal thought that Oria wouldn't have said something so foolish. Not only unfair to Natly but probably untrue. He'd known Natly for years and Oria for two conversations. If Natly could still surprise him, Oria would likely obliterate his idealism.

"It looks good," he told Arnon, putting a hand on his brother's shoulder, belatedly aware it was his father's gesture.

Arnon, however, didn't seem to notice. He folded his arms, surveying the construction with a faint smile of pride. "It should work."

With his gaze on the scaffolding of waterfalls, Lonen frowned at what he'd thought were clouds gathering over the peaks, as they did most afternoons in the heat of autumn, though they rarely produced rain as they had in years past.

Not clouds, perhaps but…smoke? He traced the line of it behind low hills, where the harvested grains were stored. Fear crawled down his spine. As if called, a messenger came sprinting up.

"King Lonen!" The messenger barely gasped the words on the last of his breath as he ran up, then dropped to his knees. The scent of char wafted from him and instant dread curdled Lonen's gut.

All these days and weeks of working, he'd anticipated this moment. Much as he'd tried to focus on the positive, to count the blessings rather than the curses, a vague foreboding had plagued him. Not unlike the nearly nightly dreams of Oria casting black magic spells, ripping him asunder—obvious metaphors for his fears of what the Bárans might yet do to the Destrye.

Without hearing the words, Lonen knew.

"Dragons…searing…eating the dead…" The messenger heaved out the news in toxic clumps. "The grain silos, everything, burning."

Beside him, Arnon cursed viciously. "It's not possible!"

But it was. Worse, it had been inevitable, if the nightmares were to be believed.

Now none of that mattered. A greasy chill rolled over him, as if the mummified thing had already dissolved his bones.

"How long ago and are they still there?" Lonen demanded, willing the man to breathe.

"Just past noon. Sire, I—" The man broke off on a strangled

scream as the shadow of a dragon passed across the platform where they stood, Natly's cry of unmitigated horror as chill as the shadow. Without thinking, Lonen thrust her behind him. In the same movement, he drew the iron axe he'd never quite lost the habit of carrying. She'd teased him about that, too, that he kept the ugly thing ever with him, when he should be wearing his father's shining sword of Destrye kingship. Call it superstition, but he'd felt better with his battle-axe at hand. Besides that, he couldn't face the finality of his father's passing by taking up the sword of office.

The dragon swooped past again, low enough for the creature on its neck to look them over, raising a hand as it had in the council chambers at Bára. A strange greeting from a soulless creature. Arnon stood at his shoulder, iron sword in hand, and it comforted Lonen that his brother shared his preference for the ugly weapons.

The dragon wheeled away again, followed by a phalanx of others, smoke drifting in their wake.

Like locusts settling on a verdant farm, they set down and the Trom riders began filling those endlessly thirsty barrels of water from the freely flowing aqueducts.

"YOU CAN'T GO alone." Arnon sounded very reasonable, but his face showed the strain of worry. "It's suicide."

"If it is, taking more Destrye with me will only get more warriors killed. This way I risk only myself."

"I don't want to be king," Arnon ground out, jaw tight, as he paced. "Don't make me have to be king."

Lonen waited until his brother made the circuit of the room and had to stop before him or dodge around. When Arnon seemed about to do just that, Lonen grasped him by the shoulders. "The treaty was between me and Princess Oria. If she violated the terms, then she owes me a follow up on her promises."

"*If* she violated the terms?" Arnon threw up his hands, breaking his brother's grip. "Of course she did! The Bárans are without honor of any kind. How many times must she break her word to you before you see her for the evil, greedy sorceress she is?"

"I don't like it either," Natly put in. She sat at the table, hands clasped around a hammered metal goblet of wine. If Lonen were a thoughtful lover, he would have brought her one of those delicate transparent vessels Oria used. A pretty gift for the faithful woman who'd waited for him at home. Natly had finally stopped crying, but her face showed the ravages of her hysterical tears. "Have I won you back from the Hall of Warriors only to lose you again? This Báran sorceress could take your love for me and twist it backwards."

Perhaps that had happened already, and that was why Lonen no longer felt as he once had for Natly. Why it was Oria who prowled through his dreams. Why he looked forward to seeing her again with an almost savage glee that gnawed at his heart—though that came from hatred. All through the counting of the dead, the damage to the precious crops, the senseless destruction, he'd fumed over Oria's betrayal and relished the moment he'd confront her.

In his saner moments, he told himself that he desired answers. Or revenge. That the fiery longing to wrap his hands around her throat came from the need to choke the pretty lies from her, not the burning need to feel her skin under his hands.

In his less sane moments, he knew only that he had no choice.

He would journey back to Bára alone and do what he could to save the Destrye.

"You'll be a good king," he told Arnon, handing him their father's sword, hilt first, aware of the relief of giving it up unworn. He started to lift the wreath from his head, but his brother stopped him.

"No," he said, with a firm shake of his head. "Wear it. Make those cursed Bárans see you for the king you are, not they barbarian they name us."

"You'll need it, if I don't return."

"If you don't return," Arnon replied with grim conviction, "none of us will need anything ever again."

~ 28 ~

"ORIA?" JULI BOWED her head in unusually somber grace, grave concern wafting off her—though the red curls springing out from behind her mask added a note of irreverence. Seeing with sgath instead of one's eyes changed the way colors appeared. The mask forced Oria into seeing more of the resonance of light on objects, with the wavelengths of the sun very different from the rays reflected by Sgatha or Grienon. But Juli's hair was a particularly impudent shade of orange, which matched her unruly character, so Oria always saw it that way in her mind.

"Come sit, Juli. Give me your news." Focusing on her task, Oria finished working seed oil into Chuffta's hide while Juli crossed the rooftop terrace. Simple tasks like that, ones she'd done so often that she could accomplish them with her eyes closed, made for good practice. She had to consciously concentrate on "seeing" her work, looking for the spots she'd missed, rather than feeling them. Working on Chuffta added an extra layer of difficulty, as he radiated magic on another spectrum entirely.

Amazing how much she hadn't seen before.

"Captain Ercole wishes to speak with you." Juli didn't sit, instead gesturing to the inner chambers. "He waits at your door. I wasn't sure of your equanimity today."

In all truth, she felt amazingly good. Tired, yes, from all the practicing and studying, but the morning sun soothed and relaxed her, so that she felt as oiled and supple as Chuffta. "Send him in. It must be important news for him to bring it himself." Or secret news.

"I hope not. We've had enough grave news to last several lifetimes," Juli tossed over her shoulder, already on her way to admit the Captain of the City Guard.

Oria watched him approach while seeming not to. Another aspect of the mask she'd never understood, that it allowed her perception to move out in every direction. Where her eyes pointed wasn't necessarily where she looked, at all. Ercole had survived the Siege of the Destrye, as the poets had come to call it, where so many had not, and she gave him credit for giving her the backing of the city guard, though he'd never admit to it. His usually vital energy thrummed with nerves. Oh yes, something had him gravely concerned.

He crossed the terrace and knelt, removing his helm and bowing his head. "Your Highness."

She managed to restrain the impulse to correct him. She wasn't queen, not yet, despite all her progress. But, finally masked, she at least stood in the way of Yar taking the throne of Bára—an effective obstacle despite the machinations of Lapo and Febe. Though she and Yar raced each other in a bizarre competition to acquire ideal mates, neither of them had yet located such a person. Having gone through the priestesses of Bára—even testing those not yet masked—Yar had departed for the sister cities to search for a bride. So far Oria had not found a priest whose touch she could abide, but as Yar's senior, she outranked him, barely. Not queen, but as close as anyone in Bára came to the status, so she allowed the fiction.

"What people believe becomes real." Chuffta's mind-voice hummed in relaxed tones.

"Captain Ercole," she acknowledged. "What a pleasant surprise."

"Not so much, I'm afraid, Your Highness. I bring unwelcome news."

Oria allowed the sudden tension to flow through and out, keeping her attention on the task of oiling Chuffta inch by inch.

Needlework, sitting still, and meditating—none of that worked for her yet, but she continued to find for herself the things that did.

"Oh?" she asked.

"A man at the gates claiming to be the King of the Destrye seeks an audience with you."

That took her aback. "Claiming? You should recall King Lonen's face well enough, Captain Ercole. Unless they have a new king?" The thought stabbed at her with surprising force. Lonen's fate shouldn't matter to her, though it seemed to. An emotion to set aside and examine later. Another trick she'd learned—to delay her emotional responses for private venting.

"I should say that the man appears to be Lonen, but he shows no sign of being the Destrye king," Ercole allowed. "He is entirely alone and without any badge of office. I'm afraid he has demanded an audience with you, formal or informal, and said to remind you that you made him a promise."

Aha.

"I advise against receiving him, Your Highness," Ercole continued. "The man seems angry to the point of derangement. He has no forces to back his demands. If you shut the gates against him, he'll have no recourse."

"Except that I did make a promise," she said gently, working her way down the soft membrane of Chuffta's wing. "I will receive him. Make certain he's given safe passage through Bára. Does anyone else know of this visit?"

Ercole glanced up at her and away. Those who didn't wear masks were discomfited by them. Sometimes that worked to her advantage. Other times…she wasn't sure. "No, my men brought the news directly to me and have kept him out of sight in the guardroom."

"Thank you. Commend them for me."

"His arrival will become common knowledge once he enters the audience chambers."

"Which is why I won't receive him there."

"Not the old council chambers?" Ercole sounded aghast, uneasy concern rippling off him. Though she'd never made it an official edict, she'd avoided using that room since the day of the Trom's arrival. Showing his bravado, Yar used it on occasion, for his "private meetings," but she discerned from his chaotic energy afterwards that he liked it no more than she did. Clearly the rest of the council felt the same way, because they'd started using a different room, never once complaining, though it was smaller and tended to swelter in the afternoon sun.

"I'll see him here. And if you would personally escort him, I would appreciate that." Which meant that he would keep Lonen out of sight of curious eyes.

Ercole hesitated. "Your Highness—I don't mean to question you, but—"

"If you don't wish to make the climb a second time, I understand." She deliberately misunderstood him. "I trust whoever you send as escort."

"I'll do it, Your Highness," he grumbled, knees creaking as he stood.

She smiled to herself, letting the amusement mingle with the piercing sorrow of missing her father, and setting to oiling Chuffta's other wing, working at seeing each fine tarsal bone while also observing the garden. The jewelbirds zipped about in the waxing heat, visiting the heavy-headed lilies. Soon the blossoms would be gone and then where would the birds go?

"They can fly away, to find other sources of nectar."

"If only the Bárans could do the same."

Slowly, carefully, like easing herself into an overly hot bath, she let her thoughts move to the anticipation of seeing Lonen. Emotions tumbled up, ready to swamp her thoughts with dread, terror, a curious tingle of excitement, and that sexual heat he'd evoked. Mostly, however, she braced herself to make good decisions.

Because Lonen could only be in Bára for one reason.

"What will you do?"

"Keep my promise," she replied absently, spreading the delicate membrane between the final two tarsals, so thin light shone through, the blood vessels hot within the skin and bone, flowing with native magic.

"That may require much of you."

"I have no choice." She wryly acknowledged to herself the irony of saying the very thing she'd chided Lonen for. As another exercise in concentration, Oria extended her perception beyond the tower. Because she expected Lonen, and via the stairs to the tower, she allowed herself the cheat of sensing in that direction only. Soon enough he impinged on her awareness, a seething sun of virulent anger, fantasies of revenge, and determination. The exuberance of his masculine energy momentarily overwhelmed her, and Chuffta wrapped the slim tip of his tail around her wrist, which felt something like a failure.

"It's not wrong to need my help. That's why I'm your Familiar."

"And I'm grateful."

The impact of Lonen's forceful personality diminished, as she allowed it to filter away, venting it through Chuffta and back into the magic below Bára. It would be a good day when she could figure out something useful to do with it, but at least by the time the King of the Destrye stepped onto her terrace, she'd regained much of her calm.

"Your Highness," Ercole intoned with more than his usual gravity, "as you requested, King Lonen of the Destrye."

"Thank you, Captain. You may go."

His rebellious need to refuse, to stay and protect her, punched out and was snuffed just as quickly. With a bow, Ercole withdrew, and Oria indulged in transferring the bulk of her attention to examining Lonen.

He felt different than before, though that burning vitality hadn't changed. If anything, he waxed brighter and stronger, vivid with frustrated impatience, threaded through with dark desire. It was like a complex bubble surrounding him, ever-shifting, confusing her newly won perceptions. To give her sgath a rest, she backed off her focus, to observe more of his surface. He'd traded his furs and cloak for lighter leathers, anticipating the climate of Bára this time, she imagined, and wore the dust of the journey.

Oddly, she wanted to pull off the mask, to look on him again with her eyes, to compare that visual with what she recalled from weeks before, when she'd been an entirely different person.

Lonen cleared his throat and she realized he thought she hadn't noticed him. Out of courtesy, she turned her mask in his direction. "King Lonen. I did not expect to meet with you on my terrace ever again."

The bubble of energy surrounding him popped, spewing entirely rage and betrayed grief. "Then you shouldn't have sent your creatures after us."

Giving Chuffta a last pat, she asked him to go to the balustrade to observe from a distance more comfortable for the Destrye. She wiped the oil off her hands, then poured juice for him into the crystal goblet she'd used when they'd met before. "I didn't."

He swore, something vile-sounding in a dialect not their common trade tongue. She needed no translation, however, given the feeling behind it. "So you deny that—"

She cut him off. "Come and sit. Take refreshment after your long journey. You can tell me what happened, so that I may confirm or deny from knowledge rather than ignorance."

He paused at that, shifting his weight, the blankness of surprise canceling out the stronger emotions for the moment. Then his decision clicked into place and he moved forward—nothing shocking there, as Lonen always seemed to surge ahead once he decided on a course of action—and he closed the distance between them in several strides. Oria steeled herself not to flinch away from the force of his physical proximity.

He stopped short of actually touching her, reeling back the impulse with palpable force of will, then sat on the bench cornered to her, with a huff of breath that sounded very like a laugh, though his face remained stony.

"You're wearing one of those masks," he said, not at all what she expected.

She handed him the glass of juice. "Yes. A mark of my new rank."

"As queen?"

"Very nearly." She didn't elaborate more, knowing he wouldn't like hearing that she'd advanced as a sorceress. And the Báran legalities that intertwined marriage, magic, and the throne would be too difficult to explain to an outsider. "As we discussed before, such things are more complicated in Bára."

"Isn't everything?"

She sighed for the truth of that, though those complications at least kept the current power struggle between her and Yar at a détente.

Lonen drank deeply of the cooled juice, a ripple of pleasure in him further dampening the sharper emotions, then held up the glass to the sun. "I have thought about these goblets, made of such a strange substance."

"We call it glass. Made from sand."

"Surely that's not so. It looks nothing like sand."

She waved a hand at the surrounding desert. "One resource we have in ample supply. It changes when melted. The golems were made in a similar way, with some changes."

The Destrye barked out a laugh. "*Some* changes indeed. Only foul magic such as you have here could create a something so obscene."

Oria sorted through the revulsion rolling off him, complicated with a black sense of betrayal and despair. He reminded her of the glass forges, seething with molten heat so fierce nothing could cool it. "Surely the golems have not attacked? There shouldn't be any outside the walls."

"Don't pretend you don't know." As Lonen's forced calm snapped, so did the glass in his hand. With an oath, he hurled himself to his feet and flung the broken goblet against the stone balustrade, sending Chuffta into startled flight.

"Oria, the Destrye is crazed," he warned.

"No." For she saw it in Lonen's mind as clearly as the sgath showed her the life signatures of everything around her, the images congealing with horror. "The Trom attacked Dru."

She collapsed back against the cushions, cold horror making chill sweat run down her back. The mask chafed and she longed to pull it off, toss it aside, and weep freely. Too late. Yar had outmaneuvered her. Her worst fears had come true.

She was forsworn again—her promises broken and scattered to the winds—and the price would be giving up her happiness forever.

~ 29 ~

THE IMPULSE TO roar his fury, to breathe fire like those fearsome dragons, battled to break free of Lonen's control. He'd been a fool three times over. All along, through the endless journey accompanied by nothing but his thoughts, he'd nursed the hope that Oria hadn't known about the Trom attack, that she hadn't broken her word and betrayed their truce yet again.

Don't let a bit of foreign pussy make you think with the little head instead of the big one. The words of Ion's ghost rattled in his heart.

All this time he'd been feeling this nostalgic sentimentality over those brief encounters with Oria. To the point of fantasizing about having her in his bed instead of Natly. And here the object of his prurient dreams and more disturbing nightmares reclined on her plush cushions, clad in crimson robes and wearing that cursed gold mask, cloaked in offensive calm. He should wrench it from her, break those delicate ribbons, so he could look into those haunting copper eyes and learn the truth.

"You made me a promise." Instead of a roar, the words came out harsh as her fragile glass breaking on stone.

"Yes," she returned with an equanimity she hadn't shown before. "And to my knowledge I kept it."

"Then how did you know the Trom attacked Dru?"

With a heavy sigh, she stood, scrubbing her palms on her thighs, leaving a smear of damp on the silk robe. He hated the thing on her—too like her sorcerous brethren who'd hurled magics at them, and those who'd died so easily under his hand. Oria walked the low wall that bordered her terrace, looking out over the city with every appearance of seeing, which made his skin prickle with unease. The white dragonlet landed beside her, mantling its wings and snaking its neck to fix him with that accusing green stare.

"I see it in your mind."

It took a moment for Lonen to catch up to what "it" she meant. When he did, he didn't much like the implication. "You *can* read my thoughts." His voice came out flat. From behind, she looked more familiar, though her glorious copper hair was all caught up and braided with ribbons as gold as the mask they held. He missed the metallic fall of it that had so bewitched him from the beginning. Then kicked himself for falling so rapidly under her spell again.

"An overly simple way of putting it, but let's agree to that." The mask made her voice strangely hollow. "I see the giant derkesthai flying overhead, a Trom greeting you. There's..." She faltered. "Char in the air. More dead."

"Worse than that." He strode up to her at the railing, intent on forcing her to deal with him honestly. "Our crops burnt to the ground. Much-needed food for the winter, gone. Yes, more Destrye dead, but more deaths to come, from slow starvation and the diseases cold and malnutrition bring. And the water—they're taking it again, in greater volumes than ever before. Foul magic."

"They took the water, too?" She sounded faint but with an edge of anger.

"Why did you do it, Oria? Why?" He stopped himself from asking a third time, from begging her not to be what he most abhorred.

The uncannily smooth mask turned to face him. "I didn't," she repeated. "I don't control the Trom."

"I'm supposed to believe that?" This time the question came out as harsh as he felt. Oria didn't flinch, exactly, but a shiver ran through her, despite the heat. "I was there the day it touched you, and you didn't die like the others. When it spoke to you and you refused to tell me what it said."

"You decide what you believe, King Lonen of the Destrye," she replied, as soft as he'd been hard. "I can only give you the truth as I know it."

"You've changed," he said, before he knew he intended to. But the tentative belief that perhaps she wasn't behind the attack gave him an absurd rush of relief.

"Yes." Not a smile in her voice, but some wry amusement. "So have you."

"Would you take off the mask so we can talk?" He sounded plaintive to himself, involuntarily raising a hand, as if to remove it.

She stepped back, deliberately out of reach. "Don't touch me." No ragged plea this time, but the cool command of a queen. "And no, I cannot show my face to anyone but close family—and then only should I choose to do so. Which, these days, I don't."

"Then how do you eat and drink?" He flung a hand at the pitcher of cool juice, belatedly realizing that she hadn't shared it and thus could have poisoned him.

"Alone," she said, and turned her mask towards the vista again, for all the world as if she saw it.

"Your ways are very strange and unnatural," he growled at her in his frustration.

She actually laughed, the sound like raindrops on tin shingles. "Oh, Lonen—you have no idea."

Absurdly, he found a smile breaking the aching stern tension of his jaw, and he rubbed it, feeling the sweat-stiffened hair of his beard, realizing suddenly how bad he must look. He should have taken the time to bathe. Or asked to visit Bára's baths before meeting with their queen. Or very nearly queen, whatever that meant. He scrubbed both hands through his hair, wishing he could at least tie it back off his neck.

"Here," Oria said, moving gracefully to the table. It had held a violet fire the night they'd talked but now appeared to be only a smooth white surface, though the glass animals still pranced along the edge. More magic. She picked something up and held it out to him. Bemused, he took it. The leather hair tie he'd worn that night.

"You left it behind," she added, as if that explained anything.

Wordlessly, he took it from her and tied back his hair, happy to have the mess of it off his neck. Though he'd been on the terrace before at night, he'd remembered it as more shaded. Looking about, he noted the bareness of the overhanging branches, the crisp brown of the vines. "Your garden is dying, Oria."

She tilted her head to the side. "I'm no longer wasting water on it."

He choked back the protest that it wasn't a waste. That was the idealist in him again, picturing her in the fantasy of the impossible garden, beautiful and outside the world. The visible evidence helped reassure him about her, though. If the Bárans were behind the latest attack and water raid, at least Oria wasn't using their ill-gotten resources. Perhaps he could trust her to uphold her promise in good faith then. The hope felt fragile, too full of idealistic wonder, but without her help, the Destrye would surely perish.

"How will you aid Dru then?"

"I've been pondering this since you arrived." Seeming restless, she paced along the balustrade. "I promised you everything in my power and I intend to keep that vow. However, while greater than it was, my power remains constricted in certain ways. I can think of one solution that is rather simple to execute, but vastly complicated in its ramifications. You won't like it."

"I don't like my people dying either."

"All right." She returned to her couch, under the gently flapping silk awning that provided the only shade. "Why don't you join me, Lonen."

He did, if only to get out of the sun.

~ 30 ~

THE MOMENT OF truth. Oria centered herself as best she could, breathing out the unexpected nerves. Being around Lonen again did strange things to her. As if he triggered the rise of different energy in herself, ones she wasn't accustomed to grappling with. If he accepted her proposed plan, that would be yet another challenge to face.

"I'm not sure this is a good plan at all."

"Nor am I, but we're in a corner."

Chuffta ruefully sighed for the truth of that. The Trom attacking Dru, taking their water, Yar haring off to the sister cities, looking for a bride with bribes in hand: It all added up to him outmaneuvering her. She couldn't possibly find an ideal mate before he did. He was at least three steps ahead of her. But the law didn't require that she have a temple-blessed husband. Just that she have a husband. A bit of a loophole in Báran law—one that existed mainly because so few would contemplate the step she planned.

Subjecting themselves to a mind-dead, magicless, and sexless marriage as well as a loveless one—a high price, even for the throne. Some sacrifices were too steep for most.

Except for her.

"Tell me," she said, pouring him another glass of juice, pleased that her hand remained steady. "Are you married?"

He sputtered on the mouthful. "Engaged. Why?"

Unfortunate but not surprising. "Why haven't you married her yet?" She sorted through the sudden gamut of his emotions—

defensiveness and guilt uppermost among them. A very beautiful woman, with masses of curling black hair and luminous dark eyes. Voluptuous and sensual, doing things to Lonen that—Oria cut off the scene, grateful for the mask that hid her flush.

"I've been a little busy keeping my people alive," Lonen growled.

"You're fond of her, but you don't love her." It shouldn't matter, but it did. Oria didn't expect love for herself, but it would be difficult to watch him wish for another.

"Reading my thoughts again?"

"My apologies. Her image rose up quite clearly to me." Along with strong feelings—conflicted ones she didn't care to examine, even if looking too closely hadn't felt overly intrusive. That he didn't love that beautiful woman would be enough. "It doesn't matter, truly, but it would make things even more difficult if it would disappoint you greatly to break your heart or hers by marrying me."

Lonen set the glass down, very carefully. He laced his fingers together and leaned forearms on his knees. Then looked at her. "Excuse me?"

She should have planned what to say better. "It would be a marriage in name only, consecrated by the temple here in Bára, but otherwise non-binding for you in most ways. You would not be required to be faithful to me, so you could continue to be lovers with that dark-haired woman, if your customs allow it." The idea gave her a surge of bitter jealousy. Still, that was only fair to him. She would never be able to be his lover—nor anyone's, as temple law would bind *her* to fidelity—but Lonen should not have to give up intimacy for the rest of his life, too. He didn't carry the burden of expiating Bára's crimes.

Lonen studied her, his dislike of her mask palpable, his astonishment grown stronger. "You want me to marry you, according to your temple laws, and keep Natly as my lover."

"I did say you wouldn't like it." Natly. It had been better before this shadow fiancée had a name.

He laughed, dropping his forehead to his knuckles, then wiping the sweat from his brow. "Nothing with you ever goes as I expect."

"I'm explaining this badly." She held up her arm, and Chuffta came to her, offering his affection and support. She scratched his breast and he leaned into her. That helped calm the strange spike of jealousy, the grief at giving up the dream of finding an ideal mate. Always a fantasy anyway. "This isn't about what I want. It has to do with…well, magic and the way that it works. I've learned a great deal about wielding magic to help Bára, and will continue to learn more. One thing I'm certain of is that I cannot extend my abilities to assist Dru without the Destrye becoming my people, too. Through you."

At least she knew that much now, after spending hours every day studying the texts available only to priestesses in the temple. She loved her rooftop terrace, drying up as it was, even more for leaving it and returning in the cooling evenings.

"Why me?" Lonen asked. He was still watching her with unnerving intensity, that male vitality pricking at her. Though she'd deliberately closed the channel, sensual energy still leaked through, warming her, despite knowing he was thinking of his fiancée. "Arnon isn't married either."

Oria shook her head, partly to dispel disappointment that he was so eager to foist her off on his brother. Of course he would be, but it still wounded her pride. "You are the king. It might have been an easy ritual that made you so, but such responsibilities are binding on planes the Destrye might not perceive."

"But the Bárans do." He sounded accusing. Something darker ate at him, some profound tension.

"Some of us. I do. And the knowledge was hard-won." He wouldn't be able to understand what it had cost her. Even if they remained married the rest of their lives, he would never know her on a profound level the way an ideal husband would. She had to resign herself to that.

"I can't marry you, Oria." Desperation filled his voice, paining her. She hadn't intended to trap him, but the way he thrashed internally confirmed that she had done so. She'd thought—well, she'd hoped—that he wouldn't hate the idea of marrying her so much. They'd had something of a tentative friendship, but apparently not enough to make even a marriage-in-name-only to her palatable. She steeled herself to persuade him.

"You can't afford not to. I can't help you any other way."

"What about heirs? I can't have a queen who won't bear me children."

"What about your brother—can his children be your heirs?"

"Possibly," he admitted. "My older brother left two sons behind when he ascended to the Hall of Warriors. By Destrye law, the crown passes to my father's children first, before going to the next generation. But if I have no sons and Arnon persists in his refusal to be my heir, then Ion's sons would be next in line." He shrugged off the musings and focused on her with renewed intensity. The image broke through her still-clumsy screening, of her beneath him, naked and writhing, her husky voice gasping his name in pleasure. "But why couldn't we be husband and wife in truth?"

"Lonen." Inadvertently she echoed her fantasy self. She knotted her fingers together, face hot under the mask. "Because I simply can't. It's not possible for me."

He was quiet a moment. "I don't understand."

"I'm not surprised, but I'm asking you to trust that I'm telling you the truth. When I ask you not to touch me, it's not because I find you unwholesome. It has to do with who I am. Not who you are. But it's so much part of who I am that it won't change. No matter how long we're married, we will never lie together as husband and wife."

"You speak as if I've agreed to this wild plan."

"Neither of us has a choice in this. You, like me, are bound to act in the best interests of your people. You can't save the Destrye from the Trom without me, and I can't defend them unless I'm their queen."

"And you'd do this, simply to keep your promise."

"Yes. And because this will also make me Queen of Bára, which will let me protect my people here, too." She didn't tell him about Yar. Time enough to judiciously admit him to Báran secrets in the days ahead. Most of the politics wouldn't be his to deal with anyway, so no need for Lonen to know. He didn't say anything, however, the silence stretching out while dark emotions rolled in waves beneath the surface, like the lethal rip currents of the sea.

"I'm sorry," Oria said finally. "Perhaps I was wrong and marriage to me will break your heart, after all." She wished the words back, because she sounded entirely too sorry for herself.

"And you—are you giving up someone or would you have never married otherwise?" he asked, surprising her. The question took her emotional breath away. Impossible to explain to him what she'd be giving up—and also placing a burden of guilt on him he didn't deserve.

Proud of herself for sounding cool and remote, she told him, "You once pointed out that my life is a strange one, to live in this tower alone. I shall simply continue to do so."

"Because of this thing where you can't touch anyone."

"Yes." Better for him to believe that than to know the truth.

"All right then," he said abruptly, standing and scrubbing his palm on his pants, then sticking out a hand. "It's a bargain."

She stood also. Folded her hands together and tried to ignore the spike of hurt and annoyance from him that she refused his hand. "Agreed."

LONEN LEFT HER to go bathe, eat, and rest, and Oria finally cut the ribbons on her mask, welcoming the breezes that cooled her skin.

"A fine time for you to ignore my advice," Chuffta said, but compassionately, without rancor.

"What else could I do?" Oria wiped the sweat from under her eyes, telling herself she couldn't possibly be weeping over the loss of a girlish dream. "I made a promise. And Bára owes the Destrye far more than the price of one woman's happiness."

"Your mother won't be pleased."

"No." Oria dreaded breaking the news to her mother. There would never be a temple-blessed marriage for her, no babies to carry on the maternal line. Though if she could prevent a daughter of hers from facing the thing in the blue light… Even the memory made her a little ill. "But this marriage will put me one step closer to the throne, and that *will* make her happy. I need to arrange to see her and make the argument. Having her support with the temple and the council could make all the difference."

"Was it worth it?" Chuffta asked, the first time he'd mentioned her ordeal in the heart of Bára's magic.

"To be able to wield sgath, instead of being at the mercy of it? Maybe. But to have the potential to keep the Trom from consuming everyone and everything, then yes. Absolutely so."

"You couldn't know Yar would send the Trom to Dru. That he'd even be able to, and so soon."

"But I might have predicted it and I missed it. Still, he also failed to predict me."

"What do you mean, Oria?" Chuffta's mind-voice bristled with suspicion.

"I won't have a temple-blessed marriage, but as queen I'll have full access to the temple knowledge—the information High Priestess Febe gave Yar to summon the Trom."

"You can't mean to do the same." Chuffta's mind-voice held a panicked edge.

"I can and I will." Oria settled into the resolve. "How else can I control what they do, what Yar attempts? I must fight his Trom with mine."

Chuffta was quiet, his tail winding around her wrist. *"You know the danger in this. Without true* hwil *you'll be subject to corruption from those dark magics. It could be your undoing."*

"But for the right reasons."

"I'm not sure that matters."

"I understand if this breaks our contract," she managed, no longer fighting the tears. "I'll release you if you feel you can't be part of this."

She felt his slight hesitation as he considered. But then he replied.

"You're not alone. I'm always with you."

"Thank you. That means more than I can say."

She would need all of Chuffta's support in the days ahead—and his company. Something told her that taking the Destrye as a husband would create as many problems as it would solve. It seemed impossible that she should feel lonelier than ever.

As the dry desert wind dried the tears on her cheeks to salt, she turned her thoughts away from the sand trap of self pity.

She had more important things to think about.

Oria's Gambit

Sorcerous Moons – Book 2

BY
JEFFE KENNEDY

A Play For Power

Princess Oria has one chance to keep her word and stop her brother's reign of terror: She must become queen. All she has to do is marry first. And marry Lonen, the barbarian king who defeated her city bare weeks ago, who can never join her in a marriage of minds, who can never even touch her—no matter how badly she wants him to.

A Fragile Bond

To rule is to suffer, but Lonen never thought his marriage would become a torment. Still, he's a resourceful man. He can play the brute conqueror for Oria's faceless officials and bide his time with his wife. And as he coaxes secrets from Oria, he may yet change their fate...

An Impossible Demand

With deception layering on deception, Lonen and Oria must claim the throne and brazen out the doubters. Failure means death—for them and their people.

But success might mean an alliance powerful beyond imagining...

Dedication

To the wonderful members of SFWA, who helped me figure out the moons. All subsequent license and errors are my fault entirely.

Thank you for reading!

Credit
Content Editor: Deborah Nemeth
Line and Copy Editor: Rebecca Cremonese
Back Cover Copy: Erin Nelson Parekh
Cover Design: Louisa Gallie

~ 1 ~

THE GOLEM'S GLASSY claws flashed, arcing through the rosy light of the moon, and sliced open his throat. Blood poured down his naked body, steaming in the chill desert air. Out it flowed, sweeping around him like the bore tides of Bára. So much of it pooled around him that he began to drown in it. He strained to lift his battle axe, to cut the golem down with cold iron, but found a flower in his hands instead.

A white lily, luminescent and fragile, somehow escaping the blood that drained his life away.

The golem struck again and he shouted at it, no sound escaping. Because he had no throat left. Because he was dead.

How could he still be standing?

The golem's claws dripped crimson and its black maw yawned, glistening with glasslike fangs. It wouldn't ever die, forever coming after the Destrye until every last one of his people were dead, unless he managed to cut it down. Out of its mouth, sickly green fire blew, a lethal wind of flame that burned the crops and aqueducts. Not a golem then, but one of the Trom. Skin over bones, a humanoid spider, it grinned, lips red as the claws, hand reaching to turn him into skin without bones, nothing but pulped flesh. No, they were fingernails, enameled and jeweled. Natly's elegant hands slicing across his throat again, lips curving in a lascivious smile. With that third swipe, his head tumbled to the ground, and as she reached for his cock with those scarlet daggers of her nails, he finally managed to shout his anguish and fury.

"Your Highness?"

Lonen jerked in the hot water, the nightmare shredding around him with the spray of droplets. The servant boy gave him a wide-eyed look. Bero. The Báran lad had attended him his last time at baths, too. He was in Bára, again, cleaning up after the journey. No Trom or golems here.

Except in his tortured brain.

"Did you need something, Your Highness? You called out, but I didn't understand the words." Bero carried a stack of the much lighter colorful clothes that men of Bára wore. *Silk*, Oria had called the fabric, another thing apparently made by insects. Despite its disturbing origins, and like the addictive and tangy sweet honey she'd also introduced him to, the cloth had an exotic loveliness, more refined than anything produced in his homeland.

Like the sorceress herself, both unsettling and compelling.

"No, I'm fine." He cupped his hands and splashed water on his face. Sloppy of him, to have fallen asleep in the city of his enemy—and then failing to awaken at Bero's footfalls as he approached. Too comfortable in the soothing waters. Too many months of short sleep. Ion would have slapped him upside the head hard enough to have his brain ringing for the carelessness. But his brother was dead and gone these many weeks, reduced to boneless pulp at the simple touch of the Trom's evil hand.

"Would you care for wine or food now, King Lonen?" Bero asked in the trade tongue, setting out the soaps and oils. "Princess Oria said you're to have anything you ask for."

Luxurious baths, booze, and fine food—an excellent strategy to lull him into meekly doing the sorceress's bidding. The nightmare had served as a timely reminder of his purpose here—to save his people from destruction, not to indulge in Oria's gifts or seductive presence. He might have agreed to her startling proposal of marriage, but he'd proceed on his terms, not hers. For the sake of the Destrye and his sanity both.

"What are the chances of a decent steak?" He meant it as a joke, though the boy wouldn't know that. The Bárans didn't eat meat as a rule and, though the Destrye did, the grave losses to their livestock and wild game meant Lonen hadn't had anything worth calling a steak since before Battles of Bára.

"Princess Oria said to tell you she sent some of the hunters to find meat for you, Your Highness. It might take a few hours, however. Until then the best she can offer is some meat kept to feed the animals, and our usual fare."

Him and livestock—both pets of the Bárans. But his stomach growled, cramping with hollow pain, so he told Bero to bring whatever, enjoying the quiet when the boy went to fetch it. It seemed like years, not weeks, since he'd last visited the baths. That evening he'd washed himself clean of the ashes of too many dead before negotiating the peace treaty with Oria. Short-lived as that peace had been.

Then, as now, the elegant beauty of the underground chambers both enchanted and intimidated him. Built of carved gold and rose stone like the rest of Bára, the baths were pools of still water, several of them at varying temperatures, going from shallow to deeper than a man could stand. Elaborately carved pillars and arches supported the shadowy ceiling, the subtle light of the sconces not quite enough to illuminate it or the far corners of the room.

For a man who'd learned to jump at shadows, he found it surprisingly lulling. As evidenced by his falling asleep deeply enough to dream, though the nightmares were nothing new. The cursed things plagued him most nights. Odd to see Natly in this one, though, rather than Oria stalking him. A facet perhaps of his dramatically changed reality—exchanging one fiancée for the other. It appeared that by agreeing to marry Oria, he'd now have Natly haunting his sleep.

At least no one else had heard him cry out. He had the place to himself on this occasion. Probably the Bárans didn't bathe in the middle of the day. The baths simply remained filled, awaiting their convenience.

A shocking waste of water.

Bero returned, setting down a platter of food and a jug of wine, along with a tray of shining instruments. "Would you like me to shave you before you eat, or after, Your Highness?"

Reflexively, Lonen clapped a hand over his beard. He had no doubt he looked scruffy from his travels, and in comparison to the Báran men who were all clean shaven that he'd seen, but…

"Is that another of Princess Oria's edicts?" He asked, not bothering to disguise the sarcasm.

Bero ducked his head, clearly chagrined. "I apologize, Your Highness. Please forgive me. I did not mean to offend. When I serve the prince and folcwitas at their baths, they—"

Lonen held up a hand to stop the increasingly penitential torrent of explanation from the already nervous boy. "No apologies. I am short-tempered." He rinsed himself one last time, then rose from the water.

"Your Highness, I did not mean to abbreviate your bath." Bero sounded even more contrite.

"You didn't. I'm clean and I don't need to lie about, indulging myself." Especially not while his people could be dying by the Trom's dragon-breath while he luxuriated in deep water and napped. Oria had said she'd stop the incursions, but she'd also promised him that very thing before this. He had no reason to trust her—and plenty of evidence otherwise. Better to be ready to fight whatever battle presented itself next.

He dried himself with the cloth Bero handed him. Not the silk of the Báran garments, but likely the same source, woven thicker to be more absorbent. Nothing like the rough cotton towels the Destrye used. Then, draping the cloth around his hips, he sat on the bench next to the platter of food, pouring wine into the delicate goblet—made of *glass*, Oria had called it, supposedly formed of the endless sands that surrounded Bára—and drank deeply. Not Oria's sweet juice this time, but a potent dark blend made from fruits of the vine. The sorceress might not be watering her formerly lush rooftop garden any longer, but whatever the reasons for her choice, the rest of Bára didn't seem to be enduring similar privations. Of course, the fruits fermented for this wine were likely grown years ago. Possibly even before Bára turned her greedy gaze on Dru's once plentiful lakes.

"Go ahead and trim my hair and beard, but no shaving," he told Bero. "That's an offense against Arill."

Bero moved behind him, setting to trimming the curls that tended to spiral wildly when untamed. "Leave it long enough to tie back," he belatedly thought to tell the boy before he scooped up a chunk of cheese, dipping it in a dish of honey before taking a bite. It drove him crazy when his hair was too short to pull back, falling into his eyes all the time. Arill knew he didn't need to go any more insane than he already had.

Probably he'd started coming unhinged during the privations of the Golem wars. Plenty of Destrye warriors had. Fighting a relentless, inhuman enemy that kept coming at you, no matter how many you'd chopped into pieces, gave even the most stalwart man nightmares. Their camps at night had often rung with the shouts of men still fighting in their sleep, causing the lookouts no end of trouble sorting real alarms from phantasms.

Not every man showed the erosion of sanity immediately. Lonen hadn't suffered from the plaguing dreams until much later. Not until after he'd lost his father, two brothers, and countless men in the Battles of Bára. Not to mention the last bloodstained fragments of his idealism.

A wonder, really, that he'd held onto it that long.

No, for him the nightmares began after he met Oria, with her fragile beauty, demonic lizardling pet, and the ability to read his thoughts more easily than Lonen could decipher his brother's plans for aqueducts to save the Destrye from starvation.

Very likely she could do far more than that with her mysterious magic. She might be able to cloud or even direct his mind. That would explain how, though he'd come to Bára to exact revenge and restitution for her crimes against Dru, he'd somehow ended up agreeing to marry the witch.

As uneasy as it made him, he'd prefer to blame his decision on her magic, rather than contemplate how much of it might spring from his strange obsession with her.

Even the exotic taste of cheese and honey on his tongue evoked her vividly. The Destrye said that all roads led to Arill's temple—which, in fact they eventually did. Apparently all of his craziness led straight back to Oria. Back home in Dru, the land of his birth that he'd nearly killed himself to return to, he'd craved that flavor with much the same unreasonable longing he'd somehow attached to the woman who'd introduced him to it.

Both of which he'd been certain never to encounter again. Wonders never ceased.

Bero trimmed his beard, then lathered and shaved his neck, throat and surrounding skin. He stepped back, watching anxiously as Lonen rubbed a hand over it. The Báran oils made the hair soft, and Bero's careful work created crisp demarcations between the hair and his skin. He probably wouldn't recognize himself reflected in still water.

"Does it meet with your approval, Your Highness?" Bero asked.

"Feels great." He nearly told the boy he didn't have to use the honorific every time—though he'd nearly gotten to the point of not looking for his late father when people used it—but he probably needed every measure of pomp he could muster among these status-conscious people. "Would you—"

He broke off at the echo of booted footsteps, and sprang to his feet, iron-headed battle axe leaping to hand. The Báran city guard who approached gave him a strange look—no doubt bemused by a nearly naked Destrye wielding the heavy, unrefined weapon in the sumptuous perfumed baths—but quickly bowed. "King Lonen, the Princess Oria would like to enter and speak with you once you've finished bathing and have dressed."

Oh sure. Exactly what he'd expected. And why in Arill not receive his erstwhile enemy and future wife in the bathing chambers of Bára?

"Tell her I'm at her disposal." At her beck and call, even, which stung his pride more than he liked. After all, he was doing this for his people, as a good king should. If he didn't find building aqueducts and shoveling manure beneath him, marrying a foreign witch shouldn't be.

The man hesitated fractionally—perhaps Lonen had snarled too much—then bowed again and stepped out.

"Your Highness, fresh clothes for you are—"

"I saw them. In a minute." He sat again, handing Bero the leather tie for his hair. His favorite one, in fact, exactly the right length and suppleness. He'd been sorry to realize he'd lost it in Bára, then bemused when Oria handed it back to him. Odd that she'd saved it all that time. The tie might be his preferred one, out of long habit, but it didn't look like much. Not like the fancy gold cords she wore in her braids. "A bit more oil in my hair, if you will, Bero, then tie it back."

He wasn't putting off dressing only to poke at Oria—or only to test how much she saw through that solid gold metal mask without eyeholes. No, he told himself, he acted out of practicality. There was simply no sense getting oil on the silk shirt, borrowed or not. If the side benefits alleviated his stinging pride, so be it.

He watched for her through the gloom, catching the exact moment she faltered at the sight of him. She didn't hesitate long, forging gamely forward, but it gave him a welcome bit of satisfaction that she saw him and that he could give her unease. Anything that awarded him an edge with the canny sorceress would be a welcome weapon.

She strode towards him in that impetuous way of hers, as if she brimmed with more energy than she could contain, crimson robes swirling about her long legs. The dragonlet, her constant companion, rode her shoulder, scales shining even whiter in contrast to the vividly colored silk, long tail wound around her arm like a series of decorative bracelets finishing at her wrist. Its green eyes shone in the dimness, as if lit from within.

Oria stopped her usual decorous and obvious distance from him, which perversely made him want to close the space between them. But he didn't, forcing himself to stay put. He'd never pressed unwelcome advances on a woman in his life, always careful of his size and strength. With Oria a slender sapling compared to the more robust Destrye women, he'd been particularly observant of her physical fragility and aware of crowding her.

Not that she credited him with any of that restraint. She wavered, well out of reach and poised to flee, as if he might seize her and tumble her to the floor. The idea had its merits—and were he another kind of man he might act on them—if only to reassure himself that she was still the same person inside. Innumerable sorceresses hid behind those featureless gold masks and the crimson robes of their office, virtually identical from any distance. He recognized Oria by her scent of night-blooming lilies, her low musical voice, and that bright copper hair that shone in the elaborately coiled braids. Also no one else carted about a winged, white dragonlet. But none of that substituted for seeing her.

When he'd met her before, she hadn't been a priestess and wore no mask. He missed Oria's lovely oval face and, most of all, her expressive eyes, so full of life and nearly the same color as her metallic hair. Maybe he'd carried anger for too many things for far too long, but all too familiar rage coiled in his gut that she'd glibly offered him marriage then coolly informed him that their alliance would be in name only, that he'd never share her bed or body.

Not only would he give up a normal marriage to a woman of his own people, he'd also never satisfy that unreasonable and burning desire to strip Oria naked and feel her slim body beneath his, to touch that fair skin, watch her extraordinary copper eyes darken with pleasure. Surely Arill had devised this torture in punishment for the many profane deeds he'd committed in the name of war, to bind him in marriage with the one woman who'd obsessed him like no other, and simultaneously ensure he'd never taste the single reward that might make tying himself to his foreign enemy bearable.

When Oria didn't speak, instead remaining rigidly silent and caressing her pet's tail where it looped around her wrist—a nervous gesture, to be sure—it occurred to him that she'd likely glimpsed that potent fantasy in his mind, along with his fury. Overheard how part of him howled to strip her of those shapeless robes and find the luminous slip of a candlelit woman who'd caught his eye in a window and reminded him of the fantastic tales of his boyhood, even amidst the blood, gore, and terror. Too late for her to unsee it, in that case. Teach her to snoop in his brain.

"You wanted to speak to me?" He prompted.

"I thought you were finished bathing." She shifted on her feet, masked face turned away, voice stilted. "I apologize for catching you undressed."

"I am finished," he told her, enjoying her unease far more than he should—though it rankled that she couldn't even bear to look at him. He was scarred yes, but he'd earned those fairly battling *her* golems, and if he'd grown overly skinny, that too was her fault. "Does it matter how I'm dressed—can you even see through that thing?"

"Bero, leave us, please," she said, instead of answering.

The boy patted the spiral tail of Lonen's hair and bowed his way out. Lonen poured more wine and held out the glass to her. "Wine? I've only the one glass and I drank from it, but you could sip from the other side, if you're concerned about catching a disease from me."

~ 2 ~

"NO, BUT THANK you for the offer," Oria managed to reply with reasonable politeness, proud of her even tone in the face of all the violent emotion whirling off him like sand thrown by a dust devil.

The Destrye king shrugged his bare shoulders, took a swig of the wine and popped some honey-dipped cheese into his mouth, chewing vigorously. His granite eyes stayed hard, studying her, his dislike of her mixing with sexual desire that carried an unsettling edge of fury.

As much as she'd come to appreciate the rational, even noble aspects to his character, it wouldn't pay to forget that Lonen, though king now, was a warrior first, and from a brutal, barbarian people. And his sexual nature affected her in improbable ways. Seeing with sgath wasn't the same as looking with her eyes. In some ways, it showed more details to her mind's eye—the physical lines of the man, yes, also layered with his shimmering personal vitality.

"You could take the mask off, if that's what's stopping you," he said. "It's good wine. So is the food, if you want some."

"Thank you, I've eaten." She sounded stiff, even to herself. Better that, though, than an emotional meltdown. "And my mask is a badge of office. I don't remove it, except with close family." Something she'd told him already.

"We're going to be family." Lonen swirled another hunk of cheese in the honey liberally, a gesture somehow suggestive, then ate it. His strong throat, skin newly shaved below his neat beard, moved as he swallowed, drawing her attention. Though she fought that fascination, better to look there than at the rest of him, so liberally displayed to her mind's eye.

He sat with his knees wide, the white drying cloth parting over one thigh, revealing shadows beneath. Strangely she longed to touch him, though she knew doing so would only overload her senses, causing devastating mental and even physical pain that could send her into a faint at best. He enticed her anyway, inciting a craving to caress that tanned skin, feel the dark hair sprinkled over his arms and legs, denser on his chest, then arrowing towards the cloth that could be so easily tugged away.

She blushed at the uncharacteristically prurient impulse, glad of the mask that hid it, though Chuffta would know her thoughts.

"And wouldn't judge you for them," her Familiar said in her mind. *"It's good to want your mate. It's the natural order of things."*

There would be nothing natural about this marriage. "We won't be family like that," she said aloud, to both of them. "We discussed that already and you agreed to a marriage in name only, King Lonen. I have good reasons for it."

Irritation flickered out of him, but he glanced down at the food tray, thick dark lashes hiding his eyes as he picked through the offerings, at last choosing spray of grapes. "But you haven't explained them. Nor did you answer my question about how well you can see in that mask. Even if we won't share a bed, we will share hopefully long lives bound together. We shouldn't have secrets between us."

She laced her fingers together, holding herself more rigid than she needed to. Oh, he had no idea of the secrets she kept. Chief and most dangerous among them that she could use male magic, the more active grien, along with sgath. Of course Lonen wouldn't know the difference as any of her people would, but he might slip up and say the wrong thing. Or use the information to deliberately betray her, if it became useful for him to do so.

Execution could be a handy way to dispose of an unwanted wife.

If her own people did the deed for him, so much more convenient.

Since she'd gained her mask, she'd gotten much better at handling the emotional energy that she absorbed from other people as passively as she did from all living things and the deep source of magic below Bára. But dealing with it effectively meant venting the accumulated energy as grien—something she needed not only privacy, but quiet and concentration to accomplish. All of which did not come easily around the larger-than-life Destrye with his exuberant masculinity.

"Let me help." Chuffta leaned his angled cheek against the patch of skin behind her ear bared by her upswept hair, where the mask did not cover. The derkesthai's buffering abilities took the jangling energy down several notches.

"Thank you." This time she kept her reply to her Familiar private. The way Lonen's flinty eyes went to Chuffta, however, showed he suspected they conversed. Something he didn't at all like. She might be more efficient to catalog what he *did* like and consign the rest to beyond her control.

"We *will* have secrets between us," she corrected the Destrye. "For many reasons. Not all the secrets are mine alone, and the temple guards hers closely. Only those who have taken the mask may know them. Not only by sacred law, but because of a ... a need for maturity in ability to absorb the information."

A wry, humorless grin cracked his face, teeth white in the dim, golden light and the darkness of his beard. "Did you just say that I'm too stupid to understand the answers to my questions?"

It sounded bad, put that way. Oria herself had only recently proved herself a master of *hwil*, a state of such perfect, inviolable peacefulness of mind and spirit that she could be trusted with the dangerous secrets of manipulating magic. Never mind that she'd lied to the priestesses and faked *hwil* well enough to pass their tests. Something else impossible to explain to an outsider, much less this brusque warrior.

Lonen could never hope to penetrate the temple's secrets. In fact, he'd be far safer and likely happier not knowing the dark side of Báran magic.

She couldn't tell him as much, however. They might be virtual strangers, but it didn't take long familiarity with the man to know he wouldn't take any explanation along those lines at all well.

She deliberately laced her fingers together again, mimicking a serenity she'd never feel, choosing her words carefully. "Even though you'll be my husband, you will still be Destrye and I will be Báran. There are worlds of things we'll never know or understand about each other. We must resign ourselves to that reality now."

His intention sharpened, giving her warning, but he still surprised a gasp out of her when he lunged to his feet and closed the distance between them with only a few athletic strides. Chuffta spread his wings and hissed, though he didn't breathe fire. Oria held her ground—barely—and Lonen flicked a dismissive gaze at her Familiar.

"Rest easy, dragonlet," he murmured. "I won't harm your mistress."

"I told you before—his name is Chuffta."

Lonen didn't acknowledge that, sticking up three fingers, his thumb and pinky tucked into his palm. "How many fingers am I holding up?"

"Lonen—"

"You're not telling me any of your precious temple secrets." He seethed with a dark combination of frustration and desire. Probably he wouldn't harm her. Not intentionally, but his longing to touch her was as palpable as the scent of warmed oils on his damp hair and skin—and as vivid as those sexual images that burned through his mind like meteors. An outsider like him might never understand what harm he could do her with the intensity of his thoughts alone, intentionally or not.

"How many fingers, Oria?" he grated out the question, his angry impatience even harsher than the sound. "It's a simple question. One I'd ask any of my men who got knocked upside the head."

It wasn't simple. None of this was.

"Three," she answered, knowing that only satisfied one question among many, but nevertheless hoping he'd let at least this go.

He nodded, confirming something to himself. Then circled around her, holding up his hand behind her. No such luck that he'd drop the subject so easily. "How many now?"

Ignorant of Báran magic, perhaps, but a canny man. Another priestess might lie, might keep the temple secrets from a foreigner, but she couldn't bring herself to deceive him more than she already had. He did deserve to know something of who—and what—he'd agreed to bind himself to.

"One."

"Is the dragonlet telling you that? It's looking at me. You can talk to it, can't you?"

"Chuffta?" She emphasized her Familiar's name.

Lonen made an aggravated sound. "Fine. Chuffta."

"He's protective. He doesn't like you behind my back. And yes, we communicate. Go over to the bench, Chuffta," she said aloud, for Lonen's benefit. "And look the other direction."

Chuffta grumbled without words, but did as she bid, settling on the bench, folding his wings, and delicately sniffing at the haft of Lonen's axe propped there. Her Familiar understood that she needed to build trust with her future husband—had, in fact, been lecturing her on the topic.

"Advising you," Chuffta corrected. *"Which, I might point out, is my job."*

"Yes, yes—now let me do mine."

She had to force herself to hold still as Lonen drew up close behind her, the fine hairs prickling on the back of her neck. "You're holding up two fingers, one on each hand."

The man moved soundlessly, but even without sgath revealing the energies around her, his masculine aura would impact her from even much farther away. This close, it enveloped her as surely as a physical embrace, the complicated interplay of his thoughts and emotions strumming over her nerves. As disastrous as that would be, she found she ached for his touch on her skin, her body heating and throbbing as if he already had. He'd brought that out in her from the beginning, though it made no sense. Only her ideal mate—a priest, masked and trained in grien—could interact with her the right way, without harming her.

She'd only completed the first stages of testing—meshing auras to evaluate compatibility. None of the priest candidates had affected her like this. Though that could be because none had met the initial requirements either. Perhaps an ideal husband would affect her this way?

Not that it mattered. These feelings for a foreigner were ... unnatural. A perversion born of her adolescent fascination with the gruesome illustrations of the barbaric Destrye warriors carrying off naked women to do vague and illicit things to them. She could never explain why those stories mesmerized her—before the priestesses snatched them away as inappropriate—no more than she could prevent her body from rousing to Lonen's presence and the potent sexuality that surrounded him.

However, though she might not have true *hwil*, she created the appearance of it well enough to fool the High Priestess. She could and would just as easily fool this magicless Destrye and prevent him from ever knowing how he affected her.

Allowing any glimpse of her weakness would only encourage him to pursue the topic of bedding her, and that could never happen. He'd touched her once—on the wrist—and she'd been unconscious for a week. She couldn't imagine what sexual intimacy would do to her. No matter how much this newly discovered, recklessly sexual side of her wanted it.

"What do you want, Oria?" Lonen breathed the question close to her ear, startling her into thinking for a moment that he'd turned the tables and read *her* mind. "Why did you come here?" he clarified. "I thought it was difficult for you to leave your tower."

Grateful to be back to non-sexual and non-magical business, she seized the opportunity to step away and turn to face him. She didn't need to, of course, but it helped diffuse that heady intimacy, the implicit trust of having him behind her, his body heat warm on her back, his breath on her exposed nape.

"I can leave my tower more often than when you knew me before. I am … stronger now."

"Because of the mask."

"It's more that I have the mask because I'm stronger."

He contemplated that, studying her. "Is the hair part of it?"

She stumbled mentally. "The hair?"

Lonen waved his hands, indicating her elaborate hairstyle by wiggling his fingers, transmitting a fair amount of Destrye disdain for all things Báran. "The braids and stuff."

She put a hand to the intricately woven style, though she hardly needed to confirm its existence to herself. "It's just easier, with the mask ribbons, to tie it all together. Well, and it's traditional."

"I liked your hair better when you wore it down."

Dropping her hand, she straightened. "I'm not a decoration that exists to please you, King Lonen."

"Not in bed, nor out of it," he replied, both musing and taunting.

"Enough of that." She was losing patience for this … sparring match. That's what it was. "It's not too late to back out of the deal. Don't marry me. I understand if this one caveat is too much to ask." She sneered a little though, when she said it. He could have all the women he wanted. She'd be the one committing herself to a life of never knowing the touch of another person besides her mother.

"And me."

"A human person," she amended with a mental caress of affection. Again she was glad of the mask that hid her smile. Lonen had folded his arms, glaring at her. He would only grow more annoyed if he thought she laughed at him or took their predicament lightly.

"Hardly one simple caveat. However, as you so succinctly pointed out," he was saying, biting out the words, "I don't have a choice in this. You can't save the Destrye from the Trom unless you're married to the Destrye king, because that's how the magic works." He freed a hand to wave it in the air, much as he had in describing the braids, making the magical rules seem equally fussy.

That's what she'd told him, a convenient half-lie. In truth, getting him to marry her had a great deal more to do with becoming Queen of Bára, granting her access to the innermost secrets that would enable her to summon the Trom and wrest control of them from Yar. Guilt chewed at her, though. She'd been thinking on her feet. How much of her conniving Lonen into marriage came from her strange attraction to him?

It worried her that she'd made the decision, not out of integrity and the resolution to live up to her promises, but out of self-indulgence. A family trait and failing, perhaps. One that had led Bára into taking so much at the cost of others.

She should face this potential corruption of her moral fiber. She did feel that, when Lonen wasn't pissed at her, they shared some common ground, besides this impossible attraction. Though they'd admittedly conversed very little—and she'd spent an awful lot of her life alone so she had little to compare—she liked talking with him better than anyone else she'd met.

"Besides me."

"A human person!" But she laughed in her head, no doubt as Chuffta intended.

"You're laughing at me." Lonen flung the accusation at her, granite eyes flat.

"No!" She retorted, too fast, surprised into being defensive. He knew it, too, narrowing his eyes at her. Worse and worse. She scrambled to explain. He wouldn't much like the truth, but he'd flustered her too much to think up a good excuse on the spot. "Chuffta and I do more than communicate—he talks to me. And sometimes he's … he makes jokes. In my head."

Chuffta flipped his wings at Lonen's incredulous stare. "You're saying the dragonlet is a smartass?"

She couldn't help it—maybe it was all the tension—but she laughed in truth. Lonen transferred his bemused stare to her, anger lightening. "I've never heard you laugh before."

"Surely you have."

"Not a real laugh, like that one, instead of those little huffing noises you make when you find something ridiculous." A mischievous smile tugged at his mouth, one she recalled from when he'd teased her about using that sword she could barely lift.

"I do not make huffing noises," she protested, and he pointed a finger.

"There. Exactly like that one."

"How did you even know I was laughing at what Chuffta said? I didn't make any sound, huffing or otherwise."

He cocked his head slightly, his smile fading and his face growing serious again. "You may be wearing a mask and that ugly shapeless robe, but I can still see the lines of your body, how you move and hold yourself."

Oh. She didn't know what to do with that information. His own way of sensing emotion, she supposed. A warrior's way of reading an opponent. He stood there, relaxed hands on towel-draped hips, and watched her, waiting for her to speak next.

She should tell him the truth, that she could marry his brother and it should work magically. That she'd misled him because she herself would rather marry a man she knew and felt affinity for. Her feelings weren't important. She was forsworn and must make recompense. It didn't matter that it had been Yar who had broken her promise that the Trom, the ancient guardians of Bára, would leave the Destrye in peace. Only a recreant would try to dodge the guilt by claiming it wasn't her fault. It fell to her to make good on the promise, not to find a path through her penance that pleased herself.

Time, however, *was* of the essence. If Yar returned from one of their sister cities with an ideal mate, he'd make a temple-blessed marriage and his claim to the crown would trump hers. If she could get Lonen to marry her that very evening, she might beat Yar to the crown. Under false pretenses. But for the right reasons. It was all a mire deeper than the muddy Bay of Bára when the tides receded.

To give herself time to mull the ramifications, she moved over to Chuffta, stroking his arched neck.

"Here—come meet Chuffta officially. He's a derkesthai and does not much like you calling him a dragonlet or a lizardling. You can touch him."

"Did I say I wanted to?"

"You said you wanted to know more about me. Here's something to know."

Trepidation colored Lonen's energy, until he shook it off. He drew near, then extended a fingertip and traced the luminously white scales. The anger evaporated entirely for the moment, leaving behind a shimmering wonder. "He's soft," he said reverently. "And intelligent?"

"Very. He has a tendency to lecture."

"My job," Chuffta reminded her unnecessarily.

"He scolds you?"

"Yes, as he's reminding me now that it's his job as my Familiar."

"I've never heard the word used that way—what does it mean?"

"It means that he's family to me, that he ... helps me." So difficult to explain to this hard man all the ways she was fragile, how Chuffta buffered the worst of the impacts of incoming energy. "It's a special relationship."

"Do you remember the first time I saw you?" Lonen asked, voice rapt as he stroked Chuffta's curved neck.

Though an apparent non-sequitur, his question made perfect sense to Oria. It had been the first time she saw him, too. "Through the window." She'd been transfixed by the sight of him, blood-drenched axe in one hand, knife in the other, as he slaughtered the priestesses on the walls, helpless in their trances as they fed sgath to the battle mages. They'd died easily because none of those women had active grien as the men did. As Oria did, against all nature and common sense—a secret no one but her mother and Chuffta could know.

Unless Yar had guessed, which could spell disaster.

"I'd never seen anything like you in my life." Lonen wasn't looking at her, his emotional energy turning warm, a youthful, wondering feel to him, his voice almost dreamy. "You and your derkesthai, like something out of an illustration in an old storybook. Fantastical and ethereal. Magical."

She stroked Chuffta's wing, holding her breath against confessing that Lonen had looked to her like something that stepped out of a book, too. Ironic that his vision had an innocent, even romantic purity to it while hers had carried darkly sexual overtones—particularly given their current opposition where she'd play the eternal virgin and he could cat about as much as he pleased.

"Why can you touch Chuffta and not me?"

His question caught her by surprise and she realized he'd transferred his gaze to her face, focus intent on her, as if he tried to see through the mask.

"It's an … energy thing," she replied, far too breathlessly. Not a useful trick, long term, to hold her breath as a way of holding her tongue. She'd have to find something else.

"An energy thing." His hand strayed much too close to hers on Chuffta's hide.

She snatched hers away and tucked both hands behind her back. "Well, energy and magic and … emotion."

"That goes through the skin." His voice had hardened, a step short of calling her a liar.

"I tried to explain that you wouldn't understand."

"I touched you once before, at the city gates when you surrendered to me."

Something about the way he said that made heat wash over her. "I surrendered Bára to you, not myself."

"You're one and the same, just I am myself, and also the Destrye and also Dru."

"Whatever you're driving at, even after we're married—should you decide to go forward with that plan—you will never be able to touch me without hurting me, so decide carefully."

His attention sharpened, a hint of dismay to it. "Did I hurt you before?"

Better to be candid. "Yes."

"And that's why you fainted—and were ill for a week."

Tempting to tell him yes and put a forever end to this line of inquiry, but she didn't like lying to him. Not outright. Not more than she had to. "That was part of it, but not all."

"Because I made you go outside the walls."

"Yes, that was another part. I can't leave Bára."

He stilled, outraged astonishment buffeting her. "Then how do you propose to be Queen of the Destrye?"

It hadn't occurred to her that he'd had some idea of taking her with him to Dru. "I—I don't know," she replied, far too faintly.

"I'm to tell my people their queen will never set foot in their forests?" His voice rose in volume on the question, his incredulous frustration hammering at her.

Oria threw up her hands, giving in to the urge to pace, to release the restless feelings he stirred up, a mirror to his. A break in *hwil*, but he wouldn't have any way to know that. "Don't tell them you married me at all! I don't care. Marry your Natly and have her play your queen."

"You said it matters to the magic, that you are bound to the Destrye king."

"It does. But what occurs on the magical plane doesn't have to be exactly replicated on the human one. What matters is that you marry me in our temple, that we're bound by oath and magic. I don't care if you marry Natly, too…in whatever kind of temple you have."

He stared at her for one more long, incredulous moment, then appeared to snap. With an abrupt turn, he stalked over to the pile of clothes, tossed aside the drying cloth, and yanked on the pants with furious gestures.

Though Oria averted her gaze automatically, her sgath worked largely on a subconscious level, constantly feeding her information about her surroundings—including a far too detailed vision of how Lonen looked naked.

"Arill take you, Oria," he snarled. "You sure know how to piss me off."

How she longed for a swig of that wine.

~3~

HE'D NEVER FIGURED himself for a romantic. Even when he was merely a prince and third in line for the throne, he'd known that although he didn't have to marry for duty—the Destrye did not engage in complicated politics, as the Bárans did—any bride he chose would have been subject to his father's blessing. Sure, he and Natly had talked about marriage, but looking back, he could see that he'd felt safe coaxing her about it, indulging in the flirtation of it, knowing she'd never say yes. Her ambitions had looked higher than that. She'd sulked for weeks when his oldest brother, Ion, married Salaya.

After that she'd worked her wiles on the second-oldest, Nolan, until he firmly rebuffed her flirtations—not only because King Archimago had decidedly *not* approved of her. Only then had she returned to Lonen. He hadn't minded her fickle games. Natly was beautiful, with an arsenal of sensual tricks that turned a man's mind, and he enjoyed her playful company. But chasing her had been a good deal more fun than having her. Those weeks in Dru after he returned home from the war, reluctantly taking up the crown that should never have been his in the natural order of things, Natly had affixed herself to his side, talking of nothing but the midwinter wedding ceremony he'd never quite agreed to. He hadn't really meant to lie to Oria by calling Natly his fiancée. After all, Natly figured them to be engaged and he'd never directly disabused her of the notion. He'd simply never found the energy to make a decision one way or the other.

He'd put it down to exhaustion—mental and physical—from tackling the Destrye's many problems. More than enough decisions to make there, few of them optimistic. That soul-deep weariness from all he'd done had made Natly's lighthearted ways, the ones he'd once prized, seem somehow tawdry and frivolous.

He'd already been battling the realization that it would be irresponsible of him as king to make Natly queen when Arnon put it into words. *You can't marry her. She would have made a decent princess, but she won't make a good queen.* Part of him had even felt relief at finding a way out. Arnon didn't outrank him, but his brother had a good brain and knew how to use it. It would take substantial conviction to ignore his one remaining brother's advice. Perhaps he also channeled their father's stern ghost.

He'd agreed to Oria's extraordinary proposal in part because he knew she *would* make a good queen, even if she was a Báran sorceress who'd bewitched him. She'd demonstrated the resolve, courage, and selflessness to sacrifice herself for any people she took as her own. It had seemed fitting to him, a restoring of balance, that she'd step in to take responsibility for the Destrye when King Archimago had died taking responsibility to protect vulnerable Bárans.

It hadn't occurred to him that she didn't intend to act as queen for anyone but the Bárans.

And now she glibly announced that she didn't care if he took another wife, if another woman pretended to be the Destrye queen in her place. That was the final snowflake to bring down the tree limb.

He pulled the shirt over his head, settling the wide collar, and found she'd stopped her pacing and regained her regal poise, handing him a full glass of wine.

"Perhaps you'll explain your anger to me," she said, all polite elegance. "A calm and rational conversation should not be too much to ask."

Taking the glass, he swallowed a healthy portion. Finding himself unable to match her reserve just yet, he stalled. "Just why *are* we standing in the baths having a long conversation, Oria?"

She gestured to the many benches. "You are welcome to sit. I came here to discuss next steps with you in private, as I had other tasks nearby, and I thought to save you the trouble of climbing to my tower again."

He grimaced at that. It had taken a good quarter-hour to ascend those endless curving stairs to her terrace atop the tallest tower in Bára. "What next steps?"

Spreading her palms wide, she huffed her exasperation. He supposed she made that sound when it wasn't a half-laugh, too. Before, when she hadn't had a metal mask hiding her face, she'd kind of puffed out her lips when she did it, blowing out her breath as if she released some tension. "The next steps are moot, Lonen, if we're not going to marry."

"Oh, we're getting married all right." His turn to pace. "We agreed already. But mark me on this: I will not be in violation of my vows by marrying or bedding anyone besides you. I can't imagine what you think of my honor as a man and a king, but I don't make promises, then turn around and break them."

"I don't either," she said quietly.

"Don't you? You promised to be Queen of the Destrye then informed me you'll never go to Dru and you're fine with a false queen on the throne, regardless of how well she'd serve the people."

Oria's golden mask seemed to ripple with flame as she swung her head to face him. He imagined her pretty mouth hanging open in an O of surprise. "I hadn't thought of it that way." To her credit, she sounded chagrined, which helped mollify him.

"Clearly." He polished off the wine, then grabbed a hunk of bread to help soak up the alcohol in his blood. The Bárans made excellent bread, he had to give them that.

"Though I did assume, when you said you were engaged, that you'd chosen a fiancée who'd make a good queen," she pointed out, with cool logic that stung a little. He couldn't explain that he hadn't given it much thought without sounding like the idiot he was, so he made a show of chewing the bread.

"I thought you'd be pleased enough to keep Natly as your lover—or wife according to your customs—and go on your way," Oria continued, in a tone of infinite patience that didn't fool him for a moment. "Some barbarian cultures allow a man to have multiple wives and concubines, I understand. A marriage of state that benefits you politically while not tying you down personally should be welcome to you."

He decided not to touch the condescending "barbarian cultures" remark. Particularly since the Destrye had maintained such practices in the past.

"For someone whose name you heard once, you've certainly mentioned Natly numerous times." He couldn't help taunting her with that. Oria might not want him to touch her, but she didn't like the idea of Natly having him either, much as she protested otherwise.

"Because she's constantly in the forefront of your thoughts," Oria retorted.

He shook his head at her, pleased to have caught her out. "Oh, Oria. Now that's a lie."

She didn't reply immediately. "That doesn't matter. I concede the point—if we decide to go ahead with this marriage and you want me to truly be Queen of the Destrye, I'll do what I can. I've learned a great deal, maybe I can eventually find a way to travel there. You're correct—I owe that much to you and Dru. But have you thought of how your people will feel about having a Báran sorceress among them, affecting their laws, passing judgment on them?"

"If you manage to drive off the Trom and put food in their mouths, they'll be happy enough." He repressed a shudder at the thought of those skeletal monsters who could at that moment be riding their fire-breathing dragons to burn the Destrye crops and buildings before they stole more of Dru's precious water. His people would put up with more than a foreign queen to be rid of that curse. "If the price is marrying their king to you so you can work your magic to protect them, then even Arill cannot deny your fitness to wear the wreath of royalty."

She sighed and held out a hand. For a moment his heart tripped in ridiculous pleasure; he thought she invited him closer. But no, the dragonl—Chuffta—flew to her. The left forearm and shoulder of her crimson robe were padded, allowing the creature to land with his back talons gripping and wide white wings spread until he balanced. She scratched his breast, her body taking that intimate posture she probably wasn't consciously aware of, which betrayed that she conversed with her Familiar. To salve his disappointment and irrational jealousy that she lavished affection on her pet and not him, Lonen savagely chewed more bread. At least he wouldn't be so blazingly hungry. Not for food, anyway.

"There's something I should tell you," she said.

"Does that mean you're relenting on withholding information? Or confessing to a previous lie?" He tensed for the answer, having placed a great deal of trust in Oria's basic honesty, if nothing else. How much more a fool would he be proved to be before this was done?

"I admit haven't told you everything. I never *will* tell you everything, which might be misleading if not an outright lie, so if that's your line in the sand, we might as well call off the agreement now."

"You're awfully insistent on not getting married now," he noted. "This was your idea to begin with."

"I know. But I was not completely forthcoming with you and I should have been." She took a deep breath and squared her shoulders. "I *could* marry your brother instead. Connecting to any part of the ruling family should be the same. That would leave you free to marry Natly"—she held up a hand when he opened his mouth—"or another. Someone who would be a *real* queen for your people. It was unfair and wrong of me not to offer that."

She cast a glance at Chuffta while Lonen mulled over her words, making him wonder what her Familiar counseled.

"Then why did you insist earlier that it had to be me?'

Oria sighed, mask turned away, though with her uncanny perceptions she'd know exactly where he was, what he was doing. How he felt. Though maybe not entirely. She didn't seem to sense how much of his willingness to marry her had nothing to do with duty at all. Something that might be best to conceal from her, lest she use it as yet another weapon against him.

"Several reasons," she said, her words followed by a heartfelt sigh. "All of them self-serving. I am not Queen of Bára because I can't be crowned until I'm married. Fortunately, neither can the only other viable contender, my brother Yar, whom you no doubt remember."

He did. Yar was younger than Oria and still a boy in most respects, with a voice that cracked and the brash impetuousness of too much arrogance and too little experience. Still, Yar had helped Lonen's warriors after the Trom attack, using his truly spectacular magical skills to mold stone into bridges and shelters. An ability like that, no matter how unsettling, would come in handy for building, say, aqueducts that didn't burn.

Oria began pacing again. Chuffta hopped to a nearby bench, watching her. "Right now, Yar is away looking for a bride from one of our sister cities. If he returns with an ideal—a suitable match, he'll be married before I can be and the throne will be his."

Lonen scratched his beard thoughtfully, its trimmed and oiled softness an unfamiliar sensation. "Not to be callous about your ambitions, but would that be such a terrible thing?"

She laughed, this one bitter with a metallic echo. "You think I'm power hungry and crave the throne. I suppose that's a fair assumption on your part."

Actually he didn't think that at all. It didn't mesh with what little he did know about her, and he felt obscurely ashamed of hurting her by the implication. He opened his mouth to say… something, but she forged on in a rush, wringing her pale fingers together.

"I did not send the Trom to Dru, but someone in Bára did. The ways of the Trom are mysterious even to us, but they can be directed by their summoner. It doesn't make sense, but I think it had to be Yar who sent them. He's the one who summoned them originally and he must control them still. He has powerful allies on our council and in the temple, those who believe it's far easier to continue to steal water from the Destrye than to cast about for other options. We also face problems with our sister cities, because we've been supplying them with water—your water—and trading goods and political favors for it. That leverage is part of how Yar will be able to convince them to give him one of their priestesses for a bride. I don't have a particular yen to be Queen of Bára, but I desperately don't want Yar to be king. For the good of the Destrye, you don't either. With the power of the throne of Bára and the sister cities *and* the Trom under his command..." she shook her head. "I don't care to picture that future. I thought you might understand."

He considered the torrent of information, as overwhelming as heavy rain on parched earth. When she decided to confide, she did so full out, something that put him in mind of her restless, energetic stride.

"So your solution is to marry ahead of him and be crowned before he returns," Lonen summarized for them both. A solid plan, but what had been her intention before he turned up at Bára's gates only hours ago? She had to have had something else in mind. "Why doesn't he marry a Báran girl—priestess, that is? Or the same for you—if time is of the essence, that would be easier and faster. You claimed you didn't have another man lined up to marry. Did you withhold information there also?" A not-so-surprising twinge of possessiveness at that thought. Though he'd never truly contemplated having Oria for himself, not beyond those plaguing dreams and the occasional fantasy, not until she proposed it.

"No—that's the full truth. I don't have anyone to marry because it's not that easy." She tucked her hands in the small of her back, pacing fast enough to make the crimson silk billow around her legs.

"It's difficult to explain."

"Try," he suggested in a dry tone, and her mask flashed as she glanced at him.

"I don't think you're stupid or ignorant. But I *do* know you're skeptical about certain elements of magic and how it works."

"Acknowledged." He poured the rest of the honey over another hunk of bread, scraped the dregs with a piece of cheese and piled several more on. A slice of meat and it would be a decent sandwich. As it was, he might never stop eating.

"The temple matches us with our spouses. In the best of all possible worlds, we find a ... good fit and make a temple-blessed marriage."

"An arranged marriage."

"More than that—there's complex testing that involves magic." She waved that off as yet another thing he wouldn't understand. Probably he wouldn't, but it rankled nonetheless. "Sufficeto say Yar did not find a match in Bára. With so many of our priestesses lost in the battle with, well, with your people..." She took a breath, and he understood the feeling. The memories of that night pained him, too. He'd been the one to kill most of those priestesses, and their blood still soaked his nightmares. Oria had seen him with that blood on his hands. No wonder she didn't want them and those stains of murder on her unsullied skin.

"There are far fewer candidate priestesses in Bára now, and none satisfied the requirements for Yar, so he's casting his net wider," Oria said more briskly. "I've received my mask recently, so I've only just begun testing, but I face the same scarcity with so many of our priests fallen in battle. So far the results are not promising, which surprises nobody at all even with a reduced pool, because I'm ..."

"A princess?" He filled in, when she didn't—but she shook her head.

"Unusually sensitive, let's say." A wealth of feeling crawled beneath her dry tone. Interesting.

"But even if Yar is counting on that," he said when she didn't continue, "on you taking longer to find a match, why risk it if the throne is at stake, something he clearly *does* have his ambitions set on? Why not settle for the second- or third-best pick?" As Oria was doing in proposing to him, it suddenly hit him. A far less savory realization. The honey wasn't enough to keep the bread from going dry in his mouth.

Oria stopped in front of him, twisting her fingers together again, and he viciously wished he could see her face, read her expression. Although he supposed he didn't need to see her to know he wouldn't like her answer. "Just tell me, Oria. Truth is best."

Though he wasn't entirely sure of that.

"A mate who's a good fit is … ideal." She settled on the word with a frustrated lifting of her hands. "A temple-blessed marriage trumps one that isn't. Were Yar and I both to marry, whichever of us has the best suited partnership—as the temple evaluates such things—would be crowned."

"So not only do you need to be married first, you need to be married and crowned before Yar can return with a supposedly better marriage."

"Yes, exactly." She sounded relieved that he understood—and maybe that she'd gotten away with not telling him everything about why the Bárans sought these purportedly perfect matches. Knowing them, it had to do with power and status. And magic, more than likely. Something he did not and would never have.

He pondered letting it lie there. Couldn't. "Why haven't you stepped up your own search, gone to these other cities to find your match?"

"I was considering it," she admitted, "before you arrived. But in the first place it's much easier for men to go beyond the walls than it is for women, for complex reasons I can't explain, but they're the same ones that would make it difficult for me to go to Dru. That same … syndrome will also cause Yar delays in bringing a bride back to Bára from her home city, so that gives me breathing room."

"And in the second place?"

"I don't have the influence he does. Because I refuse to be part of trafficking stolen water."

She said it simply, but the bald integrity of her statement touched him in an odd way—more than any of Natly's declarations of love had. It hadn't been that long ago that Lonen had sat on Oria's rooftop terrace and scorned her for not knowing whose life's blood kept her lush garden alive.

"Thank you for that," he told her gravely, meaning it. She might be playing a game of omission and half-truths, but he could count on that about her, at least.

She shrugged that off, pacing away and seeming uncomfortable. He wanted to ask more about what an ideal mate for her would be, but likely it would only cause him pain to hear all the things he could not be to her. Words like that could never be unheard and would lie between them. After years of marriage, such small resentments festered and became mortal wounds. He'd seen enough of that between his own mother and father to want to avoid the same in his own marriage, if at all possible. His idealism at work again—to be contemplating a loveless, sexless marriage of state and still hoping for happiness between them. And yet perhaps it wasn't entirely blind optimism that made him think Oria pushed to marry him instead of Arnon.

"So you call your reasons self-serving because you'll get to be queen, which makes little sense since you don't really want the power or the glory."

He had the impression that she grimaced. "That—and because being queen will give me access to the highest level of temple secrets. Which will let me discover how Yar summoned the Trom, so I can do likewise. That's how I'll wrest power from Yar and relieve Dru from the Trom's incursions."

"How did Yar get access to these secrets if he's not yet king?"

She ticked a finger at him. "You're good at this. I didn't think to ask that question for some time. I'm not certain, but I think High Priestess Febe broke sacred law and gave the spell to him. Or she gave it to Nat and Nat gave it to him."

"Your brother Nat was king following your father's death, so why was that breaking sacred law?"

"Because he *wasn't* king." She made a disgusted noise and waved her hands in the air. "They told the Destrye that, but Nat wasn't married either, so the rites couldn't be performed. But Febe and the head of the non-magical side of the council, Folcwita Lapo?"

"I remember him," Lonen said with grim distaste for the overblown man.

"They both heavily favored bringing in the Trom once it became clear the city had fallen to the Destrye."

"And they now support Yar's bid for the throne."

"Not coincidentally, yes."

"So, marrying me is the expedient choice, I can see that, but how likely are they to support your claim? Why wouldn't they delay a decision for Yar's return?"

"A potential pitfall to be sure, but I have some people on my side, too. My mother, formerly queen, may have been relieved of her mask and crown, but she still holds a great deal of sway on the council, in the temple, and in the hearts of the people of Bára. Also the city guard supports her and me, which helps enormously. For example, that's how you came to be personally escorted to me without anyone else knowing you're here. Something I'd like to keep from public notice as long as possible, another reason to have this conversation here, where no one can overhear. Finally, though you declined taking a role in governing Bára when we set terms for our surrender . . ."

Her voice wavered a bit on that word, just as she'd been unsettled when he'd said it to her earlier, about having surrendered to him. She wasn't nearly as unaffected by him as she pretended to be. Perhaps he stood a chance of wearing her down on the sexless marriage concept. Surely there must be ways for their women to be touched, or there would never be babies. He might not be a Báran man, or a priest, but he knew how to pleasure a woman. If nothing else, Natly with her bold demands and sensuous nature had taught him that much.

Oria had found her composure again, her stride more measured as she paced. "The treaty might say that you did not care to exact governorship of Bára in any way, but you *are* king of the Destrye and you did conquer Bára. They won't like it, and I might have a fight on my hands, but they'll have to acknowledge that Bára, and everything and everyone in it, belongs to you, by right of the ancient laws."

A heady thought, that Oria already belonged to him. Had he been one of his rougher ancestors, he likely would have already dragged Oria back to Dru with him as a war prize, his to do with as he pleased. The lustful fantasy aroused him profoundly, appealing to some base instinct even though the more civilized part of himself stood back in horror. It made him recall fragments of those old tales though…

"There are stories," he said, pulling on the memories to bring them out, "of foreign, pale-skinned women brought home to be wives and concubines of Destrye warriors, who inexplicably faded and died. As if they starved for food none could provide. Is that what would happen to you?"

She stopped, the abrupt change in topic derailing her stride along with her thoughts, a strange cant to her body, almost as if she were in pain. Chuffta sat up higher, wings mantling as his sinuous neck moved in a sort of question. A good insight, that he reacted to Oria's thoughts and moods. Another way to puzzle her out.

"I didn't know that," she finally breathed, strain in it. "We have no such stories."

"Perhaps you wouldn't." He kept his voice soothing, nearly regretting that he'd brought it up, except that it had garnered such a telling emotional response from her. "If the women were taken away and died without returning home…"

"Yes. No one would have known what happened to them. Tell me—were they … used?"

He nearly choked at the euphemism, especially on the heels of his brutish fantasies, then wrestled with the chagrin at having to answer, to own up to what kind of people the Destrye had been before they settled in Dru, tamed by Arill's gentle hand. Maybe there was no possible way to explain. For the first time he understood what she meant, that she could give him answers, but that he wouldn't necessarily understand them. He tried to couch it gently. "If you mean, did the men who captured the women take them to bed in the marriage sense, the answer is assuredly yes."

"Of course that's what I mean," she replied in a tart tone, far better than the pained one, and amusing him that he'd tried to be delicate. "And how can you be so sure—do the stories say so?"

"Not exactly, but—" He had to clear his throat. "Why else take them?"

Her mask faced him as he answered, seeing far too much in him. "That would have contributed, too. The sex," she clarified unnecessarily, "just as it would damage me if you gave into those … impulses like you imagined just then."

Stung, he pushed to his feet. "I wouldn't," he said far too loudly, and he was further abashed when she flinched and took several steps back. He had to take a steadying breath to lower his voice. "It's not fair, Oria, that you judge me based on fleeting thoughts and emotions. People think and feel many things they don't act on. That's part of learning to be a decent human being—knowing that there are dark yearnings in your heart and being strong enough to recognize them as such and exert control. Maybe your mind is this perfect, serene place and you don't understand the human struggle to be a better person, but I'm only a man and a flawed one at that."

She swayed, seeming shocked. "I am human, Lonen."

"You don't always seem like it."

"No?" She sounded surprised and … weary. Sad and weary. "Regardless, I understand that struggle all too well. Being flawed."

"Maybe I'd know that if I could read your mind, too. But if you couldn't see so easily into my head, you would have never known I harbored any such thoughts, however temporary, to judge me so harshly for them."

She nodded, folding her hands. "I apologize for any offense. I did not mean to sit in judgment. I sense enough of you to know your better nature. If I hadn't, I wouldn't have taken this gambit. Still… this conversation has revealed much and I'm growing more certain that it would not be a good idea for us to marry."

"Because of my sexual feelings for you?" Might as well lay it all out there.

"All right, yes. That's one reason. I'm concerned by your insistence that you would not take other lovers. I know men have … needs. It's become obvious to me that yours are quite strong." She paused, a little breathless, as if flustered. "You must understand that I'll never be able to satisfy them for you."

He took the risk of moving closer to her, fascinated that she continued with a conversation that clearly discomfited her. She lifted her chin as he approached and visibly steeled herself not to step back, so he stopped where he was. "Women have needs, too, Oria."

She tilted her head. "Do they? I'm not sure it's the same. Or perhaps it's a difference between Báran and Destrye."

He couldn't believe that. "You've never felt anything at all sexual? Nothing—never wanted to be with a man or a woman? Never have been with either?" He wasn't sure if she was playing coy, dumb, or was truly that innocent. *Or alien,* part of him cautioned.

"Same sex unions are frowned on in Bára—it puts the magic balance off. And no." Her voice sounded faint and he imagined a blush stained her high, delicate cheekbones. "A Báran priestess lies only with her husband."

"And I will be your husband," he couldn't help saying, edging closer, halting when she raised her palms.

"Not like that. If you can't agree to that part of the marriage, then we have to call it off."

"And do what?" He curled his hands into fists of frustration. "I need your help for Dru, you need to be married and made queen to do it."

"I could marry your brother," she insisted. "He would have the same freedom I offered you. I would never impose on him or interfere with his life."

"He's not here, which thwarts your need for speedy action."

"A marriage by proxy then. You could command it and the council and temple will abide. The ritual magic knows no physical distance."

He rather enjoyed debating with her, especially when she forgot to be poised and starting sounding fierce. He'd never be able to step aside and let Arnon have her. Or any man. "Same distance problem in getting him to agree, however. How could I send and receive messages in a short time? It might take considerable explanation and debate."

She flung up a hand. "I don't know. Can't you simply do it and tell him later? You're the king."

He could, yes, though Arnon would make the rest of his days a misery. "Not happening," he said, instead. "There is no way I'm standing by while you marry another man. You proposed to me and I accepted. I won't allow you to back out."

"You won't allow me." Her voice had gone lethally chill. Something swirled in the air around him that reminded him of the sorcerer's magic on the battlefield. Her slim body had gone tense as a plucked bow string and he wondered, far from the first time, what form her magic took. Shards of ice, perhaps, instead of fireballs. "How, exactly, do you plan to enforce that edict?" She asked softly, in clear warning.

He leaned in. She was scary, all right, but he found her impossibly titillating at the same time. He'd totally lost his mind, but it seemed to matter less and less. "By invoking right of ancient law. As you noted, Bára and everything in it belongs to me."

"You wouldn't dare," she hissed.

"I won't have to," he returned, "because you're far too intelligent, noble, and rational to be stubborn for the wrong reasons. I'm right here, willing and able to marry you, I'll agree to a marriage in name only, with the caveat that we'll revisit if you change your mind about that aspect in the future. The rest is details. Done."

~ 4 ~

ORIA STRUGGLED TO find a reply to that, but she'd dug herself too deep into a dune and the sands of cascading reactions showered down on her, threatening to bury her in her own conniving.

She was too new at this maneuvering—in politics and with a man. Particularly this man.

"I warned you he would not be easily led." Chuffta's mind-voice at least held a note of concern. Any smugness to his 'I told you so' might have pushed her over the edge. As it was, the male grien magic she shouldn't possess—except in a quiet ladylike seed—thrummed with the need to escape, preferably to knock the cocksure Destrye warrior off his feet. *Allow* her, indeed.

"It's not a question of changing my mind about sex," she gritted out. "That is not under my control."

Lonen held up hands in mock surrender. "All right then. Why are we even fighting about this?"

She didn't even know—she'd lost track of the entire argument. The man did things to her. Mixed her up. Made her want things she couldn't have and certainly didn't have the luxury of wanting, with so many more pressing matters. That potent sexuality of his made it difficult to think clearly. And he called her rational and intelligent. Ha! She took a step back, giving herself relief from his stimulating presence, but lifted her chin, lest he think he'd cowed her. "Probably because you're wrong; I am frequently stubborn for the wrong reasons."

A grin broke across his face, his great good humor also—thankfully—cutting that sexual tension that had swamped her. It seemed that, as he triggered the response in her, she did likewise to him. They were fools to be doing this to themselves.

"So, what was your other reason?" He asked.

"For being stubborn?"

"No." He waved that off, going back to the food platter and taking the last item on it—a bowl of greens he grimaced at but efficiently spooned into his mouth and chewed. "You said you had several self-serving reasons for insisting it be me you married, but you only listed two."

"With many parts."

"None of them really self-serving, however."

"You should tell him," Chuffta counseled. *"It will cost you nothing and will ease things between you."*

"Nothing but my pride," she retorted, but her Familiar only laughed at her. "Should I send for more food? I tasked the hunters to get meat for you, but it will take some time."

"I know—Bero gave me your message." Amusement sparkled from him and he set aside the empty bowl, wiping his hands on the drying cloth and sauntering towards her. "And now I know there's definitely another reason because you're ducking the question."

"You don't know any such thing."

"Oh yes, I do. You change the subject when any of my questions come too close to what you'd prefer to keep hidden."

"That seems impossible for you to keep track of as you ask a great many questions."

"Yes, I do." He nodded, his attention intent on her. "And I'll continue to do so. You might keep your face and body hidden from me, but I'll find other ways to get inside you. Whether you are my enemy or my lover, I'm better off knowing everything about you."

The words, part promise, part threat, made her catch her breath. "I don't have to answer any of your questions. Especially if I'm your enemy."

"Oria." He lifted a hand, as if he might touch her, but hovered it near her cheek, his gaze wandering over her mask, before he lowered it again. "You asked me to be your husband so I can help you with your problems and you can help with mine. The whole point of this effort is to combine forces, to be partners, allies, maybe even friends, if not lovers. There's no reason to treat me like an enemy to be shut out."

"Then why did you say that?"

"To put it out there. We both know we dance a fine line. Let's be clear about it, if only between us."

She closed her eyes, though it didn't help her not see him, feel him in and around her. It was too late to avoid that intimate invasion. Her sgath seemed to flow toward him of its own accord. If only her mother could advise her on this. "The truly self-serving reason is that, if I can't be married to—to have a temple-blessed marriage, then at least I'd be married to someone I..."

"That you what?" he prompted, when she paused too long. He had that avid feel to him, like Chuffta when he hunted.

Pursing her lips and blowing out a breath, she stepped back. "Someone I don't abhor."

He narrowed his eyes. "That's not what you started to say."

"Well, it's what I decided to say."

"Uh-huh. Do you know that I dreamed about you?"

He had a knack of doing that—disrupting the flow of her thoughts, taking her by surprise, and destabilizing her *hwil.* "No," she replied, face hot under the mask. It was really too steamy in the baths to be wearing it. That and her priestess robes. "Why would I know that?"

"You're a sorceress. I figured one of your magic tricks might be to send me dreams." A bit of tension filled his voice. Enough uncertainty that she decided not to ask what the dreams involved. She'd had plenty of her own about him, and if his were anything like hers...

"No. It most assuredly is not." She folded her hands, then felt too prim, and dropped them. "Now, if we can discuss—"

"If you didn't send them, then I had them because I couldn't get you out of my mind," he interrupted, though his voice was quiet. "I think you were about to say at least you'd be married to someone you're attracted to—and I'm saying I'm attracted to you, too, Oria."

"I know that," she snapped, so thoroughly unsettled that she missed denying that's what she'd been thinking. "I can feel it."

"What does it feel like?" He didn't come closer, but his energy intensified so much that it expanded to flow over her, almost overwhelming. Also addicting, like being warmed by a sun that never burned.

"I just—Lonen—can we please drop this topic and discuss next steps? I've arranged to meet with my mother, to discuss this plan with her. If we're going to go ahead with this, I must go now."

"You have to schedule time with her?"

"She's … not well. My father's death was very hard on her. Her health is tenuous and my window of opportunity narrow because of it."

His warmth chilled. "We all lost a lot of people we loved."

"I know. Believe me—" She couldn't think about it. Her father dead. Ben and his sweet smile gone forever. Nat. Her lady-in-waiting. Her faithful guard. She couldn't count all the deaths and the misery they'd left in their wakes. "This is another thing that's difficult to explain to an outsider, but my father and mother shared a special bond. Her grief is no greater than anyone's, but losing him caused her … damage."

Lonen looked thoughtful. "Did they have one of these temple-blessed marriages—ideal mates?"

A warrior of such skill shouldn't be so clever, too. It simply wasn't fair. "Yes," she admitted. "And that's all I'm saying about it."

"That doesn't mean I won't keep asking." He grinned and she realized she'd made a huff of frustration. "Okay, you'll explain your plan to her and then what?"

"If she approves, she'll approach the temple and we can be married as soon as tonight, and begin proceedings with the council to make me queen, in case Yar returns sooner than I expect." And so she could begin her research into the Trom and be ready to wrest control from him.

"I cannot stress enough how much you should not hasten that step, at the peril of not only your sanity, but the wellbeing of us all." Chuffta's mind-voice held unusual sternness, but she ignored him, focusing on convincing Lonen to stop his games and think about the tasks immediately before them.

"And if she doesn't approve?" he was asking.

"Then we'll have to go with the plan of you throwing your weight around. But it would be smoother with her help."

"Makes sense."

"Tomorrow the council meets. I'll petition them to ratify us as king and queen. Once we have the marriage in place, you and I can plan our strategy with the council, if that's all right with you."

"Sounds good." He picked up his axe, the dense iron double-bladed head like a hole in her sgath vision. "Let's go."

"You're … coming with me?"

He grinned at her. "Of course. We're doing this together. Partners. *We* have a fight on our hands—not just you."

"We're not married yet."

"But that's the plan. Which means tonight is our wedding night." That wave of fierce sexuality rolled over her.

"Not in the way you mean."

"We'll figure out something to consummate the momentous occasion. Lead the way, my lovely fiancée."

Setting her teeth against several replies, she did.

LONEN COULDN'T QUITE define to himself why he enjoyed teasing

Oria so much. Maybe because it came close—a distant second, but still—to actually touching her. If he couldn't seize her and kiss her breathless, rattling that infernal poise, he could at least make her sound all faint with words.

Besides, it was fun.

For the first time since he'd accepted the king's wreath and the burden of leading the Destrye over his father's corpse, here with Oria he'd gone long minutes without giving any thought to his crushing responsibilities and the looming threat of disaster from so many directions. He couldn't do any more for his people than he was at that moment—which included giving up a normal marriage and very likely the hope of having heirs of his own. He couldn't regret that aspect too deeply. Not as far as his responsibilities to the Destrye were concerned. It would be fitting for Ion's boys to inherit the throne that their father should have had.

That he minded the loss for himself came as something of a surprise. Somewhere deep in his heart he'd nursed the idea that he'd have a loving wife and children to be his family one day. That he wouldn't always feel so alone.

Amazing that any such tender idealism had survived all he'd seen and done.

Dueling with Oria provided a most welcome distraction from such useless thoughts. Also, with every indignant retort and flummoxed response, she became less enigmatic fantasy creature and more flesh and blood woman to him. A welcome transformation. Along with the most pleasant news that he at least hadn't been alone in his strange obsession with her. There might be hope for their marriage yet. It might never be the loving union he'd dreamt of, the wife who'd listen to his foolish thoughts and deepest fears, who he'd be able to confide in when the throne demanded he keep a brave face for all others. But maybe they could make something of a friendship.

If nothing else, conspiring with her to navigate Báran politics was far better than making decisions on his own. He'd never wanted to be king of Destrye. He wouldn't refuse the path Arill set for him, but maybe along with the punishment Oria would be, the goddess also offered him someone to share the trials of that path.

Oria led him out of the baths to a back stairway, walking just ahead of him with spine straight and chin high. Chuffta rode on her shoulder, head swiveling to watch him with those discerning green eyes. Hard to believe such a small skull could contain much intelligence, though he had to admit the Familiar demonstrated more of it than a typical animal, clearly much smarter than his own hunting hounds. The Trom had ridden much larger dragonish creatures that looked much the same as the derkesthai, only in darker colors. Perhaps the adult version of her Familiar. Not a reassuring possibility.

"Is Chuffta a juvenile?" He asked.

"No, he just acts juvenile—hey!" She slapped a hand at Chuffta, freeing the braid he'd yanked with sharp teeth, her giggle like water in the desert. A fascinating woman, so remote, even stern at times, cloaked with magic that shone almost as brightly to his eyes as her copper hair, and then almost girlish in her innocence. She hadn't stepped outside Bára until he forced her to, and she evinced an almost childlike naiveté about the world even a short distance beyond the walls. More than that, she'd told him she mostly stayed in her tower, living alone but for her Familiar and visits from her mother. Why?

"Why?" Oria asked, an uncanny echo of his thoughts. It took him moment to think back.

"I thought maybe Chuffta would grow into one of those dragon creatures the Trom flew in on." Chuffta's mouth parted, showing sharply fanged teeth, long forked tongue lolling out, for all the world looking like a ferocious smile.

Apparently Oria didn't perceive *that* because she continued walking, smoothly replying, "He says not, though I wondered the same thing. He told me that would be like comparing a house cat to one of the golden desert jaguars." She breathed a laugh. "Also he wants me to tell you that he's far smarter than the Trom dragons, who he calls vile and witless beasts." At the top of the stairwell, she turned and followed a narrow interior hall, stuffy from the lack of windows that normally graced most Báran passageways.

"Is this a servants' corridor?"

"Yes." She glanced back at him, an odd habit as she clearly didn't need to. Perhaps because she hadn't had her mask long. "I hope you're not offended. I mean no insult, only to hide your presence in Bára as long as possible."

His hands twitched with the impulse to slide around her waist and pull her back against him, to kiss that delectably exposed nape and tease her about offending him. Could he really never touch her at all? If skin-to-skin contact was the problem, perhaps he could wear gloves… He had some for cold weather—unfortunately back in Dru. "No, I'm not at all offended. The Destrye are not like your Báran men, so obsessed with status. I ask out of simple curiosity."

"You seem to have plenty of that and none of it simple," she muttered, then stopped before a door, rapping on it briskly, then opening it. "Would you make sure she's alone?"

Lonen took a step to oblige, but Chuffta spread his wide white wings and took off from her shoulder, doing his mistress's bidding—much as Lonen himself had been so eager to do. Ion would be laughing his ass off. *Don't let a bit of foreign pussy make you think with the little head instead of the big one.* For once the memory of his eldest brother didn't come with a wave of fresh grief. If he watched from the Hall of Warriors, Ion would be hugely amused that Lonen had not only failed to follow what was likely very good advice, but wouldn't even enjoy the promised reward for his loss of good sense.

"All right, let's go in," Oria said suddenly, her voice and body tense. She'd probably overheard his salacious thought. Maybe she could teach him how to keep his more obnoxious fantasies hidden. It didn't seem like she heard *everything* that crossed his mind—maybe mainly the ones he was more enthusiastic about.

"Ready?" she prompted, looking back at him, something in her voice. Maybe it wasn't that he provoked her, but her own nerves over presenting her plan to this former queen Lonen had never glimpsed.

"Do I look all right?" he asked her, partly to tease, but also to give her a moment to recover her poise. "I wouldn't want to bias your mother against her future son-in-law by looking like I fell out of a tree."

Oria tilted her head slightly, facing him. She'd be wrinkling the bridge of her nose for his frivolity. "You have"—she waved fingers at his temple—"some hair that's come loose."

"Where?"

She pointed. "Right there."

Deliberately he stroked a hand over the wrong spot. "I don't feel anything."

Chuffta flew back, landing on her shoulder, and she huffed her impatience. "Really it's not important and she's waiting for us."

"Can't you fix it for me?"

"No," she drew out the word as if he might be stupid after all. "Because I can't touch you."

"You said skin to skin—this is skin to hair. They're different."

"Lonen." She put her hands on her hips, bristling with exasperation.

"Just try," he coaxed. "You said your mother's good opinion and support are important."

"You don't know that," she said in a sharp tone.

"Excuse me?"

"Not you." She waved a hand to erase the words. "I'm sorry. I was replying to Chuffta. It's not always easy with both of you talking at me at once."

He and the derkesthai exchanged rueful looks, an odd brotherhood. "He thinks you can try?"

"Yes." She sighed her exasperation. "Fine. But don't move."

He could swear her Familiar gave him a knowing nod of complicity before leaning his cheek against the smooth skin under Oria's ear. She relaxed at the contact—deriving some kind of stability or comfort from it—and stepped closer to him. With slowly tentative fingers, she reached up, caught the escaped curls, and tucked them back in with deft skill.

That close, her heady scent of lilies wafted over him and he imagined her face intent as she took care not to touch him. "Are you all right?" he asked her quietly and she stilled, her copper eyes perhaps flying to his.

"So far," she breathed, the outline of her exquisite breasts rising and falling under the silk. Though he'd called the robe shapeless and ugly, in truth it clung in exactly the right places, even if it did cover up too much. She stepped back abruptly, erecting that chill barrier between them again. "No more delays. And let me do the talking."

Happy enough with the results of that test, he bowed and gestured for her to precede him, though he reserved the right to speak up if necessary. She pivoted, her tiny behind twitching as she stalked away into a set of rooms that exceeded even his imaginings for the former queen of Bára. Sculptures made of more glass twined in shades of ice-white, gold, and rose, scattered about the room. The floor of mosaicked tiles reflected light like the treacherous ice cliffs in the sea off Dru. All of it had a cooling effect—soothing in the desert climate, perhaps—but he found he preferred Oria's sunny and lush rooftop terrace, with the vivid sails of silk catching the breezes and her fire table of violet flames.

Elegant even by Báran standards, the lavishly furnished and decorated chambers looked out through grand arched windows to the city wall just below—though across the deep chasm that divided the palace grounds from the city proper—and then to the wide, desolate plain and distant hills beyond. When he wasn't baking in the landscape, Lonen could appreciate its austere appeal, the clean, simple lines and radiant colors reminding him of Oria.

All thoughts led back to Oria. His particular goddess and doom.

This, then, was the window he'd glimpsed her in that night, as he'd run along that very wall. Now, as then, her Familiar took a perch upon the sill, green eyes knowing.

A woman rose from a chair by that window, dressed more richly than the common women who strolled the paths of Bára, but not in the crimson priestess robes or even as grandly as Oria had for state occasions on his previous visit. She also wore no mask, her eyes a deep enough brown to contrast with her golden hair, but neither as spectacular a color as Oria's. Their kinship shone clear, however, in the widely set eyes framed by delicate brows and arched cheekbones, fine lines accenting her fair skin, and in her slight, willowy build. She looked as his wife would decades from now, a strange glimpse of the future. If he ever saw Oria's face again.

The intensity of her gaze had Lonen forcing himself to continue forward, despite the uncanny prickling of his scalp. Had his neck not been freshly shaved, those hairs would be standing up, too.

"What is this about, Oria?" The woman's eyes flashed with hatred that seemed to crawl across his skin like fireants, but she drew her daughter into a gentle embrace, holding her a moment before releasing her and facing Lonen. Without waiting for Oria's explanation, she launched her attack. "Destrye. I can't imagine what brings you back to Bára—surely you've pillaged enough. We have nothing more to sacrifice to your bloodthirsty lusts."

If she only knew about those lusts.

"Mother," Oria inserted herself between them. "You did not have the opportunity to meet before. This is King Lonen of the Destrye—not the king who led their armies to Bára. He's a good man and an honorable ruler, doing his best as we are, to salvage something for the future from this terrible conflict. He's come here in peace, to ask for our help."

A pretty speech and not entirely accurate—as he was far from good and honorable—but he wouldn't object even silently as Oria calling him that made up for any bending of the truth. He did send a mental apology to his father, however, for not defending his honor. As the former queen's hard gaze came back to him, he tried to look like a good and honorable king, and not a giddy lad flattered by a pretty girl's sweet words.

"King Lonen"—Oria inclined her head—"my mother, Rihanna, former queen and priestess of Bára."

No title for the woman now, apparently, but he bowed to her anyway. "I greet you, lady mother of Bára, and thank you for your hospitality under such trying circumstances."

"What do you want of us?" The former queen's face remained still and remote as a carved statue, but her dark eyes held dread. "We have nothing left to give."

"Mother." Oria took her mother's hands, skin to skin, Lonen noted. So it could be done. "The Trom have attacked Dru and again stolen water."

Though pale as ice already, the former queen blanched, then eased herself into a chair. "Oh, Yar," she whispered.

"It has to be." Oria went with her, keeping her hand and kneeling at her mother's knee. "There's only one path left to us. I must become queen as soon as possible, both to hold the throne against him and find a way to … take control myself."

Oria didn't look his way, but her mother did, gaze flicking to ascertain how much he understood. "Yourself? You can't mean you propose to try to summon *them*?"

"I do. I see no other way. As queen, I'll have access to all the temple secrets. I have to try this."

"And if you break?" Cagily, Oria's mother looked at him and away again. "We need to discuss your plan without this barbarian present."

"I've proposed to King Lonen that we wed," Oria interrupted. "And he's agreed. If you'll support my choice with the temple we can marry tonight and petition the council tomorrow."

The former queen's expression didn't falter from its smooth serenity, but Lonen didn't miss how her knuckles whitened as she gripped Oria's hands. "This extremity is not what I had in mind when we discussed the necessity of a marriage for you, my daughter." The words seemed to hold a wealth of subtext, enough to fuel a furious urge in him to lay about with his axe and cut through all the stultifying politics. They discussed marriage to him, not a death sentence, though you wouldn't know it from the former queen's dire expression.

"I know what I'm doing."

The former queen shook her head. "I don't know that you do. Are you doing this out of some misplaced guilt?"

Oria's slim shoulders moved in a shimmy of discomfort. "It seems someone here should be shouldering that very well placed guilt."

"Becoming my honored wife and queen of the Destrye is hardly a punishment," Lonen grated out, harshly enough to startle both women out of their communion.

Oria stood hastily and brushed a slim hand over her immaculate braids, as if caught with a hair out of place. "My apologies, King Lonen. We intended no insult. I am indeed honored to wed you and become your queen, as Bára is privileged to claim you as king."

A pretty speech—she was good at those—but her mother's mouth tightened over unspoken words. "This is why we should discuss this in private, Oria." She raised meaningful brows.

"No." Oria straightened her shoulders and moved to align herself beside him. Not touching him, naturally, but close enough that he could if he forgot himself and tried. "King Lonen is part of this. He's aware that some temple mysteries will remain secrets from him, so speak as you will."

"Is that so?" Rhianna gestured at him with a languid hand, but her eyes bored into him dark and hard as a rare moonless winter night. "Then is he *aware* that he can never bed you? Their barbarian race thinks nothing of rape."

Oria moved slightly in front of him at his growl, forestalling his retort. "We've discussed it. Barbarians they may be, but the Destrye are also a race of disciplined warriors. He will not harm me. He has agreed to a marriage in name only."

"Until he loses self-control." Rhianna's gaze bored into him, as if he'd already defiled her daughter in truth, rather than only in fantasy. "You are innocent of many of the harsher realities of the world outside our walls, Oria. You cannot risk this. Not for any reason."

"The Destrye have a long and bloody history, it's true," Lonen told her, unwilling to remain silent on the topic any longer. "As do your people—something I'm sure must be as well-documented in your texts as in ours. We also have a tradition of protecting women, who are sacred to the goddess Arill. I would allow no one to harm my wife—not even myself."

Oria didn't turn his way, but something about the softening of her posture made him think she paid close attention. Perhaps she mentally read the truth in his words, so he strengthened that sentiment, pushing it towards her.

"Protecting women?" Rhianna's lip curled, emotion cracking her visage. "Is that why you murdered defenseless priestesses in cold blood, one after another, like the animals you slaughter without care?"

Lonen didn't physically flinch, but only through dint of great will. That night, the first priestess he'd killed—the way her wondering eyes went dark with death—had reminded him of the first doe he'd shot. Murder. Yes, it had felt that way, had gone against everything he believed in. Nothing like the fair fight of the battlefield. He'd done it out of extremity, yes, but how to defend an indefensible act?

"I am—"

"You don't deserve a treasure like my daughter," Rhianna spat. "You have no idea what she proposes to do and worse, you mind-dead brute, you won't be able to help her when she needs it most. You'll destroy her instead, like the monster you are."

~ 5 ~

STRUCK HARD BY the wave of guilt and remorse from Lonen—along with a vivid memory image of a dying doe and blood on his hands—and with surprising, strong protective feelings of her own, Oria wrestled the potent emotions. He'd meant every word of what he'd said about not harming her, and about holding the female sacred—a fascinating and foreign image in his mind of a fertile goddess bestowing blessings. The truth resonated in him regardless of the rest.

She deeply regretted bringing him to this meeting.

Once a model of *hwil*, the former queen had become like the bay beyond Bára, her emotional state as unpredictable as the bore tides, and as lethal in their ability to swamp the unwary.

"Enough, Mother," Oria said, venting some of the emotional tension with some judicious grien that took the form of a dust devil swirling past the window, briefly whipping the sheer silk curtains that hung limply by the sides. "We've all committed grave sins in the name of war. You and I may not have held the knife blades, but we've drunk the water bought with the blood of Destrye children. Something you confessed you knew was happening and that you did nothing to stop. None of us are innocent."

She caught a flash of surprised gratitude from Lonen, glad then that she'd stood up for him in that rare moment of weakness. He seemed so strong, so fierce—even brutal in his anger at times—but he possessed a tender heart under that muscled chest.

"Something you detected in him all along, hmm?"

Ignoring Chuffta's too-smug observation, she forged on. "You've left this to me, Mother. Unless you wish to reclaim your mask and your crown, in which case I'll gladly step aside for you, I need you to support me in this decision."

"So much of this is my fault, the result of my many failures to act..." The former queen nearly chanted the words, sounding like those prematurely aged out of sanity. Oria put a finger to her temple, in lieu of putting her face in her hands. Sometimes her mother seemed like her old self, her mind as incisive as ever, then suddenly...

Lonen brushed the sleeve of her robe, carefully not touching her skin, but putting her on alert regardless. He had an inquiring feel to him and an image formed of a person tending to her mother. Was he silently asking if the former queen needed a healer? She shook her head minutely, just in case. Her mother was beyond help.

"Then don't fail to act now." She said it crisply, as her mother might once have prodded her, adding a nudge of grien. "You promised to help me. This is how you can. I need you to do this."

Rhianna lifted a tear-streaked face, her sgath hanging about her like tattered rags. "I wanted so much more for you, my beautiful and powerful daughter. You should have an ideal match, a man who will treasure you and know you as you deserve to be known, give life to your magic, bring you wealth and glory, and provide you children. No one less than the most powerful of Báran kings deserves you, not this mind-dead—"

"Will you intervene with the temple or not?" Oria cut her off as she should have done much earlier. No anger wafted off Lonen, however—at least, not more than the dark, brooding fury that seemed to underlie most of his thoughts. Had he always been of that nature or had the war done that to him? An intensely curious interest prowled over her that tasted distinctly of him. No doubt he'd have more questions for her. Joy.

Then disappointment crushed her relatively minor aggravation.

"I won't do it." Her mother lifted her chin, an echo of the proud queen she'd been. "I won't cooperate in sending you to your doom. Not even to save Bára. The sacrifice is too great."

"This is my marriage, my decision, my life."

"Don't ask me to help you ruin it. I love you too much." Her mother fulminated with dark sgath, much of it reaching towards Lonen like the shadowy tentacles of the wyrms that lurked in the damp cellars of Bára. Time to get him away from her. No telling what her unstable magic could do, even as passively as sgath typically worked. Oria had seen her mother blur those lines, too.

She set her teeth, keeping the flawless façade of *hwil*. "I won't ask it then. But I will marry him and petition the council for the crown tomorrow. Will you support me then?"

Rhianna turned her face to the window, face once again remote, seeing only the past. "I am not well." Her voice wobbled and she swallowed hard.

"I know, Mother." Oria's heart thudded dully with the pain of seeing her like this. For a while it had seemed she'd recover, but lately she only seemed to fall further into the depths of her mind, her sanity fracturing more with every descent. "Don't fret. I'll visit you in the morning and we can talk."

Her mother didn't reply, so Oria beckoned to Chuffta, who flew to her shoulder. The winding of his long tail around her arm gave her comfort.

"It was a bad day. Perhaps she'll be more lucid tomorrow," he said as they withdrew. Lonen paced stoically at her side, his emotions tightly reined, thoughts unusually opaque.

"She was lucid enough for a while there—enough to recognize what a terrible idea this is."

"I don't think it's a terrible idea."

"You don't?" Her toe caught the hem of her robe in her moment of inattention. *"But you said that—"*

"That the Destrye king would not be easily led. I think he is a good mate for you."

She rolled her eyes behind the mask. *"Like you'd know."*

He gave her the mental equivalent of a shrug. *"You like him. The rest can be overcome."*

"Now you sound like him."

"Attempting to summon the Trom yourself, however," he continued, turning severe, "that *is a terrible idea. Even your mother retains enough wit to know that. You run the risk of—"*

She bumped her shoulder to interrupt the lecture, making her Familiar spread his wings for balance. *"I'm not discussing this right now."*

"You could be having this conversation with me, you know," Lonen commented.

They emerged into the servants' corridor and Oria paused, both undecided about the direction they should take and chagrined at Lonen's remark. "I apologize." She made herself face him. "I'm in the habit of being with Chuffta and talking to him, not with…"

"Another human being?" he supplied, a ripple of humor beneath it.

Why that made her blush, she had no idea. His body heat, perhaps, like a coal brazier in the narrow, enclosed hall. "Right," she replied, determined to leave it at that.

"What happened to her?" Lonen asked, with so much gentle concern it nearly undid her.

"I explained already. My father's death damaged her."

"You said because of this ideal mate business."

"Yes." She braced herself for a barrage of more questions.

He pondered, however, hand stroking thoughtfully over his beard. "It seems to me that if I make guesses, then you're not technically telling me secrets."

"Lonen…" She hated the helpless sound in her voice, but she didn't know what she could possibly say to explain any of it. The encounter with her damaged mother had left her wrung dry and facing High Priestess Febe felt beyond her. They should go to the temple and do that next, but she couldn't quite find the impetus to leave the stuffy, shadowed corridor. Perhaps all of it had been a stupid, hopeless plan. She was so tired of fighting.

"Give me some rope here and see if I can climb on my own." Lonen leaned against the wall and crossed his ankles, still stroking his beard as he studied her. She didn't object because at least she could hide a little longer. "Your mother called me 'mind-dead,' which I assume refers to my not being a sorcerer."

"I'm really sorry about that," she whispered in furious embarrassment. "She's—"

"You apologize too much. I'm not offended, though I gather that's an insult. I know as well as you do that I don't have magic. I don't consider this a failing. I don't want it, except maybe to help build aqueducts."

Bemused, she parsed the word. "Build what?"

"Never mind. An idle thought, and something we can discuss later, when you come with me to Dru."

"Which I can't promise that—"

"Yes, yes, I know. Never mind that, either. What's important at the moment is that I gather that is this ideal mate thing would connect you mentally to your husband, and there's some sort of magical component, too. Which your mother and father had and she's distressed to the point of refusing to help you marry me because she places such a high value on wanting that for you."

"It's not really that—"

"'The sacrifice is too great'—her exact words."

"Stop interrupting me!" She nearly stamped her foot with the frustration at both the Destrye and Chuffta snickering in her head.

"Then stop saying things that don't matter," he fired back, shocking her. "This is an important conversation."

"That we're having in a servant's corridor," she pointed out.

He chuckled at that, that welcome sunny humor of his dispersing some of her emotional gloom. "When we celebrate our two decades' anniversary, we can recapitulate this day and meet each other entirely in baths and hallways."

"We did talk on my rooftop terrace earlier, as well, when I proposed marriage." Which seemed like days ago, not hours.

"Good point. I'm adding rooftop terraces to the list, though if we're in Dru we might have to substitute a treehouse."

"A house in a tree?" Something that had never occurred to her, partly because she'd never seen a tree big enough to hold an entire house. But the image in his head showed a forest of enormous trees, the leaves so dense they blocked the sun, and a structure of wood in the crux of a network of branches. The image changed so it seemed she stood inside it, looking out, the forest floor as far below as the streets of Bára from her terrace. It struck her that he'd changed the 'view' deliberately, to show her another angle.

"Are you doing that on purpose?"

"What—picturing things for you to see in my mind? Yeah. I figure if you're going to read my thoughts anyway, I might as well take advantage of it. It could be a handy secret weapon for us."

A laugh escaped her, lessening the tightness of grief and despair. "You're unlike anyone I've ever known."

"Good." He grinned, but under it a surge of possessive lust intensified the simple approval. "As I'm the only husband you'll ever have, mind-dead and unable to give life to your magic as I might be, I'll have to make it up in other ways."

"I'm really sorry she said those things."

"Another apology, and for something you can't control. I don't mind, Oria." He pushed off the wall and it seemed he might reach for her, but he stopped himself. "I'd much rather know the unvarnished truth of how it will be between us. No secrets to fester. If you're making a grave sacrifice by marrying me—one I approve of as it will save both our peoples—then I want to know exactly what you're giving up, so I can do what I can to compensate for it. I'd like to think I can offer you some happiness, if not exactly what you were expecting."

"Oh." The corridor was too hot. That was why she felt a little faint.

"Your mother is wrong." Lonen sounded gravely determined,

that warrior's resolve enfolding her, an image in his mind of him taking her in a gentle embrace that very nearly felt real. "I will treasure you, Oria, and I'll do my best to know you, but you have to let me in."

"I don't need that. That's not why we're doing this."

"I need it." His emotions, complex and shifting with layers, intensified.

"But why?"

He shrugged, impatient with the question, but continued to refine the image of holding her in his mind. "Maybe I've had plenty of misery, too much blood and loss and death. We might be marrying for political reasons, but that doesn't mean we can't bring something bright to each other's lives. That we can't take care of each other." The sense of his arms around her made it almost believable.

"How are you doing that?"

"If you sense how I feel, what's in my head, then I can give you this much. If I can't hold you and comfort you, then there's this, yes?"

"The Destrye is wiser than he seems at first."

Oria didn't know what to do with Chuffta's seemingly sudden and enthusiastic approval of Lonen, so she ignored him.

"I know it hurt you to see your mother that way," Lonen continued in a gentle tone. "It would be painful for anyone. My father, King Archimago, when my brother Nolan fell into a crevasse on the battlefield… in some ways he never recovered from that."

"I'm sorry," she whispered.

"Stop," he replied, but with a kind of tenderness. "As you said in there, we've all done things. I've done things I'll carry the stain of to my grave. But what I'm trying to tell you is that if your mother is in this state because her ideal mate died, then perhaps it will be a strength for you, that you won't be exposed to that danger with me."

She lifted her head in surprise, amazed at the way his masculine vitality had filled the narrow space, embracing her, weaving in with her sgath. "I'd never thought of it that way."

"See?" He was all smug male then. "You can learn things from me, too."

She huffed at him, not even caring that it made him grin. "I'm not convinced of that, Destrye."

"That's all right. I'll be convinced for both of us." He lifted a hand, moving close enough to trace the fall of one of her braids, though he kept a whisper distance from it. His granite-colored eyes seemed silver bright viewed with her sgath, like the white-hot heart of a glass forge. "Maybe I should be sorry that I won't be the husband you deserve, but I'm not. I'd hate to see you like that, with your fire dimmed and your sharp mind dulled."

"She used to be so much more."

"I saw glimpses of it. She must have been a formidable woman and queen. I regret I didn't meet her before."

"We all carry regrets," Oria echoed his earlier words. "And I, for one, am tired of wallowing in them. You're right—you and I are about moving forward. No more apologies, yes?"

"Works for me."

The moment felt oddly intimate. So much so that she moved away, putting safer distance between them. "I suppose that moving forward means going to the temple and convincing High Priestess Febe to marry us."

"Time for the strategy that Bára and everything in it, including you, belongs to me?" Lonen's energy took on a feral, sharp edge—one that strangely put her in mind of the iron axe he carried on his back.

"As a gambit only," she told him, bringing her own mettle to it. "Don't go getting the wrong idea about me."

He only nodded and gestured for her to lead the way. "This time, you'll leave the talking to me."

~ 6 ~

ORIA REMAINED SUBDUED, but seemed less crushed than when they'd left her mother's chambers. Lonen congratulated himself for both distracting her from her troubles and also making inroads on earning her trust. Her secrets would not become like the fanged and clawed Báran golems, tearing at their entrails until they resented each other rather than rightfully hating the pain instead. As he had with the golems, he'd hunt those secrets down, one by one, and destroy them. His iron axe cut through the magical creatures; he could cleave her magical secrets into dust as well.

Once he'd ferreted them out. Including the one her mother had alluded to: *And if you break?* Something about Oria's plan worried him—and had upset her mother, too. He'd thought no price would be too high to pay to save the Destrye, but… No. What was he thinking? His first loyalty belonged to his people. No matter his other interests in Oria, his softer regard toward her—all of that fell into the same set of considerations as his own happiness. They'd both do whatever it took for the greater good.

But he *would* find out what she faced, and what the stakes would be.

He listened as Oria explained in hushed tones how the temple hierarchy worked and the path they'd take to where the High Priestess would receive them. As soon as they emerged from the servants' corridor, word of his presence in Bára would fly ahead of them, faster than jewelbirds.

"What are jewelbirds?"

He got the impression she rolled her eyes at him, considering the question irrelevant. "I'll show you one, in my garden. They're small, fast and beautiful—they come to the flowers."

The flowers that died inch by inch without water under the scorching sun. Another thing Oria loved that would be lost to her. Nothing compared to what the Destrye had lost, but it bothered him still.

They arrived at a small waiting chamber and she sent a guard to bring her a substantial escort. There would be no surprising the High Priestess, she'd explained, so they might as well take the public halls. At that point, the more people who knew what was going on, the better. She seemed to believe the people would support her. From what he'd seen when she'd offered the city's surrender, he agreed.

Though privately he thought they'd love her better without the mask and crimson robes of the very temple they all so clearly feared.

"And your role in this battle?" he asked. "Will you be the frightened virgin terrorized into marrying her conqueror?"

She actually laughed, a lighthearted musical sound, however brief. "While I'm largely regarded as fragile, none of the priestesses would believe I could be terrorized, even by a man as intimidating as you. I shall play the nobly resigned daughter of the house of Tavlor and Rhianna. With luck, Febe will be so pleased to see me brought low and consigned to a mind-dead marriage, she'll agree to your demands for that reason alone."

"You find me intimidating?" The concept both startled him and made him absurdly proud. And here he'd thought Oria the one with all the power in her slim, magical hands.

"I can't believe that's what you focused on from everything I said."

He went to an unglassed window that overlooked one of the yawning chasms that cracked through Bára, making her towers seem that much taller by comparison. It probably didn't speak well of him that it salved his pride to know she found him intimidating, especially as it wouldn't necessarily contribute to happy relations between them. "What about me intimidates you?"

"You're big." She said it with a shrug in her voice. "And you carry a great big battle-axe that could chop me into little wriggly bits."

Wriggly bits. The more he came to know her, the more he glimpsed what might be a playful, even whimsical personality. And perhaps much of her bravery came from a rash disregard for her own wellbeing. Which brought him right back to whatever foolhardy plan she entertained.

"What did your mother mean about you 'breaking' if you try to summon the Trom? What magic is involved there?" He watched her carefully, so he caught how she stiffened defensively, lacing her fingers together as if that might hide from him what she planned.

"That's nothing I can explain to you." *Destrye.* She didn't say it aloud, but the haughty tone conveyed the slamming of temple doors against the outsider.

"Can't or won't?" he growled back. If she put him in mind of a housecat, all fluff and hiss, then he'd meet her posture for posture.

She inclined her head regally. "They are functionally the same. And regardless, this place is not private enough to discuss the situation, even if I could. It's best for you not to mention the Trom or my magic at all. I can hardly trust you with my secrets if you insist on discussing them indiscreetly. Don't worry about the magical aspects of this plan, King Lonen, I'll see to my end of the bargain."

He set his teeth against his irritation. "At what cost to you?"

"What's it to you?" she fired back. "Enough with this protective and solicitous charade you've adopted. Expiate your guilt some other way. Yes, you killed our priestesses and no, you didn't want to. But you can't bring them back by saving me any more than you can resurrect that poor doe whose throat you cut because your arrow missed her heart."

The sally struck his own heart, thudding into the old wound

with painful accuracy. "I shouldn't be surprised you saw that in my head, but it's harsh and cold of you to use that against me. If my size and axe intimidate you, then just imagine what it's like for me to have you prowling about in my secret soul, unearthing pains no one would know about otherwise."

She lifted a hand to Chuffta, stroking him for her own comfort, he surmised, a tremor in the gesture. "I know you told me not to apologize anymore, but I'm offering one anyway. My abilities are … new to me and somewhat ungovernable. I've also spent little time around people and you—well, I don't mean to see these things. But you're right that it was wrong to try to hurt you with that information."

"Is that what you were doing?" He studied her, the tense lines of her shoulders making the silk robe look as if it hung on hooks, not soft flesh. "I think that whatever you're planning is dangerous, and you don't like anyone pointing that out to you."

Chuffta fixed him with a gimlet green stare and Lonen could swear the Familiar practically nodded at him.

For her part, Oria had curled her fingers into tiny fists. "My goal is to help *your* people. That's why you came to me and that's the reason we're doing all of this. You have your part; I have mine. Don't you dare question how I intend to go about it."

"You mean, how you go about expiating your own guilt?" His taunt, throwing her words back at her, hit home he was sure, but she barely showed it.

"Don't pretend to know me, Destrye," she said softly, with surprising menace. Her magic curled around him, a palpable thing. The sensation might once have revolted him, but it had become part of being in Oria's presence, along with her scent and beguiling figure. Perversely, he even liked that she threatened him. She had that much correct—no one would believe her as the terrified virgin.

But he did come to know her. In time, he would know her even more. Once he'd bound her to him in marriage, she'd have no escape. Threaten as she might, she would never actually harm him, no more than he'd take his axe to her. He snorted out a laugh, making her turn from her restless pacing.

"You laugh?" she hissed.

"Wriggly bits, indeed," he replied, shaking his head.

It made her pause, and then her escort of armed City Guard arrived to escort them to the temple, ending further argument between them.

They walked side by side, the guard flanking and following, deeper into the palace than he'd been before. As with all of Bára, the halls were open and spacious, with regular windows open to the breezes that relieved the intense heat of afternoon. As Oria had predicted, people noted his presence with variations of shock and alarm, any number of young servants and the occasional crimson-robe figure dashing off to spread the news. He imagined them like Oria's jewelbirds, zooming about from flower to flower.

They emerged from the far side of the public areas of the palace and onto a bridge that spanned a smaller chasm to yet another set of towers, built entirely of rose-colored stone carved in circles, tiled with blue-white moons in various phases. A tribute to the moons Sgatha and Grienon.

At the far end of the short span, the high priestess stood flanked by two priests. Though they all wore the smooth golden masks of their office, the high priestess had become familiar to him with her extravagantly braided white hair, and the priests recognizable as male by their bulk. Such as it was—the Báran men stood taller than Oria, but generally slight in stature compared to Destrye warriors. Even starved and overworked, Lonen likely outweighed these men by half again.

No wonder Oria found him physically intimidating. Yet another way he'd never be the husband she'd expected to have, in yet another aspect totally out of his control.

"Destrye." The High Priestess's voice rang like a hollow gong. "You are not allowed within the sacred temple of Bára. Princess Oria, what is the meaning of this intrusion?"

"High Priestess, I—"

Without thinking, Lonen grasped Oria's upper arm, stopping her and asserting his command of the situation. This, he *could* control. She stiffened with a gasp, but Chuffta didn't leap to her defense, so it seemed his touch over the robe didn't harm her, or at least not overly much. Nevertheless, he loosened his grip.

"You will address me as Your Highness," he informed the High Priestess in a cool tone that should convey both his rank and her trespass. "Or King Lonen. I'm here to invoke the ancient right of conqueror. I claim Princess Oria as mine. You will bind her to me under your laws."

Oria had gone quiet and still, barely breathing, and he would have given a great deal at that moment for her trick of reading thoughts and emotions. High Priestess Febe betrayed nothing of her reaction, but the sense of magic thickened. Nothing like battles with mages to teach a warrior to pay attention to impending attack of an uncanny nature. Magic built much like static charges in still air heralded a bolt of lightning. The wise man took cover in such circumstances.

If only he could.

He shook Oria's arm, trying to make it look forceful without requiring a tighter grip. "Command them to stand down. You've acknowledged my claim as lawful—and you've been warned of the consequences should your people attempt to do me harm."

"It's true," she blurted, her voice strained. Concerned that he might be hurting her through the thin silk, he let go under guise of thrusting her forward. She stumbled slightly on the too-long hem of her robes, but caught herself, straightening proudly. *Nobly resigned daughter of the house of Tavlor and Rhianna.* He had to force back the smile, concentrating on his deep well of anger, although the rage didn't leap to mind as eagerly as usual.

"The Destrye king has returned to claim me as his. He's willing to make me his wife under Báran law." Oria managed to sound infuriated, frightened, courageous, and forbearing all at once. Quite the woman, his Báran sorceress. "His armies wait beyond the bay, as a token of good faith, but if he does not signal them at set intervals, they will invade Bára and this time they won't leave again."

Febe surveyed him, taking her time, but a flick of her fingers had the sense of impending lightning dispersing. "How has King Lonen entered the city without my knowledge? His Highness wears the clothes of a Báran man, so it appears he's been here long enough to be tended."

"Your knowledge?" Oria's tone went scathing. "I'm unaware of a change in protocol that would have the City Guard notifying the temple of a high-ranking visitor before the royal family."

"Indeed, High Priestess Febe," Captain Ercole, a stalwart and canny soldier who'd led the resistance against the Destrye and won Lonen's respect as few Báran fighters had, stepped forward. "King Lonen arrived and requested an immediate audience with the ruling family. With Prince Yar out of the city and the former queen Rhianna unable to receive visitors, I escorted him to Princess Oria. Our scouts have verified the presence of his armies on the far side of the bay," he added smoothly, as if they'd practiced the deception. Lonen appreciated Oria's cleverness in protecting him. In retrospect, bringing an army—or even a small guard—would have been smarter. Arnon had argued viciously for it. But Lonen had been unwilling to lead yet more Destrye into conflict and possible death. That reluctance might prove to be his great failing as a king. Or one of them. So many to choose from.

"Why now, Your Highness?" Febe turned her attention to him, her manner more obsequious. "We thought you satisfied with the treaty you made and required nothing more of Bára. Certainly not her most treasured daughter."

He allowed himself to smile, ever so slightly. If they shared Oria's abilities they would sense something of his emotions. So he allowed the feelings of lust and possessiveness—even obsession—for Oria to rise up. With a careful hand he picked up one of her long, perfectly plaited braids, running it through his fingers. It glinted in the sunlight like finely wrought copper chain. "I discovered I could not forget a certain Báran princess. The Destrye have a long, much celebrated history of taking women from Bára and your sister cities to serve us. It occurred to me that with the defeat of Bára, it's time to resurrect the tradition. A trophy, if you will, as lasting memory of our triumph and your defeat."

"Our Trom bloodied you and yours, Your Highness. But for Princess Oria's concessions to you, Bára might have called it your defeat."

"Is that so?" He made it sound bored, the texture of Oria's hair finer than silk, his fingers itching to unplait it all and run his fingers through the coppery shimmer of it. As he'd hoped, it seemed she easily tolerated his touch to her hair, her breathing quiet and Chuffta peaceful. "Perhaps you need another demonstration of Destrye might. Call your Trom and drive us out again if you can."

One of the priests murmured to Febe, his mask inclined towards hers, and she turned away with some irritation. Good thing that Oria had told him their threats would be empty with Yar away from the city.

"Perhaps it need not come to that, Your Highness," Febe spread her hands, all accommodation. "The temple acknowledges your right as conqueror to claim a woman of Bára, and we accept that it is Princess Oria who has seized your attention. But you need not marry her. If you wish to take her away, back to your homeland, we will be unable to prevent you. We ask only that you take her and go in peace, without troubling the people of Bára further."

~ 7 ~

THE TRAITOROUS BITCH. Of course she should have realized High Priestess Febe would seize the opportunity to be rid of Oria and her unknown potential that bothered the other woman so. *Ponen*, the Trom had called her. At least Oria had accurately predicted that the priestess would be pleased to see Oria consigned to such a terrible fate—indeed, smug delight radiated through the woman's *hwil*, with hints of stronger, darker emotions beneath—but she'd miscalculated the depth of the high priestess's ambition and disregard for Oria's wellbeing. She'd cheerfully send Oria off to be a sex slave to the Destrye king, knowing full well how quickly it would kill her, never mind the rest. With not even slim protection a temple marriage would afford her.

She scrambled to think of a way to persuade Febe that marriage would be necessary, but Lonen was, again, ahead of her. Fortunate, as his gentle caress on her braid sent distracting heat through her. And not of the painful, distressing variety. Seductive and soothing at the same time, the sensation made her want to lean into him for more. A very bad idea as it would turn destructive in the blink of an eye.

"You think me unworthy of marrying a Báran princess, High Priestess?" Lonen was saying, his voice as dark and edged with violence as the anger fulminating at the forefront of his mind. At that moment he seemed every bit as ruthless and terrifying as the illustrations of his Destrye ancestors, delighting as they burned and pillaged. "I don't propose to help myself to a random assortment of

Bára's wealth—though that idea holds appeal, also—I want Princess Oria as my bride, forever cementing that Bára belongs to Dru. She'll be my queen and I shall be King of Bára."

Febe didn't quite look to Oria, but her smugness had gone carefully avaricious. "Is this agreeable to you, Princess Oria? We all know what you'd be sacrificing, taking the Destrye king as your husband. Bára would hate to see you leave her walls forever. It's unfortunate His Highness is so impatient, or we'd await Prince Yar's return, so he could witness the ritual."

A strategically worded message—that still managed to avoid acknowledging that the high priestess would send Oria to a short life of sexual servitude that would eventually kill her. If going outside the walls didn't take care of that sooner rather than later. Febe knew perfectly well that Lonen marrying Oria wouldn't automatically make him King of Bára. Her mistake, however, was in believing Oria would be in collusion with her to mislead him—and that Yar would inevitably return with an ideal bride to put paid to the Destrye's ambitions. Febe might be thinking that Lonen and Oria would be long gone by the time Yar returned, in which case Lonen's assumption that he was King of Bára would last awhile with no information to contradict that belief. In the scenario Febe likely envisioned, he might labor under that misapprehension far longer than Oria would survive.

"Like my mother and father before me, I'm bred to my duty to Bára," Oria replied, holding to her role of resignation to her terrible fate to yet again save her city, all handled with a demonstrable exercise of *hwil*. Febe thought her a fool for it, but then she'd never contemplate making any sort of sacrifice, much less of the level that Oria proposed to suffer, for anything but her own self-advancement. "I ask only that we get this over with as quickly as possible. No offense intended to Your Highness."

Full of the lust Lonen so determinedly radiated, though not completely manufactured she felt sure, he tugged on the braid he still held. "A man likes an eager bride."

Though she knew he'd said it to sustain and enlarge on the ruse they perpetuated, the insinuation still made her face go hot. Febe actually leaked some vestiges of sympathy through her *hwil*. It was to her credit that she could at least feel pity for what she imagined Oria would endure. Hopefully Rhianna would never have occasion to tell Febe of the agreement she and Lonen had made. Oria regretted telling her, especially as it had made no difference and potentially exposed them to trouble.

"You'll have to leave that outside, however." High Priestess Febe pointed at Lonen's axe with a gesture very like the Destrye one against magic. Oria had never noticed that similarity before.

"Not a chance, lady," he growled.

"It's an offense against the source of magic."

"Which is why it doesn't leave my body. I've had enough of Báran magic."

"Fine then. But you'll have to remove it for the ceremony itself."

"As long as I have it close to hand," he told her, his posture and energy showing how willingly he'd use it against her if she tried anything to harm him or Oria.

"Enter the temple, then," she intoned, "and we will join you as the moons intended."

Lonen didn't move, though he released Oria's braid. "Just like that? There are no ceremonial preparations?"

"Such as?" High Priestess Febe had already turned to go in, Oria ready to follow on her heels before anyone saw through to the flaws in their story.

"Shouldn't Oria—the princess, that is—have a special gown? Attendants or some such?"

Febe cocked her head at him, puzzlement and suspicion faint on the air. "Come now, Your Highness is good to be solicitous of his captured bride, but this ceremony will simply bind her to you under our laws. I understood you to be in something of a demanding mood. It will not be a temple-blessed marriage, if that's what you're hoping for." Her voice held sudden suspicion.

Oria willed Lonen to play dumb. As if he'd heard her, he said, "What is that?"

Mollified, the high priestess inclined her head. "Merely a local custom, something idealistic young women pine for. The ceremony I shall conduct will be equally binding."

"Proceed then." Lonen retreated to his curt and lustful conqueror role, following in Febe's wake, the priests behind them at a decorous distance, the City Guard remaining outside.

"He is a smart man. Pays attention," Chuffta mused.

"Why is the Destrye king suddenly your new best friend?" It annoyed her more than it should. She'd never had to share Chuffta's affections with anyone.

"I still love you best," he soothed her, *"but he is also concerned about you taking on the Trom and wants to protect you. I like him for that."*

"Then the two of you can sit around and console each other when I do the summoning."

Chuffta tsked at her. *"Such temper."*

"This isn't exactly the best day of my life," she snapped at her Familiar—and then felt bad about it. Just as she had when she'd used Lonen's buried pain to punish him. She'd thought she'd been handling all the changes and challenges so well, but then she combusted into a ball of emotion. Having to ruthlessly suppress any hint of grien—and maintain the façade of *hwil*—around the temple priests and priestesses strained her fragile control even more. Still she didn't need to be full of self-pity. This path had been her idea. She started to apologize to Chuffta, then remembered Lonen's chiding about how she apologized too often, and stopped herself.

But that left her at a loss. How was she supposed to never apologize for anything?

"Maybe by not doing anything worth apologizing for in the first place." It could have sounded huffy, but Chuffta said it like a peace offering, his tail a comforting bracelet around her wrist.

They entered one of the smaller temple ritual spaces, simple and sacrosanct, even though it might not be as grand as the main sanctuary where she would have celebrated her temple-blessed marriage, had it not been for Lonen.

Of course, before the Destrye came, she'd been nowhere near attaining her mask, so a temple-blessed ceremony had remained a distant ambition. Important to keep that firmly in mind.

Febe positioned the two of them before the altar, waited for Lonen to unstrap his axe from his back, instructed them to kneel, then retreated behind the altar. Lonen looked about, then laid the axe by his left hand. To Oria's surprised pleasure, Febe did not banish Chuffta. The temple honored the derkesthai in general, though their relationship to the temple hierarchy tended to be more like Grienon's rapid passage through the skies, his phases ever shifting, now brightly present, then abruptly gone. To Oria, her Familiar was like Sgatha, ever present, looming large in her mind.

Much as Lonen did, occupying her senses and attention. It would be welcome when he finally departed, giving her some peace of mind again. Mental quiet had never been her forte, but the man had a knack for agitating her.

As the High Priestess assembled her tools, saying prayers over the various unguents, consecrating the wine to Sgatha, the grains to Grienon, Lonen spoke to Oria under his breath.

"How does this go?"

"I don't know." She kept her reply barely audible, but the Destrye warrior was not so easily put off.

"How can you not know?"

"I've never seen the ceremony. It's always private. Now, shh."

He didn't like that answer, his energy restive and seeking. "You could have warned me," he had to mutter, which unfortunately made her want to laugh. Exercising firm resolve, she managed not to, but the mask was what saved her from exposing the amusement so not appropriate to a nobly resigned captive bride.

"Maybe not the worst day of your life either," Chuffta noted in the idle tone he liked to use to tease her.

"You hush, too."

"Take a moment to meditate," High Priestess Febe intoned. "Clear your minds. Settle your emotions. Seek *hwil* in your hearts and contemplate the step you take today, with Sgatha and Grienon as your witnesses."

Oria folded her hands together and bowed her head, stilling her sgath so it pooled peacefully, creating the appearance of deep meditation.

"Would you like me to lead you into a true meditative trance?"

"Not now, thank you. I'd rather have my wits about me."

"Done correctly, meditation should result in greater alertness through a relaxed and open mind."

"Yes, well, we've established that I'm terrible at meditating. Leave me alone. It's my wedding day."

Chuffta snorted at that, but let it go.

"What are we supposed to be doing?" Lonen whispered, though High Priestess Febe had left the room.

"Meditating," she hissed back.

"Yes, I heard that part. What in Arill does that mean?"

"Like… praying to your goddess. *Silently,*" she emphasized.

He was quiet for a few breaths, no more. "Now what?"

She tried to suppress the laugh, but failed so it choked out in a most unladylike sound. Lonen flashed a grin at her and she shook her head. "Keep doing it. And be quiet—she could come back at any time."

"Why would I keep doing something I already did?"

"You're supposed to be contemplating!" She tried to sound stern, but his complaints so closely echoed hers through the years that she couldn't manage it.

"Contemplate what?" he groused. "I already made the decision about the step I'm about to take. There's no sense revisiting it."

"Then pretend. It won't be that much longer."

He stayed quiet for a bit more, though he shifted restlessly, looking around the room and studying the various representations of the moons, looking at her from time to time. That insatiable curiosity of his built, feeding into her sgath, slowly intensifying. She was so keenly aware of him, she knew he'd speak the moment before he did.

"You don't mind?" he asked.

"You talking when we're supposed to be meditating?"

"Do you always do what the temple tells you to do?"

"Hardly ever," she admitted. "But appearances are critical. Especially now."

He sighed and was quiet for a while. But his question remained between them, tugging at her like Chuffta pulling her braids when he wanted attention. And it might be some time before Febe returned. She reached out with her sgath to keep tabs on the high priestess, who was indeed still in one of the inner sanctums, no doubt also meditating and preparing herself for the ritual.

"We have a little time and I'll give us warning," she relented. "Do I mind what?"

"Not having a special dress, a big celebration. I don't have a *beah* for you."

"What is a *beah*?"

"A Destrye gifts his bride with a *beah* and she wears it as a symbol of their marriage. I thought I'd have time to find something to stand in place of it until I can give you a proper one. And that we'd have time to change clothes."

"You look fine—I told you before."

"I look like a Báran," he grumped, then glared, annoyance sparking when she giggled. "It's not funny."

"Báran clothes look good on you," she soothed, much as she would Chuffta's offended dignity. Perhaps males of all species were the same.

"Hey!"

She ignored Chuffta's indignant response. Lonen did look appealing in the silk pants and short-sleeved shirt, even though her sgath mainly showed her his exuberant masculine presence.

"Well, you deserve something better than that robe," he replied.

"And more than this hasty ceremony. Arill knows, Natly went on enough about the details of planning…" He trailed off, chagrin coloring his thoughts.

"Yeah," she drawled. "Maybe better to not bring up your fiancée during our actual wedding ceremony."

"Former fiancée," he corrected. "Really not even that. And this isn't the ceremony yet—this is waiting around for it to start. My knees are getting sore."

"And here I thought you were the big, bad warrior."

"I am. Big, bad warriors don't kneel. We charge about, swinging our weapons."

She laughed, shaking her head at him. That good humor of his flickered bright, charming her, banishing his perpetual anger to the shadowed corners of his aura. In the back of her mind, Febe moved. "She's coming back. Not much longer. Try to school your thoughts."

He muttered some Destrye curse at that, but subsided. Oria did her best to still her thoughts. It would be comforting to know ahead what the ceremony entailed, but the temple liked their surprises. The mystery was part of all rituals—intended to catch a person in honest reactions, particularly those that revealed a failure of *hwil*. Something, she now understood, to prevent the inevitable gaming of the system. Whatever the magical binding of the marriage ceremony, it would likely be uncomfortable, perhaps even painful for her. With any luck, Lonen's insensitivity to magic should prevent him from suffering from it.

High Priestess Febe entered the small chapel, bringing such a powerful charge of sgath with her that Oria's illicit grien leaped to devour it, forcing her to choke it back. The High Priestess had been drawing heavily on Bára's magic, using her female sgath to store it up. Priest Vico followed her, taking his place beside her at the altar, his male grien soaking up the sgath and activating the magic. They did not have an ideal partnership, but long practice and Febe's powerful sgath allowed him to perform feats usually reserved for priests of much higher rank. Fortunate, as all of those highly ranked priests had died when the Destrye attacked.

"Princess Oria, you come to the temple to beseech the moons to give you a husband. Is this so?"

"I do." Oria spoke the words firmly. Magic responded to intention and she would start this marriage with a firm one.

"King Lonen has proposed himself to be your husband, to channel your sgath to grien, to be both your walls and your guide to the world. Is he an acceptable choice?"

Ironic, all the truths and untruths in the ritual words. "He is."

"You come as a priestess to the temple and will leave as wife to King Lonen. Remove your mask so you come before him barefaced, and so that he may gaze on the face of his beloved, forevermore known only to him."

She should have expected that, but hadn't. Priest Vico came around behind her with a bowl, a platter for her mask, and bearing the small silver knives the masked used at meal times to cut the ribbons. He set the platter to her left and Oria covered her mask with her palms to hold it in place. Priest Vico cut the ribbons at her temples, sliding them from the knots in her braids. She lowered the mask to the platter, not looking at Lonen, feeling terribly shy though he'd seen her face before she gained her mask. Even so. Quickly she took the cool, scented cloth from the bowl and wiped her face with it, deeply understanding the need for this part of the ritual. It gave her time to compose her expression—and hopefully not look too sweaty or red-faced.

Lonen's comments about her having a pretty gown or time to make herself beautiful as Natly would have done niggled at her. But he wasn't marrying her for her appearance, or out of affection. Better for him to see her truly, without anything prettified between them. *Come before him barefaced.* It took more courage than she'd have thought, but she lowered the cloth to the bowl, and raised her eyes to meet his.

He smiled at her—not that cheeky grin full of mischief, but a more solemn one, gaze roving over her face. A vivid image of him caressing her cheek, then kissing her lips, came from him, and she blushed.

She waited. Knowing the temple, the next phase would likely test her sorely.

"King Lonen," High Priestess Febe intoned, her voice echoing with ripples of sgath, even as Priest Vico's grien seized Oria in a fierce mental grip, "take your bride's hand."

Oria braced herself. Oh, this would be bad indeed.

~ 8 ~

LONEN HESITATED, STARTLED out of his joy at seeing Oria's face again—so much more exotically beautiful even than he'd remembered, her eyes an even brighter coppery brown than in his dreams—taken aback by the strange request.

Much as he'd been hoping to find a way around the restriction against touching Oria's skin, he believed her that it would be painful for her, even damaging. And surely her temple brethren knew this. The twin masks of the priest and priestess behind the ornate altar both seemed to frown at him. These Bárans couldn't do anything simply. Everything had to be tied up in magical ritual and other assorted nastiness. Oria should be able to put on a pretty dress, accept his *beah* before Arill, and then dance the night away in his arms. Before spending the rest of it in his bed.

Not … whatever it was that loomed ahead of them, putting his short hairs on end.

Oria solved his dilemma by taking his hand, lacing her slim fingers between his in a grip as fierce as her bones were delicate. A small sound escaped her, she swayed, and Chuffta coiled more of his tail around her other wrist, even wrapping his sinuous neck around hers.

"Get on with it," Lonen growled at Febe, grateful his role as rampaging conqueror allowed him to force things along.

The priestess didn't like it, her posture full of disapproval, but she similarly joined hands with the priest who'd returned to her side after cutting away Oria's mask, and he raised his other hand in a gesture Lonen knew well. From the battle mages it had meant a fireball or earthquake soon to come, and he had to throttle back his now-instinctive reach for his axe.

Instead something strong, yet not entirely painful, grabbed him, darkening his vision until he seemed to be in another place. Almost like a dream, one of those surreal ones when Oria had visited his nights, prowling through his mind and consuming him body and soul. She was there in this place, too, holding his hand and—not exactly smiling at him—but looking deeply into his eyes, her copper gaze bright and sparking like candle flames. Lines of pain bracketed her pretty mouth and he tried to let go of her. She held on as tenaciously as in any of his dreams, when he'd been unable to muster the will to stop her from milking his cock or devouring his heart.

He was marrying this woman. A woman of foreign ideas and powerful magic. They'd be bound together for the rest of their lives. The yawning chasm of that future opened beneath his feet, black with terrifying and exhilarating possibilities.

Febe and the mysterious priest appeared in the dream also, golden masks glowing with otherworldly light, their crimson robes dark as old blood. Chuffta seemed to hover nearby, a blaze of white.

The priest held a shining blade in his hand, a knife made of glass that radiated a light as brightly silver blue as Grienon at full face. Oria turned their joined hands so her wrist faced up and his down. The blade struck, slicing first her fair skin where the blood showed in a delicate blue tracery, then his browner flesh from beneath, a breathtakingly bright pang. She never flinched—perhaps because she could no more move than he could—but her copper eyes darkened, the lines around her mouth deepening with the sharp pain.

It burned him, both her suffering and the hot flow of blood from his wrist. The priest handed the glass blade to the priestess, and reached out, placing a palm over each of their wounds. Oria screamed, a thin and weak sound, and Lonen tried to reach for her, still unable to move. Then the burn overtook him too, climbing up his arm until it struck his heart like a tree viper's poison. His turn to shout the agony of it, his heart racing nearly to burst.

But he couldn't break from Oria's gaze, her ever-darkening eyes filling his vision, her blood arcing into his, then flowing back, her heart pounding in staccato beats, humming like the jewelbirds she'd spoken of.

They'd become so black, her eyes, that they lost every glint of copper, going flat and dull, densely matte. With a chord of terror, he recognized those eyes, that life-sucking gaze. Identical to the Trom that had killed his father and brother.

The scene from the council chambers roared back at him, a crystal clear memory—Oria confronting the thing even as Lonen fought Arnon's restraining grip, trying against all reason to save her, his enemy, from that lethal touch that turned men to boneless pulp. The Trom had caressed her cheek, spoken to her in some tangled tongue. And nothing happened to her.

She alone had survived the monster's instantly delivered death.

Now the thing's eyes looked back out of her and once again he couldn't move to reach her. He fought the suffocating clutch of magic. Though he should be terrified of her, his heart didn't understand that. He fought, not to release her hand, but to bring her closer.

"Oria!"

Her name echoed without sound inside his skull.

And abruptly they were back in that temple room, his knees aching from the stone steps. Oria grasped his hand, fingers still interlaced with his, eyes once again lustrous copper, stared into his, wide with shock.

"Your bride is yours to do with as you wish." The voices of the priest and priestess came as if from another realm. There they stood, once again behind the altar—or had they ever truly moved?—speaking the words in unison, some aspect of the magic giving them a strange harmonic. "Her magic is yours to use, her body yours from which to draw succor and heirs."

They had to be ritual words because they knew perfectly well Lonen had no ability to access magic. But it confirmed what the Destrye had suspected, long ago on that battlefield when they'd decided to kill the masked sorcerers on the walls, in hopes of stopping the flow of magic to the battle mages. *Her magic is yours to use.* Though he couldn't use it as a Báran man would, guilt plucked at him, as he intended to use her just as ruthlessly. To save his people, yes, but he'd treat her as a tool as surely as any of these sorcerers would have. Just in different way. *Yours to use.*

Oria's hand trembled in his, her eyes blank, her face pale. Something nudged at Lonen's fingers and he started, glancing down to find the pointed tip of Chuffta's tail wedging gently between their joined hands. Mortified, he yanked them apart. Like a child's doll suddenly discarded, Oria crumpled to the stone floor. Lonen barely caught her in time, carefully touching her only over the silk, even though one of Chuffta's wings abruptly spread for balance buffeted his face.

He sat back, adjusting her so her head pillowed on his thigh, wanting more than anything to smooth back the damp tendrils of coppery hair plastered to her temples, her skin so waxy translucent that the shadowy foramina of her skull showed through. It seemed a terrible omen, this death's head, so like all the decomposed dead he'd seen over the last years.

Chuffta crawled gently onto her bosom, using the thumb claws at the bend of his wings to steady his progress. He'd done that before, when Oria lost consciousness outside the gates of the city. Hopefully he'd help her recover this time as well.

"What's wrong with her?" Lonen hardened his voice, so as to sound demanding, rather than pleading. Although he could likely drop the charade. They were married and that couldn't be reversed. The Báran ritual might be cruel, but it did seem to work on a deeper level than a Destrye marriage. Or so he assumed. None had mentioned anything like this following Arill's ceremony. The permanence of the bond resonated even in his mind-dead skull. Oria lurked in there, a part of him now. Odd, but also reassuring to sense her life force when she looked so very close to death.

"The Princess Oria is fragile." The High Priestess assumed a tone of apology, though she seemed nearly gleeful. "Perhaps we should have warned you better, King of the Destrye—your prize may not be long lived. Best to enjoy her while you can."

"Better to read your own histories, Your Highness," the priest advised, sounding more somber. "The Báran women taken by your kind are like tropical flowers consigned to eternal winter. Princess Oria will never bloom in your harsh land. Take your pleasure of her if you must. We cannot stop you from claiming your right. If she survives the night, however … I ask Your Highness to consider that it would be a kindness to leave her here." He paid no attention to Febe's intake of breath, though she otherwise showed little sign of her disapproval. "You have no cause to love Bára, King Lonen," he continued, "and much reason, perhaps to hate us and Princess Oria along with our people. But she has done you and the Destrye no wrong."

"I know that," Lonen replied, speaking only to the priest. "You are a good and loyal subject to speak for her at this time. I'll remember you to her."

High Priestess Febe remained where she was, but the priest came around to hold a hand over Oria, murmuring something that sounded like a prayer. Chuffta didn't bridle at the man, so Lonen trusted he only helped, not harmed. Indeed, Oria's face, while it didn't exactly regain color, at least looked a bit more like she belonged to the land of the living and not as if her spirit lingered in whatever witchy realm they'd traveled to for the wedding ritual.

"Take her to her tower," the priest murmured. "Priestess Juli will be there as her attendant and will know what to do for her." With a last wiggle of his fingers, he nodded to Lonen and left.

Taking the advice to heart, Lonen strapped his axe onto his back, careful not to jostle Oria unnecessarily, then gathered his unconscious wife into his arms, keeping the silk robes between his hands and her slight body. Chuffta took wing to make it easier for him. As the time before, it struck him how little she weighed, like a jewelbird herself, all brilliantly colored feathers over hollow bones.

"We need to stop doing this," he muttered at her, rising to his feet. He braced himself for Chuffta's piercing talons as the derkesthai landed on his shoulder, prehensile tail snaking out to coil gently around Oria's throat, the slim white column exposed by her laxly tipped back head. He'd have to get padded shoulders for his garments, too, as it seemed the Familiar would become a fixture in his life.

High Priestess Febe stood before him, golden mask remote. "Take your bride and go." She set Oria's mask, still on the little tile they'd put it on, onto Oria's breast.

"I intend to." Though if Febe assumed he'd leave Bára immediately, she'd be in for a surprise. One he'd enjoy. Forcing her to call Oria queen would be a well-earned triumph. "Shouldn't you tie the mask on her again, if I'm the only one to see her face forever more?"

The priestess checked a small movement, then inclined her head. "Those words are a formality, not meant to apply to other close family or temple ceremonies, but as you say, Your Highness." She retrieved a covered box, opening the colorful lid to show a spool of golden ribbons within. With deft, practiced movements, she cut away the threads of the ribbons still attached to Oria's mask at three points—the temple, cheek and jaw—then attached new ones, moving behind and around Oria, weaving the ribbons into her braids.

"It seems like it would be easier to simply untie them than to cut them every time and have to fetch new ones," he commented, as the process took some time.

"You understand nothing of magic, Destrye," the High Priestess replied in an absorbed tone, without rancor, but something of that otherworldly hum to it. "Which may well be your future undoing. You trifle with powers beyond your reckoning. If you want my advice, take your prize and go back to Dru. Against all odds you have achieved a short victory over your betters. Savor that, yes, in the tradition of your ancestors, but do not linger. Bára will only bring you grief. In your land you might have something of a pleasurable life as King of the Destrye. But you will never be King of Bára."

"Am I to believe that's some sort of magical prophecy?" He allowed a sneer, and for his deep dislike of this woman to rise up. Hopefully she'd detect it in him as Oria would.

Finished, the High Priestess stepped back and laced her fingers together over her belly. "You would be wise to recognize it as such, Your Highness, but from what I've witnessed, wisdom is not a virtue Grienon bestowed upon you."

Perhaps not. Nolan had been universally acknowledged as the most intelligent of King Archimago's sons, and he'd died first. Ion had been the most courageous, the heir and all that the Destrye could wish for in their next king, and he'd died too, gone in an instant. Lonen might never make a wise or noble king, but he was what the Destrye had. Arnon would serve, in the event of Lonen's demise, but his younger brother would make an even more reluctant king, far happier with his building plans, designs, and aqueducts.

But, though he might lack wisdom, Lonen knew a snow job when he saw one. The future belonged to those who took it by the throat and made it what they wanted it to be. Oria knew that, too.

"With all respect to your office, High Priestess," he said, allowing a feral grin to bare his teeth, "you can consign your supposed prophecies—and your wretched advice—to the nearest chasm."

Turning his back on the woman, he carried Oria up to her tower.

THE CLIMB, OF course, took forever. Fortunately, during their time in the temple the sun had set and Sgatha risen, shedding her soft rose light. Which meant they'd been in there for hours. Another reason to dislike magic—it distorted the senses. But the night breezes cooled the air, blowing in the open arched windows that riddled Oria's tower, making it look more like lacework than stone from below. Chuffta had thankfully resumed his station on Oria's breast, watching her face with devotion worthy of any hunting hound.

By the time he reached the summit of the endlessly spiraling stairs, Lonen gave thanks that he'd ignored Natly's protestations that manual labor was beneath the dignity of a king. All those trenches dug, beams lifted, and sacks of seed hauled given him the endurance for the climb. Even Oria's slight body felt like the heaviest bag of grain, his legs wobbly with effort when he finally reached the top stair.

He stood there stupidly a moment—his brain almost unable to grasp that the unending ascent had, in fact, ended—uncertain of his next move. The ceremony had perhaps taxed him far more than he had felt at the time. He almost envied Oria her deep sleep.

"King Lonen." A crimson-robed, golden-masked priestess appeared before him as if by magic. "Bring her in here. What happened to the princess?"

He followed her, impossibly weary, through the high-ceilinged hall that lead to Oria's rooftop garden. Instead of going straight through, however, the priestess turned into a branching corridor, opening a set of doors into an airy chamber, bright and ethereal as Oria herself. The woman drew gauzy curtains aside from a bed unlike any he'd seen. He lowered Oria onto it, feeling absurdly like some hero out of a tale.

Only in those the hero rescued the princess, rather than being the cause of her injuries.

"Are you Juli?"

"Yes, Your Highness." She curtseyed to him with grave ceremony. Something, however, about the red curls escaping her braids to form a sprightly halo around her mask made him think she wasn't always so decorous.

"The wedding ceremony," he told her. "It required us to hold hands. Oria suffered from my touch and collapsed immediately after. She hasn't been conscious since. The priest said you would know how to help her."

"Yes, Your Highness. I'll do what I can." She set to gathering supplies, working with deft efficiency. "You are wed then—the binding worked?"

He hadn't been aware there was any question of that. "According to High Priestess Febe, yes. Is there something I should know?"

Juli shrugged, a graceful gesture like a dancer's. "Surely Your Highness understands that Bárans don't wed foreigners. So, no, there was no certainty, even though Princess Oria believed her own magic would be enough to seal the bond, and give her access to the relationship you hold with your people."

"I'm a king crowned on the battlefield. There's nothing magical about that." Feeling worse than useless, he sat in a chair that looked too spindly to hold his weight. It creaked perilously, but held. For the time being.

"All life holds magic," Juli replied, brewing some potion with meticulous measurements. "Only of different potencies. Here in Bára, we've condensed and refined it to our purpose. In Dru, you have trees as tall as our towers, isn't it true, Your Highness?"

"Some of them nearly so, yes."

"And yet they come from a seed I could fit in the palm of my hand. How is that not magical? Here now, Master Chuffta, scoot a bit so I can reach her." The Familiar obliged with a rustle of wings and Juli used a small silver knife to cut the ribbons on Oria's mask. With an attitude of reverence, she set the molded gold thing on a tile next to the bed, clearly kept there for exactly that purpose. Strange people, the Bárans, with their masks and wasteful practices.

He watched Juli tip the fluid between Oria's lips, feeding it to her in delicate sips, all the while careful not to touch her. "Your touch harms her also?"

Juli nodded, the curls springing like coiled lamplight. "Not as much as yours, Your Highness—no insult intended—because I am first Báran and second highly trained in *hwil*, which is why I was chosen to attend her. But she's been pushed past her breaking point, so I won't add to the strain."

"What is *hwil*?" Might as well seek to extend his knowledge while he sat about being useless to his wife. And possibly to the Destrye. If Oria didn't recover, all of this would be for naught. He didn't know what he could do then, except perhaps to go home and at least die with them.

Not a pleasant option.

"It's a core teaching of our temple," Juli was explaining. "It means achieving a peaceful state of mind that allows us to contain our emotional energies. My excellent *hwil* makes me a restful person for her to be around."

Which meant, by reverse logic, that he himself would not be restful to Oria. He had zero idea how one went about containing their emotional energy. Or how to know what it was in the first place. He spread his hands, looking at them for any indication of what came out of his skin that affected Oria so. On his right wrist, a livid scar pulsed an angry red—and yet far more healed than it ought to be already. He knew how to wield his battle axe, how to lead his warriors, maybe something of the endless cascade of decision-making that made up being king, even something of farming and building aqueducts, now, but he didn't know how to keep from harming his own wife with those hands.

"Will she be all right?" He sounded plaintive and for once he didn't care. Exhaustion had him by the balls and he suddenly felt he couldn't rise from that chair, much less help Oria or anyone else. Never had he felt his own mortality so keenly.

"I believe so, Your Highness. She recovered from a far graver condition before, and she's much stronger now in her magic than she was then."

"The other time I touched her."

"Well, yes and no, Your Highness—many stresses conspired to cause Princess Oria's collapse at the surrender of Bára." She said it as if it were part of a legend. Probably it was. Wonderful. He'd go down in Báran history as the worst of fiends. Not that he didn't deserve it.

"You might as well call me Lonen. As your mistress's attendant, you'll likely be in my company a great deal. The Destrye don't much stand on ceremony."

"Then you plan to stay in Bára? The rumor mill had you riding off with the princess before Grienon rose."

He snorted at that. One thing the Bárans and Destrye shared—a love of gossip, particularly about the royal families. "We're here to stay for the time being." He stopped there, unsure of how much of Oria's ambitions she'd shared with her waiting woman. "You're not much like the others," he noted.

"No, Your Highness? How not?"

"Oria is forever telling me the answers to my questions are temple secrets. She confides very little." He waited to see if Juli would reveal how much Oria had confided in her.

Juli straightened, rubbing her palms briskly on her robes, as if drying them, or shedding dirt. "May I speak frankly, Your Highness?"

"Lonen. And please do. I've had a surfeit of secrets and Báran double-talk." He rubbed a hand over his brow, his eyelids heavy. Oria seemed to be resting a more natural sleep, however, and even Chuffta dozed, green eyes slitted as he crouched beside her on the fancy of a bed.

"Forgive me, Your—Lonen." Juli began mixing several new potions, measuring them into various containers, then combining them into a single goblet. "I should have realized the wedding ceremony would exhaust you also. This will be restorative and also let you sleep."

She handed him the pretty Báran glass and he studied it dubiously. Ion would have knocked it from his hand, lest the foreign sorceress seek to poison him. Or kill him in his sleep. "I should stay awake. Keep watch."

Juli put her hands on her hips, conveying an affectionate exasperation that reminded him of his mother, though the priestess couldn't be much older than himself. "You rode straight here from Dru, yes? Probably sleeping little on the journey and starting well before dawn today."

When he grudgingly nodded, she pointed at the glass he still held. "The temple ceremonies drain even the most stalwart, those in the best of health. There will be no staying awake for you. The tower is well protected. I'm sure you noted the guards below as you entered."

He had, bemused by their crisp, deferential salutes, instead of challenges, and total lack of surprise that he carried their unconscious princess.

"And Master Chuffta himself is no minor obstacle. Rest is what you and Oria both need."

"Not until you tell me whatever frank words you sought permission to say."

She faced him, cocking her head. "She has to be careful of you, Lonen. I say this as her friend as well as her serving woman and priestess attendant. Oria has not been much among people outside her family and priestesses like myself, all of whom have served her with perfect *hwil*. She is powerful, yes, but that power comes with a price that requires a delicate balance. Wedding you is an extraordinary step for her to take. One might say it's a choice so courageous as to be foolhardy. You could easily kill her—or worse. There you sit, hesitating to drink a healing potion from me because you fear poison. Surely you must see that you seem no less dangerous to us."

She had a point. And, he supposed, he'd already made a choice—one Ion would have beaten him bloody for considering—in marrying Oria and living among the Bárans at least as long as it took her to access those secrets she needed.

Lonen drained the glass, grimacing at the bitter flavor, handed it back to Juli, and wrapped one fist in his other hand, feeling the pull of the new wound. "Am I so terrible?"

"You are…" She hesitated.

Big, came Oria's voice in his head. *And you carry a great big battle-axe.*

"Formidable," Juli decided, and he thought she smiled behind her mask. "You radiate emotional energy as fierce as the sun's heat in summer."

"I don't know how stop doing that." He set his jaw in frustration, though it bled quickly away into lassitude. Juli's potion worked fast.

"Let me help you, Your Highness." Juli knelt at his feet, removing his slippers, then helped him sit up in the chair, nimble fingers finding the buckles of the shoulder harness, freeing him of it. She wedged a shoulder under his and levered him to his feet, though he tried to resist.

"My touch won't hurt you?" His words came out slightly slurred.

"Some." Her voice held strain, though that could be from his weight. She possessed a surprising amount of strength, her frame far sturdier than Oria's, walking him around to the far side of the bed, between Oria and the doors. "But my *hwil* protects me and I have nothing like Oria's sensitivity. It is both her blessing and her curse."

"Seems like mostly a curse to me."

"Only because she has yet to fully grow into her abilities—and you've seen very little as yet that she's already capable of. She will be a sorceress beyond compare, and a queen to go down in legend."

So, Oria had shared her plans. That was good. Though he couldn't recall why. Befuddled, he sat on the side of the bed and Juli undid the ties at his throat, then pulled the shirt over his head. "I'm sleeping here?"

"Yes." She eased him back on the pillows, the silk cool against his hot skin. A breeze scented with Oria's lilies wafted from the terrace. His eyes closed of their own accord. "Keep the sheet between you, but it's good for you to be with her. You're Oria's husband now. We're counting on you to take good care of her."

She draped another silk sheet over him, again reminding him of his mother, and days of boyhood long gone, when he'd slept without fear of dreaming. He might be dreaming already, Juli's voice a musical whisper like the moonlit breeze.

"Sgatha knows, no one else will."

~ 9 ~

SHE FLOATED THROUGH gray mists, remembering them from before. Which helped her not fight them. Instead, she accepted the way the mists wrapped her in cocoons of enshrining silk that healed her, as if she were a butterfly, soon to emerge with damp wings and no more duties than kissing flowers. That might be lovely—a life of nothing but the sugar offered by flowers and the sun on her colorful self, bringing a sigh of joy to someone's lips.

"Until a bird snapped you up."

She knew that wry mind-voice, too. Chuffta, her Familiar. Memories came back faster this time, too—good. Cracking open dry eyelids, she squinted at his triangular face, the large eyes green as new leaves in spring, his white scales shining iridescent in the rising sunlight.

"Welcome back to the land of the living," he said.

She tried to think back, recover more from the blank mists. "Did I break again?"

"Well, really you just chipped a little. Juli patched you up so the cracks don't even show and you only slept a good long night rather than days."

"What happened? Did the—"

A jagged snore interrupted her and she flipped her head on the pillow to take in the darkly haired and burly Destrye on the other side of the bed. Lonen. Her—

"Husband. Congratulations on your felicitous union. Worst wedding night in history, however."

"Oh hush."

It was good to see him again with her physical eyes. Lonen lay on his back, face relaxed so the scar that cut from his forehead, over one eye and down his cheek didn't pull to the side as it did when he was awake. More scars criss-crossed his chest and concave belly—funny that her sgath didn't show them. She tried looking with both sights at the same time, something she hadn't quite mastered the trick of. The overlapping images tended to make her dizzy. No one else admitted to it, but she nursed a theory that the temple had developed the custom of the masks exactly because they helped prevent that sort of double-vision.

Relinquishing sgath sight again was far more restful. Besides, she liked seeing Lonen with her actual eyes. Her husband. The bond resonated in the deepest part of her. Unreal.

His black hair curled in wild disarray, a dark contrast to the pale silk of the pillows. Dressed only in light trousers, and with one arm flung over his head, his body looked long and powerful—and his manhood tented those trousers dramatically, making her yank her gaze away again.

Something else to put on the list of intimidating things about him.

Just then he drew in another rumbling snore, which cut off in a mutter of blurred words, and she rolled her eyes at Chuffta. *"I slept through that?"*

"He didn't do it all night. He's been making more sounds and thrashing around just in the last little while. Dreaming, maybe? It seemed to be what woke you up."

As if to verify the words, Lonen kicked at something, then shouted. "Go on! Get out of here!" The hand flung over his head clenched into a fist, his muscles flickering, though the arm barely moved. He shouted again, anger and fear coiling around him, his words unclear, as if he spoke through deep water. Then he growled, more like a beast than a man. His eyes rocketed under his lids and he made a strangled cry.

Not knowing what to do, Oria sat up and reached out a tentative hand. She'd touched his hair before—and he hers—without any effect, but she could hardly tug on that to wake him. It seemed far too callous.

"What should I do?"

"I wouldn't want to be having that dream, whatever it is."

Okay then. "Lonen," she called softly—and with no result. He tossed his head on the pillow, crying out broken, inarticulate sounds, that pierced her heart. Jagged images of blood, death, and pain danced through the turmoil of emotions. Those dark things didn't belong in the dancing light of morning. "Lonen…" she tried louder. To no avail. Could he even hear her?

"Lonen!" she nearly shouted, layering in imperious command. "Wake up!"

His eyes flew open, seeing the dream still, one hand snapping to his side, before he went entirely still, the hard granite of his gaze taking in the ceiling, then landing on her, and softening while a smile spread across his face. "Oria." He breathed her name like a meditative chant. "You're better."

His gaze dropped to her breasts, making her realize she wore nothing but her very thin chemise. Juli must have taken off her priestess robes and loosened the ties of the undergarment, because the neckline gaped open, showing a substantial amount of skin. Self-conscious, she drew the cloth together and pushed her hair back from her forehead, snagging it in the tangled braids. She'd slept in them, which would make them an unholy mess to desnarl.

The least of her problems, really.

Giving it up, she drew up the sheet higher, using the movement to scoot back a little from his rapidly intensifying sexual energy. "You were dreaming."

He grimaced, then sat up, too, and scrubbed his hands over his scalp. The curls sprang back in the same bountiful disarray as before, but he didn't seem to notice. "Yeah. I do sometimes. Sorry if I disturbed you."

"More like you disturbed yourself." She wasn't sure if a hard man like him would welcome comfort. "It sounded bad."

"Sometimes they are." He shrugged it off, chagrin and irritation both rippling off him with the gesture. "Made Natly crazy. Said she couldn't sleep with me fighting golems all night. Yelling and kicking and such like."

Ah, so she'd shared his bed. Though, of course Oria had known that—had glimpsed their lovemaking in Lonen's head, much as she hadn't wanted to. Of course they'd slept together afterwards.

"So she stopped—sleeping with me, I mean." Lonen watched her with gray eyes gone clear and calm, now that the dregs of the nightmare had left him. "And I didn't much care, I found."

Curious. "Why not?"

"Because a lot of those dreams weren't fighting golems, but were having sex with you." He grinned. "It kind felt disloyal to be longing for you *and* keeping her from a good night's sleep while doing it. Ah, there it is. I like being able to see you blush again."

She clapped hands over her cheeks, which did feel hot. "I should put on my mask."

He stopped her as she reached for it, carefully catching the trailing cuff of her undergarment. "Don't. Not yet. During the… ceremony, or whatever in Arill you'd call that thing we endured, Febe said I alone get to see your face, something about a husband's privilege."

Of course that would be customary. Her own parents had always removed their masks once private with each other, and with their children. She hadn't thought of that aspect. She and Lonen would not have children to share her face with, but she would have him. She drew her hand back, leaving the mask where it sat, though she felt exceptionally exposed.

The wedding ritual had been something to endure, for sure, and she wouldn't blame him for being unsettled, even frightened by it. Much as in her own testing, something in the binding light had looked out at her. Like the Trom and yet not. It spoke to her without words, though she imagined the hissing voice. *Princess*

Ponen. She shuddered at the memory and Lonen tipped his head, studying her. "Cold?"

As if. The morning heat already sat heavy on the day, not a breeze stirring. "We should get up."

"Should we?"

"I should summon Juli. We'll need to eat."

"We have time for that. The council meeting isn't until this afternoon, right? And Juli said you were to rest."

Well, yes. But it felt… dangerous to be in bed with him, with his masculine exuberance sizzling hot on her skin and his gaze wandering over her, seeing more than anyone ever had. She wasn't at all sure how to handle him, what one did with a husband in one's bed in the morning. When one couldn't do the normal thing. Even then. "Do you want to tell me about your nightmare then?"

He gave her a curious look. "I figured you would have seen it in my head."

"No. Just fragments and … feelings." She fidgeted with the sheet. "I really do try not to prowl about in your mind. It's more that you sometimes project images rather forcefully—as you know, since you've discovered how to do it deliberately."

He grinned, unrepentant. "Seems only fair, to balance out the power. But I don't project the same way when I'm asleep and dreaming?"

"Perhaps it's the nature of dreams—nothing coherent came through."

"I have some privacy there then."

"Yes." She twisted the sheet in her fingers, choking back the apology that wanted to spill out.

"I was fighting the Trom," he offered. "They were at the door, trying to get in and I was afraid they'd get to you. And then I turned, and you were one of them, coming at me with your hand upraised, and I knew you'd kill me."

By Sgatha's light, it wouldn't be so. "It was only a dream," she managed to say around a tongue gone thick and dry.

"I know that. And still it seemed—I don't know. During that ritual I thought I saw something odd about your eyes."

"I barely remember anything about that ritual." She laughed, but it came out far too ragged and breathless.

It worked well enough to distract him, though, because he smiled with her. "That was a hell of a thing, wasn't it? You'll like our wedding in Arill's temple much better. It will actually be pleasant. Fun even. I have to tell you, Oria—you Bárans do *not* know how to have a good time."

"Yes, well, dealing with the magics that we do, we have to be a disciplined people. The temple and its rituals safeguard us in myriad ways. We observe rules to make sure the magic doesn't destroy us, or that we don't destroy each other."

"Disciplines like *hwil*." He studied her face intently for a reaction and she regretted that her mask sat so far away.

"What do you know about *hwil*?" She sounded, and felt, stiff.

"Juli told me some, last night when I brought you here."

"Juli shouldn't have—"

"Juli realizes that I'm going to need to know some of these things that you think to withhold from me. This is an important aspect of your life—and of any possibility that we'll be able to touch each other—so I think it's obviously valuable for me to be aware of its properties."

"Understanding *hwil* won't change anything, Lonen." She realized she'd clenched her hands into fists by the bite of her nails into her palms. "I can't just *learn* to bear someone else's touch."

"How do you know—have you ever tried?"

"What I've tried is to explain that I haven't had much opportunity to practice any of this!"

"Don't get all huffy with me." He pushed a few pillows into a better position and leaned back against them, stretching lazily and then putting his hands behind his neck, displaying his furred chest to excellent effect. "Tell me what *hwil* feels like."

"How am I supposed to do that?"

"First of all, relax. We're just having a conversation."

"In bed." Practically naked.

His smile stretched across his face as lazily as the rest. "A good place for it. How about this—do you have a hair brush?"

"Why?"

"Your braids are all messed up and it looks uncomfortable. Maybe you'll feel better if I take them down for you."

"You're obsessed with my hair." Though the snarled things *were* pulling uncomfortably.

He shrugged a little, gray eyes dancing with that mischief that sparked in blue stars from him. "I can't deny it. Get your hair brush, Oria."

She huffed out an impatient sigh, but got out of bed to retrieve the thing—though taking a moment to tie the neckline of her undergarment closed. The man was as relentless as Chuffta chewing a bone.

"Hey!"

"You know you are. Speaking of, have you hunted recently?"

"Want some alone time with the new mate, huh? I can do that." The derkesthai stretched his wings, yawned mightily, then took off out the open terrace doors.

"Where's Chuffta going?"

"To hunt. Since we'll be here for a while." She stood uncertainly, holding the brush, arrested by Lonen's intent expression and a wave of particularly intense desire from him. "What?"

"With the light behind you like that, your gown is nearly transparent. I can see all the lines of your body."

She grabbed up her gown, wrapping it tight around her.

"Don't do that, Oria," Lonen coaxed. "You're so beautiful. I love seeing you."

A whisper of pleasure ran through her at that. Ah, vanity. "Well—I shouldn't give you … ideas."'

"I'll tell you a secret." His smile went crooked and he lowered his voice to a loud whisper. "I already have the ideas."

She had no response to that, so she indicated a chair with the brush. "Want me to sit here?"

Lonen spread his legs and patted the sheet covering him between them. "You come here."

"I can't—"

"I won't touch your skin," he said, calm and insistent, but a challenge glittering in his gaze. "Trust me."

"Fine." Aware she'd huffed again, making him laugh at her, she smacked the glass handle of the brush into his palm hard enough to sting, then climbed onto the bed to sit cross-legged between his spread thighs, carefully adjusting the long chemise so it covered her. He waited for her to settle, then began carefully plucking at the braids, unwinding them and undoing the ribbons that held the ends.

"My mask knife is right there," she said, "if you want to cut the ribbons instead."

"Why not just untie them? It's wasteful to be cutting them all the time."

She didn't have a ready reply. "I never thought about it. You think about wastefulness more than I do."

"A Destrye trait, I suppose. We don't have all the riches you do in Bára, so we're careful of what we do have." He had one braid unplaited already, picking up the brush again to smooth it through the loosened locks. "I've never seen hair like yours before. It looks like metal, hammered to a bright polish. I'd like to have your *beah* made of copper just like this, to match, if that's all right with you."

Uncomfortable, she shrugged a little. "It doesn't matter to me."

"It matters to me." His voice stayed even, but annoyance seeped from him.

"Lonen…" She tried to think of a way to explain without making him angry. "I see what you're trying to do here and—"

"What am I trying to do?" he interrupted. Not irritated, but drawing her out with the teasing tone.

She pressed her lips together. She would not amuse him further by huffing. "You know perfectly well."

"Yes, but I want to know what *you* think I'm doing, as I'm not able to read *your* thoughts and emotions." He had more braids undone, and worked at a stubborn one, tugging a little. "Sorry—these are very tangled."

"I'm sure. I don't usually sleep in them. I can call Juli. You don't have to do this."

He kept a hold of the braids when she started to move away. "Oh no, you don't. You're not wriggling out of this so easily. Besides, I'm enjoying myself." He was good at it, too, surprisingly deft.

"I wouldn't think a man like you would want to tend a lady's hair."

"A man like me?"

"You know. Big, strong warrior."

His amusement went sharp, desire heightening. "Not any woman. You. What do you think I'm trying to do?"

"You never give up, do you?"

"No, so you might as well capitulate, my captive bride."

That shouldn't give her a shiver of answering desire. Likely it came of being so close physically, surrounded by his feelings, his usual intense sexuality more sensual, echoing his lazy mood.

"I think you're trying to seduce me," she finally said.

"Of course I am."

"I can't believe you admit it."

"Stop wiggling—I don't want to cut your hair by accident and this ribbon is too knotted to untie. There's no 'admitting' to it. You're my wife, Oria, I want us to be easy together. I want you to trust me."

She sighed for his obstinacy. "It's not a real marriage. Ow!" She clapped a hand to the braid he'd tugged sharply.

"Then don't say untrue things. You were there for that Arill-cursed ceremony. I might be mind-dead but I can feel the bond to you inside me. We're married as married gets and I'm not spending the rest of my life tied to a woman who dances around me like a deer darting into the shadows at every movement."

She wanted to protest that she didn't do that, but she probably did. "It's not you, though. It's because of how I am."

"You said I intimidate you."

"Badgering me into staying in bed with you and letting you brush my hair while we're both nearly naked is not making me feel less intimidated," she snapped.

He laughed, a low and sensual sound. "Yes it is, because you're all imperious princess again instead of skittish doe. Besides," he leaned close enough that his breath wafted over her ear as he spoke, "we could be a lot more naked than this."

"No, thank you," she replied, making herself stop knotting her chemise, deliberately smoothing it out.

"Nothing to make a person less intimidating than the intimacy of nakedness," he murmured, his voice doing strange things to her.

"There's no point in it," she protested, but she didn't sound nearly firm enough.

"Sure there is. You're a beautiful woman and you're mine. I want to be able to see you in all your loveliness. It will be an enduring delight to me."

"You don't know that."

"Oh, I have a pretty good idea." He nearly purred with sensual confidence and her body seemed to hum along.

He'd gotten all the braids undone and slowly dragged the brush through her hair with one hand, combing the fingers of his other hand through it in alternating strokes. So soothing. How it could feel totally different than when Juli performed this service, she didn't know. But it did. Determined to stay on point, she ignored the melting sensations.

"I understand that you're determined to find a way to have sex with me, but this will only lead to frustration and heartbreak for us both. You saw for yourself what happened from only holding hands with me."

He was quiet a bit, the only sounds the hiss of the hairbrush and the ebullient morning songs of the birds in her garden.

"Juli said it wasn't as bad this time, that you're stronger than you were."

"Obviously not strong enough." The bitterness crept into her voice, curse it. So much self-pity. "Believe me—I don't like being this way." *Worst wedding night ever.*

"Then we find a way to make you stronger."

"Things aren't that easy, Lonen. I can't just wish up being like your copper metal instead of badly blown glass, riddled with flaws. Magic doesn't just make things appear from thin air."

"How does it work?"

"It depends on the kind of magic."

"What kind do you have?"

"My kind." *Princess Ponen.*

"You're avoiding answering my questions."

"Yes. You're not the only stubborn person in this bed."

He burst out laughing, the rush of delight showering around her like a cooling rain. "I'll tell you a story then. When we left Dru to come to Bára and try to end who or what had sent the golems to attack us, I figured I'd never make it home. None of us did. We barreled up all the food and water we had left—which wasn't much—and sent it with everyone who wasn't a warrior on what we called the Trail of New Hope. Mostly the women and children, but also our scholars, artists, scribes, and a few fighters in case the golems pursued them."

"Where were they going?"

"Somewhere new." She felt the shrug in the rhythm of his hands. "We couldn't stay in Dru any longer, so they went in hopes of finding a place where they could live. My father, brothers, and I took all the warriors to Bára, certain that we'd die trying to fight you. Theirs was a journey of hope and ours of hopelessness in the face of an impossible task. Our main goal was to maybe take enough of you with us to ensure the others could escape."

"I'm sorry," she whispered, daunted by the waves of remembered angry despair coming from him.

"Don't be," he said, sharply. Then the strength of the emotion dimmed. "Is that better?"

"How did you know I was feeling it?"

"You get all tense in your neck and shoulders, and flinch away from me. I'm trying to learn to notice when I'm affecting you and pull it back. Did it work?"

"Yes," she answered, surprised. "Much better."

"See? There are many ways to undo knots. Now, I didn't tell you that story so you'd apologize, yet again, for something you didn't do. I told you so that you'd understand that I already accomplished the impossible. I not only lived, but the Destrye emerged victorious from our hopelessness. My people returned to Dru and we have a fighting chance at surviving the winter. Well," he amended, "we will when my brilliant and powerful sorceress queen makes sure of it."

"You put a lot of faith in me."

"Yes," he replied, in that implacable tone. "And in me. Because, my lovely Oria, I no longer believe in the impossible. I've already seen it shattered. So, I do believe that, while it may not be easy, you and I will find a way to be husband and wife in truth. We will put you on the throne of Bára, save the Destrye, and go on to live long and happy lives, with many copper-haired children to dote us on us in our old age."

"And the drought? Will you also command the monsoons to return?"

"Of course not. That's your job. Mine is to keep you safe while you work your sorcery."

She had to laugh. "Not to mention tending my hair."

"It's like silk—and now it's all kinked from being in those braids, so each little bump catches the light. I'm torn on whether your *beah* should be plaited copper or smooth like when your hair is straight."

"A grave dilemma indeed."

"Very much so. I will have to see your hair both ways, many times before I can make such an important decision. I've discovered that's what being king mainly involves—making good decisions." His breath whispered over her ear again. "I intend to make very good ones with you, Oria, which means I'll tend you with great diligence."

Despite herself, she giggled at this playful side of him. "Well thank you for this. I do feel better having the braids out."

"You're welcome. Want to do me a favor in return?"

~ 10 ~

HE ALMOST REGRETTED asking the question, because she stiffened warily. Not, however, as much as she would have even a short time before, so he was making inroads on earning her trust. Maybe enough to push her a little further. And, if he hadn't gotten as far as he hoped, how she responded to this request would let him know where the boundaries lay. All the better to strategize how to shift them.

"Want me to brush your hair in return?" she asked, in that prim voice that told him she didn't want him to know how she felt.

He laughed. "Spoken like a person with straight hair. I have to use a comb on mine, with lots and lots of oil."

"I know how to use a comb, Lonen."

"All right, then that would be welcome." In fact, he might greatly enjoy having her tend him in turn. "But that's not what I'm asking for right now."

"What then?" she prompted, with some impatience. Wanting to get it over with, perhaps, and clearly suspicious.

He put his lips close to the delicate curve of her ear. She shivered so deliciously when he murmured into it that he couldn't wait to experience her response when he licked her there. And elsewhere.

"I'd like to see you naked," he murmured.

As he expected, she tried to pull away, but didn't get far with his hand firmly wrapped in her hair. "Don't fly away, Oria. I'm just asking. You can say no."

"I'm saying no." But she was breathless, a high blush on her fair cheekbones. "Let me go."

"As my queen commands." He released her hair with some regret, already missing the silky mass of it sliding through his hands. Oria immediately leapt away, putting several feet between her and the bed. To his good fortune, in her haste she also forgot that the bright sunshine from the terrace silhouetted her slender form in the thin silk gown, her hair a shining cape around her. He folded his hands behind his neck, preparing for whatever lecture she intended to deliver, and enjoying the view in the meanwhile. Particularly the enticing triangle between her shapely thighs.

"Why?" she demanded.

He dragged his gaze back up to her face, though he couldn't read much of her expression with the light behind her. "I already told you."

She threw up her hands in exasperation. "And you think this will make you happy, being able to see me naked and not being able to do anything about it."

"I wouldn't agree I can't do anything about it."

"Sometimes you seem so smart and then you constantly forget that—"

"I haven't forgotten," he stopped her there, sharply. "Enough of trying to make it seem that way. Seeing you will give me something to picture when I use my own fist for relief."

She went so still that he dearly wished to get a glimpse of her expression, but moving to see better might startle her.

"I have absolutely no idea how to respond to that," she finally said, her tone faint.

"What shocks you—that I'd use my own hand in lieu of being inside you, or that I want the image of my naked wife to fantasize to while I do it?" That triangle between her thighs drew his eyes again. He could almost make out the division of her sex.

"Both, I think." Her voice was hushed. The silence drew out. "You're looking at my silhouette again, aren't you?"

"Oh yes," he replied, pushing the image forward so she might pick it up. "See yourself in my head?"

"I already look naked."

"Almost. The real thing would be better."

"I don't know." But she wavered, one hand tugging on the ties of her neckline. "I'm not sure how to feel about you picturing me while you…"

He waited but she didn't continue. "It seems wrong to picture anyone *but* you," he argued. Maybe another push. "You don't want me imagining Natly, do you?"

"A low blow there, Destrye." She moved out of the light, coming around to his side of the bed. At least he could see her face again, and the pink blush of her nipples. The shadow at her mound—not clear if her hair there was copper, too. He needed to know with a near-desperate thirst. His cock throbbed, so erect she had to be able to see the outline through the sheet. Indeed, her gaze did go there before she yanked it away. Tempting to take himself in hand and demonstrate to her then and there.

"Would you like to see it?" He asked.

Her coppery eyes flew wide and alarmed to his face. "No! I mean, not yet, I think."

Definite progress.

"Don't you do that, use your own hand, to pleasure yourself?"

She blushed nearly crimson. "I'm not having this conversation with you."

And yet she hadn't run. She lingered, curious and drawn despite herself. "You're already having this conversation," he pointed out. "And if we'd had a normal wedding night, we would have seen and done much more with each other."

"I haven't," she said abruptly, almost defiant. "Done that. *Normally* I don't feel the urge."

"Not ever?" He was flabbergasted.

"I don't think women do," she informed him coolly. "I'm not sure all men do."

"Oh, they do," he assured her. "Believe me, almost all men *and* women do."

She put her hands on her hips, delineating her narrow waist nicely. "You don't know that."

He considered it. "Yes, I do."

"Maybe the Destrye do it."

"You Bárans might have sticks up your asses, but I'm willing to bet money even your people do it.

She actually stomped her slender bare foot, forcing him to repress a smile. "I cannot believe you just said that to me!"

"Don't be annoyed. Having things up your ass can feel very nice. I'll show you."

She grabbed a pillow and flung it at his face with an incoherent screech. He caught it in time, but could no longer hold back the laughter. By the time he wiped the tears away, she'd composed herself, standing with folded arms, tapping her foot with barely contained ire.

"I was going to let you see me naked," she informed him coolly, "but not now."

She was killing him. "Aw, don't be that way. That's not fair."

"Yes, it is." She lifted her pert chin and sniffed, as if she smelled something bad. "You don't deserve a treat like the sight of my naked body, not behaving like a barbarian."

Wait. She was actually teasing him. She looked perfectly composed, even disdainful, but something about her made him realize she was being playful. If only he could toss her on the bed and torment her into showing it. "Oria, I *am* a barbarian."

"So you've demonstrated," she retorted. "But you don't have to look like one. Come and sit. I'll comb your hair."

"Are you sure you won't—"

"Not happening." She turned crisply, hair crackling about her. "And I'm summoning Juli, so you might do something about *that*."

To his utter shock, something briefly grasped his cock, a shimmer of energy like a tiny bolt of lightning. "Arill!" he gasped, fighting not to spill his seed immediately like some oversexed adolescent.

Oria turned and flashed him a coy smile. "No, Destrye. That was me."

AS SOON AS Lonen disappeared into her private bathing room—even before sending for Juli—Oria pulled a fresh set of priestess robes from the clothespress, hastily changed her chemise, and scrambled into the far more modest clothing. No more temptation, for either of them. She picked up her mask, wanting the comfort of its obscuring help, too, but the way Lonen had asked that she not… Well, she'd apparently developed a soft spot for the Destrye king because she set the mask aside again. She seemed to have a great deal of difficulty refusing him his requests, no matter how far she strayed from her usual behavior. A dangerous sign.

Especially that lapse in using grien on him. And sexually! Really, she couldn't imagine what had gotten into her, except that it had been so satisfying to see the look on Lonen's face. Plus she'd had to do something to vent all that sensual energy she'd absorbed. He deserved it, too, teasing her so mercilessly, making her lose all semblance of *hwil*. He'd so thoroughly seduced her that she'd been on the verge of dropping her chemise and demanding he show her how he pleasured himself.

Don't you do that, use your own hand, to pleasure yourself?

The question burned in her brain. Was it true that everyone else did that? Something she really didn't want to envision, the people she knew and loved, doing… No. Banishing that line of thought.

She really shouldn't have teased him, not the least because no one could know that she could use active grien that way. Stupid and impulsive. Of course Lonen wouldn't know the difference, but he might slip up and say the wrong thing, betraying her secret. But making sure he knew enough not to meant having to explain in the first place and she really wasn't at all sure that was wise. He might be insisting that their marriage was a real partnership, but only the day before he'd called her an enemy.

He talked of wedding dances, but they truly danced along a very thin line, each of them on opposite sides of it. She needed to keep that firmly in mind—and not fall into his flirtatious games.

She couldn't imagine what had gotten into her.

A scuffing sound alerted her to his approach. He emerged dressed in his Destrye clothing again. The animal skins had been dyed dark, as all the Destrye warriors seemed to wear. Was that for war or did they never dress in colors at all? Even his shirt woven of some plant material looked nearly black in the shadowed interior. At least the leather pants did more to conceal his flagrant manhood than the Báran silk trousers did. Though, judging by his relaxed and pleased expression, that might be because he'd relieved himself while in there. Something else she didn't want to know.

"You're blushing," he commented.

"It's warm in here."

"Especially for you with those layers of robes on."

As those layers formed at least a meager defense against his seductive ways, she had no intention of taking them off again. "Sit here if you want me to fix your hair."

Lonen sat in the chair before her, then leaned closer to examine the mirror, tapping it with a curious finger. "I've never seen such a thing. Like perfectly still lake water."

"Which I've never seen. It's more glass, treated with a liquid metal on one side, so it reflects."

He sat back in the chair with an amused grunt, shifting his study of the mirror itself to her, his gray eyes intent on hers. She concentrated on pouring some oil into her palm, so her curiosity wouldn't lead her to peeking into his thoughts. Careful not to touch his scalp, she brushed her oiled palms over his curls. They were softer than they looked, though coarser than her own hair. And intriguingly exotic. Still, it made no sense that it gave her pleasure to comb her fingers through them.

"Juli is having food sent up so we can breakfast here in the garden. We do have meat for you. The council session might last a long time, so you'd be wise to eat heartily."

"Fattening me up?"

He was too thin, it was true. Thinner than he'd been before and the guilt chewed at her, thinking of the Trom burning their crops. "I'd like to visit my mother beforehand, try to persuade her to attend. This is her plan as much as anyone's. Hopefully once she sees we're married, she'll relent and accept the reality of it."

"It's something she'll be able to know, just by looking at us?"

The man thought in questions. But he knew some of this already, so it wouldn't be telling him something new. Still, each secret revealed seemed to open the windows to a dozen more, making it more and more difficult to determine where to draw her boundaries with him. That thin line. "With sgath, yes. That's how I see with my mask on."

"What's that like?" He asked it easily enough, but his eyes met hers in the mirror, that obstinate challenge in them.

"I don't know how to explain it. Don't smirk. I was thinking how to describe it." She rapped him on the scalp with the glass comb.

"Ow."

"See? The sand is blowing in your tower now."

"Fair enough." He grinned at her. "I'd like to blow more than sand in your tower, Oria."

"You're incorrigible."

He sighed, trying to look sorrowful, but his playfully sexual thoughts tugged at her. "So my mother always says."

She resisted. "Is your mother alive?"

"Uh-uh. Not letting you distract me with questions. You were thinking about how to describe seeing with sgath to me. Is that related to the moon, Sgatha?"

"Yes. We believe Sgatha governs the flow of sgath." She drew the comb gently through his tangled curls, then closed her eyes to see it with sgath. "It's like … like everything radiates a kind of light. Your hair looks different than your skin, and my hands look a different color from those. Even the comb has a little glow."

"Juli said magic comes from life, but the comb isn't alive."

Opening her eyes, she looked at him in the mirror. "It is, just not in the way you think of it. Everything has energy to it. This comb, like the mirror, are both made of sand, melted and transformed, but which used to be part of the ocean. They carry a kind of … memory of what they once were."

He frowned. "That makes no sense."

"I told you it was hard to explain."

"I know, I know—don't get all huffy. Go on."

She pulled at the curls a little harder than she needed to, but he didn't wince. "That's all there is to tell."

"Liar," he mocked, softly.

"Ask me questions then, which you're so brilliant at anyway."

He didn't even have to pause to think. "So, everyone who wears a mask can see with this sgath?"

"The priestesses," she corrected. It wouldn't do for him to insult a Báran priest by suggesting he used sgath. "The priests use grien."

"Governed by Grienon."

"There you go."

"And does grien work the same way?"

Shifting sands here. "I don't know, as I'm not a man."

He grinned, vividly picturing her standing in her chemise in the light. "Now that is a truth."

His curls reasonably tamed and oiled, she went to fetch the leather tie he'd left on the table by the bed. She handed it to him, not certain she could gather the springy stuff together well enough without risking touching his skin. He didn't take it, however. Instead he picked up a long lock of her hair where it streamed over her shoulder and coiled it around his finger. "What is it you're not telling me?"

"Besides centuries of secret temple knowledge? I can't imagine."

He tugged on her hair. "Your sarcasm makes me makes me want to toss you on that bed until you're too delirious with pleasure to think straight."

That made her head reel right there. "I had to marry a Destrye with an enormous idea of himself."

"That's not the only thing that's enormous. You'll find out someday and then I'll accept *that* apology when you tell me how wrong you were."

"Ha!" She tried to step back, but he held on, his eyes turning somber.

"Oria—I can't be your partner in this if you keep me blind and deaf. There's something there, about sgath and grien that you're not telling me."

She pulled at the leather tie, tugging it between her fingers as she'd been in the habit of doing since Lonen had left it behind. How was he reading into her? She'd faked *hwil* well enough to fool the High Priestess, she certainly should be able to hide a lie from a mind-dead foreigner. "I'm not keeping you blind and deaf. I can't imagine what makes you think I am."

No longer soft, the gray of his eyes went flinty, looking more like the granite she'd first thought of when she saw him full of battle fury and spattered with blood at the city gates. "I don't know what it is either, but it's like there's part of you in me now. Maybe you gave me some of your magic."

"That's not possible." *Was it?*

"I really hate it when you tell me something's impossible, Oria."

"Then you're in for long years of misery, because someone has to be practical in this marriage."

"You said the magic ritual bound us together," he flung back at her. "Magic. Connection. You. Me. I'm in you and you're in me. And I know when you're lying to me. Another ground rule for you—I also hate it when you lie to me."

She struggled with her rising anger and all the emotion he emanated. Too much input from him, on top of all that had gone the night before, no matter how much better she'd done. She might be faking *hwil* most of the time, but it still took a measure of equanimity to do that much. Not a state of mind being around Lonen helped her to achieve. Terrible timing, when she couldn't afford any apparent lapse of *hwil* before confronting the council. Even as she wrestled both his emotional energy and hers, the marginal control she managed eroded like sand slipping through her fingers.

She needed Chuffta and he wasn't there.

"I'm coming back. Stay steady."

Could it be some of the Destrye was in her? That would explain her uncharacteristically salacious behavior. But she had too much grien in her already—she couldn't afford to have even more. Lonen waited her out, holding her leashed by the lock of her hair, implacable, though his thumb absently stroked over it.

She took a steadying breath. "You don't listen well. There are things you can't know. That would be beyond dangerous to me to reveal to you."

He didn't like it, his brows lowering and some of that dark anger brooding in the background of his thoughts. "I wouldn't do anything to endanger you, Oria."

"You wouldn't mean to, no." She slapped the tie on the table, snagged a ribbon knife, and neatly cut of the lock of hair he held—then swiftly made good her escape. "But as both our peoples have amply demonstrated, we don't have to set out with the intention of harming each other in order to do it in grand fashion."

"It's hardly the same thing," he nearly growled.

She pointed at him. "Destrye." Then tapped her breast. "Báran. It's exactly the same thing." She turned to go.

"We're not done talking, Oria." Some of his frustrated anger snaked around her, adding to the uneven charge already building. Hopefully Chuffta would return soon. She desperately needed to vent.

"You want to be my partner? Use that anger to help me get the council to ratify me as queen. That's why we got married in the first place, not to loll in bed all morning and play sexy games. This is a marriage of state and so it will remain. We both have grave responsibilities to our peoples and you'd do well to remember that, King Lonen."

~ 11 ~

HE NEARLY LUNGED after her. Stopped himself by dint of will that had carried him through battles that stronger men than he had fallen to. How had things between them deteriorated so swiftly? All he knew was he'd undone everything he'd built.

No, *she* had cut the fragile ties of trust they'd been creating, snicking it to pieces with her little silver knife.

She might as well have plunged it into his heart. Walking away from him with that chill in her gaze, leaving only a shining lock of her copper hair behind. Metal could be cold, too. He'd do well to remember that in dealing with her.

Forcing himself to keep to a walk, he tucked the lock of hair in his pocket, and then his hands. An extra measure to ensure he didn't forget himself and touch her. Or throttle her.

He sauntered onto the terrace, scanning it. The brightly colored silk banners that provided shade hung lax in the still air, the brilliant blossoms of fabulous flowers likewise hanging off draping vines, trees and stalks. The ones that hadn't dried to brown crisps drooped, wilting in the sun. A low drone hummed around him, like heat given sound. No, it came from insects buzzing around the blooms and small birds, moving so fast as they dipped from plant to plant that their wings became a blur. The jewelbirds.

Not in the shade as a reasonable person would be, Oria instead stood in one of her habitual positions, over by the stone balustrade, gazing out at the city and the sere plains beyond. The sun glinted off her cape of hair, like the hammered copper drums of the Destrye.

She dazzled him. Seduced and infuriated him. All thoughts led to the sorceress. She'd well and truly bewitched him and yet cared nothing for him except as a player in her plans.

He was an idiot to have married her.

"You only have to put up with me a few days more," she said, still in that imperiously cool tone and not in the way he found irresistibly desirable either. "Then you can go home and be free of me."

He hadn't meant to be thinking that so loudly. "Not true," he countered with ill grace. "We will never be free of each other."

"You will be free of my immediate presence," she amended, with such equanimity that he brought up some lurid thoughts about her, just to shake her up.

"Stop that."

"Why should I? And don't you dare lecture me on my responsibilities to my people. I came here for them. Married *you*, for them. You're not the only one making sacrifices here."

"I never imagined I was," she gritted through clenched teeth.

There—not so cool and remote. *You radiate emotional energy as fierce as the sun's heat in summer.* By Arill, he'd use that to thaw her, make her deal with him as a partner, if not her equal. Barbarian and mind-dead he might be, but irresponsible ruler he wasn't. "I think you do imagine that," he taunted her.

Oria refused to look at him, but her fingers flexed on the railing. Apparently she did that a great deal because she'd worn the gritty stone smooth in places, always up in her lonely tower, secluded from the world.

"Princess Oria, all alone in her quiet world, with her flowers, her jewelbirds, and her Familiar. Well, I have news for you. You're no longer alone. You don't get to be. I'm your husband and you will not shut me out. Not out of your ambitions. Not out of your emotions." He leaned in, letting her feel all the heated desire she stirred in him. "And not out of your bed."

"Stop doing that!" She scanned the sky, looking for that pet lizard she liked so well, no doubt.

"Why should I?" he repeated the question, ruthlessly pushing her.

"Because." She rounded on him at last, face flushed from fury, the heat, or both. "You want to know a secret? Fine. Here's one for you. To receive a mask, we have to prove that we've achieved *hwil*."

"Like your golems and your blank masks," he sneered. "Creatures devoid of feeling."

"If only," she snapped back. "You wanted to know so badly what it is? Well ask some other priestess because I've never achieved *hwil*. That's right, I faked it, with my mother's help. And if they find out, they'll take my mask away, and I will never become queen. So wrap your clever brain around that concept and stop trying to get to me emotionally." Her breath caught, nearly a sob. "If you won't do it for my sake, then do it for your people. Because you're going to destroy us all for the sake of your cursed male pride."

"Oria." He caught the sleeve of her robe as she turned away again. He was an ass. "Hey. I didn't know. I can't know these things unless you let me in on these secrets. That's my whole point."

"Well now you do. There: one more in my vast array of flaws." She wiped furiously at her cheeks. "You wanted into my feelings? Here I am, a whole boggy, bloody mess of them."

Oria's sensitivity ... both her blessing and her curse.

"I don't believe you're flawed."

"What do you know of it, Destrye?" She demanded, all Báran princess at her imperious best.

He held onto his patience by a thin thread, the sun hot on his oiled hair that she'd tended with such care. A mercurial woman, restless and changeable, his sorceress wife. "Obviously not a whole lot, since you refuse to explain it to me."

She didn't reply, pressing her lips against whatever tart—or wounded—reply she'd had on the tip of her tongue. Then she gave a glad cry as Chuffta winged up, landing on the balustrade with a scrabble of talons on stone. Wings still spread, he balanced as he snaked his long neck against her throat, letting her embrace him, running slim fingers over his shining white scales.

Lonen was in a hell of his own making that he'd be fighting sick jealousy over her love for the dragonlet. His fingers itched to grab his axe and chop something up. Oria, for example. In fact, maybe he should work off some of that energy. It could only help both of them.

Leaving them to their little love fest, he went inside long enough to strip to his small clothes and grab his axe, then found another spot on her expansive terrace and set to running strengthening exercises. His muscles responded stiffly at first—the wages of too little exercise the past days of riding to Bára and negotiations and rituals—but gradually they warmed.

His faithful battle axe felt good in his grip, reassuring, steady, and real. The opposite of magic in its inert iron. That was something that wasn't alive in any way. A flaw in Oria's assertions. He ran the drills with the axe in his right hand, then switched to the left. The wise warrior prepared for all eventualities.

By the time he felt like he could operate out of a place of calm logic instead of unreasoning, jealous anger, he dripped sweat. He had to use Oria's private bathing chamber to wash off again, which only made him think again about coming in his own fist earlier, dazzling images of Oria in his head.

All thoughts led to the sorceress.

At least able to behave like a civilized man again, he found Oria in the shade of her silk sail in the seats by her fire table, though it was only smooth creamy stone, no dancing violet flames. A good thing, as a number of plates of food and pitchers sat there instead. Juli had done her mistress's hair up in the complex braids again, and Oria now wore a more elaborate set of the crimson priestess robes, kind of a cross between one of her royal gowns and the daily robes. Chuffta sat beside her, tail wrapped around her wrist like a series of bracelets. And, of course, Arill take her—she wore her cursed mask again.

He fingered the lock of her hair in his pocket. She hadn't intended it as a gift, obviously, but he'd keep it as such, having found a few pieces of cut ribbon to bind each end.

"How are you feeling?" he asked, not sure how else to open the next phase of conversation.

"I won't fall apart in the next moments, at any rate." She stroked Chuffta's wing and the derkesthai gazed at him, green eyes full of intelligence, but no accusation that he could detect.

"Master Chuffta," he greeted the Familiar as Juli had, then offered one used by the Destrye. "Did you enjoy good hunting?"

Chuffta blinked and dipped his chin, looking pleased indeed. Oria made a little sound of surprise.

"What?"

"He didn't say anything to me, just communicated directly to you. He doesn't usually do that."

Lonen sat, using a pair of glass picks to stab a piece of meat. Could be filling his griping stomach would help his mood immensely. "Probably Chuffta knows that he and I are in this together with you, so we might as well find ways to communicate with each other besides through you."

"Don't start." She sounded weary, but he couldn't let her off this climbing rope while they still dangled so far above ground.

"I'm not. I'm continuing. You and I have things to sort out before we walk into that council chamber, in order to be a cohesive fighting unit. If only to serve our grave responsibilities to our peoples."

She sighed, a rough, injured sound that grabbed at his heart. "I suppose I deserve that. But you push me, Lonen. You push and push and..." She finished on another empty breath, then filled a glass with juice, her hand shaking. Belatedly she seemed to realize she couldn't drink with her mask on and sat there, holding it.

"Here, let me help you take it off." He rose and walked behind her.

"You don't have to—"

"I might as well learn the tricks of it, right? Something I can do for you when it's just the two of us, so you don't have to call on Juli every time."

"Fine." He imagined she rolled her eyes, which was better than the defeated attitude. "There's a knife—"

"I've already found the knots and can get them." They were tucked in among the braids, cleverly hidden, but not that difficult to undo.

"You interrupt me a lot."

He opened his mouth to retort, but realized that she had a point. "You're right. I'm an impatient brute. I'll try to do better."

She held the mask in place as he worked. "Not entirely impatient. You seem to be good with knots."

A peace offering? He'd take it. "I've worked with rope a lot. Climbing trees, cliffs, that kind of thing."

"City walls," she said in a more pointed voice. So much for peace.

"Weren't you the one who said we needed to get past accusations and apologies over with?" He finished with the third set of ribbons and slipped the mask from her hands, setting it on the tile kept for it nearby. Uncovering the bowl next to it, he found one of her damp and freshly scented cloths inside and offered it to her.

Eyes flashing up to him in surprise, she took the cloth, mopping her flushed face with it. Her eyes were red and swollen from crying, which meant the few tears he'd witnessed hadn't been the end of it. Giving her a moment to compose herself, he sat again, spearing more meat.

"You're supposed to use them like this." Oria picked up a pair and demonstrated holding them both in one hand, deftly plucking a grape from a platter.

He studied her hold, emulated it and tried the same with a piece of meat. Easier to learn on that than on something slippery like a grape. On his second try he got it and Oria smiled at him. A real one, if sad. "You're good with your hands in many ways."

Not the time to tease her with the sexual remark that sprang to mind at that. "I guess so? I've always liked doing things with my hands—wood carving and such." He set down the eating picks and studied his hands. "I don't like that they give you pain."

She took a breath. "It's not pain, exactly."

"Okay." He waited, restraining the questions that annoyed her so. Instead he piled a plate with a bunch of leaves, grass, and sticks—or whatever in Arill it all was—and handed it to her. When she stared at it with a blank expression, he nudged it a little. "Eat. Long council session, remember. You don't eat enough."

"I feel guilty," she admitted, balancing the plate on her knees, sharp under the silk, and poked at the greens. "I keep thinking what it takes to grow this and where we stole the water from."

"It seems to me that you spend too much time feeling guilty about things that aren't your fault and you can't control."

"For someone who claims to want to know me better and be my partner, you criticize me an awful lot."

"It's not criticism—it's good advice. You can't lead your people to better lives if you're not strong. There's no sense in starving yourself to make up for the past."

"Is that why you've lost so much weight?" she retorted. "Because you've been eating so well, so you can be strong to lead your people?"

"Point taken. But in truth it wasn't guilt that stopped me so much as lack of opportunity and appetite for the options I had. Don't apologize for that either. You eat and I'll get us back on topic. It seems to me, as we were discussing earlier, that your sensitivity to emotional energy is also what gives you powerful magic. Juli called it your blessing and curse together."

"Juli talks too much," she muttered, but she speared up some greens and chewed. When she swallowed, she pointed the glass picks at him. "And I'm not that powerful. I'm still figuring things out. The magic is strong sometimes, but it's also hard to … direct."

He nodded thoughtfully, grabbing a platter of cheese and scooping some onto her plate. "So, you're like a young warrior after a big growth spurt. You don't know where your body is or how to make your size and strength work for you. You're learning to swing the magical equivalent of a sword, but right now you're your own worst enemy because you keep hitting your own self in the noggin with it."

She gave him a funny look. "That actually makes a weird kind of sense."

"I don't know much about magic, but I do know something about training young men—well, people—in using their Arill-bestowed gifts. Just because she gave it to you, doesn't mean you don't have to practice diligently to hone those talents into something you can actually wield with confidence. Natural born talent only gets you ten percent there. Hard work and refining your skills is the rest of the battle."

She was quiet a moment, thankfully eating with more enthusiasm. "You're never quite what I expect," she finally said.

He grunted a laugh. "Good. As you're never what I expect either. We're a perfect match."

"We're not, though." She gazed at him somberly, eyes dark with concern. "And the council will know it. Worse news is, my mother refuses to see me. Her attendants say she was so upset about my—our—marriage when I sent a message to her that she said all sorts of horrible things, then fell into a fugue state."

"I'm sorry." He couldn't imagine how that would be, though if those servants were his, he'd take them to task for passing along the ranting of a madwoman. That did no one any good. "You know that, whatever she said, she didn't mean it. You said yourself she's not in her right mind."

"I know that in my head." Oria glanced at her Familiar and rolled her shoulders. "The point is, she won't be helping."

"We'll do it ourselves then." He scooped some stuff onto her plate that looked unfortunately like maggots. Hopefully it wasn't really, but if it was... well, good protein. Maybe he could eventually talk her into eating meat. That would help fill out those waifish hollows around her collarbones.

"I don't think I can do it." She nearly whispered the words, then glanced down at Chuffta, who gazed up at her with an intent green gaze.

Practicing being the better man, Lonen gave them a few minutes to converse, using the opportunity to devour more of the really excellent meat. Some kind of venison, maybe. And there were pieces of fowl with a spicy seasoning he really enjoyed.

"Want to loop me in?" he finally asked and Oria looked over at him with a flush on her cheekbones.

"Mostly Chuffta is telling me the same things you are, that I should share more with you and trust you to help me with the council."

Surprisingly honored, he dipped his chin at her Familiar. "Good man."

Oria rolled her eyes at them both and threw up her hands, which seemed a good sign indeed. Fiesty Oria would be far better at his side than the dejected one. "Fine. I can't believe I'm going to do this. But I need to swear you to secrecy somehow. Vow to your goddess or something."

He considered her. The vow waited to be made, of course. Would have been already, had they married in Arill's temple according to Destrye custom. By altering the words slightly, they could fit his and Oria's unusual union. A risk, promising so much to her, and yet... he was already committed, wasn't he? They both were.

As he'd said to her the evening before, he'd already made the decision, and he wasn't a man to go back on that. No matter his other flaws.

He set his plate aside, going to one knee before her. In the old tradition, he picked up the hem of her silk robe, kissed it, then caught and held her gaze. "I swear by the magic that binds us, by the seed of me in you and the blossom of you in me, that I shall never betray you, my wife, whether by action or inaction."

She stared at him, lips parted, pink with the fruit she'd eaten. If only he could taste her, let her taste him, they'd be so much easier with each other. Of her own accord, she lifted a hand and carefully tucked one of his escaped curls into his tied-back hair. "Thank you," she said, seeming both moved and chastened.

Tempted to break the tension with a joke, he resisted the urge. This was an important moment between them. "We both have fealties, Oria, people to whom we owe our allegiance, but we can be united in that. Trust me to help you."

"All right," she breathed. For a moment she seemed about to touch him, but she caught herself and shooed him away. "Go sit over there. You're too close for me to keep my head straight."

He let himself grin at her then. It salved his admittedly too-large masculine pride that he affected her as much she did him. Doing as she asked, he added more food to her plate, then to his own. She shook her head at him. "This is more food than I've eaten in weeks."

"Good. Maybe you'll start making up for senselessly depriving yourself. Now, tell me what I need to know."

Putting her eating picks together, she used them as a platform to lift the maggoty things to her mouth. They didn't move, so maybe they're weren't insect larvae after all.

"This is the thing. You asked me what the Trom said to me that day, why its touch didn't kill me." She gazed at him steadily, no waffling now, but studying his reactions, probably reading his emotions, too, so he kept his mind calm and still as the lakes of Dru. "It called me Princess *Ponen*, which my mother—during a fortuitous lucid period—explained is a very old word that means powerful potential."

She set her plate aside and scrubbed her palms over her knees, probably unaware that she left sweat marks from them. The memory bothered her far more than she wanted to let on.

"What it turns out to mean for me is that I have both sgath and grien." She lifted her chin, daring him to comment.

"So you have the male kind of magic, too."

"Yes." She waited, maybe for him to be horrified or something, but he kept to the placid lake image. No judgment from him. If that made her more powerful, all the better for the Destrye. "You have to understand," she continued, her face very serious. "Sgath is passive. Priestesses absorb magic, we gather and pool it, then feed it to our priests. *They* make it active, using grien to build things."

"Or make earthquakes and fireballs to destroy things," he noted wryly, then regretted breaking his own rule about not referencing past wrongs. She didn't seem to notice, however.

"Exactly. It's ... beyond unseemly for a woman to be able to wield grien. It's anathema. If anyone finds out, they won't just take my mask and deny me the throne, they'll execute me."

Something hard and mean stirred in him at that. "They'd have to go through me."

She gazed at him in momentary astonishment. "I don't think you—"

"It's not a matter of debate, and I'm sorry I interrupted you again, but I'm not going to argue about this. If any of those red-robed golem wannabes make a move to lay a finger on you, I'll burn down Bára before I let that happen." The anger felt good. She wanted him to channel it? There it was. "You're mine now, Oria, which means I'll protect you with the last breath in my body."

"What about your responsibility to the Destrye?" she challenged.

"Don't give me that. You're my queen now and the best hope of saving my people. My loyalty is one and the same. I'll wield my axe for you as I would for them."

"Some things can't be resolved with brute strength." Her eyes flashed as she said it and he began to see the sides of her she'd described. Both the sensitivity that allowed her to read his thoughts, feel his emotions, and even absorb some of those energies, and also the direct ferocity in her restless nature, the courage and willingness to fight.

"I know that," he replied calmly. "That's why I came to you, after all."

"I thought you came to me with the intention of throttling me for supposedly breaking my word to you." She said it with the same tone of challenge, but a hint of mischief lurked in her composed expression.

"A good warrior is ready for all eventualities—back up plans are key."

"A salient point, as we need one for the council session, in case things go awry."

"Sound reasoning. Are the three of us the only ones who know about the grien in you?"

Looking thoughtful, she scratched her Familiar's breast, who seemed to be for all the world, smiling at him. A strange sight on a lizard's face. "Chuffta will never tell. But there's also my mother."

"Who loves you and would never put you in jeopardy, even if she's upset about this marriage."

"Hopefully, unless she gets it in her head that she's helping somehow, in her fugue state. She's not the greatest danger, however." Oria grimaced apologetically. "Yar might guess."

~ 12 ~

"YAR?"

Lonen knew he must be gaping at her, but ... "Yar? As in your brother who's battling you for the throne and can be expected to use any and all weapons against you to win—that Yar?"

"It's not like there are others," she bit out and stood, picking up her mask.

He held out a hand for it and she sighed, coming to sit beside him, giving it to him. He studied the pattern of the braids, looking for places to weave the ribbons back in. Maybe he could learn to do the braids also, if she insisted on keeping them, so he could take her hair down as often as he liked, then help her get ready for public appearances, too.

"As zealously as you guard this secret," he said, "I'm assuming you did not confide in him."

"No. Not at all. In fact—I didn't know I had grien magic until a confrontation with him."

"A confrontation?" He kept his voice neutral, focusing on making the ribbons tight enough to hold the mask on, but not make her uncomfortable. She must have washed her hair, too, while he was working off his mad, because she smelled of a different flower now. And he should have killed that officious twerp when he had the chance.

"Don't think I can't detect those thoughts beneath that pretty mountain lake and musing about my hair. It's honeysuckle and, yes, Yar and I had a fight and I attacked him with my grien magic. He ran away. It's over. I defended myself and won, so you can forget about those revenge fantasies you're brewing."

"The lakes of Dru are very beautiful, lovely to swim in during the hot summer months. I'll take you to my favorite." His favorite that still existed, as the first two were nothing but holes in the ground, but he wouldn't burden her with that guilt as well.

"I don't know how to swim." She sounded bemused.

The ribbons took a lot longer to weave in than to undo. "You don't?"

"I've never seen enough water in one place to be able to swim in it. The baths are as deep as it gets around here."

"What about the bay?"

She shook her head minutely, so as not to disturb his work. "Outside the city walls, remember?"

"So what's up with that aspect—what does it do to you to go outside them?"

"You saw." She made a disgusted sound. "I don't know how it works, but somehow the city walls shield the priestesses. They allow us to focus on the sgath beneath Bára, to absorb what's described as a concentrated, clean magic, rather than the chaotic variety in the outer world. Outside, we kind of overload."

"Just as you do with skin-to-skin contact with someone who's not shielded with *hwil*."

"You do pay attention."

"And here you say I don't listen. So I'm also thinking this is why the priestesses were on the walls for the battle—because they can't go past them."

"That and the source of magic is below Bára and we can't go far from it."

"You said sgath comes from Sgatha."

"It does, but via her communion with the earth. Bára sits on a special place—as do our sister cities—where the sgath filters through the rocks and soil, becoming harmonized in a way, so that we can take it in without damage. We have to learn to do that judiciously, so we don't overload."

"Thus your high lonely tower."

"Thus my high, peaceful, and quiet tower, yes."

He let that go. "But you can't use this chaotic magic in the greater world that you mentioned?" Two ribbons down, one more to go. The intricate task helped him order his thoughts and questions.

"I think it's like trying to light a candle with a lightning bolt. But nobody tries, that I know of, because we can't leave the sgath provided by our cities."

"What happens if you do?"

"What happens to a plant without water?"

A too apt analogy, sitting in her dying garden. She hadn't been exaggerating about the impact of her trying to go to Dru. Ah well, that road lay over the next rise.

"So, Yar might guess and would surely use this knowledge to undermine your bid for the throne, but he's not here. Do you think he told anyone?"

"I don't think so—it would be to his advantage to keep the knowledge to himself. Also, I can't see the temple not acting on it if he told anyone there, and I'm clearly not dead. But I do think that's part of his hurry to find a bride. With an ideal partner, he'd have more than enough power to handle me. Failing that, he might try to expose me if I'm not crowned before he returns."

"Why not expose you after that point—get the temple to execute you and take the crown once you're gone?"

"The queen—or king—trumps the temple. They would not be able to act against me."

"All the more reason to succeed this afternoon then. There. All tightly masked again."

"Thank you." She adjusted to face him, but didn't move as far away as she might have once. "I know the mask repels you, so I appreciate your helping me with it."

Slowly, so she'd have time to stop him, he raised his hand and ran a fingertip along the cheekbone of the metallic face, just as he'd longed to do with her. "There's one advantage. At least I can touch this."

"You're obsessed with touching me," she said, but without her usual exasperation.

The metal was strangely cool, not as hot from the sun as he might have imagined. "I'm a man of the physical. Maybe I need to feel things to believe in them."

"Maybe I'm not real." A bit of whimsy from her, but also hints of darker pain beneath.

"Sometimes I wonder." Sometimes all of it seemed like a dream, that he might be still standing on that wall, blood dripping from his hands, while he glimpsed her, a vision from fantasy, candlelit in a window. He tapped the mask. "But this feels like it."

"And it allows me to fake *hwil*," she replied, all seriousness. "That's what you need to know if you're going to help me. If I lose that façade in the council session—and it's entirely possible because I'm already bursting with sgath and I can't vent to grien—then I'll lose all chance at being queen."

"So, you'd faint again?"

"Possibly. Or worse."

She meant exposing herself as a wielder of grien. "Maybe we should wait. Let you rest another day or two."

She wrung her hands together. "We can't afford the time. Yar could return at any moment."

"I don't like risking your health."

"That's not important."

"It is to me. It should be to you."

She waved that off, though Chuffta rustled his wings in a way that made him think the Familiar agreed. "I've survived similar crises so far. But I mean that the real worst case scenario is that I could accidentally use grien like I did with Yar," she said, confirming his speculation.

"Then you'd be forced to lay about with that battle axe of yours and that can't end well."

He smiled grimly for her little joke, but didn't let it distract him. "Then why not get rid of some on purpose now, before we go? Vent it like you say. Bleed off the energy."

She stood, scrubbing her hands together. "Because I'm afraid of hitting myself in the noggin with my own sword," she admitted ruefully. "Women aren't taught to control grien, only sgath. I have no idea what I'm doing. I've only ever used it impulsively, out of emotion, not *hwil*."

"You used it on me." The realization dawned on him. "You nearly made me come right there and then when you used it on my cock."

"Lonen!"

"Hey sorceress—you're the one who did it. I'm just talking about it."

"Is there nothing you won't give voice to?"

He pretended to think about it, then grinned at her. "No."

"Well, I shouldn't have done that." She gestured wildly, crimson rippling in the breeze of her pacing. "It was irresponsible and impulsive and wrong. That's why it's really bad that I don't have real *hwil*. I could have hurt you."

"Felt amazing, in truth. Feel free to yank that particular chain any time you get the urge."

She stomped her foot, a gesture he was beginning to love. "This is a serious conversation."

"I'm always serious."

She paused her pacing, mask swinging to him in a posture of utter astonishment. "Liar," she said softly, exactly as he'd said it before.

He held up his palms in surrender, laughing. "Guilty."

"How can you laugh at a time like this?"

"It feels good to laugh. A kind of tension release, don't you think?" She didn't answer, simply tapped her foot, so he forged on. "In all seriousness, you have too much sgath and that pushes you to overload. Chuffta helps manage that, doesn't he?"

She considered him. "He does, yes—kind of like a buffer, but it only goes so far. Transforming the sgath to grien and releasing it, that feels best."

"So manly things would work to release it, huh? A good physical workout always helps me."

"I noticed," she replied in a dry tone.

"Did you—were you watching me earlier?" The thought pleased him immeasurably.

"I could hardly help it," she sniffed, but she resumed pacing.

"Did you like what you saw?"

"I saw you naked before," she pointed out. "In the baths."

"Doesn't answer the question."

"This is a pointless direction. It won't help me figure out a way to vent."

"I don't know." He stretched out his arms on the seat back. "A good orgasm always works for me that way. Very relaxing."

She actually clapped her hands over her ears. "I'm not hearing this."

"Yes, well—it's not a good solution anyway, since you won't pleasure yourself and I haven't completely determined how to give you a climax without touching you. I have ideas, but there's not enough time to implement them."

"Oh, I'm sorry—were you talking? I couldn't hear you."

She was wound up all right. Judging by the angle of the sun, they needed to begin the long descent from her tower soon, too. He mulled the problem.

How would he help the young warrior of his analogy?

ORIA SIMMERED MOLTEN as glass in a forge, running through with hot colors. At least Lonen wasn't deliberately provoking her any longer—not energetically anyway—which she had to admit was an excellent reason to have let him in on some of her weaknesses. She still felt unsettlingly exposed to have the Destrye know so much about her, but that vow he'd made her…

It had the force of magic, something she couldn't make sense of.

Especially with so much else on her mind.

"I have an idea." Lonen stood and came towards her, looking far too potent via sgath. In many ways, it was easier to look on him with her physical eyes. She perceived less of the coiling energies around him that so distracted her. She held up hands to fend him off and he darkened with displeasure. "Relax, I'm not going to do anything to you. I'll save that for tonight," he added, sensual energy snaking towards in that way that went right through her every time.

"There might be the coronation ceremony tonight," she reminded him, pointedly stepping back. "In fact, we'd better be hoping there is."

His naughty good humor faded. "What does that entail?"

"I don't know—I've never seen one."

"Will it be like the wedding ceremony, impacting you as badly?"

"Or worse. I really don't know, but we should be prepared for that eventuality."

He crackled with lashing impatience. "How can you not know these things?"

"The temple isn't exactly forthcoming with its secrets. And that's part of the test—if you know what's coming, a person can prepare for it."

"Seems being better prepared would ensure fewer failures."

She held up her palms, acknowledging the point. "Arguably, if we fail the temple's tests, then we can't be trusted with the power of the temple's secrets. If I can't survive the coronation ceremony, then I don't deserve to be queen."

He gazed at her a long moment. "And you call us a brutal people."

"There's all kinds of brutality in the world," she informed him softly.

"True." He shook it off, surveying her with the intent perspective of a warrior. Funny how he shifted so clearly to her sgath vision, from lover to king to fighter. "I've got an idea. Let's get at it this way. You had three brothers, all grien users. I know you spent a lot of time in your tower, but I also know what sisters are like. Surely you hung around them some, listening to them talk. Boys like to screw around with what they can do—did you ever watch them play fireballs versus earthquakes or anything like that?"

She nearly laughed at his phrasing, but...

"Yes!" A kaleidoscope of memories crashed through her. So many times that Ben, Nat, and Yar had argued over meals, boasting of their new tricks and challenging each other. She'd hated those conversations because of how left out she'd felt. Particularly after Ben, who'd been the last of her brothers to take the mask and thus her partner in being the slow student, had joined their ranks. But she'd also listened with the sick envy of someone who believed she'd never be as good as they were.

And Nat, back when she was younger, he'd entertained her by juggling fireballs. He'd spent weeks working up the trick—which meant a fair number of fireballs had gone astray. Then there was the time Yar widened a chasm to trip up Ben and nearly got them both killed. Father had been furious.

"Yes, they played games all right, but..." She hissed a little between her teeth, thinking about it. "I'm afraid I'll break something."

"That's the female in you talking."

"What?" Infuriated, she clenched her fists, wanting nothing more than to smash one into his easy, taunting mien.

"I'll let you in on a male secret, Oria. Boys, particularly younger ones who've just figured out that they have strength they didn't have before, don't think about what they might break. They just mess around and forget about consequences. This is not always a good thing," he added, "which is why they need to be kept occupied and on a short leash by people who *are* aware of the consequences, but in this case I think the stakes are high enough that you should forget about breaking something."

"Young male derkesthai are the same. When they first come into their flames, no nest is safe."

She shook her head at Chuffta and relayed the words to Lonen.

He tossed a little salute to her Familiar. The interactive energy between them had changed, overlapping in interesting ways. Ones that she'd have to study later, at her leisure. Should that day ever come.

"Okay then," Lonen said. "So just let it go. Swing that sword and stop fretting."

"I'm not fretting."

"If you were a guy, I'd call you chicken. But I don't want to hurt your tender female feelings."

"Don't you taunt me, Destrye."

He pursed his lips and blew her a little kiss, a potent spark with it. "Chicken," he called.

It would serve him right if she let loose on him, but she still had little idea what affinity her grien would take, other than a kind of green fire, sometimes knocking things over, or stirring up dust devils. Still—female fretting or not—it seemed unwise to simply unleash all that sgath she'd built up into just any random manifestation of grien magic.

It would really help if she knew more about grien.

But there was something—a passing remark from one of her teachers who'd sought to reassure her about taking so long to master *hwil* and find her sgath. The priestess had said grien magic was easier to learn because it burgeoned in young men as part of their youthful vitality, pushing up like the sap in the trees in springtime. They had to practice restraint, focus, and release, while women's magic worked in the reverse. Instead of exploding outward, sgath drew in and received.

She had no time just then to learn restraint, focus, and release—

but she knew something about trees and the sap rising in them. Looking around at her dying garden, it seemed she could hardly do more damage to it than withholding water had done.

"Okay, gentlemen, both of you get behind me. This could get messy."

Lonen didn't argue for once, moving quickly behind her with an aura of excited anticipation. Chuffta took wing, landing on the stone balustrade.

"Want me to be on you, instead?"

"No. I don't want to risk catching you in the backlash."

"This is fun."

"It's not fun, it's necessary."

"It can be both."

"This is going to be great," Lonen said.

Men.

"You know you love us."

Chuffta's smug reply tugged her in a funny way, but she screened that out, concentrating on her task. Using what little *hwil* that came to her easily, letting go of worry about her inadequate control—fretting, indeed!—she focused her mind on the trees in her garden, their crisping leaves and bare branches, the wilted blossoms and the husks of others littering the stones around them. It hurt her heart to see them die.

So she released sap. Sending it to them in a rush of sorrowful love for all the shade they'd given her, the flowers that scented her nights and the fruits that graced her mornings. The grien left her in powerful gush, a blessed release from pressure, one that ached with pleasurable pain, much like voiding a much-too-full bladder.

Naked branches tossed in a wind he couldn't feel, brown leaves and dried petals spiraling in tornadic frenzy, skittering up into the brilliant blue sky. A groaning, creaking sound muttered over the terrace. With a series of sharp booms, the stone planters burst, one after another, exploding rock shrapnel everywhere.

Behind her, Lonen laughed like a crazy man, exultant and wild, his excited energy shoring her up, like the sun at her back, Chuffta's steady presence in her mind a cool white counterpoint. Roots burst out of the planters, twining, lashing for purchase. The trunks thickened, writhing as they did, then shooting up, branches proliferating and leaves bursting into green vivid life. Blossoms followed, an induced spring racing faster than Grienon through the sky, followed by full summer, fruits burgeoning, weighing the branches even as they continued to thicken.

At this rate, they'd collapse. Or tear down her tower and them with it.

"It's too much!" she shrieked, suddenly panicked, which only made a shower of vines burst into radiant blossom.

"Then pull it back in. You know how." Chuffta's calm and rational mind-voice steadied her.

At the same time, something pinged against her mask. Lonen, tapping her metal cheek. "Enough, Oria," he said with implacable firmness. "Knock it back." His presence stabilized her, too, with his granite bedrock beneath the sunshine of his vivid personality.

Like releasing a handful of petals to the wind, she let go, the sgath and grien that had somehow combined into one power condensing, drawing back, and settling like a gentle rain.

Lonen kissed his fingertips and pressed them to the mask, just over her mouth, his aura bright with emotions, both extravagant and affectionate.

"You're a hell of a woman, Oria. And you're going to be a sorceress beyond imagining. Now let's go make you queen."

~ 13 ~

IT WASN'T HOW she'd expected to face the council, to demand to be ratified as Queen of Bára with a Destrye warrior at her side and her hands tingling from unleashing grien magic that still rattled the leaves of her garden.

Of course, she wasn't at all sure what she *had* envisioned, except that her mother was supposed to have handled this, as it was her plan and she was the former queen. She was supposed to have mastered the skill of envisioning a result so that it would manifest as she chose. Oria hadn't indulged herself with many expectations, as they'd inevitably led to disappointment. Time enough to learn all of that, she'd thought, if she ever mastered *hwil*. She'd never imagined things would happen so fast, one upon the next.

Or that her personal scale of sorrows and successes would alter quite so dramatically.

The nine-person council—composed of two priests, two priestesses, four folcwitas, who managed all nonmagical aspects of running Bára, headed by Folcwita Lapo, and High Priestess Febe—all seemed to frown at her as one. Captain Ercole, representing the City Guard, stood to the side as a non-voting consultant only. Though as Oria understood it, the council didn't exactly vote so much as attempt to persuade the titular heads of the body, those being the senior folcwita and high priest or priestess, to then advise the king or queen. With the current balance, it seemed that Febe had placed herself in the role of royal by adding an extra temple representative.

"Princess Oria," Folcwita Lapo puffed with the suspicion of an embattled man, "this is most irregular. Why are you here, bringing that Destrye—"

"King Lonen," she corrected in a cool, cutting tone.

"Not my king," he snapped back.

"Your king, yes, and your conqueror. Or have you forgotten so soon?" Lonen's voice rumbled at his most intimidating. Even his energy seemed larger, filling the room. Did he do it consciously? Probably not. Or maybe he did, having learned rapidly from her. Regardless, he affected them all, magically gifted and not.

Folcwita Lapo rose and steepled his hands on the semi-circular stone table, inclining his head at Lonen. "The council apologizes for the misunderstanding, King of the Destrye, but the treaty you believed valid is not. As Bára has no one on the throne at present, we are not in a position to pass binding law on anything." Yellow frustration oozed from him in light wisps.

"Your laws are irrelevant to me," Lonen replied, "except as my wife and I determine to uphold them."

Lapo glanced at Febe, puzzled. "His wife?"

"Behold your new queen," Lonen overrode any other reply. "Queen Oria of Bára."

Lapo laughed, while Febe continued to be silent, her sgath drawn tightly about her. The other priests and priestesses held physically still, impassive in their *hwil*, but the three junior folcwitas fell to whispering among themselves, one opening a tome of Báran law.

"The council has not ratified—"

"The council has no power to ratify anything without a royal on the throne of Bára," Oria cut in again. "You said as much yourself, Folcwita Lapo. I'm sure my father would express his gratitude to you, if he could, for holding this council and city together in this state of emergency. The burden has no doubt been great. However, I'm now ready to relieve you and High Priestess Febe of the mantle that should never have fallen upon you so heavily. I'm here to rule

Bára as queen, as I was born to do and as my power and marriage entitles me to. Of course, I hope to retain all of you, for your good counsel for the benefit of all Bárans—less one priestess, naturally. It appears some imbalance has been introduced."

"Princess Oria," Febe said, not standing or moving at all, a statue of a priestess. "We all understand the strain that—"

"Queen or Your Highness," Oria stated. "You will address me properly."

Folcwita Lapo looked between them, then bent to speak into the ear of the folcwita with the law book.

"You are not queen until the temple crowns you as such." Febe's voice oozed with warning.

Oria waved a negligent hand. "Exactly. Which is why we are here. Truly I didn't expect you all to be so obtuse. My father, King Tavlor, always spoke so highly of this council's wisdom."

"The temple cannot seal the throne to—"

Folcwita Lapo held up a hand, tapping the law book. "No disrespect, High Priestess, but the law is very specific. In the absence of any of the royal family on the throne, when the first masked progeny of the previous ruler is married and presents themselves to the council, the temple is required to crown them as ruler of Bára. If Prin—Queen Oria has indeed been married by the temple, then all is in order."

"It's not an ideal marriage," Febe gritted out. "Not temple-blessed. He's a Destrye!"

"Were His Highness King Lonen and Her Highness Queen Oria duly married by the temple?" inquired the folcwita with the book, seemingly unaware that he pedantically repeated information already on the table.

"Yes," Febe conceded with ill grace, "by Priest Vico and myself, yesterevening, but they are obviously not an ideal match. His Highness is mind-dead. Her magic will go nowhere, possibly even turn back on itself."

Folcwita Lapo stewed with excitement. Febe had been injudicious, perhaps, in trying to overbalance the council in the temple's favor. It seemed she might have an unexpected ally in this. "Magic is the province of the temple," he said, bowing in Febe's direction. "As the keepers of Báran law, we note that the law books do not specify the magical quality of the marriage, only that there be one. Captain Ercole—what does the City Guard advise?"

"The guard stands with the law and the royal family," Captain Ercole replied, a solid, steady presence. "We support Queen Oria, naturally, as we supported her father and mother before her. The people will rejoice to have order restored after so long, and so much out of balance."

"Queen Oria." Febe kept her voice even, but her *hwil* cracked here and there. "Surely Your Highness does not wish to be Queen of Bára when your destiny lies with your new husband in Dru. We understand His Highness wishes to leave immediately for his homeland. We would not wish to delay you, King Lonen."

"I've changed my mind." Lonen sounded almost lazy, brushing a hand over Oria's braids, making one of the priestesses come alert with surprise beneath her *hwil*. In his determination to make a powerful show, he forgot to restrain himself and burned brightly with lust. But either she was becoming accustomed to his energy infiltrating hers, or because she'd burned off enough sgath, she absorbed it with relative ease. Even Folcwita Lapo's brash presence, which had buffeted her severely in the past, seemed little more than an uncomfortably hot breeze.

"I've come to like Bára," Lonen continued. "After all, it is mine, along with everything—and everyone—in it. Why not take my leisure to enjoy all my city has to offer?"

"You cannot be King of Bára, Your Highness," Febe said with considerable strain. "Only someone who's taken the mask can rule our city, by sacred law. You can only be the queen's consort."

The folcwita with the law book nodded, glancing up with an apologetic mien. Their excitement still hummed with bright hope, though Folcwita Lapo bowed to Lonen, showing his concern. "No dishonor to Your Highness, King Lonen."

"I am not concerned with such details," Lonen replied, attention on Oria and the braid he fingered. It was for show this time, however, not sending those waves of potent lust into her. Thankfully. "I have my kingdom, and yours. Oria can be Queen of Bára and I shall rule her. All the same in the end."

Insufferable oaf. He'd better have said that for show or they'd have words about it.

Febe rose slowly to her feet now. "Queen Oria, I beg of you. Bára begs you. You may not realize it, but your honored brother Prince Yar seeks an ideal bride. He'll return to Bára at any moment with her and they can rule as Sgatha and Grienon intend, as an ideal partnership, in a temple-blessed marriage. Bára needs this. You know it in your heart. Don't allow the Destrye this final victory over us. Our throne, the very bedrock of our lives, will be forever tainted."

Oria very nearly felt bad for the older woman. She truly believed in what she said, and had served Bára and the temple all her life. But she'd also been in favor of calling in the Trom, risking disaster with her remorseless drive to preserve those beliefs at all costs.

In the end life was more precious than any belief.

"Yes. You've grown wise, Oria."

"I try. Soon I'll be lecturing you."

Chuffta laughed, sending affection through her.

"Yar is not here and I am," she answered, speaking to them all. "For all we know he may not return with an ideal bride, who would still be foreign to Bára regardless. He might not return at all, as so many have not. My father would expect me to shoulder my ancient responsibility. My mother does expect it."

"The former queen is not here to support your claim," Febe protested. "You put words in her mouth."

"Are you calling me a liar, High Priestess?" Oria held onto her grien, but allowed her sgath to slide up against Febe's. "As your queen, I take exception to your tone. Perhaps the temple is in need of new leadership."

"You can't do that." The woman's *hwil* cracked a bit more, enough so one of the priests took note, moving in his chair. "You are not queen until I crown you."

"Then you had best crown me, or I'll put someone in charge who will."

Febe looked to Folcwita Lapo who radiated smug satisfaction at this point. He held up his palms. "Temple business falls to the temple and the royal family, as has been pointed out to the folcwitas many times. We keep secular law and all is in order. The folcwitas, the city guard, and—I feel confident in presuming to say—the people of Bára acknowledge Rhianna and Tavlor's daughter as queen. I see no reason for the temple to delay the final ritual."

Stiff necked, Febe inclined her head to Oria. "Very well. Though, as High Priestess, keeper of the sacred magics of Bára, I express grave reservations. Mark my words. This will be the day our revered city truly falls to the Destrye. You all seal our doom."

~ 14 ~

ONCE AGAIN, LONEN followed Oria through the palace halls to the temple. The Bárans, with their convoluted, even circular, laws and elaborate posturing sure came up short on preparations for rituals. No pomp and ceremony for this coronation.

Though he supposed he and Oria had that in common, as he'd taken his own father's wreath and sword on the battlefield. They'd never celebrated his ascent to the throne either, with so much work to do back in Dru. In truth, celebrating had been the last thing on his mind.

Still, hopefully that would change. He and Oria would not have to forever labor under the sawing need to address one crisis after the next. One day they would be in a better place, with their peoples fed and stable. With the gifts Oria had demonstrated on the rooftop, she could grow the crops the Destrye needed for several winters in the course of an afternoon. The impossible could be made possible indeed.

He eyed her slim, straight back as she preceded him, head held regally high. She'd looked incredible in the throes of working her magic. She'd nearly glowed with it, the force palpably sizzling against that internal part of him so sensitized to her. Other parts, too. He still throbbed with the arousal she'd incited. And from the vicious triumph that he'd not only found a way to save the Destrye from the Trom, but in the same victory acquired a sorceress to feed them and a wife for himself replete with magical beauty. Had he been able, he would have seized her in a crushing kiss, barely leashing himself to only press one to her mask.

If they didn't find a way for him to bury his cock in her, he might lose his mind. Oh right—he'd already done that. Perhaps madness occurred in stages, growing ever worse. Cheerful thought.

Oria canted her head slightly in his direction, giving him the distinct impression of reproof. If he didn't need to help her keep it together through whatever Arill-cursed trial her people intended, he would have shared some of those salacious images. As it was, he would come up with a reasonable plan to give her pleasure as it was his duty to Arill to provide his wife. For himself, he might be thrown back to bitter youth, taking himself in hand several times a day while fantasizing about the woman he couldn't touch.

Probably a deserved fate, though that didn't mean he wouldn't fight it with every trick he possessed. He'd gotten very good at fighting.

High Priestess Febe paused at the bridge to the temple, stone-stiff in every line of her body. "Only the masked may enter the temple," she intoned, in what he'd come to think of as her priestess voice. It always seemed to bode ill. "King Lonen, you must remain without."

"Not happening," he replied in a level tone and taking Oria's sleeve, keeping her from leaving him. "I entered the temple before."

"For your wedding. The unmasked may enter at five times in their lives, the wedding is one."

He was not letting Oria face this alone. He'd much prefer, in fact, if Oria had appointed a new temple head to perform the coronation ceremony. It seemed to be a foolish risk to have this woman, who so clearly resented and feared the prospect of Oria as queen, to have any power over her. She knew Oria's particular fragility and how to capitalize on it. What would stop her from gaming the ritual against Oria? From Oria's shoulder, Chuffta's eyes gleamed green and knowing. Could her Familiar read his thoughts, too? Regardless, it seemed they understood one another.

"What are the other occasions?" he inquired of the high priestess.

"The temple secrets are not yours to—"

"These are not temple secrets, High Priestess," Oria cut the woman off with that regal poise she'd put on as easily as she'd donned her mask. "This is something any Báran child knows. I apologize for our priestess, Your Highness. She is clearly overwrought and forgetting herself. The occasions are five, as on the fingers of a hand. The temple receives any and all at birth, byrebod, monahalgian, marriage, and death. Those with magical ability also may enter certain areas for instruction."

"What are byrebod and monahalgian?"

"Apologies, Your Highness—they are old terms, with no trade tongue correlations. They mean essentially presentation as an adult and consecration to the moons, respectively."

"I'm pledged to Arill, so there will be no consecration to the moons for me. What's involved in the other?"

Febe's featureless mask, for all the world seemed to smirk at him. "For men, it involves a ritual where he proves his manhood by demonstrating his fortitude, and by sealing a covenant."

That didn't sound bad, but Oria murmured, "Monahalgian would be easier on you. Surely your goddess will not mind a small transgression."

"I am loyal to all of my women, wives and goddesses," he muttered back. "Presentation as an adult for me, then I remain for the coronation."

"This is most irregular," Febe protested. "Are we to become a people who follow only the letter of the law and not the spirit of it under your reign, Queen Oria?"

Oria didn't exactly flinch, but the accusation clearly hit home—something he felt in his own gut—so he spoke up before she could waver.

"As Bára is mine, so am I hers. It's fitting that I present myself to the temple as every boy of the city does upon reaching his manhood. I consider this a covenant with Bára, which should be sufficient spirit to satisfy anyone."

Oria moved ever so slightly closer to him, relaxing the tautness of the silk sleeve he gripped, conveying her appreciation with the subtle gesture. Crazy how happy it made him that he'd pleased her. Though making her happy meant better fortune for the Destrye. He'd just think of it that way.

"Your Highness." Priest Vico stepped up. "While I'm delighted to perform your byrebod, particularly given the reasons you state, you should be aware that, ah, blood must be drawn." He tilted the mask significantly. "To seal the covenant," he added, not at all elucidating. "As a, uh, man."

"All right," Lonen replied slowly. The Bárans seemed to love drawing blood for their little rituals. The priest seemed to be waiting still, and it dawned on him. "Draw the blood from where?"

"Your ... manhood," the priest answered in a much lowered voice, as if that added delicacy to it.

Lonen found himself gaping, then looked to Oria. "You went through this?"

"Women produce their own blood, don't they?" She said in a tart voice, clearly discomfited. "You needn't do this, Your Highness. Take your leisure and await me."

Barbarians, the lot of them. But Arill knew he'd shed plenty of blood. He'd just hoped never to be wounded there. Still, if the Báran boys could withstand it, a full Destrye warrior certainly could. Besides, he'd already made a pretty speech about it and couldn't very well back pedal on that. "We'll proceed as I outlined. Priest Vico will do my byrebod ceremony, followed by the coronation."

Priest Vico bowed. "As you will. Follow me, Your Highness."

"Queen Oria will come with me." The High Priestess turned to lead her away.

"No. The queen doesn't leave my sight," Lonen declared, letting himself growl over it, venting some of the aggravation over his impending ordeal. "She belongs to me and by my side she stays."

Priest Vico coughed and the high priestess went rigid. "Women do not attend a boy's byrebod," she declared.

"Or vice-versa," Vico added, not at all helpfully.

"I would assume that a boy has his byrebod well before he's married, yes?" At the priest's nod, Lonen continued. "A wife knows everything about her husband and her magic belongs to him, along with the succor of her body. Of course she would attend this important ceremony, should they occur in the reverse order."

"Most logical," Oria agreed.

Stymied, Febe bowed—stiffly, of course—and glided away. "I will await you in the ceremonial hall then, Your Highnesses."

Priest Vico gestured them to follow, but Lonen tugged Oria's sleeve so she'd hang back.

"They don't cut off any important bits, do they?" he whispered to her.

"I wouldn't know, would I?" she hissed back. "As I'm not a *boy*."

"I can't believe your brothers wouldn't have hinted."

"Unlike you," she replied in a prim tone, lifting her chin, "they did not discuss their male parts with all and sundry."

"I don't discuss my cock with all and sundry—just with you, especially as you're so interested in it."

Her gasp of outrage took the edge off his nerves—and hers, he hoped—Chuffta's eyes glittering at him with what had to be amusement. The priest led him into a small chapel room, similar to the one they'd been married in the evening before. This one, however, looked entirely dedicated to Grienon, with representations of the small, dynamic moon in all his phases.

Priest Vico cleared his throat. "Normally, Your Highness, a boy is accompanied by his father, who has explained the ritual in advance. Or, failing that, another male relative."

"Just tell me what to do, man," Lonen answered. "Let's get it over with so we can move on."

"All right." He cleared his throat again. "Perhaps Queen Oria might wish to turn away and cover her ears?"

"Oh, for Sgatha's sake," she snapped, "I can muffle my eyes and ears and sgath will still show me—" She broke off abruptly, her mask swiveling to the sky beyond the stone temple ceiling. "No," she whispered, putting a hand to Chuffta's tail wrapped around her wrist.

"What?" Lonen asked. Then grabbed her sleeve when she only shook her head. "What is it?"

A sound broke through his words. He knew that sound, like the dull roar of a bonfire. The giant fire-breathing draconic cousins to the derkesthai, mounts of the Trom.

"Too late," Oria said, her voice hard, echoing against the metal mask.

He wasn't sure if she meant for him, or for them all.

~ 15 ~

"MAYBE THAT'S A riderless dragon roaring. Or could it be Yar returning?" Lonen asked her, unstrapping the battle axe from his back.

"I don't think it's either." She didn't sense Yar anywhere near the city. But that densely powerful black sun her sgath revealed was familiar. She hadn't been skilled enough before to get so much detail about their magical signature, but she recognized them just the same. "Yar may be behind this, however. They have not returned since you left, but I think the Trom are here now."

"They are here, yes." Chuffta's mind voice shivered with trepidation. Very little frightened the derkesthai, but his larger cousins certainly seemed to.

"The High Priestess," Priest Vico said, fear leaking through the *hwil*. "Febe would have summoned them, rather than give you the crown."

Oria stared at him in stunned surprise. "She is the summoner?"

His mask bobbed. "She and Yar both, as priest and priestess. I, myself, do not possess enough grien for the task She worked with him to do it."

"You could have warned me." Anger burned in her. Along with the terror. The feeling of that thing touching her. Those matte black eyes staring into her heart and finding a mirroring darkness. *Princess Ponen.*

"I wanted to, but we were sworn to tell only the king or queen. Since you're effectively queen now…" he trailed off, voice weakening.

Wonderful. Oria spun to the doors, hissing when Lonen brushed the skin of her hand before he clamped his own on her forearm over her sleeve. "Sorry for that. Clumsy of me, but you're not racing out there."

She struggled back the near overwhelming surge of his emotional energy that the brief touch sent rocketing through her nervous system. An intense stew of terror, love, battle rage, despair, determination, hope, and more than she could sort even with the luxury of hours, not moments.

"What choice do I have?" She tried to pull away, but he held on, his touch burning through the layers of silk. "You're hurting me."

He let go, but moved his big body between her and the doorway. "I'm not letting you confront those creatures."

"You know what they'll do! You've seen it with your own eyes. I can't let them kill my people just to get to me." All those piles of lifeless flesh… she couldn't bear for it to happen again.

"How do you know they won't kill you too?" Lonen shimmered large in her sgath, full of furious frustration.

"They won't. Or can't. You saw that too. I'm something to them. I don't know what, but they won't kill me. I have to confront them."

He seethed with conflict, the image slamming into her of him picking her up and carrying her off to some safe bower. "If you're going, I go with you."

"Lonen—they *can* kill *you*. Don't make me stand by while you're turned nothing but boneless heap before my eyes."

"I won't attack. They don't kill if we show no aggression."

"You can't be sure of that."

"Just as you can't be sure that they won't kill you this time."

Stymied, she fumed at him. "Please stay here. I'm asking this of you."

"No. I said that you don't leave my side and I meant it." He touched her masked cheek and managed a lopsided smile. "At least this keeps the priest's knife away from my jewels a little longer."

She shook her head, amazed he'd made her laugh under such dire circumstances. "I can't believe you were going to let him do that in the first place."

"Nothing gets between me and a goal. I told you that."

Yes, he had. And what Lonen said, he meant—and made happen. She could use that.

"Then remember this," she said, leaning as close to him as she dared, keeping his full attention. "You've said over and over that you're going to find a way to bed me."

Desire rode high in his gamut of emotional energy, though he responded evenly enough. "What are you getting at?"

"You'd better keep that in mind, because that's a goal and if you let the Trom kill you, it'll never happen. Think on that."

His stunned and grudgingly admiring amusement did a great deal to take the edge off her nerves. She began to understand why he enjoyed teasing her. He kept himself in front of her as she walked, a pace ahead with his signature big, bold strides as they hurried out the front doors of the temple. He carried his battle-axe two-handed, a black hole of a barrier before her.

"Leave the axe behind," she urged.

He didn't hitch even momentarily, but his incredulity swamped her. "Not even if Arill Herself asked me."

She had to run to do it—Chuffta half spreading his wings to keep balance on her shoulder—but she managed to draw level with him, grabbing onto his leather-clad arm, glad of his thicker Destrye clothes that buffered some of the impact from her impetuous move. He glanced down at her in some surprise, all of him softening, and he slowed somewhat. "Don't fret. I learned my lesson, too. As long as I'm not aggressive towards it, I should be fine."

"Last time you insisted that *I* put down *my* sword!"

"Because you could hardly lift the cursed thing," he retorted grimly. "I don't know what in Arill you were thinking. If we survive all this, I'm going to teach you to use a weapon your own size."

"I don't need a weapon. I'm a sorceress. Magic is all I need."

"Then this would be an excellent time to use it." He came to a halt, swiftly sheathing his axe on his back. Not one, but three Trom stood at the bridge to the temple. The sight of them turned her stomach, their magic like Chuffta's, but as much greater in intensity as the dragons were to him in size, nearly blinding her sgath with the radiance of it.

She'd been too mind-blind to see it before, their charismatic immensity. To the physical eye, they looked like desiccated husks of humans, skin as dry as old leaves stretched over bones, like corpses left to dry in the desert. As if to make up for all they lacked in robust humanity, concentrated magic filled them out on the non-physical plane. It extended inward also, each of them seeming to carry a black star of contained power and paradoxically infinite magic.

It made them hard to look at, the way their magic moved both out and in, as if they existed in multiple places at once, giving her a vague sense of nausea and dislocation.

"I did not see it before, either, but I do through you now. Most ... disconcerting."

"What does it mean?"

"Nothing good."

"Steady, Oria," Lonen said as she swayed on her feet, briefly cupping the back of her head over her braids. A fleeting touch that nevertheless heartened her. "I'm taking cues from you now."

Of course he handed her the decision-making power when she had no idea what to do. The Trom saved her from deciding, however.

"Queen Ponen," the one in front greeted her with its mouthless voice that emanated from its entire being. "It gladdens us to see you've taken not one, but several steps farther down your path."

She hated to contemplate what that might mean. "Bára greets you. We did not expect you to return."

The Trom couldn't smile, of course, and yet it seemed to. Much in the same way that expressions sometimes conveyed themselves from the masked priests and priestesses. She suppressed a shudder and Lonen shifted towards her, his desire to wrap her in his arms palpable. It helped, oddly enough.

"We come when summoned. Though it's true it was not your call we answered. Someday you will call to us and your understanding will deepen."

No doubt that day would come—had to, if she planned to wrest control of them from Yar and Febe—but she dreaded discovering what that deeper understanding boded for her. No sign of either of those summoners, cowards that they were, so she took the situation in hand. "None stands here who summoned you, so you may leave again."

They didn't move. "You do not yet command our obedience," the leader replied, just as it had when they met before. If it was, indeed, the same being. Difficult to discern.

Silence whistled through the chasm, a hot wind kicking up a swirl of sand on stone. Lonen's desperate curiosity to know what the Trom said reminded her that they spoke a language he didn't know but she somehow understood.

"Mind to mind," Chuffta said.

Ah, yes.

"We will see the one who summoned us, as required." The Trom spoke as if observing the weather, without inflection.

Much as she disliked Febe, Oria couldn't stomach watching her turned to pulp by the Trom, nor did she wish to hand power to the High Priestess in case the dread guardians would respond to her commands.

"The priest you seek is not within the city," she replied, willing the honesty of that to suffice to convince them to leave.

"But I am." Febe stepped before them, her sgath shivering with her temerity, her *hwil* strained. Both afraid and tremulously delighted with herself. "As Summoner, I invite you to enter the temple."

Lonen swore at that, able to understand those ritual words from the previous ceremonies, though he did not draw his axe, his hands clenching into fists and rage going black. "Stay behind me, Oria."

And watch him die? Never. She didn't move, staying right beside him as the three Trom crossed. "Summoner," the lead Trom greeted the high priestess. "What do you require of us?"

"Kill this one." Febe pointed at Oria.

~ 16 ~

EVERYTHING BLURRED INTO a high, colorless whine in his head. Even as Lonen reached for his axe determined to die protecting Oria if he had to, Chuffta spread his wings, breathing green fire that raised the already broiling temperature on the exposed bridge to unbearable levels. Oria's magic, too, as familiar on his skin now as her scent in his head, billowed up. Tornadic gusts spun into life, catching Chuffta's fire into swirls.

The Trom remained untouched by any of it, as if encased in one of Oria's transparent drinking glasses. The leader regarded Oria and Chuffta, then stepped closer without concern for the fire, unbuffeted by the wind and sand that scoured Lonen's exposed skin. Axe in hand, he moved to intercept the thing's lethal caress.

And found himself immobilized. By Oria's magic, Arill take her.

"Oria!" he shouted, fighting her grip that held him as surely as chains. "Release me, curse you."

She shouted an unintelligible reply, her voice harsh as a carrion bird's.

The Trom spoke, strange words he couldn't parse. But Chuffta stopped the defensive fire and Oria lowered her hands, seeming stunned. Whatever it said, Febe understood and clenched her fists in impotent rage.

"If you won't kill her, then kill him," she screeched over the howling wind.

"No!" To his terror, Oria imposed her slim form between his frozen one and the Trom.

"Defend him and die at their touch," Febe crowed her victory. "Lose him and join your broken mother as a widow who will never gain the crown."

Oria raised her hands. "I'll take option number three." As it had on the rooftop, her powerful grien magic surged, gaining that sharp edge, and struck the high priestess like a giant fist.

She staggered. "Impossible!" the woman nearly howled. "Abomination! You'll die for this. Kill her. Protect me and kill the foul grien user."

"Not me, not today," Oria said, quietly enough that he almost didn't hear it. Abruptly her magic released him as she drew it back, her braids snapping in the unfelt wind of it.

With a cry of despair, Febe fell, punched again by the fist, then scrabbled for purchase, fingers sliding on the sand as an invisible grip dragged her to the edge of the chasm.

"Mercy, I beg you!" she sobbed.

Then Febe plummeted over the edge, her long, wailing cry echoing back before attenuating into nothing.

Brutally reminded of his brother's death by the same unending fall, horror crawled through Lonen's heart. But he still had Oria to defend. She recklessly still stood between him and the Trom.

"The Summoner is dead," she declared, her voice reverberating with strange harmonies. "You may depart."

All three inclined their heads to her and the first spoke. They turned and walked over the bridge, disappearing back into the palace. Moments later, three dragons lifted into the sky and wheeled out of sight.

Suddenly realizing by the scream of his straining shoulders that he still held the axe mid-swing, Lonen lowered it, then spoke to Oria's back. "If you ever do anything like that again, I'll kill you myself."

ORIA, UNBELIEVABLY EXHAUSTED, could barely keep to her feet. Not in the overloaded, close to breaking sense, but in a different way, one she'd never experienced before. Her mask moved slickly over her sweating face and she longed to be rid of the thing—especially as her sgath showed the world only dimly, as if through a haze of smoke. Empty and aching, she turned to face Lonen.

"I could say the same back to you."

"It's not funny." He sounded weary, too.

"I didn't mean it as a joke. But it's irrelevant now. They're gone." *For now*, she didn't say, though the unspoken words hung in the air between them.

Lonen acknowledged that with a grunt. "Are you all right?"

"Yes." Though she wasn't sure of the truth of that. She felt... odd. But physically unharmed.

"What did they say to you—why didn't it kill you when Febe commanded it?"

"I—" She didn't want to give voice to it any more than she already had. That the Trom had told Febe they could no more kill her than one of their own. And it wasn't clear if they'd meant they actually couldn't or if they didn't want to. "I'll tell you about it later. We must go through with the coronation."

"You're clearly exhausted," he said in a neutral enough tone, though his concern and frustration with her snapped and snarled like two dogs fighting over the last piece of meat. "You have to rest and build up your reserves, or you might not survive whatever the ritual involves."

"We don't have time." It ticked away inside her, the imminence of Yar's return.

"That's not the most important consideration at this point," he insisted.

"You were the one who came to me for help." She would have snapped it, but she didn't have the energy. Really she wanted to sit. If she could just sit on the ground for a moment or two. Or lie down...

Lonen snapped fingers in front of her mask. "You're dead on your feet. Let's go back to your tower."

"I can't help you if I don't have control of the Trom, and I can't do that unless I'm queen. We're so close—let's just go in the temple and get it over with."

"Oria." Lonen spoke her name sternly enough to command her attention, if not her obedience. "Arill knows I was willing to let that priest near my cock with a knife so you could get that crown on your head, or whatever you Bárans do, but you won't be any good to Dru or Bára if you're dead. I am not letting you do this right now."

"You don't get to boss me around, Destrye."

"He has a good point, Oria—you're very tired and you have very little sgath in you."

"It's not fair," she complained to both of them, vaguely aware that she sounded pitiful and whiny. "Either I have too much energy in me or not enough. I'm sick to death of being fragile."

Lonen laughed. "Right—so damn fragile that you knocked that priestess into the chasm like a woman sweeping dirt off the porch."

She choked back the remorse. Febe had tried to kill her, but Oria had never thought she'd be capable of murder. Though once the priestess had realized the truth about Oria's grien magic... Well, there had been no choice.

"Come on." Lonen said more gently. "Let me be strong for you. I can carry you up, if you'll let me."

"It's too far," she protested. "Even you can't climb all those stairs carrying me."

"How do you think you got up there last night?" A few mischievous sparks made it through to her weakened sgath vision. "Besides, you weigh no more than a kitten."

"A kitten!" She sputtered, unable to come up with a retort.

"A drowned kitten." He leaned in, wrapping her in his bracing energy, for once only a comfort and not at all too much to bear. "All fur and spitting feistiness."

"You did *not* just call me feisty." She thought that had put up her back enough to rally, but she swayed on her feet.

"Better to retreat and rest to fight tomorrow, than to surely suffer defeat today."

"And if Yar arrives?"

She'd asked Chuffta, but Lonen replied. "Then we cut down that tree when we come to it. Let me carry you, Oria." He pulled his mantle off his shoulders, setting it around her, then strapped his axe again to his back. "That will be hot, but will protect you from my touch. Say yes."

"Fine," she replied, if only because she'd run out of energy to argue. Maybe even to stand, the way she swayed on her feet. "With the sun going down, I'm a little chilled anyway."

"Only a Báran could say such a thing. Chuffta, man, do a buddy a favor and either fly or ride on my shoulder."

"He says he'll fly so he won't score your flesh, but that if you get padding, he'd ride your shoulder in the future." She drew the cloak around her, making sure it covered her skin. "I'm ready."

She braced herself for the searing contact, but he slipped gentle arms familiarly beneath her shoulders and knees, easily lifting and tucking her against his muscled chest. With easy strides, he crossed the bridge and carried her through the palace.

Dreamily, she let her sgath vision go, closed her physical eyes, too, and simply absorbed the scent and feel of him. So familiar already. "This is so easy for you," she remarked.

"I'm getting quite a lot of practice," he replied in that wry tone of his.

She winced, opened her mouth to apologize, remembered she shouldn't, and sighed instead. "I wish I wasn't like this."

"I understand why you say that, but don't. Your blessing and your curse. Without this, you can't have the other—and your sorcery is fantastic to behold. I wouldn't change a thing about you." To her surprise, he pressed a kiss to her mask over her forehead, his energy swirling with a tenderness that disarmed her. "Well, maybe I'd change that stubborn temper of yours. And your reckless bravery."

"And the fact that you can't bed me," she reminded him.

"Oh, I'll find a way to bed you, Oria. Mark my words on that. You promised me if I survived the Trom, that would happen."

"I'm sure I never said such a thing." She yawned.

"That's how I heard it." He sounded insufferably pleased with himself.

"And you call me stubborn. You're worse."

"Oh yes, my lovely sorceress. More stubborn than you are by a far stretch, so you might as well give up and succumb to my manly charms."

They were just passing through the main doors of the palace, about to take the turn to her tower when he halted. Then cursed, using Arill's name.

"What?" She reached to see with sgath. Like lighting a too-short candle wick, it sputtered, then died, leaving her effectively blind. She reached for the magic below Bára, but it trickled in far too slowly to replenish her stores anytime soon. Much as she hated to acknowledge it, Lonen had been correct about not facing the coronation ceremony.

"Oria—there's an entourage at the bridge to Ing's Chasm. I think it's—"

"I think Yar has returned," Lonen spoke at the same time.

~ 17 ~

"PUT ME DOWN," Oria commanded. Because she sounded more like her imperious self and not the bone-weary waif of before, he acceded. But he kept a hand near the small of her back, in case she fainted.

"I'm not going to faint," she said irritably, making him smile.

"At least you're feeling spry enough to read my mind again. I've been thinking all sorts of things that you missed."

"Perhaps I chose not to sully my own mind by looking," she replied in that lofty, prim tone. If her odious brother hadn't been crossing the bridge to the palace, he'd have sent her an image to make her lose that composure. Chuffta winged in, angling through the open palace doors to accommodate his wide wingspan, sinuous neck snaked back in flight like the great fishing birds that frequented the lakes of Dru. Oria held up her left forearm and he landed there as neatly as any tamed raptor might.

The three of them waited in resigned silence, with increasing resignation, as it became clear that the young prince had indeed brought a priestess with him. The pair led a joyful procession up from the gates below, both in their golden masks, though hers was of a slightly different style, and she wore yellow silk robes instead of crimson. They walked arm in arm, sleeves drawn back and her forearm laid over his, their hands laced together. A posture even Lonen recognized as a blatant display of their compatibility. He'd never thought to experience a jagged bolt of envy for another man's fortune with a woman, but he hated that Yar and his future bride already enjoyed what remained a distant promise for him and Oria.

Unfair to them both, but Arill bestowed Her blessings according to wisdom known only to Her.

"Steady, Destrye," Oria murmured, her usual epithet sounding more like an endearment. Was she even aware of the shift? For a moment she leaned into his hand resting lightly on the cloak covering her. A gesture as potent as the most intimate caress.

Yar caught sight of them, hitched, then strode forward at an increased pace, his priestess fiancée losing some of her grace as she hustled not to be dragged along by the impetuous boy. "Oria," he called. "What is the meaning of this? Why is this bar—"

"Prince Yar," she cut him off, "allow me to present my husband, King Lonen of the Destrye."

All fell silent. Captain Ercole hastened up. "Forgive me, Queen Oria, I would have sent word, but you were in the temple."

"No apologies needed, Captain, I—"

"*Queen?*" Yar's voice rose perilously, the priestess still on his arm flinching away ever so slightly. She wore her very blond hair in two big plaits that wrapped up to form a sort of crown. "You cannot be queen—I am King of Bára now!"

"I married in Bára's temple first," she replied implacably. "I greet you, my future sister."

"Greetings, future sister, Queen Oria" the priestess inclined her head. "Thank you for—"

"Don't call her that," Yar strangled over the words. Lonen imagined the prince's face going red and purple with impotent rage. "It can't be a temple-blessed marriage. Not married to that barbarian, mind-dead Destrye."

"Yar!" Oria's tone was cutting. "You are being unforgivably rude to your brother, His Highness King Lonen."

"No insult taken," Lonen replied, giving them all the lazy smile—and attendant image—of the forest cat cleaning its claws. "I am at peace with being both mind-dead and Destrye, though it seems others than myself demonstrate barbaric behavior. Greetings, future sister. Are you gifted with a name?"

"I am Gallia of Lousá. Greetings Your Highness."

"My marriage trumps yours," Yar spoke over his bride-to-be with newfound confidence, earning a twitch of annoyance from Gallia. "Especially as you clearly have not yet been crowned. Sloppy of you, dear sister. Otherwise you might have won the race. I admit you've surprised me with this ... unorthodox move. But you've sacrificed your lifelong happiness along with any chance your progeny may have had to hold Bára for nothing. You married in the temple first, but High Priestess Febe will join us in a temple-blessed marriage for our ideal match."

"High Priestess Febe is dead, Prince Yar." Priest Vico stepped up with smooth manners, bowing as he delivered the news.

Yar paused, reassessing. "How is this possible?"

"The Trom killed her," Oria supplied, lying with admirable ease. "She summoned them and they killed her." She rubbed Chuffta between the eyes, appearing to be completely relaxed. Faking her *hwil* most likely. Then she lifted her mask to face Yar's. "At least we now know who the Summoner was, which means we shall not be disturbed by them again. I might rest easy, yielding the throne to you—perhaps even retiring with my husband to Dru—knowing that the Trom will never be called on, for any reason."

She layered meaning into her words, delivering both a promise and a subtle warning. No one there need know of Yar's culpability, if he agreed to suspend his attacks on the Destrye. Though Gallia remained still and apparently serene, Lonen thought she paid very close attention to the exchange. Yar covered his fiancée's hand with his, stroking her skin, clearly taunting Oria with the gesture.

"I don't need Febe. I have another priestess and her magic will be mine," he said with soft menace. "I shall call on whatever power I wish. For the good of Bára. Your loyalties are questionable, my sadly delicate sister. Perhaps your recent… difficulties have made you mentally unstable. There's precedent for that in the females of our family, as all have witnessed."

The folcwita from the council session who'd been the keeper of the law books cleared his throat. He spoke sofly to Priest Vico, who nodded with interest. "It seems," the priest said in a voice that carried through the hall, "that there is provision for equally qualified married couples to demonstrate their compatibility and abilities to the temple leadership, who then judge who will be crowned."

"Nonsense," Yar snarled, hand tightening on Gallia in a way that made Lonen twitch to stop him. "We will be king and queen. You'll marry us immediately."

"I will marry you now, yes, but tomorrow both couples will present themselves for my judgement. As is my sacred responsibility as High Priest of the temple of Bára."

"I'll replace you," Yar said.

"Only the king or queen can do that," Priest Vico replied implacably, "and neither you nor Princess Oria can claim that rank as yet."

"That solution is satisfactory to me," Oria inserted, sounding unconcerned, but the way she leaned into his supporting hand made her think she wearied. "King Lonen and I will meet you tomorrow. Congratulations on your wedding, to you both. I regret that we cannot attend the post-celebration."

"Prince Yar," Gallia spoke up. "As you know, the journey between cities strained me considerably. I'd prefer to—"

"What?" Yar cut her off. "You'd prefer to let my sister be crowned and leave you without the throne you left Lousá for? Your family and temple would be greatly displeased, especially to lose the many bride gifts I offered."

She inclined her head graciously. On Oria's arm, Chuffta ruffled his wings, the tip of his tail twitching where it dangled off her wrist, the only indication of her disquiet.

"Don't worry, my sweet." Yar gathered himself and stroked Gallia's hand, with a glee that was nevertheless avaricious. "It will require very little to demonstrate the superiority of our marriage. Look at them—she cannot even bear his touch skin-to-skin, much less give him any magic. We can win the throne, be crowned, and return to our wedding bed. I have heirs to beget."

"Of course," Gallia murmured.

"To the temple then," Priest Vico said, leading the way.

Oria wouldn't want to show weakness, so Lonen offered his sleeved arm to lean upon, glad that she took advantage of the support as he escorted her away from the less-than-joyful couple. Once her guard locked the doors to her tower behind them, she sagged and Chuffta took wing. Without asking, Lonen swept her up in his arms, and she sighed with relief, letting him carry her without protest.

~ 18 ~

SHE LIKED BEING in Lonen's arms, all safe and comfortable—which were not things she'd expected to ever feel with him. He ascended the stairs with tireless stamina, seeming as if he could carry her forever. Maybe he could.

"I never thought I'd feel sorry for an ideally matched couple," she finally said, after he'd climbed for some time. Without either her sgath or her physical sight, she couldn't be sure how far they'd come, but it felt like nearly halfway.

"I figured you for asleep."

"No—just thinking. All my life I wanted that, what Gallia has. It's what every girl dreams of. The perfect husband and an ideal marriage. All a lie."

"What Gallia has is a vicious idiot for a husband. I don't suppose you could have stopped it."

"Yar is young…" And she was running out of excuses for him. "But no. She would not have thanked me for intervening. Yar is correct that her family and temple would ostracize her for refusing an ideal match, especially one that will make her Queen of Bára. At least it seems as if she'll make a good queen, from the little I saw of her."

"You're so certain we'll lose tomorrow?"

"Of course we'll lose." He'd surprised her. Even in his eternal optimism, he had to recognize that they couldn't possibly triumph in a contest of that sort.

"Priest Vico favors you. If he can, he'll call it for you."

"*If* being the operative word. We'll likely have to demonstrate physical contact, as Yar and Gallia did so blatantly."

"Is that not usual?"

"Bárans are formal about physical contact in public, for obvious reasons. Yar's display wasn't quite obscene, but it was rude. Especially with a priestess new to our people. He did not accord her the respect he should have."

He made a mental note of that, to show Oria respect according to her customs, which were far more formal than those of the Destrye. "What else will the testing involve?"

"Almost certainly performing feats of magic. Meaning you would have to use grien, drawing on my sgath. Two impossible obstacles, right there—and don't take that as a challenge," she added emphatically, immediately regretting using that word at all.

"Too late." Lonen sounded far too cheerful. "You've set the stakes for me, my sorceress fair."

She groaned. "Lonen, we can't win this. We'll have to find another way to help the Destrye."

"Keep talking—every disclaimer makes me want to triumph that much more."

"Put me down. I can walk."

"Not so tired now?"

"I'm feeling more energized." Indeed, Lonen's bracing proximity refilled her empty spaces with surprising rapidity, her sgath vision returning with, if not its usual clarity, a very decent level considering she'd been cleaned out not long before.

"Excellent news," he said, not putting her down. "But save your strength. I have plans for it."

Her face went hot. "You can't be thinking that—"

To his credit, he waited for her to finish the sentence until it became clear she wouldn't. "Exactly."

"Lonen."

"Oria," he echoed in the same tone of exasperation.

She wouldn't reward his mischievous behavior by laughing.

"Look," he said. "Part of the deal tomorrow is demonstrating our compatibility and the solidity of our marriage, yes? How can we do that if *you* don't believe I can be a real husband to you?"

"I think I have very good reasons for my doubts," she said quietly, not wanting to dampen his spirits, but whatever he had in mind, he would come away disappointed.

"That's why I need to convince you." He pressed a kiss to her mask, as he had before, but pausing in his climb to let it linger. "Say you'll give me the chance to try."

"Will you encase me in metal then?" She meant to sound scathing, but it came out breathless. This close to him, the ardent energy of his desire flowed through her in inescapable waves.

"Something like that. Will you trust me?"

"I don't know."

He stopped entirely. "Yes or no. And before you answer, let me remind you of how much you've trusted me already. This is a small thing compared to your life."

"It doesn't feel like a small thing." Her heart thudded in dread. Or anticipation? So difficult to know.

"Are you afraid?"

"I'm not an idiot. Of course I'm afraid of that pain."

"Am I hurting you now?"

"Well, no, but—"

"I'm going to interrupt that 'but.' It will be pleasure only, Oria." He swarmed with earnest hope and desire, steely determination beneath. "Pleasure that Arill bestows upon us, so that people who love can share themselves intimately. Let me have that with you."

She couldn't resist him, and she suspected he knew it. "Fine." She blew out the capitulation on a long breath, and he resumed climbing with an increased, even jaunty stride. No telling what she'd just agreed to.

"I don't suppose Chuffta hunts at night?" he asked.

"I will give you privacy," her Familiar immediately chimed in. *"I will not be listening, so call loudly should you need me."*

She felt unexpectedly bereft. Chuffta hadn't been away from her thoughts since she was a child.

"I'm still only a loud thought away. And you're a woman grown. You deserve a little private joy."

"Thank you. I love you."

"And I love you." He withdrew from her, with one last affectionate and wordless thought.

"He's giving us privacy," she told Lonen.

"Good man. I wondered if your connection to him is part of why you never experimented with pleasuring yourself."

She had to keep from squirming, knowing he'd feel it. "I really don't want to discuss that."

"Oria, sweetheart—you just gave me permission to do a lot more than talk about sex with you. And we have a bit of a climb still. Help me understand you. Having sex with me will be a lot more intimate than talking about it."

She was afraid of that, which meant she might as well start conditioning herself to this exposure. Not unlike learning to be around people in the first place. "I'm sure that's part of it, but I also never really felt the urge."

"Never? Not even a little?" He sounded entirely dubious.

"No." Except those books. They'd made her feel this way, too, which was entirely wrong.

"Tell me what you're thinking," Lonen murmured.

"Are you certain you can't read my thoughts?" She could understand why it discomfited him that she could read his.

"Not exactly, but your body reveals a great deal—especially when I'm holding you like this."

"I really could walk."

"Not happening. I'm enjoying myself too much. What were you thinking?"

"Oh, it's wrong and awful and embarrassing. I can't say."

He was quiet a moment. "Does it have to do with how much it aroused you to talk about surrendering to me?"

If she hadn't been wearing her mask, she would have clapped her hands over her face. "Lonen…"

"You might as well tell me," he said, with those teasing sparks, but also with soothing images of cuddling her and keeping her safe. "You know I won't stop asking questions until I wear you down."

That was the truth. "I can't believe I'm going to tell you this."

"I can believe it. If nothing else, you at least trust me to take care of you."

Also true, rational or not. How it had happened that she trusted a Destrye warrior with her emotional well-being more than her mother or brother… Her world continued to alter, not content with upending, but also insisting on twisting sideways and in all sorts of unpredictable directions. Why not this aspect, too?

She took a steadying breath, reaching for *hwil*. "When I was young, I saw these illustrations in the history books."

"Yes?" he prompted when she faltered. "What of?"

"Of Destrye taking women captive, tied up with rope, and—ugh—I felt things then, which is horrible of me." She waited for his reproof, seething with humiliated shame, an echo of the priestess's scorn when she caught Oria rapt over those books, taking them away and advising her that meditation would do far more to build *hwil*.

"I thought as much." He said instead, full of male satisfaction.

"But I don't want that," she hastened to make sure he understood. "I don't know why it affected me. I don't want it to happen, I'm only saying that's the only time before that I felt any … urges."

"Before what?"

"Recently," she said, hoping to stop things there. No such luck, of course.

"Before meeting me?"

"Maybe," she muttered, but he only grew more pleased with himself.

"You get under my skin, too. For a long time I thought it was magic, that you'd somehow bewitched me."

She sat up a little straighter, indignant. "I would never!"

"Don't spit, kitten. I know that now. More important, I understand something of those desires you speak of and can give you a taste of them."

"If you try to rape me, I will use everything in me to kill you," she warned him, chill dread mixing with the heat of longing.

Absurdly, he laughed. "I have no doubt you could and would, my sorceress wife, with those weapons you wield so well. I promise you—no rape. No pain or fear. Only a glimpse to open that window, to allow you to feel what made those illustrations so compelling."

"I still don't understand how you can possibly do this without touching my skin," she muttered, rebellious and intrigued.

"I'm an inventive man when I want something."

~ 19 ~

GAINING THE TOP of the tower, he carried Oria straight to her bedroom. Their bedroom, he supposed. Far from feeling tired from the climb, his body surged with fevered excitement. Oria would be his at last. A wedding night to remember, if somewhat delayed. He set her on her feet where she remained, watching him light candles in the glass lanterns, suspicion in every line of her body.

"Lonen..." she started as he gently turned her by the shoulders, facing her away from him.

"I'm only removing your mask and taking down your hair," he soothed her.

She laughed, a little ragged. "I should have known that would be first."

"Indeed you should have," he agreed, working more quickly this time, having tied the knots himself. "Whenever we're alone, this will be first. Can we agree to that?"

"I suppose that's not too much to ask." She handed him the mask to set beside the bed, trading him for one of the cool cloths that Juli left for her in the covered jar. Oria used it to mop her face—and to keep it shielded, he suspected, as he took down her braids and brushed out the rippling copper mass of her hair.

"What are you thinking?" she whispered.

"Aren't you listening?"

"I'm trying not to do that as much."

"I don't mind," he told her, discovering to his surprise that he really didn't. "In fact, I'm finding I like having you in my head." He drew his hands through her hair, savoring the silky heft of it. "A way of being close to you, since I can't yet be inside your body."

She relaxed fractionally. "Then you won't..."

"Won't hurt you. I know what the limits are. Trust me."

Letting out a breath, she set the face cloth aside. "I do."

"Enough to take off your robes?"

She hesitated fractionally, then nodded, first untying his mantle and giving it back to him. Bemused, he tossed it aside, watching her. It would be so much easier if he could first kiss her, seduce her with gentle caresses. But she wasn't a woman to be cozened regardless. She had her own style of boldness, once she set herself on a course of action.

She blushed, eyes hooded, but unfastened the robes without faltering further, shedding the layers of them, until she stood only in that thin white chemise, in a pool of crimson silk. Still not looking at him, she pulled at the ties, then dropped the undergarment as well, standing naked before him.

Arill had blessed him with such a glorious woman. If She also gave him the challenge of being unable to touch his wife's skin, then he accepted that as the price.

Slim as a sapling, skin luminous in the candlelight with her radiant cape of metallic hair surrounding her, Oria took his breath away. Her breasts were tipped with small nipples, a rose as delicate as Sgatha's light, and the hair at her mons glinted a copper so smooth and straight he ached to taste her with his tongue.

Someday, they would find a way.

She studied his reaction, probably reading his emotions, so he let her feel it—the astounding desire and awe of her exotic beauty. Receiving the message, she smiled. Tentative, even shy at first, then blooming with all her radiance.

"I am relieved to be pleasing to you," she said quietly, surprising him.

"How could you have doubted it?"

Her shimmy of a shrug made her breasts bounce enticingly. Clearly Arill planned to test his restraint and self-control severely. He'd asked Her for a penance to cleanse his spirit of the taint of his deeds and She had delivered. Hopefully he'd emerge from it a better person, if somewhat crazed.

"I've never been naked for a man," Oria was saying, so he dragged his fascinated gaze up to her face. "And I know I am not at all like Nat—your Destrye women."

Because she'd seen Natly in his mind. Arill only knew what all she'd seen of Natly there.

"Nor am I like your Báran men," he returned, then caught himself, struck. She'd said he intimidated her with his size, and he was darker, hairier than any Báran he'd seen. "Do I revolt you?"

She gave him a curious smile. "Those illustrations, remember?"

How perfect that she'd shared that with him. It made many things easier, and he hoped to deliver on that long-held fantasy. "On that note, hold out your wrists, crossed in front of you." He picked up one of her many silk scarves and drew close enough to scent her heating skin.

She eyed him uncertainly, but those eyes also showed her arousal, her dark pupils wide. "We're really doing this?"

"It ups the tension, speaks to your fantasy—and mine, I might add—and has the bonus of keeping you still so I won't accidentally touch your skin with mine."

She took a deep breath and held out her crossed wrists, gaze on his face. Not the dying doe, life bleeding away at his hands, but an ardent woman trusting him to deliver on his promises. The absolution he'd looked for. Wrapping the silk in and around her wrists, tying the knots just so to keep her delicate bones from crushing together, he vowed to never destroy that look in her eyes.

A FINE TREMBLING ran through her as Lonen bound her wrists. *Hwil* danced far beyond her grasp as those shameful adolescent desires assaulted her, jumbling with the new ones that centered entirely on Lonen. Naked before her Destrye warrior, vulnerable and at his mercy. He stood close enough that she could turn her hands and run them over his chest, open his shirt and tangle her fingers in the hair beneath. His eyes—a gray so dark they looked almost black in the golden light—flicked up to study her face, the gentle concern a contrast to the raging storm of violent desire beneath. He affected her profoundly on multiple levels, his physical presence amplifying the vivid fantasy images rolling through his mind, of her gasping beneath him, crying out his name, their skin sliding together so slickly she almost felt it.

"If I could," he murmured, voice rasping over her nerves as he walked her backwards, holding only the ends of the silk, "I would be kissing you now. I'd start with light ones, like butterfly wings on your lips, lulling you in until you felt safe enough to open your mouth. Yes, just like that. Your lips wet and plump and pink from meeting mine."

The backs of her thighs hit the edge of the bed, but he kept her from instinctively sitting. Instead he raised her hands above her head, looping her scarf over the rods that held the gauzy bed curtains. Hot blood rioted through her, unruly, exultant, needy. "Lonen…" she whispered.

"You're okay. Just feel. I've got you. By now you'd have opened your mouth to me. My tongue would be inside you, tangling with yours." He left her standing there, arms relaxed, but tethered to the bed. Picking up another scarf from her basket of them, he pressed it to his lips. They looked fuller, more enticing than she'd ever noticed, framed by his glossy black beard. Lifting the scarf to her mouth, he caressed her lower lip with the silk where he'd kissed it, slightly damp from his, tasting of him. "Is this okay?"

So far, yes. Tentatively, she tasted it with the tip of her tongue, finding some of him there. He groaned, eyes hot. "Kitten tongue. I'd pull that into my mouth, maybe nipping at it until you squirmed, begging me for more."

She did squirm, as if his words evoked it, tugging against the silk that only tightened, making her flesh bloom with desire around it. "More. Please give me more."

"Oria," he grated, his hands fisting in the silk. "You might be the death of me."

"Pleasure me, Destrye," she demanded. "Prove your worth to a sorceress of Bára."

He breathed a laugh. "Sweet captive bride, you will writhe for me and, before we're done, you'll scream my name in pleasure."

She wanted to already, convulsing when he drew the silk across her taut nipples. They'd never been so sensitive, her breasts swelling like molten glass, full of breath and fire. Lonen dragged the silk over and around the skin of them, teasing her, while her breath grew ragged.

"These are my lips on you," he told her, picturing it so she would, "licking all this delicious flesh." He stepped back and flicked the ends of the silk against her, drawing incoherent cries in response. "I might use my teeth, too. Do you like that?"

"Yes. Oh, yes." She nearly sobbed the words, unable to take and keep a decent breath. "Whatever you want, warrior."

"Because you belong to me." He loomed large before her, fierce and feral.

Only one answer. "Yes."

"These are my hands on you." Tying the scarf around her rib cage, he knotted above and between her breasts, crossing it up and over her shoulders, then bringing the ends around and beneath, tying them off to the center knot. He took his time, teasing her nipples with the free ends. Picking up her container of mask ribbons, he tied them to the scarves, meticulously making sure not to brush her skin with his, tightening them around her breasts with nearly painful pressure. "I have big hands," he told her as he worked. "Barbarian hands, rough from fighting and manual labor. They scrape your soft white Báran skin and you love it."

"I love it," she agreed, longing for that very thing. "Touch me, Lonen."

"I am. I'm squeezing your breasts. Do you feel that? Taking my fill of you, as is my right."

He tightened the ribbons and she cried out, writhing against the bonds.

"Hold still," he ordered in a harsh voice. "Don't make me bind you further. All your pleading won't save you."

Understanding, she did her best to hold still, transfixed as he made a loop with a thin strip of ribbon, then slipped it over the tight peak of her nipple. His eyes caught hers. "Your teeth chewing your lip—that's me, devouring your mouth, your nipples." Slowly, he tightened the little noose and she gasped at the intensity of it. He smiled, a cruel, ruthless enjoyment of her predicament. "See? Many uses for those ribbons you squander so freely, Princess."

He did the same to her other nipple, all the while describing what he'd be doing to her, until he'd reduced her panting and begging. "Please, Lonen," she chanted.

"You want me between your legs?" he asked, leaning close so his breath caressed her cheek. "Touching you there, making you pump those pretty hips until you can't hold back."

"Yes, yes, yes." She ached there as never before. "Touch me please."

He dropped to his knees, eye level with her sex and she watched him, rapt, abruptly aware that he'd never undressed. "Take off your shirt," she told him.

With a half-smile, he complied. "As you command, Princess." He picked up another scarf, threading it between her ankles and holding the ends in each hand, one in front of her and one behind. Working as slowly as before, he wisped the silk up the inside of her thighs, tantalizing her into edging her feet apart. When he reached the apex of her thighs, he dragged the scarf between her slick nether lips, sliding against her so she whimpered at the intensity of it.

"This is my hand, parting your folds," he whispered. "There, yes?"

She had no words, only moans of encouragement as slipped against her, making her move her hips with it, just as he'd promised. "That's it my hot little princess," he crooned, "take your pleasure from me. My hand stroking you. You feel so good. Here's my mouth on you."

He imagined it, inhaling her scent, and she groaned at the sight of his dark curls between her thighs as the silk worked her. The tension built and she struggled against the mounting pressure. "I want," she panted. "I need."

"Take it then," he rasped. "Let go. Let go of all of it."

"No." She closed her thighs around the silk. "I want all of it. Take me, all the way."

"It's easier to give you pleasure this way and—"

"I don't care. The first time, I want this with you. Make me yours, Destrye."

He rose to his feet, expression intent, ardor swirling about her as if he ran his hands over her flesh indeed. "Shall I plow between your pretty virgin thighs? Take your innocence and make you mine forever more?"

"Yes!" she urged him, all concept of dignity, of reserve in *hwil* vanished. She'd become a wild thing. "Take me. I'm yours to ravish."

He lifted a hand to hover near her cheek, but checked himself from touching her. "So beautiful, my powerful sorceress. So helpless before me." His hand dove into her hair, winding it around his fist and tugging remorselessely so her head tipped back exposing her throat. "Spread your legs for me," he growled.

With a sob, she complied, the opening rocking her apart, with all of her so vulnerable to him. Something touched her thigh, cool and smooth, making her tense. What was it? He tugged her hair and slid it between her nether lips, making her moan, making her forget.

"This is my cock." His voice came harsh and uneven. He pressed it against her aching flesh and pictured crawling between her spread thighs and pushing back her knees, positioning himself at her entrance. "I'm going to take you, my lovely Oria."

"Yes. Lonen. Yes."

He nudged it into her, spreading her slowly, working it back and forth, so she adjusted to the invasion. "This is me, fucking you." In the fantasy he turned her over, holding her hair like the reins of a horse, making her arch her neck even as he pulled her hair in reality, pushing the thing in and out of her. "Keep those pretty thighs spread wide," he cautioned, "or I'll tie them apart. Don't make me hurt you."

Or his hand could brush her skin there, even as carefully as he moved. It felt so good, the filling and stretching, her body quickening, picking up where it had been. She moaned. "I don't care. I want you in me for real. Fuck me for real, Lonen. I don't care if it hurts."

He breathed a wild and ragged laugh. "You would tempt the purest of men to such depravity. Sweet as it will be to sheath myself in you, that day has not yet come. But you're mine just the same. Tell me so."

"I'm yours." She felt it, too, in the syncing of their bodies, the fantasies he fed her and she drank in, pumping back to him with her cries of need and the undulations of her naked body. "With me." The words cracked, so she repeated the demand. "Take yourself in hand and be with me."

With a muttered oath, he released her hair, reaching to undo his leather pants. Avidly she watched him grasp his cock, fisting it as he pumped a like phallus in her. She caught his gaze, the gray catching silver sparks, and poured some of her sgath into him, just a taste, enough to feed his fires. He snarled and pumped harder, a spur of the phallus in her grinding a sensitive spot.

Eyes locked on his, she let go of all reserve. He grunted as he came and—just as he'd promised—she screamed his name when her world split apart.

~ 20 ~

LONEN FELL TO his knees with the power of the climax, Oria shuddering with the aftershocks of her own orgasm, gleaming like a goddess of fire, her body slick with sweat and sex. His goddess. His queen.

Carefully he slid his dagger hilt from her sweet sex, beyond glad that the wide guard had shielded his hand from her intimate tissues. He'd forgotten himself there at the end, in his excitement, slamming it into her. No blood on her thighs, though, so he'd been right on judging the size. Smaller than his own girth, so easier for her than if he'd penetrated her for the first time. Perhaps by the time they found a way for her to tolerate contact with him, she'd be accustomed enough that he wouldn't hurt her. A good thing, as he'd promised.

Oria smiled at him, stray wisps of hair plastered to her cheeks and temples, her face a perfectly erotic blend of sensuality and satisfaction. Setting the dagger aside, he rose to free her, releasing her from the bed post so she could sit, then untying the bonds around her wrists. She sighed as she plucked the ribbon ties from her nipples and wiggled out of the binding scarves, then flopped back with a gusty breath. Bemused, he watched her as he wiped himself and then the floor where he'd spilled his seed.

Perhaps his seed once parted from his body wouldn't hurt her, but he hadn't been sure. A man's seed contained a great deal and who knew how it would affect his sensitive Oria. Something they could test, however, in judicious amounts. He might be able to spill his seed on her and work it inside. With something better than his knife hilt. Perhaps he could speak to one of her glass forgers to create a phallus for the purpose. Several of various sizes would be useful, to determine which best pleasured her.

That would be an interesting conversation.

Still, the thought of Oria bearing their heirs lit a fire of hope in him. They would find a way.

Moving carefully, he edged himself onto the bed around her. Lazily, she turned her head, her coppery eyes owlish and sated. "Why aren't you naked?" she asked.

Raising his brows at her, he sat up, shucked off the pants he'd just fastened, along with the boots he'd never gotten around to removing, and rejoined her, obligingly naked as she.

"Lie on your back," she commanded, and he did, bemused, watching her look at him.

"I thought you'd already seen me naked," he reminded her.

"Yes, well." She gave him an impish smile—a delightful one he'd never before seen, that curved her luscious lips and brought dimples to her cheeks—and returned to her scrutiny. "I may have exaggerated. I tried not to look."

"And now?"

She raised her gaze to his again. "I like looking at you. I understand now why you wanted to see me." She gestured at his flaccid cock. "Good thing you didn't have a wound there to tend after all."

He winced at the prospect. "I'll do it, but I won't say I'm not savoring the reprieve."

"I think I could do what you did to yourself," she said, a hint of shyness in her smile. "Maybe by wrapping cloth around my hands or some such."

His cock stirred at the image. "In Dru we have thick garments for our hands, called gloves, that we wear for warmth. I've thought of that for both of us."

She cocked her head with interest. "I'd like that." She sobered then. "I thought about using grien to touch you, but …."

"Yeah." He grinned and picked up a lock of her trailing hair, winding it around his finger. "Maybe after you've practiced a bit more. I wouldn't want to be emasculated by my sorceress bride. Think of what the other guys would say."

"Good incentive for you to mind your smart mouth, Destrye," she replied in a tone so arch he wanted to pull her down and drown it with a kiss. She read it in him, her eyes wandering over his face. "I know you don't want me to apologize, but I'm sorry you can't do that, kiss me and touch me for real."

"This is real," he returned. "And it's more than I knew to hope for. You are the burning fire in my heart, Oria."

Her gaze went dewy. "This is more than I imagined to hope for, too."

"Even if I'm not a perfect match for you?" he teased.

She shuddered lightly, a delicious sight on her naked form. "I can't even imagine being like this with anyone but you. Thank you for making this so good for me."

"It's all you, Oria." He fingered the lock of hair. "This would be when we'd cuddle. I'd pull you close against me and hold you in my arms. I'd whisper how sweet and lovely you are, and you would tell me what a huge cock I have."

She burst out laughing and hit him with a pillow. "How about something to eat instead, and then sleep?"

He grinned at her, delighted in everything about her. "Sounds great. Big day tomorrow."

She stilled in pulling on her chemise. "What are we going to do about the contest?"

"Our best." He tugged her hair. "Between the two of us, that's not inconsiderable."

IN THE MORNING, they descended the stairs together. Oria rested her hand slightly on Lonen's sleeve, where he'd created padding by wrapping his forearms in leather strips. Both for Chuffta to land on and for her to touch, he'd explained, muttering something about similarly sharp talons on each of them that she ignored. Chuffta, riding on her other shoulder, wryly agreed.

She felt too relaxed to rise to Lonen's teasing. Too replete. Though she was sore in places, the slight pain made her feel smug, rather than injured. And not at all fragile. She'd married a man who pleased her well—and with great inventiveness. To her surprise, she discovered she'd begun to believe his assertions that they could triumph over anything. Perhaps they *could* win the contest and the end of the day would see her crowned Queen of Bára.

He'd been right, too, about their increased intimacy. After all they'd done with each other, she felt more at ease with him. Even at his greatest extremity he'd been careful of her, taking her on that wild ride of pleasure beyond anything she'd imagined. He'd relaxed, also, just what he'd declared good sex would do. Even with shadows of caution threading through his thoughts as he contemplated what they faced, his aura radiated satisfied happiness and he shone with confidence.

Also, an idea had occurred to her.

"So," she said quietly, though their voices could hardly carry out of the tower and her sgath revealed no one nearby until the guards at the bottom. The sheer audacity of the idea had her reluctant to speak it too loudly. "I've been thinking. If we're to demonstrate a partnership of sgath and grien, perhaps I can do both. Any grien tricks required of you, I can do, and you can pretend to be generating them."

He gave her a sideways look. "They'd never believe I can work magic. They'd have to know it was you."

She shook her head. "That's it—a woman with grien magic is even more unlikely than a Destrye with it. If they see, they'll believe. There won't be any other explanation."

"Too much risk. We don't dare expose that talent of yours."

"I agree. Too dangerous," Chuffta chimed in, unsolicted.

"This is worth the risk," she argued with both of them. "Otherwise we're certain to lose and I won't be able to wrest control of the Trom from Yar, and both Bára and Dru will be doomed."

Neither of her men liked it, but neither could come up with a better solution.

"Maybe it won't come to that," Lonen said, but the words lacked his usual optimistic confidence.

"I'll save it for a last resort only, I promise."

"I never thought I'd wish for magic," Lonen muttered, then subsided into increasingly brooding thoughts for the remainder of their descent.

Yar and Gallia met them in the courtyard between the palace and temple, along with Priest Vico and a considerable assembly of onlookers from all walks of life. Apparently everyone wanted to witness the show. Juli, who'd been up to help Oria dress and braid her hair, bowed and came to stand behind her as an attendant. No sign of Rhianna, if the former queen had even been told what was going on.

Just as well if not. Even with her aggravation with Yar and disappointment in Oria, it would have to be impossibly difficult to watch your only remaining children duel. For that reason, Oria hadn't sent a message. No matter how this day turned out, their mother would face grief, which she had no ability to withstand.

Another turnabout, for Oria to be strong and her mother so fragile.

Gallia looked as beautifully composed as she had the night before, but her sgath had dimmed, streaked with unhappiness and a sickly pain.

"Are you well, sister?" Oria asked her, after the formal greetings, which Yar rushed through, shimmering grien snaking about him.

Gallia started with surprise. "Very well, thank you. Bára's magic is yet unfamiliar to me. I would not have expected it, but I assimilate

Báran sgath differently. It has a … different flavor."

Oria wouldn't have expected that either, but it was interesting. So rarely did the priestesses travel to their sister cities that little information was available regarding such things. "We can postpone the contest if you—"

"Do you seek to delay, sister dear?" Yar ostentatiously took Gallia's bare hand in his. "Perhaps you are afraid and seek to avoid the certain humiliation of defeat. We will accept your forfeit."

"No forfeit," Oria replied, though she didn't like his lack of concern for his new wife. Had Yar always been so self-involved, so callous to the needs of others? Perhaps so. Sometimes what seem to be the flaws of youth are truly the chasms of personality.

"Prepare to be defeated then. Priest Vico—we are ready to begin!" He dropped Gallia's hand as abruptly as he'd seized it, striding over to address the priest.

"Quickly," Oria bent to Gallia. "Whatever should happen today, you will find a champion in our mother, the former queen. She has bad days and good. More of the former than the latter. But visit her regularly, talk with her. You'll learn to anticipate the good days. And if Yar doesn't treat you well, take your appeal to her. She'll help you."

Gallia seemed briefly taken aback before her cloak of *hwil* settled. "I appreciate your concern, sister, but I am content."

Oria doubted it, but she let the woman maintain that façade. Deliberately, she set it aside. She couldn't think of her new sister's plight and maintain the appearance of her own *hwil*.

Lonen brushed a hand over her braids. "She is a sorceress like yourself, not powerless. She'll find a way to handle him."

"Arill make it so," she replied, just so he'd smile. "The onlookers will leave," Priest Vico declared. "Contestants and attendants to remain. Master Chuffta, you may sit to the side."

"The creature helps her," Yar protested. "It's an unfair advantage."

Oria didn't say that she had to be in contact with her Familiar for most of the benefit. If Yar didn't realize that, all the better.

Priest Vico considered. "The derkesthai have a long history of assisting Báran kings and queens. If Princess Oria's Familiar gives her an advantage, then that would go towards her duties as queen as well, and should be ascertained as such. Master Chuffta may remain."

Oria breathed an internal sigh of relief to at least have Chuffta with her.

"Always. Even when I'm not physically present, I am with you."

"Unless I'm intimate with Lonen and you're not listening," she reminded him.

"Naturally." He managed to keep his mind-voice free of even the least hint of sarcasm. He hadn't commented on her belated wedding night this time, for which she was grateful. Some things weren't for sharing with anyone else. What had passed between her and her Destrye warrior would remain their private secret.

"The contest," announced Priest Vico, "consists of three parts. We begin the first, the demonstration of compatibility."

JUST AS ORIA had predicted. She'd explained to him that the initial testing of compatibility between prospective spouses began with proximity, progressed to casual skin-to-skin contact, and then probably to some form of more intimate contact. She didn't know about the last as she hadn't made it that far with anyone. It perversely pleased him that she hadn't, even though rationally it would be better if she had, and could have known what to prepare them for.

Regardless, this portion would likely be the most difficult for Oria. Her powerful magics weren't in doubt—at least to his eye—only her ability to withstand her husband's touch.

After the onlookers departed at Priest Vico's command, Juli

stepped up to cut the ribbons to Oria's mask, while Yar and Gallia's attendants did likewise. For the first time, Lonen looked on Yar's face, studying his enemy. He had the gawky looks—and unfortunately pimpled skin—of a beardless boy, his eyes strangely dark beneath beetling red brows. Gallia was a lovely woman, with blue eyes and skin more golden than Oria's cream. She took her time blotting her face, her hands unsteady.

"The journey took a toll on her," Oria murmured to him.

"Perhaps last night also," he agreed. It bothered his wife to think of her brother mistreating a woman, though it hardly surprised him, given what he'd seen of Yar's selfish character. Even if he hadn't been deliberately cruel to her, the boy had no compassion in him, no sensitivity to the needs of another person. On top of his likely inexperience with a woman, it made for a bad combination for a virginal bride. Drawing on the hard heart he'd built over years of warfare, he pushed the sympathy aside. "It may sound callous, but if her exhaustion helps our cause…"

"I know." But Oria sounded glum.

"This battle was forced upon us. We didn't choose it, but we'll fight it anyway." If the Destrye had learned nothing else from the Golem Wars, they'd come to understand that truth all too well.

Oria flexed her fingers on his sleeve. "And yet we've both discovered the myriad regrets of the actions we've taken to win those battles. I'd prefer to find a victory that doesn't require another's crushing defeat."

He winced at the reminder that many Bárans had been equally forced into conflict. Now who was selfish? He was saved thinking up an optimistic reply to that by Priest Vico.

"Please embrace your spouse."

Lonen brought Oria into his arms, carefully touching her over her clothes, postponing the inevitable impact on her. They'd been close when he carried her, but still nothing like this, the lines of their whole bodies folding together. She turned her cheek to lay it against his chest, wrapping slender arms around his waist and nestling against him. Her soft breasts and thighs snuggled into him as if made for him, a slim dagger fitting perfectly into the sheath of his body. Holding her like this reminded him of the first time she'd handed him one of her delicate glass wine vessels—that he might fail to temper his strength and shatter her out of carelessness.

"This is proximity?" he murmured, brushing his lips over the braids crowning her head.

She breathed a laugh. "He skipped a few phases since it's clear we are able to be near each other without suffering."

Indulging himself in the rare luxury, he ran his hands along the elegant line of her spine and dainty curve of her waist. "Is it truly better with me then than it was—being near?"

She raised her face, giving him a small smile. "Better than I ever imagined."

"Remain in physical contact, but take each other's hands, please," Priest Vico instructed.

"Here we go," Lonen muttered, and Oria drew composure about her like a cloak of winter chill.

"Whatever happens, just keep going," she told him. "Don't worry about me. I'll be fine."

He doubted that, and reserved the right to act to protect her according to his own judgment, but he dropped his hands to his sides as she did, lacing his fingers carefully with hers, as if being gentle with her would make any difference. She shuddered, closing her eyes as lines of pain formed around them. She slowed her breathing in a way he recognized now as a method for mastering difficult input. Not unlike a wounded warrior steeling himself against the surgeon's knife.

From what he could tell, she seemed to be doing better than during their wedding ceremony, though that could be entirely false optimism. Especially as bewildering as that experience had been.

Over her head, he met Chuffta's intent gaze, exchanging wordless hope and concern.

Priest Vico might be helping her as Lonen hoped, because he

wasted little time making Oria endure the contact. "And now a kiss, maintained until I ask you to stop."

Number three. At least the trial would stop at a kiss. Not what Lonen had hoped for their first kiss, but so it went in their star-crossed marriage. Oria raised her face, lines of strain between her brows and bracketing her lovely mouth. "Stop fretting," she taunted. "Chicken."

Arill, how he loved this woman. Delay only made it worse, so he brushed her lips with his, unable to savor the sweetness of her with the incoherent sound of pain she made. Doing his best to shield her, he held back his emotions as he would on the battlefield. Her heart pounded in frantic beats, shuddering into him, and he kissed her softly, soothingly, if only to make that aspect as bearable as possible.

A scuffle and cry in the background. "Beast!" Gallia cried. Adhering to the rules, Lonen kept the kiss, ignoring whatever had happened. If Yar and Gallia forfeited, so much the better.

"You may desist," Priest Vico called in a placid tone as if nothing had happened.

Oria broke away from him, gasping for breath, clutching her hands to her stomach as if she might be ill. He checked his impulse to reach for her, to comfort her, clenching his hands into fists instead. So wrong that what should be good between them was the worst thing for her.

"Both marriages pass the compatibility test," the priest declared.

"Are you insane?" Yar thrust a finger in Oria's direction. "Look at her. She's staggering from the impact of that barbarian's foul touch."

"Look to your own bride, Prince Yar," the priest replied. "Impacts occur on many levels. However, I concede that Prince Yar and Priestess Gallia demonstrate greater compatibility, so far as magic is concerned."

A fine point, as Gallia, while not obviously physically stressed as Oria, looked miserably unhappy, a trickle of blood at the corner of her mouth. She took the cloth her attendant offered, wiping it away and seemed grateful to don her mask again.

Oria did too, quietly talking with Juli as she did so. With a pang that he refused to accept as foreboding, he watched her face disappear behind the featureless metal again.

LONEN WORRIED FOR her palpably, his concern tugging at her, but she couldn't reassure him. At this point, she could only grit through. He'd been as gentle as possible with her, but the contact, particularly mouth to mouth, had burned like acid, hollowing her out as surely as if he'd taken his axe to her. If she thought about it too much, she'd become depressed at the unlikelihood of them ever being able to touch with pleasure. A small consideration, perhaps, given the far more daunting obstacles they faced, but one that had become strangely important to her.

"Yesterday you were certain you could not lie with him at all and you have. Give it time. You're doing brilliantly well."

Grateful for her Familiar, she sent him a loving thought and straightened, moving to Lonen and putting her hand on his padded forearm.

"I'm so sorry," he murmured.

"No apologies," she reminded him.

He growled under his breath but subsided when Vico spoke.

"For the second part, the priestesses will demonstrate their sgath. Please, gather your sgath and offer it to Grienon through me. Would either of you prefer to go first?"

"I'll go first," Oria said, ignoring Lonen's muttered protest. Yes, she was giving Gallia time to sort herself, but she couldn't do less. Even though Oria had focused on Lonen's kiss, trying to ignore the pain of contact in favor of the surprisingly lovely tickle of his beard on her face, the shocking tender heat of his mouth—her sgath had relentlessly revealed how harshly Yar had kissed his new bride. Lonen was likely right that she should treat Gallia as the enemy, but her heart ached for her sister.

And she was so very weary of having enemies.

Also, this part at least came easily to her now. Accumulating sgath had never been the problem for her—quite the opposite. Until the night before when she'd completely depleted herself. For the most part, once she'd learned how to see and hold it comfortably, all those lessons on connecting it to a priest fell into place. Breathing in the clean, clear, and familiar magic of Bára, Sgatha's gift, she let it well up into a serene pool, and presented it to Priest Vico. In the same way, the priestesses of the city had offered their collective sgath to the battle mages.

Priest Vico sipped from it, then bowed in thanks, and spoke the ritual words. "A powerful gift, indeed. I thank you, priestess, for sharing with this humble priest."

Yar seethed, his grien energy sparking and swirling in her mind's eye. Her own grien wanted to rise to battle it, but she restrained it. Soon enough. He nudged Gallia forward. "Show him. Gallia is the most powerful junior priestess of Lousá. She will make a great queen."

Perhaps so, but at that moment her sgath hung in a ragged mist. Oria choked back her sympathy for the woman as she tried to reach for Bára's unfamiliar magic. It seemed to slip away from her the moment she reached for it, like a skittish kitten uncertain of a stranger and unwilling to be petted just yet. What she did manage to gather, the dark cavities of the journey's strain devoured as quickly as she built it up. Yar was an idiot to have pushed her so fast. She finally pulled together enough to offer Priest Vico, who thanked her as he had Oria.

"While Priestess Gallia's sgath is present, Priestess Oria's strength of sgath is far greater. This part goes to her and King Lonen."

Yar took Gallia's arm, shaking her slightly as he spoke in an undertone to her. His grien lashed about her, but she appeared unmoved. Enviable *hwil*.

"For the third part, the priests will demonstrate their grien," Vico declared. "Please, focus your grien and release it according to your affinity, but in a way that all might observe, to please Sgatha. Would either of you—"

"I might as well go." Yar swaggered as he stepped forward. "As we know how this will end."

He raised his hands, his powerful grien streaming out. With careless effort, he drew from the stone of the chasm and the rock spires behind the temple's towers, sculpting a column, then refining it.

Into a statue of himself as king.

Safe in the anonymity of her mask, Oria rolled her eyes at his hubris. She couldn't stand by and allow him to take the throne. That had long been her resolve, but the day's events—and seeing how he abused the woman he should cherish—only reinforced her certainty. Even if they lost this trial, she would find another way to defeat her brother.

Not only for the Destrye, for Lonen, and for Bára, but for the good of the world.

Yar twirled and bowed, making an insult of the demonstration. Priest Vico acknowledged his grien with the ritual words neutrally enough, but her brother's accomplishment spoke volumes. Even among her family, even compared to their father the king, Yar's gift had stood out in both its strength and his skill with it. If only he had something of Lonen's character, he might be worthy of such power.

As it was, the prospect of him with the rule of Bára and full access to the temple secrets soured her gut. She simply could not fail. The stakes were far too high.

"King Lonen?" the priest invited.

"Why bother?" Yar sounded bored. "He's a mind-dead barbarian grunt. He has nothing to demonstrate. I've won. Two out of three."

"Not true," Oria answered the challenge. She'd learned the value of magic well-faked. "The Destrye have magic of their own and King Lonen will demonstrate it."

"Oria, no," Lonen urged in a low voice, his emotions anything but quiet. "It's not worth the risk. We'll find another way."

"I'm doing it," she replied in an even tone. "Play along or you will have blown it for us before we've begun."

~ 21 ~

HE WANTED TO fight her on it, but recognized the utter futility. Perhaps he'd been wrong in thinking—bragging even—that he possessed more stubbornness. Obstinacy or will, Oria had cultivated an ability to forge ahead regardless of the consequences to herself. And now her survival depended on him making a convincing show of working Destrye magic.

His father and brothers must be howling with laughter as they watched from the Hall of Warriors. At least he provided entertainment for them. A Destrye pretending to be a sorcerer. If the poets didn't write ballads proclaiming him a fool for taking a Báran sorceress to wife, they surely would for this fiasco.

With no idea what he'd do—he should have realized Oria would insist on this reckless strategy and planned ahead—he unstrapped his battle axe and began swinging it in the basic training cycle, chanting a nonsense rhyme of Destrye children, which would hopefully sound like a magical incantation. More fodder for that future ballad.

"Heya naya, frahm frahm frinny. Naya heya, frinnah say say."

He repeated it, moving the axe from hand to hand, adding in foot stomping as if he danced to Destrye drums. The sweep of Oria's magic filtered through him, tingling as it had when she'd teased his cock with it, but passing through and to the laughable edifice Yar had created. It creaked and shivered, then burst with vines, twining and trailing with rapid growth. Huge indigo flower buds swelled, then burst in blossom. The vines turned woody, encasing and obscuring the sculpture's lines until it was unrecognizable.

Drawing the line there, lest Oria take it in her head to do more and even further risk exposing herself, Lonen set down his axe and wiped his brow.

Priest Vico regarded him, surprise in the lines of his shoulders. "Bára will benefit from nature magic such as yours, King Lonen. I've never seen its like, not even in the temple annals. The Destrye appear to have secrets of their own. Both men have demonstrated the application of magic. While Prince Yar's grien is more powerful and he demonstrated more refined skill with it, King Lonen's is unique and much needed in this time of privation. This part goes to—"

"Wait." Yar held up a hand, regal command in his voice, all trace of the arrogant boy gone. "Oria, forfeit. Do it now or I will speak the truth of this."

Dread coiled in Lonen's stomach. Yar did know, as Oria had feared, and he would use that knowledge to win. So be it. At least her brother had shown some filial compassion and given her an out.

"I have no intention of forfeiting," Oria replied, equally cool, devastating Lonen with the words. "The contest will be won fairly or not at all."

"Don't make me do this." Yar actually sounded human again. A boy not ready for the pressures he'd shouldered. "I don't want your death. Forfeit."

Priest Vico looked between them. "Her death?"

"Last chance, Oria. Forfeit or die."

Lonen turned to Oria, mentally urging her to do it with everything in him, speaking as loudly as he dared. "We'll find another way, Oria. It's not worth it. Take the out. Forfeit."

"Is that what you would do?" she replied under her breath. "You who stormed the walls of Bára by yourself? I think not. I refuse to be a coward."

No time to argue he'd not been entirely alone. "It's not cowardice to retreat in the face of doom, to leave the field of battle to fight another day. You can't fight him if you're dead."

"He can't prove anything," she insisted. "It's a bluff."

He couldn't take the chance. Not with her life and not with the future of his people hanging in the balance. "I'm sorry to do this, but I can't let you risk this."

"Don't you dare!" she snarled, her magic whipping at him.

He ignored her, raising his voice. "We forfeit."

But Priest Vico shook his head. "The contest is between Prince Yar and Princess Oria. Only they can forfeit. Do you wish to forfeit, Princess?"

"No. Pronounce your determination."

"Very well, the contest goes to Queen Oria and her consort King Lonen. May you reign in—"

"Remember that you forced my hand, Oria," Yar cut through. "The grien is hers." The words thudded flat into sudden, shocked silence.

Priest Vico visibly floundered. "The… the what you say?"

"The grien. It's hers. She's an abomination and should be executed as such. High Priestess Febe knew it and Oria killed her to keep the secret. Oria used it against me before today and like a sentimental fool I protected her and did not report it to the temple. I take full responsibility for my lapse."

"Ridiculous," Oria sneered. "No woman can use grien. It's not an abomination; it's an impossibility."

"Examine her," Yar told the priest. "If you look closely, you can see it in her. I can see it now. Revolting and against nature, but there."

Oria stiffened as Priest Vico approached her. "Forgive me, Princess, but temple law compels me to be certain that such an anomaly has not occurred."

HER PREVIOUS CONFIDENCE bled away, leaving fear behind. Much of it came from Lonen and she abruptly regretted her foolhardy bravado. If she failed this examination, she'd fail again to keep her word to aid the Destrye—and this time through her own actions.

All because she simply could not force herself to swallow her pride and forfeit to Yar.

"Can you help me?" she sent to Chuffta, fully aware she grasped at sand already blown away.

"I don't know how I can." His mind-voice sounded afraid also. *"Be still and serene as possible. Focus on sgath, bring that aspect up as strong as you can."*

She did her best, silencing the frantic whispers of her oversensitized nerves that hadn't at all settled from the stress of the compatibility test. Beating frantically against her ribs, her heart thrummed like a trapped jewelbird. Though Lonen tried to drown his emotions behind the image of that serene lake, his worry threaded toward her. She couldn't think about him.

Except that if she died, he'd at least be free to marry Natly and have a normal wife he could bed. No, that thought didn't help because she wasn't that generous. Lonen was her husband and she wanted to live, to keep him and see that lake for herself, to learn to swim in it.

Besides, without her Yar's Trom would kill them all. She had to win this. She was on the side of the good and right. Surely that meant something.

It wasn't fair that they'd lose because she couldn't conceal a simple bit of magic. The silence stretched on. Then Priest Vico's astonishment and deep regret flooded her senses.

"Former priestess Oria," he said at last, his voice hushed and hoarse. "You are disqualified from this contest. I must ask that you surrender your mask."

Gallia made a sound and Oria appreciated her new sister's sympathy. Or perhaps it was revulsion. In the end, it likely didn't matter. She tried to think of a solution, a defense, some way to extract herself from this, but came up with nothing nothing nothing.

With fingers as numb as her brain, she fumbled at the ribbons, grateful when Lonen stepped up to undo the knots for her, his bedrock strength as steady as ever. Juli took the mask, her sgath curling in comforting tendrils. Vico accepted it from her and turned his back decisively on Oria.

"King Yar and Queen Gallia, may you reign in peace," he declared.

Yar's grien rocketed in bolts of triumph, lashing out to shiver over the stone statue of himself, fragments of stone sifting down and taking her leaves and blossoms with them. The cleaned stone stood starkly clean when he'd finished, its sterility an apt foreshadowing of their futures.

"I only regret that my first action as king will be my sister's execution." He almost managed to sound sorry about it. "It's your fault, Oria, for driving me to this."

"An ill omen to begin a new era," Priest Vico noted, without emotion, his *hwil* perfect.

"Is it?" Yar rounded on the priest, his voice and grien turned snarling. "You dare criticize me? I say it's a good omen. We begin my reign on a fresh page, with Bára cleansed anew of the abominations perpetuated on our fair city. I will make Bára great again!"

"Be careful, kingling," Lonen ground out from just behind her shoulder. "You are still my subject, Bára belongs to Dru as Princess Oria belongs to me. I am the final law here and you will not gainsay me or I will bring devastation down upon you and destroy your city, great or not."

Oria nearly protested, but Lonen put a firm hand on her shoulder, and she subsided. He'd given her room to do what she thought best and she'd failed him. She owed him whatever steps he wished to take now.

"Your words are but sand on the breeze," Yar returned. "You have no idea of the power I wield, Destrye. Run home to your pitiful forests and ruined crops. Plant more. I'll simply burn them again. I care not for your fate."

With a snarl of rage, Lonen stepped around her, axe at the ready. Yar met it with a blast of grien that made the Destrye stagger. Snapping out of her fog of stunned grief, Oria put herself between them, creating a wall of grien of her own to protect them.

Yar clenched his fists and howled in frustration. "Gallia! Feed me sgath. We cannot allow this renegade abomination to escape." He reached for her, but Gallia stepped back, releasing the sgath she'd replenished in the interim, sending it to Oria through a path so subtle only another woman would be able to detect it.

"I'm sorry, my husband," she answered in a thready voice, as if terribly weakened. "I hate to fail you, but I have nothing to offer. I cannot help."

Yar rounded on her, fist upraised, but she knelt in apology. Her mind-voice whispered into Oria's, astonishing her. *"Run, sister. Take your life and go. Survive outside the walls. Bára and Lousá await your return."*

"That's our cue." Even as Lonen spoke the words, he swept Oria up, tossing her over his shoulder and taking off at a run, axe still in hand. Had she been able to appreciate the irony of it, she would have laughed at the image they must make. Straight out of the illustrations. Except for Chuffta faithfully winging behind them, fierce and ready to burn anyone who tried to stop them.

"But where will we go?" she gasped, the words stuttering out with his pounding strides. Even in his haste, he carefully didn't touch her skin. *Survive outside the walls. Bára and Lousá await your return.* Was it possible? Did she have any choice?

"Anywhere but this place," he snapped back. "Just hold the cursed wall so he can't follow. You do your part, I'll do mine."

It was, she supposed, what they'd agreed to all along.

The Tides of Bára

Sorcerous Moons – Book 3

BY
JEFFE KENNEDY

A Narrow Escape

With her secrets uncovered and her power-mad brother bent on her execution, Princess Oria has no sanctuary left. Her bid to make herself and her new barbarian husband rulers of walled Bára has failed. She and Lonen have no choice but to flee through the leagues of brutal desert between her home and his—certain death for a sorceress, and only a bit slower than the blade.

A Race Against Time

At the mercy of a husband barely more than a stranger, Oria must war with her fears and her desires. Wild desert magic buffets her; her husband's touch allures and burns. Lonen is pushed to the brink, sure he's doomed his proud bride and all too aware of the restless, ruthless pursuit that follows…

A Danger Beyond Death…

Can Oria trust a savage warrior, now that her strength has vanished? Can Lonen choose her against the future of his people? Alone together in the wastes, Lonen and Oria must forge a bond based on more than lust and power, or neither will survive the test…

Dedication

This one is for Carien Ubink, aka Sullivan McPig, aka Voodoo Bride.
First and best reader, amazing assistant, and without whom I'd be utterly lost.
(And forget easily half of my obligations.)

Acknowledgements

Many thanks to the wonderful readers who generously—and creatively!—suggested names for Lonen's warhorse. I loved these:

Aloeus, from Colleen Champagne;
Draevvon, from Tommi Crow; and
Shajae, from Evergreen.

Ultimately, I went with my assistant Carien's choice, though she made it half in jest. Once she said it, all the conversations between Lonen and Oria about it jumped to life in my head. After that, no matter how much I loved them, no other name would do. Because Carien ran the contest to pick a name, we decided she couldn't win a prize and we'd award to the honorable mentions instead.

All she gets is the above dedication.

Thank you for reading!

Credits
Content Editor: Deborah Nemeth
Line and Copy Editor: Rebecca Cremonese
Back Cover Copy: Erin Nelson Parekh
Cover Design: Louisa Gallie

~1~

ORIA HELD THE barrier against her raging brother.

At least, she did the best she could with her magic draining by the moment, its potency attenuating with distance and diminishing with the lack of opportunity to replenish her sgath—or to even take a full breath. Of course, her upside-down position, bouncing over Lonen's shoulder as he ran headlong through the palace, did nothing to make any of it easier.

"We may be in luck," Chuffta, her Familiar, reported. *"Yar's magic is running low also. He's sent for more priestesses to feed him sgath, as Gallia can't."* He paused to mentally cough at that. Oria's Familiar had also telepathically received Gallia's urgent message for them to run. As Yar's wife—particularly a newlywed in a temple-blessed marriage—only Gallia should be feeding Yar sgath to fight the magical barrier Oria had erected to save herself from execution, and Lonen from retribution. But Gallia had only recently arrived in Bára and, unused to the city's native magic, so different from her home at Lousá, she had not reached her full power.

But Gallia was stronger than she'd claimed. As a sister in magic, Oria could judge quite precisely how much Gallia had been capable of channeling. Oria's new sister had exaggerated her weakness—in a move shockingly disloyal to her new husband and against all expectation—to allow Oria to escape. If all went well, Yar would never discover the deception. Between his unstable temper and Gallia's status in Bára, that could turn out badly for her sister sorceress. Hopefully, she'd take Oria's advice and appeal to her and

Yar's mother, the former Queen Rhianna, for assistance.

"I can't imagine Priest Vico will allow other priestesses to feed sgath to Yar. It's against temple law if his ideal wife is alive and well," she replied to Chuffta.

"Yes, but it depends on what Vico considers to be 'well.'"

She framed a reply—speaking mentally took concentration—then grunted in pain as Lonen ducked around a corner, the sudden shift in direction making his shoulder dig into her belly. It looked so much more romantic in the illustrations. In reality, being carried off over a barbarian's shoulder left much to be desired.

"Sorry," Lonen shot the word out between panting breaths. "Unavoidable."

She didn't reply. Couldn't. It would be handy if she and Lonen could speak mind-to-mind the way she could with Chuffta—and unexpectedly with Gallia—particularly under circumstances like this. He might not like it, though. At the moment, all of his considerable personal energy was focused away from her, no doubt on fighting them free of Bára. At least that saved her having to screen out his emotions along with everyone else's.

"You are correct," Chuffta reported from his vantage, flying well above Yar's group. Her Familiar seemed to be enjoying his spy activities. *"They are arguing about it. Yar is most put out. He's losing focus and less able to fight your barrier. Vico is gently suggesting he check his* hwil, *which has not gone over well."* No, Yar would not do well with the suggestion that he might be showing any loss of the crucial equanimity that allowed the priests and priestesses of Bára to handle their dangerously powerful magic. Loss of *hwil* could be grounds for the temple taking back the mask that was their badge of office. With no mask, Yar could not be king. Could she somehow use that to her advantage—push Yar into losing *hwil* entirely?

"No, Oria." Chuffta's mind-voice was both sorrowful and deadly earnest. *"Without your mask, you cannot be queen either. And now that they know you can use grien, your life would be forfeit, regardless. It's not worth the risk."*

It might be, though. If only to save Bára and Dru both from the devastation that would be Yar's rule.

"I won't let you sacrifice yourself. Neither will Lonen," Chuffta added.

"I'm already regretting that I encouraged you two to become friends," she grumbled. Though it warmed her heart that her two men—albeit one a Destrye barbarian warrior and the other a derkesthai winged lizard—cared so much about her. They were her only allies in this mad escape to nowhere. Where would they go? *Anywhere but this place,* Lonen had said. Which meant leaving Bára and lethal exposure to the wild magic that would kill Oria within hours of leaving the walled city. Unless…

"Wait!" she shouted, and hammered her fists against Lonen's muscled back when he didn't even pause. She might as well be spitting into a sandstorm for all the good it did. She began kicking and wriggling against his powerful grip, which only tightened.

"Cut… it… out," he panted in time with his strides. He sent her a fierce mental image of him paddling her backside and dropping her into a chasm. As he happened to be racing toward the bridge over Ing's Chasm, which divided the palace grounds from Bára proper, he certainly could try. Not that he would. Most likely. The barbarian was hard to predict.

Not that he'd have a chance in Sgatha against her. She might give him the courtesy of staying out of his head, but she *would* use her magic against him if she had to. She'd become his wife, not his possession.

To get through his thick skull—and with Chuffta's report that Yar was otherwise occupied arguing with the High Priest—she diverted some of her active grien magic into a sharp smack on Lonen's ass.

He shouted in surprise, dropped her in an undignified heap on the ground, and whirled on his unseen attacker, brandishing his iron battle-axe in both hands. If she hadn't been trying to get her breath back, both from the jouncing ride and the fall—and if the circumstances had been less extreme—she'd have laughed at the look on his face.

With his warrior's reflexes, his consternation didn't last long, and he rounded on her with a thunderous expression. "That was you!"

"Yes, curse you." She was struggling to her feet, gracelessly tangled in her priestess robes. Despite his annoyance with her, Lonen moved quickly to help with a hand under her elbow, judiciously touching her only over the silk. She appreciated the assist, but quickly stepped out of his reach before he could toss her over his shoulder again. "You weren't listening to me."

"I was busy saving your life if you hadn't noticed," he bit out, and reached for her with one hand, holding the heavy axe in his other with easy strength.

She barely nipped back in time, holding up her palms to fend him off. "Not so fast. I stopped you because I want to go see my mother."

He stared at her with almost comical disbelief, the scar that jagged from his forehead and down one cheek ticcing with his ire, the emotion swirling around her now wholly pointed in her direction along with his incredulous attention. "I married a crazy woman," he said in an almost reflective tone. "Arill has cursed me with an insane wife, because I wasn't losing my mind fast enough on my own."

Oria threw up her hands and moved to go back into the palace. She made it one step before Lonen thrust his bulk between her and the doorway.

"Don't try it, Oria," he warned. "I don't want to hurt you, but I'll risk skin contact with you if it means saving your pretty neck from the executioner's blade."

"We don't have time for this!"

"Thank Arill—she's regained her sanity." Lonen moved to grab her again and she danced back, nearly tripping over the long hem of her formal robes.

"Listen to me, you thickheaded Destrye barbarian. Chuffta is watching them from above. Yar is out of power for the moment. We have breathing room and I need to see my mother."

"We don't have time for a heartfelt goodbye, you softhearted Báran sorceress," he snarled.

"I may be naïve, but I'm not stupid," she snarled back. "I need her advice if I'm going to find a way to survive outside the walls. Even you have to admit it will do me no good to escape execution only to succumb to the wild magic within hours of leaving the city. There has to be a way to do it because Gallia survived the journey here, but I don't know the trick. My mother might. *Think!*"

"I'm not stupid either. But at the risk of being cruel, I ask you to recall your mother's state of mind only two days ago." He took a deep breath, his emotional aura dampening. Something he was rapidly learning to do in being gentle with her. "She's beyond helping you."

"She has good days," Oria insisted. "And if she's in a fugue, then I promise we'll leave immediately with little time lost. It's worth the risk if you want me to be of any use to the Destrye."

Lonen possessed a quick intelligence and an enviable ability to adapt his strategy quickly to changing circumstances, so he didn't argue further. He also put the welfare of his people above all else. He slid the axe into its sheath on his back and stepped aside. "Walk fast. The moment Chuffta reports any change, you tell me immediately."

"Yes, Your Highness," she snapped, moving at a half-run down the grand hall to her mother's rooms. With his longer stride, Lonen kept up easily.

"I like the sound of that," he told her. "Finally, a little respect and humility from my scary sorceress wife."

"You wish," she retorted and he laughed, that big, rich sound. The Destrye king had a remarkable ability to find humor in the most dire circumstances. Perhaps all Destrye were like that, but somehow she didn't think so.

"All still okay?" she asked Chuffta, mostly to check on him. Certainly not because Lonen had ordered her to.

"They've gone into the temple and I think it best not to follow. I'll wait to see if anyone emerges to give the order to stop you."

Perhaps Vico planned to delay Yar long enough to let her escape. He'd taken her mask, as temple law compelled him, and she'd distinctly read his shock and revulsion at the discovery that she could wield male grien magic in addition to her appropriately female sgath. But he'd also acted before this to support her claim to the throne of Bára. She might be anathema due to her using male magic, but Yar posed an entirely different kind of threat. Not everyone supported her over Yar, but at least the people she most respected seemed to recognize the danger of his power-mad ways.

"Your mother refused to see you this morning," Lonen pointed out. "How will you get in now?"

"No she didn't. I never asked her to come to the trial."

"What?" Lonen's anger snapped brisk at her. "You could have used her support—and you lied to me that you sent her a message about it."

"I implied," she answered, refusing to feel guilty about it. "I couldn't ask her to watch her two remaining children fight over the throne, possibly to the death."

"We're going to have words about this, Oria," he gritted out.

"Sure!" she said, with a confidence she didn't feel. "If I live, we can fight all you like about how I don't have to do what you tell me to."

She was spared his response—a blistering one it would have been, too, by the feel of him—as they arrived at her mother's chambers to find them barred, and the guards with swords drawn against them.

"What's the meaning of this?" she demanded, using her best affronted-princess tone. The city and palace guard were on her side in the conflict with Yar. At least, they had been before this.

Lonen loomed at her back, the shadow cast by the bright sun

outside the window revealing that he brandished his axe again. The double-headed blades stood out stark and black against the golden rose stone of the wall. An ill omen.

"None are to enter the former queen's chambers," one of the guards said sternly enough, but the fear and uncertainty she read easily in his mind betrayed him, along with an image of Yar's face.

"According to whose orders?"

The guards exchanged glances. "Ah, King Yar's orders, Princess Oria," he answered.

"He's not king yet. If he said so, he lied."

"No, but… he will be, since you lost the contest. And we have to live here, Princess."

She shouldn't question how they knew the outcome of the magic trial. Vico may have banished the audience, but more sorcerers and sorceresses than she possessed the ability to magically spy on events. Knowledge was gold in Bára and gossip the fastest way to capitalize on it.

"If they're incapacitated, they can't be blamed for dereliction of duty," Lonen commented, in an eerily even tone. That deep, boiling rage in him fulminated near the surface, and she had no doubt he'd kill them without trouble. Her warrior might not relish killing, but he did it well.

"Choose, gentlemen," she ordered, trying to match Lonen's chill. "Death or unconsciousness—or you can yield and I'll make sure Captain Ercole knows you acted on my command." Ercole, at least, would stay loyal to her. The lay folk of Bára wouldn't care so much about her unseemly magic. She hoped. It wasn't as if there was historical precedent. No woman could actively wield grien magic, just as men couldn't passively absorb sgath. That was the natural order of things.

It just figured that she'd be the unnatural one.

"Only so far as you know," Chuffta chided. *"Why would the temple have a law against an impossible thing? There must have been those who came before you, to cause such a law to be put into the scrolls."*

An interesting point. *Princess Ponen,* the Trom had called her, on two occasions. An old word that meant potential, her mother had explained during one of her more lucid moments. Perhaps Oria's strange abilities related to that. But then the alien and terrible Trom could hardly be trusted. Summoned by Yar, the monstrous guardians killed with the least touch—any who still defied them after their giant dragon mounts reduced all in their path to ash with their fiery breath. But the Trom had deferred to Oria in an odd way. A profoundly discomfiting way, and their touch had no effect on her. Especially counterintuitive since she couldn't bear skin-to-skin contact with any but family and those with perfect *hwil.*

Someday you will call to us and your understanding will deepen. The memory of the Trom's words to her was enough to make her shudder, but time enough to deal with the Trom and the ongoing threat they posed *after* they escaped.

The guards meanwhile hesitated only a moment longer, eyeing Lonen with trepidation. He'd gained quite the reputation among the soldiers of Bára during the assault of the city. She didn't care to contemplate how many Bárans he'd killed personally, not to mention all the defenseless priestesses he'd murdered. Her people had slaughtered far more of his. Besides, she and Lonen had agreed to stop apologizing to each other for the transgressions of the past.

The present took up enough of that kind of thing.

With hasty bows, the guards stepped aside, ostentatiously looking the other direction. "Thank you, gentlemen," she said, including Lonen in it with a glance over her shoulder. He acknowledged the courtesy with a wry half smile, his gray eyes stony as the granite traded to Bára by one of her sister-cities. If she hadn't been able to sense the turmoil beneath, she'd have imagined him emotionless. "We're still in the clear—and this won't take long."

"It had better not," he muttered, following her in through the outer chambers, "or I'll knock *you* upside the head and carry you out of this cursed place."

She ignored him, long practiced at it from paying no attention to

Chuffta's lectures.

"To your chagrin, on many an occasion," Chuffta noted.

"And great peace of mind on many more."

He snorted mentally, though his worry threaded beneath. Oria picked up her skirts and her pace, hustling through the elegant chambers. The former queen sat in her usual spot by the window, alone, which was not usual at all.

"Mother!" Oria called out. "Where are your waiting women?"

Rhianna slowly moved her gaze from the window. Her brown eyes focused on her daughter, first puzzled, then with dawning awareness as she saw Lonen also. Her vacant expression crumpled into agonized grief. "You did it. You married the mind-dead barbarian. The worst has come to pass."

They'd been through this once already and Oria had no intention of subjecting Lonen to her mother's doom-filled predictions again. She knelt and took her mother's hands in hers. They were far too thin, and cold despite the growing midday heat. "I married him, yes. But the bond between us is strong—if you can perceive it, you know that much. It will be all right. He hasn't hurt me."

Rhianna seemed to look through her. "Not yet. Not until he tires of being married in name only and forces you into his bed—and to your death. You don't know how horrible men like him can be."

Lonen didn't make a sound, but his outrage at the accusation crawled over her skin. Justifiably so. He'd been excruciatingly careful with her, finally understanding the devastating implications for her of skin-to-skin contact. And he'd still found a way to consummate their marriage—however unconventionally—and the memory of the intimate moments of the night before would make her blush if she allowed it. She no longer had her mask to hide such inappropriate emotions, however, so she tucked those thoughts away where her mother couldn't feel them.

Oria could fake *hwil* like a High Priestess.

"I'm fine, mother. Don't worry. King Lonen is a good man. He'll take good care of me."

"He's a barbarian! A mind-dead—"

"Let's move this along," Lonen interrupted, using a mock-pleasant tone that didn't fool her for a moment. He simmered with impatience to be gone and in a few moments more, her barbarian would snap and resume bodily hauling her out of Bára.

"Mother, I can't explain, but I have to leave Bára. I have to go beyond the walls."

The former queen's face contorted in horror and she gripped Oria's hands. Once she would have shown no emotion, her *hwil* as a senior priestess and queen without flaw. All that had changed since her husband fell in battle to the Destrye forces. "You can't!" Rhianna wailed. "It will kill you."

"It won't." Oria kept her voice calm, ignoring Lonen's urgent worry tugging at her. "Yar brought a bride here from Lousá. Her name is Gallia, and you'll like her. Be good to her, help her if you can."

"Gallia came from Lousá?" her mother echoed.

"Yes. So there must be a way to travel between cities. How do the priestesses do it and live?"

She'd hoped to have time in the secret temple archives to discover such mysteries for herself, but she'd flat run out of that luxury.

"You're traveling to Lousá?" It didn't seem possible, but her mother gripped harder, grinding Oria's finger bones together. "Yes! My brilliant daughter, you're so clever. Go to Lousá and find an ideal husband there. One who will set your magic free. You cannot imagine the perfection of an ideal marriage. It's what you deserve."

Better to let her mother believe that, rather than that Oria fled in the face of execution at her brother's order. "Exactly, mother. But I need to know how to do it. How do I keep the wild magic from eroding my mind and *hwil*, from making me break?"

Her mother frowned, cocking her head. "Where is your mask?"

"I am here alone with you and my husband," Oria improvised. "I set it right over there. How do I travel outside the walls?"

"This is taking too long," Lonen murmured at her. "Better to take the chance and go."

"Just a few minutes more. We're still clear."

"Not so much. Servants have emerged from the temple and sgath is building within. Yar may have won the argument."

Sgatha take Yar and all his minions. "Mother, if you love me, tell me now."

Her mother's face cleared. "You should appeal to High Priestess Febe for the lesson. That's the proper protocol. You know that."

Internally Oria groaned. That protocol might be just a titch difficult to manage as Oria had killed Febe the day before. "You always explain things so much better, Mother. Please? As a gift to me."

"You promised to tell Lonen when things changed."

"No, he ordered. I never agreed."

"You said, 'yes, Your Highness.'"

"That was sarcasm." Out loud, she repeated, "Please. Tell me what I need to know."

Her mother released her hands, looking sorrowful, then framed Oria's face in her palms. "You were such a beautiful little girl. The image of my aunt Tania. Did I ever tell you that?"

"No." She didn't even know she had an aunt Tania.

"So powerful. So ambitious and determined. Don't be like her, Oria. Find an ideal husband and channel your magic through him. Don't try to do it alone. Don't be like Tania. Promise me."

"All right. I promise. How do I survive the wild magic?"

"Oria, it's time to go. She can't help you." For as grim as he sounded, Lonen's hand on her shoulder remained gentle. His intense energy burned through the silk, but not painfully so.

"He's right, Oria—you're out of time."

"A minute more," she urged them both. Lonen's hand tightened on her, aware as he so uncannily could be that she conversed with her Familiar also.

"Did Chuffta give warning?"

"Mother, please!"

"I'm coming there. If you won't tell Lonen, I will."

Her mother smiled, leaned in, pressed a kiss to her cheek—and whispered a few cryptic words of advice.

~ 2 ~

LONEN WRESTLED DOWN the twin urges to throttle Oria for her stubbornness and to simply toss her over his shoulder again.

He should never have put her down, no matter the provocation. That had been his first mistake, followed by a whole sequence that ended with letting her talk him into this fool's errand.

Worse, he couldn't pin down where the presentiment came from, but he strongly suspected she was lying to him about passing along Chuffta's warnings. She got a certain look and feel to her when the lizardling spoke to her and, if his instincts didn't miss, the derkesthai had been chattering away. Probably with bad news, as all news in Bára seemed to be. He tightened his hand on her slim shoulder, the bones so frail beneath he could crush them if he wasn't careful.

Totally in contrast to her personality, which might crush *him* if he let her. Especially if anything happened to her because of it. He'd already faced losing her several times that day, which was plenty for one morning. And they had a great deal to get through before the day ended. He needed her to save his people, never mind his personal feelings.

"Oria, time's up. Come willingly or I'll take steps."

She resisted with surprising strength in that delicate frame, staying poised with her mother's lips against her cheek. A flutter at the window had him leaping back and drawing his axe in the same movement. Chuffta landed on the stone sill, wide wings buffeting the sides of the arch, which was by no means narrow. Though the derkesthai's body was no longer than Lonen's forearm, his wings were each double that, with thin white webbing that showed sunlight between fine bones, like the fingers of a hand. As if the wings were indeed the animal's forelegs, he possessed no others—only taloned hind legs he used to grip the sill.

Chuffta's brilliant green eyes fixed on him with uncanny intelligence and there was no missing the urgency in them.

"That's it. We're leaving." With no more warning, he bent down, wrapped an arm around Oria's slender waist and hauled her unceremoniously off her feet. She wailed pitifully and he hardened his heart. The former queen reached for her daughter, tears streaming down her cheeks.

"Oria, wait! Take me to Lousá with you! I'll help you find a husband worthy of you."

Setting his teeth, Lonen carried Oria away, Chuffta winging close above.

"I'll be back, Mother," Oria cried. "I promise."

Manfully, Lonen didn't comment on the likelihood of Oria keeping that promise. If he had anything to say about it—and he most certainly would—his wife wouldn't set foot anywhere near Bára again.

"You can put me down," Oria said loudly, maybe not for the first time, as they reached the outer doors. "It might look better for me to walk instead of you dragging me along like some captured slave girl."

He carried the burden of guilt for many things, Arill knew, but he wouldn't be ashamed over this one, no matter how she needled him. He'd also take the higher road and not remind her how much her slave-girl-captured-by-the-Destrye-barbarian sexual fantasies had played into their very hot wedding night. She'd could have used her magic to stop him, as she'd done earlier, and she hadn't. He'd probably behave just as badly if torn away from his one remaining loving family member, too, so he'd give her the rope.

He set her on her feet and Chuffta landed neatly on her padded shoulder, rubbing his triangular head against her cheek as she dashed her own tears away. "Stay right here while I check the corridor," he instructed her, as if she were someone who listened to sense.

Fortunately, the way was clear—the guards had absented themselves. If Arill watched over him and Oria, the guards had simply run off to avoid punishment, not for other, more sinister reasons. Reaching back through the doorway, he nearly forgot himself and took Oria's hand, diverting to her sleeve at the last moment. "Come on. Move fast."

She trotted beside him, face flushed, breathing too hard. "Can you keep up?" he asked.

Her extraordinary copper eyes flashed to his, her expression smoothing into something like her favored remote mask. His haughty foreign sorceress. "I'm not a child, Destrye."

"No bigger than one," he said in a dubious tone sure to fire her up.

She glared in fury—and picked up her pace, her tears drying. "When I make you pay for all of this, the price will be dear indeed."

"I look forward to it," he replied in all sincerity. At least she was talking as if she planned to survive, which was all that mattered for the moment.

They hurried over the bridge from the palace into the city proper, the denizens turning in surprise at their hasty passage. Because of the way various chasms—all without fences or railings of any kind—riddled the city, rather than take the far-too-exposed main bridge from the palace doors, they had to travel past the guard barracks to reach a bridge to take them over. They crossed and retraced their steps on the other side, weaving amongst the people traveling the path between the chasm and the towers and various associated buildings. Lonen glimpsed the palace guard pouring out the grand doors, weapons bristling.

"Through here." He tugged Oria through a doorway into a dark pub he recalled from the days the Destrye occupied the city. The proprietor, a genial Báran man, gaped at them. "Princess Oria!" he called out. "And King Lonen? Is all—"

"I'm fine," she answered, all graciousness, pausing to wave at the people. "Taking a stroll through the city. Such a lovely day."

She was an abysmal liar, but a decent actress. The man relaxed and the people summoned a cheer. They all supported Oria's claim to the throne. Because they weren't idiots.

"Back door open?" Lonen asked, and winked at them. "Better to keep the princess off the main paths."

"Of course, I—"

But Lonen was already hustling Oria in that direction, taking her through a storeroom with wine—and water—casks, and out again into the scorching Báran sunlight.

"How did you know that place had a back door?"

"Most of your dwellings do. All those open doors and windows you riddle every damn building with."

"For cross-ventilation."

"I get it."

"But you knew *that* place in particular."

"They serve that honey ale. The men liked it. I chased down more than a few of mine there, who thought to use that back door to duck me."

"I had no idea."

"It was a long week that you slept through."

She pressed her lush mouth over whatever retort she planned, so he suppressed his grin at her expense. "Where are we even going?" she asked instead. "The city gates are that way. And Yar has the palace guard after us."

"I saw them," he replied grimly. "We're going to the barracks to get my horse."

"You have a horse?"

"Did you think I walked from Dru?"

"I hadn't thought about it." She had that faint tone, the one she got when she ran up against her unfamiliarity with the world outside Bára. So fierce in so many ways, so powerfully magical, and yet she'd also spent far too much of her life sequestered in her tower. Even without the challenge of withstanding the wild magic outside the walls, the coming journey would be a trial for her.

She said nothing more as they wove through the puzzle of back alleys and jagged lanes that made up the less polished side of Bára. Here merchants unloaded wares and the occasional work golem performed some manual task, an unsavory sight. The Bárans didn't like to use animals for labor, a nicety Lonen found ironic given how easily they dismissed the humanity of the Destrye they'd slaughtered for the precious water they hauled about in casks. Besides, though the city golems were innocuous cousins of the ones he'd battled as they attacked the Destrye in relentless waves, and though they lacked the razor-sharp teeth and claws of their fiercer versions, the things still sent a rill of terror through him.

Old habits die hard. Especially when they haunt your nightmares.

Every single person they passed stared in astonishment at the sight of their beloved princess—unmistakable with her metallic copper hair, intricately braided in the priestess style. In retrospect he viciously wished he'd thought to roll her up in a blanket. Easier to transport, less trouble, *and* not so obvious.

Swiveling his head on his sinuous neck, Chuffta gave him a bright-eyed stare that seemed to be full of humor.

"I don't suppose you can work magic to cloud people's minds, make them forget they saw you?" he muttered at Oria.

She glanced up in surprise. "Why would I do that?"

He noted in the back of his mind that she hadn't denied having that ability—something he'd long suspected. She'd only assured him that she hadn't sent him dreams while they were apart, not that she hadn't influenced his thoughts while they were together. "We won't exactly be difficult to track," he pointed out, gesturing in frustration at the many onlookers.

Pursing her lips, she blew out a huff of exasperation. It was absurdly entertaining to him to see the gesture again. He'd hated the golden priestess mask that had hidden her face. Though he knew it wounded her pride that Vico had stripped it from her, he couldn't summon up much regret. He liked seeing her face. She might be able to read his mind with ease, but reading her expressions gave him at least a few clues to understanding his enigmatic sorceress.

"There's only one way out of Bára," she said. "It's not a mystery which way we'll go."

Grimly, he acceded to the truth of that. It had made the city both impregnable from most assaults and then almost ridiculously easy to take, once they found the key. "Assuming we make it out of the gates, how far will Yar chase you?"

She considered that with a bemused expression—though some of that could be for the city guard barracks they'd entered. "I've never been here," she commented, confirming his speculation.

"The stables are through here, at the other end. Answer my question."

She shrugged. "If we make it through the gates, he won't. He knows I'll die out there. Why bother chasing me beyond the walls?"

Fear stabbed at him, but he put it away. No sense thinking about that. She was certainly dead if they stayed. He turned down a narrow corridor—and several of the guard appeared, blocking their passage, swords drawn, postures clearly belligerent. Wonderful. Thrusting Oria behind him, he brandished his battle-axe. Chuffta flew up to hover above them, hissing, wings working furiously.

"Princess Oria," the one in front called out. "We are to escort you back to the palace. Please step back while we dispense with this barbarian. We'll protect you."

Lonen choked back a curse as she slipped in front of him, as if her slight body gave him protection. The light-framed men of Bára posed no great threat. Even their fighters had become weak in comparison to the Destrye, sheltered too long by their magical overlords. Once they'd disabled their sorcerers, the Destrye armies had dealt with the men at arms with comparative ease.

Something of Oria stirred deep inside him, however, in that place that had come alive following their grueling ritual of a wedding ceremony. A bright place she seemed to occupy, like a candle in a window at night. Normally a slim spark, the sense of her grew, glowing like a torch gaining fire, eating the fuel and getting hotter, burning.

He'd felt something of it before at the temple, though this was as the sun to the small moon Grienon in its intensity. Was this her magic?

"Stand down," she commanded. "You will not block us."

"Princess, by order of King Yar, we—"

"He is no king of mine, nor of yours." She cut them off, face pale in the murky interior. The low buildings in the shadow of the city wall had no windows to let in the light and air—none of the cross-ventilation of which the Bárans were so proud—like the towers did. More defensible, no doubt. Or the barracks didn't rate the consideration. "Yar has usurped my throne. I won the contest fairly. But rather than plunge Bára into civil war, I seek to leave peacefully."

Had he thought her a bad liar? She'd spun that one skillfully enough.

"You speak treason," one guard said, his lips white, eyes widening in horror.

"She does," came a deeper voice. The tall form of Captain Ercole came up the dim corridor. "And the punishment for treason is exile. Let them go."

The men put down their weapons without argument, stepping aside to let them pass. If nothing else, the Báran guard did have good discipline. Lonen would have snorted in disgust at their painting Oria's actions as treason if it didn't allow for their easier escape. The complicated tensions between their Temple—which awarded priesthood to those judged capable of controlling their magic, and thus eligibility for the throne—and the ruling council still gave him headaches. The throne should have been Oria's. But for arcane Temple rules that ousted her, it would have been.

She didn't have a treasonous bone in her body.

"Thank you, Captain," Oria said, but the man shook his head, disappointment writ clear on his face.

"I don't pretend to understand what's happening. All I know is what I see before my eyes—a daughter of the royal house, hope of her people, abandoning the city in its hour of need."

Though her spine remained straight, chin high, something in Oria sagged. Lonen might have felt it more than he saw it. Chuffta landed on her shoulder, wings folding with a snap, prehensile tail snaking down her arm in a series of coils, glittering like ivory bracelets. Lonen set his hand at her waist to brace her on the other side. A low and vicious verbal blow from Ercole, who'd been one of her strongest supporters. And after Oria had sacrificed so much of herself for Bára. Would they only be happy when she gave up her very life for them?

Oria held up her hand, stopping him from speaking before he knew he'd been about to voice the thought. "So be it then," she said quietly, and pushed past Ercole, giving him and the guard the wide berth she needed around the non-magical, the tense set of her face revealing how their harsh emotions must be affecting her. For her sake then, he reined back his own anger and outrage, moving between her and the men.

"You should know, Captain," she said over her shoulder, "that I said goodbye to my mother, after forcing our way past the guards at her door who sought to keep her from me. They should not be held to fault for that." Her tone strongly implied she held Ercole responsible for their safety.

"Princess," Ercole called after them. Oria took several more steps before she halted, looking back without fully turning.

"We'll guard your back this last time," Ercole said, with a grave nod. "The least we can do is see you safely into exile. Go swiftly and in peace."

She dipped her chin and turned swiftly away, hurrying to keep up with Lonen, not meeting his gaze. It didn't take long to reach the outbuildings between the guard barracks and the towering wall. Lonen's stallion stood at the near end of the room, having long since scented his approach.

"I didn't know horses were so big," Oria gasped.

"My stallion is particularly large. And trained to be aggressive. Stay back until I have him suited up. Keep clear of both his front and back—he bites and kicks."

Oria gazed about the slapdash construction, made mainly of cannibalized casks that had seen better days, a slight wrinkle to her pert nose. For his part, Lonen worked quickly, retrieving the stallion's tack and fitting him with it—a task made no easier by the horse, restive from days of inactivity.

"This room is made of wood," Oria said, a question in her voice.

"Yes. Bára had no stables when we occupied originally, so Ion"—he managed to say his late brother's name without any special emphasis, proud of himself for the neutral tone—"had this built for the few horses we needed to keep in the city. The rest, of course, stayed with the encamped army. Arill take you, horse! Hold still." He elbowed the stallion's shoulder. It would feel like a gnat bite to the massive warhorse, but Oria cried out a protest.

"Don't hurt him!"

Lonen, holding aloft the heavy leather saddle to slide it onto the horse's back—not easy with the stallion's shoulder level with the top of his head—scowled at her. Normally several grooms would have helped with this. "He knows better. He's being a brat because he's mad at being cooped up all these days and we don't have time for his dramatics. Oria, no! Don't go near his—"

He dropped the saddle and lunged for her, but Oria moved fast when she made up her mind. Recklessly brave—and with much of the same impetuous nature that drove Yar—she stretched up on tiptoe to lay her hands on the horse, bracketing his jaw. Having expected the vicious stallion to bite through her delicate fingers, Lonen checked himself as the horse stilled immediately, then snuffled Oria's braids and nickered, a sound he'd never heard from the warhorse.

Chuffta, still on Oria's shoulder, arched his neck back like a striking snake staying clear, nostrils flaring as he surveyed the stallion with bright-eyed interest.

"What's his name?" she asked.

"He's a horse—he doesn't have a name."

"Don't be stupid. Everything that's alive has a name, if only to itself."

"Then ask him."

"He doesn't think that clearly. But there's something... Something you call him sometimes. He likes it."

"We don't have time for—"

"If you want him to hold still, I need his name. What is it? I can hear it just on the edge of your thoughts... Aha! Buttercup."

"His name is not—"

"I would hate being cooped up, too, Buttercup," Oria was murmuring, blithely ignoring him. "You like to run and fight and be free, just like your master, don't you? But if you'll be still a few moments longer, we can all go. Won't you like that, Buttercup? I think you can finish now, Lonen."

Shaking himself out of the spell it felt like she cast on him, too, Lonen took advantage of whatever magic she'd wrought to calm the warhorse. He couldn't help sneaking peeks at her, however, her slim form inclined against the muscled bulk of the big black steed, her white hands like fairy wings against the stallion's massive jaw that Lonen had seen chomp through far sturdier bones. Though some of her braids had come loose from the elaborate weave hanging in coppery tangles down her back, and her robes were dusty and ragged from the magical duel and their mad flight through the city, she looked beyond beautiful.

The image reminded him sharply of the first time he saw her, framed by candlelight in a window, looking like something out of an old storybook. Now, as then, the sight stirred something deep in him he'd thought long lost to countless dead and the relentless tread of clawed golem feet.

Some part of him that still believed that magic brought light and hope, not devastation.

That happy endings could be real.

~3~

"LET'S GO." LONEN'S command came gruff, abrupt, and Oria dragged herself from the fascinating communion with Buttercup's thoughts. They weren't as sharply formed as Chuffta's, not shaped into words as he could do, but they shared a certain quality. An immediacy. A vividly intense experiencing of life.

"Is that how I seem?" Chuffta seemed equally bemused by Buttercup.

"In different way."

"Oria!" Lonen raised his voice, making her start. He sat astride Buttercup, bending over and holding out his crooked arm for her. "We're escaping, remember? Focus, please."

"Ercole let us go, and his men are watching our backs," she replied, releasing Buttercup's head with reluctance, but keeping a thread of contact to his thoughts so he wouldn't start dancing around again, threatening to step on her with those hooves the size of her head. Later she'd think about the crushing disappointment in her that had radiated from Ercole. The bitter sense of betrayal that she'd abandon Bára for the Destrye king.

A daughter of the royal house, hope of her people, abandoning the city in its hour of need.

Lonen shook his head, black curls springing with the movement, escaping the tie-back. Frustrated exasperation from him. He thrust his angled forearm at her as if she hadn't noticed it the first time. She eyed both it and the daunting distance to Buttercup's back. Was she meant to climb him like a tower?

"Can't you hear the fighting? Yar has guards loyal to him and they've obviously engaged Ercole's." Lonen bit out the words. "Ercole will do what he can, but we have to get out of Bára immediately. Take my hand. Now."

She didn't mean to back up, but the slap of his harsh emotions took her by surprise. He was a man of action and she thwarted him doing what he needed to—getting her safely away so she could help rescue his people. She understood that.

But a desperately cowardly part of herself shouted in alarm that as soon as she took his arm, this part of her life would end forever. She'd be on a Destrye warhorse, plunging through the gates of Bára and into the wild magic of the outer world. Despite the information her mother had whispered to her, Oria wasn't at all sure she could implement the advice. It would take time and practice to hone those skills.

Until then, it would be as it had been before, when she'd stepped through the gates and it had felt as if a tower had dropped onto her head, breaking open her skull and dashing her brains to the stones. The memory of that pain froze her, and she wasn't brave enough to face it.

That and the days of gray fog, the wandering through nothingness, neither dead nor alive.

She might not emerge from it sane, if she emerged at all. What if she spent the rest of her days with her body an empty husk and her consciousness forever trapped in that formless realm?

Execution, at least, would be quick.

"It shouldn't be so bad this time. You're more skilled, stronger, and in better mental and emotional condition. The time before you were already stretched thin enough to break before you stepped through the gates."

"I know... but this won't end. There won't be any going back inside to my tower to rest and recover. I'll have no refuge. It will batter me until I break."

Her head spun with it, and cold sweat dripped down her back. Outside the walls, under the huge sky with nowhere to hide, she might fall off the edge of the world, with nothing to cling to.

"Oria." Lonen ground out her name. "If you don't take my arm right now, I'm going to—"

"Don't shout at me!" she shrieked, though she knew, in the rational part of her mind, that he hadn't been.

With a curse, he slid off of Buttercup and seized her.

Not to toss her over the saddle as she expected. But to wrap her in his arms and pull her close against him. Chuffta took off from her shoulder and Lonen cupped her head in one big hand, carefully touching only her hair, and held her cheek against his chest, murmuring soothing words at her, not seeming to care that she stood there rigidly, arms straight down her sides to clenched fists.

"Oria, I'm sorry. I'm sorry. I didn't think."

He wrapped her, too, in soothing, reassuring affection, imagining a cozy bed with furs and a crackling fireplace; outside freezing cold. The scene changed to a platform in a tree, with the cool green rustling leaves of summer all around. It helped, even given the strange array of images, and she found herself able to take a breath again.

"No, I'm sorry," she said against him. "I don't know what happened."

"You panicked," he replied. "If I'd been thinking, I would have realized." He lifted his head, body tensing. She heard it now, too. Shouting in the distance and a clatter of swords. But he didn't move.

"We have to go," she said, but she didn't move either.

"Can you?" He put his hands on her shoulders and moved her away from him. "Look at me, Oria."

Not understanding why it was so difficult, she raised her eyes to meet his flinty gray gaze. Behind him, Chuffta perched on Buttercup's saddle, watching her. Lonen studied her, too, assessing, nearly seeing into her heart as the Trom had. "I don't know why I'm so afraid," she whispered, as if not giving full voice to the fear would make it less real.

"Because you're a smart woman. The outer world, leaving Bára, it all holds real danger for you. Fear gives us warning. We listen to it and make decisions accordingly."

The shouting grew closer and his fingers tensed on her shoulders. But he kept up the soothing images. In his vision the leaves of the tree parted to show a distant lake, blue as the sky, still and serene. "The outer world holds beauty, too. And here you face certain death."

"Okay," she said on a thin breath.

"Are you sure? I'll hold you, but you have to try not to struggle against me if you panic again. I need a hand free to defend us against attackers, too."

The sounds of pitched fighting grew closer. He was right and she begged the unreasoning part of her to listen. To stay in Bára was to die. Whatever happened outside, not matter how painful, at least she had a chance to live.

"I'm sure. Let's go." Before she succumbed to panic again.

With a quick smile, he let her go and vaulted up the saddle again with admirable ease. Chuffta took wing to make room. Tamping down her trepidation, she reached to grasp his muscled forearm.

"Put your foot on mine," he instructed, all calm radiating from him. He lifted her as she bent her knee, helping her reach, then swooping her the rest of the way onto his lap before she realized it. Nestling her across his strong thighs, he wrapped one arm around her waist, holding her tightly against him, and drew his axe with the other. "You'd think Ion would have built more than one exit. One thing is certain, we're not going back out the door and into that melee."

"What will we do?"

He grinned down at her. "Nice thing about wood is, it breaks." His thighs flexed and he shouted a command.

Buttercup didn't move.

A hint of alarm leaked through Lonen's studied calm. He tightened his thighs again, giving the command, but Buttercup still didn't move. "What in Arill?" he growled.

"Oh! Sorry." Belatedly she thought to remove her mental hold on the stallion and the warhorse leapt forward, jolting them. Lonen kept his seat though, holding her secure.

"Hang tight!" he shouted, and she wrapped her arms around his waist. Buttercup galloped headlong for the far wall. They would crash into it. What in the name of Sgatha was he—

At the last moment, Buttercup reared up onto his hind legs, front hooves cracking against the wood, sending splinters flying. In the same arc of movement, he leapt through the opening into bright daylight, Lonen ducking over her to protect their heads. His cheek grazed her ear, sending a hiss of destabilizing and painful energy through her. She breathed it out, knowing it would only grow worse.

HE ONLY HOPED the city gates would be open. They should be at this time of day. Unless Yar had ordered them closed against Oria's escape. They'd delayed far too long, cutting it much too close. He should have run straight for his horse to begin with. Preferably with Oria unconscious.

At least then she wouldn't have had time to contemplate the enormous, tremendously difficult step—and leap of faith in him—that she took by leaving her home.

He'd seen Oria under many pressures before. She'd surrendered the city to him, white with strain and dread. He'd seen her furious, grieving, shedding tears of frustration and despair. He'd even seen her waxy pale with overload to the point of collapse.

But he'd never seen her panicked like she was now, her pupils mere pinpricks so the copper disks of her eyes appeared huge in her face gone ghostly as the dead, her voice a thin screech of utter terror.

He'd make it up to her. Somehow, someday.

If he could get her out of Bára.

The warhorse galloped headlong for the gates. Bárans of all stripes crowded the narrow streets. Common folk going about their business, a cluster of healers haggling at a stall, even a priest or priestess, androgynous in the gold mask and shapeless crimson robes. Some flung themselves out of the way, and the well-trained horse neatly dodged those who didn't. As Lonen urged him for even more speed, the rested—and restive—stallion readily complied, his footing never slipping even on the tight turns around towers, avoiding the deep chasms that snaked through the city. Time enough later to conserve their resources. If the gates stood open, they needed to get through as fast as possible. If not…

Well, Lonen had experience with those doors—and the huge bar that barricaded them that could be moved only by magic. No mortal warhorse, not even one of his stallion's fearsome strength, could hope to batter them down.

The swung onto the main road that led to the gates, the horse's hooves hitting the paving stones with a clatter and people—merchants, guards, and passersby alike—scattering with screams of shock and terror.

The gates had been closed. No welcoming daylight. The enormous bar in place.

He cursed, viciously. For all he'd hoped Arill rested her hand on their escape, the goddess could be a fickle bitch and dearly loved to punish him for his many sins.

"Keep going!" Oria shouted at him. Sideways across his lap, she looked forward, her profile calm, intent, and still. Chuffta flew just above and to the left of them, guarding their undefended flank. He showed no signs of slowing.

All right, then. Speaking of leaps of faith.

They plunged straight for the gates, strong and firm in the shadowed arch. Guards stood to either side, not risking themselves beneath the warhorse's thundering hooves, but ready to cut them down once they were trapped.

The torch of Oria's magic swelled in his breast, heating him from within. Ten horse-lengths away. Nine.

"If you're going to do something, do it now!" he shouted.

Five lengths.

Three.

The bar lifted, sailing over the wall and the doors burst outward with a boom and flash, as if struck by lightning. Already under the arch of stone, they thundered through a rain of rocks and rubble. A shard clipped Chuffta's wing and he screeched, bobbling in the air, but recovering. He shot ahead, a white projectile, into the blue sky above the sere plain beyond.

Oria gasped and at first Lonen thought it was the wild magic taking its toll. Then he saw what had alarmed her—an old woman pulling a handcart, stopped in the middle of the road that ascended through the soft dunes from the gates of Bára. No way they could go off the paved road, the big horse would flounder in the deep sand and they'd be done for.

Cueing the stallion, who responded with the ease of his perfect training, Lonen felt the steed's muscles bunch, spring—and they sailed over the woman's head, handcart and all—landing on the far side.

Oria's whooping laughter flew though the bright sunshine also. A welcome sound.

A hopeful one.

~ 4 ~

LONEN PRESSED ON, not slowing their pace for some time, though the warhorse grew slick with sweat, his huge lungs working like the bellows of Bára's glass forges.

Hot as those blazing forges, too, with the afternoon sun beating mercilessly down on them.

"The next time I plan an escape from a desert city," he said aloud, "it's going to be at night."

Oria didn't reply and he didn't expect her to. She'd lost consciousness not long after they'd left the walls of Bára behind. Though she sagged against him like a flower wilting without water, he kept talking to her, in case she could hear. For all he knew she hovered near death and he carried her dying body away from the only place that could save her.

Except that they'd execute her first, he reminded himself. He'd made the only decision he could—no sense revisiting it. Oria always liked to accuse him of eternal optimism in the face of impossible odds. Then so be it, he'd hold on to the hope that she'd recover. Keeping his mind active helped preserve his own sanity and alertness, too. So as they rode onward, he worked the problem.

He could add to lessons learned that in the future he'd actually *plan* the escape at all. Had he thought about it, he could have predicted the strong likelihood of things going this badly. Oria had speculated that Yar might know of her ability to wield grien magic—and had warned him the temple held such a thing to be anathema, punishable by death. If he hadn't been so dazzled by her, so head-in-the-trees at being able to slake a bit of the obsessive lust she stirred in him, he might have taken some steps against the worst-case scenario. Supplies of water, for example. Or those potions Oria's serving woman had brewed to restore her health after the wedding ceremony—those would have been incredibly handy to have along. Then he might have been able to do something to help her recover from the impacts of this magic.

The only thing that kept him from despairing that she'd already died was the spark inside his heart where Oria's flame remained lit, if weak and fluttering. Well, that and Chuffta, who'd long since folded himself into the space between Lonen and Oria, banding the skin of her wrist with his tail, and laying his cheek to hers. At the thought, Chuffta turned his head to angle one green eye at him, the translucent lid closing slowly from the bottom up, then descending again.

It was almost as if the derkesthai winked at him in reassurance. Lonen would take it that way.

Once away from the city, they passed very few other travelers. It was always this way, with not many willing—or foolhardy enough—to brave the drifting sands of the alkali desert to make the journey. After they turned off the road and in the direction of Dru, they encountered no one at all.

Of course, around Bára itself, nothing thrived. When he'd traveled to the walled city only days before, full of violent thoughts of revenge and retribution, only he and the warhorse moving under the harsh blue sky, he'd entertained himself with the fancy that Bára had sucked the life out of everything surrounding her. The magic-wielders inside the walls wore elegant, colorful silks and dined on honey and exotic fruits, but they did so on the backs of the Destrye—draining the lakes of Dru, leaving her people starving or burnt to ashes.

As desolate as the desert surrounding Bára.

Now, against all probability, he carried Bára's greatest treasure in his arms, and his heart was full of bewildered affection for the enemy he'd once thought he'd hated. He hadn't expected to return to Dru with a foreign sorceress as his wife, but he'd hoped he would ride home with some chance of saving the Destrye from further Trom incursions. The Trom had caused their dragons to burn many of the Destrye's crops and aqueducts, but Lonen's people had saved some. If the Trom hadn't returned in his absence, if Oria could prevent them from returning in the future, he supposed that hope still lived.

As long as Oria did.

He slowed the horse to a walk as they neared the Bay of Bára, where the bore tides left scars of salt on the baked soil and fine sand drifted in sere waves, a mockery of the distant sea. No one had pursued them, just as Oria predicted. But, though the sun lowered to the horizon, he'd vastly prefer to cross before resting, rather than be pinned between Bára and the treacherous mud. Just in case.

Scowling at the sky, he looked for the moons. Sgatha hung low, swallowing the western horizon with her broad, rosy crescent. She'd remain there, in that phase, for weeks yet, finishing her steady, stately progress across the sky before sinking for the winter months. No sign of Grienon at all, which could change at any moment. The smaller, brighter moon rose and set several times a night, whirling through his phases, like a young man never satisfied to sit still for long.

It made sense to him, that the Bárans associated female magic with Sgatha and male magic with mercurial, intense Grienon. And it bothered him to find any lucidity to the Bárans' magic.

Still, he had no idea how to calculate the ebb and flow of the bore tides. He reined the stallion up on a sharp rise overlooking the flat, expansive bay. A thin stream of water ran from what had once been a mighty river through the silt, connecting to the sea some leagues down. The crossing grew only more treacherous nearer the ocean—the Destrye scouts had learned that to their sorrow when they'd first approached Bára.

The stream running through the middle—all that remained of

the once great river that had formed the bay, now no more than a sad trickle that wouldn't even qualify as a creek in Dru—had carved steep banks into the rocky ground beneath the sand. Occasional paths wended down firmer sections here and there, mostly worn by wildlife, though Lonen pitied any creature relegated to drinking from it. The water ran bitter and so brackish that it had immediately sickened the Destrye who'd tried it. Once the river must have been fresh water, carrying snowmelt and rainfall out of the stone mountains beyond Bára. Now, however, it had dried up along with all the land in the region, cursed by whatever force baked away all their rain. The salts and minerals in the soil saturated the pitiful stream, poisoning what flowed from the hills.

The bore tides from the sea took care of the rest, infusing the channel with salt water, sometimes several times daily.

One of his brother Arnon's clever engineers had charted the flow of the tides when the Destrye army had crossed before. It had to do with the moons and their phase, and how they combined their forces, male and female, sometimes fighting each other, sometimes working together. And just as difficult for the inexperienced to predict. It was too much to remember. Each time they'd needed to make the crossing Arnon had consulted the complicated charts the engineers had drawn up. Though Sgatha moved slowly and changed faces with similar stateliness, Grienon's mad dashes across the sky, waxing and waning as he did, collided with her influence. They pushed and pulled the tides up and down the flat river channel. Sometimes the bore tide rushed in with thunderous certainty, flowing well past the crossing. Other times it aborted in mid-surge, turning back to the sea.

Impossible for Lonen to figure alone.

When he'd crossed on the way to Bára, he'd taken his chances. He'd been too consumed with anger over Oria's supposed betrayal to care for his own life. He and his horse had run when they could, then trudged through the deeper silt when they couldn't—the stallion sinking to his knees in places, even without Lonen's additional weight, and Lonen to his hips. If the bore tide had caught them in those moments, he certainly would have died. The stallion, with his height, could likely wait out the shallow surge. Lonen had entertained a half-formed plan of climbing to the saddle in hopes of holding his head above water long enough to survive until the waters receded again.

But Arill had watched over him and they'd crossed without incident.

Carrying his precious burden, however, he could not cavalierly trust to luck—or Arill—again. Not twice in a row. Arill might cast her blessings according to her own wishes, but she rarely showered them twice in the same way. The man who hoped for the exact same extraordinary blessing was nothing more than a fool.

He rarely wished for Arnon's gift with math—and patience for calculating the arc of the moons' passage, confirming the numbers with his engineers—but it would be convenient to trust in a skill at this point. Maybe two hours left before the sun set. Enough time to make the crossing, even if they got bogged down and had to go slowly. Far better than chancing it with less light, when he might not be able to spot the treacherous sinkholes. He glanced down at Oria, as if she might have suddenly recovered, offering some magical solution to the problem, as she had with the truly spectacular exploding open of the city gates.

She'd said she had no idea what affinity her grien had, as she'd only recently discovered she possessed it and, as a woman, had naturally not been trained to use it. The Báran sorcerers used their magic in particular ways. Yar moved and molded stone. Others he'd seen in battle hurled fireballs or opened chasms in the earth. Or bringing golems to life.

Oria, though—so far, besides blasting open the doors or smacking him with her grien, she'd brought blooming, fruiting life to dying plants. And grown vines out of stone at the trial. She'd also communicated with his horse, holding him still with a thought. Perhaps it wasn't unreasonable to think she could hold back the tides.

But her eyes remained stubbornly closed. The tracery of blue veins in her eyelids deepened to purple shadows around her eyes, her complexion like the thin, translucent skin between the concentric layers of a pungent root vegetable.

She was dying in his arms. And he could do nothing to save her. Just as he'd been unable save Nolan from dying on the battlefield, or his father and Ion crumpling to boneless jelly before his eyes at the Trom's lethal caress.

And if they failed to return, he wouldn't be able to prevent the Trom from destroying the Destrye utterly. The outcome that nearly everyone he loved had given their lives to prevent.

Chuffta rustled his wings, catching Lonen's attention. This time the derkesthai's gaze held challenge. The dragonlet opened its narrow mouth, showing several rows of sharp teeth, lips drawing back as if in a grin—and a narrow lick of green flame shot out, singeing the skin on his hand that held the warhorse's reins.

"Hey!" The stallion jumped at his pained exclamation, lifting his head from his resting droop. Oria's Familiar simply stared at him, unapologetic. "Yeah, yeah. Okay," Lonen muttered. "No more self-pity."

They might as well just go for it and trust in Arill to keep generous. She had been thus far, after all.

A distant roar rumbled through the air, shaking the ground beneath their feet with enough force to make the stallion dance in place. It sounded like a storm advancing at high speed, racing toward them. Grienon popped above the horizon, sailing through the sky, his blue-white face bright and full. As if drawn by a string, the bore tide followed.

It arrived in a wall of deceptive froth, bright as the down of the geese the Destrye plucked for warm comforters, but with a crashing force that sent dust and silt flying upward, darkening the sky and turning the lowering sun bloodred. Within breaths the water filled the wide channel, brim to brim with tossing waves that quickly settled into a smooth, serene bay.

Not unlike the lakes of Dru.

And he and the horse had spent many a time swimming—both in training and play.

Without giving himself a chance to hesitate longer, taking the event as a gift from Arill, he said to Chuffta. "Better take wing, man." Oria's Familiar disentangled himself from her and pushed into the sky with whuffing wing beats. Lonen signaled the warhorse to go. As unquestioningly as Buttercup had run for the closed doors of the gates of Bára, the stallion leapt.

They plunged into the water, sinking briefly before the horse struck upward, swimming in mighty strokes. They could not have stood on the bottom and hoped to hold their heads above water. Never before had the water been deep enough to allow the horse to swim freely. If the water receded before they made it across, they would be mired in the fresh silt, possibly drowned in sinkholes. If they fell from the horse's back, the stroking hooves would drag him and Oria under—a force even the most powerful swimmer would be hard pressed to escape.

He wouldn't let any of that happen. He held on with all his might, giving the warhorse his head, trusting in his training as Lonen had so many times, and concentrating on holding Oria's face well clear of water. The initial dive had drenched her, but her chest rose and fell with regular breaths, if shallow ones.

They surged on through the ephemeral sea.

The crossing seemed to take forever. The sun lowered to the horizon; Chuffta flew overhead, a white sentinel in a red sky; Oria remained unmoving as death in his arms. And the stallion swam on, his breathing growing labored, shudders wracking his great body. Lonen could have swum on his own, but he had no way to ensure Oria wouldn't drown, so he watched his great steed's strength weaken, until he feared the warhorse would fail entirely.

Silently he encouraged the horse, praying to Arill with everything in him, in a way he seldom ever did with any serious intent.

He didn't know how Oria had spoken to the stallion mind to mind—and he was only a mind-dead Destrye—but he focused on the brain between the pointed ears, imagining cool lakes and green mountain pastures for the steed, just as he'd learned to project those soothing places for Oria. Did it really matter that he called the animal by a name? Of course Oria would have had to pick *that* name out of his head. Buttercup, the teasing name he'd used to taunt the colt when he'd been an impatient, much younger man—and carelessly cruel as young men could be.

"That all you got in you, Buttercup?" he'd said. "I should turn you out with the fillies, Buttercup." *Buttercup*. Was it possible the young horse had heard and understood, perhaps thinking that his actual name? And here the warhorse had carried him so valiantly all these years. Lonen could have given him a name of strength, like Aloeus, Shajae, or Draevvon. But he hadn't. He'd called him a scathing nickname and then nothing at all. *Something you call him sometimes. He likes it.*

Well, then.

"Good job, Buttercup." He coughed a little, his throat full of salt and grit. But the warhorse seemed to prick up his ears, perhaps swim a little harder, so he tried again. "Buttercup, if you get us safely across and home, I'll never coop you up in a shack again. You can run as you please, stuff yourself with hay and cover all the pretty mares that catch your eye."

The verdant fantasy sucked him in, too, and he indulged in imagining taking Oria to such a place. His favorite lake. They would picnic on the shore while Buttercup grazed and Chuffta fished in the glassy waters. He'd teach Oria to swim and then caress her soft, naked skin, making love to her in the water and again on the bank. She'd look glorious on the green grass, her hair spread beneath her like a blanket of hammered copper, outshining the sun.

A thumping shocked him out of the dream. Again. Jarring him so he had to tighten his grip on Oria, hoping her soaked silk robes wouldn't convey more of his damaging touch to her skin.

Thump. Thump thump. Thump.

Buttercup's hooves hitting the bottom.

Lonen peered through the deepening dusk, spotting the steep rise of the far bank, a darker silhouette against the deep violet sky. The warhorse's hooves hit with more regularity now, struggling to find purchase on the shifting surface. To save the last of the stallion's lagging strength, Lonen swung a leg over and slid off his back. Water briefly closed over his head, but he pushed up off the bottom, holding Oria high in his arms as he treaded water. Buttercup floundered to the shallows and climbed onto a flat rock, standing there, blowing out water, nose nearly touching the ground.

Lonen found purchase with his boots, his own legs unsteady, but he managed to stand, beyond thankful that the warhorse had found a solid section of the bank. He was tempted to lay Oria down on the broad, flat rock, just so he could rest a moment. After just a bit of rest, he could continue.

Something white hovered before him, twin green stars glowing. Chuffta. The Familiar gazed steadily at him, then his tail snaked down to curl around Lonen's arm, tugging him forward.

Right—it would be foolhardy to stay where they were. The waters had receded considerably, which meant the tide could return at any moment, according to its capricious schedule, and wash them all away.

Forcing himself forward, he managed to climb the bank. After a few moments, the scrabbling clop of Buttercup's hooves reassured him that the warhorse followed. He staggered to a high, dry area. This side of the bay had less sand and more hard ground. Scrappy evergreen shrubs dotted the landscape in bunches, though many had gone rusty with dried needles. The few clumps of deciduous trees were naked skeletons of their former selves, littering the banks like the corpses of thieves hung to warn of disaster ahead.

But they—and the driftwood washed up by the ferocious tides from distant lands—would make for good firewood, and Oria was cold as death.

Laying her on the ground, he risked skin-to-skin contact, checking the pulse in her throat. After all, his touch could hardly harm her if she were in fact dead. The flickering flame inside him said she lived, but part of him wondered if he wouldn't carry that piece of her for the rest of his life, even if she had passed into Arill's arms.

But her heart still beat, pushing the blood through her body, however feebly, her damp skin chill in the thin desert air. The land around Bára grew as cold at night as it scorched in the day, something that never made sense to him. Though not much in that city of sorcerers did.

"I have to build a fire, to warm her up," he told Chuffta, who'd landed on a piece of driftwood nearby. He scraped out something of a shallow in the baked soil to hold the fire and provide a bit of protection to bank the coals through the night. Then he began dragging over fallen logs and driftwood, using his battle-axe to chop some into smaller pieces. His armsmaster would chew him up and down for abusing a weapon so, but Lonen was simply glad to have that instead of a sword.

To his surprised pleasure, Chuffta had gathered a significant pile of good-sized twigs and kindling by the time Lonen was satisfied with his supply. "Good man," he said.

Glad of the muscle memory that had carried him through many a time after his battle-numbed brain had given up, Lonen stripped Buttercup of his tack, talking to him all the while and apologizing for not doing it sooner. The horse slept on his feet, an enviable skill, and barely stirred as Lonen moved around him. They were all mud-caked, but no remedy for that right then. He'd have to find water and sustenance for him and Oria the next day. The Destrye horses had stomached the bitter brine just fine—an enviable ability at this point. Hopefully Chuffta could, too. All of that would have to wait.

Thank Arill, his furred cloak had been stowed in his saddle packs, and was only somewhat damp. If only they'd been stocked with fire-making tools. He could do it with the available stones, it would just take longer. He assembled a small cone of kindling and began working to create a spark, when Chuffta nudged Lonen's shoulder with his pointed chin, politely, it seemed. As soon as Lonen pulled his hands back, Chuffta breathed a lick of flame that set the kindling to merrily burning. Happy to leave it to the expert, he set Chuffta to fanning the flames with gentle strokes of his wings, coaching the winged lizard to add larger sticks as the fire grew.

Meanwhile he stripped first Oria, then himself of their soaked clothes, laying them out on the still-warm rocky soil to dry during the night. He'd seen her naked before, but even if she objected, she could castigate him later for it. He'd actually enjoy that. It would be a happy day when she'd recovered enough to exercise her fiery temper on him.

With some bemusement, he noted that his optimism had returned. The black despair from the far side of the bay had faded, washed away in the tides of Bára, perhaps. Or maybe just from leaving that soul-sucking landscape behind, walled off by that bitter sea. Oria would eventually wake, he'd bring her home to Dru, and they'd find a way to defeat Yar and save the Destrye.

"Chuffta, man." His voice grated hoarse. "How's the wing?"

Chuffta, standing on one leg, wings mantled for balance, tucked a good-sized chunk of wood into the fire by manipulating it with one set of talons, his mouth and tail. The derkesthai blinked at him, for all the world seeming to smile. Okay then.

With the last of his strength, Lonen wrapped Oria in the cloak, furred side in. It covered her from her feet to over the top of her head. Making sure their skin didn't touch, Lonen laid himself beside her, drawing the loose side over him.

"All right then. I'll just rest a moment," he told Chuffta, "and get her warm. Just a short rest. Wake me in a couple hours."

And fell into oblivion.

~ 5 ~

SHE COULDN'T BREATHE. The gray mists swaddled her so thick and tight that she couldn't fight free of them. Though far too familiar to her, the misty place at least meant she lived. It also meant, however, that she'd collapsed, that the magic had overwhelmed her physical body. Bad, yes, but when she'd broken before, she'd always come back to herself first in the realm of the timeless fog. This was—more or less—normal. She'd begun to think of it as a cocoon, from which she'd emerge stronger, ready to fly. It should be a good thing, in the long view.

Not this time.

Now it seemed the chrysalis trapped her, a prison of her own making from which she'd never emerge. It constrained her, making her feel that no matter how she might continue to grow inside it, that would only worsen her situation. She'd end up beating her wings in a frenzy until the heat sent the whole thing up in flame, burning her to nothing. Just like all those people seared by the dragons to ash that blew away like so much sand in the winds of Bára.

The Destrye crops, too. They'd burned in the images in Lonen's mind—the living plants bursting into flame as if they were cured leaves, along with the curious wooden structures. And the people. So many people dead. She been supposed to do something, save them, somehow. Something important. Urgent.

But what?

She flailed against the suffocating mist, fragments of images tormenting her, fighting the terror of being trapped in that formless void forever. Something must have happened. Not the wedding ceremony—she'd wakened from that. The trial, the battle with Yar?

No, after that. She'd won. And then had the victory snatched away.

An enormous black horse, like nothing she'd ever seen. Cold sweat and grien magic exploding, oh so satisfying. Perhaps that had burned her. That explained the heat, the suffocating shroud. Perhaps she had died after all and even now lay on her funeral pyre, her body burning, burning to ash, until it too blew away on the hot winds.

I'm not dead! She screamed in her mind. *I'm not really dead, don't burn me!*

"A great relief to us all, I'm sure," came Chuffta's dry mind-voice, soft and rustling as his white scales under her hand. *"I kept the fire going, see? It's only a little one. Not enough to burn a body."* He showed her an image of an orange-flamed fire, the ground around it stretching out flat, sere, and empty.

She stilled, processing information as her senses began working again. It was ever thus. First she became aware of the mists, then fighting to escape them. Chuffta's mind-voice talking to her, then sound, light, and sensation from the outside world. Only after all that could she move her body again. She breathed into it, letting the panic dissipate.

It would be incredibly helpful if she could remember this early on.

"I don't know what I'd do without you anchoring me to the world," she told Chuffta. *"It's like finding the city wall in a blinding sandstorm."*

"Maybe that's one reason your mother asked me to be your Familiar."

It would be nice to believe that. Her mother hadn't always been so broken. Before Oria's father fell in battle, Queen Rhianna had been as constant as Sgatha, ever serene, powerful, and wise—and knowing more about Oria's abilities than she'd said, subtly guiding her path. Losing that compass had been as if the moon herself dropped out of the sky. But her mother had at least given her a final gift, in those last few moments, whispering the secret to surviving outside the walls.

And Oria *had* survived. At least, she wasn't quite dead, much as she might feel like it.

It might be better to say 'not yet.' Already the wild magic flowed into her again, jangling through her pores, as if that sense awoke along with sight, sound, and touch. Not always easy to sort the difference, what her magical portals brought in versus the physical ones. Like seeing with her body's eyes and sgath simultaneously—a fast path to overload and a debilitating headache. Not necessarily in that order. From what Lonen had said of the old Destrye tales, the priestesses captured by the Destrye had lived for a while, their death a slow attenuation.

She opened her eyes, working against the stiff movement of her eyelids, but still saw only muffling darkness. Night?

"You're wrapped in Lonen's cloak, to keep you warm. I fed the fire." Chuffta sounded enormously pleased with himself.

"Thank you—I'm impressed."

"I'm learning new skills, too."

She chuckled mentally at his boasting, judiciously trying a small amount of sgath to see what her physical eyes could not. Then reeled it back with a groan. All that wild magic—wow. Her sgath sight practically blinded her. She shut it down to the narrowest possible window, closing the sgath portal with it.

As Sgatha wanes, so does sgath. Put it in shadow. Narrow the crescent.

Like most temple teachings, her mother's advice hadn't been straightforward, but the imagery helped. Eventually she could maybe separate the two—still use sgath sight without allowing the wild magic to pour in like the relentless fury of a bore tide—but for now she'd be conservative. As in, locking herself up tight.

Paying attention to other physical senses, she became aware of a gentle snore, then the weight of an arm holding her. Lonen. He'd stayed with her, wrapped her in the cocoon of fur. No wonder she couldn't breathe. Tentatively she wriggled her fingers, unable to feel much of the motion, then flexed her hands, clumsily worming them along the furry interior of the cloak, seeking an opening to the outside air.

It had to be there somewhere.

Feeling increasingly desperate to breathe, she pushed at the smothering stuff around her face, finding that some of it was her braids, damp and stiff with salt. What in Sgatha had happened to her? She dragged them off her face as best she could, her skin covered in grit. Some fell into her dry mouth, astringently bitter. She sneezed, then coughed—which made her stomach lurch, salt water burbling up her throat to burn in her nose, making her cough harder.

The arm pinning her tightened convulsively, which didn't help her master the cough in the least. Just as abruptly, the pressure released. Bright daylight made her clench her lids closed, and blessed fresh air rushed in. She threw herself onto her side, gasping for air between coughs, then ignominiously vomiting up bitter salt.

The furry cloak pressed up against her belly, as Lonen supported her, the arch helping to open her throat and chest. He also thumped her gently between the shoulder blades through the cloak. In a distracted part of her mind, she wondered how he'd learned such useful tricks. At the forefront, she burned with humiliation that he should see her under such conditions. Surely other newlywed brides were able to preserve the mystery and romance a while longer.

Though, one thing she'd learned over the past days, from not only her marriage, but also Gallia's, was that the reality of being married did not in any way match the fantasy.

"Water," she croaked through her scorching throat.

"I wish," Lonen's voice came from just behind her ear. "Sorry, I hoped to have some when you woke, but I fell asleep. You were supposed to wake me," he said in an accusing tone.

She only realized he didn't mean her when Chuffta replied.

"He needed sleep. I fed the fire."

She tried to tell Lonen that, but it only made her stomach heave again and sent her head throbbing—though the final spasm seemed to kick out the rest of the vile stuff she'd somehow swallowed. Exhausted, unable to hold herself up any longer, she flopped onto her back, finding Lonen—looking more like a barbarian than ever, and strangely appealing for all that—leaning over her.

His hair and beard were caked with mud, streaked with dried salt, and what hadn't dried in mats against his scalp, temples and jaw stood out in mad curls. Smears of black and brown covered his face. Only his gray eyes were clear and unsullied. They roved over her face with a bright wonder incongruent with how terrible she must look. An unexpectedly tender array of emotions curled around her. His or hers, she didn't know. That, too, had become increasingly difficult to tease apart.

"You're alive," he whispered. Something about the intensity of his expression made her abruptly shy and she had to look away—unfortunately taking in the length of his nude body poised above her. Her face heated.

"You're naked," she blurted out. Then realized she felt either fur or sunshine all along her body, too. She covered herself, though clumsily, her arms felt so weak. "I'm naked!"

Lonen laughed, shaking his head at her. "We've seen each other naked before."

This was different. "We're outside."

"Yes," he replied in a grave tone, nodding solemnly, but humor sparked through it. "I should make you a scout for the Destrye, with such keen observation skills."

He didn't understand—but then he didn't know what it was like to wake up from the nothing, not remembering what had happened, naked, vulnerable.

"I know what happened—I can be your memory. And we're both here to protect you."

"Thank you," she replied, carefully shielding the rest of her thoughts from her Familiar. She didn't want to hurt his feelings by betraying that none of that made her feel more secure. Fortunately,

he seemed preoccupied.

Groaning, she struggled to sit, body creaking in protest from every parched tissue. Lonen helped lever her up and she clutched at the cloak with those nerveless fingers to keep some semblance of modesty, though the blazing sun several hands above the horizon made that uncomfortably hot.

She recognized nothing. All around, the land stretched bare and flat, only clumps of leafless trees and brown shrubs scattered about. A wide, shallow crevice cut through nearby, stretching as far as she could see in either direction—though the distant orange peaks on one horizon might be the Enchantment Mountains that rose behind Bára. No sign of the city. The sky arched in a pitiless, endless void above and she acutely felt her miniscule nature, a fragile creature easily swallowed by it all.

Unable to bear it, she cast about in the other direction, where Buttercup—also filthy—nuzzled at some bush that hardly seemed edible. Closer by, Chuffta worked intently to drag what looked like a tree limb to a blazing bonfire. He had his wings spread and managed it by half-flying, half-hopping on one leg, and wrestling the thing with mouth, tail and the free foot.

"What are you doing?" she asked aloud, for Lonen's benefit, though the words scraped her raw throat.

"I'm feeding the fire," he chirped happily. *"Keeping you warm!"*

Lonen groaned. "Hey, man. Enough with the fire. You'll roast us."

"No?" Chuffta paused, releasing the limb with foot and mouth, but keeping his tail wrapped around it. He sounded terribly disappointed. He cocked his head at the fire. *"Maybe just one more?"*

"No more, please, Chuffta." She rubbed at her gritty, sensitive eyes, though it only made them water more. She certainly wasn't weeping. She blinked them open to find Lonen grinning and grimacing at once. "I don't know what's gotten into him," she said, ducking her face so he wouldn't see.

"I like fire! It's hot."

"His first time with fire?" Lonen suggested. "Other than your purple magic kind."

"Could be." She must have sounded dubious, because he shrugged.

"Some people are like that, obsessed with fire. Why not a derkesthai?"

"I've never played with fire before," Chuffta confirmed. *"It's not like breath-flame, that runs out. As long as I keep putting wood, in there, it goes and goes."*

"You can build another one when we sleep tonight, how's that?" she suggested. Chuffta grumbled, but agreed. He stayed by his fire, though, tail lovingly wrapped around the limb he'd wanted to add.

"How are you feeling?" Lonen asked as he rose and went to gather something from the ground. She thought she couldn't be hotter, but a rush of embarrassed heat washed over her at the sight of him striding around naked, hairy buttocks flexing as he bent over. It seemed impossible to feel both ill and an uncomfortable surge of desire, but there it was.

"You could put some clothes on," she croaked, clapping a hand over her eyes. Then dropped it and stared at him aghast. "Do we have clothes?"

He laughed and held up her crimson robes, bringing them to her. "Considerably worse for wear, but yes."

To avoid looking at him, she busied herself with sorting through the ragged, stiff and muddied mess of her priestess robes tangled with her formerly white chemise, now a mottled mix of pink and brown. Her fingers, numb and enervated like the rest of her, wouldn't work properly. The last time she'd broken, she'd awakened perfectly energized. Though that had been a smaller episode. The time before that had been much worse, and she'd put the state of her body down to sleeping for a week. Perhaps that hadn't been the only reason, which did not bode well for her current prospects. Nor did the continued cramping of her stomach.

She swallowed down the foul taste in her mouth, clearing her throat again. "My robes are filthy and so am I—I think I'll go wash in that stream down there."

Lonen squatted before her, making her hastily avert her gaze. "Not a good idea. The bore tides come without warning. You could be mired and drown."

"The bore tides?" she echoed, meeting his somber granite eyes if only to keep from looking at the rest of him. "That's… the Bay of Bára?"

"I don't think there's more than one," he teased gently. His vitality and good humor grated on her. Not fair for him to be bouncing around and teasing when she felt as listless as the silt in the sullen bay.

"Why did you bring us here? We can't cross the bay. No one can cross it and live."

"We already did. Last night. People can cross—how do you think the Destrye got to Bára in the first place? Crossing that thing is how we got so wet and muddy, not to mention you with a belly full of brine. I'm sorry about that," he added, brow furrowing in concern. "I had no idea you'd swallowed so much. How are you feeling?" This second time he asked the question with pointed emphasis, as if he guessed she'd dodged answering before.

"I'm fine," she replied, coolly cloaking the lie with *hwil* as best she could. "I'd like to get dressed though."

"So dress." He didn't move.

"Could you give me a little privacy?" She wasn't sure how she'd manage the robes—or easing her roiling gut—but no way would she let him to see her so ill, weak and clumsy.

He cocked his head, studying her. "Why are you acting so strangely with me? We're husband and wife. You know I undressed you. I know that you're *not* fine. Arill take you, Oria—more than once I thought you were dead. We may yet be dead if we don't find some water and Dru is a long journey yet."

"Dru?" She couldn't go to Dru. She needed to go to one of Bára's sister-cities, where they could heal her. She hoped.

"Exactly, which is quite a journey still. So this isn't a time for lady games."

She choked on her rising ire, startled into a half laugh. "Lady games?" she repeated incredulously.

He waved a hand at her and stood, manhood flagrantly swinging as he did. "Acting all prim and embarrassed, as if we haven't been as intimate as a man and woman can be."

"Well, not exactly as—"

"*Lying* to me," he interrupted, "about how you feel."

"I feel thirsty," she snapped.

"What else?" he demanded, fists on hips.

"I can't talk to you when we're naked."

He yanked the robes from her hands, tossing them out of her reach. "Let's test that theory."

"Hey!" She wanted to reach for them, but they were hopelessly distant.

"You can have them back when you tell me the truth."

"Don't you dare threaten me, Destrye!" She would have surged to her feet, but the wobbly weakness in them told her she'd just collapse. Even more ignominious.

"Technically that's blackmail, not a threat," he replied, as if that were a reasonable response. "How. Are. You. Feeling?"

She wrapped her arms around her knees under the robe. "Naked."

"Truthful, at least. What else?"

Miserable, ill, weak, feeble, supremely incapable of dealing with any of it. Both overloaded with magic and completely without useful resources. She felt thrown back to all those years of being useless, too fragile for anything. She was afraid. And she really needed to answer the call of nature and she was pretty sure she couldn't even stand. She was paradoxically both excruciatingly lonely and desperate to be left alone for a few moments. She wanted to lie back and weep, which would solve nothing.

"I'm here. Can I help?"

"I don't think so. I just need to rest a bit. And deal with the Destrye."

Lonen muttered something that sounded foul, tossed her robes at her again, then began yanking on his own clothes. She clutched the filthy silks, too hot in the cloak, but unable to muster the energy to move. Fully dressed, Lonen sat in front of her again, then took her hand through the thick fur, prying it away from her knees to do so. "Talk to me, Oria. Help me out here."

"I don't know what you want me to say." Her voice came out as small as she felt and cold sweat dripped down her spine, though she could have sworn her parched body had no water in it.

He studied her. "How about just spitting out whatever you're trying to hide from me. Then you won't have to spend the effort lying about it, when you're already clearly weak as a baby bird fallen from the nest."

"I'm not weak," she spat at him, her vision going a little black at the edges. Chuffta finally abandoned his beloved fire and hopped to her side. Lonen frowned slightly at her Familiar, then transferred the scowl to her.

"Do you need help getting dressed?" he asked more gently and she cringed at the thought. All those days after her first collapse, her mother and Juli had sponge-bathed her, helping her remember how to power her limbs, dressing and undressing her. Here, in the middle of nowhere, with no food or water, and no one but this Destrye warrior for leagues, she couldn't afford the luxury of such delicacy.

Nor could she imagine asking him for such intimate assistance.

"I need privacy," she muttered, mortified.

He sighed, studying their joined hands. "I'll tell you what. You show me you can stand on your own, and I'll give you some time alone."

She pressed her lips together, raised her chin and stared him down. "You'll do as I tell you, Destrye."

With a grim half-smile, he shook his head slowly. "Not a chance, Princess. You're weak as a newborn, aren't you? This is why you were abed for a week after that first collapse when we went out the gates. That's what it does to you, being out here." He squeezed her hand through the cloak. "What I don't understand is why you don't want me to help you."

She gazed over his shoulder miserably, fixing her gaze on the horizon, clenching her teeth against the chattering of incipient tears. She had no words.

"Is it pride?" He asked. He wouldn't give up. She knew that about him. There was no getting past him. She'd have to have his help to pee, to dress, probably even to eat and drink—if they found water—as the alternative was to sit there and die under the scorching sun. It should be an easy decision and yet… *Pride.* It sounded so superficial, but if she gave that up, too, what would she have left?

"I hate this," she finally whispered.

"Yeah." He nodded, still squeezing her hand. "You and I—we're not people who ask for help easily. We like to be strong and independent. But sometimes we're sick and hurt and need the help. So come on—don't you need to piss?"

She choked a little, certain her face had gone as crimson as the silk still wadded in her lap. "Yes, but—"

"This might surprise you, but I figured even elegant Báran princesses do that, too." He scooped her up, cloak, clothes and all, giving her a warm smile. "Let's set you on a log you can hang that pretty behind over, so you can do your business."

~ 6 ~

BY ALTERNATELY COAXING and bullying her, he got Oria tended and dressed. Once she gave in and let him help her, it amazed him she'd managed to sit up straight as long as she had. She was clearly miserable. Her muscles had no strength and her coppery eyes shone glassy with fever. He kicked himself for not realizing how much of the poisonous water would have flowed into a throat lax with unconsciousness. He'd spat it out every time he took a mouthful and his gut made him feel as if he'd eaten bad meat.

Thank Arill, he'd found a flask in Buttercup's packs with a small supply of water. He gave it all to Oria, who sat on his cloak—upright, but barely—sipping at it. His own thirst raged, but he could last a while longer without. Listlessly she watched him brush the warhorse down, a cloud of dried mud billowing around them.

"Why bother when he'll only get dirty again?" she asked, the first thing she'd said to him since admitting she needed his help. He sympathized with her embarrassment, his usually regal and poised foreign princess so reduced. But it also pissed him off that she acted as if she couldn't trust him. They might not yet be lovers in truth—though that was only because she couldn't bear the touch of his skin, or he'd have long since plumbed her depths—but she *had* allowed him to pleasure her with various implements. And had watched him take himself in hand with all apparent delight.

Now she was acting as if they'd never spent that passionate night together. As if she barely knew who he was. Erecting barriers around herself like a miniature version of her walled city where only she lived inside.

"If there's sand and dirt between the tack and his hide," he told her, "it will rub and cause sores. I should have done it last night, but I was nearly as exhausted as you are. This won't take much longer and then we can get going. If we move at a good pace, there's an oasis we can reach by mid-afternoon."

She was quiet a moment, eyes cast down. Chuffta surreptitiously tucked another twig onto the fire and she didn't reprimand him. A real firebug, the derkesthai had turned out to be.

"You'll like it there," he continued, as if they were having a real conversation. "There's a pool deep enough to submerge in. We can take your braids down and you can wash. You'll feel better then."

She muttered something, almost too quietly for him to hear. Recross the bay? Surely he had mistaken her words.

"What's that?" He drew the brush over Buttercup's glossy black coat, letting the regular movements soothe his ire, steeling himself for the fight that would be over quickly. Oria was in no shape to battle him.

"We have to go back across the bay," she said more loudly.

"I'm going to pretend you didn't say that," he told her easily.

"I can't go to Dru."

"I think you'll find that you can, because that's where I'm taking you."

"You're taking me to Lousá. Or one of the other sister-cities. I'm not sure which is closest."

"Uh huh." Finished with the stallion's grooming, Lonen checked his hooves for any remaining packed mud or rocks. Buttercup complied with unusual placidity. They were all exhausted. Or the cursed creature really did like his name. "And you know the way to these cities?" He asked Oria, keeping the tone light and conversational, knowing full well she didn't.

"Well… no." She frowned into the distance. "But there must be a way to find them. There are roads."

"Which ones?"

"I don't know, Destrye, but we're going back across the bay."

"I'll tell you what, Princess." He paused to beat the dirt from the saddle blanket and draped it over Buttercup's back, then hefted the saddle up. Once he had it all cinched in place, he went to crouch in front of Oria. Her mud and salt encrusted braids snarled around her narrow, high-cheekboned face, reminding him of the stories of the snake-haired goddess. As in those illustrations, Oria's eyes burned with a scathing otherworldly determination. If she weren't also pale as death and wracked by a fine trembling, he'd fear for his extremities. Once she recovered her powers, he'd have to watch himself. Until then…

"I'll tell you what," he repeated, meeting her stare without flinching. "If you can walk across that bay under your own power, then sure, I'll go with you and we can wander around the desert searching for those sister-cities."

Her lush mouth thinned. "You know I can't. That's low, Destrye, even for you."

"Nice to know there's new depths for me to sink to," he replied with false cheer. "I wouldn't want to think I've topped out at my age. Guess that means we're going to Dru. Chuffta, man, make yourself useful. Quit feeding the Arill-cursed fire already and kick some sand over it. We're heading out."

"It's not like it could spread to anything," Oria pointed out in a bitter tone as Chuffta set to the new task with enthusiasm, sweeping his wings to brush sand into the shallow pit.

"Habit," Lonen admitted. "We're wary of fire in Dru. Everything is built of wood there, not stone. A loose flame can cause great devastation in only moments. Up you go."

He scooped her up, trying not to be alarmed at her frailty. If she'd reminded him of a furious kitten on previous occasions—all fur and spitting feistiness—now she felt like a broken-winged bird. She didn't fight him, likely couldn't, but refused to meet his gaze as he lifted her to Buttercup's back. "Hold on to the saddle there until I climb up. If you can do that mind-trick again to hold him still that would be good. He's calm today—tired, to tell the truth—but just in case."

"I can't," she said in a small voice, slouching in the saddle like a crumpled flower.

"Why not?" At least she admitted that much and he preferred to keep her talking—and to keep an eye on her as he shook out and folded the cloak to pack it away. "You were amazing yesterday. Controlling Butter—the warhorse, blasting the city gates. You were something to see."

"Stop trying to flatter me. I know I'm a pitiful mess. It's the wild magic," she clarified, an edge to her voice. Better that than the defeated tone. "To shut it out I have to close up everything."

"Nothing in, nothing out, huh? Makes a kind of sense." As much as magic ever did. It explained why she still lived. He gathered up the rest of their things, wedged them into the packs, and prepared to mount. "Hold still so I don't touch your skin by accident." Vaulting up behind her, he caught her slight body against him as she swayed. Despite her mean-eyed looks and barbed replies, she leaned back against him, closing her eyes and relaxing, a sigh passing her cracking lips. He needed to get her to water. "You okay being this close to me? I figure you don't want anything heavier between us, what with the heat, but..."

She shook her head. "It's better, actually, with my magic senses closed. I don't feel near as much from you."

Good and bad, he supposed. Probably base of him that his brain went to the sexual possibilities. If she mastered this shutting-down trick, maybe they could be husband and wife as Arill intended. Not an admirable thing for him to consider with Oria so ill. But if they made it through this, then... something to look forward to. Arill had made him an optimist for a reason. He nudged Buttercup into motion, Chuffta flying up to pace above them.

"You can't take me to Dru," Oria said without opening her eyes.

"Oria..." He sighed. "I can't take you anywhere else."

She didn't reply, her body motionless against him. With any

luck, they'd make it to the oasis in half a day.

ORIA DRIFTED IN a dream of gray fog, swaddling mist, and scorching heat. Her body had long since gone completely numb, but so had her other senses. For the first time in her life, she felt nothing at all from the world around her. Always it had been a question of too much. Too many emotions, too much intense energy pouring in from all directions, the restlessness filling her, needing to be vented.

Now she felt like the blossoms of her rooftop garden, which she'd likely never see again. Wilting, drying up to a husk under the withering sun.

What happens to a plant without water?

She'd asked Lonen that question, by way of explaining what happened when a priestess left the sgath source beneath her city. When she'd said it, she thought to end the argument over whether she could ever go to Dru to serve as queen of the Destrye.

Now he was taking her there.

When her thoughts assembled with any coherency, she fulminated with fury at his high-handedness. Yes, they'd had to flee Bára, but she'd never agreed to go to Dru. She couldn't. And Lonen knew that. He'd been the one to tell her their old stories, of captives like her, withering away to nothing before they died. She'd thought, here and there, that he cared about her. Had felt something of it. And maybe he did on some level. But he cared more about his own people. Not that she blamed him for that. He saw her as the key to saving the Destrye—and once that might have been the case.

No longer. With that bleak thought her ire bled away into nothingness.

Before she'd thought it had been overload that killed her long ago ancestresses—both from the wild magic beyond the walls and the corrosive effects of intimate contact with their barbarian captors. Through the hazy lethargy, she understood that she'd had the situation turned on its head. She would die, not from taking in too much wild magic, or even too much of Lonen's exuberant masculine energy, but through starvation. She couldn't digest the wild magic and with every league they went farther from the purified magic of the cities that could sustain her.

Yar would have his way, as she'd unfortunately predicted. She'd die out here in the wastes, and he would triumph. How ironic, that she'd lived so much of her life feeling worthless because she couldn't master enough *hwil* to manage the tides of magical and emotional input and now she'd be even more useless without them. The idea filled her with listless fury. She'd come so far that it seemed brutally unfair for her to fail now.

And just as she'd finally married—and discovered the great pleasure that could bring.

Creaking open her crusty eyelids, she gazed up at Lonen. He'd turned her so she sat sideways on his lap, holding her against him with one strong arm, so she wouldn't fall. Every once in a while, he shifted her to the other side, apologizing for waking her. She didn't bother to explain that she wasn't sleeping. Couldn't. As if she'd lost that ability, too.

He looked as terrible as she felt, his jaw set and tense, lines of strain radiating from his creased eyes as he watched the horizon. Though she couldn't sense his emotions, the worry in his face told her all she needed to know of how he felt.

"Can you find your way back?" She reached out to Chuffta. *"To your people, should I die?"*

"You're not going to die," he replied with equanimity, the pulse of his wings part of the rhythm of his mind-voice. He sounded tired, too. *"We're almost to the water and then you'll be fine."*

She didn't bother to argue. *"Come ride with us. Rest your wings."*

"Buttercup is tired, too, so even my weight adds strain. Lonen would walk, but he's afraid you'll fall off without him holding you. I'm all right."

Hazily, she contemplated that. *"You can hear his thoughts?"*

"It seems to help that he's in proximity to you. He's concerned that we've not found the oasis yet. Some of the markers he followed have gone."

Oh. *"But you said we're close."*

"I scent water on the wind, yes."

"Can you go look for it, and lead us there?"

"Yes. But I don't want to leave you. I promised I never would."

"You're not leaving me any more than if you went hunting. Just for a little while."

"Your thoughts are very quiet, Oria. I can't hear you unless I'm close and I listen very hard. If I go, I won't be able to hear you at all."

"That's all right. Lonen will protect me, like you said. Go. Find the water."

"All right. Hang on, Oria. I love you."

"And I love you. Fly and be well."

She waited until she didn't sense him, Lonen frowning at the derkesthai's departure.

"Lonen," she said. But her voice emerged without sound. She tried again. "Lonen."

He glanced down at her, eyes brightening. "You're awake. Are you feeling any better? We're almost there."

That he'd lie to comfort her nearly broke her heart. "Lonen..."

His expression sobered, seeing something in her face. "What do you need?"

"Leave me here."

"Not if Arill Herself asked me to."

"You, Buttercup—you're better without my weight. I'm dead anyway. Leave me."

"I hate to tell you this, Oria. You're a beautiful woman, but you're skin over bone at this point. You weigh practically nothing."

"Chuffta... he said you'd walk if you didn't have to hold me on. Leave me. Save yourselves."

"Oh, I see now. You sent him off, didn't you? That explains it. But your brain has clearly baked in this heat because even if I were daft enough to dump you here, Chuffta would simply find you and he'd sit here and die right with you."

A tear leaked from the corner of her eye at the image he painted. It burned on her cheek as it tracked down.

"Don't cry, Oria." All the harshness left Lonen's face and voice. "Arill knows your willingness to sacrifice yourself is a fine and noble quality, but we love you too much to leave you here."

"I'm a burden."

"You won't be. You're going to save the Destrye, remember? We need you. I'm taking you to Dru if I have to drag you there, pouring water down your throat every step of the way. Do you understand me?" He asked the question with such fierce determination that it was more of a demand.

She wanted to answer him, but couldn't. She'd used up all she had left, arguing with the barbarian. No longer fighting to keep her eyes open, she let her lids fall and the gray mists take her.

~ 7 ~

ORIA LAPSED INTO unconsciousness again. Just as well, as he'd be hard put to continue to disguise his helpless rage from her. He kept picturing calm lakes for all he was worth—though that only made him thirstier—but beneath he fumed with his inability to help her.

He was an idiot twelve times over. Why in Arill hadn't he rechecked the markers on the journey from the oasis to Bára? Because he'd known the way *to* Bára, had made the journey back and forth several times over during the various battles and restagings. He'd been grossly overconfident. Worse, on the journey to Bára, he'd been so full of revenge fantasies—and, if he were honest with himself, as a doomed man ought to be, so consumed with lust to see Oria again—that he hadn't given any thought to the return journey. He'd grown soft already in his kingship, relying on his scouts and lieutenants to mark the way and guide the armies.

It was one thing to follow an army. Another to find one's way alone across an empty landscape.

He would figure something out. He would not allow Oria—or Buttercup, who valiantly continued on—to die in this remorseless desert like jerky smoked too long over the fire. Chuffta could make it for sure. The winged lizard seemed to be in his element, never too hot, apparently unaffected by the lack of water. Surprising that Oria had been able to persuade her Familiar to leave her, but she could be convincing when she set her mind to it.

Not that it worked on him. Leave her, indeed. He'd strap her to

Buttercup and send her on without *him*, if he thought they'd make it. His was the much greater weight, even scrawny as he'd gotten over the last years of privation. If he'd had anything to tie Oria to the saddle with, he'd have long since done it. Over the last excruciating hours, he'd contemplated cutting the furred cloak into lengths to use as rope. It might work.

If he could muster the strength. Dubious at this point, as he barely clung to the saddle himself. Everything in him focused on holding onto Oria, and keeping them both on the horse.

Buttercup, head down, stumbled—and Lonen caught his breath, anticipating the fall. Once they went down, they'd all stay down. He knew it in his gut.

But the valiant steed recovered, pausing only a moment and blowing out froth before continuing on. Lonen adjusted Oria so her face would be shaded from the sun. Her formerly lush lips were thin and dry as old leaves, her breath barely whispering through them. Still so beautiful, her bones elegant arcs. And such a strong and noble heart. Arill had given him a treasure in this woman and he'd bumbled it, as careless as if he'd dropped one of her glass figurines to shatter on the stones of her rooftop terrace.

To distract himself from despair, he drew on his memories of her in her high garden, surrounded by exotic blooms, a violet cast to her face from the flames of her magical fire table. He might have started to fall in love with her then. Or before that, when she rode dressed all in white to surrender Bára, full of prickly pride and pragmatic resignation. She deserved more from him than this. So did he. If they survived this, he'd find a way to recreate her garden and her violet fire. He would give them both the romance they'd had no time for.

Something hit his head and he loosed a hand to bat at it. It ducked him, then the something wrapped hard around his wrist, yanking. Lonen pulled back, hard, making a fist to punch the cursed thing—and it bit him.

The sharp pain penetrated the fog of his erotic daydreams.

Chuffta.

"Hey, man." His voice came out gritty as the sand that coated his throat. "Thought you ditched us."

The derkesthai, tail wrapped around his wrist still, flapped his leather wings, hovering there. Holding Lonen's gaze, Chuffta then turned his head deliberately in a direction angling to the left and behind them.

His thoughts tumbling clumsy as unpolished stones, Lonen tried to grasp what he might mean. Chuffta released his wrist, flew in that direction, and back again, eyes bright green with intent.

"Water?" Lonen asked—and Chuffta bobbed up and down in an aerial dance of agreement. "Can't kill us any deader to go back, I guess. Lead the way."

He turned Buttercup, who obeyed dully, going back the way they'd come, though at an oblique angle. If Chuffta had found the oasis, then Lonen had seriously fucked up in passing it by. They might have reached it hours ago. If it took that long to get there, then…

Ah well, at least he hadn't died by dragon breath or at the Trom's hand. Arnon would make a good king. If anyone could find a way to defeat Yar and his monstrous minions, clever Arnon would. He'd cling to that hope, rather than face that he might have doomed more than Oria and himself in his terrible carelessness.

Buttercup stumbled again, nearly going to his knees, barely catching himself.

Nothing in sight. Only the heat haze and those corpses of trees. Once this had been a forest like in Dru, the histories said. Now the sun and sand ate everything that passed here. An omen he should have heeded.

Buttercup caught his foot a third time. Rocks skittered away, clattering, and the stallion scrambled for purchase, throwing up his head and nearly unseating them. Only long practice had Lonen's thighs gripping, holding them on.

Then he caught sight of it.

A smear of blessed green. Buttercup nickered, catching the scent of water in the desert, picking up his pace. Chuffta swooped around them, making a whistling sound that could only be joy.

"ORIA."

Sweet water coated her lips, sliding down her throat, a strange and foreign sensation after being dry for so long. It felt as if she floated in water. Cool, not like the baths. A delightful, impossible fantasy. Or she'd died and this was the afterlife. If so, being dead might not be so bad.

"Oria, drink the water."

She knew that voice. Lonen. He'd made it an order, but sounded ragged, desperate. That wasn't right. He should be happy and float in the water, too. She smiled at him. "Come on in. Feels good." Then she frowned at the sharp pain of her lips cracking. Had he even heard her? Maybe they were both dead, ghosts who could never talk to each other, much less ever hope to touch each other. She gasped over the sharp grief of that thought.

He made a sound, inarticulate, and more water dribbled over her lips. She lapped at it. Tasted so wonderful. Like no water she'd had in her life. Not salty or bitter. Not even like the water at Bára, which seemed like some faint-hearted cousin of this one.

"That's it, love," he murmured. "Drink the sweet water."

She turned her face, loving the feel of it. She was floating. And not in gray mist, but in the real world. Definitely not the baths, though—instead a dusky violet sky arced above. So funny. She giggled.

"Drink, Oria. You'll feel better."

"Chuffta?"

"Always."

"I sent you away." Memory rushed back. She'd told him to go so he wouldn't grieve if she died.

"Yes. We'll have words about that. For now, drink."

Another time she might have laughed at how much her Familiar sounded like Lonen, promising they'd have words. But drinking the water sounded like excellent advice. She turned her face—she *was* floating—and gulped, the shock of the cool water hitting her empty belly and making it cramp.

"Not too fast. You'll make yourself sick." Lonen's laugh skated over the words. Not his musical, delighted bellow, instead he sounded somewhat unhinged with relief.

Oria squinted her eyes open, then ducked her head back to let the water run over them, washing away the grit and stinging salt. Lonen sat beside her, cross-legged in the shallow water of what appeared to be a small lake, Chuffta on his shoulder, peering at her with concern. Buttercup stood fetlock deep a bit farther on, black nose submerged in the water, silvery bubbles rising around. Feathery looking trees ringed the edges, making the sky a smaller pink- and orange-shot circle of dusky blue above. Sunset. Grienon, in a widening crescent, stood high in the sky. No sign of Sgatha, but she'd be near the horizon, behind the trees. How odd not to be able to see past them. A different world.

"Where are we?" she asked.

"The oasis." Lonen choked a little, his voice breaking on the second word. He scooped up a handful of water and drank it down, his thick throat working as he swallowed. Scooping up another handful, he splashed it over his face and head, shaking the water droplets free and sighing in pleasure. He'd succeeded only in smearing the dust and dried mud around, so his eyes looked crystalline light in comparison.

"You look awful," she said, though it wasn't entirely true. He looked like he'd been dragged across the desert, but also deeply appealing. Maybe that came from the rush of gladness to be alive, the wrenching gratitude that he'd saved them. She had no energy, could barely swallow, and yet she still wanted to lick the water droplets from his strong throat. "Why don't you wash? And drink more."

He gave her a wry half-smile, unamused. A firm pressure at her back made her aware he supported her with a hand under her. "I'm keeping you from drowning. You're welcome."

Oh. Chagrined, she tried to sit up, managing only a half-baked sort of flail that had her head going under, making her choke and sputter.

"Hey, hey, hey," Lonen soothed. "It wasn't a complaint. I'm sorry. There's plenty of time to drink all the water we want and to get clean. I've got you. That's all I meant. Relax."

"Sometimes your humor escapes me, Destrye," she grumbled, attempting to relax again, to find that nice floating place.

He wiped his face with his other hand again. "Believe me—it's not just you. Nolan always complained that I had a warped sense of humor."

"The brother who fell into one of Yar's crevasses on the battlefield." She'd said it as a touchstone to the memory, regretting it when Lonen's smile dimmed. She wasn't in her right mind still, to be so careless. "I'm sorry."

"Don't apologize, remember? It's okay. I'm impressed you recalled that detail. And that's no surprise—I figured it had to have been Yar's doing."

"Only he could have worked such a powerful stone magic," she agreed with remorse. She restrained herself from apologizing again. She turned her face, drinking more water, trying to think what the right thing to say would be, how to recover some sense of dignity. Being able to keep her own self from drowning would be a good place to start.

"It's actually good to think of him that way again." Lonen scratched his beard, gazing at the sunset sky, the gray of his eyes taking on an indigo cast from it. "You know—with all the war and grief, it seems like the normal life stuff gets swallowed up by the violence and intensity. But just then, I remembered him giving me a hard time about my black humor. He said I'd never win a bride that way." Lonen slanted her a look at that, a bit of his cocky grin returning.

"He couldn't have guessed that a bride would manipulate you into marrying her."

"Is that what you think happened?"

She didn't know what she thought. Mostly she felt. The coolness of the water restoring something of life to her body. Experimentally she moved her arms and legs, swishing them. It seemed maybe she had more control again. She might even feel more energized. That part of her that measured the level of sgath seemed to register something. Not a lot, but more than the emergency empty warning there'd been on the verge of the Bay of Bára. Extending the experiment, she opened a sliver of a crescent, bracing for the chaotic impact of the wild magic.

Instead, much like the water surrounding her, a pure and fresh magic streamed into her. She drank it in along with more water. Not like Bára's magic, but also not jangling and jarring like the kind outside the walls. Giddy relief rose in her.

"I told you that you wouldn't die. Since you're better, I'm going to build a fire for us!" With that, Chuffta took off with a clap of leathery wings, zooming out of sight beyond the trees.

She laughed aloud and Lonen frowned at her, making her realize that laughing at his last question wouldn't be an appropriate response at all. "Chuffta wants to build a fire," she explained.

Lonen scanned the small lake. "Where did he go? He can't just build it anywhere—he'll risk setting fire to the trees or undergrowth."

"I'll tell him to wait for you. Go show him where."

"Keeping you from drowning, remember?" He rubbed her back through the silk of her robes and chemise, darker concern dampening his thoughts. Nice to feel something of them again. That, too, grounded her. Amazing how much she'd relied on sensing the direction of his emotions behind what tended to be a brooding visage—when he wasn't amused at her expense. Surprising, too, how familiar in a comforting way sensing that connection with him had become.

"I think I can maybe sit up. It's shallow enough here, right?"

"Are you trying to get rid of me again?"

"I should apologize for that. My earlier behavior was—"

"Understandable. I don't even feel bad about interrupting you on that one, since you broke the rules by apologizing."

"That was an apology for something I *could* control. It doesn't count. But never mind. Would you please help me sit up? I think I can. And then I can tend myself a little while you get Chuffta going with the fire. Unless you don't want him to build one?"

"No, we'll certainly need it. Already the air grows chillier."

"I see Buttercup still has his tack on. I'm sure you want to take care of him and clean up yourself."

Lonen followed the direction of her gaze to where Buttercup still happily stood fetlock-deep, now apparently snoozing. "Yes, he deserves tending. Though forgive me if I wanted to get water into *you* first." He smiled at her, relaxing into the relief that they'd made it. "Are you sure you can do this?"

"Let's try and if I can't, then we'll know."

It took more effort than she'd expected—or maybe more than she'd hoped. Floating in the water with Lonen supporting her had been deceptive, leading her to overestimate her vitality. When she tried to move on her own, her muscles quavered, at first not obeying. Lonen couldn't help her as much he clearly wanted to, pushing with the one hand at her back, the other repeatedly waving around as he began to take hold of her, then stopping himself. She floundered about, throttling back the humiliation, even as Lonen's frown darkened.

"Oria, give it a bit more time. I can—"

"No. I want to try to do this." She would master herself and free him to take care of more important things.

"Fine, but let's be more methodical about it. Lie still a moment." He moved so he knelt over her, straddling her body with his big thighs. He slipped his other hand behind her back, gathering a handful of the crimson silk of her robes as they billowed in the currents they made. "Brace your hands on my shoulders so you don't fall into me."

She could do that much, though clumsily, pressing her palms to the soaked leather of the vest he wore. An oddly intimate gesture, especially considering the reason and the circumstances. Feeling shy, she looked at him through her lashes, to find him watching her with that wry half-smile of his. "On three," he said, seeming as if he said much more. Not trusting her voice, she nodded.

"One. Two… Three." Gently he pulled her up and she balanced against his chest, grateful for the support as her head went woozy with the changed posture. Finding her position in space again, she centered more over her hips, even managing to draw her knees up so she sat cross-legged. "I think you have it," Lonen murmured.

And she glanced up with a delighted smile. To find him so close, his face only a hand's length from hers, gray eyes glittering nearly silver with the lowering light. His gaze fell to her mouth. Thinking of kissing her? Yes. His desire misted around her. Not really possible and yet… they had shared that one kiss, during the trial, to prove they could. The touch had burned her, yes, scorching her magical senses but also deeper, sensually female ones.

He cleared his throat, yanking his gaze away and replacing that trickle of emotion with the image of a still lake. "Let's try it without any support. Ready?"

Swallowing back the absurd disappointment—quite the turnabout that he'd become more careful of touching her than she remembered to be about it—she nodded again.

She swayed as he slid his hands slowly away, so she put her hands down, finding smooth, rounded stones lining the bottom. The instability seemed to come almost as much out of being bereft of his closeness as the loss of physical support. Silly thought.

And perhaps desperation. It would be really wonderful not to feel so absolutely alone.

"Forgetting me?"

"No." Though even Chuffta felt not quite as close as he once had. Probably a result of narrowing her portals so completely. It was better now that she'd opened up to the oasis magic. *"You're waiting for Lonen before you build the fire, yes?"* He'd already told her he would and she believed he'd abide by that, but she asked by way of distracting him.

"Yes." His mind-voice held a distinct grumble. *"I'm piling up wood while I* wait.*"*

"I think I'm okay," she told Lonen. "And Chuffta grows impatient."

He frowned at her, digging both hands through his hair to push the filthy mess out of his face. And maybe to restrain himself from grabbing onto her again. His impulse to do so came through clearly. "Your well-being is more important than Chuffta's obsession with fire. Or Buttercup's tack for that matter. They can wait a while longer."

"Have already waited forever…*"*

She giggled—and it occurred to her that Chuffta might be providing distraction also. Much better not to be scrutinizing every twitch of her weak and uncooperative body. For both of them, as Lonen hovered much too anxiously.

"Really, I'm fine." She layered more asperity into her voice than she felt. "A little breathing room would be welcome, Destrye."

She didn't fool him, because he gave her a wry smile. But he also stood, brushing water from his soaked clothes before pointing a commanding finger at her. "No moving. No going deeper. Call Chuffta if you feel at all faint."

"I will." She tried to sound meek.

"I mean it, Oria. People can drown in a few inches of water."

"Babies and invalids," she retorted. "Even this desert girl knows that much."

"I am not touching that one," he replied evenly. "I'll be back in a moment to help you take your hair down."

She nearly protested out of reflex that it wouldn't be necessary, but in truth her scalp crawled with the pulling tightness of the filthy braids and itched to be clean. Hopefully there wasn't anything else in there crawling around to make her itch. With a last glance to be sure of her obedience, Lonen waded to the shore a few feet away, calling for Chuffta.

Leaving her blessedly alone in the still silence of the lake.

~ 8 ~

THOUGH WEARINESS DRAGGED at him more heavily than his water-sodden leathers, Lonen forced himself to go on. Despite the temporary satiation of the water, his gut crawled up his spine with twisting emptiness. He'd managed to put on a strong show for Oria, but his thoughts came in disconnected bursts. They'd found water, but they needed food. Something not plentiful at the oasis, unfortunately.

He'd been on some other errand, however. It would come to him. Checking over his shoulder, he verified Oria had stayed put. At least her fiery will remained intact, though that's about all she had. Anyone else—even the mightiest Destrye, much less a slight, city-bred foreigner—would have long since given up their grip on mortality and taken refuge in the Hall of Warriors. Dread that in her fragility she might tip over and drown scuttled through his gut. No—that was hunger. They needed food.

What had he come up on the beach to do?

"Show me where to build the fire. Then I can hunt for you and you can cook the meat."

"Oria?" In his bafflement, he turned again—but she sat docilely enough, the water eddying in blue-silver circles around her waist as she scrubbed at her face, scooping up water to alternately drink and splash herself.

"No, idiot. Me." Chuffta hovered in front of him, in midair.

"Who?" He *was* an idiot. Or delirious. He'd heard of this—men hearing voices, seeing things that weren't there. Nightmares invading the waking world. He focused on Chuffta, certain the dragonlet's green eyes burned with exasperation. "I'm hearing you in my thoughts?"

"Obviously."

"How? I never did before."

He got the definite impression of a mental shrug. *"It's not like I wasn't talking, so it must be that you weren't listening."*

That didn't sound exactly right but he couldn't pull together the brain power to argue the point.

"So..." The voice in his head slowed down to an exaggerated degree. *"Show me where to build the fire. Then I can hunt for you and you can cook the meat."*

"You can hunt for us?" He repeated, knowing it sounded stupid, but somehow unable to move his head past that.

"Yes. I'm not excited about spending the rest of my days living alone in this oasis with your rotting corpses. Where. Fire. Barbarian idiot."

"Hey!" He began to understand some of Oria's reactions to her Familiar now. Still, Chuffta's ire snapped through his daze somewhat. As Oria appeared to be still upright in the water—and would be getting cold soon—he scanned the shore for a campfire ring. Spotting one, he directed the derkesthai to it. "See? In places like this previous travelers, if they're responsible, choose good locations and build a semi-permanent ring. Go ahead and clear out some of that old ash, so it won't suffocate our fire."

Chuffta set to the job with enthusiasm—and without further comment, thankfully—while Lonen whistled for Buttercup, who came trotting, happy enough to be finally divested of his tack. "Sorry, Buttercup," Lonen murmured to the warhorse. "I'll take better care of you, I promise. Thanks for carrying us through the desert. You have the heart of a lion."

The stallion bobbed his head as Lonen removed his halter, giving him the uncanny impression that the animal heard and agreed. Although, there he was, talking to the creature as if it could understand. He was beginning to sound like Oria. At least he hadn't "heard" Chuffta speak to him again. That had been beyond the pale. A sorcery no Destrye should experience. Perhaps he'd imagined it.

After brushing down Buttercup and sending the horse off to happily graze on some grasses, Lonen went to build the kindling start, surprised to find Chuffta already nursing a small fire burning with a green flame.

"I watched you last night," he said, giving Lonen what looked like a smile, complete with sharp teeth, a lolling forked tongue, and a wisp of green fire. *"How did I do?"*

"Not bad at all. I'll chop some bigger pieces for you."

"Get the fire hot and I'll go hunt. Tend to Oria. She needs you."

She needed someone better than him, but the lizard had already taken off. What the derkesthai would be able to take down at his size that would feed them, Lonen didn't know. Any number of critters should come in for water, so perhaps the lizardling would get lucky. Arill make it so.

With the fire burning bright, he laid out his furred cloak to warm before he returned to Oria. They'd want it to curl up in. She sat where he'd left her, face tipped up to the sky, eyes closed. Had she returned to her dream state? She sat upright, so he didn't think so.

"Are you all right?" He asked, resisting the urge to touch her cheek, gilded on the edges by the firelight.

She opened her eyes, shadowed, haunting with the flickering flames. "Do you hear them?" she whispered.

Senses going alert, he crouched beside her, drawing his hunting knife as he'd left the battle-axe by the fire. Thickheaded and careless. "What?" He kept his voice hushed, as it would carry over the water.

"The stars," she replied in a dreamy tone. "They're singing. Do you hear them?"

He relaxed fractionally, though it boded ill that she hallucinated, too. At least Chuffta and Buttercup had their wits. Then he shook his head at the absurd thought. "Come on, let's undo your braids so we can wash and dry off." He set the point of his knife to one of the knots, rather than untie the ribbons. It chafed his thrifty heart to do it, but she shouldn't need the cursed things anymore anyway, and he wanted to get her dry.

"Just cut all the braids off," she replied with brisk irritation, scrubbing at her scalp with such vigor that he very nearly did slice through a few.

"No need," he replied. "And keep still, lest I slice your pretty skin."

"You and my hair," she scoffed, but at least subsided. "It would grow back, you know."

"A few moments of work and it won't need to," he answered in as even a tone as he could manage. It did wonders for his heart, to hear her speaking of the future again, that she teased him for his foibles. "How are you feeling?" he dared to ask.

"Better," she replied, surprise in her voice. "I don't know why, but I'm not going to question it. Here, you keep cutting the ribbons—at least you'll concede this much to efficiency—and I'll untangle them." In demonstration she plucked a braid from his hands and began working the plaited hair free, splashing it with water to help it along.

"What would be efficient is to cut all the ribbons, then take you into deeper water so you can soak the mud and salt out."

"Oh." She sounded taken aback and glanced over her shoulder at him, a slight smile curving her lips. In the dim light, the scabbed cracks in them barely showed. "And you'll… help me with the not-drowning part, will you?"

The wistfulness of her expression disarmed him, and he tugged lightly on the braid he held. "Always."

Her smile altered slightly—a bemused twist to it—and she turned away again, dropping her hair. "That's what Chuffta says to me, too."

Uncertain what had changed her mood, he sorted through the stiff mass of braids, aware of a similar stiffness between them. He very nearly told her that Chuffta had spoken in his head, but he wasn't sure if that would please or further upset her. Besides—he wasn't sure if it had been real or the product of fever, starvation, and all the strangeness of recent events.

He also considered asking if she was still angry that he'd refused to take her back across the bay, that he'd nearly killed her already dragging her over the desert to Dru. But no sense resurrecting *that* argument either. So he worked in silence.

"There," he finally said.

"Will you help me stand?" she asked, in a tone so neutral he might have missed how much she disliked asking, if he hadn't been through that with her before.

"I could carry you," he offered.

She shook her head, pulling the braids out of his grip where he still reflexively caressed them. "I want to stand on my own, Lonen."

Which said everything about her and their relationship, right there.

"All right." He made an effort to push back his annoyance, focusing on the peaceful lake, and stood. "I'll get behind you and lift you to your feet." And they would see how well she stood. At least that way he'd be ready to catch her.

If he remained standing, himself.

"No, I want to try something. Take my hands."

He studied her, but she seemed rational. "Are you sure?"

"If I'm wrong, we'll know quickly."

She said that so matter-of-factly, as if he hadn't felt every agonized shudder his touch wracked her with. "Why stress yourself further when you—"

"Give me some credit, Destrye. I know something of what I'm about here."

She sounded tart enough, but he'd come to know her better over the last days and recognized when she brazened her way through things. She'd confessed to him that she'd managed to fake *hwil* well enough to fool her temple busybodies. Besides, not long ago she'd been muttering about death and lapsing in and out of consciousness, not to mention the crazy bit about the stars singing just a few moments before.

"Fine," she snapped. "Don't help me."

"Arill save me, woman," he growled back. "I'm not in the best of shape either. Give me a chance to catch up. Here." He thrust his hands at her. "Take them if you're so determined to. I suppose you can only die once."

"That's a matter of some debate," she muttered, slipping her cool, damp hands into his. Hesitating only a moment, she clasped him tighter and tried to stand. She wobbled considerably, nearly falling back, so he gripped her and pulled—ready to let go and catch her by the shoulders or waist if needed.

He watched her face for signs of strain, for those distinctive brackets of pain around her mouth that came with physical contact, but she remained serene except for a grimace when her leg threatened to give. Checking himself, he squeezed her hands, savoring the delicacy of her hands with their fine bones. "How can we be touching?"

She opened her mouth to reply, then wobbled dangerously. "Cursc it," she grated out as her legs went. He caught her in time, sweeping her up in his arms, as she should have let him do in the first place. Blinking at him with some surprise, she smiled, though it was more a grim twist of her mouth. "Admirable, those warrior reflexes."

"Handy for dealing with stubborn sorceresses." Wasting no more time—and hoping to prevent an argument from that hasty observation—he waded deeper into the water, carrying her with no effort despite his own fatigue. Though he wished he'd taken the time to shuck his boots. They were already soaked, from his precipitous dunking when they finally made it to the oasis, but the rounded stones the ancients had paved the bottom of the pond with made for uneven footing. Keeping his balance on the precarious surface took such concentration that Oria's hand caressing his face nearly shocked him.

She had that dreamy look again, dragging her fingertips lightly through his beard. "It's so soft. How can it look rough but feel soft?"

"Many things are not as they appear. You should be the queen of knowing that."

"And yet I'm queen of nothing. A shade forever cursed to live beyond the walls and tides of Bára."

Not a good time to remind her that she would be Queen in Dru. It wouldn't have made him feel better either, were their positions reversed. He stopped in water deep enough for her soak herself, but shallow enough to stand should she insist on trying that again. She dipped her head back with a sigh, her braids swirling into a halo, but she didn't relinquish her grasp on his beard.

"How can you be touching me, Oria?" he asked softly, unsure if he wanted to know the answer. It could be a bad sign, that she'd gone so far in her steps to the Hall of Warriors that she'd lost sight of what might injure her further.

"My mother gave me the key," she replied just as quietly, without opening her eyes, stroking his beard so he leaned his cheek into her hand. It would feel marvelous if it didn't make him sick with worry. "To fend off the wild magic I… closed all the portals for it to enter. That means it closes off everything else, too. I can touch you—and you can stop picturing that cursed lake, because I can't read your thoughts anyway."

"If you can't read my thoughts, how do you know I'm picturing it?"

A faint line formed between her brows. "I don't know. I'm still getting something. As if it comes from another place. The water? I don't know. But if I wasn't getting magic from somewhere, I'd already be dead."

Though he thought he'd already faced that possibility, her words struck cold terror through his heart. "Maybe you should open up more of those portals then. Feed yourself from the magic."

"It is more coherent here," she admitted, then opened her eyes, the copper uncannily bright even in the dimness, as if lit from within. "And I am doing some of that. But I like touching you. We could have sex, for real. Finally. It's what you've wanted."

He bit back a vicious retort. She wasn't in her right mind so he wouldn't take offense at the implication he lusted for her so badly that he'd take her even though it meant her death.

"Let's get us both cleaned up first," he said. "Can you float?"

She frowned at him and let her hand fall, turning her face away. "I don't know how."

"Standing then—the water should help buoy you." He lowered her legs, transferring his supporting grip to her waist. "Or you can hang onto me and I can loosen the braids."

"You do it." She held onto his shoulders and tipped her head back into the water again. The movement exposed the long, graceful line of her neck, and with her silk robes plastered to her skin, outlined her small, perfect breasts, nipples taut from the cool water. She might have his number after all because his cock stiffened at the sight. He did crave her, beyond reason.

But he wasn't a monster. He might have behaved like one in the past, entertained dark-edged lustful thoughts about her that she'd unfortunately glimpsed in his mind, but he could be a better man than that. He wouldn't act on them. Especially with her so fragile.

As gently as he could, he combed his fingers through the braids, loosening the salt and caked dirt, freeing the silken strands of her hair to float like seaweed. Recalling how she'd complained of them itching and pulling at her scalp, he judiciously massaged that too, watching her face for any hint of pain.

"Help me undress, too," she murmured.

He paused in his scrubbing. No hint of mischief or guile in her face, but he suspected her of continuing an ill-advised seduction. "I thought you didn't like being naked outside."

She lifted her head, eyeing him somberly—and sliding her hands from his shoulders to the back of his neck. The light caress of her fingers proved a fatal distraction, and he fought his darker nature that wanted to take her up on the implicit offer. "I told you I'm sorry for how I behaved. I was just…" She shook her head, sleek as a seal, the copper dark as the water that soaked it. "You wouldn't understand, but I was afraid—and being naked was somehow part of that."

"I understand better than you think. I sometimes dream of riding into battle naked, carrying a feather instead of my battle-axe."

Her mouth quirked. "That makes sense, in a way."

Why had he told her that? He hadn't told anyone of those particular nightmares. Natly, his former almost-fiancée, would have laughed at him outright and he wouldn't have blamed her for it. In the light of day, he understood the meaning, how it reflected the eternal anxiety of being unprepared for a fight. And yet the vulnerability of those dreams bothered him on some deep level.

"If you won't help me, will you at least keep your promise to keep me from drowning while I undress myself?" She quirked a brow at him, her tone going acerbic, some accusation in it. Had he just thought to himself that he began to understand her? Not for the first time he wished for the ability to see into *her* mind.

"I'll help you," he replied mildly. "But I'm not having sex with you, so you can forget that idea."

She was quiet, hanging onto his shoulders again, as he loosened the ties of her robes. The knots had tightened from soaking in the water, so it took slow, steady attention. He ignored the gleam of her fair skin in the moonlight as he peeled back the layers, the wet crimson silk nearly black in contrast.

"The chemise, too," she said, when he pulled away the last of the robes, draping the sodden mass over his arm so they wouldn't sink or float away.

He didn't bother to argue. The cursed garment showed every detail of her body anyway. He pulled it off over her head and she shook out her hair, dipping again to sleek it back out of her face. So she was naked. He'd seen her naked before. He could ignore that.

"It's amazing, being in water so deep," she said. "I get what you mean about floating. Here, I can hold my clothes while you undress and wash off."

Handing them over, he kept an eye on her, though she showed no sign of going under. He'd be able to catch her quickly enough if she did. Toeing off first one boot, then the other, happy to get the Arill-benighted things off his feet. He threw them to shore, in the vicinity of the cheerful campfire that blazed, Chuffta's dark silhouette of half-spread wings beside it. He ducked his head, scrubbing at his own scalp with considerable relief. The chill of the water helped cool his feverish brain, too. "Can you walk to shore, or should I carry you?" he asked, hoping that she'd be able to walk, so he wouldn't face the test of carrying her naked body against him.

"Do you realize those are the first words you've spoken to me since you delivered your no-sex verdict?"

He hadn't noticed—but he wasn't surprised, given how tightly he'd reined in his tongue and all reactions to her. "It's not a verdict."

"What is it then? And you still have your clothes on."

"They're clean enough from being on me in the water."

"Lonen. Don't be ridiculous. Take them off and rinse them so we can let them dry by the fire."

He was being ridiculous—and he was a warrior, for Arill's sake. He could control himself, clothed or naked. Working quickly, he stripped out of his shirt and the water-shrunk leathers. His turgid cock sprang free of the confining pants with a surge of blood that nearly emptied his head. What little had remained up there.

In case Oria got ideas, he took a few judicious steps back, using the excuse of swishing the clothes to rinse them. Then he slung them over his shoulder and turned back to face Oria—who'd snuck up on him and stood far too close. Under the water, her slim hand fastened around his erect cock, choking the breath out of him.

He fisted his hands to keep from seizing her in turn. This was the sorceress who'd haunted his dreams, her beautiful face a play of light and shadow, those copper eyes reflecting the firelight, full of erotic knowledge.

Knowledge she did not possess. Her confidence was an illusion—one that could kill her if he believed in it.

Desperate, he knocked her hand aside.

~ 9 ~

SHOCKED—AND PUSHED OFF balance by the unexpected blow, gentle though it was—Oria staggered in the water. Lonen caught her, of course, strong hands bracketing her waist and holding her head easily above water. His face had gone stern and remote, his jaw tight, eyes flinty.

All determined Destrye warrior now.

But for a moment, when she'd grasped his cock, he'd reacted to her as he once had—expression lighting with lust, his member moving in her hand in heated welcome. At least that part of him still wanted her. She might be hideously underweight, her lips cracking painfully if she moved her mouth too quickly, but at least she was clean. Of course, she probably resembled a Trom, all scaled skin over bones. Still, she couldn't be that revolting if his body reacted to her.

Trying one more time, she moved into the embrace he didn't offer, sleeking her naked body against his and gasping at the startling sensation of skin on skin. He echoed the sound, hands flexing on her waist, heart drumming under her ear as she wrapped her arms around him. This. This was what she'd missed all her life. She wanted to burrow into him, take him inside her and wrap herself all around his masculine strength and vitality.

"Lonen." She breathed his name instead of the plea. Tipping back her head, she found him staring at her, a contorted expression on his face. His emotions simmered behind that cursed lake image, a turbulent mix of desire and alarm, all encased in resolute steel. If she could, she would've plundered his thoughts for clues. Why wouldn't he take her as he'd said he longed to?

"Kiss me," she coaxed. Okay, begged, but she had no pride anymore.

As if he struggled against a fierce wind, he slowly lowered his mouth to hers, pausing before reaching her. He hesitated so long that she opened up some of the portals, just a hair more, but enough poured in through that slim breach that his roiling emotions slammed through her. Too much to sort, except that dread and regret rode the crest.

She struggled to slam the lid back on, just as he pulled back again, eyes fastened still to her mouth. "Your lips are cracked," he said, and released his hold on her.

Bereft of the stunning contact, she lifted a hand to her mouth. Scaled, cracked lips, indeed—and a tang of blood where a split reopened with her prodding. Lonen watched her, his face stony again. "Am I that revolting?" she whispered through her fingers, and his expression softened.

"No, love. You are beyond beautiful. But you're so fragile I think I could crush you with one hand. I am not making love to you. Not tonight. No matter how much I might want to."

Might want to. Not did want to. "I don't want to be a virgin anymore." The words came out pitiful and pleading, but there it was.

"You're not, remember? Our wedding night."

"That was an… implement. Not you. I want you inside me. I want to at least taste that pleasure before I die."

That did it. His jaw firmed and he looked past her, remote as granite. "Then you're in luck because you're not going to die anytime soon—and certainly not at my hands. Now, walk or be carried?"

"I'll walk." Apparently she did have pride left. She began wading through the water toward the campfire on the shore, helping herself along by pulling her arms through the water, the robes she held swishing with them, creating drag. The round stones rose smooth against her feet, but also made her footing difficult. She staggered here and there, slipping. And as she made it to the shallows, losing the support of the water, her legs trembled, threatening to give way as they had before.

Lonen put his arms around her waist, but she pushed him away. "Don't. I can do it."

"Pride again, Oria?" His voice came grimly mocking from behind her. "I thought we were past this."

That had been before he rejected her. Rationally, she knew he was right, but she'd hoped that passion would override such considerations. Perhaps if she knew more about seducing a man...

"Come to the fire and rest, Oria. You're tired and need to eat." Chuffta's mind-voice sounded unusually gentle and solicitous. He should be chiding her, which meant he thought she couldn't take it. She stood in the waist-deep water, trembling with fatigue. It seemed that no matter how far she came, she always faced this point of being too delicate to even be alive. She trembled with vicious anger at herself for being so pitifully weak.

"Oria." Lonen put a hand on her shoulder, stroking her arm. "Let me help you."

"Fine. Carry me." She sounded dull to herself. He picked her up as if she weighed nothing, which she probably did, even after drinking all that water, and had her to the fire in several quick strides that put all her floundering to shame. Setting her on his furred cloak, he took her wet silks, and handed her something else. One of his shirts, quite worse for wear.

"Dry yourself with that, then wrap up in the cloak so you don't get cold." Naked buttocks flexing, he moved to the ring of trees nearby, hanging her clothes and his from the branches.

She wanted to ask him how he could stand her when she couldn't stand herself—but obviously he couldn't. Numbly, she did as he told her, using the shirt to dry her skin, then wringing out her hair and mopping at it. She combed her fingers through it, spreading it to the warm fire. The heat and light relaxed her weeping muscles.

Chuffta slid another log onto the fire, quite proficient at it. Satisfied, he picked his way over to her, sliding up her arm and snaking his tail around her waist, his scaled body warm and soft against her skin.

"You're doing amazingly well," he said in her mind, with great gentleness. *"I know it's hard feeling weak and powerless, but only hours ago you couldn't sit up by yourself. Pay attention to how far you've progressed, rather than how far you have to go."*

"I thought I was supposed to put my attention on the result I want," she replied aloud, too tired to try to form the thoughts that would let her to speak to him mind-to-mind.

"What's that?" Lonen asked, returning to the fire with knife in hand, his cock no longer erect. He poked at something in the shadows, grunted, then began wedging a couple of forked branches into the sand on either side of the fire. As if nothing had occurred between them. Okay, she could do that, too. Politely pretend.

"I was talking to Chuffta. It's a teaching of the temple. That we're supposed to focus our intentions on the results we want so the magic goes that direction. Probably nonsense."

He looked thoughtful. "Makes sense, actually. Arill teaches something similar—be hopeful for what you want. Don't dwell on what you dread."

Like all that dread she'd sensed in him. She nearly called him on his own dwelling, but what did it matter? She stroked Chuffta's breast where he had a hard time scratching and he purred in her mind. Lonen picked up something furry and limp, with long ears. Her stomach rolled in piteous empathy.

"What is that—is it dead?"

"I'm not sure what it is—a rodent something, but dead, yes."

"Are you going to bury it?

He slanted her a look she couldn't read. "No. I'm going to skin it and cook it over the fire so we can eat it."

Not a joke. "I'm not eating another living being."

"Then you're in luck with this also because it's not living—it's dead."

"You know what I mean. Bárans don't eat flesh. I never have. It's unclean and wrong."

Lonen's expression became all too easy to interpret. "Oria. You are going to eat this if I have to sit on you and force each bite down your throat."

"I'll just throw it up again!"

"Then I'll make you eat that, too," he retorted, voice and face implacable.

"You wouldn't."

"Test me and find out." He picked up the poor animal and carried it into the shadows. At least she wouldn't have to witness this "skinning."

"I caught it for you." Chuffta sounded apologetic. *"And for Lonen, too, because he's so hungry that he didn't think he had the strength to hunt. I looked for fruit, but didn't see any. And there are no grains or things like that. I'm not sure if the leaves here make good salad."*

"It's all right." She stroked the arch of his wing, more to assuage the stab of guilt than to please her Familiar. Lonen always seemed so strong. It hadn't occurred to her that he might be hungry and tired, too. "How did you know how Lonen felt?"

"He talked to me," Lonen said out of the darkness. Not so far away. "In my head."

"He did?" She looked at Chuffta who returned her surprised stare, green eyes wide and mind radiating innocence. "Why didn't you tell me?"

"I just did." Lonen returned to the fire, setting a stick spitted with several small bodies over the brackets. "Chuffta, man—I left the guts in a pile over there for you if you want them."

"Tell him thank you for me."

"Tell him yourself." But Chuffta had already gone for his gory feast. "He says to say thank you."

It shouldn't bother her that her Familiar had talked mind-to-mind with Lonen. Even though he'd only ever done so with her before. She'd always known he could hear the thoughts of others than her—though, true, she'd thought it was only other magic bearers—but she'd somehow gotten the idea that they shared a special bond that allowed him to talk only to her.

Lonen glanced at her through the hair falling over his eyes. He hadn't tied it back again. Hopefully he hadn't lost his favorite leather tie. An irrelevant concern, given all they faced. She didn't know why she thought of it. "I didn't tell you when it happened because I wasn't sure how you'd take it. I didn't want to upset you."

"And now you don't care if you upset me?" She said it lightly, but looked into the fire instead of at him, pulling her hair over the other shoulder and angling to dry it, too.

He didn't reply immediately, adjusting the roasting of the dead animals. The smell made her think of the funeral pyres after the Destrye army left, as the bodies that had been pulped by the Trom and not burned by their dragons had been dealt with. He'd no doubt follow through on his threat to force her to eat, but she didn't understand how anyone could stomach it.

"I think," he finally said, slowly as if he were thinking as he spoke, "that as much as we sometimes miscommunicate, it's still better to speak honestly with each other than withhold information."

She snapped her gaze up to find him watching her intently. "I'm not withholding information."

"Aren't you?" He held her gaze. "You hadn't told me your mother explained how to manage the wild magic."

"We haven't exactly had time for conversation."

He nodded thoughtfully. Turned the spit. Juices dripped into the fire, making it hiss, and she had to look away. "Fair enough. Then explain to me what's going on with you. The portals of magic and so forth."

"I'm too tired." Indeed, she was inexpressively weary.

"It will keep you awake until it's time to eat. Then you can sleep all you like."

Her gorge rose at the thought of eating that meat. If her stomach hadn't been hollow as a dried gourd, she might have emptied it.

"Oria." He sighed and raked his hands through his hair. "If I'm going to keep you alive long enough to get you to Dru, I need to know how to help you."

Of course. The man never forgot his mission. Get her back to Dru to stop the Trom from their depredations and save his people. She couldn't blame him for caring about that above all things. Even when he'd been her enemy she'd found that attractive in him, his devotion to leading wisely, standing up to his responsibilities. Once she'd felt the same way. Only days ago, when sgath filled her with magic, making her feel powerful even when she hadn't known how to channel it. Maybe what she experienced now was how ordinary magicless people felt all the time. What a grim existence that would be. And yet Lonen seemed filled with vitality, even having struggled with the same privations as she.

"Remember that we promised to be partners?" He asked, more quietly. "We're married, which means we need to trust each other. When you won't talk to me, it makes me think that you don't trust me."

Annoying, when he didn't trust her, either. At least, not enough to believe that she wanted him to touch her. She nearly said that, but the look in his eyes, softer gray now with earnest feeling, changed her mind. They were exhausted and starving. Maybe people didn't always get along so well under these circumstances. She certainly wasn't holding up so well to the challenge. And what would it hurt to confide in him? The temple had banished her from its ranks. She owed their secrets no allegiance. She did owe Lonen, much as she hated admitting how dependent she was on him. But he'd confided in her, hadn't he? Telling her about that dream of riding naked into battle, a hint of embarrassment shadowing the words, though he'd kept his tone light and joking.

"I don't understand it myself," she told him, acutely aware she was telling him something she'd never spoken of to anyone but her

Familiar. "It's kind of funny. When I was younger, all those years in my tower—well, even right up until you and the Destrye arrived—I thought that if I could just master *hwil*, everything would fall into place. If only I could quiet my mind, learn to meditate properly, then I wouldn't be such a mess. I could go out in public for as long as I wanted to, without having to run back to my tower before whatever event I attended was even over. If I could master *hwil*, I'd get my mask, I'd manage my sgath and be a priestess, and..."

"And everything would be perfect," he finished for her, when she didn't, eyes glinting with shared understanding.

"Well, not perfect, maybe." Because that sounded even more naïve than she'd been. Though she'd had a vision of herself in her robes and mask, perfectly self-possessed, strong, and unassailable. Naïve, indeed. "But much better than I had been."

He gave a lopsided smile, shaking his head absently at something. "It *is* funny, how the goal always seems to move. I once thought that when I got big and strong enough to fight the golems, then they wouldn't scare me so cursed much. Then I thought if only we could win the war, everything would go back to normal. Then it was, if only we could build the aqueducts before winter, grow enough crops, bring in enough water, then next summer we'd be fine."

He glanced at her again, pushing back his hair from his eyes. "We know what became of that hope."

The Trom had burned the crops and their clever aqueducts. "And now your goal is to get me to Dru alive."

He studied her a moment. "It's a good interim goal, anyway. Shorter term than that is figuring out how to get you to eat this meat so you won't waste away on me."

"I'll eat it," she said, though her stomach revolted. Maybe if she closed her eyes. She owed him that much. She'd made vows to help him save the Destrye and she wouldn't be foresworn again. "Thank you for cooking it for me. It was ungracious of me to say otherwise."

Lonen smiled at her, warmth in it. "I think we can cut you extra rope given the circumstances. I'm sure I'd be far more than ungracious, were I in your tree."

She had no reply to that, so she waited, steeling herself for the unpleasantness ahead. Lonen pulled some of the meat off the spit and put it on a utensil he'd pulled from the saddle bags, working intently with his knife. Coming around the fire, he sat beside her on the cloak, and handed her what turned out to be a plate, but made of metal instead of glass. "Here's a flask with water to wash it down with if you need to," he said. "I cooked it really well and pulled it into slivers so you don't have to chew it much. You can pretend it's those grubs you like to eat."

"Grubs?" She kept her eyes firmly on his face, so as not to look what in her lap. He didn't seem to be joking. "I don't eat grubs."

"Those white, wormy looking things you ate for our big meal before the council meeting, when you went in and kicked ass, forcing them to agree to make you queen."

She nearly laughed at how he kept trying to build up her ego. She must seem pitiful indeed if he felt he needed to put so much effort into it. "Is that how it happened?"

"That's how I remember it." He reached up and tucked a lock of hair behind her ear, trailing a finger down her cheek. "You were spectacular. Still are."

She swallowed against the tightness in her throat, surprised at how much she'd needed to hear that. Pitiful, yes. "Thank you."

"You're welcome." He nodded at the plate. "Eat your grubs."

"It was grain."

"This is just like grain. Just a little more processed down the line."

"What a way to think of it. I will never understand you and your barbarian ways."

"Back at you, sorceress. Eat."

"I can't while you're watching me."

"Tough. Do it anyway. If you stall any longer, I will make good on my threat. At least sitting on you will be fun for me."

"You're such a bully," she muttered, but at the resolute glint in his eyes, she pinched up some of the meat, held her breath and shoved it in her mouth. It kind of felt like grain to her fingers, but tasted… ugh. Like blood and char. She didn't have to chew much—he was true to his word on that—so she swallowed as hastily as possible.

He raised a thick brow in question. "First bite down."

"And I didn't even puke on you."

He laughed and ran a hand down her hair. "You'll do, sorceress. Are you cold—do you want the cloak on you?"

"No—the fire is really warm. Trying to cover me up?"

"If only." He got up and went to the other side of the fire again, unspitting another little carcass. "If you've got enough so far, I'm eating this one."

"Please do." He did look far too gaunt. More so than ever, and he'd arrived back in Bára skinner than he'd been on his first visit. Despite his muscled chest and shoulders, and the ridged lines of his abdomen, his hip bones stood out sharply and she could see his lower ribs. Of course, his leanness only served to define the lines of his muscles and sinews, tempting her to run her fingers along them, to explore him as she hadn't been able to before. "Have all you like," she said with fervor, quickly swallowing another pinch of the meat. If she didn't look at the cooking bodies—or inhale the smell too deeply—she could kind of forget what it was.

"Don't think you're off the hook." Lonen leveled a stern look at her. "You'll get more for breakfast."

Relieved that he apparently wouldn't make her eat more than he'd already given her, she ate what she had as fast as possible. It did fill her stomach, the warmth of the food welcome.

"You were telling me about the magic and how you thought things would fall into place once you had your mask," he reminded her.

"And you never forget a question once you've asked it."

He grinned, eyes sparkling. "See? You do understand me and my barbarian ways."

She huffed out an exasperated sigh, which only broadened his grin. At least talking let her not think about the animal she ate. And what its name to itself might have been. Finer sentiment apparently flew out the open window when it came to survival. "I thought that once I had my mask I'd understand all the temple lessons. That everything would make sense and I would know what I was doing all the time."

Lonen grunted a laugh. "Good luck with that. I'm still waiting to know what I'm doing."

"You too? Some king and queen we make."

"If only our subjects could see us now."

He surprised the laugh out of her. Somehow he managed to do that—make her laugh at the most absurd moments, even at her lowest, like this night. She shook her head ruefully, the silken slide of her drying hair an unusual sensation on her bare skin. Lonen stared at her a moment, rapt, before yanking his gaze away. Maybe he did still find her attractive. Another irrelevant thing to be wondering about, though these things seemed to be looming large in her heart and mind.

"Sometimes we focus on the small things because the big ones are too much to contemplate all at once," Chuffta said as he landed by the fire, looking sleek and satisfied. *"And the rodent things didn't have names. I asked and they didn't answer."*

She nearly choked on her mouthful, Lonen giving her a quizzical look. "Chuffta," she said by way of explanation. "Trying to make me feel better. Anyway, to answer your question, I have no idea how this works. We left the city and the wild magic hit me hard, just like the last time. Mother told me to remember sgath comes from Sgatha and to make it wane like her crescent until it went dark to the new moon. So I did."

"And promptly passed out," Lonen noted in a wry tone.

"Well, I think that would have happened anyway. Then, when I woke up later, all that feeling of magic coming in was gone."

"But you were weak. Could barely move."

As if she needed reminding of how he'd had to help her. Perhaps being up close and personal with her more unattractive body functions had served to repel him. She couldn't blame him there. "I had thought that was because of the backlash of the wild magic. That's how it affected me the last time. But now I think some of it is because I began to starve, being away from Bára's magic."

He nodded. "That's what you said. Like a flower without water, you wilted. You're better now, though. And getting stronger all the time."

"The food helped." She set the plate aside, surprised to find it empty. "Thank you."

"My pleasure to feed my wife."

"Me and Buttercup. You take good care of us."

He winced. "Don't tell anyone that name, okay? It's beneath a warhorse's dignity. And don't dodge the subject. It's more than the food."

"Yes, but I don't know what. It's like there's a coherent kind of magic here that I can absorb. But my portals are still closed because I can't read your thoughts, much, and I don't overload when you touch me. Which is why we should have sex while we're here, because we might not have another opportunity."

"Now who won't drop the topic she's interested in pursuing? I'm not doing it, Oria, so let it go."

"You were the one to go on about it, how much you wanted me and that you'd find a way," she snapped, full of ire again. And the sting of humiliation that he'd rejected the offer yet again.

"And we will. *When* you're healthy again."

"What if I'm never healthy again, Lonen—have you thought of that? What if this is the best I'll ever be? We could leave this oasis and I'll begin to starve again."

He set his jaw stubbornly. "I refuse to believe that. However, *if* that should happen and we can't find a way to reverse it, then I'll bring you back here to get strong. Then you can believe I'll make love to you until you can't see straight. Something to look forward to."

She didn't return his crooked grin. "I know this is your thing, your way of looking at life, to be all idealistic and proclaim we'll 'climb that tree when we come to it,' but have you considered, *really* thought about the fact that maybe I'm no longer the sorceress I was? Even if I can manage to live, my relationship with magic might have forever changed." Her voice caught on that, but she refused to shed any more tears of self-pity. "Not only might I be useless in helping you fight the Trom, it's entirely likely I could become a stone around your neck. The forever sickly wife who is nothing but a burden. You should think long and hard on this, Destrye—and before you decide to expend the effort to drag me across the rest of the desert."

He stared into the fire, then at her through the screen of his dark lashes. "Is that what the sex thing is about? You're wanting to give me something in exchange for taking care of you."

"It seems only fair." She sounded bitter. Better than pitiful, though. "I don't have anything else to offer."

"I would be severely pissed about that," he said in a conversational tone, wrapping up the meat and stowing it. "Except I'm too tired. And neither of us is in any state to be rational. Still, I'm going to point out that I married you with every intention of keeping my vows. That's what marriage is about: being partners and helping each other when we need it. I want to make love to you, yes, but not as some sort of equivalent exchange of favors, so you can get that out of your head. You might not think better of me than that, but I do."

"I didn't mean it like that." She'd made a miserable mess of it. She couldn't seem to do anything right. "I... want you, too. I wanted to touch you while I'm able to."

"We can do that, Oria." He finished his tasks, scrubbing his hands clean in the sand. "Chuffta, you'll mind the fire? Not too hot.

Keep it low, just like this."

Her Familiar spread his wings and imitated a bow, happily setting a proprietary talon on the topmost log on the ready pile of wood. Lonen came around the fire to her. "Lie down, love—let's get some sleep. Things will look brighter in the morning."

It felt good to do so. To give up the effort of sitting upright and stretch out on the warm fur. Lonen lay down behind her, drawing her back up against his bare chest, hot from the fire and his inherent vitality, and cupped his body around hers. "Lift your head," murmured.

She did and he moved her hair, smoothing it over her shoulder and moving his arm under her head. His biceps made a surprisingly good pillow, the hairless skin of his underarm soft against her cheek. He drew the fur around them and she melted into the comfort of it all. Sleep—real sleep—not the dragging weight of unconsciousness suffused her mind.

"I might have been an idealist once." Lonen's voice came softly, dreamy and reflective. She might have thought he spoke only to himself, but he kissed her hair, his other hand resting on her belly, softly caressing her with quiet fingers. "But I lost it along the way. I only found it again when I saw you, Oria. My world had become a bleak, sterile place that housed only cruelty and desperation. You brought magic into my life. That's everything."

In that interstitial place between waking and dreaming, his words meant everything to her, too.

~ 10 ~

HE CAME AWAKE all at once, as he'd acquired the habit of doing on the long campaign trail. A good and bad skill. He gained alertness rapidly—critical in case of attack—but it also gave him a disorienting jolt. Gone were the days of slow, drowsy awakening, gradually remembering his dreams and the events of the night before, idly pondering plans for the coming day. Instead his heart thundered into readiness to fight, his body tensed to spring, long before his brain caught up.

Fortunately, long habit also helped him catch up quickly so he didn't disturb Oria, still sleeping deeply in his arms. Which also allowed him to ease his hips back from her delicious bottom before she woke and discovered how he'd been grinding his morning erection against her. She didn't need more reminders of his burning lust to have her—nor did he need another seduction attempt from her to test his resolve.

They still lay exactly as they'd fallen asleep and the sun had risen to long past anything he could call morning—a testament to their deep exhaustion. Probably only the growing heat had awakened him. He felt hugely better, however. Nothing like water, food, and rest to restore a man. And a beautiful woman to salve his soul. Oria's hair gleamed copper bright in the midday sun and he indulged himself by winding a lock of it around his finger like a ring. It looked quite fine. When they reached Dru—and he refused to contemplate any other outcome, if that made him an idealist, so be it—he'd have Oria's *beah* made of copper in exactly this shade.

Smooth or plaited, he wasn't yet certain.

Her breathing changed from the deep evenness of sleep and she stirred, so he risked caressing her. Pushing the already too-warm cloak back, he stroked a hand down her slight waist and the curve of her hips, then back up her concave belly. Far too thin, but so soft and sweet. She had a point about indulging in touching. Though he'd never get enough of her, never saturate himself with her presence to satisfy that craving.

She lifted a hand to rub at her eyes, frowned, then turned in his arms, blinking at him. A reflection of his own awakening, remembering what had happened before she slept, though with all the drowsy dreaminess he'd lost somewhere on a corpse-strewn battlefield.

"Hello," he said, softly, to help her along, restraining himself from asking how she felt as it seemed to annoy her. Probably he wouldn't like that first thing when he awoke either.

"Hi." She frowned a little. "We're at the oasis still, right?"

He suppressed a smile, lest she think he laughed at her. "Yes. Just since yesterday evening."

She narrowed her eyes, the softness of sleep quickly vanishing as the coppery awareness sharpened. Some of her magic swirled through him, sparkling and sure. She'd recovered a great deal during her sleep. "You laugh at me," she noted in a tart tone, "but just try going in and out of consciousness for several days and you'd get paranoid about lost time, too."

"I wasn't laughing, Oria." He smoothed a hand along the arch of her spine, her hair falling silky over it. "At least not *at* you. It only amused me that it was your first question."

"The first one I articulated anyway." In a rapid shift of mood, she curved into him, pressing her slim body into his, her nipples taut pebbles against his chest and he bit back a groan. Awake, she lost that fragile quality, the vibrancy of her personality somehow transforming her from warm coal to blazing bonfire against him. A miscalculation there in savoring her sleeping presence instead of getting up before she awoke, putting him firmly in danger of forgetting her well-being and succumbing to his savage nature. Greatly recovered or not, she needed much more rest and gentle caring—not the debauched array of what he longed to do to her.

He wouldn't again make the mistake of mishandling this precious gift from Arill.

Oria, however, had other ideas. She tangled her fingers in the hair of his chest, tugging at it with a playful glint in her eye. "My first question was 'who is this magnificent man in my bed?'"

He put a hand over hers, steeling himself to withstand the temptation she presented—along with the ridiculous rush of pleasure that she found him attractive, and the very good sign that she felt good enough to flirt. He hadn't always been sure. She'd dropped hints here and there, but the Báran girl he'd married only days before had been reticent in her naïveté, and the sorceress canny in what she revealed to him. Both far easier to deal with than this temptress determined to seduce him.

"Had you forgotten me already?" He asked lightly, in the same teasing tone.

"I thought perhaps one of the llerna had snuck into my bed to claim tribute for the water and sanctuary." She wriggled against him, sliding a slender thigh along his as he fought to keep his groin well back.

"Are there such creatures?"

She raised her brows, thankfully distracted by the question. "Who do you think built these oases?"

"We didn't know. We'd didn't even know where Bára was until we followed the golems back. Our scouts found the oases along the way. What are these llerna?"

"Builders and guardians. They gathered together the water as the great rivers dried to trickles, concentrating them in sacred spots, where only the thirsty could enter." She spoke the words like she recited an old lesson.

"That explains why they weren't drained like everything else," he mused. "I'd wondered how—" He broke off on a gasp as her clever hand wrapped around his hard cock. "Oria."

Her eyes glinted with sensual mischief, but her expression was resolute. "Don't use that tone with me. You want me. This tells me that." She stroked him up and down, and his hips helplessly followed. "Am I wrong?"

"I want you, of course. More than water in the desert." He gritted his teeth and took her wrist in a firm grip. She held on, her delicate hand astonishingly strong, the squeeze sending bolts of lust up his spine to fog his brain. "Arill, take it—I refuse to hurt you!"

"You were able to give me pleasure without intercourse," she crooned, watching his face. "I can do the same for you. Let me do this."

He thrust through her hand, already slick with his fluids, unable to stop himself, trying to muster the argument. "Oria," he breathed, bereft of other words. "Love. I—"

"Shh. Let me. I want to." She pushed closer, working his cock in her tenacious grip, sliding her limber leg higher on his hip. With a groan, he gave up and pushed his thigh between hers. The slick heat of her sex shocked him—but not into sense. Instead he lost himself to her, grasping her by her hips and holding her in place to ride his thigh. She moaned, the most enticing of sounds, throwing her head back, face suffused with pleasure, and he was helpless to do anything but drink it in.

He kissed her, a vague thought of keeping it gentle fleeing before the crashing lust. She opened her mouth as sweetly as her legs, offering him everything and, Arill save him, he took it. Their skin slicked with sweat, gliding together, tongues entwining like their bodies.

He wouldn't last long, he was so starved for her, but she was close, too, both thighs clamped around his as he ground against her soft woman's flesh. She broke their kiss with a cry of pleasure, throwing her head back again as her body convulsed and arched. Her hand tightened almost painfully on his cock with it, but that only worked to send him flying, the power of the orgasm blowing through him and shattering him entirely.

THE SENSATION OF the powerful Destrye warrior coming apart in her grip filled Oria with a heady rush of power. His hard thigh pressed up against her sex drove her wild with pleasure—as much as any of his meticulous techniques when they'd consummated their marriage—but this, this pushing him beyond the brink of control…

An amazing experience. One that went some way to restoring her sense of herself as a potent woman.

They lay there for a time, panting, breaths mingling along with sweat. He seemed to need a moment to recover, gently staying her hand from moving any more, making a sound of relief when she stopped. For her part, she wasn't sure what to do with the sticky emissions coating her palm—and it would be better if he didn't know that the small exertion had made her a little dizzy, her vision gray at the edges. It had been worth it.

"I know about it." Chuffta chided.

"I thought I told you to go away and give us privacy."

"I did." Her Familiar's mind-voice carried a distinct tinge of huffy self-righteousness. *"But when I felt you getting weak, I thought I'd better check on you. I don't care what you do with your mate."*

"At least I'm strong enough to talk to you this way again. That's a good sign, right?" Her mental tone sounded firm to herself. Much better. Chuffta, however, did not reply, which she took to be a diplomatic denial. Ah, well.

Lonen laughed breathlessly and opened his eyes, the gray sparkling clear. "That was—" He broke off with a frown. "Arill, take it, your mouth is bleeding."

He pulled away from her, sitting up and wiping his own mouth with the back of his hand, observing the smear of blood, then scrutinizing her. "How else did I hurt you?"

"You didn't," she snapped, wiping her own mouth, with her clean hand. She still wasn't sure what to do about the other, and she didn't sit up, just in case the dizziness became too obvious. In a moment she'd feel better and go to the water to wash. "I'm fine. I know my stupid lips are cracked and it's revolting, but I have no blood-borne diseases, if that's what you're worried about."

Lonen sighed, frustrated exasperation wafting around her, and scrubbed his hands through his hair. He hadn't oiled it after they'd bathed the night before, and it stood out in wild curls. "Why would you say such a thing?"

"You said something very similar to me once."

"That was before."

"Before what?"

"*This.*" He gestured back and forth between them. "And it should be obvious that is *not* what I'm worried about. You've heard my thoughts, for Arill's sake. Must you always read the worst interpretation into what I say and do?"

Stung, she did sit up, ruthlessly clamping down on the dizziness. "I don't do that."

"You do it a lot," he retorted in a dark tone, glaring at her.

"Well!" She stumbled on the tart reply that hovered on her tongue. "Maybe I do. I'm sorry. I don't have much experience with having a husband. Before *this.*" She imitated his gesture.

His expression immediately shifted as he smiled, the sun breaking through the sandstorm, and he reached out to caress her cheek. "And I have little with a wife or a fearsome sorceress, let alone both at once. I'm sorry, too. There. That's our quota of apologies for the day."

She kept her own smile firmly in place. She'd already dwelled far too much on whether or not she retained any of her abilities. "We're allowed one each per day now?"

"It seems practical until we get better at navigating these new trails with each other. But only for current issues. Apologies for the past are still off the table," he explained cheerfully, stretching his arms and groaning. "I'm stiff as a deer smoked over a ten-day fire."

"Ugh." She grimaced at the image. "Can't it be stiff as a tree or something?"

"That will work," he allowed, standing and flexing, then twisting at his waist and pumping his arms so his chest rippled impressively, filling her with heady warmth. She wanted more of him. Perhaps she could seduce him further. She seemed to be getting better at the skill. "I'm going to take a dip before we head out again," he said, dashing her hopes.

"Isn't it too late in the day for us to journey?"

He shook his head. "It's good timing, actually. Better for us to ride at night anyway. Less parching. Want to join me for that dip?"

"I will soon," she said, working to contain her disappointment. The blood stained her fingers accusingly. "You go ahead."

He stopped his gymnastics and frowned at her. "Are you avoiding telling me you can't stand?"

"I can stand." She hoped. Stowing her pride, she made the effort, figuring it would be better if he was there to catch her, if her own optimism outpaced reality. Fortunately, she managed, though her head swam a little and she popped out in a cold sweat. "I thought I'd visit the trees in privacy," she told him with as much dignity as she could muster, given she was naked and dizzy.

"You're wobbly," he countered, then held up a hand when she opened her mouth. "But if you say you can do it, I'll trust you, okay? Just don't let your Arill-cursed pride get in the way. Call me if you need me. Or send Chuffta." He gestured at the derkesthai who perched by the fire, surreptitiously poking it with a stick.

"You say that like someone who isn't full of pride, too," she groused, but he only grinned back easily.

"Of course—that's how I recognize it at work. After we bathe, we'll eat and go. Unless you think it will help you if we stay here longer?"

She nearly said it would, if only because it would be lovely to stay at the oasis. Alone with Lonen and Chuffta, avoiding the challenges that lay ahead. But her magical instincts told her otherwise. That internal gage that seemed to monitor the ebb and flow of sgath indicated that she no longer operated at a loss, but neither would she absorb any more. The magic of the llerna restored her, but otherwise wasn't there to build up a surplus.

With those refreshed senses, too, she clearly sensed Lonen's restlessness to be home, to find out what might be going on in Dru. So much of his hopeful optimism resting on her. They might actually make it there and what then? But she had to try. She'd promised.

So, she shook her head. "Being here… it's like a kind of stasis for me. It's brought me back to baseline at least, but no more than that."

Avoiding the concern in Lonen's too discerning gaze, she walked to the water and rinsed off her hands. Hopefully it wasn't an insult to his manliness, to rinse away the seed. If so, better to know. And he wasn't the kind to not say so if he did feel that way. It occurred to her briefly to try to put some inside herself, to see if the seed would take. Becoming pregnant with her Destrye husband's baby, however, would be an exceedingly bad idea at this juncture, if she even could. From what little she knew of it, pregnancy wreaked havoc on a priestess's *hwil* and sgath both. More than one priestess had given up her mask during the difficulties of gestation and sometimes for some time after.

The priests sometimes joked that no one lost *hwil* faster than a priestess with a newborn. For their part, the priestesses in question did not find such remarks amusing and those priests found themselves decidedly lacking in free priestesses willing to feed them sgath.

Lonen did not say anything, but the silence thickened. Deliberately opening more of her awareness, she felt for his change of mood. Desire, thick and sweet. She rose from her crouch—carefully, so she wouldn't wobble—and turned to face him.

He hadn't moved, but still stood there watching her, the concern in his expression replaced by the intensity of lust. And his cock had thickened again, rising to point at her, as if indicating the direction of his thoughts. A little embarrassed, though Lonen clearly wasn't, she cast a glance at Chuffta—who had apparently abandoned all subterfuge and was enthusiastically building the campfire into a blazing inferno.

"You're a beautiful woman, Oria," Lonen said, as if that explained anything. Which, she supposed, it must for him.

"Maybe we *should* stay here another day or two," she offered, hopeful that he could be tempted, hesitant to face another rejection. "Until I'm physically stronger, too, and so we can have actual sex."

"We have had actual sex, Oria," he replied gently. "We just did. It's not as if some kinds count and others don't."

"You know what I mean."

"I suspect I do. Which is why I'm going to keep on this point. What we've done together, what we will do—it's all good by me. Never feel like I need more than that."

Uncomfortable with the intensity of his gaze, and quite certain that, as much as he might wish to mean that, he wouldn't always, she looked down at her knotted fingers. "That's not what you said before."

"That was before I understood your ... how it is for you."

What word had he been about to use? Fragility. Limitations. Devastating weakness. It all came down to the same, in the end. "Still. You had more than that with Natly."

To his credit, he looked puzzled. "Natly? What does she have to do with any of this?"

"Lonen." Exasperated she spread her hands. "If we make it to Dru—"

"*When* we make it to Dru," he interrupted.

"Natly will be there."

"Yes, because she lives there," he replied in that tone of infinite patience.

"She's your fiancée!"

"Was. I'm married to someone else now."

Oria stamped her bare foot at his deliberate obtuseness, then felt ridiculous. "She doesn't know that! For all you know she's been planning your royal wedding in Arill's Temple, waiting only to slip you into the groom's robes, and then to be crowned queen. Have you considered at all what it will be like to arrive with me in tow, a foreign queen you can't even bed, much less get heirs on?" One who might even lack the magic he'd sacrificed a normal marriage to gain advantage for his people.

"That's our business and no one else's." He came to her and gathered her close, with infinite tenderness, hands roaming over her skin. It helped reassure her, as annoying as it was to need to be reassured. "And it's a joy to be able to touch you as Arill intended, but none of that is what's most important. Our marriage is consummated. No one will question it. Leave Natly to me. I'll worry about her—she's not your problem."

Oria let out a long breath. "I'm not worried about her. I just think this won't be as easy as you seem to believe."

He was quiet a moment. "None of this has been easy. It's all just versions of what's more or less difficult. All I know is, I couldn't remain here any longer than absolutely necessary not knowing what's going on in Dru. At best, they're fighting the approach of winter, trying to stock enough food and water to get us through until spring. At worst…"

He trailed off, so she said it for him. "At worst Yar has sent the Trom after them. You're right. I only meant—"

He kissed her, stopping the words in the loveliest way, a nurturing, soothing sort of kiss. They wouldn't have that again, once they left this place. Breaking away, he gave her a tender smile that made her heart turn over. "I know what you meant and I want that, too. You once pointed out to me, however, that we are more than just ourselves. We have our responsibilities. I can't stay here in paradise with you while the Destrye suffer. I simply… can't."

"I know." She returned the smile so he wouldn't think her feelings were hurt, because of course it wasn't about that. He desired her, yes, but nothing compared to his love of his people. Which was as it should be. If she still had people, she'd feel the same way. And she'd lost that through no fault of Lonen's. They'd married out of political expediency—part of her grand plan that had seemed like such a good one at the time—and that must continue to reign supreme for them both. Regardless of how it turned out for her.

She needed to give up this longing to have more of him. It sprang from the loneliness of exile and nothing more. She'd been clinging to him like a rock in the rushing tides of events and that was unfair of her.

She simply had to endure. If she could make it to Dru, then she'd find out if she could do anything to help the Destrye. She'd hoard every last bit of magic the oasis had restored to her and use it if she could to strike a last blow at Yar, a final revenge for condemning her to this banishment.

It might cost her remaining health, probably her life, but she had no use for either anymore. She refused to be the anchor that dragged Lonen down. Her story would reach its fated end, the one she'd been moving toward all along with relentless momentum. She'd enter the tales after this, be one of those sorceresses stolen away from the desert cities, to languish and fade away with the Destrye. The irony would be that she hadn't been carried off as a prize, to be used for sex as she had imagined in her lurid fantasies. *Why else take them?* Lonen had said.

Why indeed.

"Oria?" Lonen reached for her, but she nipped out of his grasp. "Are you all right?"

"I'm fine. I need to visit the trees. Then I'll be ready to go."

~ 11 ~

ORIA REMAINED SUBDUED. Too much so for someone of her typically bright and restless nature, but Lonen supposed he should be glad to have her conscious, if not exactly talkative. His efforts to draw her into conversation were met with the explanation that she needed to concentrate on keeping her portals closed—both to screen out the wild magic and conserve the magic she'd acquired at the oasis.

Fair enough, except he didn't quite believe her. One thing about Natly—she'd always made it abundantly clear when she'd taken offense, no matter how slight, and never failed to detail exactly what he needed to do to make it up to her, which usually cost dearly. He'd developed some skill at seeing the storm on the horizon and taking appropriate steps to dodge the worst of it.

Not so with Oria. He'd done or said something wrong, that was certain, but instead of dressing him down as Natly would have, she'd withdrawn. She drew that regal pride around her as securely as the enveloping robes that swaddled her from chin to toe. She'd even drawn a flap of the silk over her hair—which she'd braided into a single rope—and tucked her hands within.

He missed the gloriously naked woman who'd unselfconsciously knelt at the water's edge, her hair sliding in streams of copper that parted to reveal her exquisitely fair skin. She rode astride behind him, nearly in physical contact—though she held onto his belt rather than wrapping her arms around him as he'd have liked—and she'd gone as distant as the brilliant stars in the sky overhead. Chuffta winged in from time to time, flying in from the darkness like a white ghost from stories to ride on her shoulder, which meant they likely conversed.

Not that it bothered him. Well, not that it should.

He didn't exactly resent her relationship with her Familiar, but without the derkesthai, Oria would be forced to deal with him, if only out of loneliness. Of course, she'd spent most of her life in a tower, so she was the queen of being alone. Probably she didn't even feel the sting of it. Not like he did, so long accustomed to being surrounded by his boisterous brothers and then also crammed in with so many refugee Destrye in the impromptu city that had grown around Arill's temple like the shelves of fungus that burgeoned on the shady side of trees.

The silence as they rode through the desert night left him too much alone with his thoughts, which circled endlessly and inevitably back to Oria. All thoughts led to the sorceress just as all roads led to Arill's temple.

Oria had wanted to stay at the oasis. Maybe for more reasons than her health, which would be a potent one. Of course, she hadn't wanted to leave Bára or its environs, either.

Nothing to be done for any of it. If he could get her to Dru, he would marshal Arill's best healers to help Oria, Báran physiology or not. He'd been thinking, too—Oria had said sgath came from all living things and the forests of Dru were a massive living thing, both the individual trees and the collective. Arill knew he'd sensed the vitality of the forest innumerable times. It felt more magical to him than any of Bára's stones ever had. If the wedding ceremony had connected Oria and him enough to allow her to use her magic to aid the Destrye, then it should give her a similar conduit to the forest's vitality. She hadn't been to a forest, so she didn't know.

He just had to get her there, and perhaps marry her in Arill's temple, to cement the connection from the other direction, in case such magic worked for the Destrye also. Oria had a point about Natly's likely fury at such an event. Frankly he'd forgotten about her until Oria evoked her. It said a great deal about the tenuous connection he had to his former almost-fiancée.

Natly had never consumed him as Oria had and did. She'd be better finding a man who loved her with that kind of consuming passion.

No, taking Oria all the way to Dru would be the lasting solution, no matter how tempting it had been to stay at the oasis. Even she couldn't live on magic alone and those rodent things Chuffta had found wouldn't be enough to sustain two adults for long. He'd have thought all sorts of wildlife would come in for the water, but that didn't seem to be the case. The Destrye scouts had noted that before, the strange lack of animal life in the oases that studded the desert, like sterile jewels in a barren crown. Perhaps to do with those llerna Oria had referenced. Chuffta had likely found the creatures out in the desert, which was paradoxically far more full of life than the verdant oases.

Magic. Always replete with questions and lacking solid answers.

Reaching Dru might end up being the best thing for Oria. Never mind what happened to the sorceresses in the old tales. Who even knew if those contained the least grain of truth? His warrior ancestors had been a brutal lot on many fronts, by all accounts. Besides the sexual contact that would have eroded the *hwil* of Oria's sisters in magic, those men had likely deserved the moniker of "barbarian"—and every other insult a Báran princess could think to heap upon them.

They would not have been gentle men. And even if they hadn't been brutal enough to cause the women to suffer and die from physical abuse alone—which certainly could have occurred—the mental and emotional trauma for the women, on top of being ripped from their homes, would have eroded their will to live.

Not a good line of thinking, as Oria had too much in common with those women. But he hadn't raped her. Would never treat any woman so shamefully. The Destrye had changed under Arill's taming hand. The roving bands of pillaging warriors had learned to treat women as sacred as the Goddess herself. Now, Arill knew that Lonen lacked the temperament to be Her acolyte. He was far from the Goddess's chosen—and never further from that blessed state than when he'd slaughtered the Báran priestesses with his own hands—but he tried his best. He'd visited Arill's temple and asked to atone, made his sacrifice to Her.

And his path had led directly to taking Oria as his bride, however unlikely that development had seemed at the outset. Perhaps Arill set him to make up for the many sins of his past brethren against Oria's sister sorceresses. Whether that was Arill's intention or not, and though he'd been pressed to restrain himself as much as he had, he felt sure he'd be cursed if he ever treated the fragile Oria at all roughly. He'd be careful with her and never unleash the violent lusts that surged at the least thought of her.

Which seemed to be all his thoughts of late. Where all thoughts led, after all.

Full circle, yet again.

At least out of the oasis they again had to contend with the proscription against skin-to-skin contact. The more barriers against his darker nature, the better. He could wish for more distance from his brutish ancestors. There were tales that Destrye warriors who strayed too long from Arill's temple reverted, like domestic wolves going feral in the woods—and like those, even more dangerous for it. As if the brief taming caused a backlash into savagery, like a fire once banked finding new kindling.

Perhaps his long journeys accounted for the restless savage growing inside him. From his first glimpse of her, Oria had obsessed him, occupying his mind waking and sleeping, testing his control of the barbarian that lurked in the hot blood of his darkest heart. If they could only get to Dru, then he wouldn't be so much with her. Better perhaps that she refused to converse with him, saving it all for that silent communion with the derkesthai. Probably no less than he deserved.

He sighed heavily, Buttercup echoing the sound.

LONEN DROVE THEM on like a man possessed by demons. After badgering her for the first few hours of their ride, he'd finally subsided into a sullen silence. At least so Oria presumed. She tried to be like the new moon, Sgatha in her dark phase, holding all her light and power within. Thus she read nothing of the Destrye's thoughts, only interpreting his mood from the rigid line of his back and the tension of his muscles. She knew him somewhat, having tasted the brooding anger that seethed in him, a familiar flavor on the back of her tongue. He possessed a dual nature it seemed—both the sparkling humor and the smoldering ire. For now, the latter worked in him, like one of his campfires banked so the embers glowed hot.

That was fine. He didn't need to be happy with her. In fact, it would be better for him to remain unattached.

"He's already attached. The Destrye worries for you. You're being willfully dense if you don't perceive that."

She might not be able to read thoughts, but Chuffta projected his easily enough into her mind. They'd reverted to him speaking mind-to-mind to her and she unable to respond except vocally—which she wouldn't do where Lonen could overhear and get ideas about drawing her into conversation—and with very strong thoughts.

Unfortunately, Chuffta tended to pick and choose which of her thoughts he responded to. She'd never been sure how much of that depended on the thoughts themselves, or if he could hear everything in her mind if he wished to and the picking and choosing simply gave her the illusion of privacy. When she was a girl, he'd seemed to be entwined in her consciousness far more than he was now. Perhaps the attenuation she'd perceived as she got older had less to do with her growing control of *hwil*, as she attributed it with great hopefulness, and more to do with his circumspection.

"You know I don't listen to everything you think. You're not that *interesting."*

She thought very hard about yanking his tail. Either he didn't get the image or he ignored her.

"And I don't lecture. It's my job to give you advice, as you and I both know. It doesn't matter that you've left Bára and are no longer a priestess. You weren't a priestess when we bonded. I agreed to be your *Familiar, not a priestess's or the future queen of Bára's or any of those things you've been thinking."*

But he had agreed because her mother—and his derkesthai family, too—all had believed she had some great destiny. Not one where she'd perish in a foreign land after ignominiously wasting away.

"It would make for an excellent tragic ballad."

She thought fiercely at him to stop his teasing, but he blithely ignored her, his mind-voice taking on the melodramatic, ringing tones of a court minstrel. *"The once-powerful, orphaned princess of Bára, exiled beyond the foul deserts to the cruel land of Dru, foully abused by her barbarian warrior husband, died upon a bower of flowers, her faithful derkesthai Familiar by her side. With her last breath, she extolled his wisdom, charm, and loyalty. 'If only I had listened to your advice,' she gasped, coughing up a spot of blood, 'if only! I might have led a happy and healthy life. Instead I'm dying because I'm a self-pitying idiot and I—'"*

"Stop it!" she snapped.

Lonen instantly halted Buttercup—who danced in place at the abruptness of it, Chuffta exploding off her shoulder in a clap of wings, too—and Lonen had leapt off, reaching up for her before she knew it. The man moved like lightning when alarmed.

"What's wrong?" He demanded, already lifting her down with big hands around her waist. "Are you ill?"

"No," she gasped, steadying herself by bracing against his chest. "No—I'm sorry. I was..." She was embarrassed to admit it. "Chuffta was haranguing me and I couldn't stand it any longer."

"Snapped you out of that miserable funk." Chuffta's mind-voice oozed smug, self-satisfaction, and she glared at the white blur of him

in the sky. *"You were making* me *want to kill* myself.*"*

"If only," she muttered. "I'm sorry. We can keep going."

"That's two surplus apologies for the day." Lonen had a hint of amusement in his voice, but he let go of her and stepped back. "I'll have to exact a penance for it."

"Surely it's well past midnight, so one of those can count for today. Tell you what—apply the other to the day after." She wouldn't apologize to him for anything more.

"Cranky," Chuffta observed.

She'd show them cranky.

"Better than self-pity."

"All right," Lonen sounded wary. "Since we're stopped, let's take a little rest. Eat. I could stretch my legs."

At least with the darkness she could wander off a short way to relieve herself. She gratefully drank the water Lonen handed her, and less happily choked down more of the meat. It sat in her gut heavily, but the more she ate of it, the better she seemed to digest it. When Lonen lifted her back onto Buttercup, she grasped his forearms for stability, the play of his muscles through his sleeves reminded her forcefully of their sexual interlude at the oasis. His skin had burned beneath her touch, the surprising softness of the skin of his cock an exciting contrast to the rigidity beneath. Most of all, she missed that closeness they'd had at that moment, how they'd moved together in a mutual understanding. She hadn't needed to read his thoughts or feel his emotions to know his mind. Now he seemed as far from her as Bára. And just as unreachable. Behind walls she'd erected herself and had no idea how to breach.

"What?" he asked, and she realized she'd held onto him, staring down into his shadowed face.

"Nothing." She let go.

"Nothing," Chuffta sang in mimicry.

In self-defense, she closed Chuffta out of her thoughts, though he likely already knew what lay in her secret heart. She knew she was being difficult—but she didn't know how to stop. *Is this pride?*

Lonen's voice mocked her. Almost certainly. Still bereft of all else, she clung to that. She wouldn't lay the onus of her feelings on him, along with responsibility for her very life.

She'd rather be miserable company in her prideful ways, than a clingy burden Lonen would come to resent. He refused her sexual favors, fine. Then she needed to concentrate on providing the only value she did hold for him: using her magic to save the Destrye.

If she could manage that, perhaps she could even hope for something more than a slow death in a foreign land. Once she'd served her purpose to Lonen he'd be happy to let her go, so he could move on to a healthier woman, like the sensuous Natly. He'd been right to hold her at arm's length. She could withstand succumbing to this sapping affection for him that made her want to hide in his arms and forever avoid facing the world. He'd become another tower for her, another refuge from all the things she lacked the fortitude to fight.

This feeling that she cared more deeply for him than a refuge came from fear and insecurity. It had to. She couldn't have succumbed to such foolishness as to love a man who'd married her only for expediency.

She couldn't let it happen, this desire to give in to having Lonen take care of every little thing for her. Taking care *of* her. Enough already. She was the daughter of Rhianna, great-niece of the mysterious but powerful Tania, a descendent of great sorceresses. *Princess Ponen.* She'd faced the Trom and resisted their lethal touch. She alone had done that.

She could and would do better.

And she'd do it on her own, too, as was her fate.

~ 12 ~

THEY STOPPED ONLY for short rests like that one, Lonen determined to make the next oasis before dawn. Oria gave in to the dragging need for sleep, dozing against Lonen's back—though the Destrye seemed tireless. No, that wasn't exactly right. He seemed as weary as she, but pressed on regardless. Though his eyes reddened, with shadows beneath, he did not admit to his obvious exhaustion. She would have given him grief for his own stubborn pride, but she hated to play the hypocrite.

She was also profoundly grateful for his extraordinary endurance. His and Buttercup's. Besides, it felt so good to lean on him while she had the excuse to do so.

"Oria!" Chuffta's warning call penetrated her sleepy haze. "Stop! *Be quiet, but tell Lonen to stop."*

A strike of fear thudded through her at the alarm in Chuffta's mind-voice. "Stop!" She tugged at Lonen's belt to emphasize her hissed warning. "Lonen, Chuffta says to stop and be silent," she clarified, though he'd already halted Buttercup with some command that had the big horse utterly, eerily still. Just as soundlessly, Lonen drew his big knife. He'd affixed the battle-axe to the saddle packs in order to make room for her.

He twisted in the saddle, putting an arm around her waist and his lips near her ear. "I hear you," he said, words barely above a breath. "Can he tell me in my head?"

"No. That might have been an oasis thing."

She shook her head, pressing her lips together.

"Does he say what it is? Don't whisper—that carries—voice it as quietly as possible."

"Golems. Many, many of them, marching your way. These are not like the city golems. These have fangs and claws, like the ones Lonen said they fought outside the walls." And in Dru, he didn't have to add.

Golems? *"But Priest Sisto died. How can his creations persist?"*

"I only know what I see."

Following Lonen's directions, she relayed the information, murmuring in his ear, his hair tickling her cheek. Absurd that she'd notice the savory scent of his skin at such a moment. He dipped his chin sharply, not arguing as she had. "Is there a way to avoid them?"

"Tell him to angle toward where Grienon sets."

She did, then held her breath for fear of making any sound as Lonen gave some undetectable signal that had Buttercup moving silently in that direction. How the big warhorse could pick his way across the rocky soil without striking anything with his massive hooves, she didn't know. No longer the least bit sleepy, she stretched her senses—a trick without opening her portals to the magic, like patting her head and rubbing her belly at the same time, but onc she seemed to be improving at with practice—trying to detect the presence of the magical constructs.

She sensed nothing magical, but with Buttercup walking so stealthily the ambient sounds of the desert swelled around her. For such a barren place, a surprising amount of life emerged at night. Various insects clicked, buzzed, and hummed. Some sort of bird sent a lonely sounding call through the chill air. And just after, the hoot of perhaps an owl. Something furiously rummaged in a mound of succulent-covered rocks as they passed. Perhaps one of those rodent things Chuffta had caught.

As Grienon plunged to the horizon in his impetuous way, the night grew more shadowed, only Sgatha's rosy light emanating from her waning crescent, barely a sliver now, which meant the stars bloomed ever brighter, a dizzying array of brilliant colors. She'd only ever seen the like when both moons were in dark phase and around the curve of the horizon. Still, they hadn't been like this, with none of the light of Bára to steal their glory.

Perhaps she should have tried to stay awake, with such a sky to see.

Buttercup picked his way through the heavy dark near the ground, Lonen's body flexing here and there to guide him, both of them able to see what she could not, apparently. When Grienon disappeared with a final blue-white flash, leaving a quickly dissipating glow behind, the night grew even thicker, Sgatha barely touching the dim. How would Lonen know the direction?

Then, something rustled against her senses. Invisible, inaudible, a breath of magic blowing across her nerves like the first breeze stirring after a baking afternoon. She wrapped her arms around Lonen's waist, squeezing to alert him, not sure what else to do, but absolutely certain she shouldn't speak. With his warrior's awareness, he had stopped Buttercup. He didn't speak either, slowly turning his head as he scanned the night, projecting questioning emotion at her.

He'd really gotten quite good at that. If only she could project into his mind. Though she didn't know what she'd say. Could be she'd imagined that brush of awareness, just as she'd often imagined—wishful thinking, her lady-in-waiting Alva would say—those longed-for cooling breezes. She should tell Lonen it had been a false alarm. She shouldn't have stopped their progress with her fancies in the first place.

"The golems have shifted. Moving your direction, Oria. Straight for you."

Sgatha curse them. She needed to tell Lonen. He looked over his shoulder at her, though she couldn't read his expression in the dark. "They're headed this way," she said, as softly as she could.

"Can we avoid?" he asked, so she barely heard him, even so close. He seemed calm, but his emotional energy grew both tense and still, radiating with increasing power so she felt it without trying.

"No. They're moving in behind you, too. I'm coming there."

"We're surrounded."

He didn't curse—not out loud—but she felt it in him. "I need my axe," he told her, not bothering to be so stealthy, holding her steady with a familiar hand on her hip and reaching around to unstrap the battle-axe from behind her. Then pressed his big knife into her hand. "Stay on Buttercup. No matter what happens. Only use this if you have to."

"Why aren't we being quiet anymore?"

"They already know we're here. No choice but to fight through it," he replied tersely.

"Wait, can't we run for it?"

He swung a leg over Buttercup's head and vaulted down. "Clearly you haven't seen your Báran monsters in action. They run faster than a horse and they never stop. Our only hope is to chop them to pieces. Does Chuffta say how many there are?"

"More than there are towers in Bára."

"Dozens, maybe," she temporized. With Lonen off his back, Buttercup shifted, restless, and she grabbed for the reins. "Counting isn't his strong suit. Aren't you in more danger on the ground?"

"Buttercup will protect you, but I can't effectively swing the axe with you on his back, too."

"Then I'll get down." Before she lifted a leg, Lonen was there, free hand gripping her knee.

"Don't. You. Dare." He sounded darker, more stern and threatening than she'd ever heard him. "You stay on this horse no matter what happens. Use the knife if you have to. I'll draw the golems away, then you make a break for it."

Her naïve brain finally caught up. "No. You're not sacrificing yourself for me."

"Of course not," he replied too easily, releasing his grip to pat her knee. Then took the reins from her and knotted them loosely to a ring on the saddle. "I've killed hundreds, maybe thousands of these things. I'll clear a path for you, draw them off and chop them up, then meet you at the oasis. Have Chuffta guide you there."

As if called, Chuffta glided in, wings fully spread to catch the thick, cool air, soundless as the ghost he resembled. Surprising her, he landed on Lonen's shoulder, green eyes shining in the night. *"I'll fight with Lonen, then we'll find you."*

Tears rose up to choke her throat, her eyes burned with them, but she throttled them back. "I'm staying here with you," she told them both.

"No, you're not."

"No, you're not."

They spoke the words, aloud and mind-voice together in an uncanny echo of each other, their united certainty reverberating on several levels at once.

"You have to make it to Dru, Oria," Chuffta told her firmly.

"The Destrye need you more than they need me," Lonen said, stroking her thigh now, much as he'd reassure Buttercup. "At this point, you're the only one who can save them. My job was just to get you there."

"You're their king!" she gritted fiercely through the teeth she'd locked to hold back the overwhelming tide of emotion. Hers and his, twined together. "They need *you*."

"Not if they're dead, they don't." He sounded so calm, so resolved. "My brother Arnon can be king, but only if you make it to Dru and stop your brother."

The magic whispered across her nerves, sand eddying over rock in a restlessly building breeze. Familiar. The golems of Bára.

"Nearly upon us." Chuffta confirmed. He took wing, shooting up to circle above them.

"Lonen." She said it pleadingly, unable to think of anything else to say to convince him. Surely he couldn't die like this, but how could one man fight off so many? He'd killed thousands, perhaps, but even she knew that had been with his men all around.

"Don't worry, love," he said, squeezing her thigh through the silk of her gown. His grief and fear came through clearly as the brilliant stars. He did intend to sacrifice himself for her. "I've survived worse than this. And Chuffta will help me. I'll give Buttercup the signal. Your job is to stay on. Cling like one of your Arill-cursed burrs to the saddle. Chuffta and I will find you."

A lie. He didn't expect to survive this.

"I don't want to lose you," she managed, aware that she'd utterly failed to hold back the emotion, her chest aching with the effort to suppress it. No *hwil* whatsoever.

The magic of the golems sang louder, almost as strong as being in Bára again. All around them. She risked taking Lonen's hand, the contact searing her, but she welcomed the pain, bending over and pulling him to her. His mouth received her kiss, harsh and full of desire. He wanted to live, but he wanted her to live more, for his people to live. His beard scratched her face, his hand releasing hers to cup her head and hold her tight there as he drank her in.

Then wrenched himself away. He stepped back, well out of reach.

She floundered internally, scrabbling to rebalance after taking so much of him in. It helped that she'd been relatively empty, but the sudden influx was as if someone had suddenly lit a too-bright torch in a dark room. The presence of the golems all around flared across her newly sensitized senses.

The shadowy silhouette that was her husband lifted his battle-axe, swinging it in a circle over his head. "Fare well, my powerful queen," he said. "It's been the privilege of my life to be wed to you. Take care of my people."

So much for his protestations that he'd catch up to her.

"Don't you dare die, Destrye!" She ordered, sgath rising in her as it hadn't for a long time. Not since they'd left Bára. In the darkness, ghostly white gleamed, like fog crawling in across the sand from the sea. Golems. "I love you, you cursed barbarian."

His teeth gleamed with his unexpected grin. "I know you do, sorceress."

~ 13 ~

ORIA'S SUPPRESSED SCREECH of inarticulate frustration did his heart good. Of course, hearing her admit she loved him, despite all the ways he'd failed her—and despite her own wishes, he suspected—did a great deal to bolster him, too.

He'd won the regard of the most amazing woman he'd ever encountered. Something for the tales right there. Perhaps he'd finally satisfied his debt to Arill. Or would, by saving Oria and sending her safely to Dru.

Stupid of him, to forget the golems might be out there. Low light confused their senses, but they still roamed at night. He'd been so focused on crossing the desert, so certain Yar had not pursued that he hadn't thought to watch for the golems. Of course, Oria had insisted they'd all perished with their foul creator. He was sure she had not lied about that, which meant she'd been misled.

No matter. This he knew how to do. It wasn't entirely true that the warhorse couldn't outrun the monsters. He could—but not with two on his back. Oria didn't need more reasons to hesitate, however.

The salt from her tears still lingered on his lips from that incredible kiss. She loved him. The knowledge filled him with power, and he burned to take down the golems.

Oria screamed when the first leapt at him from the blackness of night, Buttercup dancing her out of the way. Hopefully she'd manage to stay astride—she did have a reasonably good seat, considering she'd never seen a horse before. Something to do with her magical communion with animals, he assumed. The scream had been for him. She clung to the saddle as he'd hoped, through Buttercup's rearing when he struck out with iron-shod hooves, knocking aside the golems in his path. Hopefully they'd cleave a path for her quickly enough that she wouldn't have to see him overcome.

'Dozens,' indeed. More like a hundred. But he had Chuffta to help, the derkesthai wheeling about to guard his back and the flanks he opened to attack as he swung the axe two-handed. The iron cleaved through two at once with the powerful stroke, sending the halves falling to the shadows at his feet. The things had no brains; the Destrye had learned that early on. It did no more good to cut their heads from their necks than to cut off a limb. They just kept coming.

No, what worked best was to chop them at mid-chest level, separating the clawed hands and fanged mouths from the ambulatory body. The sharp parts couldn't move and the relatively harmless body could only bump into him—until he stomped them with his iron-soled boots. Treacherous for wading in stone-bottomed oasis lakes. Perfect for battle with unnatural creatures.

One part of him kept track of Oria, safe behind him thanks to Buttercup's careful maneuvers. The training was meant to save injured soldiers but worked just as well for a foreign sorceress with no fighting skills. The rest of him focused on methodically cutting through the golems—and leading them away, back down the slight ridge they'd ascended. More of them around him meant fewer for Oria to flee, so he welcomed the onslaught.

Liberating, too, in a way, not to have to reserve any of his strength.

All out, in this final battle of his.

Three golems snaked in on his unguarded left flank, claws sharp as broken glass slicing through his side. He turned the pain into a bellow of fury, continuing the swing to the right and using the momentum to bring the axe around. Before he did, Chuffta dove in, the green fire hitting the three attackers, their fanged maws melting, their globous heads following. They staggered past, clawed hands waving in the air almost comically, until Chuffta's fire finished them.

Lonen laughed, exultant at their demise. Each one demolished put Oria one step closer to Dru and safety. He would die, but she would live. And she loved him. It was enough for any man's life.

He kept moving farther from Oria, judiciously at first, wary of her being cut off from him. Fortunately, the golems had ignored Oria for the most part. Were struck by the powerful hooves of the warhorse when they didn't. The Destrye had seen this before. Though the mindless things would go through anything in their path—men, women, children, livestock and pets alike—they tended when attacking to focus on the warriors. Some instruction embedded in them, no doubt.

Who knew? Perhaps something in them recognized Oria as Báran and thus not to be attacked unless necessary.

And there. On that side, the tides of golems thinned. He whistled, catching the warhorse's attention, then signaled. Before his hand dropped, Buttercup leapt, clearing several golems and trampling others. In the clear, he disappeared into the night, Oria's white face turned back, looking for him.

BUTTERCUP GALLOPED THROUGH the night and Oria clung to his back, holding to the saddle with both hands—still awkwardly hanging onto the knife, too—not even attempting to take the reins. The battle receded in their wake, all sounds of it fading into one more background desert noise. It had been eerily silent anyway, the golems making no sound, only punctuated by the hot rush of Chuffta's fire, the hollow whumps of his beating wings, and Lonen's bellows of pain and fury.

She'd hear them for the rest of her life.

Clenching her jaw to keep her teeth from clacking together, she thought furiously. No way could she leave them behind. Lonen would die—if he hadn't already—overcome by those endless waves of attacking golems.

They did look very like the menial worker golems of Bára. Those had become practically invisible to her eye, always a part of the background on the rare occasions she'd descended from her tower. Some priests had an affinity for glass, just as Yar had for stone, and some long-ago inventive sorcerer had employed his ingenuity to transform his relatively unglamorous talent for making drinking goblets and plates into forming creatures from the same materials. Not only glass replicas of animals, like those Oria had collected and had left behind with all her things, but living facsimiles of people.

Close enough, anyway. Due to the nature of glass, the worker golems were mainly tubes with smooth-featured, globular heads, and attenuated arms and legs, finishing in fringes of fingers for grasping and manipulating. Possessing less intelligence than most animals, the worker golems could be set to perform repetitive tasks, usually those too boring or distasteful for Bárans to do themselves.

Some, she knew, had been tailored to specific tasks. The ones set to cleaning the sewers and removing blockages tended to be smaller and skinnier, to fit more easily into the pipes. But none of them were like the ones that had attacked them.

She'd seen them in Lonen's mind before, but that somehow didn't quite match the reality. Those gaping maws that took up most of their heads, overfilled with sharp-edged fangs with no purpose but to rend and kill. Those fringes of fingers made into scythes of claws good for nothing but slicing at living flesh.

When her mother had explained the battle golems in the aftermath of Bára's fall to their Destrye conquerors, she'd insisted that no one had intended them to kill the Destrye. *Sisto claimed he'd found a way to create the golems with a kind of ongoing spell. It acted like a packet of sgath. He embedded them with both the command to carry out the task—to fill the barrels with water and bring them back—and also with the magic to keep them animated. No one realized that would result in them going through anything—or anyone—who stood in the way.*

Trained by the temple, Oria had excellent recall and she remembered those words clearly. The creatures she'd seen this night, however—they'd obviously been constructed to kill. She'd weep for what Sisto, and Bára, had done, but she'd left her tears behind with Lonen. His battle rage had swirled around him in arcs larger than the concentric circles he cleaved with his axe. With Chuffta weaving in and out of the pattern, they'd formed a kind of lethal dance, demolishing the golems and leading them away from her.

But there had been so many. More and more pouring in from all around, filling the air with magic.

They would be too much, even for a warrior as mighty as Lonen. And she was hurtling away from any hope of saving him.

Not that she could do anything. Bereft of her own magic, so weak and—

No. That wasn't true. She felt tremendously better. Singing with sgath, in truth. But how could that be?

...a kind of ongoing spell ... like a packet of sgath ... provided them with the magic to keep them animated.

Packets of sgath from Bára. Each of those golems carried one. She summoned the memory, hearing her mother's voice. *...the Destrye began to fight back. They discovered that iron would kill Sisto's golems by neutralizing the packet of sgath. He felt them die.*

The iron didn't neutralize the packets of sgath—it released it. And she'd been right there, in a monsoon of sgath, as Lonen's axe dropped the golems. No wonder she'd absorbed so much—even with her portals as closed as she could make them.

Opening a narrow channel and reaching, she found Buttercup's mind. Some wild magic leaked in around the edges, but she could withstand that for a time—because she must, if for no other reason. The hot-blooded gallop of thoughts from the stallion greeted her and her suggestion that they return to the fight with a rush of gladness. He bore great affection for his master and looked forward to battling beside him again.

In truth, she did, too.

She'd had enough of this being weak and worthless. If she couldn't save the man she loved, then the rest meant nothing. Not even revenge.

~ 14 ~

THOUGH HIS ARMS—NO, his entire body—had begun to fatally tire, Lonen fought on. The longer he stayed on his feet, the better chance Oria had of making it clear. He poured every drop of the unrealistic optimism she'd chided him for harboring into believing she could and would make it. The golems hadn't come to the oasis, so maybe whatever magic kept wildlife away would also serve to keep her safe there. She'd find something to eat—or Chuffta would help her.

After the next oasis, she'd be able to find naturally occurring fresh water before much longer. Buttercup would be her guide there. She'd make it to Dru, maybe even lead a long and fruitful life there. The Destrye would treat her… well, with honor, if nothing else.

Green fire roared too close to his side, and he caught himself from stumbling farther into Chuffta's line of attack. Claws sliced through his calf muscle above his boot, the pain penetrating the haze. Not claws. Fangs—a bodiless golem head clung to his leg by its razor-sharp teeth alone.

Had Alby been here, he would have taken care of that kind of cleanup, and Lonen missed his squire dreadfully. Of course, had Alby been with him, Lonen would have sent him to protect Oria.

In his moment of distraction, another golem leapt at him, sinking its fangs into his forearm as he hastily deflected the Arill-cursed creature. Long claws swiped at him—giving his throat a near-miss—so he jammed the haft of the battle-axe in the thing's face, popping it free, taking a good chunk of flesh with it.

Reversing the thrust, he batted the head off his leg, sending it spinning away into the ring of dismembered corpses all around him. The bits and pieces waved claws and gnashed fangs, looking oddly like a field of summer wheat waving in the morning light. Two more golems crawled spider-like over that rim, fangs and claws glinting with golden radiance. The sun was rising. In the tales, this would mean some magical surcease from the attack, but in the real world no such serendipity would save him.

He staggered again and the wounded leg gave, taking him to one knee. More than that recent bite getting to him, perhaps. He bled from dozens of lacerations. As many as there were towers in Bára, he thought to himself without humor. Just his fate, to be thinking of that cursed city as he faced his death. Instead he summoned Oria's face, with her otherworldly beauty and sheen of fantastical magic. Or was that Arill's face? The goddess, coming to take him the Hall of Warriors.

Perhaps his transgressions had been forgiven after all.

The white-winged derkesthai hovered before him, piercing green eyes replacing the vision.

"Go," he told Chuffta. "It's over. Go to Oria, where you belong."

The Familiar swooped up, then circled around his head. A group of three golems joined the first two, spreading into a loose circle to surround him. They'd grown smarter somehow, nearly like wolves in their intelligence, forming simple strategies to harry him until he'd grown too weak to defend himself.

He wobbled, concentrating on staying upright, not bothering to wipe away the blood that dripped into his eyes. At least he still held his axe. He'd die with it in hand. And Oria—she would live. Too bad he had no hope that she carried his child. Even his optimism wouldn't take him that far. Unless Arill had performed a miracle?

He'd fix on that. Arill had not only absolved him, she'd seen to it that his seed made his way into Oria. With her grit and determination, she'd see the pregnancy through. He could picture her as in the paintings of Arill as mother, her belly round and skin glowing with health and happiness. There. Oria would laugh at him for pulling out such an extraordinary feat of wishful thinking.

Hazily, though the sweat and blood, he saw the golems approach, cautious, but with bladelike claws at the ready. Behind them someone human climbed the golem heap. His brothers Ion and Nolan, come to escort him to the Hall of Warriors. He should have known they wouldn't let him die alone. No—it was Ion and their father. King Archimago frowned at him, holding out the wreath and sword of kingship. The image wavered, then resolved into one person, a flash of copper and crimson, blowing in a wind he couldn't feel.

"Nooo," he moaned, struggling to his feet. Impossible that she'd returned. She'd be slaughtered and he'd have to watch. His legs failed, that final effort robbing him of the last of his strength. Blackness swam up, dragging him back to the ground. As he fell, it seemed that the world spun, the golems whirling into the air, dancing like translucent leaves glittering with ice.

Then gone.

FOR ONCE, HE didn't come alert as he awoke. Instead, he groped groggily for where in Arill's green earth he could be. He ached in every fiber of his being, head swimming with … blood loss? Yes, that was it. He'd been fighting the golems and they'd been closing in for the kill.

Why hadn't they finished the job?

Or had they? He'd always imagined death would take away pain, but perhaps Arill intended for him to suffer a while longer. Because he hadn't saved Oria after all. She'd come back.

Or had that been a vision? Please, Arill, let it have been a dying man's selfish wish and not true.

Sun beat hot on his eyelids, so he opened them, squinting against the too-bright blue of the desert sky. He rolled his head, his neck creaking. All around, the heaps of waxen golem bodies still ringed him, though they seemed... deflated somehow. No longer waving like wheat in a summer breeze. They'd collapsed into inert and rigid heaps, the edges crumbling here and there into glittering sand. If people went back to ashes and dust, he supposed the golems went back to glass and sand.

His neck hurt, so he rolled his head the other direction, hoping to loosen it.

Oria.

Her copper braid gleamed bright, her crimson robes swirling in some breeze that also tugged tendrils of her hair, Chuffta on her shoulder. She bent and touched a golem.

Panic roared through him.

"Oria!" He barely croaked out her name, but he pushed at it. "No—don't!"

She whirled, her face a pale blur as his head pounded with the rising dark. He fought it down. His battle-axe. It should be there. He yet lived, which meant he could still protect her.

"LONEN. LONEN, LISTEN to me. Lie still." Somehow she was beside him, bending over him so that the coppery strands that had escaped her braid hung around her face like the fine chain jewelry the Destrye women wore. He lifted a hand to touch one, but his arm dropped back to the ground. So weak. Too weak. His addled brain caught up again.

"Don't go near the golems," he begged her, voice broken like the glass shards strewn around him. "There's still a chance. Flee this place."

"Shh. Have some water." She held something to his mouth, but he turned his head. They didn't have time.

"Buttercup. You have to run," he insisted.

"It's okay," she said in soothing tones that made no sense. Didn't she understand the danger? Even now a golem could be sneaking up behind her. "Just rest. Drink the water."

"No!" He knocked the thing from her hand, struggling to sit, but the blackness roared up. Roared like dragons come to burn the crops and the Destrye. "The dragons are coming—you must run!"

She'd disappeared. Good. Maybe she'd listened and fled at last. Or she had been a vision his dying mind had conjured up. Who knew it would take so long to die? He'd always imagined it fast, over before he knew it. A surprise hit and then he'd be entering the Hall of Warriors. Though he'd seen men linger for days or weeks before finally yielding to Arill's dark kiss. Nolan… maybe he'd lain like this, somewhere in that unnatural crevasse, with not even the blue sky to gaze on, dying slowly of thirst and his injuries.

Like himself. So thirsty. Had Oria offered him water? No, that had been a vision. Oria was safe in Dru, learning to swim and ride horses and growing ripe with his baby.

"Look, Destrye." Her lovely face came into view again, mouth set in stern lines, copper eyes full of fire. "You're going to drink this or *I* will sit on *you*."

He blinked at her, confused. "Drink what?"

She huffed out a sigh of exasperation and pushed the hair off her pained face, smearing it with blood. "Water, from this—"

He knocked it aside, reaching for her. "You're bleeding!"

"No." She drew out the word with infinite patience. "This is *your* blood. Now drink this cursed water so you don't shattering die on me!"

She put the cup to his lips, and he let her, watching her over the rim as cool, sweet water filled his mouth. She looked tired, worried—and angry with him, but he could handle that—but also better. The sheen of magic glowed around her, the tendrils of her hair rustling with it.

"Good," she said. "I'm getting more."

"Wait—" he reached for her, but he was too cursed slow, and she was already gone. He stared up at the sky, feeling horribly alone. Where had she gone? A weight settled on his chest, bright green eyes peering at him from Chuffta's triangular face. "You were supposed to go to her," Lonen chided him, his voice clouded with water. And maybe blood. The derkesthai only regarded him solemnly, and Lonen missed hearing his words in his head.

"He says to tell you to lie still and do everything I say and you'll be fine," Oria said, kneeling beside him and putting the cup to his lips again.

He drank, finishing it quickly, but took the precaution of snagging her sleeve before she could leave him again. "He did not say that."

Her lips left their grim line to smile slightly. "What do you know? I say he did." She moved to rise.

But he held on. "Don't leave me."

She softened, brushing back his hair from his forehead. "Never. I came back, didn't I? I'm just getting more water. If only I had more than this little cup." She turned her head, meeting Chuffta's gaze, making a sound of surprise. "Oh, good idea—I should have thought of that."

Her magic, green as her Familiar's eyes, surged around him, just as it had that day in her rooftop garden. He knew it as well as he did her scent and the silk of her hair. It moved past him, to the pile of decomposing glass rubble, then faded away. She looked a bit dimmer, but pleased.

"What did you do?" he asked her, feeling like he looked for the answer to a much bigger question.

She reached over him and held up something from a translucent handle that looked for all the world like a bucket used for toting water, but made of glass. "Made something bigger. I'll be right back."

"Don't go," he said, holding on, thinking vaguely that he'd asked her that once already and that he should be embarrassed for himself.

She gently disengaged her sleeve from his grip. "Only for a moment. Chuffta is with you. See?"

She left him with only the lizardling's too discerning stare for company. "No bonfire to tend, huh, buddy?"

The derkesthai cocked his head, then lifted his wings in a half-mantle and rustled them like a human shrug while turning down the edges of his mouth in an approximation of a pout.

Lonen rasped out a laugh at the sight, which had Oria smiling more naturally on her return, lugging the far-too-heavy bucket and setting it down with a relieved sigh.

"I should help you—"

"Oh right. You may be a big, strong, immortal Destrye warrior, but right now you're flat on your back and you're not helping anybody." She dipped the cup in the bucket and held it to his mouth. "Drink."

Chagrined, he followed her order. She had a point. The water was reviving him, but with that came the awareness of his body. So many wounds, all seeping blood. He swallowed down the water. "Bandages," he muttered, more to himself than her.

"I put some on the worst, but that's next, now that you're not on the brink of death." She pushed the scraggling tendrils off her brow and he realized that she was sweating and she'd rinsed the blood from her face and hands.

"It's hot," he told her, again with the feeling that he wanted to communicate more, but lacked the facility with words.

"And you gave me grief for my keen observation skills," she retorted. "Maybe next time I'm in your position you'll remember this and be nicer to me."

"I try to be good to you, Oria." He'd bumbled so much, done so poorly with the gift Arill had bestowed on him. "I really do…"

"Shh." She dipped a white cloth in the bucket of water and wiped his face, her coppery gaze going abstract as she carefully cleaned the cuts. "You are good to me. Better than I deserve. I'm sorry I said that. You're wonderful. Much nicer to me than I am to you."

"You love me."

Her eyes narrowed as they flicked to his again, her expression wry. "Trust you to remember something I blurted out in a moment of crisis."

"It helped, knowing that. Helped me keep fighting so you could get away. But you came back."

"That's right. And you're glad I did or you would be dead. Close your eyes." She dribbled water over his face, dabbing with the cloth. "This wound looks bad, but it's pretty shallow. You don't think he'll lose the eye, do you?"

Lonen started to ask how he'd know, then realized she conferred with Chuffta.

"Yes, I agree," she continued. "The side is the worst. The one on his neck looks bad, but I think it's stopped bleeding for now, so I'll leave it packed for last. I need to gather more sgath though. Lonen?" Something nudged at his mouth. More water. "Drink some more, then you can rest."

Obediently, he drank. "Where are you going?"

"Just over here. Not far."

"Stay away from the golems," he said, remembering his fear at seeing her reaching for one. "They look dead, but they're unnatural—they keep coming and coming and coming, even the pieces, and..."

They'd been endless, coming at him.

Had he died?

"Everything is all right," Oria soothed. A cool damp cloth draped over his eyes and forehead, and he sighed at the relief from the searing sun. "Trust me. Rest."

"The oasis..."

"Yes. Soon. Take a nap and then we'll go."

"All right. A short nap." Sleep dragged at him, but he fought it. "You won't leave me?"

"Never. I'm right here."

~ 15 ~

ORIA STOOD, STRETCHING her lower back against the painful cramp. She should have made the bucket smaller. In her enthusiasm she'd made it too heavy and filled it too full.

"You could make another one."

"I'd better conserve my sgath. Once I've used up all these packets, I'm out again."

"Unless we find more golems. Maybe we can attract and trap some."

"Interesting thought. Perhaps a plan for later." She spoke out loud to her Familiar partly to conserve her mental energy, but also because it seemed to soothe Lonen to hear her voice. Reassurance that he wasn't alone, probably. Something she understood, that profound lonely neediness of swimming up from the depths of near-death unconsciousness. He'd lapsed back into a more normal sleep now, his breathing deeper and steadier than it had been. His face remained starkly pale, whiter than the scrap of her chemise she had soaked and put over his eyes—and that angry slash that nearly followed the path of his previous scar. To be fair, though, the chemise had long since gone past being white, now a permanent brownish pink from encounters with mud and blood.

Still. *"You're sure he won't die?"* She asked Chuffta mind-to-mind, just in case Lonen could overhear.

"His life force is strong and you've stopped most of the bleeding. Once you've washed and bandaged his wounds—make sure they're clean so he won't get infection—then he should heal. The worst danger is over."

"I don't know how you're so sure," she muttered at him, moving over to a pile of still-waving golem appendages. Lonen had a point that she had to be careful of them. When she'd first arrived to find him on his knees, the ring of golems about to deal the death blow, she'd overreacted, blowing his attackers away in a blast of ill-considered grien.

"Understandable, really. And quite effective." Chuffta aimed a trickle of flame to melt the scything claws of a downed golem. *"Here's a good one. Still mostly intact."*

The best ones were those that still had most of their torso—particularly if Chuffta took care of the claws for her. In that first frenzy of squandering her accumulated sgath on saving Lonen, she'd turned to the nearest downed golem to steal its packet of sgath, and got sliced across the forearm for her trouble. Even now the three shallow cuts kept opening to ooze bright blood. A small lie to tell Lonen the blood wasn't hers. It had worked to calm him and, compared to the blood he'd shed, her wounds were nothing.

The man looked like he'd bathed in blood. If he hadn't been upright, she'd have been certain he could not have survived.

She pushed the haunting image aside, clearing her mind and emotions in order to absorb the sgath from the golem's packet. It was a good one indeed. Chuffta had an eye for the really fresh, intact ones.

"Now that I know what to look for, I can kind of detect in them what I feel in you, then search for that. It's not enough just to locate the least chopped up ones, though that's a start."

"A good thing, as most of them are pretty well diced."

"Lonen is a skilled and determined warrior."

Didn't she know it. How many men could have defeated an unkillable enemy in such devastating numbers? The immense pile of golem parts staggered her. He hadn't only dispatched them; he'd kept chopping them into smaller bits.

At least at first. The pile told its own chronology of his desperate battle, with the smallest chunks at the bottom—and in the trail leading away from her—with nearly intact golems missing only their feet on top.

The implicit story of what he'd been through brought up emotions she couldn't afford. With an effort, she cleared her mind again, letting go of the terror and worry. Grimly amusing, after all this time, that *hwil* actually came in handy. It wasn't some steady state of never feeling anything as she'd imagined all those years. Instead it had become more of a tool, a way of calming herself enough to become like that still lake Lonen always pictured, allowing the sgath to flow from the golems into her.

It wasn't a rush, like the streaming geyser of sgath below Bára. That flowed with its own power, gushing in whether she'd wanted it or not. This... this felt more like sipping from one of Lonen's flasks. Tip it too much and it splashed out all over her, wasting itself by vanishing into the parched ground. Fail to pull on it enough and the stream broke off. She'd also discovered that once she began she needed to keep the draw going, or the connection was lost and the remaining sgath snapped back to wherever it had come from—bound so deeply that she could no longer reach it.

She'd wasted part of several promising packets until she got the hang of it. And then the one she'd walked away from the moment she'd heard Lonen call her name, his blast of terror reaching her even before his voice. She never wanted to hear that again. Nor his broken words begging her not to leave him. Because she had left him. Alone there to fight those golems and die beneath their monstrous claws and teeth. She didn't care that he'd told her to do it. No one should suffer what he had.

She should never have left him and she never would again.

If she hadn't realized the significance of the sgath packets the golems carried and released to Lonen's cold iron blade... It didn't bear thinking about.

"Then why torture yourself by dwelling on it?"

"Hush," she told Chuffta, returning to the slumbering Lonen. She'd have to wake him to feed him more water, but for the time being she'd take advantage of his unconsciousness to tend the terrible hole in his side.

"He was happy, in a way, during that fight," Chuffta said more gently, landing on Lonen's chest and spreading his wings to shade the Destrye's face. *"He was thinking about you, imagining you happy and safe."*

"And the Destrye, too, I imagine." The wads of her chemise that she'd packed into the wound had dried there. Dipping the cup into her bucket, she poured water to soak the cloth away, so as not to break the fresh scabs.

"That too, but mostly he pictured you pregnant."

She choked at that, having to clear her throat. "You're making that up."

"No—it was very sweet. You were all fat and happy. You make a cute mother."

"That will be the day." Still, she snuck a glance at Lonen's lax face. He'd mentioned children, more than once. Apparently it was a fondly held wish of his. One she might not be able to satisfy for him. One among many. She eased the cloth away and put it in the bucket to rinse. When he awoke, she'd fetch fresh water for drinking. This batch would go to blood removal. A stroke of luck to have so much available for once. "Look at this—does it need more cauterizing?"

Chuffta snaked his head down to peer at it. *"I think it's good. You don't want it totally closed, or the bad fluids won't be able to exit. Also, if I burn him now, he'll feel it and awake."*

That seemed likely. The only saving grace of Lonen's dead faint after they rescued him was that it allowed Chuffta to cauterize the worst of the bleeding without him being aware. Something else she'd thought better not to mention right away.

Working methodically, she stripped him, tossing away the worst of the ragged and bloodied clothes, making a pile of the rest that might at least be salvageable for bandages. She washed him with care, using water liberally since she could, touching him only with the silk that had once been her chemise. The stinging pain and enervation when she accidentally brushed his skin sapped the sgath she'd so carefully scavenged, so she slowed. No sense jeopardizing that.

As she worked, learning his body as she hadn't been able to—the way a wife would—she channeled the sgath judiciously into the growing grien that had made her dying plants bloom. She didn't know much about living flesh, but all life felt more or less the same through that lens. His body would do the work of knitting itself together, Chuffta advised, if only she made sure each wound was as clean as possible, and then gave him a boost with extra growing ability.

Lonen woke once or twice, still disoriented, but better each time—drinking down the water she offered, watching her with gray eyes gone almost silver with fatigue. After that first time, he no longer pleaded with her not to leave him.

A good thing, as her heart couldn't take that again.

And each time, once he fell back to sleep, she and Chuffta sought out more golems to feed her reservoir of sgath, leaving the drained ones as heaps of once-again inanimate glass. The ones 'dead' the longest had begun to disintegrate into sand again.

By early afternoon she'd done all she could for Lonen—short of putting him on Buttercup's back and taking him to the shade of the oasis. She'd blown the golems away in that initial fit of fury, with the power of her grien, yes, but that had been instinct. She didn't think she could hold Buttercup still and exert enough power and finesse to lift Lonen into the saddle. She certainly wasn't going to be carrying him physically.

"Why not make shade for us?" Chuffta asked, a yawn in his voice. She glanced at him sharply, alarmed to see him visibly drooping. The derkesthai always seemed so indefatigable, she hadn't thought to tend him. Though she'd noticed his flame growing thinner and weaker with every visit they made to the golem junk pile.

"Are you all right? You must be exhausted."

"I am tired. And hot, even. I'll have some of that water and a nap. Shade would be lovely."

If he'd been less tired, that would have come out even more pointed, she suspected. "I don't want to waste the sgath."

"The remaining golems will keep. They're not going anywhere. This can be our oasis, with shade. We have enough water, thanks to the golems. It is not wise, I think, to skimp on our recovery now for fear of the future. Let's survive the present."

"Always so practical," she replied. A little stung by the rebuke and that, absorbed in Lonen's condition, she'd failed to pay attention to her Familiar or to tend Buttercup, she cleared her mind. The sgath from the golems wasn't anything like having the magic below Bára to use. It felt somehow stale, like water that had been stored in barrels as compared to the bright taste of the oasis water. But, just like barrel-water, it worked for the purpose well enough.

This wasn't the brilliant billow of grien she'd unleashed on her garden or in the marriage trial, or even the blast she'd leveled at the remaining golems. This stream she shaped with cool *hwil*, directing it into the glass heaps that had been Sisto's creations—and that still vaguely resonated with his personality. It helped, in truth, that the substance had been shaped by grien before, as if it retained a certain affinity for it. Which could help to explain priestly affinities, but she set that thought aside for later consideration.

Instead she worked with meticulous care, smoothing the glass into a bubble, as she'd seen the glass-blowers do once on one of her rare excursions to the forges. She'd asked how glass was made and her father took her there—with her brothers all crowding around—the king explaining to his progeny where Bára's famous glass came from, a treasure to forever safeguard, one that could not be measured as the value lay in the skill of their artisans, not in piles of treasure.

That had been before the monsoons stopped altogether, a change in the world she hadn't marked at the time, but which had led to this moment, to her building a glass dome over her Destrye husband. To nurse him back to health so they could resume their journey to Dru, where she would reign as queen.

And live to strike a devastating blow to the King of Bára.

If only her father could have predicted things would come to such a pass. Would he have made different decisions?

"Would you?" Chuffta, curled up in the shade of the now opaque dome beside the sleeping Lonen, asked the question in a mind whisper, eyes half lidded, tail wrapped around himself so many times he resembled a coiled snake, chin propped as if to strike.

"I don't know," she replied, but he'd already fallen asleep.

~ 16 ~

"How do you feel?" Oria sounded highly amused to be asking the question. Lonen blinked the grit of sleep from his eyes, then rubbed at them, absently noting that—although stiff and painful—his arm responded to his brain's commands. Oria sat beside him, Buttercup dozing head-down behind her, all of them under some kind of shelter while dusk fell outside. She proffered a cup. "Water?"

His thirst raged like a chained beast, so he levered up on one elbow—holy Arill, his side hurt!—and took the water, drinking it down. Without a word Oria took the cup from his hand, dipped it into a bucket and handed it, dripping, back to him. He drank that, too, taking a moment to assess her and their situation.

"Where did you find water?" he asked, handing the cup back for more.

She smiled, surprisingly dazzling—a way she hadn't smiled since before they escaped Bára. Since the morning after their wedding night. Intimate and relaxed. "I'd made a bet with myself what your first coherent question would be." She handed him another full cup.

"And were you correct?" he asked, bemused by this radiant Oria, sitting serenely, her hair unbound and streaming around her shoulders.

"It was in my top five." As he sipped at this cupful more slowly, she stroked the curved back of Chuffta coiled beside her, a gleaming white spiral wrapped in folded wings and a tail. He didn't think he'd ever seen the derkesthai asleep. "The golems," Oria said. "They had several barrels of water with them. I managed to hack into one of them—the barrel, not the golem—and it's all good water. We must have run afoul of them on a water-gathering mission." She met his gaze somberly, both of them too familiar with what that might mean.

"You hacked into a barrel…" he mused, struck by the image of delicate Oria hacking into anything—then struck again with a further incredulous thought. "With my axe?"

"Sgatha, no!" She looked appalled. "I can't even lift that thing. It's there by your side, where you dropped it when you, also, dropped."

Further bemused, he looked to where she pointed. Indeed, the axe lay by his side, haft still caked with dried blood from his own hands. "I wasn't sure—I know your penchant for wielding weapons too heavy for you to lift."

"Ha ha."

He glanced up at the ceiling. No, a dome? Like a rigid tent, it curved overhead, gleaming with rose and gold from the setting sun. "If I'm lying where I fell"—and it certainly felt like it, though she'd clearly undressed, washed, and tended him—"then where did this come from?"

Oria beamed, mouth curving again in a proud smile. "I made it."

"You… made it?"

She nodded, full of a youthful enthusiasm she rarely exhibited. "With grien. I used grien magic, Lonen! To make this shelter, so we'd be in the shade."

He returned her grin and levered himself painfully to a sitting position. "You figured out how to process the wild magic."

"No such luck." She grimaced and waved a hand out the opening of the dome. "I took it from the golems. Each one carries a kind of a reserve of magic inside—like you carry water in flasks—that's how they keep going away from Bára. When you cut them with your axe, it released the sgath and I soaked some up. I only realized after a while what had happened. That's when I came back."

Fury and terror rose up in him. He set the cup carefully down. "Which I expressly ordered you not to do."

"You're welcome." She scowled at him. "I forget—did we have the argument yet where I tell you that you don't get to order me about?"

"Probably." He tried to remember, then laughed, surprising her. Then reached out to take a lock of her hair, letting the silk slide through his fingers. "Thank you for saving my life, my powerful and resourceful sorceress wife. Where do you stand on being touched now?"

"Oh no, you don't." She pulled her hair from his hand, reminding him of the time she'd cut off a lock, to escape his grasp. He still had it somewhere in his things. "Even if I could withstand it—which I probably can't for long, as the intake of sgath has sensitized me again—*you*, my battered barbarian, are in no condition for frolicking."

"Frolicking?"

"And so forth." She scooted back as he reached for her again, and his side grabbed.

"Ow! Holy Arill." His hand came away bloody and … charred? He held it up to the dimming light to see the crisped flakes of skin better. "How did I get burned—Chuffta?"

"A few of the wounds we had to cauterize." She sounded apologetic, her face scrunched up in sympathy. "I'm sure it hurts like anything, but I didn't have many options."

"No, you wouldn't have," he replied absently, surveying his body in greater detail. He was a mess, a crisscross of bloodstained bandages, purpling bruises, and scabbed over lacerations. In places, like the forearm the golem had gnawed, fresh blood seeped into the bandages from his movements, but all things considered… "Is it the same day?"

"Yes—I found you an hour or so past dawn and it's just evening."

"How am I so healed? These scabs look at least a day old, maybe two—and the deeper wounds are only seeping."

She rolled her eyes at him and shook her hair back. "You would be an expert on wound healing."

"I've had some experience." Particularly with the sort caused by the glass-knifed claws and fangs of the golems, he didn't have to add, because Oria already looked pained at the reminder.

"I helped the healing along," she said softly, watching him with wide, uncertain eyes. "It worked better than I expected."

"You have healing powers, too?" The possibilities there could be phenomenal.

"Not exactly… It's more like what I did with the plants. I kind of added energy to your natural healing process."

"That explains why I'm so ravenous." Over the years of privation, especially the last months, he'd grown accustomed to being hungry. Now that he'd slaked his thirst, his body demanded food like a bear fresh out of hibernation.

"Sorry. I'd hoped to have food for you by the time you awoke, but Chuffta has been sleeping." She stroked the derkesthai again, who didn't move. "He was exhausted from the battle he fought alongside you, and then helping me all day. He even ran out of green flame and I didn't know he could. I don't think he did either."

Lonen stretched carefully. The side hurt like a demon, but he felt reasonably strong—and surprisingly energized. Now that he thought about it, he could feel Oria's blend of bright feminine and fruitful zest flowing through his body. He tapped one of the bandages. "Was this your chemise?"

She wrinkled her nose. "Unfortunately. You're wearing all that's left of it. And those are what's left of the clothes you were wearing. Your saddle packs are there, though, if you have more. I didn't want to rifle through your things too much."

He raised a brow at her, grabbing a pack and dragging it over, though it made his side pull painfully. That would take some getting used to. "At this point I'd say they're our things. How did you get the tack off the horse?"

"*Buttercup* told me how."

He paused, arrested by that. "I thought you said he doesn't think that way?"

She shrugged a little. "He doesn't so much. But that's a familiar routine for him and the tack was uncomfortable. He's used to you taking it off when he's not working, so he kind of… expected it, I guess is a way to put it. So I just followed his expectations."

"Your abilities are truly remarkable." Unaccountably, she blushed at that, glancing away. "I really wish I could kiss you right now, Oria."

Her gaze came back to his, less shy, the copper burning with heat. "I'd like that, too," she said quietly. Almost an admission, which for her he supposed it was.

"You love me," he said, mostly to himself, still assimilating that startling information, but the warmth in her eyes turned hard and hot.

"Are you going to hold that over my head forever?"

"Pretty much," he returned cheerfully. At least his iron-shod boots had survived intact. "When dealing with a hugely powerful sorceress who can melt you in your boots, it's definitely an advantage if she's too softhearted towards you to blast you when you aggravate her."

"What are you doing?"

"Getting dressed."

"I see *that*. Why?"

"We need food, so I'm going to hunt."

"No, you are not. That spot on the ground was very nearly your death bed. Look at all that blood soaked into the ground. You need to rest and build your strength."

"We need to eat, Oria," he told her gently, but firmly. Though it was true, lifting his hips to pull on his pants about took his breath away. He'd have to avoid using those abdominals as much as possible. "I need food to fuel this healing, and so do you and Chuffta. You two helped me. Now it's my turn. Besides," he added, with a wary eye at the thickening dusk, "what if more golems find us?"

"I think I might actually be of help there," she said tentatively.

That shouldn't surprise him. "Good news. I'm happy to leave the dealing with magical creatures to your capable hands then." He stood, the dome plenty high enough to accommodate the warhorse's height, much less his. The world spun a little, but he remained upright. Oria studied him, a line between her brows. "I'm not an idiot," he reassured her. "If I'm going to pass out, I'll sit."

"Good, because I won't be catching you if you fall." She stood, straightening her robes. The silk clung to her slender form.

"So, you're naked under there, huh?" he couldn't help teasing her.

She gave him an arch look. "I was always naked under my chemise, too. This is hardly different."

He shook his head slowly, letting some of his desire for her leak in her direction. Like his hunger, he'd become somewhat accustomed to feeling it all the time, in the background of his thoughts—until moments like this made it rage. "Trust me, love, it's different."

"You must be feeling better," she observed, bending to gather some things and put them in the packs.

"Now what are *you* doing?"

"Packing up. If you're not going to rest, and now that you can get on Buttercup under your own power, then we might as well load up and get going. I know you want to keep heading to Dru. You can watch for some hapless creature to kill on the way."

"What about Chuffta?"

"I'll hold him. If he wakes, he can hunt for us."

It was a solid plan, so he helped her pack things away. Lifting the saddle would have been a struggle, but the warhorse unexpectedly knelt, making it much easier. When he glanced at Oria in question, she lifted her hands, palms up. "What can I say? I wasn't lifting that thing off his back. I couldn't even reach it, so Buttercup and I worked out an arrangement." The horse nodded his head at her and whuffed in affection—a sound he hadn't made since he was a colt.

The sight of the fearsome warhorse acting like a puppy dog tamed to his mistress's hand took Lonen aback. On the one hand, yes—it made saddling up much easier, given his injuries. On the other, the stallion should be meaner and tougher than that. The comparison to his own vulnerability to the foreign sorceress's taming was unavoidable.

Although the goddess Arill had done the same for all the rough Destrye warriors, hadn't She? Perhaps She approved. Still. He could just hear what Ion would have said. What smart remarks Arnon and the other warriors would toss about once they reached Dru, if they overheard Oria explaining her deal with his horse.

"You need to give him a different name," he muttered, slapping the warhorse's flank in a signal to rise to his feet again.

"Why?" Oria sounded surprised. "That is his name."

"It's a name I called him in jest. You know, like men call each other flower names to taunt them into being tougher."

"Buttercup is a flower?"

"Yes. Small, yellow, and sweet. The opposite of this horse."

"Hmm. Because flowers aren't tough. Or manly."

"Exactly," he agreed, relieved that she seemed to understand. Though a certain tone in her voice made him decide to leave the topic there. He climbed into the saddle, giving in and pressing the heel of his hand hard into the aching wound. Hopefully he wasn't aggravating the healing process by moving too soon. But neither was he going to sit idly by and helplessly watch while Oria tried to defend them from more golems while the two of them steadily weakened from hunger. He'd take the gift of her saving his life and use it to better ensure she made it safely to Dru. "Hand me Chuffta."

She scooped up the sleeping derkesthai and handed him up, then took his proffered forearm and climbed into the saddle behind him. "I can take him now."

"I've got him." The lizardling made for a warm and comforting weight in his lap. "You concentrate on holding on."

"My seat has gotten much better," she replied tartly, but she snaked an arm around his waist on the good side. Well, the less injured side, anyway. "Does that hurt?"

It did some, but he wasn't giving up the delicious feel of her slim body and soft breasts snuggled up against his back. "I'm good. And I meant that you can help keep me in the saddle. Though if I do pitch over, just let me fall. Don't hurt yourself getting crushed."

"Oh right. I'll just wave my hands in the air while you get hurt."

He let that go. If she didn't understand by now that he'd pay any price to preserve her well-being…Well, it wasn't worth arguing about. He gazed around at the litter of broken glass ringing the uncanny dome, all gleaming in the blue-white light of Grienon climbing the sky, waxing rapidly to full. "I guess we just leave this here?"

"Maybe someone will be glad of the shelter," she offered. "And the remaining barrels of water. Not like we can carry them."

Much as he hated to leave so much useful water behind, he had to agree. Once they made it home, he could send people back for it. Turning Butter—the warhorse's head towards Dru, they rode out.

~ 17 ~

FOR THE NEXT couple of days and nights, they rode mostly without incident, stopping to sleep for a few hours, then continuing on, not even staying at the last oasis for long. True to Lonen's predictions, the landscape soon began to change, the scrubby desert vegetation giving way to lusher bushes, then to copses of trees with needle-like leaves. Evergreens, he called them. They were able to refill their flasks from small springs that flowed with sweet water, then even from little ponds, surrounded by moss-covered rocks, like naturally occurring oases. They took forever to fill even a small flask but didn't accumulate enough to fill a golem's barrel, so had escaped their depredations, but they were plenty to sustain the four of them.

The waiting while the flasks filled gave them time to rest, which even Lonen took advantage of, his face gray with weariness.

The weather also grew colder as they left the desert behind, making her shiver so much in her thin silks that Lonen insisted she wear his furred cloak, and wouldn't hear of them sharing. She worried about his slowing recovery. For all that he'd healed rapidly at first, he'd barely recovered more than that. He refused to let her use any of her energy to boost the process, saying—not at all nicely—that he'd healed without her before and could do it again. She'd learned not to ask him about it, as he tended to bite her head off. Had she been this awful to deal with when she felt terrible?

Probably.

So she found other ways to surreptitiously support him. Chuffta, once again bright-eyed and full of flame, hunted for them, saving Lonen that effort. While she couldn't bring herself to skin and gut the unfortunate creatures—usually those same rodents, though birds also fell prey to the derkesthai's skills—she did learn to cook them. That way she could pretend to eat more while giving most of it to Lonen. He needed the food far more than she did.

For her part, she kept her portals tightly closed and hoarded the sgath she'd taken from the golems, having sucked every last one dry while Lonen slept that long first afternoon. With Chuffta also asleep, her head had been far too quiet. She'd missed both her Familiar's running commentary and Lonen's teasing. She might have regretted having blurted her feelings to Lonen, except that it seemed to please him so much. Still, she was already so dependent on him, she had to fight a gaping sense of vulnerability. He wouldn't mistreat her, she trusted in that. And he'd repeatedly demonstrated that he was committed to their marriage and would be a devoted spouse.

Still, it would be nice if he felt more than lust for her. The nearer they came to the forests of Dru, the more she imagined Lonen's regret when he laid eyes on his lost love Natly again. Perhaps his distance came from that regret already.

Every time she thought that, she thrust it aside as foolish. He behaved gruffly because he was in pain. She'd been unpleasant to him, too, when she was so sick.

So she left him to his grim silence, resisting the urge to probe his mind. She didn't need to be sniffing out his thoughts and feelings, especially when she needed every last drop of sgath to stay alive long enough to help the Destrye. How she'd stop the Trom, she still didn't know, but it certainly would require magic. Lots of sgath. Chuffta's idea of luring golems to feed her from their packets could work.

With that power in reserve, hopefully she could devise a way to summon the Trom that wouldn't require her to spend all she had, letting her assume command and order them away. With Gallia a possible ally, she could hope was that her new sister would sabotage any efforts of Yar's to summon the Trom back to his side.

If so, with that task accomplished, she could move on with her obligations met. What that life would be, she didn't know. But she refused to tie Lonen to her in a one-sided agreement. He shouldn't have to forever pay the price for saving his people, not even if it pleased him that she'd fallen in love.

No, she'd see her vows done, and then think of next steps. All she had to do was decipher a long-held temple secret with no help, fuel the summoning with minimal power, and be strong enough to withstand whatever the Trom asked in return.

"Remember your mother's cautions about doing this on your own," Chuffta inserted into her thoughts, unnecessarily.

"I rather think becoming like my aunt Tania, whoever she might have been, is the least of my worries." Better to use up some mental energy than give Lonen one more thing to worry about.

"I think it's a very real concern, Oria. What's if there's more to the temple prohibition against women using grien magic than superstition or fear? The Trom were very interested in you—and that can't be a good thing. If 'ponen' means potential, that could be potential for power as corrupt as theirs."

"But there are two faces to all magic, yes? Sgath and grien, absorbing and thrusting. Where there's potential for corruption, there must be potential for ... whatever the reverse of corruption would be."

"Growth? Restoration? Healing?"

"Yes. Nurturing, not decomposition." She'd used her grien that way before, to grow things. How could that be wrong—or even corrupt? *"I've managed to survive in ways we couldn't have predicted, back in Bára. Perhaps I'll even find other ways to access magic."*

"You have ideas?"

"I'd like to suggest to Lonen your idea of luring in some golems and using them. Also, I've been thinking—I could maybe harness the wild magic."

Chuffta pondered that, his thoughts sifting quietly. *"I don't know if anyone ever has,"* he finally offered.

"Yes, well, we didn't know a sorceress of our people could survive be-

yond the walls either. If we're to help Dru, I'll have to think of other outside-the-walls ideas. Harnessing wild magic is an obvious possibility."

Not that she wanted to try it any time soon. Even still it made her shudder, thinking of the sheer chaotic enormity of the wild magic when she'd opened her senses to it. Now that she'd found a way to shut it out, she could maintain that default reasonably well. Sometimes, though, the wild magic sneaked through while she slept deeply, warping her dreams and then jerking her awake with the jangling input until she slammed shut her portals again. Fortunately, Lonen hadn't noticed. He slept apart from her—on the other side of the fire he and Chuffta unfailingly built to keep her warm—citing his half-healed wounds and claiming that he'd only cause her pain if they touched and keep them both from sleeping.

She missed the closeness of how they'd cuddled at the oasis, and tried to remind herself that it didn't mean Lonen was distancing himself from her. True, she shouldn't have put him on the spot by confessing her feelings, but there were many good reasons for them to sleep apart besides that.

Touching skin-to-skin wasn't possible regardless since her sensitivity to touch, if not quite back full force, was still a very real problem. Also, the way he jerked and shouted in his sleep reminded her of that nightmare she'd wakened him from that first night in her bed, when he'd sheepishly confessed to having bad dreams about the golems—and her. She strongly suspected the golem battle that nearly killed him had stirred up those nightmares again and he sought to hide it from her.

"Or the vision he had of you with Trom eyes. Like Yar's."

"A dream only."

"Summoning could do that to you. It did something to Yar. Maybe to Febe, too."

"They were rotten to begin with. We don't know it will affect me the same way."

"We don't know that it won't."

"Do you have another suggestion for saving the Destrye from the

Trom's attacks?"

Chuffta didn't reply so she considered the argument concluded. At least he didn't pry into her bruised feelings. No advice for the lovelorn.

SHE WAS DOZING against Lonen's back, enjoying being close to him and the soft, lulling warmth of the afternoon. Amazing, truly, that the sun could be so different from the one in Bára. That was, she knew it to be the same sun, but it seemed to have a totally different character. Soft and gentle, never scorching. And most welcome after the bitter nights and chilly mornings.

"Look, Oria," Lonen said, the first words he'd spoken in hours. He tended to fall into his taciturn silences and she left him alone, remembering well how she'd preferred to stay quiet with her energy flagging, feeling like she was dying by finger-widths. Though Lonen wasn't dying.

Was he?

She studied him where he'd turned in the saddle to get her attention. His color wasn't good. Far too pale—even a little gray-green—with violet shadows under his eyes.

"Not me," he said with impatience, just as she opened her mouth to ask how he felt. "There." He indicated a small spring that steamed amid a copse of evergreens, surrounded by the moss that seemed to always accompany them. The sheer amount of green everywhere continued to astonish her, but this one also sported small yellow flowers. Short and velvety looking, they shone like little stars in an emerald sky. "Buttercups," he explained, with a little smile, holding out his forearm so she could use it to climb down. "The heat from the spring keeps it warm enough for them to bloom."

Because he'd rest if she did, she dismounted, Chuffta winging in to land on her shoulder, stroking her cheek with his in affectionate greeting. Behind her, Lonen grunted as he lowered himself from Buttercup's back, but she resisted turning around to check on him as he'd only growl at her. She knelt on the soft moss and caressed the silken petals of one of the small blossoms, relieved when Lonen sat beside her.

He plucked one and handed it to her, bowing slightly, and she didn't miss the wince of pain that crossed his face, though he banished it quickly. "For my lady," he said, a hint of breathlessness beneath.

She watched him surreptitiously as she sniffed it, finding the scent only that of a living plant, no particular fragrance. Buttercup the horse nuzzled her shoulder and she held the blossom up to him to lip.

"Don't let him eat that," Lonen said sharply. "They're poison."

"Are they?" She examined the pretty flower and mentally nudged Buttercup to go graze on some water weeds instead. "Hmm. Kind of tough and dangerous after all, then."

Lonen opened his mouth to retort, then closed it and shook his head. With a sigh, he lay back on the moss in the shade and closed his eyes. "You never give up once you've set your mind on something, do you?"

"Much like someone else I know," she agreed, sending Chuffta off to splash in the spring as he liked to do. Not as good as building a fire, but still fun. "Which is why we're going to talk about the fact that you're not only not getting better, you're getting worse."

"Oria." His tone was oppressive. "There's no point in—"

"Is this pride, Destrye?" she cut in, making the tone mocking enough that he cracked open an eye to glare balefully at her. "The sand is blowing in *your* tower now."

"You don't have to sound so Arill-cursed pleased about it," he growled, closing his eyes again, obviously beyond weary.

"I'm not pleased, Lonen." She searched for the right words to get through to him. Gave up. "I'm worried about you. The wounds are infected, aren't they?" She'd tried so hard to clean them well, but she'd clearly missed something.

He grunted and she thought that might be the only reply she'd get. Then he turned his head and opened his eyes to gaze at her, the gray silver-bright with fever. "It seems our fate that one or the other of us is sick."

"The wound in your side?" she persisted, guessing, as that had been the worst and the hardest to clean. The first to be cauterized as he'd been losing so much blood from it.

He nodded, slowly, keeping his eyes on her. "But there's nothing to be done about it."

"Let me see."

"No." He held up a hand when she moved toward him, hardening his voice. "No, and I mean that, sorceress. You can't help me without hurting yourself, and even then there's not much to be done. We're nearly to Dru. The healers at Arill's Temple will help me."

She knotted her fingers together, certain he lied to her. *"Can you read his thoughts, tell me if he's lying?"* she asked Chuffta privately.

"Don't try going around me to the lizardling," Lonen sharply.

How could he always tell?

"He keeps picturing the lake, but…" came Chuffta's slow and thoughtful reply.

"But what?"

"Oria! I mean it. You promised me the privacy of my thoughts," Lonen struggled to sit, his face going decidedly gray. She pushed him back down with ease.

"He's sure he's dying," Chuffta confirmed. *"I can see it clearly now. He's hoping to live long enough to get you to Dru."*

"Stupid. Stubborn. Barbarian. Thick-headed. Idiot." She chanted the words, tearing at Lonen's shirt while he feebly tried to stop her. The effort exhausted him and he gave up, staring up at the leaves, sweat rolling in greasy rivulets down his temples into his hair. She gasped when she got the shirt pulled up. The bandage she'd put on him only two days before had completely corroded, soaked through with blood and pus, black lines radiating out with menace. "Oh, Lonen..."

He laughed, of all things, breathless and resigned. "Now I know it's as bad as I thought."

"I'm sorry, I shouldn't have—"

"No apologies, remember?"

"That's my one for the day," she snapped, reaching for the bandage. Stopped by the pain of his hand closing around her wrist. She snatched it back, holding it to her breast, bewildered.

"I'm sorry." Lonen's breathing was labored. "There's my one for the day. You can't remove the bandage."

"It's covered in pus," she reasoned. "Let me wash the wound and then I'll make a fresh bandage."

"No." He stared up at the leaves again, but she thought he didn't see them. "Washing won't help. Something in my gut got nicked and the dirt comes from there. I've seen it before, belly wounds like this. The flesh all around it weakens. Your bandage is the only thing holding my guts in."

She sat there, impotent, holding her wrist against her breast, trying to think of a solution.

Lonen rolled his head, looking for her. "You couldn't have changed it. I was doomed the moment that claw got me."

"And you knew all along," she hissed at him, full of unreasoning fury. "You hid it from me."

"Yes." He nodded, then changed it and shook his head. "I wasn't sure at first, only felt it later. And the last time I looked, well..."

"It's obvious." Her whisper turned over and over in her mind. *Obvious. Obvious. Obvious.*

"I thought I could get you all the way to Dru, but..." He trailed off, staring at the leaves again. Or maybe the sky. "This might be as good a place as any. Tell Arnon to put up a marker for me, later, when there's time." He laughed again, at a joke only he understood.

"I'm not leaving you here," she told him, suddenly aware of how hard she gripped her own wrist. Deliberately she let go.

"I'm not sure you have a choice, love," he replied, his tone abstract. "I probably shouldn't have gotten off Buttercup. There won't be any getting back on. Not even with your circus tricks. You go, take Chuffta and Buttercup. You can reach the borders of Dru by nightfall."

"I thought you didn't want me to leave you." If he'd been more lucid, he would have caught the dangerous edge in her voice.

"You won't be." He lifted his fingers as if reaching for her, rolling his head to look for her. "Ride for Dru and bring back the healers. That's my only hope."

"I'm not falling for that again."

"Wise. He will not live for us to return."

"I'm only amazed that he managed to conceal it this long."

"He is most stubborn, it's true."

"Tell me about it," she said out loud. Time to conserve her energy for what needed doing. What she should have done in the first place. Steeling herself, she knelt up and laid her hands on Lonen's bare skin.

He yelped as if burned himself, and grabbed her wrists. "What in Arill are you doing, Oria?"

She used all her strength to resist him, opening the channel between them that the wedding magic had created back in Bára. At least she had that, a direct conduit that the wild magic couldn't infiltrate. "One advantage," she gritted through her teeth, "of you being so cursed stubborn and prideful is that you're too weak now to fend me off. I'm not letting you die." Ruthlessly, she connected the channel from him to her carefully sealed reservoir of sgath. The cool magic flowed eagerly into him, as if as drawn to Lonen as Oria herself.

"If you do this, you'll die," Lonen protested, sounding desperate.

"Not necessarily. We're close to Dru and you've been certain all along that I'll be better once there. Maybe I believe in your optimism finally." She tried giving him a cocky grin, though it likely came out distorted, his terrible agony filling her along with all the jangling input, even as the life-sustaining sgath drained from her.

"Oria," he pleaded with her now, his voice in the distance.

But he was gaining strength—both a good and bad thing. Good that her scheme was working. Bad that he might be able to wrest her away from him. She redoubled her efforts, opening her channels so fully that the wild magic started to pour in, too.

"Don't do this," he gritted, managing to lift her hands from his skin. "You need your magic to save the Destrye."

"Your goddess Arill can take the Destrye for all I care!" She shrieked her defiance, at him, at the fate that had lost her the crown and her home in one brutal swoop, at the sheer agony of the magic coursing through her.

"Is that so?" came a cool voice from behind her. "I'm quite certain she holds us in Her hand already. Take your foul hands off my brother, sorceress, before I cut them off."

~ 18 ~

LONEN GRAPPLED TO identify that voice, to make his vision, grown dark and blurred, work for him, give him the truth. Or rather, to refute what his ears told him.

It couldn't be. His brother had died, months and months before. Swallowed up by the earth on the battlefield outside Bára.

Hadn't he?

"Nolan?" Perhaps his brother was a figment come to carry him to the Hall of Warriors. He'd been there before, with Ion. But no—that had been their father, King Archimago. And then it hadn't been real at all, because it had been Oria arriving to save him.

A man shouldn't have to grapple with so many death visions.

And now she'd done it again, saving him at great cost to herself. They would have words about this. If she survived.

"Yes, brother," Nolan was saying. "I'm glad you haven't forgotten me in your... conquests. Unhand him, sorceress. And undo whatever twisted magic you work upon him, or I shall simply shoot you and cheerfully bear the consequences of killing a woman."

Oria, of course, determinedly ignored him. Or couldn't hear—her mouth was set in a flat line as she emptied her life energy into him. Her eyes had gone opaque, the copper shadowing to a matte black that alarmed him.

"Stand down," he ordered. Enough of his strength had returned that he lifted her palms from his body, now he managed to change his grip to touch her over the silk sleeves. "She's helping me."

Astonished silence greeted that declaration. If only he could see their faces. If only he could stand and explain rationally. He squeezed Oria's wrists with no response from her. She might not even be aware of what was going on. "Oria. Love. Stop. Close your portals. We're rescued. Save some sgath for the journey."

Something flickered in her face. Then Chuffta landed beside him, wrapping his tail around the bare skin of her wrists.

A shout of alarm from the men. "A monster! Kill that thing!"

"No! As King of the Destrye, I forbid you." He managed to lever himself up—something that had been impossible before, so she had indeed worked a miracle—and pulled Oria against him, angling his shoulder to deflect any attack on the derkesthai. A good thing, too, as several of the Destrye, including Nolan, had arrows trained on them, points wavering now.

His brother. Thinner, worn, and wan. His dreamer's smile gone hard and ruthless, his once elegant beard a wild tangle. But alive.

"Nolan," he breathed.

"King?" Nolan raised a dubious brow. There was the incisive intelligence, the wit that could load a single word with ten thousand questions—and make you feel you couldn't answer any of them. Belatedly, Lonen realized that Nolan, as his elder, should be king instead. That he likely didn't know of their father and Ion's deaths.

"A great deal has happened," he offered, a weak explanation, but how to deliver such news, all at once? "And we thought you were dead."

"I nearly was." Nolan's face was set in grim lines. "We all were. Sucked into the earth by the foul magic of the Bárans, our enemy—one of whom, if I'm not mistaken, you now hold to your breast. Is she your captive?"

He nearly said yes. It would be much easier and get them past difficult explanations. But one look at her wide, unseeing eyes as she lay against him, hands curled against her breast, covered in gore from saving his life, decided him. He'd made her a vow. Several of them, and he'd never dishonor her by even temporarily granting her a lesser status among the Destrye.

"She is my wife," he said, as ringingly as he could, having only just been snatched back from the path to the Hall of Warriors. "And thus your Queen. You will all treat her with the appropriate respect and deference."

Nolan's piercing blue stare didn't waver, nor did his stern expression alter. He'd always had an intense gaze, but one softened with laughter. At least, he had before the golem wars. Had he changed gradually over time and Lonen hadn't noticed—or just since the earth opened up and ate him? In the end it didn't matter.

They all had changed irrevocably.

"You don't wear the wreath or Father's sword," Nolan noted. Not in challenge, more in the manner of a man wrestling with new information.

"The wreath is in my saddlebags," Lonen replied, feeling his weariness now that the battle energy faded. Oria was a limp weight against him. Arill curse her for her foolhardiness. "The sword I left with Arnon, in case I did not return."

Nolan dipped his chin, not sending a man to check for the wreath as Lonen half expected. "So Ion and Father are dead then," he said, as if noting that the day grew warm. He finally unnocked his arrow and tipped it to his forehead in a salute. "Long live the king," added in a wry tone.

Lonen winced. "Brother, no one had any inkling that you lived. Had I any idea—"

But Nolan shook his head to stop him, tucked his arrow back in the quiver, shouldered his bow and set his men to work with hand signals too quick to follow. "My tale is a long one and it seems yours is, also. There will be time to talk. When my king is not half dead. And my queen," he added, in a tone so neutral it shouted his disapproval. "I assume you're headed home? I *hope* you're headed home. If so, let us take care of you and get you there."

"Yes." Almost unable to believe they'd actually make it, he dropped his head back to the comforting moss he'd expected to be his grave. "Thank you. Please take us home."

"I'M GOING TO save you the trouble of wondering by telling you up front that we're safe in Dru," came Chuffta's mind-voice, both gentle and dry with amusement. *"And welcome back."*

Oria opened her eyes to a large, round room so strange she immediately appreciated her Familiar's warning. She lay in one bed among many, all narrow and evenly spaced at intervals, like spokes in a wheel. A few were occupied, sounds of sleeping and misery wafting to her as birdsong once had. In the center, the massive trunk of what appeared to be a living tree rose up and through the roof. Enormous limbs arched, holding up a ceiling that seemed to be both made of wood and made to look like limbs. The illusion made her frown, trying to discern where the tree ended and the man-made structure began. Cracks of light shone through here and there, with glimpses of what might be a gray sky. Not the deep flint gray of Lonen's eyes, but a chill off-white. Actual leaves, large as her hand and in astonishing shades of amber, scarlet, and gold, grew from the limbs. Or fell from them. As she watched, one released its grip with an almost audible sigh, then spun in lazy spirals to land light as a butterfly on the fur covering her.

Chuffta, lying curled up against her side, nosed the leaf. It must be dying, to be that color and have fallen so. The thought filled her with formless sorrow. Her nose was cold, so she snuggled deeper under the cozy fur as best she could with the lassitude of her body. Perhaps she'd stay in bed forever.

"A cycle only, one more pronounced here. The leaves die and fall off during winter, but grow again in spring."

"How do you know that?" Her mental tone sounded reasonably firm, which was a good sign. But she couldn't feel much of anything at all, not even that connection to Lonen she'd mercilessly exploited, which was likely a very bad sign. She didn't remember the gray mist

at all, and wasn't sure if *that* was a good sign or a bad one. So many questions to ask Chuffta—how she got to Dru, where was Buttercup, if Lonen had died, why she wasn't dead—but she took refuge for a few moments longer in a simple question about leaves and seasons.

Cycles only. Should that make death less sad?

"Derkesthai stories," Chuffta replied, his soft tone matching her melancholy mood. Or just fitting himself to it, the same way he fit under her arm against the curve of her body.

"So many of those."

"This is true. We don't have piles of books like you do, nor do we build cities to live in, so we pass the time telling stories of other places."

"And one of those places was Dru?"

"I'm not sure." He sounded as if he'd been contemplating it. *"It's cold here—do you feel it? We Derkesthai wouldn't like to be long outside shelter. And, of course, we don't have the same place names that you do, unless one of us has been a Familiar there."*

She nearly asked him to tell her more, about those other Familiars, though he tended to give her sketchy tales about them for some reason. Asking for stories would be continuing to avoid facing the hard truths, however, and she'd spent far too much of her life staying protected and remote from those.

"Tell me quick—did Lonen die?"

"No!" Chuffta sounded surprised. *"I would have told you right away if that were so."*

"No, you wouldn't have. You would have waited until you thought I was strong enough to handle the news." The rush of relief at hearing Lonen lived made her a little giddy. Maybe she would leave this bed someday.

"I suppose there's truth in that," Chuffta admitted, his mind-voice colored with some chagrin. *"Something I hadn't considered, since I didn't have to give you such dire news."*

"Then tell me the rest. What aren't you saying? He's still sick from his injuries."

"The both of you, yes. Lonen's brother Prince Nolan managed to get you both to Dru. You're in their capital city—which is nothing like Bára, by the way—in their Temple of Arill, which is where their healers also are. From their thoughts, I gather that Lonen is somewhere else, his chambers perhaps, with the healers going to him."

"Nolan. I remember him arriving as I was healing Lonen."

"And interrupted you. Both good and bad, as you didn't finish, but you also lived. That was a great risk you took, Oria."

She gazed up at the ceiling. It hadn't felt like a risk. It had felt like the necessary thing to do. But her magic gauge read severely low, matching the enervation of her body. Her system seemed both exhausted and overloaded at once, as if she'd been buffeted by a sandstorm for hours, leaving her both flayed and without reserves.

"Has he been to see me?" She asked that instead of what she really wanted to know, which was where they stood with each other.

"No. I haven't seen him since we arrived and they brought you here, but it seems he's been quite ill. I'm not sure he could have, even if..." Chuffta aborted that line of thought. *"Once you're better, you can go see him. Something to look forward to."*

"Do you even know if he'll get better? You haven't gone to look. Maybe he's died and you don't know, and—" Galvanized, she pushed at the fur blankets.

"Please." Chuffta's voice oozed scorn. *"You know as well as I do that he lives. Look inside yourself. And naturally I didn't go look. I wasn't leaving you alone here."*

Guilt pierced her. *"Have you eaten at all? Oh, Chuffta."*

"I can last a while without food. The cold helps." He sounded so sour about it that she might have laughed, if she hadn't been so upset.

"I see our patient is awake." The feminine voice saved her the excoriating reply that burned in her mind. Chuffta probably heard it anyway. The woman moved into her range of vision—the first female Destrye she'd seen—and snagged the beautiful dying leaf, tossing it toward the floor. With dark, curling hair barely tamed by a deep green veil, the woman possessed strong features like Lonen's, with the same hard chin, though her nose was more hawklike. "How are you feeling?" she asked. The inevitable question.

"I am …" How to answer this foreign woman who understood nothing of her particular ailment? "I am well enough, considering. Thank you for caring for me."

The woman's lips thinned and she felt Oria's brow with the back of her hand. Oria flinched as the touch seared like hot water on burned skin, clenching her jaw to keep from whimpering. Under the fur, Chuffta's tail wound around her wrist in soothing coils. "Arill does not permit that we turn away those in need, no matter who they might be," the woman replied.

Oria kept herself from stiffening at the hostility coming from the healer. No honorifics, either. Not that she'd banked heavily on being queen in Dru, but being a beggar for life-sustaining care would make for a ghastly future. Far better to have given her life saving Lonen.

"I don't know what to do for you," the woman continued, going to a basin to wash her hands. "You have no fever, no wounds, no apparent illness, and yet you've slept for nearly a week." She made it sound like sheer laziness. "Prince Nolan reports that you remained unconscious for the journey before that, too. If I may speak frankly, we did not expect you to ever awake. If not for the King's strict orders, we would have ceased care and let you die peacefully."

"I would not have let them do that."

She stroked Chuffta's tail in fervent gratitude, very clear on why he'd refused to leave her. "Then Lonen has been awake?" she asked.

"*His Highness*," the woman emphasized, "has been gravely ill. I realize that you were in his company, and we have followed his instructions regarding you as relayed by Prince Nolan, but that does not entitle you to information about the king." Her tone—and the aftertaste of her thoughts and emotions from the brief contact—made it clear the woman thought Oria's care had been wasted effort.

"How is he—is he recovering from his wounds?"

"That's not the business of a foul magic-user."

"I will see him." She tried moving, but the room spun in lazy circles.

"You need to eat."

"That's not possible. When His Highness has recovered, you may apply for an audience through the regular channels. If the king wishes to grant you an audience, he will send for you." She made that sound highly unlikely.

Oria summoned all her will—all the effort she'd expended over the long years to master *hwil*, to overcome the debilitating effects of magic on her being, and the casual scorn of those physically stronger—and levered herself up, sitting as straight as possible. They'd dressed her in some sort of high-necked, long-sleeved sleeping gown, and put curious knitted things on her feet. She welcomed them because with the fur pushed aside the chill of the room made her shiver. Chuffta hopped onto her shoulder, spreading his wings and looping his tail down her arm.

Pulling her best regal attitude, Oria leveled the woman with a stare. "I've been patient with you, healer, because I appreciate your care, however grudgingly rendered. However, I am King Lonen's wife, duly married, and thus your queen. You will address me as such, and you will escort me to see my husband with no further delay."

"Husband," the woman spat. "We've seen no evidence of any such marriage and plenty to suspect you laid a spell on our king to force him to bring you here. You will not be allowed to cause him further damage. If you're well enough to get up, then you will be escorted into the forest to live or die as Arill intends."

"Is that how it stands? If you fear my power so much, then I wonder you aren't more wary of what I'll do to you for thwarting me. Shall I demonstrate?"

The woman took an actual step back, making a sign Oria remembered from the Destrye warriors at the gates of Bára when she surrendered the city. A warding off of ill luck, if she wasn't mistaken.

The way the woman avoided looking directly at Chuffta confirmed it.

"They tried to make me leave, so I burned them until they stopped." He sounded most pleased with himself, so Oria made a show of scratching his jaw. If she couldn't have respect, she'd take fear.

"Go find where Lonen is. Maybe you can lead me there if she won't."

"Are you sure?"

"Yes. I'll be all right for a few minutes while you look."

Chuffta winged off with an unnecessary but gratifying flourish of green flame, then slipped through the edge of a shade covering one of the windows. The healer moved, opening her mouth, likely to call guards.

"Don't make me cast a spell on you," Oria said in quiet, firm warning.

The healer gasped, one hand going to her throat. "Arill will protect me!"

"Will She? Did your goddess protect you when the golems came?"

She sputtered in fear and fury. "You—you cannot—"

"I absolutely can. More than that, I will. Don't trifle with a sorceress of Bára. And you will address me as 'Your Highness.'"

The healer, though she paled, narrowed her eyes in scorn and opened her mouth to retort.

A bellow cut through whatever the healer had been about to say. A ringing demand that echoed against the wooden ceilings. Even with the distortion, Oria's heart leapt at the familiar voice. And the relief that she wouldn't have to make good on her bluff. Chuffta had been right about the food. Trying to stand and walk might have had her in an ignominious heap on the floor.

The healer leapt into motion, green veil flying as she dashed across the wide room to the door as it slammed open, somehow managing to both block the entry and bow at the same time. "Your Highness! You should not be out of—"

"Where is Oria?" Lonen snarled. Never had she been so happy

to hear his bad-tempered growl.

"This is the woman's ward, by Arill's command, and even you—"

"I'll answer to the goddess, but I *will* see my wife. Where is she?"

"Lonen—I'm here," Oria called, sick with relief. Or from lack of food. No, mostly that he'd come for her. That he hadn't abandoned her. He pushed into the room, one hand pressed to his bad side, Chuffta perched on his good shoulder. Then paused, totally arrested.

~ 19 ~

"ORIA," HE BREATHED. "Arill take it—I thought you'd died and they hid the news from me."

"No." Her voice caught with emotion. He'd been so ill—still gaunt with it and wearing some sort of hastily donned robe—but he strode toward her with a semblance of his old vitality. Just seeing him felt like—how had he put it? Like water in the desert. "I only just awoke or I would have—"

She broke off when he seized her, pulling her against him and burying his face in her hair. Even as overwrought as he was, he made sure not to touch her skin. "I kept asking for you," he whispered brokenly. "At first they said you wouldn't come, and then that you couldn't. Until I saw Chuffta, I thought…"

He trailed off, so she tugged at his hair, tipping down his face so he'd look at her. They'd cleaned him up, trimmed his beard, and tied back his hair. The new scar on his face had healed some, though it still pulled with angry red. And the flinty gray of his eyes held the dampness of grief. "You knew that was a lie. There's never a time I wouldn't come to you if I could."

A crooked smile twisted his mouth. "Because you love me."

She sighed in exasperation. "You'll never let me forget I said that."

"No. It means too much to me." He stroked a hand over her hair. "You only just awoke—are you all right?" He looked around the room, seeming to notice it for the first time. "Why are you in the ward for Arill's Blessings?"

She laughed, beyond happy just to see him alive and well. "Just awoke, remember? And I don't even know what that means." Over his shoulder, several of the other patients had sat up, eyeing them with curious dark gazes—including the healer, whose face was aghast. "But we do have an audience."

He didn't even look. "We won't for long. I'm taking you to my chambers. Can you stand?"

When she hesitated, he moved to scoop her up—she barely stopped him. "Your side, Lonen. I can tell it pains you."

"Not having you with me pains me more."

"Your Highness." The healer stepped up, gathering her authority of common sense that outranked even a king. "The…your wife is correct. You shouldn't even be out of bed. You cannot risk opening the wound again or you will risk being abed another week. Or longer."

He rolled his eyes at Oria, and she ducked her face close to him so the healer wouldn't see her smile at his irreverence. "She's right," she said to him. "But I'm all right here. Get some food in me and I'll be good to stand and walk soon."

"They haven't fed you?" His expression went thunderous.

"It's hard to feed a sleeping person. But I'm tough and stubborn, as you know."

"I do know. Your stubbornness will be the end of me, I swear to Arill. But you can be as stubborn as you like in my bed. Talya—send for a litter to carry Her Highness to my rooms."

The healer, apparently named Talya, hesitated long enough for Lonen's face to go to stone. He turned and gave her one look—and she stalked off to do his bidding.

"She's not happy that I'm here," Oria noted. The other faces that watched them, including Destrye who'd clearly followed Lonen here and lingered outside the doorway, talking in consternation and gesturing at her, all looked unhappy. She'd warned him of this, that the Destrye would not be pleased to have one of their sworn enemy among them. "None of them are. They think I've cast a spell on you."

"Ask me if I care what they think."

"Lonen, seriously!"

"I am being serious." He looked at the crowd by the door. "Leave us. Unless you're carrying a litter for my queen or food for her, be gone. Enough of this." With a grunt, he picked her up. "Chuffta, man, clear the way."

"Lonen!" she snapped. His limp was obvious as he strode after her Familiar, the hall now empty. "If you make yourself worse again, I'll—"

"Nurse me back to health?" He turned his head to grin at her, then nuzzled her hair. "That could be fun."

She sighed. "You're incorrigible."

"I'm happy to have you with me. You're never leaving my sight again. I'm taking you where you belong and then I promise to rest. After I see that you're fed."

The hallways, strangely narrow and twisting, all in forms of wood, some with leaves and branches, sometimes open to the cold sky, flew past as he carried her. "Will you sit on me?" she teased.

"If necessary." His tone made it obvious he didn't find it all funny. He carried her into a grand chamber, dominated by a large bed and huge fireplace, all familiar for some odd reason. Then she realized—one of the soothing images that he used to reassure her. Setting her on the bed, he called for servants to stoke the fire and bring soup. Shivering, she crawled under the furs, these so soft she couldn't resist stroking them. Chuffta, with mind-trills of delight, went to the fireplace.

"This is much better. You'll get well here. Soon you'll be stronger than ever."

If only. Lonen, paler, hand holding his side, sat beside her on the bed. "What? What's that expression?"

"And you say you can't read my thoughts."

"I can't." He looked supremely annoyed about it, too. "I couldn't even feel you inside me. I'd lie in this bed, dreaming of you and the golems, and I'd wake up and not know where you were."

"You've had a fever."

"Yes. Cursed infection. But see?" He gave her that optimistic grin. "We made it to Dru. I told you we'd do it. Everything will be okay."

Not everything. "Lonen."

His smile dimmed. "Save it. Whatever you're about to say, we'll talk about it when we're well."

"No, I have to say it now. You couldn't feel me because my magic is gone. There's none left and very likely no way for me to get it back now. I can't help the Destrye. You married me for no reason."

His face went deathly still. "What are you saying?"

"You're not listening to me. We married for specific reasons that no longer exist."

He shrugged that off. "Things change. Those reasons don't matter. We made vows to each other."

Exactly what she'd thought. She drew herself up. "Your people put me in that charity ward because that's what I am. I'm not even a decent trophy anymore. I can't go home, but neither will I be a burden on you."

He sighed heavily. "Arill knows, you *are* a burden."

She tried not to let that hurt, because she'd known it. Fragile Oria. Always potentially something, never more than a not-quite-good-enough. "Look. Out in the desert when I tried to get you to leave me behind, we talked about this. And you said that you were determined to get me to Dru no matter what so I could save the Destrye. But I *can't*."

He stared at her, incredulous. "I said that to give you a reason to live, to dig in, because you were so het up to sacrifice yourself. That's not why I wanted you to live, to come to Dru."

"Of course it is. I understand that. It's not like you love me. And there's Natly to consider, so I'm willing to release you from—"

He cut her off with a raised hand. "Stop right there. Of course I love you. I tell you so all the time."

Her mouth dropped open, temper rising that he'd make such a claim. "You have not. Never once have you said so."

"All the time," he repeated evenly. "I call you 'love' all the time."

"I didn't know that's what you meant," she floundered. When had he first called her that? Ages ago. In the desert, maybe. Or the oasis.

He raised his gaze to the ceiling. "Arill give me patience with this woman. What, Oria, *did* you think 'love' meant?"

"I don't know!" She threw up her hands. "For all I know you Destrye call your cattle 'love' before you slaughter them. Maybe you mean 'juicy little snack.'"

He lowered his gaze to her, the flinty frustration lightening with blue sparks. "Well, you are that, so I agree it could be a valid interpretation."

His words shouldn't have warmed her, but they did. "Does it matter, though?" she persisted. "There's so much to be overcome."

"Be still," he said. Then, tucking his robe around himself, he got into the bed behind her, adjusting her so she lay back against him, the furs over them and his arms tight around her. "Be still and listen. I love you, Oria. You love me. It doesn't matter what brought us to this moment. It doesn't matter what the future will bring. All that matters is us, being together. Everything else is just a part of that story."

"The story they'll tell about us in the history books?" she asked, drowsy with warmth and his comforting nearness. With feeling his love wrap around her.

"Yes, complete with illustrations. The mighty-thewed Destrye king and his powerful, copper-haired Báran sorceress queen."

"You'll need to eat better, to build up those thews again," she murmured.

"We'll work on that, too." He kissed her hair.

"And their faithful derkesthai companion" Chuffta inserted, belly up

in front of the fire.

She relayed that to Lonen, and he laughed. "Along with their fierce warhorse, Black Buttercup."

She smiled at the image. In that moment it all seemed possible.

Read on for the first chapter of

The Forests of Dru

Sorcerous Moons – Book 4

~ 1 ~

"WE WON THE war and this is still the best the king's table can command?"

Nolan poked at the meat with a sour scowl, and Arnon clapped him on the shoulder. "Not much of a homecoming, huh? You could have brought us game from the far forests and done better."

"I brought the King of the Destrye instead." Nolan shrugged him off. "That seemed more useful at the time."

Lonen, that selfsame King of the Destrye, didn't adjust his position to ease his aching side, lest his brother misinterpret that as a sign of discomfort with the topic of conversation. Nor did he miss the sidelong glance from Nolan that suggested he might be reconsidering Lonen's inherent usefulness. Not that Lonen could argue much otherwise. Being laid up in bed recuperating for more than a week didn't lend itself to high-profile—or even marginally effective—rule. Nevertheless, some remnant of his youthful self cringed, wishing he could do something to earn his older brother's approval rather than his scorn.

Mostly, though, he longed to be back in that bed, under the furs with Oria, sharing her warmth, basking in the surety that she slept beside him. To be there when the strange dreams woke her.

Oria hadn't wanted him to be up and about yet, but Nolan—believed lost in battle, now miraculously returned and restless with unsatisfied expectations—had decided he'd waited long enough for explanations. Rather than risk having Nolan barge into his bedchamber and interrogate Oria, Lonen had conceded to the lesser of the evils and gotten himself to this private dinner with his two remaining brothers. The last three of Archimago's line, sadly diminished in robustness of every kind.

But three was one more than they'd thought they had.

That had to be a good thing. A blessing from Arill herself. Somehow, though, under the sharp scrutiny of Nolan's piercing blue stare, Lonen nursed a few doubts.

He gave in and shifted, easing the pinch in his gut. The infection no longer poisoned him, but the massive tissue damage had yet to replace itself—however much ever would—despite Oria's foolhardy attempt to give her life to heal him. That side of his body sagged inward, as if part of him had been carved out.

Which, come to think of it, it pretty much had.

With a grimace for that, he forced himself to finish the slice of stringy roast on his plate, then picked up his warmed wine and drank, hoping to mute some of the ache.

"It's not good for you to be upright in a chair like this," Arnon said, frowning at him. "I can see it pains you."

"Father would say a warrior can suffer far more than a bit of pain, especially in the service of Dru," Nolan replied, gaze never wavering from Lonen. "He would have expected his successor to be sitting the throne and handling the pressing issues of the Destrye, not lying abed with a foreign mistress."

"You mean Her Highness, Oria, Queen of the Destrye?" Lonen didn't raise his voice, but his tone carried all the iron resolve of his battle-axe. Enough that Nolan sat back slightly, a hint of surprise flickering through his eyes before they sharpened again. *That's right. I am not the same little brother you knew before the war.* He might not be ruling impressively, but neither was he a pushover. Not anymore.

"She is Báran," Nolan said flatly, tempting Lonen to remark on his brother's powers of observation. But this was no time for levity. This conversation had been a long time coming and Nolan clearly intended to have it out now. So be it—and Arill hold him in her hand for this battle.

"I'm fully aware of that, Nolan, as I met her in Bára, where she is in fact, a princess and should be queen of her people by her own right."

"What exactly happened there?" Arnon put in, full of curiosity. "What?" He gave Nolan's frown a scowl of his own. "You're not the only one who's been sitting on questions while Lonen concentrated on *not dying*," he added pointedly. "You've dragged him out of bed for this, so we might as well get the whole story."

"I'm not interested in this Báran princess's *story*," Nolan snapped. "What I want is to break this foul spell she's employed to ensorcell our brother and king. We needed to get him away from her devious influence if we're to have a hope of that. *Stories* can wait."

"I am not ensorcelled."

"She's a witch, Lonen—you know this."

"A sorceress, actually." Surreptitiously, Lonen scanned the shadows near the ceiling. Sure enough, the emerald gleam of Chuffta's eyes shone back from a high perch, his iridescent white body stretched into a low profile along the upper curve of a ceiling beam. Oria had sent her Familiar to spy on the conversation, even though Lonen had asked her to keep her friend and guardian close. He didn't like her to be alone. Not after what had happened to her without his protection when they'd arrived in Dru.

"You call it a pine, I call it an evergreen," Nolan replied. "It's the same Arill-cursed tree."

Lonen regarded his brother calmly. One benefit of battling hordes of golems, running out of water in the desert, and countless other ways he'd nearly died horrifically—it had become abundantly clear to him that arguments over minor details like semantics paled significantly as anything to get excited about. He'd have thought Nolan would have learned that lesson, too, during his trials and journeys.

"Trees are sacred to Arill," Arnon put in, ever the pedant, "so it's not technically correct to call it an 'Arill-cursed' tree."

Nolan turned on Arnon with a snarl, proving that temperance had not been one of the lessons he'd learned. Ironic, as Nolan had been the dreamer and thinker before the Golem Wars. Whereas Lonen, solidly third in line for a throne he'd thought he'd never have to sit, had been the irresponsible, playful one their father had despaired of teaching discipline to. Perhaps tragedy and the horrors of war worked to change people. Fire tempered some weapons to greater strength and destroyed others.

"Queen Oria is a sorceress, yes," Lonen said before his brothers could come to blows. "She wields powerful magic, but she does so with heart and conscience." He eyed Chuffta in the shadows, certain her spy would be faithfully relaying the conversation, and chose his words carefully for both audiences. "Instead of staying in Bára as their queen, Her Highness married me and journeyed here at great risk to herself, sacrificing her own throne out of a sense of responsibility to the Destrye, in order to help us." And to keep a personal vow to him, but that should remain exactly that—personal. He held her promises to him close to his heart, treasuring them alongside her confession that she loved him. Precious gifts from a prickly and dangerous woman. They did not need to be scrutinized by others.

Particularly those who couldn't—or wouldn't—understand what lay between him and the foreign bride who'd brought a bright face to the terrible magics wreaked in the wars, and light into his own darkened heart. She might have made the difference in him becoming the tempered weapon, rather than the warped one.

Nolan sighed heavily. Pushing his plate aside and leaning elbows on the table, he laced his fingers together except for the index fingers, which he pointed at Lonen. "Your obvious sentiment aside, let's discuss the legality of this marriage."

"It's a legal marriage, Nolan."

He waved that off. "Only according to Báran law, which is not ours. We do not recognize it."

"I recognize it, and I was there." The onerous ritual had nearly knocked him unconscious and had left Oria in a dead faint. The magic connection hummed between them, Oria a warm flame inside him. The only time since their marriage that he hadn't felt it was when they'd been separated, both near death. Something he never intended to endure again—and something else he wouldn't attempt to explain. Before he'd experienced it for himself, he wouldn't have understood it either. Nolan opened his mouth and Lonen held up a hand. "A moot point anyway, as I intend to rectify any lingering legal qualms by marrying Oria in Arill's Temple, just as soon as we can both stand upright for the entire ceremony." *And dance afterwards,* he promised himself. Oria would see how a wedding—and wedding night—should be properly celebrated.

He flicked a glance at Chuffta, hoping Oria had gotten that particular message. She could be stubborn, but he'd have his way in this.

"Well, let's discuss that," Nolan said.

"No."

Nolan made an impatient sound. "I want you to hear me out on this."

"No."

"There is no need for you to marry her, Lonen! Keep her as a trophy of war, if you must. Our warriors have a history of that. It's somewhat outdated, but the tradition is an old and stirring one that celebrates Destrye victory. We can play it to the people that way and they'll see you as all the stronger and more vital for it. Don't ask them to accept a foreigner—the enemy!—as their queen. There's no reason to do so and it makes you look weak. Your people deserve a Destrye woman as their queen."

Lonen shrugged. "They won't get one."

"Can she even quicken with your seed? We have no way of knowing if Destrye can breed with her kind. She could leave you without heirs."

"There are Ion's sons, if so."

"It's one thing for that to be a last resort, another for you to go in knowing she won't give you heirs."

"What man knows such things for certain when he marries?"

"What about Natly?"

Lonen tightened his jaw. "She's irrelevant to this conversation."

"Hardly. She waited for you to return, believing the two of you to be engaged. She could still be your queen."

At Nolan's suggestion, Arnon dropped his face into his hands. He and Lonen had spoken about Natly before, with Arnon arguing strongly against Natly as an appropriate queen.

"It seems to me," Lonen said slowly, measuring Nolan, "that you, yourself, rejected Natly as a suitable queen."

His elder brother had the grace to wince. "Yes, well. It need not be Natly, but—"

"It's a moot point. I've made vows and I intend to keep them. Would our people want a king who breaks his vows?"

"You mean like your betrothal to Natly?" Nolan shot back.

Lonen clenched his teeth against returning the bite. "I never promised. She assumed."

"Perhaps you are becoming the politician, parsing terms and dividing rope fibers."

"Perhaps so," Lonen returned, ignoring the sneer in Nolan's voice. The accusation was a fair one. "But I *am* king. I realize I shouldn't be. Arill knows our father died too young and this crown should be his." Lonen waved a hand at the wreath of hammered metal leaves he'd worn to the dinner. He didn't much care for it, and he'd worn it mainly as a reminder of his authority to his elder brother. At least it was light, even if he felt vaguely like an imposter wearing the thing. "Ion should have lived to succeed him, as we all believed he would. And yes, Nolan—you should have been king in his stead. Would have been, had we but known you lived."

Nolan's jaw flexed and he sat back, crossing his arms. "It wasn't as if I had a way to send a message. It took us weeks to find our way out of those caverns. If not for the underground lake that cushioned our fall, we would have died of thirst." He shook his head, a ghost of his old smile crossing his mouth behind the neat beard. "I tell you, it pissed me off mightily that I might die of *drowning* of all things."

"What did you do for food?" Lonen asked.

"You haven't gotten to hear this tale." Arnon poured them all more wine, clearly cheered by the turn in conversation. "It deserves to be set down as an epic ballad of its own."

"You tell it." Nolan took his cup, staring into it. "I'm weary of it, myself."

Arnon, who never met a topic that wearied him, grinned with enthusiasm. "So, there they were, Nolan and his regiment, on the north flank of the city. Fireballs hurtling through the air, golems everywhere, whirlwinds whipping through the center of the battlefield, while lightning forked overhead."

Lonen adjusted his position, sitting back to enjoy his brother's tale—and not bothering to point out that he'd been there, too. No sense interrupting the story's rhythm. He kept an eye on Nolan, however, darkly brooding over his wine.

"Then *crack*!" Arnon slapped his hands together, making both of his brothers jump and grinning at it, Arill take him. "The ground shook and opened up. Nolan and his men raced away from the edges, but no man can outrun the earth itself. The ground disappeared beneath their feet, and they fell, plummeting to certain death."

Nolan wiped a hand over his forehead and Lonen nearly called a halt to the story, but Nolan caught him looking and pierced him with a stare so challenging he knew it would only give insult. Instead he silently toasted his brother's bravery. After a slight hesitation, Nolan dipped his chin.

Oblivious to the exchange, Arnon continued. "Our hero, Prince Nolan, managed to grab a handhold and cling to it, as did a few other men. But the ground continued to shake, crumbling beneath their hands, while horses, supplies, even golems rained around them. They fell, too, sending a prayer to Arill to guide their steps to the Hall of Warriors."

"My prayer was nothing so coherent," Nolan interrupted.

"Shut up, this is my tale now," Arnon replied easily. He was doing this on purpose then. Telling the elaborate story to defuse tensions. Good on him. "But instead of waking in the Hall of Warriors, our hero plunged into icy water, cold and black as the sea. He drove for the surface, hampered by the rocks, men, horses, and supplies also teeming in the water."

"Grim," Lonen said, and Nolan raised his brows in acknowledgment of the observation. There. A bit of connection. Lonen would have to tell his brother the story of swimming through the bore tides of the Bay of Bára, carrying an unconscious Oria, nearly drowning all of them.

Or perhaps better not to.

"No light penetrated so deep in the earth," Arnon described with ghoulish glee, "but Arill held our hero in her hand, guiding him to swim to an unseeable shore."

"I mainly tried to swim *away* from flailing hooves and falling rocks," Nolan pointed out acerbically.

"Do *you* want to tell the story after all?" Arnon rounded on him.

"No, no—you go ahead. Never mind the fact checking."

"Thank you. Prince Nolan, chilled to the bone, exhausted and aching from the fall, at last dragged himself onto a dry shelf of stone. A few other men made it also, along with several horses—still with their packs, thank Arill."

"How many men?" Lonen asked out of habit before he caught himself. "Never mind, it—"

"About three dozen survived the fall," Nolan answered, gaze glittering. Out of a regiment of more than a thousand warriors. Horrifying indeed. Of course, they'd thought none had survived the chasm at all, so there was that. "Ten of those didn't survive the first few hours, and we lost three more on the journey to Dru. I brought fewer than two dozen home."

Lonen closed his eyes and sent a prayer to Arill to fete the lost soldiers well in the Hall of Warriors—and to forgive him that he felt some relief at the smaller number of bodies to feed and keep warm through the winter.

"You're jumping the story," Arnon accused.

"Apologies, brother." Nolan at least sounded less dour.

Arnon grunted, but continued. "Only three dozen men survived the fall," he intoned, "and ten of those didn't survive the first few hours."

Lonen passed a hand over his mouth to hide his smile.

"In the blackness of the caves, they might have been lost had Prince Nolan not been an educated man, as well as an experienced woodsman and hunter. Discovering that a phosphorescent fungus grew on the rocks, he reasoned that, like the moss on trees in the forests of Dru, it might grow more densely on the north face, and he navigated accordingly."

Lonen whistled, impressed, and Nolan refilled his goblet, shaking his head slightly, but not interrupting.

"As they continued, they discovered a well-worn passage. One that led more or less directly to Dru, and in fact emerged into a dry lake bed somewhat north of us." Arnon waited, expression expectant.

The wine evaporated on his tongue and Lonen found himself sitting upright, the pain in his side a minor consideration. "Wait—an underground passage from Bára to Dru?"

Nolan gave him a long look. "At least to the region north of Dru, but it appears so."

"That's how their golems traveled here. And how they drained the lakes so quickly before we became aware, sending the water back to Bára."

"The passage might have acted like an aqueduct, an underground river carrying water from our lakes to theirs until it had drained completely. They might have made others over however many years, with many routes to the surface, which would explain how the golems managed to pop up so unexpectedly and disappear again," Arnon agreed.

"Why didn't you tell me about this before?" Lonen demanded.

So many possibilities. How could they use this to their advantage? Of course, they'd thought the golems had been eliminated following the fall of Bára and that their major problem now lay in incursions by the even more deadly Trom, who needed no underground passages, instead flying in on their enormous dragons that scorched crops and Destrye alike. But he had nearly died under the fangs and claws of a band of golems he and Oria had encountered on their journey. "If we could—"

"*Why didn't we tell you?*" Nolan interrupted in a tone as scathing as dragon fire. "There was the small problem of an enemy princess in your bed. She of the people who sent the cursed goblins. We could hardly discuss such sensitive matters in her hearing. Arill only knows what her plans are or what information she'd send back to—"

"Oria is a not a spy." Lonen set his teeth against saying more. Steeled himself not to look up at her actual spy, concealed in the beams above.

"How do you know that?" Nolan demanded, angry and bewildered. "*Think*, man! You acknowledge she's a powerful sorceress. She could easily work magics to cloud your mind. She could be here to finally and completely undermine Dru. What better way than to capture the attention—and, incredibly enough, the hand in marriage—of our king? How is it possible this has *not* occurred to you?"

"Because I know her," he snapped. And he knew the many reasons she'd fought against him bringing her to Dru. Ones not at all politic to divulge. "I know what goes on in her heart and mind."

Nolan threw up his hands. "No man knows what goes on in the heart and mind of a woman, and that's if she's Destrye and not a foul Báran sorceress."

"Be mindful how you speak of your queen."

"I have pledged that woman no fealty."

"You will," Lonen replied evenly, putting the weight of command behind it. "Or do you mean to challenge me as king?"

"And bring civil war to Dru, on top of everything else? Oh, that's a grand idea."

"Are you asking me to abdicate in your favor?"

Nolan's face was perfectly neutral, an impenetrable mask. "Are you offering?"

"It's been suggested that I should abdicate in favor of Ion's son, Mago. His claim takes precedence, even over yours."

"That was before the Trom attacked," Arnon cautioned. "We discussed it as a peacetime proposition because we believed the war had ended—and because Salaya campaigned for it. I never thought it was a good idea, even if it might ease her widow's grief, and would not support that measure now. We are as much at war as ever and Mago is too young to bear such a heavy responsibility. In times of war, a warrior must lead."

"I am a warrior, and not too young." Nolan gave them both long and pointed stares. If all had gone as it should, he would have been crowned king. It never should have been Lonen and they all knew it.

"By Destrye law, I became king the moment my father and older brothers died," Lonen spoke slowly, feeling the weight of it himself. "I believed you dead and grieved your loss, brother, with never a thought that you might have survived." Not exactly true, but the haunting terror that his brother might be trapped beneath the earth, broken, bleeding, and slowly dying without succor wasn't worth plaguing them with. "I took the sword of the Destrye from my father's dead hand. A hand that had been turned to jellied flesh by a monster so heinous it dropped my father and his heir with a touch, reducing every bone in their bodies to pulp. I had to wipe the hilt clean of unnameable substances just to keep my grip."

He paused to gather himself, his brothers watching with ill-disguised horror.

"I didn't want it, never sought to be king, but I took that responsibility," Lonen told Nolan. "I assumed the weight of it over their dead bodies, as my heritage demanded I do, and I negotiated our truce with the Bárans." He put down the wine goblet with a thump when Nolan opened his mouth. "It doesn't matter that the truce was violated by *some* of their people. I did my best by the Destrye, as our father would have wanted. We came home to a decimated people, but I kept going. It was on me to find a way to save us and by Arill, I have tried."

"You've done more than most men could have," Arnon said. "The aqueducts. Planting the late crops. Rationing food and water. Planning for winter. Nolan, he nearly killed himself, and this after a long and exhausting campaign."

"I don't question any of that," Nolan replied.

"But you question my competency now."

"I think you should consider that you might be compromised."

Silence fell among them, sharp-spined and treacherous to navigate.

"And you, Arnon—what do you think?" Lonen asked his younger brother.

"We don't know her," Arnon said quietly. "You ran off to Bára to demand answers, to hold this princess to her vow that they would observe the peace and no longer attack us, steal our water, burn our crops. I looked at that sword every cursed day and made myself consider that you would likely never return for it. Every time I made a decision in your name, I dreaded the day we'd reconcile ourselves to your death, and I'd have to hold the throne for Mago. If the Destrye survived long enough to for him to grow up.

"And then you returned—more than half-dead and apparently married to this Báran sorceress—who for all we know sent those attacks, who has swayed your heart and mind to the point that you snarl at us for asking the simplest of questions. We try to give you space to recover without her influence, and you barge into the ward for Arill's Blessings—the women's ward, even, where men are expressly forbidden to enter—you terrify our head healer, roar orders in all directions, install the sorceress in your bed, and refuse to admit anyone but a few servants. If not for them we'd wonder if the sorceress yet lived. You won't even admit our healers to tend you, though you need it badly."

"That was you who ordered Oria sent to that charity ward, who kept her from me?" Lonen gripped the arms of his chair, rather than strangle Arnon.

"We decided together," Nolan said, jaw tight.

"You had no right to—"

"This is the first time since you've returned that we've been able to talk to you." Arnon thumped a fist on the table in a rare show of frustrated temper. "What in Arill do you expect of us, Lonen?"

"I expect you to believe in and support me. If not because I'm your brother, then because I am your rightful king, whether any of us are happy about that situation or not."

"It's not that, Lonen, dammit." Arnon raked his hands through his already messy brown curls. "If it were one of us, you would do the same. If you believed we'd been captured and controlled by a sorcerer—and up until recently, you agreed their magic was an abomination against Arill, too—then you would fight to help us also."

"And I'm telling you that I am not controlled and I don't need your help. Oria is here to help *us*, to protect us from the Trom. You'll see."

"See what?" Nolan spread his hands wide. "They're gone and the damage has been done. You lost most of the unharvested crops. We have no nearby fresh water supplies for all these people hunkered down for the winter under the wings of Arill's Temple. You've made little progress in shoring up what was supposed to be emergency construction and not long-term housing. And there's no indication these 'Trom' and their 'dragons' will return. We have nothing left worth taking."

"Any number of people can bear witness to what the Trom and their dragons did," Lonen said. "Don't try to make it sound like a child's tale."

"My point is that we have bigger problems than you dreaming up some implausible cause for your sorceress wife. If I were king, I—"

"But you're not." Lonen cut him off and Nolan's piercing gaze flashed with anger before he directed it ferociously at his wine. Lonen choked back the temper and sighed. "We're all stuck with me being king, like it or not."

"There is legal precedent," Nolan said, not looking up, but staring into his cup, "for a king to be deposed by another with an equivalent or more potent claim to the throne."

"That civil war you mentioned?" Lonen tried to keep it light, but the implicit betrayal stung.

Nolan flicked a sharp glance at him. "Nothing so large scale or destructive. A duel would allow Arill to select her champion, according to the old ways."

Arnon drew a sharp breath. "Lonen is barely out of his sickbed. He cannot duel with you, even if Arill's priestesses agree to such an archaic ritual."

"If you wanted me murdered, brother," Lonen replied, holding Nolan's gaze, "you would have done better to leave me at the spring. I could have died in peace and you would not have had to sully your hands with my blood."

"I've thought back to that day." Nolan's eyes were dark. "And sometimes regretted my part in it. Particularly that I brought that viper of a sorceress here instead of leaving her there to fertilize the forest as I should have."

"I would have killed you for abandoning her."

"A dying man held no threat to me."

"I'm not dying now."

"And you may yet get the opportunity to try to kill me," Nolan replied, with no apparent emotion.

"Brothers—" Arnon began.

"I've had enough." Lonen cut him off. He drained his mug and eased to his feet, no longer bothering to hide the wince of pain. "Such a heartening interlude this has been. So worth leaving my sickbed for."

"Go back to her then," Nolan called after him. "She is pretty enough to distract you for a while. But you have to get out of bed sometime."

"Lonen." Arnon caught up to him, expression earnest, eyes grave. "Let the healers tend you. Give us that much."

"Not Talya," he growled. If he saw the woman, he might strangle her.

Arnon held up his hands. "Fine. Not Talya. Who?"

A fine question. "Baeltya."

"Isn't she a junior healer?"

"Yes. And she tended me when I was but a junior prince. She has a good manner." A quiet one that might not disturb Oria too greatly. "Send her."

"I will." Arnon gripped his shoulder. "We're on your side, brother."

"Then show it." He shrugged out of Arnon's grasp and strode away.

Alby, Lonen's lieutenant, met him outside the doors. He made no comment, but stayed closer than usual. Perhaps he thought he needed to be ready to catch Lonen if he fell, which meant he must look nearly as bad as he felt. Lonen would not let himself fall, however. They walked slowly down the long hall, as Chuffta slipped in through a crack in the ceiling and winged his silent way ahead of them.

About Jeffe Kennedy

Jeffe Kennedy is an award-winning author whose works include novels, non-fiction, poetry, and short fiction. She has been a Ucross Foundation Fellow, received the Wyoming Arts Council Fellowship for Poetry, and was awarded a Frank Nelson Doubleday Memorial Award.

Her award-winning fantasy romance trilogy *The Twelve Kingdoms* hit the shelves starting in May 2014. Book 1, *The Mark of the Tala*, received a starred Library Journal review and was nominated for the RT Book of the Year while the sequel, *The Tears of the Rose* received a Top Pick Gold and was nominated for the RT Reviewers' Choice Best Fantasy Romance of 2014. The third book, *The Talon of the Hawk*, won the RT Reviewers' Choice Best Fantasy Romance of 2015. Two more books followed in this world, beginning the spin-off series *The Uncharted Realms*. Book one in that series, *The Pages of the Mind*, has also been nominated for the RT Reviewer's Choice Best Fantasy Romance of 2016. The second book, *The Edge of the Blade*, released December 27, 2016.

Her other works include a number of fiction series: the fantasy romance novels of *A Covenant of Thorns*; the contemporary BDSM novellas of the *Facets of Passion*; an erotic contemporary serial novel, *Master of the Opera*; and the erotic romance trilogy, *Falling Under*, which includes *Going Under*, *Under His Touch* and *Under Contract*.

She lives in Santa Fe, New Mexico, with two Maine coon cats, plentiful free-range lizards and a very handsome Doctor of Oriental Medicine.

Jeffe can be found online at her website: JeffeKennedy.com,

every Sunday at the popular SFF Seven blog, on Facebook, on Goodreads and pretty much constantly on Twitter @jeffekennedy. She is represented by Connor Goldsmith of Fuse Literary.

jeffekennedy.com

facebook.com/Author.Jeffe.Kennedy

twitter.com/jeffekennedy

goodreads.com/author/show/1014374.Jeffe_Kennedy

Titles by Jeffe Kennedy

OTHER FANTASY ROMANCES

A COVENANT OF THORNS

Rogue's Pawn
Rogue's Possession
Rogue's Paradise

THE TWELVE KINGDOMS

Negotiation
The Mark of the Tala
The Tears of the Rose
The Talon of the Hawk
Heart's Blood
For Crown and Kingdom

THE UNCHARTED REALMS

The Pages of the Mind
The Edge of the Blade

SORCEROUS MOONS

Lonen's War
Oria's Gambit
The Tides of Bára
The Forests of Dru

CONTEMPORARY EROTIC ROMANCES

Exact Warm Unholy

FACETS OF PASSION

Sapphire

Platinum

Ruby

Five Golden Rings

FALLING UNDER

Going Under

Under His Touch

Under Contract

MISSED CONNECTIONS

Last Dance

EROTIC PARANORMAL

MASTER OF THE OPERA E-SERIAL

Master of the Opera, Act 1: Passionate Overture

Master of the Opera, Act 2: Ghost Aria

Master of the Opera, Act 3: Phantom Serenade

Master of the Opera, Act 4: Dark Interlude

Master of the Opera, Act 5: A Haunting Duet

Master of the Opera, Act 6: Crescendo

Master of the Opera

BLOOD CURRENCY

Blood Currency

BDSM FAIRYTALE ROMANCE

Petals and Thorns

OTHER WORKS

Birdwoman

Hopeful Monsters

Teeth, Long and Sharp

Thank you for reading!